P9-DUK-489

JOHN STEINBECK

JOHN STEINBECK

NOVELS AND STORIES 1932–1937

The Pastures of Heaven
To a God Unknown
Tortilla Flat
In Dubious Battle
Of Mice and Men

THE LIBRARY OF AMERICA

The paper used in this publication meets the
minimum requirements of the American National Standard for
Information Sciences—Permanence of Paper for Printed
Library Materials, ANSI Z39.48—1984.

Distributed to the trade in the United States
by Penguin Books USA Inc
and in Canada by Penguin Books Canada Ltd.

Library of Congress Catalog Number: 94-2943
For cataloging information, see end of Notes
ISBN 1-883011-01-9

First Printing
The Library of America—72

Manufactured in the United States of America

ROBERT DeMOTT
WROTE THE NOTES AND
ELAINE A. STEINBECK
WAS SPECIAL CONSULTANT FOR THIS VOLUME

Contents

THE PASTURES OF HEAVEN

TO MY FATHER AND MOTHER

I

W HEN the Carmelo Mission of Alta California was being built, some time around 1776, a group of twenty converted Indians abandoned religion during a night, and in the morning they were gone from their huts. Besides being a bad precedent, this minor schism crippled the work in the clay pits where adobe bricks were being moulded.

After a short council of the religious and civil authorities, a Spanish corporal with a squad of horsemen set out to restore these erring children to the bosom of Mother Church. The troop made a difficult journey up the Carmel Valley and into the mountains beyond, a trip not the less bewildering because the fleeing dissenters had proved themselves masters of a diabolic guile in concealing traces of their journey. It was a week before the soldiery found them, but they were discovered at last practising abominations in the bottom of a ferny canyon in which a stream flowed; that is, the twenty heretics were fast asleep in attitudes of abandon.

The outraged military seized them and in spite of their howlings attached them to a long slender chain. Then the column turned about and headed for Carmel again to give the poor neophytes a chance at repentance in the clay pits.

In the late afternoon of the second day a small deer started up before the troop and popped out of sight over a ridge. The corporal disengaged himself from his column and rode in its pursuit. His heavy horse scrambled and floundered up the steep slope; the manzanita reached sharp claws for the corporal's face, but he plunged on after his dinner. In a few minutes he arrived at the top of the ridge, and there he stopped, stricken with wonder at what he saw—a long valley floored with green pasturage on which a herd of deer browsed. Perfect live oaks grew in the meadow of the lovely place, and the hills hugged it jealously against the fog and the wind.

The disciplinarian corporal felt weak in the face of so serene a beauty. He who had whipped brown backs to tatters, he whose rapacious manhood was building a new race for California, this bearded, savage bearer of civilization slipped from his saddle and took off his steel hat.

"Holy Mother!" he whispered. "Here are the green pastures of Heaven to which our Lord leadeth us."

His descendants are almost white now. We can only reconstruct his holy emotion of discovery, but the name he gave to the sweet valley in the hills remains there. It is known to this day as *Las Pasturas del Cielo*.

By some regal accident the section came under no great land grant. No Spanish nobleman became its possessor through the loan of his money or his wife. For a long time it lay forgotten in its embracing hills. The Spanish corporal, the discoverer, always intended to go back. Like most violent men he looked forward with sentimental wistfulness to a little time of peace before he died, to an adobe house beside a stream, and cattle nuzzling the walls at night.

An Indian woman presented him with the pox, and, when his face began to fall away, good friends locked him in an old barn to prevent the infection of others, and there he died peacefully, for the pox, although horrible to look at, is no bad friend to its host.

After a long time a few families of squatters moved into the Pastures of Heaven and built fences and planted fruit trees. Since no one owned the land, they squabbled a great deal over its possession. After a hundred years there were twenty families on twenty little farms in the Pastures of Heaven. Near the centre of the valley stood a general store and post office, and half a mile above, beside the stream, a hacked and much initialed school house.

The families at last lived prosperously and at peace. Their land was rich and easy to work. The fruits of their gardens were the finest produced in central California.

II

To the people of the Pastures of Heaven the Battle farm was cursed, and to their children it was haunted. Good land although it was, well watered and fertile, no one in the valley coveted the place, no one would live in the house, for land and houses that have been tended, loved and labored with and finally deserted, seem always sodden with gloom and with threatening. The trees which grow up around a deserted house are dark trees, and the shadows they throw on the ground have suggestive shapes.

For five years now the old Battle farm had stood vacant. The weeds, with a holiday energy, free of fear of the hoe, grew as large as small trees. In the orchard the fruit trees were knotty and strong and tangled. They increased the quantity of their fruit, and diminished its size. The brambles grew about their roots and swallowed up the windfalls.

The house itself, a square, well-built, two-story place, had been dignified and handsome when its white paint was fresh, but a singular latter history had left about it an air unbearably lonely. Weeds warped up the boards of the porches, the walls were grey with weathering. Small boys, those lieutenants of time in its warfare against the works of man, had broken out all the windows and carted away every movable thing. Boys believe that all kinds of portable articles which have no obvious owner, if taken home, can be put to some joyous use. The boys had gutted the house, had filled the wells with various kinds of refuse, and, quite by accident, while secretly smoking real tobacco in the hayloft, had burned the old barn to the ground. The fire was universally attributed to tramps.

The deserted farm was situated not far from the middle of the narrow valley. On both sides it was bounded by the best and most prosperous farms in the Pastures of Heaven. It was a weedy blot between two finely cultivated, contented pieces of land. The people of the valley considered it a place of curious evil, for one horrible event and one impenetrable mystery had taken place there.

Two generations of Battles had lived on the farm. George

Battle came west in 1863 from upper New York State; he was quite young when he arrived, just draft age. His mother supplied the money to buy the farm and to build the big square house upon it. When the house was completed, George Battle sent for his mother to come to live with him. She tried to come, that old woman who thought that space stopped ten miles from her village. She saw mythological places, New York and Rio and Buenos Aires. Off Patagonia she died, and a ship's watch buried her in a grey ocean with a piece of canvas for her coffin and three links of anchor chain sewn in between her feet; and she had wanted the crowded company of her home graveyard.

George Battle looked about for a good investment in a woman. In Salinas he found Miss Myrtle Cameron, a spinster of thirty-five, with a small fortune. Miss Myrtle had been neglected because of a mild tendency to epilepsy, a disease then called "fits" and generally ascribed to animosity on the part of the deity. George did not mind the epilepsy. He knew he couldn't have everything he wanted. Myrtle became his wife and bore him a son, and, after twice trying to burn the house, was confined in a little private prison called the Lippman Sanitarium, in San Jose. She spent the rest of her existence crocheting a symbolic life of Christ in cotton thread.

Thereafter the big house on the Battle farm was governed by a series of evil-tempered housekeepers of that kind who advertise: "Widow, 45, wants position housekeeper on farm. Good cook. Obj. Mat." One by one they came and were sweet and sad for a few days until they found out about Myrtle. After that they tramped through the house with flashing eyes, feeling that they had been abstractly raped.

George Battle was old at fifty, bent with work, pleasureless and dour. His eyes never left the ground he worked with so patiently. His hands were hard and black and covered with little crevices, like the pads of a bear. And his farm was beautiful. The trees in the orchard were trim and groomed, each one a counterpart of its fellows. The vegetables grew crisp and green in their line-straight rows. George cared for his house and kept a flower garden in front of it. The upper story of the house had never been lived in. This farm was a poem by the inarticulate man. Patiently he built his scene and waited for a Sylvia. No Sylvia ever came, but he kept the garden waiting for her just the same. In all the years when his son was growing up, George Battle paid very little attention to him. Only the fruit trees and the fresh green rows of vegetables were vital. When John, his son, went missionarying in a caravan, George didn't even miss him. He went on with the work, yearly bending his body lower over his earth. His neighbours never talked to him because he did not listen to talk. His hands were permanently hooked, had become sockets into which the handles of tools fitted tightly. At sixty-five he died of old age and a cough.

John Battle came home in his caravan to claim the farm. From his mother he had inherited both the epilepsy and the mad knowledge of God. John's life was devoted to a struggle with devils. From camp meeting to camp meeting he had gone, hurling his hands about, invoking devils and then confounding them, exorcising and flaying incarnate evil. When he arrived at home the devils still claimed attention. The lines of vegetables went to seed, volunteered a few times, and succumbed to the weeds. The farm slipped back to nature, but the devils grew stronger and more importunate.

As a protection John Battle covered his clothes and his hat with tiny cross-stitches in white thread, and, thus armoured, made war on the dark legions. In the grey dusk he sneaked about the farm armed with a heavy stick. He charged into the underbrush, thrashed about with his stick and shouted maledictions until the devils were driven from cover. At night he crept through the thickets upon a congregation of the demons, then fearlessly rushed forward, striking viciously with his weapon. In the daytime he went into his house and slept, for the devils did not work in the light.

One day in the deepening twilight John crept carefully upon a lilac bush in his own yard. He knew the bush sheltered a secret gathering of fiends. When he was so close that they could not escape, he jumped to his feet and lunged toward the lilac, flailing his stick and screaming. Aroused by the slashing blows, a snake rattled sleepily and raised its flat, hard head. John dropped his stick and shuddered, for the dry sharp warning of a snake is a terrifying sound. He fell upon his knees and prayed for a moment. Suddenly he shouted, "This is the damned serpent. Out, devil," and sprang forward with clutching fingers. The snake struck him three times in the throat where there were no crosses to protect him. He struggled very little, and died in a few minutes.

His neighbours only found him when the buzzards began to drop out of the sky, and the thing they found made them dread the Battle farm after that.

For ten years the farm lay fallow. The children said the house was haunted and made night excursions to it to frighten themselves. There was something fearsome about the gaunt old house with its staring vacant windows. The white paint fell off in long scales; the shingles curled up shaggily. The farm itself went completely wild. It was owned by a distant cousin of George Battle's, who had never seen it.

In 1921 the Mustrovics took possession of the Battle farm. Their coming was sudden and mysterious. One morning they were there, an old man and his old wife, skeleton people with tight yellow skin stretched and shiny over their high cheek bones. Neither of them spoke English. Communication with the valley was carried on by their son, a tall man with the same high cheek bones, with coarse-cropped black hair growing half way down his forehead, and with soft, sullen black eyes. He spoke English with an accent, and he only spoke his wants.

At the store the people gently questioned him, but they received no information.

"We always thought that place was haunted. Seen any ghosts yet?" T. B. Allen, the storekeeper, asked.

"No," said young Mustrovic.

"It's a good farm all right when you get the weeds off."

Mustrovic turned and walked out of the store.

"There's something about that place," said Allen. "Everybody who lives there hates to talk."

The old Mustrovics were rarely seen, but the young man worked every daylight hour on the farm. All by himself he cleared the land and planted it, pruned the trees and sprayed them. At any hour he could be seen working feverishly, half running about his tasks, with a look on his face as though he expected time to stop before a crop was in.

The family lived and slept in the kitchen of the big house.

All the other rooms were shut up and vacant, the broken windows unmended. They had stuck fly-paper over the holes in the kitchen windows to keep out the air. They did not paint the house nor take care of it in any way, but under the frantic efforts of the young man, the land began to grow beautiful again. For two years he slaved on the soil. In the grey of the dawn he emerged from the house, and the last of the dusk was gone before he went back into it.

One morning, Pat Humbert, driving to the store, noticed that no smoke came from the Mustrovic chimney. "The place looks deserted again," he said to Allen. " 'Course we never saw anybody but that young fellow around there, but something's wrong. What I mean is, the place kind of *feels* deserted."

For three days the neighbours watched the chimney apprehensively. They hated to investigate and make fools of themselves. On the fourth day Pat Humbert and T. B. Allen and John Whiteside walked up to the house. It was rustlingly still. It really did seem deserted. John Whiteside knocked at the kitchen door. When there was no answer and no movement, he turned the knob. The door swung open. The kitchen was immaculately clean, and the table set; there were dishes on the table, saucers of porridge, and fried eggs and sliced bread. On the food a little mould was forming. A few flies wandered aimlessly about in the sunshine that came through the open door. Pat Humbert shouted, "Anybody here?" He knew he was silly to do it.

They searched the house thoroughly, but it was vacant. There was no furniture in any rooms except the kitchen. The farm was completely deserted—had been deserted at a moment's notice.

Later, when the sheriff was informed, he found out nothing revealing. The Mustrovics had paid cash for the farm, and in going away had left no trace. No one saw them go, and no one ever saw them again. There was not even any crime in that part of the country that they might have taken part in. Suddenly, just as they were about to sit down to breakfast one morning, the Mustrovics had disappeared. Many, many times the case was discussed at the store, but no one could advance a tenable solution.

The weeds sprang up on the land again, and the wild berry vines climbed into the branches of the fruit trees. As though practice had made it adept, the farm fell quickly back to wildness. It was sold for taxes to a Monterey realty company, and the people of the Pastures of Heaven, whether they admitted it or not, were convinced that the Battle farm bore a curse. "It's good land," they said, "but I wouldn't own it if you gave it to me. I don't know what's the matter, but there's sure something funny about that place, almost creepy. Wouldn't be hard for a fellow to believe in haunts."

A pleasant shudder went through the people of the Pastures of Heaven when they heard that the old Battle farm was again to be occupied. The rumour was brought in to the General Store by Pat Humbert who had seen automobiles in front of the old house, and T. B. Allen, the store proprietor, widely circulated the story. Allen imagined all the circumstances surrounding the new ownership and told them to his customers, beginning all his confidences with "They say." "They say the fellow who's bought the Battle place is one of those people that goes about looking for ghosts and writing about them." T. B. Allen's "they say" was his protection. He used it as newspapers use the word "alleged."

Before Bert Munroe took possession of his new property, there were a dozen stories about him circulating through the Pastures of Heaven. He knew that the people who were to be his new neighbours were staring at him although he could never catch them at it. This secret staring is developed to a high art among country people. They have seen every uncovered bit on you, have tabulated and memorized the clothes you are wearing, have noticed the colour of your eyes and the shape of your nose, and, finally, have reduced your figure and personality to three or four adjectives, and all the time you thought they were oblivious to your presence.

After he had bought the old place, Bert Munroe went to work in the overgrown yard while a crew of carpenters made over the house. Every stick of furniture was taken out and burned in the yard. Partitions were torn down and other partitions put in. The walls were repapered and the house re-roofed with asbestos shingles. Finally a new coat of pale yellow paint was applied to the outside.

Bert himself cut down all the vines, and all the trees in the yard, to let in the light. Within three weeks the old house had lost every vestige of its deserted, haunted look. By stroke after stroke of genius it had been made to look like a hundred thousand other country houses in the west.

As soon as the paint inside and out was dry, the new furniture arrived, overstuffed chairs and a davenport, an enameled stove, steel beds painted to look like wood and guaranteed to provide a mathematical comfort. There were mirrors with scalloped frames, Wilton rugs and prints of pictures by a modern artist who has made blue popular.

With the furniture came Mrs. Munroe and the three younger Munroes. Mrs. Munroe was a plump woman who wore a rimless pince nez on a ribbon. She was a good house manager. Again and again she had the new furniture moved about until she was satisfied, but once satisfied, once she had regarded the piece with a concentrated gaze and then nodded and smiled, that piece was fixed forever, only to be moved for cleaning.

Her daughter Mae was a pretty girl with round smooth cheeks and ripe lips. She was voluptuous of figure, but under her chin there was a soft, pretty curve which indicated a future plumpness like her mother's. Mae's eyes were friendly and candid, not intelligent, but by no means stupid. Imperceptibly she would grow to be her mother's double, a good manager, a mother of healthy children, a good wife with no regrets.

In her own new room, Mae stuck dance programs between the glass and the frame of the mirror. On the walls she hung framed photographs of her friends in Monterey, and laid out her photograph album and her locked diary on the little bedside table. In the diary she concealed from prying eyes a completely uninteresting record of dances, of parties, of recipes for candy and of mild preferences for certain boys. Mae bought and made her own room curtains, pale pink theatrical gauze to strain the light, and a valance of flowered cretonne. On her bedspread of gathered satin, she arranged five boudoir pillows in positions of abandon, and against them leaned a long-legged French doll with clipped blonde hair and with a cloth cigarette dangling from languid lips. Mae considered that this doll proved her openness of mind, her tolerance of things she did not quite approve. She liked to have friends who had pasts, for, having such friends and listening to them, destroyed in her any regret that her own life had been blameless. She was nineteen; she thought of marriage most of the time. When she was out with boys she talked of ideals with some emotion. Mae had very little conception of what ideals were except that in some manner they governed the kind of kisses one received while driving home from dances.

Jimmie Munroe was seventeen, just out of high school and enormously cynical. In the presence of his parents, Jimmie's manner was usually sullen and secretive. He knew he couldn't trust them with his knowledge of the world, for they would not understand. They belonged to a generation which had no knowledge of sin nor of heroism. A firm intention to give over one's life to science after gutting it of emotional possibilities would not be tenderly received by his parents. By science, Jimmie meant radios, archeology and airplanes. He pictured himself digging up golden vases in Peru. He dreamed of shutting himself up in a cell-like workshop, and, after years of agony and ridicule, of emerging with an airplane new in design and devastating in speed.

Jimmie's room in the new house became a clutter of small machines as soon as he was settled. There was a radio crystal set with ear phones, a hand-powered magneto which operated a telegraph key, a brass telescope and innumerable machines partly taken to pieces. Jimmie, too, had a secret repository, an oaken box fastened with a heavy padlock. In the box were: half a can of dynamite caps, an old revolver, a package of Melachrino cigarettes, three contraptions known as Merry Widows, a small flask of peach brandy, a paper knife shaped like a dagger, four bundles of letters from four different girls, sixteen lipsticks pilfered from dance partners, a box containing mementos of current loves—dried flowers, handkerchiefs and buttons, and most prized of all, a round garter covered with black lace. Jimmie had forgotten how he really got the garter. What he *did* remember was far more satisfactory anyway. He always locked his bedroom door before he unlocked the box.

In high school Jimmie's score of sinfulness had been equalled by many of his friends and easily passed by some. Soon after moving to the Pastures of Heaven, he found that his iniquities were unique. He came to regard himself as a reformed rake, but one not reformed beyond possible outbreak. It gave him a powerful advantage with the younger girls of the valley to have lived so fully. Jimmie was rather a handsome boy, lean and well made, dark of hair and eyes.

Manfred, the youngest boy, ordinarily called Manny, was a serious child of seven, whose face was pinched and drawn by adenoids. His parents knew about the adenoids; they had even talked of having them removed. Manny became terrified of the operation, and his mother, seeing this, had used it as a deterrent threat when he was bad. Now, a mention of having his adenoids removed made Manny hysterical with terror. Mr. and Mrs. Munroe considered him a thoughtful child, perhaps a genius. He played usually by himself, or sat for hours staring into space, "dreaming," his mother said. They would not know for some years that he was subnormal, his brain development arrested by his adenoidal condition. Ordinarily Manny was a good child, tractable and easily terrified into obedience, but, if he were terrified a little too much, an hysteria resulted that robbed him of his self-control and even of a sense of self-preservation. He had been known to beat his forehead on the floor until the blood ran into his eyes.

Bert Munroe came to the Pastures of Heaven because he was tired of battling with a force which invariably defeated him. He had engaged in many enterprises and every one had failed, not through any shortcoming on Bert's part, but through mishaps, which, if taken alone, were accidents. Bert saw all the accidents together and they seemed to him the acts of a Fate malignant to his success. He was tired of fighting the nameless thing that stopped every avenue to success. Bert was only fifty-five, but he wanted to rest; he was half convinced that a curse rested upon him.

Years ago he opened a garage on the edge of a town. Business was good; money began to roll in. When he considered himself safe, the state highway came through on another street and left him stranded without business. He sold the garage a year or so later and opened a grocery store. Again he was successful. He paid off his indebtedness and began to put money in the bank. A chain grocery crowded up against him, opened a price war and forced him from business. Bert was a sensitive man. Such things as these had happened to him a dozen times. Just when his success seemed permanent, the curse struck him. His self-confidence dwindled. When the war broke out his spirit was nearly gone. He knew there was money to be made from the war, but he was afraid, after having been beaten so often.

He had to reassure himself a great deal before he made his first contract for beans in the field. In the first year of business, he made fifty thousand dollars, the second year two hundred thousand. The third year he contracted for thousands of acres of beans before they were even planted. By his contracts, he guaranteed to pay ten cents a pound for the crops. He could sell all the beans he could get for eighteen cents a pound. The war ended in November, and he sold his crop for four cents a pound. He had a little less money than when he started.

This time he was sure of the curse. His spirit was so badly broken that he didn't leave his house very often. He worked in the garden, planted a few vegetables and brooded over the enmity of his fate. Slowly, over a period of stagnant years, a nostalgia for the soil grew in him. In farming, he thought, lay the only line of endeavor that did not cross with his fate. He thought perhaps he could find rest and security on a little farm.

The Battle place was offered for sale by a Monterey realty company. Bert looked at the farm, saw the changes that could be made, and bought it. At first his family opposed the move, but, when he had cleaned the yard, installed electricity and a telephone in the house, and made it comfortable with new furniture, they were almost enthusiastic about it. Mrs. Munroe thought any change desirable that would stop Bert's moping in the yard in Monterey.

The moment he had bought the farm, Bert felt free. The doom was gone. He knew he was safe from his curse. Within a month his shoulders straightened, and his face lost its haunted look. He became an enthusiastic farmer; he read exhaustively on farming methods, hired a helper and worked from morning until night. Every day was a new excitement to him. Every seed sprouting out of the ground seemed to renew a promise of immunity to him. He was happy, and because he was confident again, he began to make friends in the valley and to entrench his position.

It is a difficult thing and one requiring great tact quickly to become accepted in a rural community. The people of the valley had watched the advent of the Munroe family with a little animosity. The Battle farm was haunted. They had always considered it so, even those who laughed at the idea. Now a man came along and proved them wrong. More than that, he changed the face of the countryside by removing the accursed farm and substituting a harmless and fertile farm. The people were used to the Battle place as it was. Secretly they resented the change.

That Bert could remove this animosity was remarkable. Within three months he had become a part of the valley, a solid man, a neighbour. He borrowed tools and had tools borrowed from him. At the end of six months he was elected a member of the school board. To a large extent Bert's own happiness at being free of his Furies made the people like him. In addition he was a kindly man; he enjoyed doing favours for his friends, and, more important, he had no hesitancy in asking favours.

At the store he explained his position to a group of farmers, and they admired the honesty of his explanation. It was soon after he had come to the valley. T. B. Allen asked his old question,

"We always kind of thought that place was cursed. Lots of funny things have happened there. Seen any ghosts yet?"

Bert laughed. "If you take away all the food from a place, the rats will leave," he said. "I took all the oldness and darkness away from that place. That's what ghosts live on."

"You sure made a nice looking place of it," Allen admitted. "There ain't a better place in the Pastures when it's kept up."

Bert had been frowning soberly as a new thought began to work in his mind. "I've had a lot of bad luck," he said. "I've been in a lot of businesses and every one turned out bad.

When I came down here, I had a kind of an idea that I was under a curse." Suddenly he laughed delightedly at the thought that had come to him. "And what do I do? First thing out of the box, I buy a place that's supposed to be under a curse. Well, I just happened to think, maybe my curse and the farm's curse got to fighting and killed each other off. I'm dead certain they've gone, anyway."

The men laughed with him. T. B. Allen whacked his hand down on the counter. "That's a good one," he cried. "But here's a better one. Maybe your curse and the farm's curse has mated and gone into a gopher hole like a pair of rattlesnakes. Maybe there'll be a lot of baby curses crawling around the Pastures the first thing we know."

The gathered men roared with laughter at that, and T. B. Allen memorized the whole scene so he could repeat it. It was almost like the talk in a play, he thought.

III

EDWARD WICKS lived in a small, gloomy house on the edge of the county road in the Pastures of Heaven. Behind the house there was a peach orchard and a large vegetable garden. While Edward Wicks took care of the peaches, his wife and beautiful daughter cultivated the garden and got the peas and string beans and early strawberries ready to be sold in Monterey.

Edward Wicks had a blunt, brown face and small, cold eyes almost devoid of lashes. He was known as the trickiest man in the valley. He drove hard deals and was never so happy as when he could force a few cents more out of his peaches than his neighbours did. When he could, he cheated ethically in horse trades, and because of his acuteness he gained the respect of the community, but strangely became no richer. However, he liked to pretend that he was laying away money in securities. At school board meetings he asked the advice of the other members about various bonds, and in this way managed to give them the impression that his savings were considerable. The people of the valley called him "Shark" Wicks.

"Shark?" they said. "Oh, I'd guess he was worth around twenty thousand, maybe more. He's nobody's fool."

And the truth was that Shark had never had more than five hundred dollars at one time in his life.

Shark's greatest pleasure came of being considered a wealthy man. Indeed, he enjoyed it so much that the wealth itself became real to him. Setting his imaginary fortune at fifty thousand dollars, he kept a ledger in which he calculated his interest and entered records of his various investments. These manipulations were the first joy of his life.

An oil company was formed in Salinas with the purpose of boring a well in the southern part of Monterey county. When he heard of it, Shark walked over to the farm of John Whiteside to discuss the value of its stock. "I been wondering about that South County Oil Company," he said.

"Well, the geologist's report sounds good," said John Whiteside. "I have always heard that there was oil in that section.

17

I heard it years ago." John Whiteside was often consulted in such matters. "Of course I wouldn't put too much into it."

Shark creased his lower lip with his fingers and pondered for a moment. "I been turning it over in my mind," he said. "It looks like a pretty good proposition to me. I got about ten thousand lying around that ain't bringing in what it should. I guess I'd better look into it pretty carefully. Just thought I'd see what your opinion was."

But Shark's mind was already made up. When he got home, he took down the ledger and withdrew ten thousand dollars from his imaginary bank account. Then he entered one thousand shares of Southern County Oil Company stock to his list of securities. From that day on he watched the stock lists feverishly. When the price rose a little, he went about whistling monotonously, and when the price dropped, he felt a lump of apprehension forming in his throat. At length, when there came a quick rise in the price of South County, Shark was so elated that he went to the Pastures of Heaven General Store and bought a black marble mantel clock with onyx columns on either side of the dial and a bronze horse to go on top of it. The men in the store looked wise and whispered that Shark was about to make a killing.

A week later the stock dropped out of sight and the company disappeared. The moment he heard the news, Shark dragged out his ledger and entered the fact that he had sold his shares the day before the break, had sold with a two thousand dollar profit.

Pat Humbert, driving back from Monterey, stopped his car on the county road in front of Shark's house. "I heard you got washed out in that South County stock," he observed.

Shark smiled contentedly. "What do you think I am, Pat? I sold out two days ago. You ought to know as well as the next man that I ain't a sucker. I knew that stock was bum, but I also knew it would take a rise so the backers could get out whole. When they unloaded, I did too."

"The hell you did!" said Pat admiringly. And when he went into the General Store he passed the information on. Men nodded their heads and made new guesses at the amount of Shark's money. They admitted they'd hate to come up against him in a business deal.

At this time Shark borrowed four hundred dollars from a Monterey bank and bought a second-hand Fordson tractor.

Gradually his reputation for good judgment and foresight became so great that no man in the Pastures of Heaven thought of buying a bond or a piece of land or even a horse without first consulting Shark Wicks. With each of his admirers Shark went carefully into the problem and ended by giving startlingly good advice.

In a few years his ledger showed that he had accumulated one hundred and twenty-five thousand dollars through sagacious investing. When his neighbours saw that he lived like a poor man, they respected him the more because his riches did not turn his head. He was nobody's fool. His wife and beautiful daughter still cared for the vegetables and prepared them for sale in Monterey, while Shark attended to the thousand duties of the orchard.

In Shark's life there had been no literary romance. At nineteen he took Katherine Mullock to three dances because she was available. This started the machine of precedent and he married her because her family and all of the neighbours expected it. Katherine was not pretty, but she had the firm freshness of a new weed, and the bridling vigour of a young mare. After her marriage she lost her vigour and her freshness as a flower does once it has received pollen. Her face sagged, her hips broadened, and she entered into her second destiny, that of work.

In his treatment of her, Shark was neither tender nor cruel. He governed her with the same gentle inflexibility he used on horses. Cruelty would have seemed to him as foolish as indulgence. He never talked to her as to human, never spoke of his hopes or thoughts or failures, of his paper wealth nor of the peach crop. Katherine would have been puzzled and worried if he had. Her life was sufficiently complicated without the added burden of another's thoughts and problems.

The brown Wicks house was the only unbeautiful thing on the farm. The trash and litter of nature disappears into the ground with the passing of each year, but man's litter has more permanence. The yard was strewn with old sacks, with papers, bits of broken glass and tangles of baling wire. The only place on the farm where grass and flowers would not grow was the hard-packed dirt around the house, dirt made sterile and unfriendly by emptied tubs of soapy water. Shark irrigated his orchard, but he could see no reason for wasting good water around the house.

When Alice was born, the women of the Pastures of Heaven came herding into Shark's house prepared to exclaim that it was a pretty baby. When they saw it was a beautiful baby, they did not know what to say. Those feminine exclamations of delight designed to reassure young mothers that the horrible reptilian creatures in their arms are human and will not grow up to be monstrosities, lost their meaning. Furthermore, Katherine had looked at her child with eyes untainted by the artificial enthusiasm with which most women smother their disappointments. When Katherine had seen that the baby was beautiful, she was filled with wonder and with awe and misgiving. The fact of Alice's beauty was too marvellous to be without retribution. Pretty babies, Katherine said to herself, usually turned out ugly men and women. By saying it, she beat off some of the misgiving as though she had apprehended Fate at its tricks and robbed it of potency by her foreknowledge.

On that first day of visiting, Shark heard one of the women say to another in a tone of unbelief, "But it really is a pretty baby. How do you suppose it *could* be so pretty?"

Shark went back to the bedroom and looked long at his little daughter. Out in the orchard he pondered over the matter. The baby really was beautiful. It was foolish to think that he or Katherine or any of their relatives had anything to do with it for they were all homely even as ordinary people go. Clearly a very precious thing had been given to him, and, since precious things were universally coveted, Alice must be protected. Shark believed in God when he thought of it, of course, as that shadowy being who did everything he could not understand.

Alice grew and became more and more beautiful. Her skin was as lucent and rich as poppies; her black hair had the soft crispness of fern stems, her eyes were misty skies of promise. One looked into the child's serious eyes and started forward thinking—"Something is in there that I know, something I seem to remember sharply, or something I have spent all my life searching for." Then Alice turned her head. "Why! It is only a lovely little girl."

Shark saw this recognition take place in many people. He saw men blush when they looked at her, saw little boys fight like tigers when she was about.

He thought he read covetousness in every male face. Often when he was working in the orchard he tortured himself by imagining scenes wherein gypsies stole the little girl. A dozen times a day he cautioned her against dangerous things: the hind heels of horses, the highness of fences, the danger that lurked in gullies and the absolute suicide of crossing a road without carefully looking for approaching automobiles. Every neighbour, every pedlar, and worst of all, every stranger he looked upon as a possible kidnapper. When tramps were reported in the Pastures of Heaven he never let the little girl out of his sight. Picnickers wondered at Shark's ferocity in ordering them off his land.

As for Katherine, the constantly increasing beauty of Alice augmented her misgiving. Destiny was waiting to strike, and that could only mean that destiny was storing strength for a more violent blow. She became the slave of her daughter, hovered about and did little services such as one might accord an invalid who is soon to die.

In spite of the worship of the Wicks' for their child and their fears for her safety and their miser-like gloating over her beauty, they both knew that their lovely daughter was an incredibly stupid, dull and backward little girl. In Shark, this knowledge only added to his fears, for he was convinced that she could not take care of herself and would become an easy prey to anyone who wished to make off with her. But to Katherine, Alice's stupidity was a pleasant thing since it presented so many means by which her mother could help her. By helping, Katherine proved a superiority, and cut down to some extent the great gap between them. Katherine was glad of every weakness in her daughter since each one made her feel closer and more worthy.

When Alice turned fourteen a new responsibility was added to the many her father felt concerning her. Before that time Shark had only feared her loss or disfigurement, but after that he was terrified at the thought of her loss of chastity. Little by little, through much dwelling on the subject, this last fear absorbed the other two. He came to regard the possible defloration of his daughter as both loss and disfigurement. From that time on he was uncomfortable and suspicious when any man or boy was near the farm.

The subject became a nightmare to him. Over and over he cautioned his wife never to let Alice out of her sight. "You just can't tell what might happen," he repeated, his pale eyes flaring with suspicions. "You just can't tell what might happen." His daughter's mental inadequateness greatly increased his fear. Anyone, he thought, might ruin her. Anyone at all who was left alone with her might misuse her. And she couldn't protect herself, because she was so stupid. No man ever guarded his prize bitch when she was in heat more closely than Shark watched his daughter.

After a time Shark was no longer satisfied with her purity unless he had been assured of it. Each month he pestered his wife. He knew the dates better than she did. "Is she all right?" he asked wolfishly.

Katherine answered contemptuously, "Not yet."

A few hours later—"Is she all right?"

He kept this up until at last Katherine answered, "Of course she's all right. What did you think?"

This answer satisfied Shark for a month, but it did not decrease his watchfulness. The chastity was intact, therefore it was still to be guarded.

Shark knew that some time Alice would want to be married, but, often as the thought came to him, he put it away and tried to forget it, for he regarded her marriage with no less repugnance than her seduction. She was a precious thing, to be watched and preserved. To him it was not a moral problem, but an aesthetic one. Once she was deflorated, she would no longer be the precious thing he treasured so. He did not love her as a father loves a child. Rather he hoarded her, and gloated over the possession of a fine, unique thing. Gradually, as he asked his question—"Is she all right?"—month by month, this chastity came to symbolize her health, her preservation, her intactness.

One day when Alice was sixteen, Shark went to his wife

with a worried look on his face. "You know we really can't tell if she's all right—that is—we couldn't really be sure unless we took her to a doctor."

For a moment Katherine stared at him, trying to realize what the words meant. Then she lost her temper for the first time in her life. "You're a dirty, suspicious skunk," she told him. "You get out of here! And if you ever talk about it again, I'll—I'll go away."

Shark was a little astonished, but not frightened, at her outburst. He did, however, give up the idea of a medical examination, and merely contented himself with his monthly question.

Meanwhile, Shark's ledger fortune continued to grow. Every night, after Katherine and Alice had gone to bed, he took down the thick book and opened it under the hanging lamp. Then his pale eyes narrowed and his blunt face took on a crafty look while he planned his investments and calculated his interest. His lips moved slightly, for now he was telephoning an order for stock. A stern and yet sorrowful look crossed his face when he foreclosed a mortgage on a good farm. "I hate to do this," he whispered. "You folks got to realize it's just business."

Shark wetted his pen in the ink bottle and entered the fact of the foreclosure in his ledger. "Lettuce," he mused. "Everybody's putting in lettuce. The market's going to be flooded. Seems to me I might put in potatoes and make some money. That's fine bottom land." He noted in the book the planting of three hundred acres of potatoes. His eye traveled along the line. Thirty thousand dollars lay in the bank just drawing bank interest. It seemed a shame. The money was practically idle. A frown of concentration settled over his eyes. He wondered how San Jose Building and Loan was. It paid six per cent. It wouldn't do to rush into it blindly without investigating the company. As he closed the ledger for the night, Shark determined to talk to John Whiteside about it. Sometimes those companies went broke, the officers absconded, he thought uneasily.

Before the Munroe family moved into the valley, Shark suspected all men and boys of evil intent toward Alice, but when once he had set eyes on young Jimmie Munroe, his fear and suspicion narrowed until it had all settled upon the sophisticated Jimmie. The boy was lean and handsome of face, his mouth was well developed and sensual, and his eyes shone with that insulting cockiness high school boys assume. Jimmie was said to drink gin; he wore town clothes of wool—never overalls. His hair shone with oil, and his whole manner and posture were of a rakishness that set the girls of the Pastures of Heaven giggling and squirming with admiration and embarrassment. Jimmie watched the girls with quiet, cynical eyes, and tried to appear dissipated for their benefit. He knew that young girls are vastly attracted to young men with pasts. Jimmie had a past. He had been drunk several times at the Riverside Dance Palace; he had kissed at least a hundred girls, and, on three occasions, he had sinful adventures in the willows by the Salinas River. Jimmie tried to make his face confess his vicious life, but, fearing that his appearance was not enough, he set free a number of mischievous little rumours that darted about the Pastures of Heaven with flattering speed.

Shark Wicks heard the rumours. In Shark there grew up a hatred of Jimmie Munroe that was born of fear of Jimmie's way with women. What chance, Shark thought, would beautiful, stupid Alice have against one so steeped in knowledge of worldliness?

Before Alice had ever seen the boy, Shark forbade her to see him. He spoke with such vehemence that a mild interest was aroused in the dull brain of the girl.

"Don't you ever let me catch you talking to that Jimmie Munroe," he told her.

"Who's Jimmie Munroe, Papa?"

"Never you mind who he is. Just don't let me catch you talking to him. You hear me! Why! I'll skin you alive if you even look at him."

Shark had never laid a hand on Alice for the same reason that he would not have whipped a Dresden vase. He even hesitated to caress her for fear of leaving a mark. Punishment was never necessary. Alice had always been a good and tractable child. Badness must originate in an idea or an ambition. She had never experienced either.

And again—"You haven't been talking to that Jimmie Munroe, have you?"

"No, Papa."

"Well just don't let me catch you at it."

After a number of repetitions of this order, a conviction crept into the thickened cells of Alice's brain that she would really like to see Jimmie Munroe. She even had a dream about him, which shows how deeply she was stirred. Alice very rarely dreamed about anything. In her dream, a man who looked like the Indian on her room calendar, and whose name was Jimmie, drove up in a shiny automobile and gave her a large juicy peach. When she bit into the peach, the juice ran down her chin and embarrassed her. Then her mother awakened her for she was snoring. Katherine was glad her daughter snored. It was one of the equaling imperfections. But at the same time it was not ladylike.

Shark Wicks received a telegram. "Aunt Nellie passed away last night. Funeral Saturday." He got into his Ford and drove to the farm of John Whiteside to say he couldn't attend the school board meeting. John Whiteside was clerk of the board. Before he left, Shark looked worried for a moment and then said, "I been wanting to ask you what you thought about that San Jose Building and Loan Company."

John Whiteside smiled. "I don't know much about that particular company," he said.

"Well, I've got thirty thousand lying in the bank drawing three per cent. I thought I could turn a little more interest than that if I looked around."

John Whiteside pursed his lips and blew softly and tapped the stream of air with his forefinger. "Offhand, I'd say Building and Loan was your best bet."

"Oh, that ain't my way of doing business. I don't want bets," Shark cut in. "If I can't see a sure profit in a thing, I won't go into it. Too many people bet."

"That was only a manner of speaking, Mr. Wicks. Few Building and Loan Companies go under. And they pay good interest."

"I'll look into it anyway," Shark decided. "I'm going up to

Oakland for Aunt Nellie's funeral, and I'll just stop off a few hours in San Jose and look into this company."

At the Pastures of Heaven General Store that night there were new guesses made at the amount of Shark's wealth, for Shark had asked the advice of several men.

"Well anyway, there's one thing you can say," T. B. Allen concluded, "Shark Wicks is nobody's fool. He'll ask a man's advice as well as the next one, but he's not going to take anybody's say-so until he looks into it himself."

"Oh, he's nobody's fool," the gathering concurred.

Shark went to Oakland on Saturday morning, leaving his wife and daughter alone for the first time in his life. On Saturday evening Tom Breman called by to take Katherine and Alice to a dance at the schoolhouse.

"Oh, I don't think Mr. Wicks would like it," Katherine said, in a thrilled, frightened tone.

"He didn't tell you not to go, did he?"

"No, but—he's never been away before. I don't think he'd like it."

"He just never thought of it," Tom Breman assured her. "Come on! Get your things on."

"Let's go, Ma," said Alice.

Katherine knew her daughter could make such an easy decision because she was too stupid to be afraid. Alice was no judge of consequences. She couldn't think of the weeks of torturing conversation that would follow when Shark returned. Katherine could hear him already. "I don't see why you'd *want* to go when I wasn't here. When I left, I kind of thought you two would look after the place, and the first thing you did was run off to a dance." And then the questions—"Who did Alice dance with? Well—what did he say? Why didn't you hear it? You ought to of heard." There would be no anger on Shark's part, but for weeks and weeks he would talk about it, just keep talking about it until she hated the whole subject of dances. And when the right time of the month came around, his questions would buzz like mosquitoes, until he was sure Alice wasn't going to have a baby. Katherine didn't think it worth the fun of going to the dance if she had to listen to all the fuss afterwards.

"Let's go, Ma," Alice begged her. "We never went any place alone in our lives."

A wave of pity arose in Katherine. The poor girl had never had a moment of privacy in her life. She had never talked nonsense with a boy because her father would not let her out of earshot.

"All right," she decided breathlessly. "If Mr. Breman will wait 'til we get ready, we *will* go." She felt very brave to be encouraging Shark's unease.

Too great beauty is almost as great a disadvantage to a country girl as ugliness is. When the country boys looked at Alice, their throats tightened, their hands and feet grew restless and huge, and their necks turned red. Nothing could force them to talk to her nor to dance with her. Instead, they danced furiously with less beautiful girls, became as noisy as self-conscious children and showed off frantically. When her head was turned, they peeked at Alice, but when she looked at them, they strove to give an impression of unawareness of her presence. Alice, who had always been treated in this way, was fairly unconscious of her beauty. She was almost resigned to the status of a wall flower at the dances.

Jimmie Munroe was leaning against a wall with elegant nonchalance and superb ennui when Katherine and Alice entered the schoolhouse door. Jimmie's trousers had twenty-seven inch bottoms, his patent leather shoes were as square across the toes as bricks. A black jazz-bow tie fluttered at the neck of a white silk shirt, and his hair lay glitteringly on his head. Jimmie was a town boy. He swooped like a lazy hawk. Before Alice had taken off her coat he was beside her. In the tired voice he had acquired in high school he demanded, "Dancing, baby?"

"Huh?" said Alice.

"How'd you like to dance with me?"

"Dance, you mean?" Alice turned her smoky, promiseful eyes on him, and the stupid question became humorous and delightful, and at the same time it hinted at other things which moved and excited even the cynical Jimmie.

"Dance?" he thought she asked. "Only dance?" And in spite of his high school training, Jimmie's throat tightened, his feet and hands shifted nervously and the blood rose to his neck.

Alice turned to her mother who was already talking with Mrs. Breman that peculiar culinary gabble of housekeepers. "Ma," said Alice, "can I dance?"

Katherine smiled. "Go on," she said, and then, "Enjoy yourself for once."

Jimmie found that Alice danced badly. When the music stopped, "It's hot in here, isn't it? Let's stroll outside," he suggested. And he led her out under the willow trees in the schoolhouse yard.

Meanwhile a woman who had been standing on the porch of the school house went inside and whispered in Katherine's ear. Katherine started up and hurried outside. "Alice!" she called wildly. "Alice, you come right here!"

When the wayward two appeared out of the shadows, Katherine turned on Jimmie. "You keep away, do you hear me? You keep away from this girl or you'll get into trouble."

Jimmie's manhood melted. He felt like a sent-home child. He hated it, but he couldn't override it.

Katherine led her daughter into the schoolhouse again. "Didn't your father tell you to keep away from Jimmie Munroe? Didn't he?" she demanded. Katherine was terrified.

"Was that him?" Alice whispered.

"Sure it was. What were you two doing out there?"

"Kissing," said Alice in an awed voice.

Katherine's mouth dropped open. "Oh, Lord!" she said. "Oh, Lord, what shall I do?"

"Is it bad, Ma?"

Katherine frowned. "No—no, of course it's not bad," she cried. "It's—good. But don't you ever let your father know about it. Don't you tell him even if he asks you! He—why, he'd go crazy. And you sit here beside me the rest of the evening, and don't you see Jimmie Munroe any more, will you? Maybe your father won't hear about it. Oh, Lord, I hope he don't hear about it!"

On Monday Shark Wicks got off the evening train in Salinas, and took a bus to the cross-road which ran from the highway into the Pastures of Heaven. Shark clutched his bag and began the four mile walk home.

The night was clear and sweet and heavy with stars. The faint mysterious sounds of the hills welcomed him home and set up reveries in his head so that he forgot his footsteps.

He had been pleased with the funeral. The flowers were nice, and there were so many of them. The weeping of the women and the solemn tip-toeing of the men had set up a gentle sorrow in Shark which was far from unpleasant. Even the profound ritual of the church, which no one understands nor listens to, had been a drug which poured sweet mysterious juices into his body and his brain. The church opened and closed over him for an hour, and out of his contact he had brought the drowsy peace of strong flowers and drifting incense, and the glow of relationship with eternity. These things were wrought in him by the huge simplicity of the burial.

Shark had never known his Aunt Nellie very well, but he had thoroughly enjoyed her funeral. In some way his relatives had heard of his wealth, for they treated him with deference and dignity. Now, as he walked home, he thought of these things again and his pleasure speeded up the time, shortened the road and brought him quickly to the Pastures of Heaven General Store. Shark went in, for he knew he could find someone in the store who would report on the valley and its affairs during his absence.

T. B. Allen, the proprietor, knew everything that happened, and also he enhanced the interest of every bit of news by simulating a reluctance to tell it. The most stupid piece of gossip became exciting when old T. B. had it to tell.

No one but the owner was in the store when Shark entered. T. B. let down his chair-back from the wall, and his eyes sparkled with interest.

"Hear you been away," he suggested in a tone that invited confidence.

"Been up to Oakland," said Shark. "I had to go to a funeral. Thought I might as well do some business at the same time."

T. B. waited as long for elaboration as he thought decent. "Anything happen, Shark?"

"Well, I don't know if you'd call it that. I was looking into a company."

"Put any money in?" T. B. asked respectfully.

"Some."

Both men looked at the floor.

"Anything happen while I was gone?"

Immediately a look of reluctance came over the face of the old man. One read a dislike for saying just what had happened, a natural aversion for scandal. "Dance at the schoolhouse," he admitted at last.

"Yes, I knew about that."

T. B. squirmed. Apparently there was a struggle going on in his mind. Should he tell Shark what he knew, for Shark's own good, or should he keep all knowledge to himself. Shark watched the struggle with interest. He had seen others like it many times before.

"Well, what is it?" he prodded.

"Hear there might be a wedding pretty soon."

"Yeah? Who?"

"Well, pretty close to home, I guess."

"Who?" Shark asked again.

T. B. struggled vainly and lost. "You," he admitted.

Shark chuckled. "Me?"

"Alice."

Shark stiffened and stared at the old man. Then he stepped forward and stood over him threateningly. "What do you mean? Tell me what you mean—you!"

T. B. knew he had overstepped. He cowered away from Shark. "Now don't, Mr. Wicks! Don't you do nothing!"

"Tell me what you mean! Tell me everything." Shark grasped T. B. by the shoulder and shook him fiercely.

"Well, it was only at the dance—just at the dance."

"Alice was at the dance?"

"Uh-huh."

"What was she doing there?"

"I don't know. I mean, nothing."

Shark pulled him out of his chair and stood him roughly on his fumbling feet. "Tell me!" he demanded.

The old man whimpered. "She just walked out in the yard with Jimmie Munroe."

Shark had both of the shoulders now. He shook the terrified storekeeper like a sack. "Tell me! What did they do?"

"I don't know, Mr. Wicks."

"Tell me."

"Well, Miss Burke—Miss Burke said—they was kissing."

Shark dropped the sack and sat down. He was appalled with a sense of loss. While he glared at T. B. Allen, his brain fought with the problem of his daughter's impurity. It did not occur to him that the passage had stopped with a kiss. Shark moved his head and his eyes roved helplessly around the store. T. B. saw his eyes pass over the glass fronted gun case.

"Don't you do nothing, Shark," he cried. "Them guns ain't yours."

Shark hadn't seen the guns at all, but now that his attention was directed toward them, he leaped up, threw open the sliding glass door and took out a heavy rifle. He tore off the price tag and tossed a box of cartridges into his pocket. Then, without a glance at the storekeeper, he strode out into the dark. And old T. B. was at the telephone before Shark's quick footsteps had died away into the night.

As Shark walked quickly along toward the Munroe place, his thoughts raced hopelessly. He was sure of one thing, though, now that he had walked a little; he didn't want to kill Jimmie Munroe. He hadn't even been thinking about shooting him until the storekeeper suggested the idea. Then he had acted upon it without thinking. What could he do now? He tried to picture what he would do when he came to the Munroe house. Perhaps he would have to shoot Jimmie Munroe. Maybe things would fall out in a way that would force him to commit murder to maintain his dignity in the Pastures of Heaven.

Shark heard a car coming and stepped into the brush while it roared by, with a wide open throttle. He would be getting there pretty soon, and he didn't hate Jimmie Munroe. He didn't hate anything except the hollow feeling that had entered him when he heard of Alice's loss of virtue. Now he could only think of his daughter as one who was dead.

Ahead of him, he could see the lights of the Munroe house now. And Shark knew that he couldn't shoot Jimmie. Even if he were laughed at he couldn't shoot the boy. There was no murder in him. He decided that he would look in at the gate and then go along home. Maybe people would laugh at him, but he simply could not shoot anybody.

Suddenly a man stepped from the shadow of a bush and shouted at him. "Put down that gun, Wicks, and put up your hands."

Shark laid the rifle on the ground with a kind of tired obedience. He recognized the voice of the deputy sheriff. "Hello, Jack," he said.

Then there were people all around him. Shark saw Jimmie's frightened face in the background. Bert Munroe was frightened too. He said, "What did you want to shoot Jimmie for? He didn't hurt you. Old T. B. phoned me. I've got to put you where you can't do any harm."

"You can't jail him," the deputy said. "He hasn't done anything. Only thing you can do is put him under bond to keep the peace."

"Is that so? I guess I have to do that then." Bert's voice was trembling.

"You better ask for a big bond," the deputy went on. "Shark's a pretty rich man. Come on! We'll take him into Salinas now, and you can make your complaint."

The next morning Shark Wicks walked listlessly into his house and lay down on his bed. His eyes were dull and tired but he kept them open. His arms lay as loosely as a corpse's arms beside him. Hour after hour he lay there.

Katherine, from the vegetable garden, saw him go into the house. She was bitterly glad of the slump of his shoulders and of his head's weak carriage, but when she went in to get luncheon ready, she walked on her toes and cautioned Alice to move quietly.

At three o'clock Katherine looked in at the bedroom door. "Alice was all right," she said. "You should have asked me before you did anything."

Shark did not answer her nor change his position.

"Don't you believe me?" The loss of vitality in her husband frightened her. "If you don't believe me, we can get a doctor. I'll send for one right now if you don't believe me."

Shark's head did not turn. "I believe you," he said lifelessly.

As Katherine stood in the doorway, a feeling she had never experienced crept into her. She did a thing she had never contemplated in her life. A warm genius moved in her. Katherine sat down on the edge of the bed and with a sure hand, took Shark's head on her lap. This was instinct, and the same sure, strong instinct set her hand to stroking Shark's forehead. His body seemed boneless with defeat.

Shark's eyes did not move from the ceiling, but under the stroking, he began to talk brokenly. "I haven't any money," his monotonous voice said. "They took me in and asked for a ten thousand dollar bond. I had to tell the judge. They all heard. They all know—I haven't any money. I never had any. Do you understand? That ledger was nothing but a lie. Every bit of it was lies. I made it all up. Now everybody knows. I had to tell the judge."

Katherine stroked his head gently and the great genius continued to grow in her. She felt larger than the world. The whole world lay in her lap and she comforted it. Pity seemed to make her huge in stature. Her soothing breasts yearned toward the woe of the world.

"I didn't mean to hurt anyone," Shark went on. "I wouldn't have shot Jimmie. They caught me before I could turn back. They thought I meant to kill him. And now everybody knows. I haven't any money." He lay limply and stared upward.

Suddenly the genius in Katherine became power and the power gushed in her body and flooded her. In a moment she knew what she was and what she could do. She was exultantly happy and very beautiful. "You've had no chance," she said softly. "All of your life you've been out on this old farm and there's been no chance for you. How do you know you can't make money? I think you can. I know you can."

She had known she could do this. As she sat there the knowledge of her power had been born in her, and she knew that all of her life was directed at this one moment. In this moment she was a goddess, a singer of destiny. It did not surprise her when his body gradually stiffened. She continued to stroke his forehead.

"We'll go out of here," she chanted. "We'll sell this ranch and go away from here. Then you'll get the chance you never had. You'll see. I know what you are. I believe in you."

Shark's eyes lost their awful lifelessness. His body found

strength to turn itself. He looked at Katherine and saw how beautiful she was in this moment, and, as he looked, her genius passed into him. Shark pressed his head tightly against her knees.

She lowered her head and looked at him. She was frightened now the power was leaving her. Suddenly Shark sat up on the bed. He had forgotten Katherine, but his eyes shone with the energy she had given him.

"I'll go soon," he cried. "I'll go just as soon as I can sell the ranch. Then I'll get in a few licks. I'll get my chance then. I'll show people what I am."

IV

THE ORIGIN of Tularecito is cast in obscurity, while his discovery is a myth which the folks of the Pastures of Heaven refuse to believe, just as they refuse to believe in ghosts.

Franklin Gomez had a hired man, a Mexican Indian named Pancho, and nothing else. Once every three months, Pancho took his savings and drove into Monterey to confess his sins, to do his penance, and be shriven and to get drunk, in the order named. If he managed to stay out of jail, Pancho got into his buggy and went to sleep when the saloons closed. The horse pulled him home, arriving just before daylight, and in time for Pancho to have breakfast and go to work. Pancho was always asleep when he arrived; that is why he created so much interest on the ranch when, one morning, he drove into the corral at a gallop, not only awake, but shouting at the top of his voice.

Franklin Gomez put on his clothes and went out to interview his ranch hand. The story, when it was stretched out of its tangle of incoherencies, was this: Pancho had been driving home, very sober as always. Up near the Blake place, he heard a baby crying in the sage brush beside the road. He stopped the horse and went to investigate, for one did not often come upon babies like that. And sure enough he found a tiny child lying in a clear place in the sage. It was about three months old by the size of it, Pancho thought. He picked it up and lighted a match to see just what kind of a thing he had found, when—horror of horrors!—the baby winked maliciously and said in a deep voice, "Look! I have very sharp teeth." Pancho did not look. He flung the thing from him, leaped into his buggy and galloped for home, beating the old horse with the butt end of the whip and howling like a dog.

Franklin Gomez pulled his whiskers a good deal. Pancho's nature, he considered, was not hysterical even under the influence of liquor. The fact that he had awakened at all rather proved there must be something in the brush. In the end, Franklin Gomez had a horse saddled, rode out and brought in the baby. It did not speak again for nearly three years; nor, on inspection, did it have any teeth, but neither of these facts convinced Pancho that it did not make that first ferocious remark.

The baby had short, chubby arms, and long, loose-jointed legs. Its large head sat without interval of neck between deformedly broad shoulders. The baby's flat face, together with its peculiar body, caused it automatically to be named Tularecito, Little Frog, although Franklin Gomez often called it Coyote, "for," he said, "there is in this boy's face that ancient wisdom one finds in the face of a coyote."

"But surely the legs, the arms, the shoulders, Señor," Pancho reminded him. And so Tularecito the name remained. It was never discovered who abandoned the misshapen little creature. Franklin Gomez accepted him into the patriarchate of his ranch, and Pancho took care of him. Pancho, however, could never lose a little fear of the boy. Neither the years nor a rigorous penance eradicated the effect of Tularecito's first utterance.

The boy grew rapidly, but after the fifth year his brain did not grow any more. At six Tularecito could do the work of a grown man. The long fingers of his hands were more dexterous and stronger than most men's fingers. On the ranch, they made use of the fingers of Tularecito. Hard knots could not long defy him. He had planting hands, tender fingers that never injured a young plant nor bruised the surfaces of a grafting limb. His merciless fingers could wring the head from a turkey gobbler without effort. Also Tularecito had an amusing gift. With his thumbnail he could carve remarkably correct animals from sandstone. Franklin Gomez kept many little effigies of coyotes and mountain lions, of chickens and squirrels, about the house. A two-foot image of a hovering hawk hung by wires from the ceiling of the dining room. Pancho, who had never quite considered the boy human, put his gift for carving in a growing category of diabolical traits definitely traceable to his supernatural origin.

While the people of the Pastures of Heaven did not believe in the diabolic origin of Tularecito, nevertheless they were uncomfortable in his presence. His eyes were ancient and dry; there was something trogloditic about his face. The great strength of his body and his strange and obscure gifts set him apart from other children and made men and women uneasy.

Only one thing could provoke anger in Tularecito. If any person, man, woman or child, handled carelessly or broke one of the products of his hands, he became furious. His eyes shone and he attacked the desecrator murderously. On three occasions when this had happened, Franklin Gomez tied his hands and feet and left him alone until his ordinary good nature returned.

Tularecito did not go to school when he was six. For five years thereafter, the county truant officer and the school superintendent sporadically worked on the case. Franklin Gomez agreed that he should go to school and even went so far as to start him off several times, but Tularecito never got there. He was afraid that school might prove unpleasant, so he simply disappeared for a day or so. It was not until the boy was eleven, with the shoulders of a weight lifter and the hands and forearms of a strangler that the concerted forces of the law gathered him in and put him in school.

As Franklin Gomez had known, Tularecito learned nothing at all, but immediately he gave evidence of a new gift. He could draw as well as he could carve in sandstone. When Miss Martin, the teacher, discovered his ability, she gave him a piece of chalk and told him to make a procession of animals around the blackboard. Tularecito worked long after school was dismissed, and the next morning an astounding parade was shown on the walls. All of the animals Tularecito had ever seen were there; all the birds of the hills flew above them. A rattlesnake crawled behind a cow; a coyote, his brush proudly aloft, sniffed at the heels of a pig. There were tomcats and goats, turtles and gophers, every one of them drawn with astonishing detail and veracity.

Miss Martin was overcome with the genius of Tularecito. She praised him before the class and gave a short lecture about each one of the creatures he had drawn. In her own mind she considered the glory that would come to her for discovering and fostering this genius.

"I can make lots more," Tularecito informed her.

Miss Martin patted his broad shoulder. "So you shall," she said. "You shall draw every day. It is a great gift that God has given you." Then she realized the importance of what she had just said. She leaned over and looked searchingly into his hard eyes while she repeated slowly, "It is a *great gift* that God has given you." Miss Martin glanced up at the clock and announced crisply, "Fourth grade arithmetic—at the board."

The fourth grade struggled out, seized erasers and began to remove the animals to make room for their numbers. They had not made two sweeps when Tularecito charged. It was a great day. Miss Martin, aided by the whole school, could not hold him down, for the enraged Tularecito had the strength of a man, and a madman at that. The ensuing battle wrecked the schoolroom, tipped over the desks, spilled rivers of ink, hurled bouquets of Teacher's flowers about the room. Miss Martin's clothes were torn to streamers, and the big boys, on whom the burden of the battle fell, were bruised and battered cruelly. Tularecito fought with hands, feet, teeth and head. He admitted no honorable rules and in the end he won. The whole school, with Miss Martin guarding its rear, fled from the building, leaving the enraged Tularecito in possession. When they were gone, he locked the door, wiped the blood out of his eyes and set to work to repair the animals that had been destroyed.

That night Miss Martin called on Franklin Gomez and demanded that the boy be whipped.

Gomez shrugged. "You really wish me to whip him, Miss Martin?"

The teacher's face was scratched; her mouth was bitter. "I certainly do," she said. "If you had seen what he did today, you wouldn't blame me. I tell you he needs a lesson."

Gomez shrugged again and called Tularecito from the bunk house. He took a heavy quirt down from the wall. Then, while Tularecito smiled blandly at Miss Martin, Franklin Gomez beat him severely across the back. Miss Martin's hand made involuntary motions of beating. When it was done, Tularecito felt himself over with long, exploring fingers, and still smiling, went back to the bunk house.

Miss Martin had watched the end of the punishment with horror. "Why, he's an animal," she cried. "It was just like whipping a dog."

Franklin Gomez permitted a slight trace of his contempt

for her to show on his face. "A dog would have cringed," he said. "Now you have seen, Miss Martin. You say he is an animal, but surely he is a good animal. You told him to make pictures and then you destroyed his pictures. Tularecito does not like that—"

Miss Martin tried to break in, but he hurried on.

"This Little Frog should not be going to school. He can work; he can do marvellous things with his hands, but he cannot learn to do the simple little things of the school. He is not crazy; he is one of those whom God has not quite finished.

"I told the Superintendent these things, and he said the law required Tularecito to go to school until he is eighteen years old. That is seven years from now. For seven years my Little Frog will sit in the first grade because the law says he must. It is out of my hands."

"He ought to be locked up," Miss Martin broke in. "This creature is dangerous. You should have seen him today."

"No, Miss Martin, he should be allowed to go free. He is not dangerous. No one can make a garden as he can. No one can milk so swiftly nor so gently. He is a good boy. He can break a mad horse without riding it; he can train a dog without whipping it, but the law says he must sit in the first grade repeating 'C-A-T, cat' for seven years. If he had been dangerous he could easily have killed me when I whipped him."

Miss Martin felt that there were things she did not understand and she hated Franklin Gomez because of them. She felt that she had been mean and he generous. When she got to school the next morning, she found Tularecito before her. Every possible space on the wall was covered with animals.

"You see?" he said, beaming over his shoulder at her. "Lots more. And I have a book with others yet, but there is no room for them on the wall."

Miss Martin did not erase the animals. Class work was done on paper, but at the end of the term she resigned her position, giving ill health as her reason.

Miss Morgan, the new teacher, was very young and very pretty; too young and dangerously pretty, the aged men of the valley thought. Some of the boys in the upper grades were seventeen years old. It was seriously doubted that a teacher so young and so pretty could keep any kind of order in the school.

She brought with her a breathless enthusiasm for her trade. The school was astounded, for it had been used to ageing spinsters whose faces seemed to reflect consistently tired feet. Miss Morgan enjoyed teaching and made school an exciting place where unusual things happened.

From the first Miss Morgan was vastly impressed with Tularecito. She knew all about him, had read books and taken courses about him. Having heard about the fight, she laid off a border around the top of the blackboards for him to fill with animals, and, when he had completed his parade, she bought with her own money a huge drawing pad and a soft pencil. After that he did not bother with spelling. Every day he laboured over his drawing board, and every afternoon presented the teacher with a marvellously wrought animal. She pinned his drawings to the schoolroom wall above the blackboards.

The pupils received Miss Morgan's innovations with enthusiasm. Classes became exciting, and even the boys who had made enviable reputations through teacher-baiting, grew less interested in the possible burning of the schoolhouse.

Miss Morgan introduced a practice that made the pupils adore her. Every afternoon she read to them for half an hour. She read by installments, *Ivanhoe* and *The Talisman*; fishing stories by Zane Grey, hunting stories of James Oliver Curwood; *The Sea Wolf*, *The Call of the Wild*—not baby stories about the little red hen and the fox and geese, but exciting, grown-up stories.

Miss Morgan read well. Even the tougher boys were won over until they never played hookey for fear of missing an installment, until they leaned forward gasping with interest.

But Tularecito continued his careful drawing, only pausing now and then to blink at the teacher and to try to understand how these distant accounts of the actions of strangers could be of interest to anyone. To him they were chronicles of actual events—else why were they written down. The stories were like the lessons. Tularecito did not listen to them.

After a time Miss Morgan felt that she had been humouring the older children too much. She herself liked fairy tales, liked to think of whole populations who believed in fairies and consequently saw them. Within the safe circle of her tried and erudite acquaintance, she often said that 'part of America's cultural starvation was due to its boorish and superstitious denial of the existence of fairies.' For a time she devoted the afternoon half hour to fairy tales.

Now a change came over Tularecito. Gradually, as Miss Morgan read about elves and brownies, fairies, pixies, and changelings, his interest centred and his busy pencil lay idly in his hand. Then she read about gnomes, and their lives and habits, and he dropped his pencil altogether and leaned toward the teacher to intercept her words.

After school Miss Morgan walked half a mile to the farm where she boarded. She liked to walk the way alone, cutting off thistle heads with a switch, or throwing stones into the brush to make the quail roar up. She thought she should get a bounding, inquisitive dog that could share her excitements, could understand the glamour of holes in the ground, and scattering pawsteps on dry leaves, of strange melancholy bird whistles and the gay smells that came secretly out of the earth.

One afternoon Miss Morgan scrambled high up the side of a chalk cliff to carve her initials on the white plane. On the way up she tore her finger on a thorn, and, instead of initials, she scratched: "Here I have been and left this part of me," and pressed her bloody finger against the absorbent chalk rock.

That night, in a letter, she wrote: "After the bare requisites to living and reproducing, man wants most to leave some record of himself, a proof, perhaps, that he has really existed. He leaves his proof on wood, on stone or on the lives of other people. This deep desire exists in everyone, from the boy who writes dirty words in a public toilet to the Buddha who etches his image in the race mind. Life is so unreal. I think that we seriously doubt that we exist and go about trying to prove that we do." She kept a copy of the letter.

On the afternoon when she had read about the gnomes, as she walked home, the grasses beside the road threshed about for a moment and the ugly head of Tularecito appeared.

"Oh! You frightened me," Miss Morgan cried. "You shouldn't pop up like that."

Tularecito stood up and smiled bashfully while he whipped his hat against his thigh. Suddenly Miss Morgan felt fear rising in her. The road was deserted—she had read stories of half-wits. With difficulty she mastered her trembling voice.

"What—what is it you want?"

Tularecito smiled more broadly and whipped harder with his hat.

"Were you just lying there, or do you want something?"

The boy struggled to speak, and then relapsed into his protective smile.

"Well, if you don't want anything, I'll go on." She was really prepared for flight.

Tularecito struggled again. "About those people—"

"What people?" she demanded shrilly. "What about people?"

"About those people in the book—"

Miss Morgan laughed with relief until she felt that her hair was coming loose on the back of her head. "You mean—you mean—gnomes?"

Tularecito nodded.

"What do you want to know about them?"

"I never saw any," said Tularecito. His voice neither rose nor fell, but continued on one low note.

"Why, few people do see them, I think."

"But I knew about them."

Miss Morgan's eyes squinted with interest. "You did? Who told you about them?"

"Nobody."

"You never saw them, and no one told you? How could you know about them then?"

"I just knew. Heard them, maybe. I knew them in the book all right."

Miss Morgan thought: "Why should I deny gnomes to this queer, unfinished child? Wouldn't his life be richer and happier if he did believe in them? And what harm could it possibly do?"

"Have you ever looked for them?" she asked.

"No, I never looked. I just knew. But I will look now."

Miss Morgan found herself charmed with the situation. Here was paper on which to write, here was a cliff on which to carve. She could carve a lovely story that would be far more real than a book story ever could. "Where will you look?" she asked.

"I'll dig in holes," said Tularecito soberly.

"But the gnomes only come out at night, Tularecito. You must watch for them in the night. And you must come and tell me if you find any. Will you do that?"

"I'll come," he agreed.

She left him staring after her. All the way home she pictured him searching in the night. The picture pleased her. He might even find the gnomes, might live with them and talk to them. With a few suggestive words she had been able to make his life unreal and very wonderful, and separated from the stupid lives about him. She deeply envied him his searching.

In the evening Tularecito put on his coat and took up a shovel. Old Pancho came upon him as he was leaving the tool shed. "Where goest thou, Little Frog?" he asked.

Tularecito shifted his feet restlessly at the delay. "I go out into the dark. Is that a new thing?"

"But why takest thou the shovel? Is there gold, perhaps?"

The boy's face grew hard with the seriousness of his purpose. "I go to dig for the little people who live in the earth."

Now Pancho was filled with horrified excitement. "Do not go, Little Frog! Listen to your old friend, your father in God, and do not go! Out in the sage I found thee and saved thee from the devils, thy relatives. Thou art a little brother of Jesus now. Go not back to thine own people! Listen to an old man, Little Frog!"

Tularecito stared hard at the ground and drilled his old thoughts with this new information. "Thou hast said they are my people," he exclaimed. "I am not like the others at the school or here. I know that. I have loneliness for my own people who live deep in the cool earth. When I pass a squirrel hole, I wish to crawl into it and hide myself. My own people are like me, and they have called me. I must go home to them, Pancho."

Pancho stepped back and held up crossed fingers. "Go back to the devil, thy father, then. I am not good enough to fight this evil. It would take a saint. But see! At least I make the sign against thee and against all thy race." He drew the cross of protection in the air in front of him.

Tularecito smiled sadly, and turning, trudged off into the hills.

The heart of Tularecito gushed with joy at his homecoming. All his life he had been an alien, a lonely outcast, and now he was going home. As always, he heard the voices of the earth—the far off clang of cow bells, the muttering of disturbed quail, the little whine of a coyote who would not sing this night, the nocturnes of a million insects. But Tularecito was listening for another sound, the movement of two-footed creatures, and the hushed voices of the hidden people.

Once he stopped and called, "My father, I have come home," and he heard no answer. Into squirrel holes he whispered, "Where are you, my people? It is only Tularecito come home." But there was no reply. Worse, he had no feeling that the gnomes were near. He knew that a doe and fawn were feeding near him; he knew a wildcat was stalking a rabbit behind a bush, although he could not see them, but from the gnomes he had no message.

A sugar-moon arose out of the hills.

"Now the animals will come out to feed," Tularecito said in the papery whisper of the half witless. "Now the people will come out, too."

The brush stopped at the edge of a little valley and an orchard took its place. The trees were thick with leaves, and the land finely cultivated. It was Bert Munroe's orchard. Often, when the land was deserted and ghost-ridden, Tularecito had come here in the night to lie on the ground under the trees and pick the stars with gentle fingers.

The moment he walked into the orchard he knew he was nearing home. He could not hear them, but he knew the gnomes were near. Over and over he called to them, but they did not come.

"Perhaps they do not like the moonlight," he said.

At the foot of a large peach tree he dug his hole—three feet across and very deep. All night he worked on it, stopping to listen awhile and then digging deeper and deeper into the cool earth. Although he heard nothing, he was positive that he was nearing them. Only when the daylight came did he give up and retire into the bushes to sleep.

In midmorning Bert Munroe walked out to look at a coyote trap and found the hole at the foot of the tree. "What the devil!" he said. "Some kids must have been digging a tunnel. That's dangerous! It'll cave in on them, or somebody will fall into it and get hurt." He walked back to the house, got a shovel and filled up the hole.

"Manny," he said to his youngest boy, "you haven't been digging in the orchard, have you?"

"Uh-uh!" said Manny.

"Well, do you know who has?"

"Uh-uh!" said Manny.

"Well, somebody dug a deep hole out there. It's dangerous. You tell the boys not to dig or they'll get caved in."

The dark came and Tularecito walked out of the brush to dig in his hole again. When he found it filled up, he growled savagely, but then his thought changed and he laughed. "The people were here," he said happily. "They didn't know who it was, and they were frightened. They filled up the hole the way a gopher does. This time I'll hide, and when they come to fill the hole, I'll tell them who I am. Then they will love me."

And Tularecito dug out the hole and made it much deeper than before, because much of the dirt was loose. Just before daylight, he retired into the brush at the edge of the orchard and lay down to watch.

Bert Munroe walked out before breakfast to look at his trap again, and again he found the open hole. "The little devils!" he cried. "They're keeping it up, are they? I'll bet Manny *is* in it after all."

He studied the hole for a moment and then began to push dirt into it with the side of his foot. A savage growl spun him around. Tularecito came charging down upon him, leaping like a frog on his long legs, and swinging his shovel like a club.

When Jimmie Munroe came to call his father to breakfast, he found him lying on the pile of dirt. He was bleeding at the mouth and forehead. Shovelfuls of dirt came flying out of the pit.

Jimmie thought someone had killed his father and was getting ready to bury him. He ran home in a frenzy of terror, and by telephone summoned a band of neighbours.

Half a dozen men crept up on the pit. Tularecito struggled like a wounded lion, and held his own until they struck him on the head with his own shovel. Then they tied him up and took him in to jail.

In Salinas a medical board examined the boy. When the doctors asked him questions, he smiled blandly at them and did not answer. Franklin Gomez told the board what he knew and asked the custody of him.

"We really can't do it, Mr. Gomez," the judge said finally. "You say he is a good boy. Just yesterday he tried to kill a man. You must see that we cannot let him go loose. Sooner or later he will succeed in killing someone."

After a short deliberation, he committed Tularecito to the asylum for the criminal insane at Napa.

V

HELEN VAN DEVENTER was a tall woman with a sharp, handsome face and tragic eyes. A strong awareness of tragedy ran through her life. At fifteen she had looked like a widow after her Persian kitten was poisoned. She mourned for it during six months, not ostentatiously, but with a subdued voice and a hushed manner. When her father died, at the end of the kitten's six months, the mourning continued uninterrupted. Seemingly she hungered for tragedy and life had lavishly heaped it upon her.

At twenty-five she married Hubert Van Deventer, a florid, hunting man who spent six months out of every year trying to shoot some kind of creature or other. Three months after the wedding he shot himself when a blackberry vine tripped him up. Hubert was a fairly gallant man. As he lay dying under a tree, one of his companions asked whether he wanted to leave any message for his wife.

"Yes," said Hubert. "Tell her to have me mounted for that place in the library between the bull moose and the bighorn! Tell her I didn't buy this one from the guide!"

Helen Van Deventer closed off the drawing room with its trophies. Thereafter the room was holy to the spirit of Hubert. The curtains remained drawn. Anyone who felt it necessary to speak in the drawing room spoke softly. Helen did not weep, for it was not in her nature to weep, but her eyes grew larger, and she stared a great deal, with the vacant staring of one who travels over other times. Hubert had left her the house on Russian Hill in San Francisco, and a fairly large fortune.

Her daughter Hilda, born six months after Hubert was killed, was a pretty, doll-like baby, with her mother's great eyes. Hilda was never very well; she took all the children's diseases with startling promptness. Her temper, which at first wore itself out with howling, became destructive as soon as she could move about. She shattered any breakable thing which came into the pathway of her anger. Helen Van Deventer soothed and petted her and usually succeeded in increasing the temper.

47

When Hilda was six years old, Dr. Phillips, the family physician, told Mrs. Van Deventer the thing she had suspected for a long time.

"You must realize it," he said. "Hilda is not completely well in her mind. I suggest that she be taken to a psychiatrist."

The dark eyes of the mother widened with pain. "You are sure, doctor?"

"Fairly sure. I am not a specialist. You'll have to take her to someone who knows more than I do."

Helen stared away from him. "I have thought so too, doctor, but I can't take her to another man. You've always had the care of us. I know you. I shouldn't ever be sure of another man."

"What do you mean, 'sure'?" Dr. Phillips exploded. "Don't you know we might cure her if we went about it right?"

Helen's hands rose a trifle, and then dropped with hopelessness. "She won't ever get well, doctor. She was born at the wrong time. Her father's death—it was too much for me. I didn't have the strength to bear a perfect child, you see."

"Then what do you intend to do? Your idea is foolish, if I may be permitted."

"What is there to do, doctor? I can wait and hope. I know I can see it through, but I can't take her to another man. I'll just watch her and care for her. That seems to be my life." She smiled very sadly and her hands rose again.

"It seems to me you force hardships upon yourself," the doctor said testily.

"We take what is given us. I can endure. I am sure of that, and I am proud of it. No amount of tragedy can break down my endurance. But there is one thing I cannot bear, doctor. Hilda cannot be taken away from me. I will keep her with me, and you will come as always, but no one else must interfere."

Dr. Phillips left the house in disgust. The obvious and needless endurance of the woman always put him in a fury. "If I were Fate," he mused, "I'd be tempted to smash her placid resistance too."

It wasn't long after this that visions and dreams began to come to Hilda. Terrible creatures of the night, with claws and teeth, tried to kill her while she slept. Ugly little men pinched her and gritted their teeth in her ear, and Helen Van Deventer accepted the visions as new personalities come to test her.

"A tiger came and pulled the covers," Hilda cried in the morning.

"You mustn't let him frighten you, dear."

"But he tried to get his teeth through the blanket, mother."

"I'll sit with you tonight, darling. Then he can't come."

She began to sit by the little girl's bedside until dawn. Her eyes grew brighter and more feverish with the frenzied resistance of her spirit.

One thing bothered her more than the dreams. Hilda had begun to tell lies. "I went out into the garden this morning, mother. An old man was sitting in the street. He asked me to go to his house, so I went. He had a big gold elephant, and he let me ride on it." The little girl's eyes were far away as she made up the tale.

"Don't say such things, darling," her mother pleaded. "You know you didn't do any of those things."

"But I did, mother. And the old man gave me a watch. I'll show you. Here." She held out a wrist watch set with diamonds. Helen's hands shook with terror as she took the watch. For a second her face lost its look of resistance, and anger took its place.

"Where did you get it, Hilda?"

"The old man gave it to me, mother."

"No—tell me where you found it! You did find it, didn't you?"

"The old man gave it to me."

On the back of the watch a monogram was cut, initials unknown to Helen. She stared helplessly at the carved letters. "Mother will take this," she said harshly. That night she crept into the garden, found a trowel and buried the watch deep in the earth. That week she had a high iron fence built around the garden, and Hilda was never permitted to go out alone after that.

When she was thirteen, Hilda escaped and ran away. Helen hired private detectives to find her, but at the end of four days a policeman discovered Hilda sleeping in a deserted real estate tract office in Los Angeles. Helen rescued her daughter from the police station. "Why did you run away, darling?" she asked.

"Well, I wanted to play on a piano."

"But we have one at home. Why didn't you play on it?"

"Oh, I wanted to play on the other kind, the tall kind."

Helen took Hilda on her lap and hugged her tightly. "And what did you do then, dear?"

"I was out in the street and a man asked me to ride with him. He gave me five dollars. Then I found some gypsies, and I went to live with them. They made me queen. Then I was married to a young gypsy man, and we were going to have a little baby, but I got tired and sat down. Then a policeman took me."

"Darling, poor darling," Helen replied. "You know that isn't true. None of it is true."

"But it is true, mother."

Helen called Dr. Phillips. "She says she married a gypsy. You don't think—really you don't think she could have? I couldn't stand that."

The doctor looked at the little girl carefully. At the end of his examination he spoke almost viciously. "I've told you she should be put in the hands of a specialist." He approached the little girl. "Has the mean old woman been in your bedroom lately, Hilda?"

Hilda's hands twitched. "Last night she came with a monkey, a great big monkey. It tried to bite me."

"Well, just remember she can't ever hurt you because I'm taking care of you. That old woman's afraid of me. If she comes again, just tell her I'm looking after you and see how quick she runs away."

The little girl smiled wearily. "Will the monkey run away too?"

"Of course, and while I think of it, here's a little candy cane for your daughter." He drew a stick of stripey peppermint from his pocket. "You'd better give that to Babette, isn't that her name?" Hilda snatched the candy and ran out of the room.

"Now!" said the doctor to Helen, "my knowledge and my experience are sadly lacking, but I do know this much. Hilda will be very much worse now. She's reaching her maturity. The period of change, with its accompanying emotional overflow invariably intensifies mental trouble. I can't tell what may happen. She may turn homicidal, and on the other hand, she may run off with the first man she sees. If you don't put her in expert hands, if you don't have her carefully watched, something you'll regret may happen. This last escapade is only a forerunner. You simply cannot go on as you are. It isn't fair to yourself."

Helen sat rigidly before him. In her face was that resistance which so enraged him. "What would you suggest?" she asked huskily.

"A hospital for the insane," he said, and it delighted him that his reply was brutal.

Her face tightened. Her resistance became a little more tense. "I won't do it," she cried. "She's mine, and I'm responsible for her. I'll stay with her myself, doctor. I won't let her out of my sight. But I will not send her away."

"You know the consequences," he said gruffly. Then the impossibility of reasoning with this woman overwhelmed him. "Helen, I've been your friend for years. Why should you take this load of misery and danger on your own shoulders?"

"I can endure anything, but I cannot send her away."

"You love the hair shirt," he growled. "Your pain is a pleasure. You won't give up any little shred of tragedy." He became furious. "Helen, every man must some time or other want to beat a woman. I think I'm a mild man, but right now I want to beat your face with my fists." He looked into her dark eyes and saw that he had only put a new tragedy upon her, had only given her a new situation to endure. "I'm going away now," he said. "Don't call me any more. Why—I'm beginning to hate you."

The people of the Pastures of Heaven learned with interest and resentment that a rich woman was coming to live in the valley. They watched truckloads of logs and lumber going up Christmas Canyon, and they laughed a little scornfully at the expense of hauling in logs to make a cabin. Bert Munroe walked up Christmas Canyon, and for half a day he watched the carpenters putting up a house.

"It's going to be nice," he reported at the General Store. Every log is perfect, and what do you know, they've got gardeners working there already. They're bringing in big plants and trees all in bloom, and setting them in the ground. This Mrs. Van Deventer must be pretty rich."

"They sure lay it on," agreed Pat Humbert. "Them rich people sure do lay it on."

"And listen to this," Bert continued. "Isn't this like a woman? Guess what they got on some of the windows — bars! Not iron bars, but big thick oak ones. I guess the old lady's scared of coyotes."

"I wonder if she'll bring a lot of servants." T. B. Allen spoke hopefully, "but I guess she'd buy her stuff in town, though. All people like that buy their stuff in town."

When the house and the garden were completed, Helen Van Deventer and Hilda, a Chinese cook and a Filipino house-boy drove up Christmas Canyon. It was a beautiful log house. The carpenters had aged the logs with acids, and the gardeners had made it seem an old garden. Bays and oaks were left in the lawn and under them grew cinerarias, purple and white and blue. The walks were hedged with lobelias of incredible blue.

The cook and the house-boy scurried to their posts, but Helen took Hilda by the arm and walked in the garden for a while.

"Isn't it beautiful," Helen cried. Her face had lost some of its resistance. "Darling, don't you think we'll like it here?"

Hilda pulled up a cineraria and switched at an oak trunk with it. "I liked it better at home."

"But why, darling? We didn't have such pretty flowers, and there weren't any big trees. Here we can go walking in the hills every day."

"I liked it better at home."

"But why, darling?"

"Well, all my friends were there. I could look out through the fence and see the people go by."

"You'll like it better here, Hilda, when you get used to it."

"No I won't. I won't ever like it here, ever." Hilda began to cry, and then without transition she began screaming with rage. Suddenly she plucked a garden stick from the ground and struck her mother across the breast with it. Silently the house-boy appeared behind the girl, pinioned her arms, and carried her, kicking and screaming, into the house.

In the room that had been prepared for her, Hilda method-ically broke the furniture. She slit the pillows and shook feathers about the room. Lastly she broke out the panes of her window, beat at the oaken bars and screamed with anger. Helen sat in her room, her lips drawn tight. Once she started up as though to go to Hilda's room, and then sank back into her chair again. For a moment the dumb endurance had nearly broken, but instantly it settled back more strongly than ever, and the shrieks from Hilda's room had no effect. The house-boy slipped into the room.

"Close the shutters, Missie?"

"No, Joe. We're far enough away from anyone. No one can hear it."

Bert Munroe saw the automobile drive by, bearing the new people up Christmas Canyon to the log cabin.

"It'll be pretty hard for a woman to get started alone," he said to his wife. "I think I ought to walk up and see if they need anything."

"You're just curious," his wife said banteringly.

"Well, of course, if that's the way you feel about it, I won't go."

"I was just fooling, Bert," she protested. "I think it would be a nice neighbourly thing to do. Later on I'll get Mrs. Whiteside to go and call with me. That's the real way to do it. But you run along now and see how they're making out."

He swung along up the pleasant stream which sang in the bottom of Christmas Canyon. "It's not a place to farm," he said to himself, "but it's a nice place to live. I could be living in a place like this, just living—if the armistice hadn't come when it did." As usual he felt ashamed of wishing the war had continued for a while.

Hilda's shrieks came to his ears when he was still a quarter of a mile from the house. "Now what the devil," he said. "Sounds like they were killing someone." He hurried up the road to see.

Hilda's barred window looked out on the path which led to

the front entrance of the house. Bert saw the girl clinging to the bars, her eyes mad with rage and fear.

"Hello!" he said. "What's the matter? What have they got you locked up for?"

Hilda's eyes narrowed. "They're starving me," she said. "They want me to die."

"That's foolish," said Bert. "Why would anyone want you to die."

"Oh! it's my money," she confided. "They can't get my money until I'm dead."

"Why, you're just a little girl."

"I am not," Hilda said sullenly. "I'm a big grown up woman. I look little because they starve me and beat me."

Bert's face darkened. "Well, I'll just see about that," he said.

"Oh! don't tell them. Just help me out of here, and then I'll get my money, and then I'll marry you."

For the first time Bert began to suspect what the trouble was. "Sure, I'll help you," he said soothingly. "You just wait a little while, and I'll help you out."

He walked around to the front entrance and knocked at the door. In a moment it opened a crack; the stolid eyes of the house-boy looked out.

"Can I see the lady of the house?" Bert asked.

"No," said the boy, and he shut the door.

For a moment Bert blushed with shame at the rebuff, but then he knocked angrily. Again the door opened two inches, and the black eyes looked out.

"I tell you I've got to see the lady of the house. I've got to see her about the little girl that's locked up."

"Lady very sick. So sorry," said the boy. He closed the door again. This time Bert heard the bolt shoot home. He strode away down the path. "I'll sure tell my wife not to call on them," he said to himself. "A crazy girl and a lousy servant. They can go to hell!"

Helen called from her bedroom, "What was it, Joe?"

The boy stood in the doorway. "A man come. Say he got to see you. I tell him you sick."

"That's good. Who was he? Did he say why he wanted to see me?"

"Don't know who. Say he got to see you about Missie Hilda."

Instantly Helen was standing over him. Her face was angry. "What did he want? Who was he?"

"Don't know, Missie."

"And you sent him away. You take too many liberties. Now get out of here."

She dropped back on her chair and covered her eyes.

"Yes, Missie." Joe turned slowly away.

"Oh, Joe, come back!"

He stood beside her chair before she uncovered her eyes. "Forgive me, Joe. I didn't know what I said. You did right. You'll stay with me, won't you?"

"Yes, Missie."

Helen stood up and walked restlessly to the window. "I don't know what's the matter with me today. Is Miss Hilda all right?"

"Yes, Missie quiet now."

"Well, build a fire in the living-room fireplace, will you? And later bring her in."

In her design for the living room of the cabin Helen felt that she had created a kind of memorial to her husband. She had made it look as much as possible like a hunting lodge. It was a huge room, paneled and beamed with redwood. At intervals the mounted heads of various kinds of deer thrust out inquisitive noses. One side of the room was dominated by a great cobblestone fireplace over which hung a torn French battle flag Hubert had picked up somewhere. In a locked, glass-fronted case, all of Hubert's guns were lined up in racks. Helen felt that she would not completely lose her husband as long as she had a room like this to sit in.

In the Russian Hill drawing room she had practiced a dream that was pleasant to her. She wished she could continue it here in the new house. The dream was materialized almost by a ritual. Helen sat before the fire and folded her hands. Then she looked for a long moment at each of the mounted trophies, repeating for each one, "Hubert handled that." And finally the dream came. She almost saw him before her. In her mind she went over the shape of his hands, the narrowness of his hips and the length and straightness of his legs. After a while she remembered how he said things, where his accents fell, and the way his face seemed to glow and redden when he was excited. Helen recalled how he took his guests from one trophy to another. In front of each one Hubert rocked on his heels and folded his hands behind his back while he told of the killing of the animal in the tiniest detail.

"The moon wasn't right and there wasn't a sign anywhere. Fred (Fred was the guide) said we hadn't a chance to get anything. I remember we were out of bacon that morning. But you know I just had a feeling that we ought to stroll out for a look-see."

Helen could hear him telling the stupid, pointless stories which invariably ended up, "Well, the range was too long and there was a devilish wind blowing from the left, but I set my sights for it, and I thought, 'Well, here goes nothing,' and darned if I didn't knock him over. Of course it was just luck."

Hubert didn't really want his listeners to believe it was just luck. That was his graceful gesture as a sportsman. Helen remembered wondering why a sportsman wasn't permitted to acknowledge that he did anything well.

But that was the way the dream went. She built up his image until it possessed the room and filled it with the surging vitality of the great hunter. Then, when she had completed the dream, she smashed it. The doorbell had seemed to have a particularly dolorous note. Helen remembered the faces of the men, sad and embarrassed while they told her about the accident. The dream always stopped where they had carried the body up the front steps. A blinding wave of sadness filled her chest, and she sank back in her chair.

By this means she kept her husband alive, tenaciously refusing to let his image grow dim in her memory. She had only been married for three months, she told herself. Only three months! She resigned herself to a feeling of hopeless gloom. She knew that she encouraged this feeling, but she felt that it was Hubert's right, a kind of memorial that must be paid to him. She must resist sadness, but not by trying to escape from it.

Helen had looked forward to this first night in her new house. With logs blazing on the hearth, the light shining on the glass eyes of the animals' heads, she intended to welcome her dream into its new home.

Joe came back into the bedroom. "The fire going, Missie. I call Missie Hilda now?"

Helen glanced out of her window. The dusk was coming down from the hilltops. Already a few bats looped nervously about. The quail were calling to one another as they went to water, and far down the canyon the cows were lowing on their way in toward the milking sheds. A change was stealing over Helen. She was filled with a new sense of peace; she felt protected and clothed against the tragedies which had beset her for so long. She stretched her arms outward and backward, and sighed comfortably. Joe still waited in the doorway.

"What?" Helen said, "Miss Hilda? No, don't bring her yet. Dinner must be almost ready. If Hilda doesn't want to come out to dinner, I'll see her afterwards." She didn't want to see Hilda. This new, delicious peacefulness would be broken if she did. She wanted to sit in the strange luminosity of the dusk, to sit listening to the quail calling to one another as they came down from the brushy hillsides to drink before the night fell.

Helen threw a silken shawl about her shoulders and went out into the garden. Peace, it seemed, came sweeping down from the hillsides and enveloped her. In a flower bed she saw a little grey rabbit with a white tail, and seeing it made her quiver with pleasure. The rabbit turned its head and looked at her for a moment, and then went on nibbling at the new plants. Suddenly Helen felt foolishly happy. Something delicious and exciting was going to happen, something very delightful. In her sudden joy she talked to the rabbit. "Go on eating, you can have the old flowers. Tomorrow I'll plant cabbages for you. You'd like that, wouldn't you, Peter? You know, Peter, is your name Peter? Silly, all rabbits are named Peter. Anyway, Peter, I haven't looked forward to anything for ages. Isn't that funny? Or is it sad? But now I'm looking forward to something. I'm just bursting with anticipation. And I don't know what the something can be. Isn't that silly, Peter?" She strolled on and waved her hand at the rabbit. "I should think the cinerarias would be better to eat," she said.

The singing of water drew her down the path toward the

streamside. As she neared the bank, a flock of quail scudded into the brush with stuttering cries of alarm. Helen was ashamed that she had disturbed them. "Come back!" she called. "I won't shoot you. The rabbit didn't mind me. Why, I couldn't shoot you if I wanted to." Suddenly she recalled how Hubert had taken her out to teach her to shoot a shotgun. He had grown religiously solemn as he taught her how to hold the weapon and how to sight with both eyes open. "Now I'll throw up a can," he said. "I don't want you ever to shoot at a still target—ever. It is a poor sportsman who will shoot a resting bird." She had fired wildly at the flying can until her shoulder was stiff, and as they drove home he patted her. "It'll be a long time before you knock over a quail," he said. "But in a little while you ought to be able to pot rabbits." Then she thought of the leather quail strings he brought home with clusters of birds hung by their necks. "When they drop off the strings they're hung long enough to eat," he said solemnly. All of a sudden Helen realized that she didn't want to think of Hubert any more. The retrospection had almost killed her sense of peace.

It was almost dark. The night was sweet with the odor of sage. She heard the cook in the kitchen rattling the cowbell she had bought as a dinner signal. Helen pulled her shawl close and shivered and went in.

In the dining room she found her daughter before her. All traces of the afternoon's rage were gone from Hilda's face; she looked happy, and very satisfied with herself.

"My darling. You're feeling better, aren't you?" Helen cried.

"Oh, yes."

Helen walked around the table and kissed her on the forehead. Then for a moment she hugged Hilda convulsively. "When you see how beautiful it is here, you'll love it. I know you will."

Hilda did not answer, but her eyes became wily.

"You will like it, won't you, darling?" Helen insisted as she went back to her place.

Hilda was mysterious. "Well maybe I'll like it. Maybe I won't have to like it."

"What do you mean, dear?"

"Maybe I won't be here very long."

"Won't be here very long?" Helen looked quickly across the table. Obviously Hilda was trying to keep some kind of secret, but it was too slippery.

"Maybe I might run away and be married."

Helen sank back in her chair and smiled. "Oh, I see. Surely you might. It would be better to wait a few years though. Who is it this time, dear? The prince again?"

"No, it's not the prince. It's a poor man, but I will love him. We made all of our plans today. He'll come for me, I guess."

Something stirred in Helen's memory. "Is it the man who came to the house this afternoon?"

Hilda started up from the table. "I won't tell you another thing," she cried. "You haven't any right to ask me. You just wait a little while—I'll show you I don't have to stay in this old house." She ran from the room and slammed her bedroom door after her.

Helen rang for the house-boy. "Joe, exactly what did the man who came today say?"

"Say he got to see you about little girl."

"Well what kind of a man was he?—how old?"

"Not old man, Missie, not young man. Maybe fifty years, I guess."

Helen sighed. It was just another of the stories, the little dramas Hilda thought out and told. And they were so real to her, poor child. Helen ate slowly, and afterwards, in the big living room, she sat before the fire—idly knocking coals from the glowing logs. She turned all the lights off. The fire glinted on the eyes of the stuffed heads on the wall, and Helen's old habit reasserted itself. She found herself imagining how Hubert's hands looked, how narrow his hips were, and how straight his legs. And then she made a discovery: When her mind dropped his hands they disappeared. She was not building the figure of her husband. He was gone, completely gone. For the first time in years, Helen put her hands to her face and cried, for the peace had come back, and the bursting expectancy. She dried her eyes and walked slowly about the room, smiling up at the heads with the casual eyes of a stranger who didn't know how each animal had died. The room looked different and felt different. She fumbled with the new window bolts and threw open the wide windows to the night. And the night wind sighed in and bathed her bare shoulders with its cool peace. She leaned out of the window and listened. So many little noises came from the garden and from the hill beyond the garden. "It's just infested with life," she thought. "It's just bursting with life." Gradually as she listened she became aware of a rasping sound from the other side of the house. "If there were beavers, it would be a beaver cutting down a tree. Maybe it's a porcupine eating out the foundations. I've heard of that. But there aren't any porcupines here either." There were vibrations of the rasping in the house itself. "It must be something gnawing on the logs," she said. There came a little crash. The noise stopped. Helen started uneasily. She walked quickly down a passageway and stopped before the door of Hilda's room. With her hand on the strong outside bolt she called, "Are you all right, darling?" There was no answer. Helen slipped the bolt very quietly and entered the room. One of the oaken bars was hacked out and Hilda was gone.

For a moment Helen stood rigidly at the open window, looking wistfully into the grey night. Then her face paled and her lips set in the old line of endurance. Her movements were mechanical as she retraced her steps to the living room. She climbed up on a chair, unlocked the gun case and took down a shotgun.

Dr. Phillips sat beside Helen Van Deventer in the coroner's office. He had to come as the child's doctor, of course, but also he thought he could keep Helen from being afraid. She didn't look afraid. In her severe, her almost savage mourning, she looked as enduring as a sea washed stone.

"And you expected it?" the coroner was saying. "You thought it might happen?"

Dr. Phillips looked uneasily at Helen and cleared his throat. "She had been my patient since she was born. In a case like this, she might have committed suicide or murder, depending on circumstances. Then again she might have lived on harmlessly. She could have gone all her life without making any violent move. It was impossible to say, you see."

The coroner was signing papers. "It was a beastly way for her to do it. Of course the girl was insane, and there isn't any reason to look into her motives. Her motives might have been tiny things. But it was a horrible way to do it. She never knew that, though. Her head in the stream and the gun beside her. I'll instruct a suicide verdict. I'm sorry to have to talk this way before you, Mrs. Van Deventer. Finding her must have been a terrible shock to you."

The doctor helped Helen down the steps of the court house. "Don't look that way," he cried. "You look as though you were going to an execution. It's better so, I tell you. You must not suffer so."

She didn't look at him. "I know now. By this time I know what my life expects of me," she said softly. "Now I know what I have always suspected. And I have the strength to endure, Doctor. Don't you worry about me."

VI

JUNIUS MALTBY was a small young man of good and cultured family and decent education. When his father died bankrupt, Junius got himself inextricably entangled in a clerkship, against which he feebly struggled for ten years.

After work Junius retired to his furnished room, patted the cushions of his morris chair and spent the evening reading. Stevenson's essays he thought nearly the finest things in English; he read *Travels with a Donkey* many times.

One evening soon after his thirty-fifth birthday, Junius fainted on the steps of his boarding house. When he recovered consciousness, he noticed for the first time that his breathing was difficult and unsatisfactory. He wondered how long it had been that way. The doctor whom he consulted was kind and even hopeful.

"You're by no means too far gone to get well," he said. "But you really must take those lungs out of San Francisco. If you stay here in the fog, you won't live a year. Move to a warm, dry climate."

The accident to his health filled Junius with pleasure, for it cut the strings he had been unable to sever for himself. He had five hundred dollars, not that he ever saved any money; he had simply forgotten to spend it. "With that much," he said, "I'll either recover and make a clean, new start, or else I'll die and be through with the whole business."

A man in his office told him of the warm, protected valley, the Pastures of Heaven, and Junius went there immediately. The name pleased him. "It's either an omen that I'm not going to live," he thought, "or else it's a nice symbolic substitute for death." He felt that the name meant something personal to him, and he was very glad, because for ten years nothing in the world had been personal to him.

There were, in the Pastures of Heaven, several families who wanted to take boarders. Junius inspected each one, and finally went to live on the farm of the widow Quaker. She needed the money, and besides, he could sleep in a shed separated from the farmhouse. Mrs. Quaker had two small boys and kept a hired man to work the farm.

The warm climate worked tenderly with Junius' lungs. Within the year his colour was good and he had gained in weight. He was quiet and happy on the farm, and what pleased him more, he had thrown out the ten years of the office and had grown superbly lazy. Junius' thin blond hair went uncombed; he wore his glasses far down on his square nose, for his eyes were getting stronger and only the habit of feeling spectacles caused him to wear them. Throughout the day he had always some small stick protruding from his mouth, a habit only the laziest and most ruminative of men acquire. This convalescence took place in 1910.

In 1911, Mrs. Quaker began to worry about what the neighbours were saying. When she considered the implication of having a single man in her house, she became upset and nervous. As soon as Junius' recovery seemed sure beyond doubt, the widow confessed her trepidations. He married her, immediately and gladly. Now he had a home and a golden future, for the new Mrs. Maltby owned two hundred acres of grassy hillside and five acres of orchard and vegetable bottom. Junius sent for his books, his morris chair with the adjustable back, and his good copy of Velasquez' *Cardinal*. The future was a pleasant and sunshiny afternoon to him.

Mrs. Maltby promptly discharged the hired man and tried to put her husband to work; but in this she encountered a resistance the more bewildering because it presented no hard front to strike at. During his convalescence, Junius had grown to love laziness. He liked the valley and the farm, but he liked them as they were; he didn't want to plant new things, nor to tear out old. When Mrs. Maltby put a hoe in his hand and set him to work in the vegetable garden, she found him, likely enough, hours later, dangling his feet in the meadow stream and reading his pocket copy of *Kidnapped*. He was sorry; he didn't know how it had happened. And that was the truth.

At first she nagged him a great deal about his laziness and his sloppiness of dress, but he soon developed a faculty for never listening to her. It would be impolite, he considered, to notice her when she was not being a lady. It would be like staring at a cripple. And Mrs. Maltby, after she had battered

at his resistance of fog for a time, took to sniveling and ne-
glecting her hair.

Between 1911 and 1917, the Maltbys grew very poor. Junius
simply would not take care of the farm. They even
sold a few acres of pasture land to get money for food and
clothing, and even then there was never enough to eat. Poverty sat cross-legged on the farm, and the Maltbys were
ragged. They had never any new clothes at all, but Junius had
discovered the essays of David Grayson. He wore overalls and
sat under the sycamores that lined the meadow stream. Sometimes he read *Adventures in Contentment* to his wife and two
sons.

Early in 1917, Mrs. Maltby found that she was going to
have a baby, and late in the same year the wartime influenza
epidemic struck the family with a dry viciousness. Perhaps because they were undernourished, the two boys were stricken
simultaneously. For three days the house seemed filled to
overflowing with flushed, feverish children whose nervous
fingers strove to cling to life by the threads of their bed
clothes. For three days they struggled weakly, and on the
fourth, both of the boys died. Their mother didn't know it,
for she was confined, and the neighbours who came to help in
the house hadn't the courage nor the cruelty to tell her. The
black fever came upon her while she was in labour and killed
her before she ever saw her child.

The neighbour women who helped at the birth told the
story throughout the valley that Junius Maltby read books by
the stream while his wife and children died. But this was only
partly true. On the day of their seizure, he dangled his feet in
the stream, because he didn't know they were ill, but thereafter he wandered vaguely from one to the other of the dying
children, and talked nonsense to them. He told the eldest boy
how diamonds are made. At the bedside of the other, he explained the beauty, the antiquity and the symbolism of the
swastika. One life went out while he read aloud the second
chapter of *Treasure Island*, and he didn't even know it had
happened until he finished the chapter and looked up. During
those days he was bewildered. He brought out the only
things he had and offered them, but they had no potency

with death. He knew in advance they wouldn't have, and that made it all the more terrible to him.

When the bodies were all gone, Junius went back to the stream and read a few pages of *Travels with a Donkey*. He chuckled uncertainly over the obstinacy of Modestine. Who but Stevenson could have named a donkey "Modestine"?

One of the neighbour women called him in and cursed him so violently that he was embarrassed and didn't listen. She put her hands on her hips and glared at him with contempt. And then she brought his child, a son, and laid it in his arms. When she looked back at him from the gate, he was standing with the howling little brute in his arms. He couldn't see any place to put it down, so he held it for a long time.

The people of the valley told many stories about Junius. Sometimes they hated him with the loathing busy people have for lazy ones, and sometimes they envied his laziness; but often they pitied him because he blundered so. No one in the valley ever realized that he was happy.

They told how, on a doctor's advice, Junius bought a goat to milk for the baby. He didn't inquire into the sex of his purchase nor give his reason for wanting a goat. When it arrived he looked under it, and very seriously asked, "Is this a normal goat?"

"Sure," said the owner.

"But shouldn't there be a bag or something immediately between the hind legs?—for the milk, I mean."

The people of the valley roared about that. Later, when a new and better goat was provided, Junius fiddled with it for two days and could not draw a drop of milk. He wanted to return this goat as defective until the owner showed him how to milk it. Some people claimed that he held the baby under the goat and let it suck its own milk, but this was untrue. The people of the valley declared they didn't know how he ever reared the child.

One day Junius went into Monterey and hired an old German to help him on the farm. He gave his new servant five dollars on account, and never paid him again. Within two weeks the hired man was so entangled in laziness that he did no more work than his employer. The two of them sat around the place together discussing things which interested and puzzled them—how colour comes to flowers—whether there is a symbology in nature—where Atlantis lay—how the Incas interred their dead.

In the spring they planted potatoes, always too late, and without a covering of ashes to keep the bugs out. They sowed beans and corn and peas, watched them for a time, and then forgot them. The weeds covered everything from sight. It was no unusual thing to see Junius burrow into a perfect thicket of mallow weeds and emerge carrying a pale cucumber. He had stopped wearing shoes because he liked the feeling of the warm earth on his feet, and because he had no shoes.

In the afternoon Junius talked to Jakob Stutz a great deal. "You know," he said, "when the children died, I thought I had reached a peculiar high peak of horror. Then, almost while I thought it, the horror turned to sorrow and the sorrow dwindled to sadness. I didn't know my wife nor the children very well, I guess. Perhaps they were too near to me. It's a strange thing, this *knowing*. It is nothing but an awareness of details. There are long visioned minds and short visioned. I've never been able to see things that are close to me. For instance, I am much more aware of the Parthenon than of my own house over there." Suddenly Junius' face seemed to quiver with feeling, and his eyes brightened with enthusiasm. "Jakob," he said, "have you ever seen a picture of the frieze of the Parthenon?"

"Yes, and it is good, too," said Jakob.

Junius laid a hand on his hired man's knee. "Those horses," he said. "Those lovely horses—bound for a celestial pasture. Those eager and yet dignified young men setting out for an incredible fiesta that's being celebrated just around the cornice. I wonder how a man can know what a horse feels like when it is very happy; and that sculptor must have known or he couldn't have carved them so."

That was the way it went. Junius could not stay on a subject. Often the men went hungry because they failed to find a hen's nest in the grass when it came suppertime.

The son of Junius was named Robert Louis. Junius called him that when he thought of it, but Jakob Stutz rebelled at what he considered a kind of literary preciousness. "Boys must be named like dogs," he maintained. "One sound is sufficient for the name. Even Robert is too long. He should be called 'Bob.' " Jakob nearly got his way.

"I'll compromise with you," said Junius. "We'll call him Robbie. Robbie is really shorter than Robert, don't you think?"

He often gave way before Jakob, for Jakob continually struggled a little against the webs that were being spun about him. Now and then, with a kind of virtuous fury, he cleaned the house.

Robbie grew up gravely. He followed the men about, listening to their discussions. Junius never treated him like a little boy, because he didn't know how little boys should be treated. If Robbie made an observation the two men listened courteously and included the remark in their conversation, or even used it as the germ of an investigation. They tracked down many things in the course of an afternoon. Every day there were several raids on Junius' Encyclopedia.

A huge sycamore put out a horizontal limb over the meadow stream, and on it the three sat, the men hanging their feet into the water and moving pebbles with their toes while Robbie tried extravagantly to imitate them. Reaching the water was one of his criteria of manhood. Jakob had by this time given up shoes; Robbie had never worn any in his life.

The discussions were erudite. Robbie couldn't use childish talk, for he had never heard any. They didn't make conversation; rather they let a seedling of thought sprout by itself, and then watched with wonder while it sent out branching limbs. They were surprised at the strange fruit their conversation bore, for they didn't direct their thinking, nor trellis nor trim it the way so many people do.

There on the limb the three sat. Their clothes were rags and their hair was only hacked off to keep it out of their eyes. The men wore long, untrimmed beards. They watched the water-skaters on the surface of the pool below them, a pool which had been deepened by idling toes. The giant tree above them whisked softly in the wind, and occasionally dropped a leaf like a brown handkerchief. Robbie was five years old.

"I think sycamore trees are good," he observed when a leaf

fell in his lap. Jakob picked up the leaf and stripped the parchment from its ribs.

"Yes," he agreed, "they grow by water. Good things love water. Bad things always been dry."

"Sycamores are big and good," said Junius. "It seems to me that a good thing or a kind thing must be very large to survive. Little good things are always destroyed by evil little things. Rarely is a big thing poisonous or treacherous. For this reason, in human thinking, bigness is an attribute of good and littleness of evil. Do you see that, Robbie?"

"Yes," said Robbie. "I see that. Like elephants."

"Elephants are often evil, but when we think of them, they seem gentle and good."

"But water," Jakob broke in. "Do you see about water too?"

"No, not about water."

"But I see," said Junius. "You mean that water is the seed of life. Of the three elements water is the sperm, earth the womb and sunshine the mould of growth."

Thus they taught him nonsense.

The people of the Pastures of Heaven recoiled from Junius Maltby after the death of his wife and his two boys. Stories of his callousness during the epidemic grew to such proportions that eventually they fell down of their own weight and were nearly forgotten. But although his neighbours forgot that Junius had read while his children died, they could not forget the problem he was becoming. Here in the fertile valley he lived in fearful poverty. While other families built small fortunes, bought Fords and radios, put in electricity and went twice a week to the moving pictures in Monterey or Salinas, Junius degenerated and became a ragged savage. The men of the valley resented his good bottom land, all overgrown with weeds, his untrimmed fruit trees and his fallen fences. The women thought with loathing of his unclean house with its littered dooryard and dirty windows. Both men and women hated his idleness and his complete lack of pride. For a while they went to visit him, hoping by their near examples to drag him from his slothfulness. But he received them naturally and with the friendliness of equality. He wasn't a bit ashamed of his poverty nor of his rags. Gradually his neighbours came to think' of Junius as an outcast. No one drove up the private road to his house any more. They outlawed him from decent society and resolved never to receive him should he visit them.

Junius knew nothing about the dislike of his neighbours. He was still gloriously happy. His life was as unreal, as romantic and as unimportant as his thinking. He was content to sit in the sun and to dangle his feet in the stream. If he had no good clothes, at least he had no place to go which required good clothes.

Although the people almost hated Junius, they had only pity for the little boy Robbie. The women told one another how horrible it was to let the child grow up in such squalor. But, because they were mostly good people, they felt a strong reluctance for interfering with Junius' affairs.

"Wait until he's school age," Mrs. Banks said to a group of ladies in her own parlour. "We couldn't do anything now if we wanted to. He belongs to that father of his. But just as soon as the child is six, the county'll have something to say, let me tell you."

Mrs. Allen nodded and closed her eyes earnestly. "We keep forgetting that he's Mamie Quaker's child as much as Maltby's. I think we should have stepped in long ago. But when he goes to school we'll give the poor little fellow a few things he never had."

"The least we can do is to see that he has enough clothes to cover him," another of the women agreed.

It seemed that the valley lay crouched in waiting for the time when Robbie should go to school. When, at term opening, after his sixth birthday, he did not appear, John Whiteside, the clerk of the school board, wrote a letter to Junius Maltby.

"I hadn't thought of it," Junius said when he read it. "I guess you'll have to go to school."

"I don't want to go," said Robbie.

"I know. I don't much want you to go, either. But we have laws. The law has a self-protective appendage called penalty. We have to balance the pleasure of breaking the law against the punishment. The Carthaginians punished even misfortune. If a general lost a battle through bad luck, he was executed. At present we punish people for accidents of birth and circumstance in much the same manner."

In the ensuing discussion they forgot all about the letter. John Whiteside wrote a very curt note.

"Well, Robbie, I guess you'll have to go," said Junius, when he received it. "Of course they'll teach you a great many useful things."

"Why don't you teach me?" Robbie pleaded.

"Oh, I can't. You see I've forgotten the things they teach."

"I don't want to go at all. I don't want to learn things."

"I know you don't, but I can't see any other way out."

And so one morning Robbie trudged to school. He was clad in an ancient pair of overalls, out at the knees and seat, a blue shirt from which the collar was gone, and nothing else. His long hair hung over his grey eyes like the forelock of a range pony.

The children made a circle around him in the school yard and stared at him in silence. They had all heard of the poverty of the Maltbys and of Junius' laziness. The boys looked forward to this moment when they could torture Robbie. Here was the time come; he stood in their circle, and they only stared at him. No one said, "Where'd you get them clothes," or, "Look at his hair," the way they had intended to. The children were puzzled by their failure to torment Robbie.

As for Robbie, he regarded the circle with serious eyes. He was not in the least frightened. "Don't you play games?" he asked. "My father said you'd play games."

And then the circle broke up with howls. "He doesn't know any games."—"Let's teach him pewee."—"No, nigger-baby." "Listen! Listen! Prisoner's base first."—"He doesn't know any games."

And, although they didn't know why, they thought it rather a fine thing not to know games. Robbie's thin face was studious. "We'll try pewee first," he decided. He was clumsy at the new games, but his teachers did not hoot at him. Instead they quarreled for the privilege of showing him how to hold the pewee stick. There are several schools of technique in pewee. Robbie stood aside listening for a while, and at last chose his own instructor.

Robbie's effect on the school was immediate. The older

boys let him entirely alone, but the younger ones imitated him in everything, even tearing holes in the knees of their overalls. When they sat in the sun with their backs to the school wall, eating their lunches, Robbie told them about his father and about the sycamore tree. They listened intently and wished their fathers were lazy and gentle, too.

Sometimes a few of the boys, disobeying the orders of their parents, sneaked up to the Maltby place on a Saturday. Junius gravitated naturally to the sycamore limb, and, while they sat on both sides of him, he read *Treasure Island* to them, or described the Gallic wars or the battle of Trafalgar. In no time at all, Robbie, with the backing of his father, became the king of the school yard. This is demonstrated by the facts that he had no chum, that they gave him no nickname, and that he arbitrated all the disputes. So exalted was his station that no one even tried to fight with him.

Only gradually did Robbie come to realize that he was the leader of the younger boys of the school. Something self-possessed and mature about him made his companions turn to him for leadership. It wasn't long before his was the voice which decided the game to be played. In baseball he was the umpire for the reason that no other boy could make a ruling without causing a riot. And while he played the games badly himself, questions of rules and ethics were invariably referred to him.

After a lengthy discussion with Junius and Jakob, Robbie invented two vastly popular games, one called Slinkey Coyote, a local version of Hare and Hounds, and the other named Broken Leg, a kind of glorified tag. For these two games he made rules as he needed them.

Miss Morgan's interest was aroused by the little boy, for he was as much a surprise in the schoolroom as he was in the yard. He could read perfectly and used a man's vocabulary, but he could not write. He was familiar with numbers, no matter how large, yet he refused to learn even the simplest arithmetic. Robbie learned to write with the greatest of difficulty. His hand wavered crazy letters on his school pad. At length Miss Morgan tried to help him.

"Take one thing and do it over and over until you get it perfectly," she suggested. "Be very careful with each letter."

Robbie searched his memory for something he liked. At length he wrote, "There is nothing so monsterous but we can belief it of ourselfs." He loved that 'monsterous.' It gave timbre and profundity to the thing. If there were words, which through their very sound-power could drag unwilling genii from the earth, 'monsterous' was surely one of them. Over and over he wrote the sentence, putting the greatest of care and drawing on his 'monsterous.' At the end of an hour, Miss Morgan came to see how he was getting on.

"Why, Robert, where in the world did you hear that?"

"It's from Stevenson, ma'am. My father knows it by heart almost."

Of course Miss Morgan had heard all the bad stories of Junius, and in spite of them had approved of him. But now she began to have a strong desire to meet him.

Games in the school yard were beginning to fall off in interest. Robbie lamented the fact to Junius one morning before he started off to school. Junius scratched his beard and thought. "Spy is a good game," he said at last. "I remember I used to like Spy."

"Who shall we spy on, though?"

"Oh, anyone. It doesn't matter. We used to spy on Italians."

Robbie ran off excitedly to school, and that afternoon, following a lengthy recourse to the school dictionary, he organized the B.A.S.S.F.E.A.J. Translated, which it never was above a whisper, this was the Boys' Auxiliary Secret Service For Espionage Against The Japanese. If for no other reason, the very magnificence of the name of this organization would have made it a force to be reckoned with. One by one Robbie took the boys into the dim greenness under the school yard willow tree, and there swore them to secrecy with an oath so ferocious that it would have done credit to a lodge. Later, he brought the group together. Robbie explained to the boys that we would undoubtedly go to war with Japan some day.

"It behoofs us to be ready," he said. "The more we can find out about the nefarious practices of this nefarious race, the more spy information we can give our country when war breaks out."

The candidates succumbed before this glorious diction. They were appalled by the seriousness of a situation which required words like these. Since spying was now the business of the school, little Takashi Kato, who was in the third grade, didn't spend a private moment from then on. If Takashi raised two fingers in school, Robbie glanced meaningly at one of the Boy Auxiliaries, and a second hand sprung frantically into the air. When Takashi walked home after school, at least five boys crept through the brush beside the road. Eventually, however, Mr. Kato, Takashi's father, fired a shot into the dark one night, after seeing a white face looking in his window. Robbie reluctantly called the Auxiliary together and ordered that espionage be stopped at sundown. "They couldn't do anything really important at night," he explained.

In the long run Takashi did not suffer from the espionage practised on him, for, since the Auxiliaries had to watch him, they could make no important excursions without taking him along. He found himself invited everywhere, because no one would consent to be left behind to watch him.

The Boy Auxiliaries received their death blow when Takashi, who had in some way learned of their existence, applied for admittance.

"I don't see how we can let you in," Robbie explained kindly. "You see you're a Japanese, and we hate them."

Takashi was almost in tears. "I was born here, the same as you," he cried. "I'm just as good American as you, ain't I?"

Robbie thought hard. He didn't want to be cruel to Takashi. Then his brow cleared. "Say, do you speak Japanese?" he demanded.

"Sure, pretty good."

"Well, then you can be our interpreter and figure out secret messages."

Takashi beamed with pleasure. "Sure I can," he cried enthusiastically. "And if you guys want, we'll spy on my old man."

But the thing was broken. There was no one left to fight but Mr. Kato, and Mr. Kato was too nervous with his shotgun.

Hallowe'en went past, and Thanksgiving. In that time Robbie's effect on the boys was indicated by a growth in their vocabularies, and by a positive hatred for shoes or of any kind of good clothing for that matter. Although he didn't realize it, Robbie had set a style, not new, perhaps, but more rigid than it had been. It was unmanly to wear good clothes, and even more than that, it was considered an insult to Robbie.

One Friday afternoon Robbie wrote fourteen notes, and secretly passed them to fourteen boys in the school yard. The notes were all the same. They said: "A lot of indians are going to burn the Pres. of the U. S. to the stake at my house tomorrow at ten o'clock. Sneak out and bark like a fox down by our lower field. I will come and lead you to the rescue of this poor soul."

For several months Miss Morgan had intended to call upon Junius Maltby. The stories told of him, and her contact with his son, had raised her interest to a high point. Every now and then, in the schoolroom, one of the boys imparted a piece of astounding information. For example, one child who was really famous for his stupidity, told her that Hengest and Horsa invaded Britain. When pressed he admitted that the information came from Junius Maltby, and that in some way it was a kind of a secret. The old story of the goat amused the teacher so much that she wrote it for a magazine, but no magazine bought it. Over and over she had set a date to walk out to the Maltby farm.

She awakened on a December Saturday morning and found frost in the air and a brilliant sun shining. After breakfast she put on her corduroy skirt and her hiking boots, and left the house. In the yard she tried to persuade the ranch dogs to accompany her, but they only flopped their tails and went back to sleep in the sun.

The Maltby place lay about two miles away in the little canyon called Gato Amarillo. A stream ran beside the road, and sword ferns grew rankly under the alders. It was almost cold in the canyon, for the sun had not yet climbed over the mountain. Once during her walk Miss Morgan thought she heard footsteps and voices ahead of her, but when she hurried around the bend, no one was in sight. However, the brush beside the road crackled mysteriously.

Although she had never been there before, Miss Morgan knew the Maltby land when she came to it. Fences reclined tiredly on the ground under an overload of bramble. The fruit trees stretched bare branches clear of a forest of weeds. Wild blackberry vines clambered up the apple trees; squirrels and rabbits bolted from under her feet, and soft voiced doves flew away with whistling wings. In a tall wild pear tree a congress of bluejays squawked a cacophonous argument. Then, beside an elm tree which wore a shaggy coat of frost-bitten morning glory, Miss Morgan saw the mossy, curled shingles of the Maltby roof. The place, in its quietness, might have been deserted for a hundred years. "How run-down and slovenly," she thought. "How utterly lovely and slipshod!" She let herself into the yard through a wicket gate which hung to its post by one iron band. The farm buildings were grey with weathering, and, up the sides of the walls, outlawed climbers pushed their fingers. Miss Morgan turned the corner of the house and stopped in her tracks; her mouth fell open and a chill shriveled on her spine. In the centre of the yard a stout post was set up, and to it an old and ragged man was bound with many lengths of rope. Another man, younger and smaller, but even more ragged, piled brush about the feet of the captive. Miss Morgan shivered and backed around the house corner again. "Such things don't happen," she insisted. "You're dreaming. Such things just can't happen." And then she heard the most amiable of conversations going on between the two men.

"It's nearly ten," said the torturer.

The captive replied, "Yes, and you be careful how you put fire to that brush. You be sure to see them coming before you light it."

Miss Morgan nearly screamed with relief. She walked a little unsteadily toward the stake. The free man turned and saw her. For a second he seemed surprised, but immediately recovering, he bowed. Coming from a man with torn overalls and a matted beard, the bow was ridiculous and charming.

"I'm the teacher," Miss Morgan explained breathlessly. "I was just out for a walk, and I saw this house. For a moment I thought this auto-da-fé was serious."

Junius smiled. "But it *is* serious. It's more serious than you think. For a moment I thought you were the rescue. The relief is due at ten o'clock, you know."

A savage barking of foxes broke out below the house

among the willows. "That will be the relief," Junius continued. "Pardon me, Miss Morgan, isn't it? I am Junius Maltby
and this gentleman on ordinary days is Jakob Stutz. Today,
though, he is President of the United States being burned by
Indians. For a time we thought he'd be Guenevere, but even
without the full figure, he makes a better President than a
Guenevere, don't you think? Besides he refused to wear a
skirt."

"Damn foolishness," said the President complacently.

Miss Morgan laughed. "May I watch the rescue, Mr.
Maltby?"

"I'm not Mr. Maltby, I'm three hundred Indians."

The barking of foxes broke out again. "Over by the steps,"
said the three hundred Indians. "You won't be taken for a
redskin and massacred over there." He gazed toward the
stream. A willow branch was shaking wildly. Junius scratched
a match on his trousers and set fire to the brush at the foot of
the stake. As the flame leaped up, the willow trees seemed to
burst into pieces and each piece became a shrieking boy. The
mass charged forward, armed as haphazardly and as terribly as
the French people were when they stormed the Bastille. Even
as the fire licked toward the President, it was kicked violently
aside. The rescuers unwound the ropes with fervent hands,
and Jakob Stutz stood free and happy. Nor was the following
ceremony less impressive than the rescue. As the boys stood at
salute, the President marched down the line and to each over-
all bib pinned a leaden slug on which the word HERO was
deeply scratched. The game was over.

"Next Saturday we hang the guilty villains who have attempted this dastardly plot," Robbie announced.

"Why not now? Let's hang 'em now!" the troop screamed.

"No, my men. There are lots of things to do. We have to
make a gallows." He turned to his father. "I guess we'll have
to hang both of you," he said. For a moment he looked covetously at Miss Morgan, and then reluctantly gave her up.

That afternoon was one of the most pleasant Miss Morgan
had ever spent. Although she was given a seat of honour on
the sycamore limb, the boys had ceased to regard her as the
teacher.

"It's nicer if you take off your shoes," Robbie invited her, and it was nicer she found, when her boots were off and her feet dangled in the water.

That afternoon Junius talked of cannibal societies among the Aleutian Indians. He told how the mercenaries turned against Carthage. He described the Lacedaemonians combing their hair before they died at Thermopylae. He explained the origin of macaroni, and told of the discovery of copper as though he had been there. Finally when the dour Jakob opposed his idea of the eviction from the Garden of Eden, a mild quarrel broke out, and the boys started for home. Miss Morgan allowed them to distance her, for she wanted to think quietly about the strange gentleman.

The day when the school board visited was looked forward to with terror by both the teacher and her pupils. It was a day of tense ceremony. Lessons were recited nervously and the misspelling of a word seemed a capital crime. There was no day on which the children made more blunders, nor on which the teacher's nerves were thinner worn.

The school board of the Pastures of Heaven visited on the afternoon of December 15. Immediately after lunch they filed in, looking sombre and funereal and a little ashamed. First came John Whiteside, the clerk, old and white haired, with an easy attitude toward education which was sometimes criticised in the valley. Pat Humbert came after him. Pat was elected because he wanted to be. He was a lonely man who had no initiative in meeting people, and who took every possible means to be thrown into their contact. His clothes were as uncompromising, as unhappy as the bronze suit on the seated statue of Lincoln in Washington. T. B. Allen followed, dumpily rolling up the aisle. Since he was the only merchant in the valley, his seat on the board belonged to him by right. Behind him strode Raymond Banks, big and jolly and very red of hands and face. Last in the line was Bert Munroe, the newly elected member. Since it was his first visit to the school, Bert seemed a little sheepish as he followed the other members to their seats at the front of the room.

When the board was seated magisterially, their wives came in and found seats at the back of the room, behind the children. The pupils squirmed uneasily. They felt that they were surrounded, that escape, should they need to escape, was cut off. When they twisted in their seats, they saw that the women were smiling benevolently on them. They caught sight of a large paper bundle which Mrs. Munroe held on her lap.

School opened. Miss Morgan, with a strained smile on her face, welcomed the school board. "We will do nothing out of the ordinary, gentlemen," she said. "I think it will be more interesting to you in your official capacities, to see the school as it operates every day." Very little later, she wished she hadn't said that. Never within her recollection, had she seen such stupid children. Those who did manage to force words past their frozen palates, made the most hideous mistakes. Their spelling was abominable. Their reading sounded like the jibbering of the insane. The board tried to be dignified, but they could not help smiling a little from embarrassment for the children. A light perspiration formed on Miss Morgan's forehead. She had visions of being dismissed from her position by an outraged board. The wives in the rear smiled on, nervously, and time dripped by. When the arithmetic had been muddled and travestied, John Whiteside arose from his chair.

"Thank you, Miss Morgan," he said. "If you'll allow it, I'll just say a few words to the children, and then you can dismiss them. They ought to have some payment for having us here."

The teacher sighed with relief. "Then you do understand they weren't doing as well as usual? I'm glad you know that."

John Whiteside smiled. He had seen so many nervous young teachers on school board days. "If I thought they were doing their best, I'd close the school," he said. Then he spoke to the children for five minutes—told them they should study hard and love their teacher. It was the short and painless little speech he had used for years. The older pupils had heard it often. When it was done, he asked the teacher to dismiss the school. The pupils filed quietly out, but, once in the air, their relief was too much for them. With howls and shrieks they did their best to kill each other by disembowelment and decapitation.

John Whiteside shook hands with Miss Morgan. "We've never had a teacher who kept better order," he said kindly. "I think if you knew how much the children like you, you'd be embarrassed."

"But they're good children," she insisted loyally. "They're awfully good children."

"Of course," John Whiteside agreed. "By the way, how is the little Maltby boy getting along?"

"Why, he's a bright youngster, a curious child. I think he has almost a brilliant mind."

"We've been talking about him in board meeting, Miss Morgan. You know, of course, that his home life isn't all that it ought to be. I noticed him this afternoon especially. The poor child's hardly clothed."

"Well, it's a strange home." Miss Morgan felt that she had to defend Junius. "It's not the usual kind of home, but it isn't bad."

"Don't mistake me, Miss Morgan. We aren't going to interfere. We just thought we ought to give him a few things. His father's very poor, you know."

"I know," she said gently.

"Mrs. Munroe bought him a few clothes. If you'll call him in, we'll give them to him."

"Oh. No, I wouldn't—" she began.

"Why not? We only have a few little shirts and a pair of overalls and some shoes."

"But Mr. Whiteside, it might embarrass him. He's quite a proud little chap."

"Embarrass him to have decent clothes? Nonsense! I should think it would embarrass him more not to have them. But aside from that, it's too cold for him to go barefoot at this time of year. There's been frost on the ground every morning for a week."

"I wish you wouldn't," she said helplessly. "I really wish you wouldn't do it."

"Miss Morgan, don't you think you're making too much of this. Mrs. Munroe has been kind enough to buy the things for him. Please call him in so she can give them to him."

A moment later Robbie stood before them. His unkempt hair fell over his face, and his eyes still glittered with the fierceness of the play in the yard. The group gathered at the front of the room regarded him kindly, trying not to look too pointedly at his ragged clothes. Robbie gazed uneasily about.

"Mrs. Munroe has something to give you, Robert," Miss Morgan said.

Then Mrs. Munroe came forward and put the bundle in his arms. "What a nice little boy!"

Robbie placed the package carefully on the floor and put his hands behind him.

"Open it, Robert," T. B. Allen said sternly. "Where are your manners?"

Robbie gazed resentfully at him. "Yes, sir," he said, and untied the string. The shirts and the new overalls lay open before him, and he stared at them uncomprehendingly. Suddenly he seemed to realize what they were. His face flushed warmly. For a moment he looked about nervously like a trapped animal, and then he bolted through the door, leaving the little heap of clothing behind him. The school board heard two steps on the porch, and Robbie was gone.

Mrs. Munroe turned helplessly to the teacher. "What's wrong with him, anyway?"

"I think he was embarrassed," said Miss Morgan.

"But why should he be? We were nice to him."

The teacher tried to explain, and became a little angry with them in trying. "I think, you see—why I don't think he ever knew he was poor until a moment ago."

"It was my mistake," John Whiteside apologized. "I'm sorry, Miss Morgan."

"What can we do about him?" Bert Munroe asked.

"I don't know. I really don't know."

Mrs. Munroe turned to her husband. "Bert, I think if you went out and had a talk with Mr. Maltby it might help. I don't mean you to be anything but kind. Just tell him little boys shouldn't walk around in bare feet in the frost. Maybe just a word like that'll help. Mr. Maltby could tell little Robert he must take the clothes. What do you think, Mr. Whiteside?"

"I don't like it. You'll have to vote to overrule my objection. I've done enough harm."

"I think his health is more important than his feelings," Mrs. Munroe insisted.

School closed for Christmas week on the twentieth of December. Miss Morgan planned to spend her vacation in Los Angeles. While she waited at the crossroads for a bus to Salinas, she saw a man and a little boy walking down the Pastures of Heaven road toward her. They were dressed in cheap new clothes, and both of them walked as though their feet were sore. As they neared her, Miss Morgan looked closely at the little boy, and saw that it was Robbie. His face was sullen and unhappy.

"Why, Robert," she cried. "What's the matter? Where are you going?"

The man spoke. "We're going to San Francisco, Miss Morgan."

She looked up quickly. It was Junius shorn of his beard. She hadn't realized that he was so old. Even his eyes, which had been young, looked old. But of course he was pale because the beard had protected his skin from sunburn. On his face there was a look of deep puzzlement.

"Are you going up for the Holidays?" Miss Morgan asked. "I love the stores in the city around Christmas. I could look in them for days."

"No," Junius replied slowly. "I guess we're going to be up there for good. I am an accountant, Miss Morgan. At least I was an accountant twenty years ago. I'm going to try to get a job." There was pain in his voice.

"But why do you do that?" she demanded.

"You see," he explained simply. "I didn't know I was doing an injury to the boy, here. I hadn't thought about it. I suppose I should have thought about it. You can see that he shouldn't be brought up in poverty. You can see that, can't you? I didn't know what people were saying about us."

"Why don't you stay on the ranch? It's a good ranch, isn't it?"

"But I couldn't make a living on it, Miss Morgan. I don't know anything about farming. Jakob is going to try to run the ranch, but you know, Jakob is very lazy. Later, when I can, I'll sell the ranch so Robbie can have a few things he never had."

Miss Morgan was angry, but at the same time she felt she was going to cry. "You don't believe everything silly people tell you, do you?"

He looked at her in surprise. "Of course not. But you can see for yourself that a growing boy shouldn't be brought up like a little animal, can't you?"

The bus came into sight on the highway and bore down on them. Junius pointed to Robbie. "He didn't want to come. He ran away into the hills. Jakob and I caught him last night. He's lived like a little animal too long, you see. Besides, Miss Morgan, he doesn't know how nice it will be in San Francisco."

The bus squealed to a stop. Junius and Robbie climbed into the back seat. Miss Morgan was about to get in beside them. Suddenly she turned and took her seat beside the driver. "Of course," she said to herself. "Of course, they want to be alone."

VII

O LD Guiermo Lopez died when his daughters were fairly
well grown, leaving them forty acres of rocky hillside
and no money at all. They lived in a whitewashed, clapboard
shack with an outhouse, a well and a shed beside it. Practically nothing would grow on the starved soil except tumble
weed and flowering sage, and, although the sisters toiled
mightily over a little garden, they succeeded in producing
very few vegetables. For a time, with grim martyrdom, they
went hungry, but in the end the flesh conquered. They were
too fat and too jolly to make martyrs of themselves over an
unreligious matter like eating.

One day Rosa had an idea. "Are we not the best makers of
tortillas in the valley?" she asked of her sister.

"We had that art from our mother," Maria responded
piously.

"Then we are saved. We will make enchiladas, tortillas, tamales. We will sell them to the people of Las Pasturas del
Cielo."

"Will those people buy, do you think?" Maria asked scep-
tically.

"Listen to this from me, Maria. In Monterey there are several places where tortillas, only one finger as good as ours, are
sold. And those people who sell them are very rich. They have
a new dress thrice a year. And do their tortillas compare with
ours? I ask that of you, remembering our mother."

Maria's eyes brimmed with tears of emotion. "They do
not," she declared passionately. "In the whole world there are
none like those tortillas beaten by the sainted hands of our
mother."

"Well, then, adelante!" said Rosa with finality. "If they are
so good, the people will buy."

There followed a week of frenzied preparation in which the
perspiring sisters scrubbed and decorated. When they had finished, their little house wore a new coat of whitewash inside
and out. Geranium cuttings were planted by the doorstep,
and the trash of years had been collected and burned. The

front room of the house was transformed into a restaurant containing two tables which were covered with yellow oil-cloth. A pine board on the fence next to the county road proclaimed: TORTILLAS, ENCHILADAS, TAMALES AND SOME OTHER SPANISH COOKINGS, R. & M. LOPEZ.

Business did not come with a rush. Indeed very little came at all. The sisters sat at their own yellow tables and waited. They were child-like and jovial and not very clean. Sitting in the chairs they waited on fortune. But let a customer enter the shop, and they leaped instantly to attention. They laughed delightedly at everything their client said; they boasted of their ancestry and of the marvellous texture of their tortillas. They rolled their sleeves to the elbows to show the whiteness of their skin in passionate denial of Indian blood. But very few customers came. The sisters began to find difficulties in their business. They could not make a quantity of their product, for it would spoil if kept for long. Tamales require fresh meat. So it was that they began to set traps for birds and rabbits; sparrows, blackbirds and larks were kept in cages until they were needed for tamales. And still the business languished.

One morning Rosa confronted her sister. "You must harness old Lindo, Maria. There are no more corn husks." She placed a piece of silver in Maria's hand. "Buy only a few in Monterey," she said. "When the business is better we will buy very many." Maria obediently kissed her and started out toward the shed.

"And Maria—if there is any money over, a sweet for you and for me—a big one."

When Maria drove back to the house that afternoon, she found her sister strangely quiet. The shrieks, the little squeals, the demands for every detail of the journey, which usually followed a reunion, were missing. Rosa sat in a chair at one of the tables, and on her face there was a scowl of concentration.

Maria approached timidly. "I bought the husks very cheaply," she said. "And here, Rosa, here is the sweet. The biggest kind, and only four cents!"

Rosa took the proffered candy bar and put one huge end of it in her mouth. She still scowled with thought. Maria settled herself nearby, smiling gently, quizzically, silently pleading for a share of her sister's burden. Rosa sat like a rock and sucked her candy bar. Suddenly she glared into Maria's eyes. "To-day," she said solemnly, "today I gave myself to a customer."

Maria sobbed with excitement and interest.

"Do not make a mistake," Rosa continued. "I did not take money. The man had eaten three enchiladas—three!"

Maria broke into a thin, childish wail of nervousness.

"Be still," said Rosa. "What do you think I should do now? It is necessary to encourage our customers if we are to suc-ceed. And he had three, Maria, three enchiladas! And he paid for them. Well? What do you think?"

Maria sniffled and clutched at a moral bravery in the face of her sister's argument. "I think, Rosa, I think our mother would be glad, and I think your own soul would be glad if you should ask forgiveness of the Mother Virgin and of Santa Rosa."

Rosa smiled broadly and took Maria in her arms. "That is what I did. Just as soon as he went away. He was hardly out of the house before I did that."

Maria tore herself away, and with streaming eyes went into her bedroom. Ten minutes she kneeled before the little virgin on the wall. Then she arose and flung herself into Rosa's arms. "Rosa, my sister," she cried happily. "I think—I think I shall encourage the customers, too."

The Lopez sisters smothered each other in a huge embrace and mingled their tears of joy.

That day marked the turning point of the affairs of the Lo-pez sisters. It is true that business did not flourish, but from then on, they sold enough of their "Spanish Cookings" to keep food in the kitchen and bright print dresses on their broad, round backs. They remained persistently religious. When either of them had sinned she went directly to the little porcelain Virgin, now conveniently placed in the hall to be accessible from both bedrooms, and prayed for forgiveness. Sins were not allowed to pile up. They confessed each one as it was committed. Under the Virgin there was a polished place on the floor where they had knelt in their nightdresses.

Life became very pleasant to the Lopez sisters. There was not even a taint of rivalry, for although Rosa was older and

braver, they looked almost exactly alike. Maria was a little fatter, but Rosa was a little taller, and there you had it.

Now the house was filled with laughter and with squeals of
enthusiasm. They sang over the flat stones while they patted
out the tortillas with their fat, strong hands. Let a customer
say something funny, let Tom Breman say to them, as he ate
his third tamale, "Rosa, you're living too high. This rich living is going to bust your gut wide open if you don't cut it
out," and both of the sisters would be racked with giggles for
half an hour afterwards. A whole day later, while they patted
out the tortillas on the stone, they would remember this
funny thing and laugh all over again. For these sisters knew
how to preserve laughter, how to pet and coax it along until
their spirits drank the last dregs of its potentiality. Don Tom
was a fine man, they said. A funny man—and a rich man.
Once he ate five plates of chile con carne. But also, something
you did not often find in a rich man, he was an *hombre fuerte*,
oh, very strong! Over the tortilla stones they nodded their
heads wisely and reminiscently at this observation, like two
connoisseurs remembering a good wine.

It must not be supposed that the sisters were prodigal of
their encouragement. They accepted no money for anything
except their cooking. However, if a man ate three or more of
their dishes, the soft hearts of the sisters broke with gratitude,
and that man became a candidate for encouragement.

On an unfortunate night, a man whose appetite was not
equal to three enchiladas offered to Rosa the money of
shame. There were several other customers in the house at the
time. The offer was cast into a crackle of conversation. Instantly the noise ceased, leaving a horrified silence. Maria hid
her face in her hands. Rosa grew pale and then flushed brilliant with furious blood. She panted with emotion and her
eyes sparkled. Her fat, strong hands rose like eagles and settled on her hips. But when she spoke, it was with a curious
emotional restraint. "It is an insult to me," she said huskily.
"You do not know, perhaps, that General Vallejo is nearly our
ancestor, so close as that we are related. In our veins the pure
blood is. What would General Vallejo say if he heard? Do you
think his hand could stay from his sword to hear you insult
two ladies so nearly in his family? Do you think it? You say to

us, 'You are shameful women!' We, who make the finest, the thinnest tortillas in all California." She panted with the effort to restrain herself.

"I didn't mean nothing," the offender whined. "Honest to God, Rosa, I didn't mean nothing."

Her anger left her then. One of her hands took flight from her hip, this time like a lark, and motioned almost sadly toward the door. "Go," she said gently. "I do not think you meant bad, but the insult is still." And as the culprit slunk out of the doorway, "Now, would anyone else like a little dish of chiles con frijoles? Which one here? Chiles con frijoles like none in the world."

Ordinarily they were happy, these sisters. Maria, whose nature was very delicate and sweet, planted more geraniums around the house, and lined the fence with hollyhocks. On a trip to Salinas, Rosa and Maria bought and presented to each other boudoir caps like inverted nests of blue and pink ribbons. It was the ultimate! Side by side they looked in a mirror and then turned their heads and smiled a little sadly at each other, thinking, "This is the great day. This is the time we shall remember always as the happy time. What a shame it cannot last."

In fear that it would not last, Maria kept large vases of flowers in front of her Virgin.

But their foreboding came seldom upon them. Maria bought a little phonograph with records—tangoes, waltzes. When the sisters worked over the stones, they set the machine to playing and patted out the tortillas in time to the music.

Inevitably, in the valley of the Pastures of Heaven, the whisper went about that the Lopez sisters were bad women. Ladies of the valley spoke coldly to them when they passed. It is impossible to say how these ladies knew. Certainly their husbands didn't tell them, but nevertheless they knew; they always know.

Before daylight on a Saturday morning, Maria carried out the old, string-mended harness and festooned it on the bones of Lindo. "Have courage, my friend," she said to the horse, as she buckled the crupper and, "The mouth, please, my Lindo," as she inserted the bit. Then she backed him between the shafts of an ancient buggy. Lindo purposely stumbled over the shafts, just as he had for thirty years. When Maria hooked the traces, he looked around at her with a heavy, philosophic sadness. Old Lindo had no interest in destinations any more. He was too old even to be excited about going home once he was out. Now he lifted his lips from his long, yellow teeth, and grinned despairingly. "The way is not long," Maria soothed him. "We will go slowly. You must not fear the journey, Lindo." But Lindo did fear the journey. He loathed the journey to Monterey and back.

The buggy sagged alarmingly when Maria clambered into it. She took the lines gingerly in her hands. "Go, my friend," she said, and fluttered the lines. Lindo shivered and looked around at her. "Do you hear? We must go! There are things to buy in Monterey." Lindo shook his head and drooped one knee in a kind of curtsey. "Listen to me, Lindo!" Maria cried imperiously. "I say we must go. I am firm! I am even angry." She fluttered the lines ferociously about his shoulders. Lindo drooped his head nearly to the earth, like a scenting hound, and moved slowly out of the yard. Nine miles he must go to Monterey, and nine miles back. Lindo knew it, and despaired at the knowledge. But now that her firmness and her anger were over, Maria settled back in the seat and hummed the chorus of the "Waltz Moon" tango.

The hills glittered with dew. Maria, breathing the fresh damp air, sang more loudly, and even Lindo found youth enough in his old nostrils to snort. A meadow lark flew ahead from post to post, singing furiously. Far ahead Maria saw a man walking in the road. Before she caught up with him, she knew from the shambling, ape-like stride that it was Allen Hueneker, the ugliest, shyest man in the valley.

Allen Hueneker not only walked like an ape, he looked like an ape. Little boys who wanted to insult their friends did so by pointing to Allen and saying, "There goes your brother." It was a deadly satire. Allen was so shy and so horrified at his appearance that he tried to grow whiskers to cover up his face, but the coarse, sparse stubble grew in the wrong places and only intensified his simian appearance. His wife had married him because she was thirty-seven, and because Allen was the only man of her acquaintance who could not protect himself. Later it developed that she was a woman whose system required jealousy properly to function. Finding nothing in Allen's life of which she could be jealous, she manufactured things. To her neighbors she told stories of his prowess with women, of his untrustworthiness, of his obscure delinquencies. She told these stories until she believed them, but her neighbours laughed behind her back when she spoke of Allen's sins, for everyone in the Pastures of Heaven knew how shy and terrified the ugly little man was.

The ancient Lindo stumbled abreast of Allen Hueneker. Maria tugged on the lines as though she pulled up a thunderously galloping steed. "Steady, Lindo! Be calm!" she called. At the lightest pressure of the lines, Lindo turned to stone and sunk into his loose-jointed, hang necked posture of complete repose.

"Good morning," said Maria politely.

Allen edged shyly over toward the side of the road. "Morning," he said, and turned to look with affected interest up a side hill.

"I go to Monterey," Maria continued. "Do you wish to ride?"

Allen squirmed and searched the sky for clouds or hawks. "I ain't going only to the bus stop," he said sullenly.

"And what then? It is a little ride, no?"

The man scratched among his whiskers, trying to make up his mind. And then, more to end the situation than for the sake of a ride, he climbed into the buggy beside the fat Maria. She rolled aside to make room for him, and then oozed back. "Lindo, go!" she called. "Lindo, do you hear me? Go before I grow angry again." The lines clattered about Lindo's neck. His nose dropped toward the ground, and he sauntered on.

For a little while they rode in silence, but soon Maria remembered how polite it was to encourage conversation. "You go on a trip, yes?" she asked.

Allen glared at an oak tree and said nothing.

"I have not been on a train," Maria confided after a moment, "but my sister, Rosa, has ridden on trains. Once she rode to San Francisco, and once she rode back. I have heard very rich men say it is good to travel. My own sister, Rosa, says so too."

"I ain't going only to Salinas," said Allen.

"Ah, of course I have been there many times. Rosa and I have such friends in Salinas. Our mother came from there. And our father often went there with wood."

Allen struggled against his embarrassment. "Couldn't get the old Ford going, or I'd've gone in it."

"You have, then, a Ford?" Maria was impressed.

"Just an old Ford."

"We have said, Rosa and I, that some day we, too, may have a Ford. Then we will travel to many places. I have heard very rich men say it is good to travel."

As though to punctuate the conversation, an old Ford appeared over the hill and came roaring down on them. Maria gripped the lines. "Lindo, be calm!" she called. Lindo paid not the slightest attention either to Maria or to the Ford.

Mr. and Mrs. Munroe were in the Ford. Bert craned his neck back as they passed. "God! Did you see that?" he demanded, laughing. "Did you see that old woman-killer with Maria Lopez?"

Mrs. Munroe smiled.

"Say," Bert cried. "It'd be a good joke to tell old lady Hueneker we saw her old man running off with Maria Lopez."

"Don't you do anything of the kind," his wife insisted.

"But it'd be a good joke. You know how she talks about him."

"No, don't you do it, Bert!"

Meanwhile Maria drove on, conversing guilelessly with her reluctant guest. "You do not come to our house for enchiladas. There are no enchiladas like ours. For look! we learned from our mother. When our mother was living, it was said as far as San Juan, even as far as Gilroy, that no one else could make tortillas so flat, so thin. You must know it is the beating, always the beating that makes goodness and thinness to a tortilla. No one ever beat so long as our mother, not even Rosa. I go now to Monterey for flour because it is cheaper there."

Allen Hueneker sank into his side of the seat and wished for the bus station.

It was late in the afternoon before Maria neared home again. "Soon we are there," she called happily to Lindo. "Have courage, my friend, the way is short now." Maria was bubbling with anticipation. In a riot of extravagance she had bought four candy bars, but that was not all. For Rosa she had a present, a pair of broad silken garters with huge red poppies appliquéd on their sides. In her imagination she could see Rosa putting them on and then lifting her skirt, but very modestly, of course. The two of them would look at the garters in a mirror standing on the floor. Rosa would point her toe a trifle, and then the sisters would cry with happiness.

In the yard Maria slowly unharnessed Lindo. It was good, she knew, to put off joy, for by doing so, one increased joy. The house was very quiet. There were no vehicles in front to indicate the presence of customers. Maria hung up the old harness, and turned Lindo into the pasture. Then she took out the candy bars and the garters and walked slowly into the house. Rosa sat at one of the little tables, a silent, restrained Rosa, a grim and suffering Rosa. Her eyes seemed glazed and sightless. Her fat, firm hands were clenched on the table in front of her. She did not turn nor give any sign of recognition when Maria entered. Maria stopped and stared at her.

"Rosa," she said timidly. "I'm back home, Rosa."

Her sister turned slowly. "Yes," she said.

"Are you sick, Rosa?"

The glazed eyes had turned back to the table again. "No."

"I have a present, Rosa. Look, Rosa." She held up the magnificent garters.

Slowly, very slowly, Rosa's eyes crept up to the brilliant red poppies and then to Maria's face. Maria was poised to break into squealing enthusiasm. Rosa's eyes dropped, and two fat tears ran down the furrows beside her nose.

"Rosa, do you see the present? Don't you like them, Rosa? Won't you put them on, Rosa?"

"You are my good little sister."

"Rosa, tell me, what is the matter? You are sick. You must tell your Maria. Did someone come?"

"Yes," said Rosa hollowly, "the sheriff came."

Now Maria fairly chattered with excitement. "The sheriff, he came? Now we are on the road. Now we will be rich. How many enchiladas, Rosa? Tell me how many for the sheriff."

Rosa shook off her apathy. She went to Maria and put

motherly arms about her. "My poor little sister," she said. "Now we cannot ever sell any more enchiladas. Now we must live again in the old way with no new dresses."

"Rosa, you are crazy. Why you talk this way to me?"

"It is true. It was the sheriff. 'I have a complaint,' he said to me. 'I have a complaint that you are running a bad house.' 'But that is a lie,' I said. 'A lie and an insult to our mother and to General Vallejo.' 'I have a complaint,' he told me. 'You must close your doors or else I must arrest you for running a bad house.' 'But it is a lie,' I tried to make him understand. 'I got a complaint this afternoon,' he said. 'When I have a complaint, there is nothing I can do, for see, Rosa,' he said to me as a friend, 'I am only the servant of the people who make complaints.' And now you see, Maria, my sister, we must go back to the old living." She left the stricken Maria and turned back to her table. For a moment Maria tried to understand it, and then she sobbed hysterically. "Be still, Maria! I have been thinking. You know it is true that we will starve if we cannot sell enchiladas. Do not blame me too much when I tell you this. I have made up my mind. See, Maria! I will go to San Francisco and be a bad woman." Her head dropped low over her fat hands. Maria's sobbing had stopped. She crept close to her sister.

"For money?" she whispered in horror.

"Yes," cried Rosa bitterly. "For money. For a great deal of money. And may the good mother forgive me."

Maria left her then, and scuttled into the hallway where she stood in front of the porcelain Mary. "I have placed candles," she cried. "I have put flowers every day. Holy Mother, what is the matter with us? Why do you let this happen?" Then she dropped on her knees and prayed, fifty Hail Marys! She crossed herself and rose to her feet. Her face was strained but determined.

In the other room Rosa still sat bent over her table.

"Rosa," Maria cried shrilly. "I am your sister. I am what you are." She gulped a great breath. "Rosa, I will go to San Francisco with you. I, too, will be a bad woman—"

Then the reserve of Rosa broke. She stood up and opened her huge embrace. And for a long time the Lopez sisters cried hysterically in each other's arms.

VIII

MOLLY MORGAN got off the train in Salinas and waited three quarters of an hour for the bus. The big automobile was empty except for the driver and Molly.

"I've never been to the Pastures of Heaven, you know," she said. "Is it far from the main road?"

"About three miles," said the driver.

"Will there be a car to take me into the valley?"

"No, not unless you're met."

"But how do people get in there?"

The driver ran over the flattened body of a jack rabbit with apparent satisfaction. "I only hit 'em when they're dead," he apologized. "In the dark, when they get caught in the lights, I try to miss 'em."

"Yes, but how am I going to get into the Pastures of Heaven?"

"I dunno. Walk, I guess. Most people walk if they ain't met."

When he set her down at the entrance to the dirt side-road, Molly Morgan grimly picked up her suitcase and marched toward the draw in the hills. An old Ford truck squeaked up beside her.

"Goin' into the valley, ma'am?"

"Oh—yes, yes, I am."

"Well, get in, then. Needn't be scared. I'm Pat Humbert. I got a place in the Pastures."

Molly surveyed the grimy man and acknowledged his introduction. "I'm the new schoolteacher. I mean, I think I am. Do you know where Mr. Whiteside lives?"

"Sure, I go right by there. He's clerk of the board. I'm on the school board myself, you know. We wondered what you'd look like." Then he grew embarrassed at what he had said, and flushed under his coating of dirt. " 'Course I mean what you'd *be* like. Last teacher we had gave a good deal of trouble. She was all right, but she was sick—I mean, sick and nervous. Finally quit because she was sick."

Molly picked at the fingertips of her gloves. "My letter says

93

I'm to call on Mr. Whiteside. Is he all right? I don't mean that. I mean—is he—what kind of a man is he?"

"Oh, you'll get along with him all right. He's a fine old man. Born in that house he lives in. Been to college, too. He's a good man. Been clerk of the board for over twenty years."

When he put her down in front of the big old house of John Whiteside, she was really frightened. "Now it's coming," she said to herself. "But there's nothing to be afraid of. He can't do anything to me." Molly was only nineteen. She felt that this moment of interview for her first job was a tremendous inch in her whole existence.

The walk up to the door did not reassure her, for the path lay between tight little flower beds hedged in with clipped box, seemingly planted with the admonition, "Now grow and multiply, but don't grow too high, nor multiply too greatly, and above all things, keep out of this path!" There was a hand on those flowers, a guiding and a correcting hand. The large white house was very dignified. Venetian blinds of yellow wood were tilted down to keep out the noon sun. Halfway up the path she came in sight of the entrance. There was a veranda as broad and warm and welcoming as an embrace. Through her mind flew the thought, "Surely you can tell the hospitality of a house by its entrance. Suppose it had a little door and no porch." But in spite of the welcoming of the wide steps and the big doorway, her timidities clung to her when she rang the bell. The big door opened, and a large, comfortable woman stood smiling at Molly.

"I hope you're not selling something," said Mrs. Whiteside. "I never want to buy anything, and I always do, and then I'm mad."

Molly laughed. She felt suddenly very happy. Until that moment she hadn't known how frightened she really was. "Oh, no," she cried. "I'm the new school teacher. My letter says I'm to interview Mr. Whiteside. Can I see him?"

"Well, it's noon, and he's just finishing his dinner. Did you have dinner?"

"Oh, of course. I mean, no."

Mrs. Whiteside chuckled and stood aside for her to enter. "Well, I'm glad you're sure." She led Molly into a large dining room, lined with mahogany, glass-fronted dish closets. The square table was littered with the dishes of a meal. "Why, John must have finished and gone. Sit down, young woman. I'll bring back the roast."

"Oh, no. Really, thank you, no, I'll just talk to Mr. Whiteside and then go along."

"Sit down. You'll need nourishment to face John."

"Is—is he very stern, with new teachers, I mean?"

"Well," said Mrs. Whiteside. "That depends. If they haven't had their dinner, he's a regular bear. He shouts at them. But when they've just got up from the table, he's only just fierce."

Molly laughed happily. "You have children," she said. "Oh, you've raised lots of children—and you like them."

Mrs. Whiteside scowled. "One child raised me. Raised me right through the roof. It was too hard on me. He's out raising cows now, poor devils. I don't think I raised him very high."

When Molly had finished eating, Mrs. Whiteside threw open a side door and called, "John, here's someone to see you." She pushed Molly through the doorway into a room that was a kind of a library, for big bookcases were loaded with thick, old comfortable books, all filigreed in gold. And it was a kind of a sitting room. There was a fireplace of brick with a mantel of little red tile bricks and the most extraordinary vases on the mantel. Hung on a nail over the mantel, slung really, like a rifle on a shoulder strap, was a huge meerschaum pipe in the Jaegar fashion. Big leather chairs with leather tassels hanging to them, stood about the fireplace, all of them patent rocking chairs with the kind of springs that chant when you rock them. And lastly, the room was a kind of an office, for there was an old-fashioned roll-top desk, and behind it sat John Whiteside. When he looked up, Molly saw that he had at once the kindest and the sternest eyes she had ever seen, and the whitest hair, too. Real blue-white, silky hair, a great duster of it.

"I am Mary Morgan," she began formally.

"Oh, yes, Miss Morgan, I've been expecting you. Won't you sit down?"

She sat in one of the big rockers, and the springs cried with sweet pain. "I love these chairs," she said. "We used to have one when I was a little girl." Then she felt silly. "I've come to interview you about this position. My letter said to do that."

"Don't be so tense, Miss Morgan. I've interviewed every teacher we've had for years. And," he said, smiling, "I still don't know how to go about it."

"Oh—I'm glad, Mr. Whiteside. I never asked for a job before. I was really afraid of it."

"Well, Miss Mary Morgan, as near as I can figure, the purpose of this interview is to give me a little knowledge of your past and of the kind of person you are. I'm supposed to know something about you when you've finished. And now that you know my purpose, I suppose you'll be self-conscious and anxious to give a good impression. Maybe if you just tell me a little about yourself, everything'll be all right. Just a few words about the kind of girl you are, and where you came from."

Molly nodded quickly. "Yes, I'll try to do that, Mr. Whiteside," and she dropped her mind back into the past.

There was the old, squalid, unpainted house with its wide back porch and the round washtubs leaning against the rail. High in the great willow tree her two brothers, Joe and Tom, crashed about crying, "Now I'm an eagle." "I'm a parrot." "Now I'm an old chicken." "Watch me!"

The screen door on the back porch opened, and their mother leaned tiredly out. Her hair would not lie smoothly no matter how much she combed it. Thick strings of it hung down beside her face. Her eyes were always a little red, and her hands and wrists painfully cracked. "Tom, Joe," she called. "You'll get hurt up there. Don't worry me so, boys! Don't you love your mother at all?" The voices in the tree were hushed. The shrieking spirits of the eagle and the old chicken were drenched in self-reproach. Molly sat in the dust, wrapping a rag around a stick and doing her best to imagine it a tall lady in a dress. "Molly, come in and stay with your mother. I'm so tired today."

Molly stood up the stick in the deep dust. "You, miss," she whispered fiercely. "You'll get whipped on your bare bottom when I come back." Then she obediently went into the house.

Her mother sat in a straight chair in the kitchen. "Draw up, Molly. Just sit with me for a little while. Love me, Molly! Love your mother a little bit. You are mother's good little girl, aren't you?"

Molly squirmed on her chair. "Don't you love your mother, Molly?"

The little girl was very miserable. She knew her mother would cry in a moment, and then she would be compelled to stroke the stringy hair. Both she and her brothers knew they should love their mother. She did everything for them, everything. They were ashamed that they hated to be near her, but they couldn't help it. When she called to them and they were not in sight, they pretended not to hear, and crept away, talking in whispers.

"Well, to begin with, we were very poor," Molly said to John Whiteside. "I guess we were really poverty-stricken. I had two brothers a little older than I. My father was a traveling salesman, but even so, my mother had to work. She worked terribly hard for us."

About once in every six months a great event occurred. In the morning the mother crept silently out of the bedroom. Her hair was brushed as smoothly as it could be; her eyes sparkled, and she looked happy and almost pretty. She whispered, "Quiet, children! Your father's home."

Molly and her brothers sneaked out of the house, but even in the yard they talked in excited whispers. The news traveled quickly about the neighbourhood. Soon the yard was filled with whispering children. "They say their father's home." "Is your father really home?" "Where's he been this time?" By noon there were a dozen children in the yard, standing in expectant little groups, cautioning one another to be quiet.

About noon the screen door on the porch sprang open and whacked against the wall. Their father leaped out. "Hi," he yelled. "Hi, kids!" Molly and her brothers flung themselves upon him and hugged his legs, while he plucked them off and hurled them into the air like kittens.

Mrs. Morgan fluttered about, clucking with excitement. "Children, children. Don't muss your father's clothes."

The neighbour children threw handsprings and wrestled and shrieked with joy. It was better than any holiday.

"Wait till you see," their father cried. "Wait till you see what I brought you. It's a secret now." And when the hysteria had quieted a little he carried his suitcase out on the porch and opened it. There were presents such as no one had ever seen, mechanical toys unknown before—tin bugs that crawled, dancing wooden niggers

and astounding steam shovels that worked in sand. There were superb glass marbles with bears and dogs right in their centres. He had something for everyone, several things for everyone. It was all the great holidays packed into one.

Usually it was midafternoon before the children became calm enough not to shriek occasionally. But eventually George Morgan sat on the steps, and they all gathered about while he told his adventures. This time he had been to Mexico while there was a revolution. Again he had gone to Honolulu, had seen the volcano and had himself ridden on a surfboard. Always there were cities and people, strange people; always adventures and a hundred funny incidents, funnier than anything they had ever heard. It couldn't all be told at one time. After school they had to gather to hear more and more. Throughout the world George Morgan tramped, collecting glorious adventures.

"As far as my home life went," Miss Morgan said, "I guess I almost didn't have any father. He was able to get home very seldom from his business trips."

John Whiteside nodded gravely.

Molly's hands rustled in her lap and her eyes were dim.

One time he brought a dumpy, woolly puppy in a box, and it wet on the floor immediately.

"What kind of a dog is it?" Tom asked in his most sophisticated manner.

Their father laughed loudly. He was so young! He looked twenty years younger than their mother. "It's a dollar and a half dog," he explained. "You get an awful lot of kinds of dog for a dollar and a half. It's like this. . . . Suppose you go into a candy store and say, 'I want a nickel's worth of peppermints and gumdrops and licorice and raspberry chews.' Well, I went in and said, 'Give me a dollar and a half's worth of mixed dog.' That's the kind it is. It's Molly's dog, and she has to name it."

"I'm going to name it George," said Molly.

Her father bowed strangely to her, and said, "Thank you, Molly." They all noticed that he wasn't laughing at her, either.

Molly got up very early the next morning and took George about the yard to show him the secrets. She opened the hoard where two pennies and a gold policeman's button were buried. She hooked his little front paws over the back fence so he could look down the street at the school-house. Lastly she climbed into the willow tree, carrying

George under one arm. Tom came out of the house and sauntered under the tree. "Look out you don't drop him," Tom called, and just at that moment the puppy squirmed out of her arms and fell. He landed on the hard ground with a disgusting little thump. One leg bent out at a crazy angle, and the puppy screamed long, horrible screams, with sobs between breaths. Molly scrambled out of the tree, dull and stunned by the accident. Tom was standing over the puppy, his face white and twisted with pain, and George, the puppy, screamed on and on.

"We can't let him," Tom cried. "We can't let him." He ran to the woodpile and brought back a hatchet. Molly was too stupefied to look away, but Tom closed his eyes and struck. The screams stopped suddenly. Tom threw the hatchet from him and leaped over the back fence. Molly saw him running away as though he were being chased.

At that moment Joe and her father came out of the back door. Molly remembered how haggard and thin and grey her father's face was when he looked at the puppy. It was something in her father's face that started Molly to crying. "I dropped him out of the tree, and he hurt himself, and Tom hit him, and then Tom ran away." Her voice sounded sulky. Her father hugged Molly's head against his hip.

"Poor Tom!" he said. "Molly, you must remember never to say anything to Tom about it, and never to look at him as though you remembered." He threw a gunny sack over the puppy. "We must have a funeral," he said. "Did I ever tell you about the Chinese funeral I went to, about the coloured paper they throw in the air, and the little fat roast pigs on the grave?" Joe edged in closer, and even Molly's eyes took on a gleam of interest. "Well, it was this way. . . ."

Molly looked up at John Whiteside and saw that he seemed to be studying a piece of paper on his desk. "When I was twelve years old, my father was killed in an accident," she said.

The great visits usually lasted about two weeks. Always there came an afternoon when George Morgan walked out into the town and did not come back until late at night. The mother made the children go to bed early, but they could hear him come home, stumbling a little against the furniture, and they could hear his voice through the wall. These were the only times when his voice was sad and discouraged. Lying with held breaths, in their beds, the children knew what that meant. In the morning he would be gone, and their hearts would be gone with him.

They had endless discussions about what he was doing. Their father was a glad argonaut, a silver knight. Virtue and Courage and Beauty—he wore a coat of them. "Sometime," the boys said, "sometime when we're big, we'll go with him and see all those things."

"I'll go, too," Molly insisted.

"Oh, you're a girl. You couldn't go, you know."

"But he'd let me go, you know he would. Sometime he'll take me with him. You see if he doesn't."

When he was gone their mother grew plaintive again, and her eyes reddened. Querulously she demanded their love, as though it were a package they could put in her hand.

One time their father went away, and he never came back. He had never sent any money, nor had he ever written to them, but this time he just disappeared for good. For two years they waited, and then their mother said he must be dead. The children shuddered at the thought, but they refused to believe it, because no one so beautiful and fine as their father could be dead. Some place in the world he was having adventures. There was some good reason why he couldn't come back to them. Some day when the reason was gone, he would come: Some morning he would be there with finer presents and better stories than ever before. But their mother said he must have had an accident. He must be dead. Their mother was distracted. She read those advertisements which offered to help her make money at home. The children made paper flowers and shamefacedly tried to sell them. The boys tried to develop magazine routes, and the whole family nearly starved. Finally, when they couldn't stand it any longer, the boys ran away and joined the navy. After that Molly saw them as seldom as she had seen her father, and they were so changed, so hard and boisterous, that she didn't even care, for her brothers were strangers to her.

"I went through high school, and then I went to San Jose and entered Teachers' College. I worked for my board and room at the home of Mrs. Allen Morit. Before I finished school my mother died, so I guess I'm a kind of an orphan, you see."

"I'm sorry," John Whiteside murmured gently.

Molly flushed. "That wasn't a bid for sympathy, Mr. White-side. You said you wanted to know about me. Everyone has to be an orphan some time."

"Yes," he agreed. "I'm an orphan too, I guess."

Molly worked for her board and room. She did the work of a full time servant, only she received no pay. Money for clothes had to be accumulated by working in a store during summer vacation. Mrs. Morit trained her girls. "I can take a green girl, not worth a cent," she often said, "and when that girl's worked for me six months, she can get fifty dollars a month. Lots of women know it, and they just snap up my girls. This is the first schoolgirl I've tried, but even she shows a lot of improvement. She reads too much though. I always say a servant should be asleep by ten o'clock, or else she can't do her work right."

Mrs. Morit's method was one of constant criticism and nagging, carried on in a just, firm tone. "Now, Molly, I don't want to find fault, but if you don't wipe the silver drier than that, it'll have streaks." —"The butter knife goes this way, Molly. Then you can put the tumbler here."

"I always give a reason for everything," she told her friends.

In the evening, after the dishes were washed, Molly sat on her bed and studied, and when the light was off, she lay on her bed and thought of her father. It was ridiculous to do it, she knew. It was a waste of time. Her father came up to the door, wearing a cutaway coat, and striped trousers and a top hat. He carried a huge bouquet of red roses in his hand. "I couldn't come before, Molly. Get on your coat quickly. First we're going down to get that evening dress in the window of Prussia's, but we'll have to hurry. I have tickets for the train to New York tonight. Hurry up, Molly! Don't stand there gawping." It was silly. Her father was dead. No, she didn't really believe he was dead. Somewhere in the world he lived beautifully, and sometime he would come back.

Molly told one of her friends at school, "I don't really believe it, you see, but I don't disbelieve it. If I ever knew he was dead, why it would be awful. I don't know what I'd do then. I don't want to think about knowing he's dead."

When her mother died, she felt little besides shame. Her mother had wanted so much to be loved, and she hadn't known how to draw love. Her importunities had bothered the children and driven them away.

"Well, that's about all," Molly finished. "I got my diploma, and then I was sent down here."

"It was about the easiest interview I ever had," John Whiteside said.

"Do you think I'll get the position, then?"

The old man gave a quick, twinkly glance at the big meerschaum hanging over the mantel.

"That's his friend," Molly thought. "He has secrets with that pipe."

"Yes, I think you'll get the job. I think you have it already. Now, Miss Morgan, where are you going to live? You must find board and room some place."

Before she knew she was going to say it, she had blurted, "I want to live here."

John Whiteside opened his eyes in astonishment. "But we never take boarders, Miss Morgan."

"Oh, I'm sorry I said that. I just liked it so much here, you see."

He called, "Willa," and when his wife stood in the half-open door, "This young lady wants to board with us. She's the new teacher."

Mrs. Whiteside frowned. "Couldn't think of it. We never take boarders. She's too pretty to be around that fool of a Bill. What would happen to those cows of his? It'd be a lot of trouble. You can sleep in the third bedroom upstairs," she said to Molly. "It doesn't catch much sun anyway."

Life changed its face. All of a sudden Molly found she was a queen. From the first day the children of the school adored her, for she understood them, and what was more, she let them understand her. It took her some time to realize that she had become an important person. If two men got to arguing at the store about a point of history or literature or mathematics, and the argument deadlocked, it ended up, "Take it to the teacher! If she doesn't know, she'll find it." Molly was very proud to be able to decide such questions. At parties she had to help with the decorations and to plan refreshments.

"I think we'll put pine boughs around everywhere. They're pretty, and they smell so good. They smell like a party." She was supposed to know everything and to help with everything, and she loved it.

At the Whiteside home she slaved in the kitchen under the mutterings of Willa. At the end of six months, Mrs. Whiteside grumbled to her husband, "Now if Bill only had any sense. But then," she continued, "if *she* has any sense—" and there she left it.

At night Molly wrote letters to the few friends she had made in Teachers' College, letters full of little stories about her neighbours, and full of joy. She must attend every party because of the social prestige of her position. On Saturdays she ran about the hills and brought back ferns and wild flowers to plant about the house.

Bill Whiteside took one look at Molly and scuttled back to his cows. It was a long time before he found the courage to talk to her very much. He was a big, simple young man who had neither his father's balance nor his mother's humour. Eventually, however, he trailed after Molly and looked after her from distances.

One evening, with a kind of feeling of thanksgiving for her happiness, Molly told Bill about her father. They were sitting in canvas chairs on the wide veranda, waiting for the moon. She told him about the visits, and then about the disappearance. "Do you see what I have, Bill?" she cried. "My lovely father is some place. He's mine. You think he's living, don't you, Bill?"

"Might be," said Bill. "From what you say, he was a kind of an irresponsible cuss, though. Excuse me, Molly. Still, if he's alive, it's funny he never wrote."

Molly felt cold. It was just the kind of reasoning she had successfully avoided for so long. "Of course," she said stiffly, "I know that. I have to do some work now, Bill."

High up on a hill that edged the valley of the Pastures of Heaven, there was an old cabin which commanded a view of the whole country and of all the roads in the vicinity. It was said that the bandit Vasquez had built the cabin and lived in it for a year while the posses went crashing through the country looking for him. It was a landmark. All the people of the valley had been to see it at one time or another. Nearly everyone asked Molly whether she had been there yet. "No," she said, "but I will go up some day. I'll go some Saturday. I know where the trail to it is." One morning she dressed in her

new hiking boots and corduroy skirt. Bill sidled up and offered to accompany her. "No," she said. "You have work to
do. I can't take you away from it."

"Work be hanged!" said Bill.

"Well, I'd rather go alone. I don't want to hurt your feelings, but I just want to go alone, Bill." She was sorry not to
let him accompany her, but his remark about her father had
frightened her. "I want to have an adventure," she said to
herself. "If Bill comes along, it won't be an adventure at all.
It'll just be a trip." It took her an hour and a half to climb up
the steep trail under the oaks. The leaves on the ground were
as slippery as glass, and the sun was hot. The good smell of
ferns and dank moss and yerba buena filled the air. When
Molly came at last to the ridge crest, she was damp and
winded. The cabin stood in a small clearing in the brush, a
little square wooden room with no windows. Its doorless entrance was a black shadow. The place was quiet, the kind of
humming quiet that flies and bees and crickets make. The
whole hillside sang softly in the sun. Molly approached on
tiptoe. Her heart was beating violently.

"Now I'm having an adventure," she whispered. "Now I'm
right in the middle of an adventure at Vasquez' cabin." She
peered in at the doorway and saw a lizard scuttle out of sight.
A cobweb fell across her forehead and seemed to try to restrain her. There was nothing at all in the cabin, nothing but
the dirt floor and the rotting wooden walls, and the dry, deserted smell of the earth that has long been covered from the
sun. Molly was filled with excitement. "At night he sat in
there. Sometimes when he heard noises like men creeping up
on him, he went out of the door like the ghost of a shadow,
and just melted into the darkness." She looked down on the
valley of the Pastures of Heaven. The orchards lay in dark
green squares; the grain was yellow, and the hills behind, a
light brown washed with lavender. Among the farms the
roads twisted and curled, avoiding a field, looping around a
huge tree, half circling a hill flank. Over the whole valley was
stretched a veil of heat shimmer. "Unreal," Molly whispered,
"fantastic. It's a story, a real story, and I'm having an adventure." A breeze rose out of the valley like the sigh of a sleeper,
and then subsided.

"In the daytime that young Vasquez looked down on the valley just as I'm looking. He stood right here, and looked at the roads down there. He wore a purple vest braided with gold, and the trousers on his slim legs widened at the bottom like the mouths of trumpets. His spur rowels were wrapped with silk ribbons to keep them from clinking. Sometimes he saw the posses riding by on the road below. Lucky for him the men bent over their horses' necks, and didn't look up at the hilltops. Vasquez laughed, but he was afraid, too. Sometimes he sang. His songs were soft and sad because he knew he couldn't live very long."

Molly sat down on the slope and rested her chin in her cupped hands. Young Vasquez was standing beside her, and Vasquez had her father's gay face, his shining eyes as he came on the porch shouting, "Hi, Kids!" This was the kind of adventure her father had. Molly shook herself and stood up. "Now I want to go back to the first and think it all over again."

In the late afternoon Mrs. Whiteside sent Bill out to look for Molly. "She might have turned an ankle, you know." But Molly emerged from the trail just as Bill approached it from the road.

"We were beginning to wonder if you'd got lost," he said. "Did you go up to the cabin?"

"Yes."

"Funny old box, isn't it? Just an old woodshed. There are a dozen just like it down here. You'd be surprised, though, how many people go up there to look at it. The funny part is, nobody's sure Vasquez was ever there."

"Oh, I think he must have been there."

"What makes you think that?"

"I don't know."

Bill became serious. "Everybody thinks Vasquez was a kind of a hero, when really he was just a thief. He started in stealing sheep and horses and ended up robbing stages. He had to kill a few people to do it. It seems to me, Molly, we ought to teach people to hate robbers, not worship them."

"Of course, Bill," she said wearily. "You're perfectly right. Would you mind not talking for a little while, Bill? I guess I'm a little tired, and nervous, too."

The year wheeled around. Pussywillows had their kittens, and wild flowers covered the hills. Molly found herself wanted and needed in the valley. She even attended school board meetings. There had been a time when those secret and august conferences were held behind closed doors, a mystery and a terror to everyone. Now that Molly was asked to step into John Whiteside's sitting room, she found that the board discussed crops, told stories, and circulated mild gossip.

Bert Munroe had been elected early in the fall, and by the springtime he was the most energetic member. He it was who planned dances at the schoolhouse, who insisted upon having plays and picnics. He even offered prizes for the best report cards in the school. The board was coming to rely pretty much on Bert Munroe.

One evening Molly came down late from her room. As always, when the board was meeting, Mrs. Whiteside sat in the dining room. "I don't think I'll go in to the meeting," Molly said. "Let them have one time to themselves. Sometimes I feel that they would tell other kinds of stories if I weren't there."

"You go on in, Molly! They can't hold a board meeting without you. They're so used to you, they'd be lost. Besides, I'm not at all sure I want them to tell those other stories."

Obediently Molly knocked on the door and went into the sitting room. Bert Munroe paused politely in the story he was narrating. "I was just telling about my new farm hand, Miss Morgan. I'll start over again, 'cause it's kind of funny. You see, I needed a hay hand, and I picked this fellow up under the Salinas River bridge. He was pretty drunk, but he wanted a job. Now I've got him, I find he isn't worth a cent as a hand, but I can't get rid of him. That son of a gun has been every place. You ought to hear him tell about the places he's been. My kids wouldn't let me get rid of him if I wanted to. Why he can take the littlest thing he's seen and make a fine story out of it. My kids just sit around with their ears spread, listening to him. Well, about twice a month he walks into Salinas and goes on a bust. He's one of those dirty, periodic drunks. The Salinas cops always call me up when they find him in a gutter, and I have to drive in to get him. And you know, when he comes out of it, he's always got some kind of present in his pocket for my kid Manny. There's nothing you can do with a man like that. He disarms you. I don't get a dollar's worth of work a month out of him."

Molly felt a sick dread rising in her. The men were laughing at the story. "You're too soft, Bert. You can't afford to keep an entertainer on the place. I'd sure get rid of him quick."

Molly stood up. She was dreadfully afraid someone would ask the man's name. "I'm not feeling very well tonight," she said. "If you gentlemen will excuse me, I think I'll go to bed." The men stood up while she left the room. In her bed she buried her head in the pillow. "It's crazy," she said to herself. "There isn't a chance in the world. I'm forgetting all about it right now." But she found to her dismay that she was crying.

The next few weeks were agonizing to Molly. She was reluctant to leave the house. Walking to and from school she watched the road ahead of her. "If I see any kind of a stranger I'll run away. But that's foolish. I'm being a fool." Only in her own room did she feel safe. Her terror was making her lose colour, was taking the glint out of her eyes.

"Molly, you ought to go to bed," Mrs. Whiteside insisted. "Don't be a little idiot. Do I have to smack you the way I do Bill to make you go to bed?" But Molly would not go to bed. She thought too many things when she was in bed.

The next time the board met, Bert Munroe did not appear. Molly felt reassured and almost happy at his absence.

"You're feeling better, aren't you, Miss Morgan."

"Oh, yes. It was only a little thing, a kind of a cold. If I'd gone to bed I might have been really sick."

The meeting was an hour gone before Bert Munroe came in. "Sorry to be late," he apologized. "The same old thing happened. My so-called hay hand was asleep in the street in Salinas. What a mess! He's out in the car sleeping it off now. I'll have to hose the car out tomorrow."

Molly's throat closed with terror. For a second she thought she was going to faint. "Excuse me, I must go," she cried, and ran out of the room. She walked into the dark hallway and steadied herself against the wall. Then slowly and automatically she marched out of the front door and down the steps. The night was filled with whispers. Out in the road she could see the black mass that was Bert Munroe's car. She was surprised at the way her footsteps plodded down the path of their own volition. "Now I'm killing myself," she said. "Now I'm throwing everything away. I wonder why." The gate was under her hand, and her hand flexed to open it. Then a tiny breeze sprang up and brought to her nose the sharp foulness of vomit. She heard a blubbering, drunken snore. Instantly something whirled in her head. Molly spun around and ran frantically back to the house. In her room she locked the door and sat stiffly down, panting with the effort of her run. It seemed hours before she heard the men go out of the house, calling their good-nights. Then Bert's motor started, and the sound of it died away down the road. Now that she was ready to go she felt paralysed.

John Whiteside was writing at his desk when Molly entered the sitting room. He looked up questioningly at her. "You aren't well, Miss Morgan. You need a doctor."

She planted herself woodenly beside the desk. "Could you get a substitute teacher for me?" she asked.

"Of course I could. You pile right into bed and I'll call a doctor."

"It isn't that, Mr. Whiteside. I want to go away tonight."

"What are you talking about? You aren't well."

"I told you my father was dead. I don't know whether he's dead or not. I'm afraid—I want to go away tonight."

He stared intently at her. "Tell me what you mean," he said softly.

"If I should see that drunken man of Mr. Munroe's—" she paused, suddenly terrified at what she was about to say.

John Whiteside nodded very slowly.

"No," she cried. "I don't think that. I'm sure I don't."

"I'd like to do something, Molly."

"I don't want to go, I love it here—But I'm afraid. It's so important to me."

John Whiteside stood up and came close to her and put his arm about her shoulders. "I don't think I understand, quite," he said. "I don't think I want to understand. That isn't necessary." He seemed to be talking to himself. "It wouldn't be quite courteous—to understand."

"Once I'm away I'll be able not to believe it," Molly whimpered.

He gave her shoulders one quick squeeze with his encircling arm. "You run upstairs and pack your things, Molly," he said. "I'll get out the car and drive you right in to Salinas now."

IX

O F ALL the farms in the Pastures of Heaven the one most admired was that of Raymond Banks. Raymond kept five thousand white chickens and one thousand white ducks. The farm lay on the northern flat, the prettiest place in the whole country. Raymond had laid out his land in squares of alfalfa and of kale. His long, low chicken houses were whitewashed so often that they looked always immaculate and new. There was never any of the filth so often associated with poultry farms, about Raymond's place.

For the ducks there was a large round pond into which fresh water constantly flowed from a two inch pipe. The overflow from the pond ran down rows of thick sturdy kale or spread itself out in the alfalfa patches. It was a fine thing on a sunny morning to see the great flock of clean, white chickens eating and scratching in the dark green alfalfa, and it was even finer to see the thousand white ducks sailing magnificently about on the pond. Ducks swim ponderously, as though they were as huge as the Leviathan. The ranch sang all day with the busy noise of chickens.

From the top of a nearby hill you could look down on the squares of alfalfa on which the thousands of moving white specks eddied and twisted like bits of dust on a green pool. Then perhaps a red tail hawk would soar over, carefully watching Raymond's house. The white specks instantly stopped their meaningless movements and scuttled to the protecting roosters, and up from the fields came the despairing shrieks of thousands of hawk-frightened chickens. The back door of the farmhouse slammed, and Raymond sauntered out carrying a shot gun. The hawk swung up a hundred feet in the air and soared away. The little white bunches spread out again and the eddying continued.

The patches of green were fenced from each other so that one square could rest and recuperate while the chickens were working in another. From the hill you could see Raymond's whitewashed house set on the edge of a grove of oak trees. There were many flowers around the house: Calendulas and

big African marigolds and cosmos as high as trees; and, behind the house, there was the only rose garden worthy the
name in the valley of the Pastures of Heaven. The local people
looked upon this place as the model farm of the valley.

Raymond Banks was a strong man. His thick, short arms,
wide shoulders and hips and heavy legs, even the stomach
which bulged his overalls, made him seem magnificently
strong, strong for pushing and pulling and lifting. Every exposed part of him was burned beef red by the sun, his heavy
arms to the elbows, his neck down into his collar, his face,
and particularly his ears and nose were painfully burned and
chapped. Thin, blond hair could not protect his scalp from
reddening under the sun. Raymond's eyes were remarkable,
for, while his hair and eyebrows were pale yellow, the yellow
that usually goes with light blue eyes, Raymond's eyes were
black as soot. His mouth was full lipped and jovial and completely at odds with his long and villainously beaked nose.
Raymond's nose and ears were terribly punished by the sun.
There was hardly a time during the year when they were not
raw and peeled.

Raymond Banks was forty-five and very jolly. He never
spoke softly, but always in a heavy half shout full of mock
fierceness. He said things, even the commonest of things, as
though they were funny. People laughed whenever he spoke.
At Christmas parties in the schoolhouse, Raymond was invariably chosen as the Santa Claus because of his hearty voice,
his red face and his love for children. He abused children with
such a heavy ferocity that he kept them laughing all the time.
In or out of his red Santa Claus suit, the children of the valley
regarded Raymond as a kind of Santa Claus. He had a way of
flinging them about, of wrestling and mauling them, that was
caressing and delightful. Now and then, he turned serious and
told them things which had the import of huge lessons.

Sometimes on Saturday mornings a group of little boys
walked to the Banks farm to watch Raymond working. He let
them peep into the little glass windows of the incubators.
Sometimes the chicks were just coming out of the shells,
shaking their wet wings and wabbling about on clumsy legs.
The boys were allowed to raise the covers of the brooders and
to pick up whole armfuls of yellow, furry chicks which made a

noise like a hundred little ungreased machines. Then they walked to the pond and threw pieces of bread to the grandly navigating ducks. Most of all, though, the boys liked the killing time. And strangely enough, this was the time when Raymond dropped his large bantering and became very serious.

Raymond picked a little rooster out of the trap and hung it by its legs on a wooden frame. He fastened the wildly beating wings with a wire clamp. The rooster squawked loudly. Raymond had the killing knife with its spear shaped blade on the box beside him. How the boys admired that knife, the vicious shape of it and its shininess; the point was as sharp as a needle.

"Now then, old rooster, you're done for," said Raymond. The boys crowded closer. With sure, quick hands, Raymond grasped the chicken's head and forced the beak open. The knife slipped like a flash of light along the roof of the beak and into the brain and out again. The wings shuddered and beat against their clamp. For a moment the neck stretched yearningly from side to side, and a little rill of blood flowed from the tip of the beak.

"Now watch!" Raymond cried. His forked hand combed the breast and brought all the feathers with it. Another combing motion and the back was bare. The wings were not struggling so hard now. Raymond whipped the feathers off, all but the wing tip feathers. Then the legs were stripped, a single movement for each one. "You see? You've got to do it quick," he explained as he worked. "There's just about two minutes that the feathers are loose. If you leave them in, they get set." He took the chicken down from the frame, snicked another knife twice, pulled, and there were the entrails in a pan. He wiped his red hands on a cloth.

"Look!" the boys shrieked. "Look! what's that?"

"That's the heart."

"But look! It's still moving. It's still alive."

"Oh, no, it isn't," Raymond assured them. "That rooster was dead just the second the knife touched his brain. That heart just beats on for a while, but the rooster is dead all right."

"Why don't you chop them like my father does, Mr. Banks?"

"Well, because this is cleaner and quicker, and the butchers want them with their heads on. They sell the heads in with the weight, you see. Now, come on, old rooster!" He reached into the trap for another struggling squawker. When the killing was over, Raymond took all the chicken crops out of the pan and distributed them among the boys. He taught them how to clean and blow up the crops to make chicken balloons. Raymond was always very serious when he was explaining his ranch. He refused to let the boys help with the killing, although they asked him many times.

"You might get excited and miss the brain," he said. "That would hurt the chicken, if you didn't stick him just right."

Mrs. Banks laughed a great deal—clear, sweet laughter which indicated mild amusement or even inattention. She had a way of laughing appreciatively at everything anyone said, and, to merit this applause, people tried to say funny things when she was about. After her work in the house was finished, she dug in the flower garden. She had been a town girl; that was why she liked flowers, the neighbours said. Guests, driving up to the house, were welcomed by the high, clear laughter of Cleo Banks, and they chuckled when they heard it. She was so jolly. She made people feel good. No one could ever remember that she said anything, but months after hearing it, they could recall the exact tones of her laughter.

Raymond Banks rarely laughed at all. Instead, he pretended a sullenness so overdrawn that it was accepted as humour. These two people were the most popular hosts in the valley. Now and then they invited everyone in the Pastures of Heaven to a barbecue in the oak grove beside their house. They broiled little chickens over coals of oak bark and set out hundreds of bottles of home brewed beer. These parties were looked forward to and remembered with great pleasure by the people of the valley.

When Raymond Banks was in high school, his chum had been a boy who later became the warden at San Quentin prison. The friendship had continued, too. At Christmas time they still exchanged little presents. They wrote to each other when any important thing happened. Raymond was proud of his acquaintance with the warden. Two or three times a year he received an invitation to be a witness at an execution, and he always accepted it. His trips to the prison were the only vacations he took.

Raymond liked to arrive at the warden's house the night before the execution. He and his friend sat together and talked over their school days. They reminded each other of things both remembered perfectly. Always the same episodes were recalled and talked about. Then, the next morning, Raymond liked the excitement, the submerged hysteria of the other witnesses in the warden's office. The slow march of the condemned aroused his dramatic sense and moved him to a thrilling emotion. The hanging itself was not the important part, it was the sharp, keen air of the whole proceeding that impressed him. It was like a super-church, solemn and ceremonious and sombre. The whole thing made him feel a fullness of experience, a holy emotion that nothing else in his life approached. Raymond didn't think of the condemned any more than he thought of the chicken when he pressed the blade into its brain. No strain of cruelty nor any gloating over suffering took him to the gallows. He had developed an appetite for profound emotion, and his meagre imagination was unable to feed it. In the prison he could share the throbbing nerves of the other men. Had he been alone in the death chamber with no one present except the prisoner and the executioner, he would have been unaffected.

After the death was pronounced, Raymond liked the second gathering in the warden's office. The nerve-wracked men tried to use hilarity to restore their outraged imaginations. They were more jolly, more noisily happy than they ordinarily were. They sneered at the occasional witness, usually a young reporter, who fainted or came out of the chamber crying. Raymond enjoyed the whole thing. It made him feel alive; he seemed to be living more acutely than at other times.

After it was all over, he had a good dinner with the warden before he started home again. To some little extent the same emotion occurred to Raymond when the little boys came to watch him kill chickens. He was able to catch a slight spark of their excitement.

The Munroe family had not been long in the Pastures of Heaven before they heard about the fine ranch of Raymond Banks and about his visits to the prison. The people of the valley were interested, fascinated and not a little horrified by the excursions to see men hanged. Before he ever saw Raymond, Bert Munroe pictured him as a traditional executioner, a lank, dark man, with a dull, deathly eye, a cold, nerveless man. The very thought of Raymond filled Bert with a kind of interested foreboding.

When he finally met Raymond Banks and saw the jolly black eyes and the healthy, burned face, Bert was disillusioned, and at the same time a little disgusted. The very health and heartiness of Raymond seemed incongruous and strangely obscene. The paradox of his good nature and his love for children was unseemly.

On the first of May, the Banks' gave one of their parties under the oak trees on the flat. It was the loveliest season of the year, lupins and shooting stars, gallitos and wild violets smouldered with colour in the new, short grass on the hillsides. The oaks had put on new leaves as shiny and clean as washed holly. The sun was warm enough to drench the air with sage, and all the birds made frantic, noisy holiday. From the chicken yards came the contented gabbling of scratching hens and the cynical, self-satisfied quacking of the ducks.

At least fifty people were standing about the long tables under the trees. Hundreds of bottles of beer were packed in washtubs of salt and ice, a mixture so cold that the beer froze in the necks of the bottles. Mrs. Banks went about among the guests, laughing in greeting and in response to greeting. She rarely said a word. At the barbecue pits, Raymond was grilling little chickens while a group of admiring men stood about, offering jocular advice.

"If any of you can do it better, just step up," Raymond shouted at them. "I'm going to put on the steaks now for anyone that's crazy enough not to want chicken."

Bert Munroe stood nearby watching the red hands of Raymond. He was drinking a bottle of the strong beer. Bert was fascinated by the powerful red hands constantly turning over the chickens on the grill.

When the big platters of broiled chicken were carried to the tables, Raymond went back to the pits to cook some more for those fine men who might require a second or even a third little chicken. Raymond was alone now, for his audience had all flocked to the tables. Bert Munroe looked up from his plate of beef steak and saw that Raymond was alone by the pits. He put down his fork and strolled over.

"What's the matter, Mr. Munroe? Wasn't your chicken good?" Raymond asked with genial anxiety.

"I had steak, and it was fine. I eat pretty fast, I guess. I never eat chicken, you know."

"That so? I never could understand how anyone wouldn't like chicken, but I know plenty of people don't. Let me put on another little piece of meat for you."

"Oh! I guess I've had enough. I always think people eat too much. You ought to get up from the table feeling a little bit hungry. Then you keep well, like the animals."

"I guess that's right," said Raymond. He turned the little carcasses over the fire. "I notice I feel better when I don't eat so much."

"Sure you do. So do I. So would everybody. Everybody eats too much." The two men smiled warmly at each other because they had agreed on this point, although neither of them believed it very strongly.

"You sure got a nice piece of land in here," Raymond observed, to double their growing friendship with a second agreement.

"Well, I don't know. They say there's loco weed on it, but I haven't seen any yet."

Raymond laughed. "They used to say the place was haunted before you came and fixed it up so nice. Haven't seen any ghosts, have you?"

"Not a ghost. I'm more scared of loco weed than I am of ghosts. I sure do hate loco weed."

"Don't know as I blame you. Course with chickens it doesn't bother me much, but it raises hell with you people that run stock."

Bert picked up a stick from the ground and knocked it gently on the winking coals. "I hear you're acquainted with the warden up to San Quentin."

"Know him well. I went to school with Ed when I was a kid. You acquainted with him, Mr. Munroe?"

"Oh, no—no. He's in the papers quite a bit. A man in his position gets in the papers quite a bit."

Raymond's voice was serious and proud. "Yeah. He gets a lot of publicity all right. But he's a nice fella, Mr. Munroe, as nice a fella as you'd want to meet. And in spite of having all those convicts on his hands, he's just as jolly and friendly. You wouldn't think, to talk to him, that he had a big responsibility like that."

"Is that so? You wouldn't think that. I mean, you'd think he'd be kind of worried with all those convicts on his hands. Do you see him often?"

"Well—yes. I do. I told you I went to school with him. I was kind of chums with him. Well, he hasn't forgot me. Every once in a while he asks me up to the prison when there's a hanging."

Bert shuddered in spite of the fact that he had been digging for this. "Is that so?"

"Yes. I think it's quite an honor. Not many people get in except newspaper men and official witnesses, sheriffs and police. I have a good visit with Ed every time too, of course."

A strange thing happened to Bert. He seemed to be standing apart from his body. His voice acted without his volition. He heard himself say, "I don't suppose the warden would like it if you brought a friend along." He listened to his words with astonishment. He had not wanted to say that at all.

Raymond was stirring the coals vigorously. He was embarrassed. "Why, I don't know, Mr. Munroe. I never thought about it. Did you want to go up with me?"

Again Bert's voice acted alone. "Yes," it said.

"Well, I'll tell you what I'll do then. I'll write to Ed (I write to him pretty often, you see, so he won't think anything of it). I'll just kind of slip it in the letter about you wanting to go up. Then maybe he'll send two invitations next time. Of course I can't promise, though. Won't you have another little piece of steak?"

Bert was nauseated. "No. I've had enough," he said. "I'm not feeling so good. I guess I'll go lie down under a tree for a little while."

"Maybe you shook up some of the yeast in that beer, Mr. Munroe. You've got to be pretty careful when you pour it."

Bert sat on the crackling dry leaves at the foot of an oak tree. The tables, lined with noisy guests, were on his right.

The hoarse laughing of the men and the shrill cries of communicating women came to him faintly through a wall of thought. Between the tree trunks he could see Raymond Banks still moving about the meat pits, grilling chickens for those few incredible appetites that remained unappeased. The nausea which had forced him away was subtly changing. The choked feeling of illness was becoming a strange panting congestion of desire. The desire puzzled Bert and worried him. He didn't want to go to San Quentin. It would make him unhappy to see a man hanged. But he was glad he had asked to go. His very gladness worried him. As Bert watched, Raymond rolled his sleeves higher up on his thick red arms before he cleaned the grates. Bert jumped up and started toward the pits. Suddenly the nausea arose in him again. He swerved around and hurried to the table where his wife sat shrilling pleasantries around the gnawed carcass of a chicken.

"My husband never eats chicken," she was crying.

"I'm going to walk home," Bert said. "I feel rotten."

His wife laid down the carcass of the chicken and wiped her fingers and mouth on a paper napkin. "What's the matter with you, Bert?"

"I don't know. I just feel kind of rotten."

"Do you want me to go home with you in the car?"

"No, you stay. Jimmie'll drive you home."

"Well," said Mrs. Munroe, "you better say good-bye to Mr. and Mrs. Banks."

Bert turned doggedly away. "You tell them good-bye for me," he said. "I'm feeling too rotten." And he strode quickly away.

A week later Bert Munroe drove to the Banks farm and stopped his Ford in front of the gate. Raymond came from behind a bush where he had been trying a shot at a hawk. He sauntered out and shook hands with his caller.

"I've heard so much about your place, I thought I'd just come down for a look," Bert said.

Raymond was delighted. "Just let me put this gun away, and I'll show you around." For an hour they walked over the farm, Raymond explaining and Bert admiring the cleanliness and efficiency of the chicken ranch. "Come on in and have a glass of beer," Raymond said, when they had covered the place. "There's nothing like cold beer on a day like this."

When they were seated Bert began uneasily, "Did you write that letter to the warden, Mr. Banks?"

"Yes—I did. Ought to have an answer pretty soon now."

"I guess you wonder why I asked you? Well, I think a man ought to see everything he can. That's experience. The more experience a man has, the better. A man ought to see everything."

"I guess that's right, all right," Raymond agreed.

Bert drained his glass and wiped his mouth. "Of course I've read in the papers about hangings, but it isn't like seeing one really. They say there're thirteen steps up to the gallows for bad luck. That right?"

Raymond's face wore an expression of concentration. "Why, I don't know, Mr. Munroe. I never counted them."

"How do they—fight and struggle much after they're dropped?"

"I guess so. You see they're strapped and a black cloth is over their heads. You can't see much of anything. It's more like fluttering, I'd say, than struggling."

Bert's face was red and intent. His eyes glistened with interest. "The papers say it takes fifteen minutes to half an hour for them to die. Is that right?"

"I—I suppose it is. Of course they're really what you might call dead the minute they drop. It's like you cut a chicken's head off, and the chicken flutters around, but it's really dead."

"Yes—I guess that's right. Just reflex, they call it. I suppose it's pretty hard on some people seeing it for the first time."

Raymond smiled in faint amusement. "Sure. Nearly always somebody faints. Then the kid reporters from the papers cry sometimes, cry like babies, and some people are sick, you know, really sick—lose their dinner right there. Mostly first timers are that way. Let's have another bottle of beer, Mr. Munroe. It's good and cold, isn't it?"

"Yes, it's fine beer all right," Bert agreed absently. "I'll have to get your recipe. A man ought to have a little beer ready for the hot weather. I've got to go now, Mr. Banks. Thank you for showing me around the place. You could give some pointers to these Petaluma people about chickens, I guess."

Raymond flushed with pleasure. "I try to keep up with new things. I'll let you know when I hear from Ed, Mr. Munroe."

During the next two weeks Bert Munroe was nervous and extremely irritable. This was so unusual that his wife protested. "You're not well, Bert. Why don't you drive in and let a doctor look you over."

"Oh! I'm all right," he insisted. He spent most of his time at work on the farm, but his eyes roved to the county road every time an automobile drove by. It was on a Saturday that Raymond Banks drove up in his light truck and parked before the Munroe gate. Bert dropped a shovel and went out to meet him. When one farmer meets another they seldom go into a house. Instead, they walk slowly over the land, pulling bits of grass from the fields, or leaves from the trees and testing them with their fingers while they talk. Summer was beginning. The leaves on the fruit trees had not yet lost their tender, light greens, but the blossoms were all gone and the fruit set. Already the cherries were showing a little colour. Bert and Raymond walked slowly over the cultivated ground under the orchard trees.

"Birds are thick this year," said Bert. "They'll get most of the cherries, I guess." He knew perfectly well why Raymond had come.

"Well, I heard from Ed, Mr. Munroe. He says it will be all right for you to go up with me. He says they don't let many come, because they try to keep the morbidly curious people away. But he says any friend of mine is all right. We'll go up next Thursday. There's an execution Friday." (Bert walked along in silence, his eyes on the ground.) "Ed's a nice fellow. You'll like him," Raymond went on. "We'll stay with him Thursday night."

Bert picked up an overlooked pruning from the ground and bent it to a tense bow in his hands. "I've been thinking about it," he said. "Would it make any difference to you if I pulled out the last minute?"

Raymond stared at him. "Why, I thought you wanted to go. What's the matter?"

"You'll think I'm pretty soft, I guess, if I tell you. The fact is—I've been thinking about it and—I'm scared to go. I'm scared I couldn't get it out of my head afterwards."

"It's not as bad as it sounds," Raymond protested.

"Maybe it isn't. I don't know about that. But I'm scared it would be bad for me. Everybody don't see a thing the same way."

"No, that's true."

"I'll try to give you an idea how I feel, Mr. Banks. You know I don't eat chicken. I never tell anybody why I don't eat it. Just say I don't like it. I've put you to a lot of trouble. I'll tell you—to kind of explain." The stick snapped in his hands, and he threw the two ends away and thrust his hands in his pockets.

"When I was a kid, about twelve years old, I used to deliver a few groceries before school. Well, out by the brewery an old crippled man lived. He had one leg cut off at the thigh, and, instead of a wooden leg, he had one of those old fashioned crutches—kind of a crescent on top of a round stick. You remember them. He got around on it pretty well, but kind of slow. One morning, when I went by with my basket of groceries, this old man was out in his yard killing a rooster. It was the biggest Rhode Island Red I ever saw. Or maybe it was because I was so little that the chicken looked so big. The old man had the crutch braced under his arm pit, and he was holding the rooster by the legs." Bert stopped and picked another pruning from the ground. This one, too, bent under his hands. His face was growing pale as he talked.

"Well," he continued, "this old man had a hatchet in his other hand. Just as he made a cut at the rooster's neck, his crutch slipped a little bit, the chicken twisted in his hand, and he cut off one of the wings. Well, then that old man just about went crazy. He cut and he cut, always in the wrong place, into the breast and into the stomach. Then the crutch slipped some more and threw him clear off balance just as the hatchet was coming down. He cut off one of the chicken's legs and sliced right through his own finger." Bert wiped his forehead with his sleeve. Raymond was heaping a little mountain of dirt with the side of his shoe.

"Well, when that happened, the old man just dropped the

rooster on the ground and hobbled into the house holding on to his finger. And that rooster went crawling off with all its guts hanging out on the ground—went crawling off and kind of croaking." The stick snapped again, and this time he threw the pieces violently from him. "Well, Mr. Banks, I've never killed a chicken since then, and I've never eaten one. I've tried to eat them, but every time, I see that damned Rhode Island Red crawling away." For the first time he looked directly at Raymond Banks. "Do you see how that would happen?"

Raymond dodged his eyes and looked away. "Yes. Yes, sir, that must have been pretty awful."

Bert crowded on. "Well, I got to thinking about this hanging. It might be like the chicken. I dreamed about that chicken over and over again, when I was a kid. Every time my stomach would get upset and give me a nightmare, I'd dream about that chicken. Now suppose I went to this hanging with you. I might dream about it, too. Not long ago they hung a woman in Arizona, and the rope pulled her head right off. Suppose that happened. It would be a hundred times worse than the chicken. Why I'd never get over a thing like that."

"But that practically never happens," Raymond protested. "I tell you it's not nearly as bad as it sounds."

Bert seemed not to hear him. His face was working with horror at his thoughts. "Then you say some people get sick and some of them faint. I know why that is. It's because those people are imagining they're up on the gallows with the rope around their necks. They really feel like the man it's happening to. I've done that myself. I imagined I was going to be hung in twenty-four hours. It's like the most god-awful nightmare in the world. And I've been thinking— what's the use of going up there and horrifying myself? I'd be sick. I know I would. I'd just go through everything the poor devil on the gallows did. Just thinking about it last night, I felt the rope around my neck. Then I went to sleep, and the sheet got over my face, and I dreamed it was that damned black cap."

"I tell you, you don't think things like that," Raymond cried angrily. "If you think things like that you haven't got any right to go up with me. I tell you it isn't as terrible as that, when you see it. It's nothing. You said you wanted to go up, and I got permission for you. What do you want to go talking like this for? There's no need to talk like you just did. If you don't want to go, why the hell don't you just say so and then shut up?"

The look of horror went out of Bert's eyes. Almost eagerly he seized upon anger. "No need to get mad, Mr. Banks. I was just telling you why I didn't want to go. If you had any imagination, I wouldn't have to tell you. If you had any imagination, you'd see for yourself, and you wouldn't go up to see some poor devil get killed."

Raymond turned away contemptuously. "You're just yellow," he said and strode away to his truck. He drove furiously over the road to his ranch, but when he had arrived and covered the truck, he walked slowly toward his house. His wife was cutting roses.

"What's the matter with you, Ray? You look sick," she cried.

Raymond scowled. "I've got a headache, that's all. It'll go away. You know Bert Munroe that wanted to go up with me next week?"

"Yes."

"Well, now he don't want to go."

"What's the matter with him?"

"He's lost his nerve, that's what. He's scared to see it."

His wife laughed uneasily. "Well, I don't know as I'd *like* to see it myself."

"You're a woman, but he's supposed to be a man."

The next morning Raymond sat down listlessly to breakfast and ate very little. His wife looked worried. "You've still got that headache, Ray. Why don't you do something for it?"

Raymond ignored her question. "I've got to write to Ed, and I don't know what to say to him."

"What do you mean, you don't know."

"Well, I'm afraid I'm getting a cold. I don't know whether I'll be in shape to go up there Thursday. It's a long trip, and cold crossing the bay."

Mrs. Banks sat in thought. "Why don't you ask him to come down here sometime. He's never been here; you've been there lots of times."

Raymond brightened up. "By George! That's an idea. I've

been going up to see him for years. I'll just drop him a note to come and see us."

"We could give him a barbecue," Mrs. Banks suggested.

Raymond's face clouded over. "Oh, I don't think so. A close friend like Ed would rather not have a crowd. But beer—say, you should see how Ed loves his beer. I'll drop him a note now." He got out a pen and a little pad of writing paper and an ink bottle. As his pen hesitated over the paper, his face dropped back into a scowl. "Damn that Munroe anyway! I went to a lot of trouble for him. How'd I know he was going to turn yellow on me."

X

PAT HUMBERT'S parents were middle-aged when he was born; they had grown old and stiff and spiteful before he was twenty. All of Pat's life had been spent in an atmosphere of age, of the aches and illness, of the complaints and self-sufficiency of age. While he was growing up, his parents held his opinions in contempt because he was young. "When you've lived as long as we have, you'll see things different," they told him. Later, they found his youth hateful because it was painless. Their age, so they implied, was a superior state, a state approaching godhead in dignity and infallibility. Even rheumatism was desirable as a price for the great wisdom of age. Pat was led to believe that no young thing had any virtue. Youth was a clumsy, fumbling preparation for excellent old age. Youth should think of nothing but the duty it owed to age, of the courtesy and veneration due to age. On the other hand, age owed no courtesy whatever to youth.

When Pat was sixteen, the whole work of the farm fell upon him. His father retired to a rocking chair beside the air tight stove in the sitting room, from which he issued orders, edicts and criticisms.

The Humberts dwelt in an old, rambling farm house of five rooms: a locked parlour, cold and awful as doom, a hot, stuffy sitting room smelling always of pungent salves and patent medicines, two bedrooms and a large kitchen. The old people sat in cushioned rocking chairs and complained bitterly if Pat did not come in from the farm work to replenish the fire in the stove several times a day. Toward the end of their lives, they really hated Pat for being young.

They lived a long time. Pat was thirty when they died within a month of each other. They were unhappy and bitter and discontented with their lives, and yet each one clung tenaciously to the poor spark and only died after a long struggle.

There were two months of horror for Pat. For three weeks he nursed his mother while she lay rigid on the bed, her breath clattering in and out of her lungs. She watched him with stony, accusing eyes as he tried to make her comfortable. When she was dead, her eyes still accused him.

Pat unlocked the terrible parlour; the neighbours sat in rows before the coffin, a kind of audience, while the service went on. From the bedroom came the sound of old Mr. Humbert's peevish weeping.

The second period of nursing began immediately after the first funeral, and continued for three weeks more. Then the neighbours sat in rows before another coffin. Before the funerals, the parlour had always been locked except during the monthly cleaning. The blinds were drawn down to protect the green carpets from the sun. In the centre of the room stood a gilt-legged marble topped table which bore, on a tapestry of Millet's Angelus, a huge Bible with a deeply tooled cover. On either side of the Bible sat squat vases holding tight bouquets of everlasting flowers. There were four straight chairs in the parlour, one against each of the four walls—two for the coffin and two for the watchers. Three large pictures in gilt frames hung on the walls, colored, enlarged photographs of each of the old Humberts looking stern and dead, but so taken that their eyes followed an intruder about the room. The third picture showed the corpse of Elaine in its boat on the thin sad river. The shroud hung over the gunwale and dipped into the water. On a corner table stood a tall glass bell in which three stuffed orioles sat on a cherry branch. So cold and sepulchral was this parlour that it had never been entered except by corpses and their attendants. It was indeed a little private mortuary chamber. Pat had seen three aunts and an uncle buried from that parlour.

Pat stood quietly by the graveside while his neighbours shaped up a tent of earth. Already his mother's grave had sunk a little, leaving a jagged crack all around its mound. The men were patting the new mound now, drawing a straight ridgepole and smoothing the slope of the sides. They were good workmen with the soil; they liked to make a good job with it whether it be furrow or grave mound. After it was perfect, they still walked about patting it lightly here and there. The women had gone back to the buggies and were waiting for their husbands to come. Each man walked up to Pat and shook his hand and murmured some solemn friendly thing to him. The wagons and surreys and buggies were all moving away now, disappearing one by one in the distance. Still Pat stood in the cemetery staring at the two graves. He didn't know what to do now there was no one to demand anything of him.

Fall was in the air, the sharp smell of it and the little jerky winds of it breathing up and then dying in mid-blow. Wild doves sat in a line on the cemetery fence all facing one way, all motionless. A piece of old brown newspaper scudded along the ground and clung about Pat's ankles. He stooped and picked it off, looked at it for a moment and then threw it away. The sound of grating buggy wheels came from the road. T. B. Allen tied his horse to the fence and walked up to Pat. "We thought you'd be going someplace tonight," he said in an embarrassed voice. "If you feel like it, we'd like you to come to supper at our house—and stay the night, too."

Pat started out of the coma that had fallen on him. "I should be going away from here," he said. He fumbled for another thought. "I'm not doing any good here."

"It's better to get away from it," Allen said.

"It's hard to leave, Mr. Allen. It's a thing you'll sometimes want to remember, and other times you'll want to forget it, I guess. But it's hard to leave because then you know it's all over—forever."

"Well, why don't you come to supper over at our house?"

All of Pat's guards were down; he confessed, "I never had supper away from home in my life. They"—he nodded toward the graves—"They didn't like to be out after dark. Night air wasn't good for them."

"Then maybe it would be good for you to eat at our house. You shouldn't go back to the empty place, at least not tonight. A man ought to save himself a little." He took Pat's arm and swung him toward the gate. "You follow me in your wagon." And as they went out of the gate a little elegy escaped from him. "It's a fit thing to die in the fall," he said. "It wouldn't be good to die in the spring and never to know about the rainfall nor how the crops shaped. But in the fall everything's over."

"They wouldn't care, Mr. Allen. They didn't ever ask about

the crops, and they hated the rain because of their rheumatism. They just wanted to live. I don't know why."

For supper there were cold cuts of beef, and potatoes fried
raw with a few onions, and bread pudding with raisins. Mrs.
Allen tried to help Pat in his trouble by speaking often of his
parents, of how good and kind they were, of his father's honesty and his mother's famous cookery. Pat knew she was lying
about them to help him, and he didn't need it. He was in no
agony of grief. The thick lethargy still hung over him so that
it was a great effort to move or to speak.

He was remembering something that had happened at the
funeral. When the pall-bearers lifted the casket from its two
chairs, one of the men tripped against the marble topped
table. The accident tipped over one of the vases of everlastings and pushed the Bible askew on its tapestry. Pat knew that
in decency he should restore the old order. The chairs should
be pushed against their walls and the Bible set straight. Finally he should lock up the parlour again. The memory of his
mother demanded these things of him.

The Allens urged him to stay the night, but after a little
while, he bade them a listless good night and dragged himself
out to harness his horse. The sky was black and cold between
the sharp stars, and the hills hummed faintly under a lowering
temperature. Through his lethargy, Pat heard the clopping of
the horse's hooves on the road, the crying of night birds and
the whisk of wind through the drying leaves. But more real to
him were his parents' voices sounding in his head. "There'll
be frost," his father said. "I hate the frost worse than rats."
And his mother chimed in, "Speaking of rats—I have a feeling there's rats in the cellar. I wonder if Pat has set the traps
this year past. I told him to, but he forgets everything I tell
him."

Pat answered the voices. "I put poison in the cellar. Traps
aren't as good as poison."

"A cat is best," his mother's whining voice said. "I don't
know why we never have a cat or two. Pat never has a cat."

"I get cats, mother, but they eat gophers and go wild and
run away. I can't keep cats."

The house was black and unutterably dreary when he arrived. Pat lighted the reflector lamp and built a fire in the

stove to warm the kitchen. As the flame roared through the wood, he sank into a chair and found that he was very comfortable. It would be nice, he thought, to bring his bed into the kitchen and to sleep beside the stove. The straightening of the house could be done tomorrow, or any day for that matter.

When he threw open the door into the sitting room, a wave of cold, lifeless air met him. His nostrils were assailed by the smell of funeral flowers and age and medicine. He walked quickly to his bedroom and carried his cot into the warm and lighted kitchen.

After a while Pat blew out the light and went to bed. The fire cricked softly in the stove. For a time the night was still, and then gradually the house began to swarm with malignant life. Pat discovered that his body was tense and cold. He was listening for sounds from the sitting room, for the creak of the rocking chairs and for the loud breathing of the old people. The house cracked, and although he had been listening for sounds, Pat started violently. His head and legs became damp with perspiration. Silently and miserably he crept from his bed and locked the door into the sitting room. Then he went back to his cot and lay shivering under the covers. The night had become very still, and he was lonely.

The next morning Pat awakened with a cold sense of duty to be performed. He tried to remember what it was. Of course, it was the Bible lying off-centre on its table. That should be put straight. The vase of everlastings should be set upright, and after that the whole house should be cleaned. Pat knew he should do these things in spite of the reluctance he felt for opening the door into the sitting room. His mind shrank from the things he would see when he opened the door—the two rocking chairs, one on either side of the stove; the pillows in the chair seats would be holding the impressions of his parents' bodies. He knew the odors of age and of unguents and of stale flowers that were waiting for him on the other side of the door. But the thing was a duty. It must be done.

He built a fire and made his breakfast. It was while he drank the hot coffee that a line of reasoning foreign to his old manner of life came to him. The unusual thoughts that

thronged upon him astounded him at once for their audacity
and for their simplicity.

"Why should I go in there?" he demanded. "There's no
one to care, no one even to know. I don't have to go in there
if I don't want to." He felt like a boy who breaks school to
walk in a deep and satisfying forest. But to combat his freedom, his mother's complaining voice came to his ears. "Pat
ought to clean the house. Pat never takes care of things."

The joy of revolt surged up in him. "You're dead!" he told
the voice. "You're just something that's happening in my
mind. Nobody can expect me to do things any more. Nobody
will ever know if I don't do things I ought to. I'm not going
in there, and I'm never going in there." And while the spirit
was still strong in him, he strode to the door, plucked out the
key and threw it into the tall weeds behind the house. He
closed the shutters on all the windows except those in the
kitchen, and nailed them shut with long spikes.

The joy of his new freedom did not last long. In the daytime the farm work kept him busy, but before the day was
out, he grew lonely for the old duties which ate up the hours
and made the time short. He knew he was afraid to go into
the house, afraid of those impressions in the cushions and of
the disarranged Bible. He had locked up two thin old ghosts,
but he had not taken away their power to trouble him.

That night, after he had cooked his supper, he sat beside
the stove. An appalling loneliness like a desolate fog fell upon
him. He listened to the stealthy sounds in the old house, the
whispers and little knockings. So tensely did he listen that
after a while he could hear the chairs rocking in the other
room, and once he made out the rasping sound of a lid being
unscrewed from a jar of salve. Pat could not stand it any
longer. He went to the barn, harnessed his horse and drove to
the Pastures of Heaven General Store.

Three men sat around the fat-bellied stove, contemplating
its corrugations with rapt abstraction. They made room for
Pat to draw up a chair. None of the men looked at him, because a man in mourning deserves the same social immunities
a cripple does. Pat settled himself in his chair and gazed at the
stove. "Remind me to get some flour before I go," he said.

All of the men knew what he meant. They knew he didn't

need flour, but each one of them, under similar circumstances, would have made some such excuse. T. B. Allen opened the stove door and looked in and then spat on the coals. "A house like that is pretty lonely at first," he observed. Pat felt grateful to him although his words constituted a social blunder.

"I'll need some tobacco and some shot gun shells, too, Mr. Allen," he said by way of payment.

Pat changed his habits of living after that. Determinedly he sought groups of men. During the daytime he worked on his farm, but at night he was invariably to be found where two or three people were gathered. When a dance or a party was given at the schoolhouse, Pat arrived early and stayed until the last man was gone. He sat at the house of John Whiteside; he arrived first at fires. On election days he stayed at the polls until they closed. Wherever a group of people gathered, Pat was sure to show up. From constant stalking of company he came to have almost an instinct for discovering excitements which would draw crowds.

Pat was a homely man, gangling, big-nosed and heavy-jawed. He looked very much like Lincoln as a young man. His figure was as unfitted for clothes as Lincoln's was. His nostrils and ears were large and full of hair. They looked as though furry little animals were hiding in them. Pat had no conversation; he knew he added little to the gatherings he frequented, and he tried to make up for his lack by working, by doing favours, by arranging things. He liked to be appointed to committees for arranging school dances, for then he could call on the other committeemen to discuss plans; he could spend evenings decorating the school or running about the valley borrowing chairs from one family and dishes from another. If on any evening he could find no gathering to join, he drove his Ford truck to Salinas and sat through two moving picture shows. After those first two nights of fearful loneliness, he never spent another evening in his closed-up house. The memory of the Bible, of the waiting chairs, or the years-old smells were terrifying to him.

For ten years Pat Humbert drove about the valley in search of company. He had himself elected to the school board; he

joined the Masons and the Odd Fellows in Salinas and was
never known to miss a meeting.

In spite of his craving for company, Pat never became a part
of any group he joined. Rather he hung on the fringes, never
speaking unless he was addressed. The people of the valley
considered his presence inevitable. They used him unmerci-
fully and hardly knew that he wished nothing better.

When the gatherings were over, when Pat was finally forced
home, he drove his Ford into the barn and then rushed to
bed. He tried with little success to forget the terrible rooms
on the other side of the door. The picture of them edged into
his mind sometimes. The dust would be thick now, and the
cobwebs would be strung in all the corners and on all the
furniture. When the vision invaded and destroyed his de-
fences before he could go to sleep, Pat shivered in his bed and
tried every little soporific formula he knew.

Since he so hated his house, Pat took no care of it. The old
building lay mouldering with neglect. A white Banksia rose,
which for years had been a stubby little bush, came suddenly
to life and climbed up the front of the house. It covered the
porch, hung festoons over the closed windows and dropped
long streamers from the eaves. Within the ten years the house
looked like a huge mound of roses. People passing by on the
county road paused to marvel at its size and beauty. Pat
hardly knew about the rose. He refused to think about the
house when he could refuse.

The Humbert farm was a good one. Pat kept it well and
made money from it, and, since his expenses were small, he
had quite a few thousand dollars in the bank. He loved the
farm for itself, but he also loved it because it kept him from
fear in the daytime. When he was working, the terror of
being solitary, the freezing loneliness, could not attack him.
He raised good fruit, but his berries were his chief interest.
The lines of supported vines paralleled the county road. Every
year he was able to market his berries earlier than anyone
in the valley.

Pat was forty years old when the Munroes came into the
valley. He welcomed them as his neighbors. Here was another house to which he might go to pass an evening. And
since Bert Munroe was a friendly man, he liked to have Pat

drop in to visit. Pat was a good farmer. Bert often asked his advice. Pat did not take very careful notice of Mae Munroe except to see, and to forget, that she was a pretty girl. He did not often think of people as individuals, but rather as antidotes for the poison of his loneliness, as escapes from the imprisoned ghosts.

One afternoon when the summer was dawning, Pat worked among his berry vines. He kneeled between the rows of vines and dug among the berry roots with a hoe. The berries were fast forming now, and the leaves were pale green and lovely. Pat worked slowly down the row. He was contented with the work, and he did not dread the coming night for he was to have supper at the Munroe house. As he worked he heard voices from the road. Although he was concealed among the vines, he knew from the tones that Mrs. Munroe and her daughter Mae were strolling by his house. Suddenly he heard Mae exclaim with pleasure.

"Mama, look at that!" Pat ceased his work to listen. "Did you ever see such a beautiful rose in your life, Mama?"

"It's pretty, all right," Mrs. Munroe said.

"I've just thought what it reminds me of," Mae continued. "Do you remember the post card of that lovely house in Vermont? Uncle Keller sent it. This house, with the rose over it, looks just like that house in the picture. I'd like to see the inside of it."

"Well, there isn't much chance of that. Mrs. Allen says no one in the valley has been in that house since Pat's father and mother died, and that's ten years ago. She didn't say whether it was pretty."

"With a rose like that on the outside, the inside must be pretty. I wonder if Mr. Humbert will let me see it sometime." The two women walked on out of hearing.

When they were gone, Pat stood up and looked at the great rose. He had never seen how beautiful it was—a haystack of green leaves and nearly covered with white roses. "It is pretty," he said. "And it's like a nice house in Vermont. It's like a Vermont house, and—well, it *is* pretty, a pretty bush." Then, as though he had seen through the bush and through the wall, a vision of the parlour came to him. He went quickly back to his work among the berries, struggling to put the house out of his mind. But Mae's words came back to him over and over again, "It must be pretty inside." Pat wondered what a Vermont house looked like inside. John Whiteside's solid and grand house he knew, and, with the rest of the valley, he had admired the plush comfort of Bert Munroe's house, but a pretty house he had never seen, that is, a house he could really call pretty. In his mind he went over all the houses he knew and not one of them was what Mae must have meant. He remembered a picture in a magazine, a room with a polished floor and white woodwork and a staircase; it might have been Mt. Vernon. That picture had impressed him. Perhaps that was what Mae meant.

He wished he could see the post card of the Vermont house, but if he asked to see it, they would know he had been listening. As he thought of it, Pat became obsessed with a desire to see a pretty house that looked like his. He put his hoe away and walked in front of his house. Truly the rose was marvellous. It dropped a canopy over the porch, hung awnings of white stars over the closed windows. Pat wondered why he had never noticed it before.

That night he did something he couldn't have contemplated before. At the Munroe door, he broke an engagement to spend an evening in company. "There's some business in Salinas I've got to attend to," he explained. "I stand to lose some money if I don't go right in."

In Salinas he went straight to the public library. "Have you got any pictures of Vermont houses—pretty ones," he asked the librarian.

"You'll probably find some in the magazines. Come! I'll show you where to look."

They had to warn him when the library was about to close. He had found pictures of interiors, but of interiors he had never imagined. The rooms were built on a plan; each decoration, each piece of furniture, even the floors and walls were related, were a part of the plan. Some deep and instinctive feeling in him for arrangement, for color and line had responded to the pictures. He hadn't known rooms could be like that—all in one piece. Every room he had ever seen was the result of a gradual and accidental accumulation. Aunt

Sophie sent a vase, father bought a chair. They put a stove in
the fireplace because it threw more heat; the Sperry Flour
Company issued a big calendar and mother had its picture
framed; a mail order house advertised a new kind of lamp.
That was the way rooms were assembled. But in the pictures
someone had an idea, and everything in the room was a part
of the idea. Just before the library closed he came upon two
pictures side by side. One showed a room like those he knew,
and right beside it was another picture of the same room with
all the clutter gone, and with the idea in it. It didn't look like
the same place at all. For the first time in his life, Pat was
anxious to go home. He wanted to lie in his bed and to think,
for a strange new idea was squirming into being in the back
of his mind.

Pat could not sleep that night. His head was too full of
plans. Once he got up and lighted the lamp to look in his
bank book. A little before daylight he dressed and cooked his
breakfast, and while he ate, his eyes wandered again and again
to the locked door. There was a light of malicious joy in his
eyes. "It'll be dark in there," he said. "I better rip open the
shutters before I go in there."

When the daylight came at last, he took a crowbar and
walked around the house, tearing open the nailed shutters as
he went. The parlour windows he did not touch, for he didn't
want to disturb the rose bush. Finally he went back into the
kitchen and stood before the locked door. For a moment the
old vision stopped him. "But it will be just for a minute," he
argued. "I'll start in tearing it to pieces right away." The
crowbar poised and crashed on the lock. The door sprang
open crying miserably on its dry hinges, and the horrible
room lay before him. The air was foggy with cobwebs; a
musty, ancient odour flowed through the door. There were
the two rocking chairs on either side of the rusty stove. Even
through the dust he could see the little hollows in their cushions. But these were not the terrible things. Pat knew where
lay the centre of his fears. He walked rapidly through the
room, brushing the cobwebs from his eyes as he went. The
parlour was still dark for its shutters were closed. Pat didn't
have to grope for the table; he knew exactly where it was.

Hadn't it haunted him for ten years? He picked up table and Bible together, ran out through the kitchen and hurled them into the yard.

Now he could go more slowly. The fear was gone. The windows were stuck so hard that he had to use the bar to pry them open. First the rocking chairs went out, rolling and jumping when they hit the ground, then the pictures, the ornaments from the mantel, the stuffed orioles. And when the movable furniture, the clothing, the rugs and vases were scattered about under the windows, Pat ripped up the carpets and crammed them out, too. Finally he brought buckets of water and splashed the walls and ceilings thoroughly. The work was an intense pleasure to him. He tried to break the legs from the chairs when he threw them out. While the water was soaking into the old dark wall paper, he collected all of the furniture from under the windows, piled it up and set fire to it. Old musty fabrics and varnished wood smouldered sullenly and threw out a foul stench of dust and dampness. Only when a bucket of kerosene was thrown over the pile did the flame leap up. The tables and chairs cracked as they released their ghosts into the fire. Pat surveyed the pile joyfully.

"You *would* sit in there all these years, wouldn't you?" he cried. "You thought I'd never get up the guts to burn you. Well, I just wish you could be around to see what I'm going to do, you rotten stinking trash." The green carpets burned through and left red, flaky coals. Old vases and jars cracked to pieces in the heat. Pat could hear the sizzle of mentholatum and painkiller gushing from containers and boiling into the fire. He felt that he was presiding at the death of his enemy. Only when the pile had burned down to coals did he leave it. The walls were soaked thoroughly by now, so that the wall paper peeled off in long, broad ribbons.

That afternoon Pat drove in to Salinas and bought all the magazines on house decoration he could find. In the evening, after dinner he searched the pages through. At last, in one of the magazines, he found the perfect room. There had been a question about some of the others; there was none about this one. And he could make it quite easily. With the partition between the sitting room and the parlour torn out, he would have a room thirty feet long and fifteen wide. The windows must be made wide, the fireplace enlarged and the floor sand-papered, stained and polished. Pat knew he could do all these things. His hands ached to be at work. "Tomorrow I'll start," he said. Then another thought stopped him. "She thinks it's pretty now. I can't very well let her know I'm doing it now. Why, she'd know I heard her say that about the Vermont house. I can't let people know I'm doing it. They'd ask why I'm doing it." He wondered why he was doing it. "It's none of their darn business why," he explained to himself. "I don't have to go around telling people why. I've got my reasons. By God! I'll do it at night." Pat laughed softly to himself. The idea of secretly changing his house delighted him. He could work here alone, and no one would know. Then, when it was all finished, he could invite a few people in and pretend it was always that way. Nobody would remember how it was ten years ago.

This was the way he ordered his life: During the day he worked on the farm, and at night rushed into the house with a feeling of joy. The picture of the completed room was tacked up in the kitchen. Pat looked at it twenty times a day. While he was building window seats, putting up the French-grey paper, coating the woodwork with cream-coloured enamel, he could see the completed room before him. When he needed supplies, he drove to Salinas late in the evening and brought back his materials after dark. He worked until midnight and went to bed breathlessly happy.

The people of the valley missed him from their gatherings. At the store they questioned him, but he had his excuse ready. "I'm taking one of those mail courses," he explained. "I'm studying at night." The men smiled. Loneliness was too much for a man, they knew. Bachelors on farms always got a little queer sooner or later.

"What are you studying, Pat?"

"Oh! What? Oh! I'm taking some lessons in—building."

"You ought to get married, Pat. You're getting along in years."

Pat blushed furiously. "Don't be a damn fool," he said.

As he worked on the room, Pat was developing a little play, and it went like this: The room was finished and the furniture in place. The fire burned redly; the lamps threw misty reflections on the polished floor and on the shiny furniture. "I'll go to her house, and I'll say, off-hand, 'I hear you like Vermont houses.' No! I can't say that. I'll say, 'Do you like Vermont houses? Well, I've got a room that's kind of like a Vermont room.'" The preliminaries were never quite satisfactory. He couldn't come on the perfect way for enticing her into his house. He ended by skipping that part. He could think it out later.

Now she was entering the kitchen. The kitchen wouldn't be changed, for that would make the other room a bigger surprise. She would stand in front of the door, and he would reach around her and throw it open. There was the room, rather dark, but full of dark light, really. The fire flowed up like a broad stream, and the lamps reflected on the floor. You could make out the glazed chintz hangings and the fat tiger of the overmantel hooked rug. The pewter glowed with a restrained richness. It was all so warm and snug. Pat's chest contracted with delight.

Anyway, she was standing in the door and—what would she say? Well, if she felt the way he did, maybe she wouldn't say anything. She might feel almost like crying. That was peculiar, the good full feeling as though you were about to cry. Maybe she'd stand there for a minute or two, just looking. Then Pat would say—"Won't you come in and sit for a while?" And of course that would break the spell. She would begin talking about the room in funny choked sentences. But Pat would be off-hand about it all. "Yes, I always kind of liked it." He said this out loud as he worked. "Yes, I always thought it was kind of nice. It came to me the other day that you might like to see it."

The play ended this way: Mae sat in the wingback chair in front of the fire. Her plump pretty hands lay in her lap. As she sat there, a far away look came into her eyes. . . . And Pat never went any farther than that, for at that point a self-consciousness overcame him. If he went farther, it would be like peeking in a window at two people who wanted to be alone. The electric moment, the palpitating moment of the whole thing was when he threw open the door; when she stood on the threshold, stunned by the beauty of the room.

At the end of three months the room was finished. Pat put

the magazine picture in his wallet and went to San Francisco. In the office of a furniture company, he spread his picture on the desk. "I want furniture like that," he said.

"You don't mean originals, of course."

"What do you mean, originals?"

"Why, old pieces. You couldn't get them for under thirty thousand dollars."

Pat's face fell. His room seemed to collapse. "Oh!—I didn't know."

"We can get you good copies of everything here," the manager assured him.

"Why of course. That's good. That's fine. How much would the copies cost?"

A purchasing agent was called in. The three of them went over the articles in the picture and the manager made a list; pie-crust table, drop-leaf gate-leg table, chairs: one windsor, one rush seat ladderback, one wingback, one fireplace bench; rag rugs, glazed chintz hangings, lamps with frosted globes and crystal pendants; one open-faced cupboard, pictorial bone-china, pewter candlesticks and sconces.

"Well, it will be around three thousand dollars, Mr. Humbert."

Pat frowned with thought. After all why should he save money? "How soon can you send it down?" he demanded.

While he waited for a notice that the furniture had arrived in Salinas, Pat rubbed the floor until it shone like a dull lake. He walked backward out of the room erasing his faint foot marks with a polisher. And then, at last the crates arrived at the freight depot. It took four trips to Salinas in his truck to get them, trips made secretly in the night. There was an air of intrigue about the business.

Pat uncrated the pieces in the barn. He carried in chairs and tables, and, with a great many looks at the picture, arranged them in their exact places. That night the fire flowed up, and the frosted lamps reflected on the floor. The fat tiger on the hooked rug over the fireplace seemed to quiver in the dancing flame-light.

Pat went into the kitchen and closed the door. Then, very slowly he opened it again and stood looking in. The room glowed with warmth, with welcoming warmth. The pewter was even richer than he had thought it would be. The plates in the open-faced cupboard caught sparks on their rims. For a moment Pat stood in the doorway trying to get the right tone in his voice. "I always kind of liked it," he said in his most off-hand manner. "It just came to me the other day that you might like to see it." He paused, for a horrible thought had come to him. "Why, she can't come here alone. A girl can't come to a single man's house at night. People would talk about her, and besides, she wouldn't do it." He was bitterly disappointed. "Her mother will have to come with her. But— maybe her mother won't get in the way. She can stand back here, kind of, out of the way."

Now that he was ready, a powerful reluctance stopped him. Evening after evening passed while he put off asking her to come. He went through his play until he knew exactly where she would stand, how she would look, what she would say. He had alternative things she might say. A week went by, and still he put off the visit that would bring her to see his room.

One afternoon he built up his courage with layers of will. "I can't put it off forever. I better go tonight." After dinner, he put on his best suit and set out to walk to the Munroe house. It was only a quarter of a mile away. He wouldn't ask her for tonight. He wanted to have the fire burning and the lamps lighted when she arrived. The night was cold and very dark. When Pat stumbled in the dust of the road, he thought with dismay how his polished shoes would look.

There were a great many lights in the Munroe house. In front of the gate, a number of cars were parked. "It's a party," Pat said to himself, "I'll ask her some other night. I couldn't do it in front of a lot of people." For a moment he even considered turning back. "It would look funny though, if I asked her the first time I saw her in months. She might suspect something."

When he entered the house, Bert Munroe grasped him by the hand. "It's Pat Humbert," he shouted. "Where have you been keeping yourself, Pat?"

"I've been studying at night."

"Well it's lucky you came over. I was going to go over to see you tomorrow. You heard the news, of course!"

"What news?"

"Why, Mae and Bill Whiteside are going to get married next Saturday. I was going to ask you to help at the wedding. It'll just be a home affair with refreshments afterwards. You used to help at the schoolhouse all the time before you got this studying streak." He took Pat's arm and tried to lead him down the hall. The sound of a number of voices came from the room at the end of the hall.

Pat resisted firmly. He exerted all his training in the off-hand manner. "That's fine, Mr. Munroe. Next Saturday, you say? I'd be glad to help. No, I can't stay now. I got to run to the store right away." He shook hands again and walked slowly out the door.

In his misery he wanted to hide for a while, to burrow into some dark place where no one could see him. His way was automatically homeward. The rambling house was dark and unutterably dreary when he arrived. Pat went into the barn and with deliberate steps climbed the short ladder and lay down in the hay. His mind was shrunken and dry with disappointment. Above all things he did not want to go into the house. He was afraid he might lock up the door again. And then, in all the years to come, two puzzled spirits would live in the beautiful room, and in his kitchen, Pat would understand how they gazed wistfully into the ghost of a fire.

XI

WHEN Richard Whiteside came to the far West in '50, he inspected the gold workings and gave them up as objects for his effort. "The earth gives only one crop of gold," he said. "When that crop is divided among a thousand tenants, it feeds no one for very long. That is bad husbandry."

Richard drove about over the fields and hills of California; in his mind there was the definite intention of founding a house for children not yet born and for their children. Few people in California in that day felt a responsibility toward their descendants.

On the evening of a fine clear day, he drove his two bay horses to the top of the little hills which surround the Pastures of Heaven. He pulled up his team and gazed down on the green valley. And Richard knew that he had found his home. In his wandering about the country he had come upon many beautiful places, but none of them had given him this feeling of consummation. He remembered the colonists from Athens and from Lacedaemon looking for new lands described by vague oracles; he thought of the Aztecs plodding forward after their guiding eagle. Richard said to himself, "Now if there could be a sign, it would be perfect. I know this is the place, but if only there could be an omen to remember and to tell the children." He looked into the sky, but it was clean of both birds and clouds. Then the breeze that blows over the hills in the evening sprang up. The oaks made furtive little gestures toward the valley, and on the hillside a tiny whirlwind picked up a few leaves and flung them forward. Richard chuckled. "Answer! Many a fine city was founded because of a hint from the gods no more broad than that."

After a little while he climbed out of his light wagon and unhitched his horses. Once hobbled, they moved off with little mincing steps toward the grass at the side of the road. Richard ate a supper of cold ham and bread, and afterwards he unrolled his blankets and laid them on the grass of the hillside. As the grey dusk thickened in the valley, he lay on his bed and gazed down on the Pastures of Heaven which was to be his home. On the far side, near a grove of fine oaks was the place; behind the chosen spot there was a hill and a little brushy crease, a stream surely. The light became uncertain and magical. Richard saw a beautiful white house with a trim garden in front of it and nearby, the white tower of a tank house. There were little yellow lights in the windows, little specks of welcoming lights. The broad front door opened, and a whole covey of children walked out on the veranda—at least six children. They peered out into the growing darkness, looked particularly up at the hill where Richard lay on his blankets. After a moment they went back into the house, and the door shut behind them. With the closing of the door, the house, the garden and the white tank house disappeared. Richard sighed with contentment and lay on his back. The sky was prickling with stars.

For a week Richard drove furiously about the valley. He bought two hundred and fifty acres in the Pastures of Heaven; he drove to Monterey to have the title searched and the deed recorded, and, when the land was surely his, he visited an architect.

It took six months to build his house, to carpet and furnish it, to bore a well and build the towering tank house over it. There were workmen about the Whiteside place the whole first year of Richard's ownership. The land was untouched with seed.

A neighbour who was worried by this kind of procedure drove over and confronted the new owner. "Going to have your family come out, Mr. Whiteside?"

"I haven't any family," said Richard. "My parents are dead. I have no wife."

"Then what the hell are you building a big house like that for?"

Richard's face grew stern. "I'm going to live here. I've come to stay. My children and their children and theirs will live in this house. There will be a great many Whitesides born here, and a great many will die here. Properly cared for, the house will last five hundred years."

"I see what you mean, all right," said the neighbour. "It sounds fine, but that's not how we work out here. We build a little shack, and if the land pays, we build a little more on it.

It isn't good to put too much into a place. You might want to move."

"I don't want to move," Richard cried. "That's just what I'm building against. I shall build a structure so strong that neither I nor my descendants will be able to move. As a precaution, I shall be buried here when I die. Men find it hard to leave the graves of their fathers." His face softened. "Why, man, don't you see what I'm doing? I'm founding a dynasty. I'm building a family and a family seat that will survive, not forever, but for several centuries at least. It pleases me, when I build this house, to know that my descendants will walk on its floors, that children whose great grandfathers aren't conceived will be born in it. I'll build the germ of a tradition into my house." Richard's eyes were sparkling as he talked. The pounding of carpenters' hammers punctuated his speech.

The neighbour thought he was dealing with a madman, but he felt a kind of reverence for the madness. He desired to salute it in some manner. Had he not been an American, he would have touched his hat with two fingers. This man's two grown sons were cutting timber three hundred miles away, and his daughter had married and gone to Nevada. His family was broken up before it was really started.

Richard built his house of redwood, which does not decay. He modeled it after the style of the fine country houses of New England, but, as a tribute to the climate of the Pastures of Heaven, he surrounded the whole building with a wide veranda. The roof was only temporarily shingled, but, as soon as his order could be received in Boston and a ship could get back again, the shingles were ripped off and eastern slate substituted. This roof was an important and symbolic thing to Richard. To the people of the valley the slate roof was the show piece of the country. More than anything else it made Richard Whiteside the first citizen of the valley. This man was steady, and his home was here. He didn't intend to run off to a new gold field. Why—his roof was slate. Besides, he was an educated man. He had been to Harvard. He had money, and he had the faith to build a big, luxurious house in the valley. He would rule the land. He was the founder and patriarch of a family, and his roof was of slate. The people appreciated and valued the Pastures of Heaven more because of the slate roof.

Had Richard been a politician with a desire for local prefer-ment, he could have made no more astute move than thus roofing his house with slate. It glimmered darkly in the rain; the sun made a steel mirror of it.

Finally the house was finished, two hired men were set to planting the orchards and to preparing the land for seed. A little band of sheep nibbled the grass on the hillside behind the house. Richard knew that his preparation was complete. He was ready for a wife. When a letter came from a distant relative, saying he had arrived in San Francisco with his wife and daughter and would be glad to see Richard, Richard knew he need not search farther. Before he went to San Fran-cisco, he knew he would marry that daughter. It was the fit thing. There would be no accidents of blood if he married this girl.

Although they went through the form of courtship, the matter was settled as soon as they met. Alicia was glad to leave the domination of her mother and to begin a domestic empire of her own. The house had been made for her. She had not been in it twenty-four hours before she had spread scalloped and perforated papers on the pantry shelves, of the exact kind Richard remembered in his mother's pantry. She ordered the house in the old, comfortable manner, the un-changeable, the cyclic manner—washing Monday, ironing Tuesday and so forth—carpets up and beaten twice a year; jams, tomatoes and pickles preserved and shelved in the base-ment every fall. The farm prospered, the sheep and cows in-creased, and in the garden, bachelor buttons, sweet william, carnations, hollyhocks settled down to a yearly blooming. And Alicia was going to have a baby.

Richard had known all this would happen. The dynasty was established. The chimneys wore black smudges around their crowns. The fireplace in the sitting room smoked just enough to fill the house with a delicious incense of wood smoke. The great meerschaum pipe his father-in-law had given him was turning from its new, chalky white to a rich, creamy yellow.

When the child was coming, Richard treated Alicia almost like an invalid. In the evening when they sat before the fire, he tucked a robe about her feet. His great fear was that something would go wrong with the bearing of the child. They talked of the picture she should look at to influence the appearance of the firstling, and, to surprise her, Richard sent to San Francisco for a little bronze copy of the Michelangelo *David*. Alicia blushed at its nakedness, but before very long she became passionately fond of the little figure. When she went to bed it stood on her bedside table. During the day she took it from room to room with her as she worked, and in the evening it stood on the mantle in the sitting room. Often when she gazed at its clean, hard limbs a tiny smile of knowledge and of seeking came and went on her face. She was thoroughly convinced that her child would look like the *David*.

Richard sat beside her and stroked her hand soothingly. She liked to have him stroke the palm of her hand, firmly enough so it did not tickle. He talked to her quietly. "The curse is removed," he said. "You know, Alicia, my people, and yours a little farther removed, lived in one house for a hundred and thirty years. From that central hearth our blood was mingled with the good true blood of New England. One time my father told me that seventy-three children were born in the house. Our family multiplied until my grandfather's time. My father was an only child, and I was an only child. It was the sadness of my father's life. He was only sixty when he died, Alicia, and I was his only child. When I was twenty-five and hadn't really begun to live, the old house burned down. I don't know what started the fire." He laid her hand down on the arm of his chair as gently as though it were a weak little animal. An ember had rolled out of the fireplace and off the brick hearth. He pushed it back among the other coals and then took up Alicia's hand again. She smiled faintly at the *David* on the mantle.

"There was a practice in ancient times," Richard continued. His voice became soft and far away as though he spoke from those ancient times. Later in life Alicia could tell by the set of his head, by the tone of his voice and by his expression when he was about to speak of ancient times. For the Ancient Times of Herodotus, of Xenophon, of Thucydides were personal things to him. In the illiterate west the stories of Herodotus were as new as though he had invented them. He read the Persian War, the Peloponnesian Wars and the Ten

Thousand every year. Now he stroked Alicia's hand a little more firmly.

"In ancient times when, through continued misfortunes, the people of a city came to believe themselves under a curse or even under disfavor of some god, they put all of their movable possessions in ships and sailed away to found a new city. They left their old city vacant and open to anyone who wanted it."

"Will you hand me the statue, Richard?" Alicia asked. "Sometimes I like to hold it in my hand." He jumped up and set the *David* in her lap.

"Listen, Alicia! There were only two children in the two generations before the house burned down. I put my possessions in a ship and sailed westward to found a new home. You must surely see that the home I lost took a hundred and thirty years to build. I couldn't replace it. A new house on the old land would have been painful to me. When I saw this valley, I knew it was the place for the new family seat. And now the generations are forming. I am very happy, Alicia."

She reached over to squeeze his hand in gratitude that she could make him happy. "Why," he said suddenly, "there was even an omen, when I first came into the valley. I enquired of the gods whether this was the place, and they answered. Is that good, Alicia? Shall I tell you about the omens and my first night on the hill?"

"Tell me tomorrow night," she said. "It will be better if I retire now." He stood up and helped her to unfold the rug from around her knees. Alicia leaned rather heavily on his arm as he helped her up the stairs. "There's something mystic in the house, Alicia, something marvellous. It's the new soul, the first native of the new race."

"He will look like the little statue," said Alicia.

When Richard had tucked in the covers so she could not catch cold, he went back to the sitting room. He could hear children in the house. They ran with pattering feet up and down the stairs, they dabbled in the ashes of the fireplace. He heard their voices softly calling to one another on the veranda. Before he went to bed, he put the three great books on the top shelf of the bookcase.

The birth was a very severe one. When it was over, and

Alicia lay pale and exhausted in her bed, Richard brought the little son and put him beside her. "Yes," she said, complacently, "he looks like the statue. I knew he would, of course. And David will be his name, of course."

The Monterey doctor came downstairs and sat with Richard beside the fire. He puckered his brow gloomily and rolled a Masonic ring around and around on his third finger. Richard opened a bottle of brandy and poured two little glasses.

"I'm going to name this toast to my son, Doctor."

The doctor put his glass to his nose and sniffed like a horse. "Damn fine liquor. You better name it to your wife."

"Of course." They drank. "And this next one to my son."

"Name this one to your wife, too."

"Why?" Richard asked in surprise.

The doctor was almost dipping his nostrils in the glass. "Kind of a thank offering. You were damn near a widower."

Richard dumped his brandy down his throat. "I didn't know. I thought—I didn't know. I thought first ones were always hard to bear."

"Give me another drink," the doctor demanded. "You aren't going to have any more children."

Richard stopped in the act of pouring. "What do you mean by that? Of course I'm going to have more children."

"Not by this wife, you aren't. She's finished. Have another child and you won't have any wife."

Richard sat very still. The soft clattering of children he had heard in the house for the past month was suddenly stilled. He seemed to hear their secret feet stealing out the front door and down the steps.

The doctor laughed sourly. "Why don't you get drunk if that's the way you feel about it?"

"Oh! no, no. I don't think I could get drunk."

"Well, give me another drink before I go, anyway. It's going to be a cold drive home."

Richard did not tell his wife she could not have children until six months had passed. He wanted her to regain her strength before he exposed her to the shock of the revelation. When he finally did go to her, he felt the guilt of his secret. She was holding her child in her lap, and occasionally bending down to take one of his upstretched fingers in her mouth. The child stared up with vague eyes and smiled wetly while he waggled his straight fingers for her to suck. The sun flooded in the window. From a distance they could hear one of the hired men cursing a harrow team with sing-song monotony. Alicia lifted her head and frowned slightly. "It's time he was christened, don't you think, Richard?"

"Yes," he agreed. "I'll make arrangements in Monterey."

She struggled with a weighty consideration. "Do you think it too late to change his name?"

"No, it's not too late. Why do you want to change it? What do you want to call him?"

"I want to have him called John. That's a New Testament name—" She looked up for his approval—"and besides, it's my father's name. My father will be pleased. Besides, I haven't felt quite right about naming him for that statue, even if it is a statue of the boy David. It isn't as though the statue had clothes on—"

Richard did not try to follow this logic. Instead he plunged into his confession. In a second it was over. He had not realized it would take so little time. Alicia was smiling a peculiar enigmatic smile that puzzled him. No matter how well he became acquainted with her, this smile, a little quizzical, a trifle sad, and filled with secret wisdom shut him out of her thoughts. She retired behind the smile. It said, "How silly you are. I know things which would make your knowledge seem ridiculous if I chose to tell you." The child stretched up its yearning fingers toward her face, and she flexed its fingers back and forth. "Wait a little," she said. "Doctors don't know everything. Just wait a little, Richard. We will have other children." She shifted the boy and slipped her hand under his diaper.

Richard went out and sat on his front steps. The house behind him was teeming with life again, whereas a few minutes ago it had been quiet and dead. There were thousands of things to do. The box hedge which held the garden in its place had not been clipped for six months. Long ago he had laid out a square in the side yard for a grass plot, and it lay waiting for the seed. There was no place for drying linen yet. The banister of the front steps was beside him. Richard put out his hand and stroked it as though it were the arched neck of a horse.

The Whitesides became the first family of the Pastures of Heaven almost as soon as they were settled. They were educated, they had a fine farm, and, while not rich, they were not pressed for money. Most important of all, they lived in comfort, in a fine house. The house was the symbol of the family—roomy, luxurious for that day, warm, hospitable and white. Its size gave an impression of substance, but it was the white paint, often renewed and washed, that placed it over the other houses of the valley as surely as a Rhine castle is placed over its village. The families admired the white house, and also they felt more secure because it was there. It embodied authority and culture and judgment and manners. The neighbours could tell by looking at his house that Richard Whiteside was a gentleman who would do no mean nor cruel nor unwise thing. They were proud of the house in the same way tenants of land in a duchy are proud of the manor house. While some of the neighbours were richer than Whiteside, they seemed to know they could not build a house like that even though they imitated it exactly. It was primarily because of his house that Richard became the valley's arbiter of manners, and, after that, a kind of extra-legal judge over small disputes. The reliance of his neighbours in turn bred in Richard a paternal feeling toward the valley. As he grew older he came to regard all the affairs of the valley as his affairs, and the people were proud to have it so.

Five years passed before her intuition told Alicia that she was ready to have another child. "I'll get the doctor," Richard said, when she told him. "The doctor will know whether it's safe or not."

"No, Richard. Doctors do not know. I tell you women know more about themselves than doctors do."

Richard obeyed her, because he was afraid of what the doctor would tell him. "It's the grain of deity in women," he explained to himself. "Nature has planted this sure knowledge in women in order that the race may increase."

Everything went well for six months, and then a devastating illness set in. When he was finally summoned, the doctor was too furious to speak to Richard. The confinement was a time of horror. Richard sat in his sitting room, gripping the arms of his chair and listening to the weak screaming in the bedroom above. His face was grey. After many hours the screaming stopped. Richard was so fuddled with apprehension that he did not even look up when the doctor came into the room.

"Get out the bottle," the doctor said, tiredly. "Let's name a toast to you for a God damn fool."

Richard did not look up nor answer. For a moment the doctor continued to scowl at him, and then he spoke more gently. "Your wife isn't dead, Heaven only knows why. She's gone through enough to kill a squad of soldiers. These weak women! They have the vitality of monsters. The baby is dead!" Suddenly he wanted to punish Richard for disregarding his first orders. "There isn't enough left of the baby to bury." He turned and left the house abruptly because he hated to be as sorry for anyone as he was for Richard Whiteside.

Alicia was an invalid. Little John could not remember when his mother had not been an invalid. All of his life that he could remember he had seen his father carry her up and down stairs in his arms. Alicia did not speak very often, but more and more the quizzical and wise smile was in her eyes. And in spite of her weakness, she ordered the house remarkably well. The rugged country girls, who served in the house as a coveted preparation for their own marriages, came for orders before every meal. Alicia, from her bed or from her rocking chair, planned everything.

Every night Richard carried her up to bed. When she was lying against her white pillows, he drew up a chair and sat by her bed for a little while, stroking the palm of her hand until she grew sleepy. Every night she asked, "Are you content, Richard?"

"I am content," he said. And then he told her about the farm and about the people of the valley. It was a kind of daily report of happenings. As he talked, the smile came upon her face and stayed there until her eyes drooped, and he blew out the light. It was a ritual.

On John's tenth birthday he was given a party. Children from all over the valley came and wandered on tip-toe through the big house, staring at the grandeur they had heard about. Alicia was sitting on the veranda. "You mustn't be so quiet, children," she said. "Run about and have a good time." But they could not run and shout in the Whiteside house. They might as well have shouted in church. When they had gone through all the rooms, they could stand the strain no longer. The whole party retired to the barn, from which their wild shrieks drifted back to the veranda where Alicia sat smiling.

That night, when she was in bed, she asked, "Are you content, Richard?"

His face still glowed with the pleasure he had taken in the party. "I am content," he said.

"You must not worry about the children, Richard," she continued. "Wait a little. Everything will be all right." This was her great, all-covering knowledge. "Wait a little. No sorrow can survive the smothering of a little time." And Richard knew that it was a greater knowledge than his.

"It isn't long to wait," Alicia went on.

"What isn't?"

"Why think, John. He's ten now. In ten years he will be married, and then, don't you see?—Teach him what you know. The family is safe, Richard."

"Of course, I know. The house is safe. I'm going to begin reading Herodotus to him, Alicia. He's old enough."

"I think Myrtle should clean all the spare bedrooms tomorrow. They haven't been aired for three months."

John Whiteside always remembered how his father read to him the three great authors, Herodotus, Thucydides, Xenophon. The meerschaum pipe was reddish brown by now, delicately and evenly coloured. "All history is here," Richard said. "Everything mankind is capable of is recorded in these three books. The love and chicanery, the stupid dishonesty, the short-sightedness and bravery, nobility and sadness of the race. You may judge the future by these books, John, for nothing can happen which has not happened and been recorded in these books. Compared to these, the Bible is a very incomplete record of an obscure people."

And John remembered how his father felt about the

house—how it was a symbol of the family, a temple built around the hearth.

John was in his last year in Harvard when his father suddenly died of pneumonia. His mother wrote to him telling him he must finish his course before he returned. "You would not be able to do anything that has not been done," she wrote. "It was your father's wish that you finish."

When he finally did go home, he found his mother a very aged woman. She was completely bedridden by now. John sat by her side and heard about his father's last days.

"He told me to tell you one thing," Alicia said. " 'Make John realize that he must keep us going. I want to survive in the generations,' and very soon after that he became delirious." John was looking out the window at the round hill behind the house. "Your father was delirious for two days. In all that time he talked of children—nothing but children. He heard them running up and down stairs and felt them pulling at the quilts of his bed. He wanted to take them up and hold them, John. Then just before he died the dreams cleared away. He was happy. He said, 'I have seen the future. There will be so many children. I am content, Alicia.' "

John was leaning his head in his palms now. And then his mother, who had never resisted anything, but had submitted every problem to time, pulled herself up in the bed and spoke harshly to him. "Get married!" she cried. "I want to see it. Get married—I want a strong woman who can have children. I couldn't have any after you. I would have died if I could have had one more. Find a wife quickly. I want to see her." She sank back on her pillows, but her eyes were unhappy and the smile of knowledge was not on her face.

John did not get married for six years. During that time his mother dried up until she was a tiny skeleton covered with bluish, almost transparent skin, and still she held on to life. Her eyes followed her son reproachfully; he felt ashamed when she looked at him. At length a classmate of John's came to the west to look about and brought his sister with him. They visited at the Whiteside farm for a month, and at the end of that time John proposed to Willa and was accepted. When he told his mother, she demanded to be alone with the girl. Half an hour later, Willa emerged from the sickroom blushing violently.

"What's the matter, dear?" John asked.

"Why, it's nothing. It's all right. Your mother asked me a great many questions, and then she looked at me for a long time."

"She's so old," John explained. "Her mind is so old." He went into his mother's room. The feverish frowning look was gone from her face and instead there was the old quizzical smile of knowledge.

"It's all right, John," she said. "I'd like to wait to see the children, but I can't. I've clung to life as long as I can. I'm tired of it." It was almost possible to see the tenacious will release its grip on her body. In the night she became unconscious and three days later she died as quietly and gently as though she had dozed.

John Whiteside did not think of the house exactly as his father had. He loved it more. It was the outer shell of his body. Just as his mind could leave his body and go traveling off, so could he leave the house, but just as surely he must come back to it. He renewed the white paint every two years, planted the garden himself and trimmed the box hedge. He did not occupy the powerful place in the valley his father had. John was less stern, less convinced of everything. Faced with an argument to decide, he was too prone to find endless ramifications of both sides. The big meerschaum pipe was very dark now, almost a black in which there were red lights.

Willa Whiteside loved the valley from the beginning. Alicia had been aloof and quiet, rather a frightening person. The people of the valley seldom saw her, and when they did, she treated them gently and kindly, was generous and careful of their feelings. She made them feel like peasants calling at the castle.

Willa liked to make calls on the women of the valley. She liked to sit in their kitchens drinking harsh tea and talking of the innumerable important things that bear on housekeeping. She grew to be an extensive trader of recipes. When she went to make a call, she carried a little note book in which to write confided formulae. Her neighbours called her Willa and often came in the morning to drink tea in her kitchen. Perhaps it was partly her influence that caused John to become gregarious. He lost the power his father had held through aloofness. John liked his neighbours. On warm summer afternoons he sat in his canvas chair on the veranda and entertained such men as could get away from work. There were political caucuses on the veranda, little meetings over glasses of lemonade. The social and political structure of the whole valley was built on this porch, and always it was built amusingly. John looked at the life about him with a kind of amused irony, and due to his outlook, there ceased to exist in the valley any of the ferocious politics and violent religious opinions which usually poison rural districts. When, during the discussions among the men, some local or national climax or calamity was spoken of, John liked to bring out the three great books and to read aloud of some parallel situation in the ancient world. He had as great a love for the ancients as his father had.

There were the Sunday dinners with a neighbour couple and perhaps an itinerant minister as guests. The women helped in the kitchen until the mid-day dinner was ready. At the table the minister felt the pitiless fire of his mission slipping away in the air of gentle tolerance, until, when the dessert was brought in and the cider drunk, a fiery Baptist had been known to laugh heartily at a bit of quiet ridicule aimed at total immersion.

John enjoyed these things deeply, but his sitting room was the centre of his existence. The leather chairs, whose hollows and bumps were casts of comfortable anatomy, were pieces of him. On the wall were the pictures he had grown up with, steel engravings of deer and Swiss Alpine climbers and of mountain goats. The pictures were so closely bound up with his life that he didn't see them any more, but the loss of any article would have been as painful as an amputation. In the evening his greatest pleasure came. A little fire was burning in the red brick fireplace. John sat in his chair caressing the big meerschaum. Now and then to oil it he stroked the polished bowl along the side of his nose. He was reading the Georgics or perhaps Varro on farming. Willa, under her own lamp, pursed her lips tightly while she embroidered doilies in floral designs as Christmas presents for eastern relatives who sent doilies to her.

John closed his book and went over to his desk. The roll top always stuck and required pampering. It gave suddenly and went clattering up. Willa unpursed her mouth. The look of intense agony she wore when she was doing a thing carefully left her face.

"What in the world are you doing?"

"Oh! Just seeing about some things."

For an hour he worked behind the desk, then—"Listen to this, Willa."

She relaxed again. "I thought so—poetry."

He read his verses and waited apologetically. Willa, with tact, kept silence. The silence lengthened until it was no longer tactful. "I guess it isn't very good." He laughed ruefully.

"No, it isn't."

He crumpled the paper and threw it into the fire. "For a few minutes I thought it was going to be good."

"What had you been reading, John?"

"Well, I was just looking through my Virgil and I thought I'd try my hand at a verse, because I didn't want to—oh, well, it's almost impossible to read a fine thing without wanting to do a fine thing. No matter." He rolled down the desk cover and picked a new book from the bookcase.

The sitting room was his home. Here he was complete, perfect and happy. Under the Rochester lamps every last scattered particle of him was gathered together into a definite, boundaried entity.

Most lives extend in a curve. There is a rise of ambition, a rounded peak of maturity, a gentle downward slope of disillusion and last a flattened grade of waiting for death. John Whiteside lived in a straight line. He was ambitionless; his farm not only made him a good living, but paid enough so he could hire men to work it for him. He wanted nothing beyond what he had or could easily procure. He was one of the few men who could savour a moment while he held it. And he knew it was a good life he was leading, an uniquely good life.

Only one need entered his existence. He had no children. The hunger for children was almost as strong in him as it had been in his father. Willa did not have children although she wanted them as badly as he did. The subject embarrassed them, and they never spoke of it.

In the eighth year of their marriage, through some accident, chemical or divine, Willa conceived, went through a painless, normal period of pregnancy and delivered a healthy child.

The accident never occurred again, but both Willa and John were thankful, almost devoutly thankful. The strong desire for self-perpetuation which had been more or less dormant in John rose up to the surface. For a few years he ripped the land with the plow, scratched it with the harrow and flogged it with the roller. Where he had been only a friend to the farm, the awakening duty to the generations changed him to a master. He plunged the seeds into the earth and waited covetously for the green crops to appear.

Willa did not change as her husband did. She took the boy William as a matter of course, called him Bill and refused to worship him. John saw his father in the boy although no one else did.

"Do you think he is bright?" John asked his wife. "You're with him more than I am. Do you think he has any intelligence?"

"Just so-so. Just normal."

"He seems to develop so slowly," John said impatiently. "I want the time to come when he'll begin to understand things."

On Bill's tenth birthday John opened his thick Herodotus and began to read to him. Bill sat on the floor, blankly regarding his father. Every night John read a few pages from the book. After about a week of it, he looked up from his book one evening and saw that Willa was laughing at him.

"What's the matter?" he demanded.

"Look under your chair."

He leaned down and saw that Bill had constructed a house of matches. The child was so absorbed in the work that he was not aware the reading had stopped. "Hasn't he been listening at all?"

"Not a word. He hasn't heard a word since the first night when he lost interest in the second paragraph."

John closed the book and put it in the bookcase. He did

not want to show how badly he was wounded. "Probably he's not old enough. I'll wait a year and then try him again."

"He won't ever like it, John. He isn't built like you nor like your father."

"What is he interested in, then?" John asked in dismay.

"Just the things the other boys in the valley like, guns and horses and cows and dogs. He has escaped you, John, and I don't think you can ever catch him."

"Tell me the truth, Willa. Is he—stupid?"

"No," she said consideringly. "No, he's not stupid. In some ways he's harder and brighter than you are. He isn't your kind, John, and you might just as well know it now as later."

John Whiteside felt his interest in the land lapsing. The land was safe. Bill would farm it some day. The house was safe, too. Bill was not stupid. From the first he seemed to have a good deal of mechanical interest and ability. He made little wagons, and, as Christmas presents, demanded toy steam engines. John noticed another difference about the boy, a side that was strange to the Whiteside family. He was not only very secretive, but sharp in a business sense. He sold his possessions to other boys, and, when they were tired of them, bought them back at a lower price. Little gifts of money multiplied in his hands in mysterious ways. It was a long time before John would admit to himself that he could not communicate with his son. When he gave Bill a heifer, and Bill immediately traded it for a litter of pigs which he raised and sold, John laughed at himself.

"He is certainly brighter than I am," he told Willa. "Once my father gave me a heifer, and I kept her until she died of old age. Bill is a throwback of some kind, to a pirate, maybe. His children will probably be Whitesides. It's a powerful blood. I wish he weren't so secret about everything he does, though."

John's leather chair and his black meerschaum and his books reclaimed him again from the farm. He was elected clerk of the school board. Again the farmers gathered in his house to talk. John's hair was turning white, and his influence in the valley was growing stronger as his age came upon him.

The house of Whiteside was John's personality solidified.

When the people of the valley thought of him, it was never of the man alone in a field, or in a wagon, or at the store. A mental picture of him was incomplete unless it included his house. He was sitting in his leather chair, smiling at his thick books, or reclining in one of the porch chairs on his wide, gracious veranda, or, with little shears and a basket, snipping flowers in the garden, or at the head of his own table carving a roast with artistry and care.

In the West, where, if two generations of one family have lived in a house, it is an old house and a pioneer family, a kind of veneration mixed with contempt is felt for old houses. There are very few old houses in the West. Those restless Americans who have settled up the land have never been able to stay in one place for very long. They build flimsy houses and soon move on to some new promise. Old houses are almost invariably cold and ugly.

When Bert Munroe moved his family to the Battle farm in the Pastures of Heaven, he was not long in understanding the position John Whiteside held. As soon as he could, he joined the men who gathered on the Whiteside veranda. His farm adjoined the Whiteside land. Soon after his arrival, Bert was elected to the school board, and then he was brought into official contact with John. One night at a Board meeting John quoted some lines from Thucydides. Bert waited until the other members had gone home.

"I wanted to ask you about that book you were talking about tonight, Mr. Whiteside."

"You mean the Peloponnesian Wars?" He brought the book and laid it in Bert's hands.

"I thought I'd like to read it, if you wouldn't mind lending it to me."

For a second John hesitated. "Of course—take it with you. It was my father's book. When you finish it, I have some others you might like to read."

From this incident a certain intimacy sprang up between the two families. They exchanged dinners and made little calls on each other. Bert felt at liberty to borrow tools from John.

On an evening when the Munroes had been in the valley for a year and a half, Bill walked stiffly into the Whiteside

sitting room and confronted his parents. In his nervousness
he was harsh. "I'm going to get married," he said. His manner made it seem like bad news.

"What's this?" John cried. "Why haven't you told us anything about it? Who is it?"

"Mae Munroe."

Suddenly John realized that this was good news, not a confession of a crime. "Why—why that's good! I'm glad. She's a
fine girl—isn't she, Willa?" His wife avoided his eyes. She
had been calling on the Munroes that morning.

Bill was planted stolidly in the centre of the room. "When
are you going to do it?" Willa asked. John thought her tone
almost unfriendly.

"Pretty soon now. Just as soon as we get the house finished
in Monterey."

John got up out of his chair, took the black meerschaum
from the mantel and lighted it. Then he returned to his chair.
"You've been very quiet about it," he observed steadily. "Why
didn't you tell us?" Bill said nothing. "You say you're going
to live in Monterey. Do you mean you aren't going to bring
your wife here to live? Aren't you going to live in this house
and farm this land?" Bill shook his head. "Are you ashamed of
something, Bill?"

"No, sir," Bill said. "I'm not ashamed of anything. I never
did like to talk about my affairs."

"Don't you think it a little of our affair, Bill?" John asked
bitterly. "You are our family. Your children will be our grand-
children."

"Mae was raised in town," Bill broke in. "All of her friends
live in Monterey, you know—friends she went to high school
with. She doesn't like it out here where there's nothing
doing."

"I see."

"So when she said she wanted to live in town I bought a
partnership in the Ford agency. I always wanted to get into
business."

John nodded slowly. His first anger was giving way now.
"Don't you think she might consent to live in this house, Bill?
We have so much room. We can do over any part she wants
changed."

"But she doesn't like it in the country. All of her friends are in Monterey."

Willa's mouth was set grimly. "Look at your father, Bill!" she ordered. John jerked his head upright and smiled gravely.

"Well, I guess that will be all right. Have you plenty of money?"

"Oh, sure! Plenty. And look here, father. We're getting a pretty big house, pretty big for two, that is. We talked about it, and we thought maybe you and mother would like to come to live with us."

John continued to smile with courteous gravity. "And then what would become of the house and the farm?"

"Well, we talked about that, too. You could sell the place and get enough for it to live all your lives in town. I could sell this place for you in a week."

John sighed and sank back against the cushions of his chair.

Willa said, "Bill, if I thought you would squeal, I'd beat you with a stick of wood."

John lighted his pipe and tamped the tobacco down in it. "You can't go away for long," he said gently. "Some day you'll get a homesickness you can't resist. This place is in your blood. When you have children you'll know that they can't grow up any place but here. You can go away for a little while, but you can't stay away. While you're in town, Bill, we'll just wait here and keep the house painted and the garden trimmed. You'll come back. Your children will play in the tank house. We'll wait for that. My father died dreaming of children," he smiled sheepishly. "I'd almost forgotten that."

"I could beat him with a stick," Willa muttered.

Bill left the room in embarrassment. "He'll come back," John repeated, after he had gone.

"Of course," his wife agreed grimly.

His head jerked up and he glanced at her suspiciously. "You really think that, don't you, Willa? You're not just saying it for me? That would make me feel old."

"Of course I think it. Do you think I'm wasting my breath?"

Bill was married in the late summer, and immediately afterward moved to his new stucco house in Monterey. In the fall John Whiteside grew restless again just as he had before

Bill was born. He painted the house although it did not need it very badly. He mercilessly trimmed the shrubs in the garden.

"The land isn't producing enough," he told Bert Munroe. "I've let it go for a long time. I could be raising a lot more on it than I am."

"Yes," said Bert. "None of us make our land produce enough. I've always wondered why you didn't have a band of sheep. Seems to me your hills would carry quite a flock."

"We used to have a flock in my father's time. That seems a long time ago. But, as I tell you, I've let the place go. The brush has got thick."

"Burn it off," said Bert. "If you burn that brush this fall you'll get fine pasture next spring."

"That's a good idea. The brush comes down pretty close to the house, though. I'll have to get a good deal of help."

"Well, I'll help you, and I'll bring Jimmie. You have two men, and counting yourself, that'll be five. If we start in the morning when there's no wind, and wait for a little rain first, there won't be any danger."

The fall set in early. By October the willows along the creeks of the Pastures of Heaven were yellow as flames. Almost out of sight in the air, great squadrons of ducks flew southward, and in the barnyard, the tame mallards flapped their wings and stretched their necks and honked yearningly. The blackbirds wheeled over the fields, uniting under a leader. There was a little early frost in the air. John Whiteside fretted against the winter. All day he worked in the orchard, helping to prune the trees.

One night he awakened to hear a light rain whispering on the slates and plashing softly in the garden.

"Are you awake, Willa?" he asked quietly.

"Of course."

"It's the first rain. I wanted you to hear it."

"I was awake when it started," she said complacently. "You missed the best part of it, the gusty part. You were snoring."

"Well, it won't last long. It's just a little first rain to wash off the dust."

In the morning, the sun shone through an atmosphere glistening with water. There was a crystalline quality in the sunlight. Breakfast was just over when Bert Munroe and his son Jimmie tramped up the back steps and into the kitchen.

" 'Morning, Mrs. Whiteside! 'Morning, John! I thought it was a good time to burn off that brush today. It was a nice little rain we had last night."

"That's a good idea. Sit down and have a cup of coffee."

"We just got up from breakfast, John. Couldn't swallow another thing."

"You, Jimmie? Cup of coffee?"

"Couldn't swallow another thing," said Jimmie.

"Well, then, let's get started before the grass dries out."

John went into the large basement which opened its sloping door beside the kitchen steps. In a moment he brought out a can of kerosene. When the two hired men had come in from the orchard, John provided all the men with wet gunny sacks.

"No wind," said Bert. "This is a good time for it. Start it right here, John! We'll stay between the fire and the house until we get a big strip burned off. It don't pay to take chances."

John plunged a kerosene torch into the thick brush and drew a line of fire along its edge. The brush crackled and snapped fiercely. The flame ran along the ground among the resinous stems. Slowly the men worked along behind the fire, up the sharp little hill.

"That's about enough here," Bert called. "There's plenty of distance from the house now. I think two of us better fire it from the upper side now." He started walking up around the brush patch, followed by Jimmie. At that moment a little autumn whirlwind danced down the hill, twisting and careening as it came. It made a coquettish dash into the fire, picked up sparks and embers and flung them against the white house. Then, as though tired of the game, the little column of air collapsed. Bert and Jimmie were running back. The five men searched the ground and stamped out every spark. "It's lucky we saw that," said John. "Silly little thing like that might burn the house down."

Bert and Jimmie circled the patch and fired it from the upper side. John and his two men worked up the hill, keeping between the flames and the house. The air was dense and blue with smoke. In a quarter of an hour the brush patch was nearly burned off.

Suddenly they heard a scream from the direction of the house. The house itself was barely visible through the smoke from the burning brush. All five of the men turned about and broke into a run. As the smoke grew thinner, they could see a thick, grey eddy gushing from one of the upper windows.

Willa was running distractedly toward them over the burned ground. John stopped when he came to her.

"I heard a noise in the basement," she cried. "I opened the door in the kitchen that leads to the basement, and the thing just swooped past me. It's all over the house now."

Bert and Jimmie charged up to them. "Are the hoses by the tank house?" Bert shouted.

John tore his gaze from the burning house. "I don't know," he said uncertainly.

Bert took him by the arm. "Come on! What are you waiting for? We can save some of it. We can get some of the furniture out anyway."

John disengaged his arm and started to saunter down the hill toward the house. "I don't think I want to save any of it," he said.

"You're crazy," Bert cried. He ran on and plunged about the tank house, looking for the hoses.

Now the smoke and flame were pouring from the window. From inside the house came a noise of furious commotion; the old building was fighting for its life.

One of the hired men walked up beside John. "If only that window was closed, we'd have a chance," he said in a tone of apology. "It's so dry, that house. And it's got a draft like a chimbley."

John walked to the wood pile and sat in the saw buck. Willa looked at his face for a moment and then stood quietly beside him. The outside walls were smoking now, and the house roared with the noise of a great wind.

Then a very strange and a very cruel thing happened. The side wall fell outward like a stage set, and there, twelve feet above the ground was the sitting room untouched as yet by the fire. As they watched the long tongues lashed into the room. The leather chairs shivered and shrank like live things from the heat. The glass on the pictures shattered and the steel engravings shrivelled to black rags. They could see the big black meerschaum pipe hanging over the mantel. Then the flame covered the square of the room and blotted it out. The heavy slate roof crashed down, crushing walls and floors under its weight, and the house became a huge bonfire without shape.

Bert had come back and was standing helplessly beside John. "It must of been that whirlwind," he explained. "A spark must of gone down the cellar and got into the coal oil. Yes, sir, it must of been that coal oil."

John looked up at him and smiled with a kind of horrified amusement. "Yes, sir, it must have been that coal oil," he echoed.

The fire burned smoothly now that its victory was gained; a field of growing flame rose high in the air. It no longer resembled a house at all. John Whiteside stood up from the saw buck and straightened his shoulders and sighed. His eyes rested for a moment on a place in the flame fifteen feet from the ground where the sitting room had been. "Well, that's over," he said. "And I think I know how a soul feels when it sees its body buried in the ground and lost. Let's go to your house, Bert. I want to telephone Bill. He will probably have a room for us."

"Why don't you stay with us? We have plenty of room."

"No, we'll go to Bill." John looked around once more at the burning pile. Willa put out her hand to take his arm, but withdrew it before she had touched him. He saw the gesture and smiled at her. "I wish I could have saved my pipe," he said.

"Yes, sir," Bert broke in effusively. "That was the best coloured meerschaum I ever saw. They have pipes in museums that aren't coloured any better than that. That pipe must have been smoked a long time."

"It was," John agreed. "A very long time. And you know, it had a good taste, too."

XII

A T TWO O'CLOCK in the afternoon the sight-seeing bus left
its station in Monterey for a tour of the peninsula. As it
moved along over the roads of the publicized Seventeen Mile
Drive, the travelers peered out at the spectacular houses of
very rich people. The sight-seers felt a little shy as they looked
out of the dusty windows, a little like eavesdroppers, but priv-
ileged, too. The bus crawled through the town of Carmel and
over a hill to the brown Mission Carmelo with its crooked
dome, and there the young driver pulled to the side of the
road and put his feet on the dashboard while his passengers
were led through the dark old church.

When they returned to their seats some of the barriers traveling people build about themselves were down.

"Did you hear?" said the prosperous man. "The guide said
the church is built like a ship with a stone keel and hull deep
in the ground under it? That's for the earthquakes—like a
ship in a storm, you see. But it wouldn't work."

A young priest with a clean rosy face and a pride in his new
serge cassock answered from two seats behind: "But it has
worked. There have been earthquakes, and the mission still
stands; built of mud and it still stands."

An old man broke in, an old and healthy man with eager
eyes. "Funny things happen," he said. "I lost my wife last
year. Been married over fifty years." He looked smilingly
about for some comment, and forgot the funny things that
happen.

A honeymooning couple sat arm in arm. The girl squeezed
tightly. "Ask the driver where we're going now."

The bus moved slowly on, up the Carmel Valley—past orchards and past fields of artichokes, and past a red cliff, veined
with green creepers. The afternoon was waning now, and the
sun sank toward the seaward mouth of the Valley. The road
left the Carmel River and climbed up a hillside until it ran
along the top of a narrow ridge. Here the driver cut his bus
sharply to the roadside and backed and pulled ahead four
times before he had faced around. Then he shut off the motor

and turned to his passengers. "This is as far as we go, folks. I always like to stretch my legs before we start back. Maybe some of you folks would like to get out and walk around."

They climbed stiffly from their seats and stood on the ridge peak and looked down into the Pastures of Heaven. And the air was as golden gauze in the last of the sun. The land below them was plotted in squares of green orchard trees and in squares of yellow grain and in squares of violet earth. From the sturdy farmhouses, set in their gardens, the smoke of the evening fires drifted upward until the hillbreeze swept it cleanly off. Cowbells were softly clashing in the valley; a dog barked so far away that the sound rose up to the travelers in sharp little whispers. Directly below the ridge a band of sheep had gathered under an oak tree against the night.

"It's called Las Pasturas del Cielo," the driver said. "They raise good vegetables there—good berries and fruit earlier here than any place else. The name means Pastures of Heaven."

The passengers gazed into the valley.

The successful man cleared his throat. His voice had a tone of prophecy. "If I have any vision, I tell you this: Some day there'll be big houses in that valley, stone houses and gardens, golf links and big gates and iron work. Rich men will live there—men that are tired of working away in town, men that have made their pile and want a quiet place to settle down to rest and enjoy themselves. If I had the money, I'd buy the whole thing. I'd hold on to it, and sometime I'd subdivide it." He paused and made a little gathering gesture with his hand. "Yes, and by God I'd live there myself."

His wife said: "Sh!" He looked guiltily around and saw that no one was listening to him.

The purple hill-shadow was creeping out toward the centre of the valley; somewhere below a pig screamed angrily. The young man raised his eyes from the land and smiled a confession to his new wife, and she smiled firmly and reprovingly back at him. His smile had said: "I almost let myself think of it. It would be nice—but I can't, of course."

And hers had answered: "No, of course you can't! There's ambition to think of, and all our friends expect things of us. There's your name to make so I can be proud of you. You can't run away from responsibility and cover your head in a place like this. But it would be nice." And both smiles softened and remained in their eyes.

The young priest strolled away by himself. He whispered a prayer, but practice had taught him to pray and to think about something else. "There might be a little church down there," he thought. "No poverty there, no smells, no trouble. My people might confess small wholesome sins that fly off with the penance of a few Hail Marys. It would be quiet there; nothing dirty nor violent would ever happen there to make me sorry nor doubtful nor ashamed. The people in those houses there would love me. They would call me Father and I'd be just with them when it was kindly to be just." He frowned and punished the thought. "I am not a good priest. I'll scourge myself with the poor, with the smell of them and with their fighting. I can't run from the tragedies of God." And he thought, "Maybe I'll come to a place like this when I am dead."

The old man stared into the valley with his eager eyes, and in his deafened ears the silence surged like a little wind blowing in a cypress tree. The farther hills were blurred to him, but he could see the golden light and the purple dark. His breathing choked and tears came into his eyes. He beat his hands helplessly against his hips. "I've never had time to think. I've been too busy with troubles ever to think anything out. If I could go down there and live down there for a little—why, I'd think over all the things that ever happened to me, and maybe I could make something out of them, something all in one piece that had a meaning, instead of all these trailing ends, these raw and dragging tails. Nothing would bother me down there and I could think."

The bus driver dropped his cigarette in the road and stepped it into the dirt. "Come on, folks," he called. "We ought to be getting along." He helped them in and shut the doors on them, but they crowded close to the windows and looked down into the Pastures of Heaven where the air lay blue like a lake now, and the farms were submerged in the quiet.

"You know," the driver said, "I always think it would be nice to have a little place down there. A man could keep a cow and a few pigs and a dog or two. A man could raise enough to eat on a little farm." He kicked the starter and the motor roared for a moment before he throttled it down. "I guess it sounds kind of funny to you folks, but I always like to look down there and think how quiet and easy a man could live on a little place." He thrust the gear lever; the car gathered speed and swept down the grade toward the long Carmel Valley and toward the sun where it was setting in the ocean at the Valley's mouth.

TO A GOD UNKNOWN

TO A GOD UNKNOWN

He is the giver of breath, and strength is his gift.
The high Gods revere his commandments.
His shadow is life, his shadow is death;
Who is He to whom we shall offer our sacrifice?

Through His might He became lord of the living
        and glittering world
And he rules the world and the men and the beasts
Who is He to whom we shall offer our sacrifice?

From His strength the mountains take being, and
        the sea, they say,
And the distant river;
And these are his body and his two arms.
Who is He to whom we shall offer our sacrifice?

He made the sky and the earth, and His will fixed
        their places,
Yet they look to Him and tremble.
The risen sun shines forth over Him.
Who is He to whom we shall offer our sacrifice?

He looked over the waters which stored His power and
        gendered the sacrifice.
He is God over Gods.
Who is He to whom we shall offer our sacrifice?

May He not hurt us, He who made earth,
Who made the sky and the shining sea?
Who is the God to whom we shall offer sacrifice?
                                        VEDA

I

WHEN the crops were under cover on the Wayne farm near Pittsford in Vermont, when the winter wood was cut and the first light snow lay on the ground, Joseph Wayne went to the wing-back chair by the fireplace late one afternoon and stood before his father. These two men were alike. Each had a large nose and high, hard cheek-bones; both faces seemed made of some material harder and more durable than flesh, a stony substance that did not easily change. Joseph's beard was black and silky, still thin enough so that the shadowy outline of his chin showed through. The old man's beard was long and white. He touched it here and there with exploring fingers, turned the ends neatly under out of harm's way. A moment passed before the old man realized that his son was beside him. He raised his eyes, old and knowing and placid eyes and very blue. Joseph's eyes were as blue, but they were fierce and curious with youth. Now that he had come before his father, Joseph hesitated to stand to his new heresy.

"There won't be enough in the land now, sir," he said humbly.

The old man gathered his shawl of shepherd's plaid about his thin straight shoulders. His voice was gentle, made for the ordering of simple justice. "What do you wish to complain of, Joseph?"

"You've heard that Benjy has gone courting, sir? Benjy will be married when the spring comes; and in the fall there will be a child, and in the next summer another child. The land doesn't stretch, sir. There won't be enough."

The old man dropped his eyes slowly and watched his fingers where they wrestled sluggishly on his lap. "Benjamin hasn't told me yet. Benjamin has never been very dependable. Are you sure he has gone seriously courting?"

"The Ramseys have told it in Pittsford, sir. Jenny Ramsey has a new dress and she's prettier than usual. I saw her today. She wouldn't look at me."

"Ah; maybe it's so, then. Benjamin should tell me."

"And so you see, sir, there won't be enough in the land for all of us."

John Wayne lifted his eyes again. "The land suffices, Joseph," he said placidly. "Burton and Thomas brought their wives home and the land sufficed. You are the next in age. You should have a wife, Joseph."

"There's a limit, sir. The land will feed only so many."

His father's eyes sharpened then. "Have you an anger for your brothers, Joseph? Is there some quarrel I haven't heard about?"

"No sir," Joseph protested. "The farm is too small and—" He bent his tall body down toward his father. "I have a hunger for land of my own, sir. I have been reading about the West and the good cheap land there."

John Wayne sighed and stroked his beard and turned the ends under. A brooding silence settled between the two men while Joseph stood before the patriarch, awaiting his decision.

"If you could wait a year," the old man said at last, "a year or two is nothing when you're thirty-five. If you could wait a year, not more than two surely, then I wouldn't mind. You're not the oldest, Joseph, but I've always thought of you as the one to have the blessing. Thomas and Burton are good men, good sons, but I've always intended the blessing for you, so you could take my place. I don't know why. There's something more strong in you than in your brothers, Joseph; more sure and inward."

"But they're homesteading the western land, sir. You have only to live a year on the land and build a house and plough a bit and the land is yours. No one can ever take it away."

"I know, I've heard of that; but suppose you should go now. I'll have only letters to tell me how you are, and what you're doing. In a year, not more than two, why I'll go with you. I'm an old man, Joseph. I'll go right along with you, over your head, in the air. I'll see the land you pick out and the kind of house you build. I'd be curious about that, you know. There might even be some way I could help you now and then. Suppose you lose a cow, maybe I could help you to find her; being up in the air like that I could see things far away. If only you wait a little while I can do that, Joseph."

"The land is being taken," Joseph said doggedly. "The century is three years gone. If I wait, the good land might all be taken. I've a hunger for the land, sir," and his eyes had grown feverish with the hunger.

John Wayne nodded and nodded, and pulled his shawl close about his shoulders. "I see," he mused. "It's not just a little restlessness. Maybe I can find you later." And then decisively: "Come to me, Joseph. Put your hands here—no, here. My father did it this way. A custom so old cannot be wrong. Now, leave your hand there!" He bowed his white head, "May the blessing of God and my blessing rest on this child. May he live in the light of the Face. May he love his life." He paused for a moment. "Now, Joseph, you may go to the West. You are finished here with me."

The winter came soon, with deep snow, and the air was frozen to needles. For a month Joseph wandered about the house, reluctant to leave his youth and all the strong material memories of his youth, but the blessing had cut him off. He was a stranger in the house and he felt that his brothers would be glad when he was gone. He went away before the spring had come, and the grass was green on the hills in California when he arrived.

2

A FTER a time of wandering, Joseph came to the long valley called Nuestra Señora, and there he recorded his homestead. Nuestra Señora, the long valley of Our Lady in central California, was green and gold and yellow and blue when Joseph came into it. The level floor was deep in wild oats and canary mustard flowers. The river San Francisquito flowed noisily in its bouldered bed through a cave made by its little narrow forest. Two flanks of the coast range held the valley of Nuestra Señora close, on one side guarding it against the sea, and on the other against the blasting winds of the great Salinas Valley. At the far southern end a pass opened in the hills to let out the river, and near this pass lay the church and the little town of Our Lady. The huts of Indians clustered about the mud walls of the church, and although the church was often vacant now and its saints were worn and part of its tile roof lay in a shattered heap on the ground, and although the bells were broken, the Mexican Indians still lived near about and held their festivals, danced La Jota on the packed earth and slept in the sun.

When his homestead was recorded, Joseph set out for his new home. His eyes glittered with excitement under his broad-brimmed hat and he sniffed at the valley hungrily. He wore new jeans with a circle of brass buttons around the waist, a blue shirt, and a vest for the sake of the pockets. His high-heeled boots were new and his spurs shone like silver. An old Mexican was trudging painfully in to Our Lady. His face lighted up with pleasure when Joseph drew near. He removed his hat and stepped aside. "Is there a fiesta some place?" he asked politely.

Joseph laughed with delight. "I have a hundred and sixty acres of land up the valley. I'm going to live on it."

The old walker's eyes lighted on the rifle which, in its scabbard, lay snugly under Joseph's leg. "If you see a deer, señor, and if you kill that deer, remember old Juan."

Joseph rode on, but he called back over his shoulder,

"When the house is built I'll make a fiesta. I'll remember you, then, Old Juan."

"My son-in-law plays the guitar, señor."

"Then he'll come too, Old Juan."

Joseph's horse walked quickly along, swishing with its hoofs through the brittle oak leaves; the iron shoes rang against protruding stones. The path went through the long forest that bordered the river. As he rode, Joseph became timid and yet eager, as a young man is who slips out to a rendezvous with a wise and beautiful woman. He was half-drugged and overwhelmed by the forest of Our Lady. There was a curious femaleness about the interlacing boughs and twigs, about the long green cavern cut by the river through the trees and the brilliant underbrush. The endless green halls and aisles and alcoves seemed to have meanings as obscure and promising as the symbols of an ancient religion. Joseph shivered and closed his eyes. "Perhaps I'm ill," he said. "When I open my eyes I may find that all this is delirium and fever." As he rode on and on the fear came upon him that this land might be the figure of a dream which would dissolve into a dry and dusty morning. A manzanita branch whipped his hat off and dropped it on the ground, and, when Joseph dismounted he stretched his arms and leaned down to pat the earth with his hand. There was a need in him to shake off the mood that had fallen upon him. He looked up to the treetops where the sun flashed on trembling leaves, where the wind sang huskily. When he mounted his horse again he knew that he could never lose the feeling for the land. The crying leather of his saddle, the jingle of his spur chains, the rasping of the horse's tongue over the bit-roller sang the high notes over the land's throbbing. Joseph felt that he had been dull and now suddenly was sensitized; had been asleep and was awakened. Far in the back of his mind lay the feeling that he was being treacherous. The past, his home and all the events of his childhood were being lost, and he knew he owed them the duty of memory. This land might possess all of him if he were not careful. To combat the land a little, he thought of his father, of the calm and peace, the strength and eternal rightness of his father, and then in his thought the difference ended and he knew that there was no quarrel, for his father and this new land were one. Joseph was frightened then. "He's dead," he whispered to himself. "My father must be dead."

The horse had left the river's forest now to follow a smooth rounded track that might have been made by a python's body. It was an ancient game trail made by the hoofs and pads of lonely fearful animals that had followed the track as though they loved even the ghosts of company. It was a trail of innumerable meanings. Here it swung wide to avoid a large oak with one thick overhanging limb where long ago a lion had crouched and made its kill and left its scent to turn the trail aside: here the track went carefully around a smooth rock whereon a rattlesnake habitually sunned its cold blood. The horse kept to the center of the trail and heeded all its warnings.

Now the path broke into a broad grassy meadow, in the center of which a colony of live oaks grew like a green island in a lake of lighter green. As Joseph rode toward the trees he heard an agonized squealing, and turning the grove's shoulder he came in sight of a huge boar with curved tusks and yellow eyes and a mane of shaggy red hair. The beast sat on its haunches and tearingly ate the hind quarters of a still-squealing little pig. In the distance a sow and five other little pigs bounded away, crying their terror. The boar stopped eating and set its shoulders when Joseph rode into its line of scent. It snorted and then returned to the dying pig, which still squealed piercingly. Joseph jerked up his horse. His face contracted with anger and his eyes paled until they were almost white. "Damn you," he cried. "Eat other creatures. Don't eat your own people." He pulled his rifle from its scabbard and aimed between the yellow eyes of the boar. And then the barrel lowered and a firm thumb let down the hammer. Joseph laughed shortly at himself. "I'm taking too great power into my hands," he said. "Why he's the father of fifty pigs and he may be the source of fifty more." The boar wheeled and snorted as Joseph rode on by.

Now the trail skirted a long side hill densely protected by underbrush—blackberry, manzanita and scrub oak so thickly tangled that even the rabbits had to make little tunnels through it. The trail forced its way up the long narrow ridge and came to a belt of trees, tan oak and live oak and white oak. Among the branches of the trees a tiny white fragment of mist appeared and delicately floated along just over the treetops. In a moment another translucent shred joined it, and another and another. They sailed along like a half-materialized ghost, growing larger and larger until suddenly they struck a column of warm air and rose into the sky to become little clouds. All over the valley the flimsy little clouds were forming and ascending like the spirits of the dead rising out of a sleeping city. They seemed to disappear against the sky, but the sun was losing its warmth because of them. Joseph's horse raised its head and sniffed the air. On top of the ridge stood a clump of giant madrone trees, and Joseph saw with wonder how nearly they resembled meat and muscles. They thrust up muscular limbs as red as flayed flesh and twisted like bodies on the rack. Joseph laid his hand on one of the branches as he rode by, and it was cold and sleek and hard. But the leaves at the ends of the horrible limbs were bright green and shiny. Pitiless and terrible trees, the madrones. They cried with pain when burned.

Joseph gained the ridge-top and looked down on the grass lands of his new homestead where the wild oats moved in silver waves under a little wind, where the patches of blue lupins lay like shadows in a clear lucent night, and the poppies on the side hills were broad rays of sun. He drew up to look at the long grassy meadows in which clumps of live oaks stood like perpetual senates ruling over the land. The river with its mask of trees cut a twisting path down through the valley. Two miles away he could see, beside a gigantic lonely oak, the white speck of his tent pitched and left while he went to record his homestead. A long time he sat there. As he looked into the valley, Joseph felt his body flushing with a hot fluid of love. "This is mine," he said simply, and his eyes sparkled with tears and his brain was filled with wonder that this should be his. There was pity in him for the grass and the flowers; he felt that the trees were his children and the land his child. For a moment he seemed to float high in the air and to look down upon it. "It's mine," he said again, "and I must take care of it."

The little clouds were massing in the sky; a legion of them

scurried to the east to join the army already forming on the hill line. From over the western mountains the lean grey ocean clouds came racing in. The wind started up with a gasp and sighed through the branches of the trees. The horse stepped lightly down the path toward the river again, and often it raised its head and sniffed at the fresh sweet odor of the coming rain. The cavalry of clouds had passed and a huge black phalanx marched slowly in from the sea with a tramp of thunder. Joseph trembled with pleasure in the promised violence. The river seemed to hurry along down its course, to chatter excitedly over the stones as it went. And then the rain started, fat lazy drops splashing on the leaves. Thunder rolled like caissons over the sky. The drops grew smaller and thicker, raked through the air and hissed in the trees. Joseph's clothing was soaked in a minute and his horse shone with water. In the river the trout were striking at tumbled insects and all the tree trunks glistened darkly.

The trail left the river again, and as Joseph neared his tent the clouds rolled backward from the west to the east like a curtain of grey wool and the late sun sparkled on the washed land, glittered on the grass blades and shot sparks into the drops that lay in the hearts of wildflowers. Before his tent Joseph dismounted and unsaddled the horse and rubbed its wet back and shoulders with a cloth before he turned the tired beast loose to graze. He stood in the damp grass in front of his tent. The setting sun played on his brown temples and the evening wind ruffled his beard. The hunger in his eyes became rapaciousness as he looked down the long green valley. His possessiveness became a passion. "It's mine," he chanted. "Down deep it's mine, right to the center of the world." He stamped his feet into the soft earth. Then the exultance grew to be a sharp pain of desire that ran through his body in a hot river. He flung himself face downward on the grass and pressed his cheek against the wet stems. His fingers gripped the wet grass and tore it out, and gripped again. His thighs beat heavily on the earth.

The fury left him and he was cold and bewildered and frightened at himself. He sat up and wiped the mud from his lips and beard. "What was it?" he asked himself. "What came over me then? Can I have a need that great?" He tried to remember exactly what had happened. For a moment the land had been his wife. "I'll need a wife," he said. "It will be too lonely here without a wife." He was tired. His body ached as though he had lifted a great rock, and the moment of passion had frightened him.

Over a little fire before his tent he cooked his meager supper, and when the night came he sat on the ground and looked at the cold white stars, and he felt a throbbing in his land. The fire died down to coals and Joseph heard the coyotes crying in the hills, and he heard the little owls go shrieking by, and all about him he heard the field mice scattering in the grass. After a while the honey-colored moon arose behind the eastern ridge. Before it was clear of the hills, the golden face looked through bars of pine-trunks. Then for a moment a black sharp pine tree pierced the moon and was withdrawn as the moon arose.

3

Long before the lumber wagons came in sight Joseph heard the sweet harsh clangour of their bells, the shrill little bells perched above the hames, that warned other teams to turn out of the narrow road. Joseph was washed clean; his hair and beard were combed and his eyes were eager with expectation, for he had seen no one in two weeks. At last the big teams came into view from among the trees. The horses walked with little humping steps to pull the heavy loads of planks over the rough new road. The leading driver waved his hat to Joseph and the sun flashed on his hat buckle. Joseph walked down to meet the teams and climbed to the high seat beside the first driver, a middle-aged man whose cropped coarse hair was white, whose face was brown and seamed like a tobacco leaf. The driver shifted the lines to his left hand and extended his right.

"I thought you'd be here earlier," Joseph said. "Did you have trouble on the way?"

"No trouble, Mr. Wayne, that you could call trouble. Juanito had a hot box and my own son Willie dropped his front wheel into a bog-hole. He was asleep, I guess. It isn't much of a road these last two miles."

"It will be," Joseph said, "when enough teams like these go over it, it'll be a good road." He pointed a finger. "Over by that big oak we'll drop this lumber."

To the face of the driver there came an expression of half-foreboding. "Going to build under a tree? That's not good. One of those limbs might crack off and take your roof with it, and smash you, too, some night while you're asleep."

"It's a good strong tree," Joseph assured him. "I wouldn't like to build my house very far from a tree. Is your house away from a tree?"

"Well no, that's why I'm telling you. The damn thing is right smack under one. I don't know how I happened to build it there. Many a night I've laid awake and listened to the wind and thought about a limb as big around as a barrel coming through the roof." He pulled up his team and wound the handful of lines around the brake. "Pull up even, here," he shouted to the other drivers.

When the lumber lay on the ground and the horses, haltered head-inward about the wagons, munched barley from their nose-bags, the drivers unrolled their blankets in the wagon-beds. Joseph had already built a fire and started the supper. He held his frying pan high above the flame and turned the bacon constantly. Romas, the old driver, walked up and sat beside the fire. "We'll get an early start in the morning," he said. "We'll make good time with empty wagons."

Joseph held his pan from the fire. "Why don't you let the horses have a little grass?"

"When they are working? Oh, no. There's no guts in grass. Got to have something stronger to pull over a road like yours. Put your pan down in the fire and let it lay a minute if you want to cook that bacon."

Joseph scowled. "You people don't know how to fry bacon. Slow heat and turning, that's what makes it crisp without losing it all in grease."

"It's all food," said Romas. "Everything's food."

Juanito and Willie walked up together. Juanito had a dark, Indian skin and blue eyes. Willie's face was twisted and white with some unknown illness under its crusting of dirt, and Willie's eyes were furtive and frightened, for no one believed in the pains which shook his body in the night and no one believed the dark dreams which tortured him when he slept. Joseph looked up and smiled at the two.

"You are seeing my eyes," Juanito said boldly. "I am not Indian. I am Castillian. My eyes are blue. See my skin. It is dark, and that is the sun, but Castillians have blue eyes."

"He tells everybody that," Romas broke in. "He likes to find a stranger to tell that to. Everybody in Nuestra Señora knows his mother was a squaw, and only God knows who his father was."

Juanito glared and touched his fingers to a long knife in his belt, but Romas only laughed and turned to Joseph. "Juanito tells himself, 'Some time I'll kill somebody with this knife.' That's the way he keeps feeling proud. But he knows he won't, and that keeps him from being too proud. Sharpen a

stick to eat your bacon with, Juanito," he said contemptuously, "and next time you tell about being a Castillian, be sure
nobody knows you."

Joseph set down his frying pan and looked questioningly at
Romas. "Why do you tell on him?" he asked. "What good do
you do by it? He does no harm being a Castillian."

"It's a lie, Mr. Wayne. One lie is like another. If you believe
that lie, he'll tell another lie. In a week he'd be the cousin of
the Queen of Spain. Juanito, here, is a teamster, a damn good
one. I can't let him be a prince."

But Joseph shook his head and took up the frying pan
again. Without looking up, he said, "I think he is a Castillian.
His eyes are blue, and there's something else besides. I don't
know how I know it, but I think he is."

Juanito's eyes grew hard and proud. "Thank you, señor,"
he said. "It is true, what you say." He drew himself up
dramatically. "We understand each other, señor. We are ca-
balleros."

Joseph put the bacon on tin plates and poured the coffee.
He was smiling gently. "My father thinks he is almost a god.
And he is."

"You don't know what you're doing," Romas protested. "I
won't be able to stand this caballero. He won't work now.
He'll walk around admiring himself."

Joseph blew wrinkles in his coffee. "When he gets too
proud, I can use a Castillian here," he said.

"But God damn it, he's a good skinner."

"I know it," Joseph said quietly. "Gentlemen usually are.
They don't have to be made to work."

Juanito got up hastily and walked off into the growing
darkness, but Willie explained for him. "A horse has got its
foot over a halter-rope."

The western range was still edged with the silver of the
after-glow, but the valley of Our Lady was filled to the
mountain-rims with darkness. The cast stars in the steel-grey
fabric of the sky seemed to struggle and wink against the
night. The four men sat about the coals of the fire, their faces
strong with shadows. Joseph caressed his beard and his eyes
were brooding and remote. Romas clasped his knees with
both his arms. His cigarette gleamed red and then disap-

peared behind its ash. Juanito held his head straight and his neck stiff, but his eyes, behind crossed lashes, did not leave Joseph. Willie's pale face seemed to hang in the air unconnected to a body; the mouth contracted to a nervous grimace now and then. His nose was pinched and bony and his mouth came to a curved point like a parrot's beak. When the firelight had died down so that only the faces of the men were visible, Willie put out his lean hand and Juanito took it and clasped the fingers strongly, for Juanito knew how frightened Willie was of the darkness. Joseph threw a twig into the fire and started a little blaze. "Romas," he said, "the grass is good here, the soil is rich and free. It needs only lifting with a plow. Why was it left, Romas? Why didn't anyone take it before this?"

Romas spat his cigarette stump at the fire. "I don't know. People are coming slowly to this country. It's off the main road. This would have been taken, I guess, but for the dry years. They set the country back a long time."

"Dry years? When were the dry years?"

"Oh, between eighty and ninety. Why, all the land dried up and the wells went dry and the cattle died." He chuckled. "It was dry enough, I tell you. Half the people who lived here then had to move away. Those who could, drove the cattle inland to the San Joaquin, where there was grass along the river. The cows died along the road, too. I was younger then, but I remember the dead cows with swelled-up guts. We shot at them and they went down like punctured balloons, and the stink would knock you down."

"But the rain came again," Joseph said quickly. "The ground is full of water now."

"Oh, yes, the rain came after ten years. Floods of it came. Then the grass came up again and the trees were green. We were glad then, I still remember it. The people down in Nuestra Señora had a fiesta in the rain, only a little roof over the guitar players to keep the strings dry. And the people were drunk and dancing in the mud. They got drunk on the water. Not only Mexicans, either. Father Angelo came upon them, and he made them stop."

"What for?" Joseph demanded.

"Well, you don't know what the people were doing there in

the mud. Father Angelo was pretty mad. He said we'd let the devil in. He drove out the devil and made the people wash themselves and stop rolling in the wallows. He put penances on everybody. Father Angelo was pretty mad. He stayed right there until the rain stopped."

"The people were drunk, you say?"

"Yes, they were drunk for a week, and they did bad things—took off their clothes."

Juanito interrupted him. "They were happy. The wells were dry before, señor. The hills were white like ashes. It made the people happy when the rain came. They couldn't bear it to be so happy, and they did bad things. People always do bad things when they are too happy."

"I hope it never comes again," Joseph said.

"Well, Father Angelo said it was a judgment, but the Indians said it had been before, twice in the memory of old men."

Joseph stood up nervously. "I don't like to think about it. It won't come again, surely. Feel how tall the grass is already."

Romas was stretching his arms. "Maybe not. But don't depend on that. It's time to go to bed. We'll be starting at daylight."

The night was cold with the dawning when Joseph awakened. He seemed to have heard a shrill cry while he slept. "It must have been an owl," he thought. "Sometimes the sound is warped and magnified by a dream." But he listened tensely and heard a choked sobbing outside his tent. He slipped on his jeans and boots and crept out between the tent flaps. The soft crying came from one of the wagons. Juanito was leaning over the side of the wagon in which Willie slept.

"What's the matter?" Joseph demanded. In the faint light he saw that Juanito was holding Willie's arm.

"He dreams," Juanito explained softly. "Sometimes he cannot awaken unless I help him. And sometimes when he wakes up he thinks that is the dream and the other true. Come, Willie," Juanito said. "See, you are awake now. He dreams terrible things, señor, and then I pinch him. He is afraid, you see."

Romas spoke from the wagon where he lay. "Willie eats too much," he said. "He's just had a nightmare. He always did have them. Go back to bed, Mr. Wayne."

But Joseph bent down and saw the terror on Willie's face. "There's nothing in the night to hurt you, Willie," he said. "You can come and sleep in my tent if you want to."

"He dreams he is in a bright place that is dry and dead, and people come out of holes and pull off his arms and legs, señor. Nearly every night he dreams it. See, Willie, I will stay with you now. See, the horses are here all around you, looking at you, Willie. Sometimes, señor, the horses help him in the dream. He likes to sleep with them around him. He goes to the dry dead place, but he's safe from the people when the horses are near. Go to bed, señor, I will hold him for a while."

Joseph laid his hand on Willie's forehead and found that it was cold as stone. "I'll build up a fire and get him warm," he said.

"No use, señor; he is always cold. He cannot be warm."

"You are a good boy, Juanito."

Juanito turned away from him. "He calls to me, señor."

Joseph drew his hand under the warm flank of a horse, and walked back to his tent. The pine grove on the eastern ridge made a jagged line across the faint light of the morning. The grass stirred restively in the awakening breeze.

4

THE FRAME of the house was standing, waiting for its skin, a square house crossed by inner walls to make four equal rooms. The great lone oak tree stretched a protecting arm over its roof. The venerable tree was tufted with new, shiny leaves, glittering and yellow-green in the morning sunshine. Joseph fried his bacon over the campfire, turning the slices endlessly. Then, before he ate his breakfast, he went to his new buckboard, in which a barrel of water stood. He ladled out a basinful, and filling his cupped hands, flung water on his hair and beard and wiped the beads of sleep from his eyes. He scraped the water off with his hands and went to his breakfast with his face all shining with moisture. The grass was damp with dew, sprinkled with fire. Three meadowlarks with yellow vests and light grey coats hopped near the tent stretching their beaks, friendly and curious. Now and then they puffed their chests and raised their heads like straining prima donnas and burst into a rising ecstasy of song, then cocked their heads at Joseph to see whether he noticed or approved. Joseph raised his tin cup and swallowed the last of his coffee and flung the grounds into the fire. He stood up and stretched his body in the strong sunlight before he walked to his house frame and threw back the canvas that covered his tools, and the three larks scurried behind him, stopping to sing despairingly for his attention. Two hobbled horses hopped in from their pasturage and raised their noses and snorted in a friendly manner. Joseph picked up a hammer and an apron full of nails, then turned with irritation on the larks.

"Go out and dig worms," he said. "Stop your noise. You'll make me want to dig worms, too. Get along now." The three larks raised their heads in mild surprise and then sang in unison. Joseph took his black slouch hat from the pile of lumber and pulled it down over his eyes. "Go and dig worms," he growled. The horses snorted again and one of them nickered shrilly. Instantly Joseph dropped his hammer in relief. "Hello! Who's coming?" He heard an answering nicker from the trees far down the road, and while he watched, a horseman issued into sight, his beast traveling at a tired trot. Joseph walked quickly to the dying fire and built it to a flame again and put the coffee pot back. He smiled happily. "I didn't want to work today," he told the larks. "Go and dig worms, I won't have time for you now." And then Juanito rode up. He stepped gracefully down, with two movements slipped off the saddle and bridle, and then took off his sombrero and stood smiling, expectant of his welcome.

"Juanito! I am glad to see you! You haven't had breakfast, have you? I'll fry you some breakfast."

And Juanito's expectant smile broke wide with gladness. "I have been riding all night, señor. I have come to be your vaquero."

Joseph extended his hand. "But I haven't a single cow for you to ride herd on, Juanito."

"You will have, señor. I can do anything, and I am a good vaquero."

"Can you help to build a house?"

"Surely, señor."

"And your pay, Juanito—how much pay do you get?"

Juanito's lids drew down solemnly over his bright eyes. "Before now, señor, I have been a vaquero, a good one. Those men paid me thirty dollars every month, and they said I was Indio. I wish to be your friend, señor, and have no pay."

Joseph was puzzled for a moment. "I think I see what you mean, Juanito, but you'll want money to have a drink when you go to town. You'll need money to see a girl now and then."

"You shall give me a present when I go to town, señor. A present is not pay." The smile was back again. Joseph poured out a cup of coffee for him.

"You're a good friend, Juanito. Thank you."

Juanito reached into the peak of his sombrero and drew out a letter. "Since I was coming, I brought you this, señor."

Joseph took the letter and walked slowly away. He knew what it was. He had been expecting it for some time. And the land seemed to know what it was, too, for a hush had fallen over the grass flats, the meadowlarks had gone away, and even the linnets in the oak tree had stopped their twittering. Joseph sat down on a lumber pile under the oak and slowly tore open the envelope. It was from Burton.

"Thomas and Benjy have asked me to write to you," it said. "The thing we knew must happen has happened. Death shocks us even when we know it must come. Father passed to the Kingdom three days ago. We were all with him at the last, all except you. You should have waited.

"His mind was not clear at the last. He said some very peculiar things. He did not talk about you so much as he talked to you. He said he could live as long as he wanted, but he wished to see your new land. He was obsessed with this new land. Of course his mind was not clear. He said, 'I don't know whether Joseph can pick good land. I don't know whether he's competent. I'll have to go out there and see.' Then he talked a great deal about floating over the country, and he thought he was doing it. At last he seemed to go to sleep. Benjy and Thomas went out of the room then. Father was delirious. I really should shut up his words and never tell them, for he was not himself. He talked about the mating of animals. He said the whole earth was a—no, I can't see any reason for saying it. I tried to get him to pray with me, but he was too nearly gone. It has troubled me that his last words were not Christian words. I haven't told the other boys because his last words were to you, as though he talked to you."

The letter continued with a detailed description of the funeral. It ended—"Thomas and Benjy think we could all move to the West if there's still land to be taken. We shall want to hear from you before we make any move."

Joseph dropped the letter on the ground and put his forehead down in his hands. His mind was inert and numb, but there was no sadness in him. He wondered why he was not sad. Burton would reproach him if he knew that a feeling of joy and of welcome was growing up in him. He heard the sounds come back to the land. The meadowlarks built little crystal towers of melody, a ground squirrel chattered shrilly, sitting upright in the doorway of his hole, the wind whispered a moment in the grass and then grew strong and steady, bringing the sharp odors of the grass and of the damp earth, and the great tree stirred to life under the wind. Joseph raised his head and looked at its old, wrinkled limbs. His eyes lighted with recognition and welcome, for his father's strong and simple being, which had dwelt in his youth like a cloud of peace, had entered the tree.

Joseph raised his hand in greeting. He said very softly, "I'm glad you've come, sir. I didn't know until now how lonely I've been for you." The tree stirred slightly. "It *is* good land, you see," Joseph went on softly. "You'll like to be staying, sir." He shook his head to clear out the last of the numbness, and he laughed at himself, partly in shame for the good thoughts, and partly in wonder at his sudden feeling of kinship with the tree. "I suppose being alone is doing it. Juanito will stop that, and I'll have the boys come out to live. I am talking to myself already." Suddenly he felt guilty of treason. He stood up, walked to the old tree and kissed its bark. Then he remembered that Juanito must be watching him, and he turned defiantly to face the boy. But Juanito was staring steadily at the ground. Joseph strode over to him. "You must have seen—" he began angrily.

Juanito continued to stare downward. "I did not see, señor."

Joseph sat down beside him. "My father is dead, Juanito."

"I am sorry, my friend."

"But I want to talk about that, Juanito, because you are my friend. For myself I am not sorry, because my father is here."

"The dead are always here, señor. They never go away."

"No," Joseph said earnestly. "It is more than that. My father is in that tree. My father is that tree! It is silly, but I want to believe it. Can you talk to me a little, Juanito? You were born here. Since I have come, since the first day, I have known that this land is full of ghosts." He paused uncertainly. "No, that isn't right. Ghosts are weak shadows of reality. What lives here is more real than we are. We are like ghosts of its reality. What is it, Juanito? Has my brain gone weak from being two months alone?"

"The dead, they never go away," Juanito repeated. Then he looked straight ahead with a light of great tragedy in his eyes. "I lied to you, señor. I am not Castillian. My mother was Indian and she taught me things."

"What things?" Joseph demanded.

"Father Angelo would not like it. My mother said how the earth is our mother, and how everything that lives has life from the mother and goes back into the mother. When I remember, señor, and when I know I believe these things, because I see them and hear them, then I know I am not Castillian nor caballero. I am Indio."

"But I am not Indian, Juanito, and now I seem to see it."

Juanito looked up gratefully and then dropped his eyes, and the two men stared at the ground. Joseph wondered why he did not try to escape from the power that was seizing upon him.

After a time Joseph raised his eyes to the oak and to the house-frame beside it. "In the end it doesn't matter," he said abruptly. "What I feel or think can kill no ghosts nor gods. We must work, Juanito. There's the house to build over there, and here's the ranch to put cattle on. We'll go on working in spite of ghosts. Come," he said hurriedly, "we haven't time to think," and they went quickly to work on the house.

That night he wrote a letter to his brothers:

"There's land untaken next to mine. Each of you can have a hundred and sixty acres, and then we'll have six hundred and forty acres all in one piece. The grass is deep and rich, and the soil wants only turning. No rocks, Thomas, to make your plough turn somersaults, no ledges sticking out. We'll make a new community here if you'll come."

5

THE GRASS was summer brown, ready for cutting, when
the brothers came with their families and settled on the
land. Thomas was the oldest, forty-two, a thick strong man
with golden hair and a long yellow mustache. His cheeks
were round and red and his eyes a cold wintry blue between
slitted lids. Thomas had a strong kinship with all kinds of
animals. Often he sat on the edge of a manger while the
horses ate their hay. The low moaning of a cow in labor could
draw Thomas out of bed at any hour of the night to see that
the calving was true, and to help if there were trouble. When
Thomas walked through the fields, horses and cows raised
their heads from the grass and sniffed the air and moved in
toward him. He pulled dogs' ears until they cried with the
pain his strong slender fingers induced, and, when he
stopped, they put their ears up to be pulled again. Thomas
had always a collection of half-wild animals. Before he had
been a month on the new land he had collected a racoon, two
half-grown coyote pups that slunk at his heels and snarled at
everyone else, a box of ferrets and a red-tailed hawk, besides
four mongrel dogs. He was not kind to animals; at least no
kinder than they were to each other, but he must have acted
with a consistency beasts could understand, for all creatures
trusted him. When one of the dogs foolishly attacked the
coon and lost an eye in the encounter, Thomas was unruffled.
He scraped out the torn eye-ball with his pocket knife and
pinched the dog's feet to make it forget the torture in its
head. Thomas liked animals and understood them, and he
killed them with no more feeling than they had about killing
each other. He was too much an animal himself to be sentimental. Thomas never lost a cow, for he seemed to know
instinctively where a straying beef would stray. He rarely
hunted, but when he did go out for game, he marched
straight to the hiding place of his prey and killed it with the
speed and precision of a lion.

Thomas understood animals, but humans he neither understood nor trusted very much. He had little to say to men; he

was puzzled and frightened by such things as trade and parties, religious forms and politics. When it was necessary to be present at a gathering of people he effaced himself, said nothing and waited with anxiety for release. Joseph was the only person with whom Thomas felt any relationship; he could talk to Joseph without fear.

Thomas' wife was Rama, a strong, full-breasted woman with black brows that nearly met over her nose. She was nearly always contemptuous of everything men thought or did. She was a good and efficient midwife and an utter terror to evildoing children; although she never whipped her three little daughters, they went in fear of her displeasure, for she could find a soft spot in the soul and punish there. She understood Thomas, treated him as though he were an animal, kept him clean and fed and warm, and didn't often frighten him. Rama had ways of making her field: cooking, sewing, the bearing of children, house-cleaning, seem the most important things in the world; much more important than the things men did. The children adored Rama when they had been good, for she knew how to stroke the tender places in the soul. Her praise could be as delicate and sharp as her punishment was terrible. She automatically took charge of all children who came near her. Burton's two children recognized her authority as far more legally constituted than the changeable rules their own soft mother made, for the laws of Rama never changed, bad was bad and bad was punished, and good was eternally, delightfully good. It was delicious to be good in Rama's house.

Burton was one whom nature had constituted for a religious life. He kept himself from evil and he found evil in nearly all close human contacts. Once, after a service to the church, he had been praised from the pulpit, "A strong man in the Lord," the pastor called him, and Thomas bent close to Joseph's ear and whispered, "A weak man in the stomach." Burton had embraced his wife four times. He had two children. Celibacy was a natural state for him. Burton was never well. His cheeks were drawn and lean, and his eyes hungry for a pleasure he did not expect this side of heaven. In a way it gratified him that his health was bad, for it proved that God thought of him enough to make him suffer. Burton had the powerful resistance of the chronically ill. His lean arms and legs were strong as braided ropes.

Burton ruled his wife with a firm and scriptural hand. He parceled out his thoughts to her and pared down her emotions when they got out of line. He knew when she exceeded the laws, and when, as happened now and then, some weak thing in Harriet cracked and left her sick and delirious, Burton prayed beside her bed until her mouth grew firm again and stopped its babbling.

Benjamin, the youngest of the four, was a charge upon his brothers. He was dissolute and undependable; given a chance, he drank himself into a romantic haze and walked about the country, singing gloriously. He looked so young, so helpless and so lost that many women pitied him, and for this reason Benjamin was nearly always in trouble with some woman or other. For when he was drunk and singing and the lost look was in his eyes, women wanted to hold him against their breasts and protect him from his blunders. It always surprised those who mothered Benjamin when he seduced them. They never knew quite how it happened, for his was a deadly helplessness. He accomplished things so badly that everyone tried to help him. His new young wife, Jennie, labored to keep Benjamin from hurt. And when she heard him singing in the night and knew that he was drunk again she prayed he might not fall and hurt himself. The singing drew off into the dark and Jennie knew that before the night was out, some perplexed and startled girl would lie with him. She cried a little for fear he might be hurt.

Benjy was a happy man, and he brought happiness and pain to everyone who knew him. He lied, stole a little, cheated, broke his word and imposed upon kindnesses; and everyone loved Benjy and excused and guarded him. When the families moved West they brought Benjy with them for fear he might starve if he were left behind. Thomas and Joseph saw that his homestead was in good order. He borrowed Joseph's tent and lived in it until his brothers found time to build him a house. Even Burton, who cursed Benjy, prayed with him and hated his way of living, couldn't let him live in a tent. Where he got whiskey his brothers could never tell, but he had it always. In the valley of Our Lady the Mexicans gave him liquor and taught him their songs, and Benjy took their wives when they were not watching him.

6

THE FAMILIES clustered about the house Joseph had built. They put up little shacks on their own land as the law required, but never for a minute did they think of the land as being divided into four. It was one ranch, and when the technicalities of the homesteading were satisfied, it was the Wayne ranch. Four square houses clustered near to the great oak, and the big barn belonged to the tribe.

Perhaps because he had received the blessing, Joseph was the unquestioned lord of the clan. On the old farm in Vermont his father had merged with the land until he became the living symbol of the unit, land and its inhabitants. That authority passed to Joseph. He spoke with the sanction of the grass, the soil, the beasts wild and domesticated; he was the father of the farm. As he watched the community of cabins spring up on the land, as he looked down into the cradle of the first-born—Thomas' new child—as he notched the ears of the first young calves, he felt the joy that Abraham must have felt when the huge promise bore fruit, when his tribesmen and his goats began to increase. Joseph's passion for fertility grew strong. He watched the heavy ceaseless lust of his bulls and the patient, untiring fertility of his cows. He guided the great stallion to the mares, crying, "There, boy, drive in!" This place was not four homesteads, it was one, and he was the father. When he walked bareheaded through the fields, feeling the wind in his beard, his eyes smouldered with lust. All things about him, the soil, the cattle and the people were fertile, and Joseph was the source, the root of their fertility; his was the motivating lust. He willed that all things about him must grow, grow quickly, conceive and multiply. The hopeless sin was barrenness, a sin intolerable and unforgivable. Joseph's blue eyes were growing fierce with this new faith. He cut off barren creatures mercilessly, but when a bitch crept about swollen with puppies, when a cow was fat with calf, that creature was holy to him. Joseph did not think these things in his mind, but in his chest and in the corded muscles of his legs. It was the heritage of a race which for a million years had sucked at the breasts of the soil and co-habited with the earth.

One day Joseph stood by the pasture fence, watching a bull with a cow. He beat his hands against the fence rail; a red light burned in his eyes. As Burton approached him from behind, Joseph whipped off his hat and flung it down and tore open the collar of his shirt. He shouted, "Mount, you fool! She's ready. Mount now!"

"Are you crazy, Joseph?" Burton asked sternly.

Joseph swung around. "Crazy? What do you mean?"

"You're acting queerly, Joseph. Someone might see you here." Burton looked about to see if it was true.

"I want calves," Joseph said sullenly. "Where's the harm in that, even to you?"

"Well, Joseph—" Burton's tone was firm and kind as he implanted his lesson, "—everyone knows such things are natural. Everyone knows such things must happen if the race is to go on. But people don't watch it unless it's necessary. You might be seen acting this way."

Joseph reluctantly tore his eyes from the bull and faced his brother. "What if they did?" he demanded. "Is it a crime? I want calves."

Burton looked down in shame for the thing he had to say. "People might say things if they heard you talking as I just did."

"And what could they say?"

"Surely, Joseph, you don't want me to say it. The Scripture mentions such forbidden things. People might think your interest was—personal." He looked at his hands and then hid them quickly in his pockets as though to keep them from hearing what he said.

"Ah—" Joseph puzzled. "They might say—I see." His voice turned brutal. "They might say I felt like the bull. Well, I do, Burton. And if I could mount a cow and fertilize it, do you think I'd hesitate? Look, Burton, that bull can hit twenty cows a day. If feeling could put a cow with a calf, I could mount a hundred. That's how I feel, Burton." Then Joseph saw the grey, sick horror that had come over his brother's face. "You don't understand it, Burton," he said gently. "I want increase. I want the land to swarm with life. Everywhere

I want things growing up." Burton turned sulkily away. "Listen to me, Burton, I think I need a wife. Everything on the land is reproducing. I am the only sterile thing. I need a wife."

Burton had started to move away, but he turned around and spat his words, "You need prayer more than anything. Come to me when you can pray."

Joseph watched his brother walk away and he shook his head in bewilderment. "I wonder what he knows that I don't know," he said to himself. "He has a secret in him that makes everything I think or do unclean. I have heard the telling of the secret and it means nothing to me." He ran his fingers through his long hair, picked up his soiled black hat and put it on. The bull came near the fence, lowered its head and snorted. Then Joseph smiled and whistled shrilly, and at the whistle, Juanito's head popped out of the barn. "Saddle a horse," Joseph cried. "There's more in this old boy. Drive in another cow."

He worked mightily, as the hills work to produce an oak tree, slowly and effortlessly and with no doubt that it is at once the punishment and the heritage of hills to strive thus. Before the morning light came over the range, Joseph's lantern flashed across the yard and disappeared into the barn. There among the warm and sleepy beasts he worked, mending harness, soaping the leather, cleaning the buckles. His curry comb rasped over muscled flanks. Sometimes he found Thomas there, sitting on a manger in the dark, with a coyote pup sleeping in the hay behind him. The brothers nodded good-morning. "Everything all right?" Joseph asked.

And Thomas—"Pigeon has cast a shoe and cracked his hoof. He shouldn't go out today. Granny, the black devil, kicked Hell out of her stall. She'll hurt somebody some day if she doesn't kill herself first. Blue dropped a colt this morning, that's what I came out to see."

"How did you know, Tom? What made you know it would come this morning?"

Thomas grabbed a horse's forelock and pulled himself down from the manger. "I don't know, I can always tell when a colt will drop. Come and see the little son-of-a-bitch. Blue won't mind now. She's got him clean by now."

They went to the box-stall and looked over at the spider-legged colt, with knobby knees and a whisk-broom for a tail. Joseph put out his hand and stroked the damp shining coat. "By God!" he cried, "I wonder why I love the little things so much?" The colt lifted its head and looked up sightlessly out of clouded, dark-blue eyes, and then moved away from Joseph's hand.

"You always want to touch them," Thomas complained. "They don't like to be touched when they're little like that."

Joseph withdrew his hand. "I guess I'd better go to breakfast."

"Oh, say," Thomas cried, "I saw some swallows fooling around. There'll be mud nests in the barn eaves, and under the windmill tank next spring."

The brothers had been working well together, all except Benjy, and Benjy shirked when he could. Under Joseph's orders a long truck garden stretched out behind the houses. A windmill stood on its high stilts and flashed its blades every afternoon when the wind came up. A long, unwalled cowshed arose beside the big stable. The barbed-wire fences were edging out to encircle the land. Wild hay grew rankly on the flats and on the sidehills, and the stock was multiplying.

As Joseph turned to leave the barn, the sun came over the mountains and sent warm white streaks through the square windows. Joseph moved into a shaft of light and spread his arms for a moment. A red rooster on the top of a manure pile outside the window looked in at Joseph, then squawked and retreated, flapping, and raucously warned the hens that something terrible would probably happen on so fine a day. Joseph dropped his arms and turned back to Thomas. "Get up a couple of horses, Tom. Let's ride out today and see if there are any new calves. Tell Juanito, if you see him."

After their breakfast, the three men rode away from their houses. Joseph and Thomas went side by side and Juanito brought up the rear. Juanito had ridden home from Nuestra Señora in the dawn, after spending a discreet and polite evening in the kitchen of the Garcia home. Alice Garcia had sat across from him, placidly watching the crossed hands in her lap, and the elder Garcias, guardians and referees, were placed on either side of Juanito.

"You see, I am not only the majordomo for Señor Wayne," Juanito explained into their admiring but slightly skeptical ears, "I am more like a son to Don Joseph. Where he goes, I go. He trusts only me with very important matters." Thus for a couple of hours he boasted mildly, and when, as decorum suggested, Alice and her mother retired, Juanito made formal words and prescribed gestures and was finally accepted by Jesus Garcia, with a comely reluctance, as son-in-law. Then Juanito rode back to the ranch, quite tired and very proud, for the Garcias could prove at least one true Spanish ancestor. And now he rode behind Joseph and Thomas, rehearsing to himself the manner of his announcement.

The sun blazed on the land as they rode up a grassy swell looking for calves to notch and cut. The dry grass made a whisking noise under the horses' hoofs. Thomas' horse skittered nervously, for in front of Thomas, perched on the saddle-horn, rode a villainous racoon, with beady, evil eyes looking out of a black mask. It kept its balance by grasping the horse's mane with one little black hand. Thomas looked ahead with eyes drooped against the sun. "You know," he said, "I was in Nuestra Señora Saturday."

"Yes," Joseph said impatiently, "Benjy must have been there too. I heard him singing late at night. Tom, that boy'll be getting into trouble. Some things the people here will not stand. Some day we'll be finding Benjy with a knife in his neck. I tell you, Tom, he'll get a knife some day."

Thomas chuckled. "Let him, Joe. He'll have had more fun than a dozen sober men, and he'll have lived longer than Methuselah."

"Well, Burton worries about it all the time. He's spoken to me about it over and over."

"I was telling you," said Thomas, "I sat in the store in Nuestra Señora Saturday afternoon, and the riders from Chinita were there. They got to talking about the dry years from eighty to ninety. Did you know about them?"

Joseph tied a new knot in the riata string on his saddle. "Yes," he said softly, "I've heard about them. Something was wrong. They won't ever come again."

"Well, the riders were talking about it. They said the whole country dried up and the cattle died and the land turned to powder. They said they tried to move the cows to the interior but most of them died on the way. The rain came a few years before you got here." He pulled the coon's ears until the fierce little creature slashed at his hand with its sharp teeth.

Joseph's eyes were troubled. He brushed his beard down with his hand and turned the ends under, as his father had done. "I heard about it, Tom. But it's all over now. Something was wrong, I tell you. It won't come again, ever. The hills are full of water."

"How do you know it won't come again? The riders said it had been before. How can you say it won't ever come again?"

Joseph set his mouth determinedly. "It can't come. The hill springs are all running. I won't—I can't see how it can come again."

Juanito urged his horse abreast of them. "Don Joseph, I hear a cowbell over the rise."

The three men swung their horses to the right and put them to a canter. The coon leaped to Thomas' shoulder and clung to his neck with its strong little arms. Over the rise they galloped. They came upon a little herd of red cows, and two young calves tottered among the cows. In a moment the calves were down. Juanito took a bottle of liniment from his pocket, and Thomas opened his broad-bladed knife. The shining knife snicked out the Wayne brand in the ears of both calves while they bawled hopelessly and their mothers stood by, bellowing with apprehension. Then Thomas knelt beside the bull calf. With two cuts he performed the castration and sloshed liniment on the wound. The cows snorted with fear when they smelled blood. Juanito untied the feet and the new steer scrambled up and hobbled lamely off to its mother. The men mounted and rode on.

Joseph had picked up the pieces of ear. He looked at the little brown fragments for a moment and then thrust them into his pocket.

Thomas watched the act. "Joseph," he said suddenly, "why do you hang the hawks you kill in the oak tree beside your house?"

"To warn off other hawks from the chickens, of course. Everybody does that."

"But you know God-damned well it doesn't work, Joe. No hawk in the world will let the chance of a pullet go by just because his dead cousin is hanging up by the foot. Why, he'll eat his cousin if he can." He paused for a moment and then continued quietly, "You nail the ear notchings to the tree, too, Joseph."

His brother turned angrily in his saddle. "I nail up the notchings so I'll know how many calves there are."

Thomas looked puzzled. He lifted the coon to his shoulder again, where it sat and carefully licked the inside of his ear. "I almost know what you're doing, Joe. Sometimes it almost comes to me what you're getting at. Is it about the dry years, Joseph? Are you working already against them?"

"If it isn't for the reason I told you, it's none of your damn business, is it?" Joseph said doggedly. His eyes were worried and his voice grew soft with perplexity. "Besides, I don't understand it myself. If I tell you about it, you won't tell Burton, will you? Burton worries about all of us."

Thomas laughed. "Nobody tells Burton anything. He has always known everything."

"Well," Joseph said, "I'll tell you about it. Our father gave me a blessing before I came out here, an old blessing, the kind it tells about in the Bible, I think. But in spite of that I don't think Burton would have liked it. I've always had a curious feeling about father. He was so completely calm. He wasn't much like other fathers, but he was a kind of a last resort, a thing you could tie to, that would never change. Did you feel like that?"

Thomas nodded slowly, "Yes, I know."

"Well, then I came out here and I still felt safe. Then I got a letter from Burton and for a second I was thrown out of the world, falling, with nothing to land on, ever. Then I read on, where father said he was coming out to see me after he was dead. The house wasn't built then, I was sitting on a lumber pile. I looked up—and I saw that tree—" Joseph fell silent and stared down at his horse's mane. After a moment he looked over at his brother, but Thomas avoided his eyes. "Well, that's all. Maybe you can figure it out. I just do the things I do, I don't know why except that it makes me happy to do them. After all," he said lamely, "a man has to have something to tie to, something he can trust to be there in the morning."

Thomas caressed the coon with more gentleness than he usually bestowed on his animals, but still he did not look at Joseph. He said, "You remember once when I was a kid I broke my arm. I had it in a splint doubled up on my chest, and it hurt like Hell. Father came up to me and opened my hand, and he kissed the palm. That was all he did. It wasn't the kind of thing you'd expect of father, but it was all right because it was more like medicine than a kiss. I felt it run up my broken arm like cool water. It's funny how I remember that so well."

Far ahead of them a cowbell clanged. Juanito trotted up. "In the pines, señor. I don't know why they'd be in the pines where there's no feed."

They turned their horses up the ridge, which was crowned with the dark pines. The first trees stood deployed like outposts. Their trunks were as straight as masts, and the bark was purple in the shade. The ground under them, deep and spongy with brown needles, supported no grass. The grove was quiet except for a little whispering of the wind. Birds took no pleasure in the pines, and the brown carpet muffled the sound of walking creatures. The horsemen rode in among the trees, out of the yellow sunlight and into the purple gloom of the shade. As they went, the trees grew closer together, leaned for support and joined their tops to make one complete unbroken ceiling of needles. Among the trunks the undergrowth sprang up, brambles and blackberries, and the pale, light-hungry leaves of Guatras. The tangle grew thicker at every step until at last the horses stopped and refused to force their way farther into the thorn-armed barrier.

Then Juanito turned his horse sharply to the left. "This way, señores. I remember a path this way."

He led them to an old track, deep buried in needles but free of growth and wide enough for two to ride together. For a hundred yards they followed the path, and then suddenly Joseph and Thomas drew up and stared at the thing in front of them.

They had come to an open glade, nearly circular, and as flat as a pool. The dark trees grew about it, straight as pillars and jealously close together. In the center of the clearing stood a rock as big as a house, mysterious and huge. It seemed to be shaped, cunningly and wisely, and yet there was no shape in the memory to match it. A short, heavy green moss covered the rock with soft pile. The edifice was something like an altar that had melted and run down over itself. In one side of the rock there was a small black cave fringed with five-fingered ferns, and from the cave a little stream flowed silently and crossed the glade and disappeared into the tangled brush that edged the clearing. Beside the stream a great black bull was lying, his front legs folded under him; a hornless bull with shining black ringlets on his forehead. When the three men entered the glade the bull had been chewing his cud and staring at the green rock. He turned his head and looked at the men with red-rimmed eyes. He snorted, scrambled to his feet, lowered his head at them, and then, turning, plunged into the undergrowth and broke a passage free. The men saw the lashing tail for a moment, and the long, black swinging scrotum, which hung nearly to the knees; and then he disappeared and they heard him crashing in the brush.

It had all happened in a moment.

Thomas cried, "That's not our bull. I never saw it before." And then he looked uneasily at Joseph. "I never saw this place before. I don't think I like it, I can't tell." His voice was babbling. He held the coon tightly under his arm while it struggled and bit and tried to escape.

Joseph's eyes were wide, looking at the glade as a whole. He saw no single thing in it. His chin was thrust out. He filled his chest to a painful tightness and strained the muscles of his arms and shoulders. He had dropped the bridle and crossed his hands on the saddle-horn.

"Be still a moment, Tom," he said languidly. "There's something here. You are afraid of it, but I know it. Somewhere, perhaps in an old dream, I have seen this place, or perhaps felt the feeling of this place." He dropped his hands to his sides and whispered, trying the words, "This is holy— and this is old. This is ancient—and holy." The glade was silent. A buzzard swept across the circular sky, low over the treetops.

Joseph turned slowly. "Juanito, you knew this place. You have been here."

The light blue eyes of Juanito were wet with tears. "My mother brought me here, señor. My mother was Indian. I was a little boy, and my mother was going to have a baby. She came here and sat beside the rock. For a long time she sat, and then we went away again. She was Indian, señor. Sometimes I think the old ones come here still."

"The old ones?" Joseph asked quickly, "what old ones?"

"The old Indians, señor. I am sorry I brought you here. But when I was so close the Indian in me made me come, señor."

Thomas cried nervously, "Let's get the Hell out of here! We've got to find the cows." And Joseph obediently turned his horse. But as they rode out of the silent glade and down the path he spoke soothingly to his brother.

"Don't be afraid, Tom. There's something strong and sweet and good in there. There's something like food in there, and like cool water. We'll forget it now, Tom. Only maybe sometime when we have need, we'll go back again—and be fed."

And the three men fell silent and listened for the cowbells.

I N Monterey there lived and worked a harness-maker and saddler named McGreggor, a furious philosopher, a Marxian for the sake of argument. Age had not softened his ferocious opinions, and he had left the gentle Utopia of Marx far behind. McGreggor had long deep wrinkles on his cheeks from constantly setting his jaw and pinching his mouth against the world. His eyes drooped with sullenness. He sued his neighbors for an infringement of his rights, and he was constantly discovering how inadequate was the law's cognizance of his rights. He tried to browbeat his daughter Elizabeth and failed as miserably as he had with her mother, for Elizabeth set her mouth and held her opinions out of reach of his arguments by never stating them. It infuriated the old man to think that he could not blast her prejudices with his own because he did not know what they were.

Elizabeth was a pretty girl, and very determined. Her hair was fluffy, her nose small and her chin firm from setting it against her father. It was in her eyes that her beauty lay, grey eyes set extremely far apart and lashed so thickly that they seemed to guard remote and preternatural knowledge. She was a tall girl; not thin, but lean with strength and taut with quick and nervous energy. Her father pointed out her faults, or rather faults he thought she had.

"You're like your mother," he said. "Your mind is closed. You have no single shred of reason. Everything you do is the way you feel about it. Take your mother, now, a highland woman and straight from home—her own father and mother believed in fairies, and when I put it up to her like a joke, she'd shoot her jaw and shut up her mouth like a window. And she'd say, 'There's things that won't stand reason, but are so, just the same.' I'll take a wager your mother filled you with fairies before she died."

And he modeled her future for her. "There's a time coming," he said prophetically, "when women will earn their own bread. There's no reason why a woman can't learn a trade. Take you, for instance," he said. "There's a time coming, and

not far off, either, when a girl like you will be making her
wage and be damned to the first man that wants to marry
her."

McGreggor was shocked, nevertheless, when Elizabeth
began studying for county examinations so she could be a
teacher. McGreggor almost went soft. "You're too young,
Elizabeth," he argued. "You're only seventeen. Give your
bones a chance to get hard, at least." But Elizabeth smiled
slightly in triumph and said nothing. In a house where the
littlest statement automatically marshalled crushing forces of
argument against itself, she had learned to be silent.

The profession of school teaching was something more
than child-instructing to a girl of spirit. When she turned seventeen she could take county examinations and go adventuring; it was a decent means of leaving her home, and her town
where people knew her too well; a means of preserving the
alert and shatterable dignity of a young girl. To the community where she was sent she was unknown and mysterious and
desirable. She knew fractions and poetry; she could read a
little French and throw a word of it into conversation. Sometimes she wore underclothes of lawn or even silk, as could be
seen when her laundry was on the line. These things which
might have been considered uppish in an ordinary person
were admired and expected in the school teacher, for she was
a person of social as well as educational importance, and she
gave an intellectual and cultural tone to her district. The people among whom she went to live did not know her baby
name. She assumed the title "Miss". The mantle of mystery
and learning enveloped her, and she was seventeen. If, within
six months, she did not marry the most eligible bachelor in
the district, she must be ugly as a gorgon, for a school teacher
could bring social elevation to a man. Her children were
thought to be more intelligent than ordinary children. School
teaching could be, if the teacher wished to make it so, a subtle
and certain move toward matrimony.

Elizabeth McGreggor was even more widely educated than
most teachers. In addition to fractions and French she had
read excerpts from Plato and Lucretius, knew several titles of
Aeschylus, Aristophanes and Euripides, and had a classical
background resting on Homer and Virgil. After she had

passed the examinations she was assigned to the school at Nuestra Señora. The isolation of the place pleased Elizabeth. She wanted to think over all the things she knew, to arrange them in their places, and from their eventual arrangement to construct the new Elizabeth McGreggor. In the village of Our Lady she went to board with the Gonzales family.

Word flew through the valley that the new teacher was young and very pretty, and thereafter, when Elizabeth went out, when she walked to school or hurried to the grocery, she met young men who, though idle, were intensely preoccupied with their watches, with the rolling of a cigarette or with some vague but vital spot in the distance. But occasionally there was one strange man among the loiterers who was pre-occupied with Elizabeth; a tall man, black-bearded and with sharp blue eyes. This man bothered Elizabeth, for he stared at her when she passed, and his eyes pierced through her clothing.

When Joseph heard about the new teacher he drew in upon her in lessening circles until at last he sat in the Gonzales parlor, a carpeted, respectable place, and he stared across at Elizabeth. It was a formal call. Elizabeth's soft hair was puffed on her head, but she was the teacher. Her face wore a formal expression, almost stern. Except that she smoothed down her skirt over her knees again and again, she might have been composed. At intervals she looked up into the searching eyes of Joseph and then looked away again.

Joseph wore a black suit and new boots. His hair and beard were trimmed, and his nails were as clean as he could get them.

"Do you like poetry?" Elizabeth asked, looking for a moment into the sharp, unmoving eyes.

"Oh, yes—yes, I like it; what I have read of it."

"Of course, Mr. Wayne, there are no modern poets like the Greeks, like Homer."

Joseph's face became impatient. "I remember," he said, "of course I remember. A man went to an island and got changed into a pig."

Elizabeth's mouth pinched at the corners. In an instant she was the teacher, remote and above the pupil. "That is the Odyssey," she said. "Homer is thought to have lived about nine hundred, B.C. He had a profound effect on all Greek literature."

"Miss McGreggor," Joseph said earnestly, "there's a way to do this thing, but I don't know it. Some people seem to know by instinct, but I don't. Before I came I tried to think what I'd say to you, but I couldn't discover a way, because I've never done anything like this before. There's a time of fencing to go through and I don't know how to do it. Besides it all seems useless to me."

Elizabeth was caught by his eyes now, and she was startled by his intensity of speech. "I don't know what you're talking about, Mr. Wayne." She had been flung from her seat of learning, and the fall frightened her.

"I know I'm doing it all wrong," he said. "I don't know any other way. You see, Miss McGreggor, I'm afraid I might get confused and embarrassed. I want you to be my wife, and you must know it. My brothers and I own six hundred and forty acres of land. Our blood is clean. I think I should be good to you if I could know what you want."

He had dropped his eyes while he talked. Now he looked up and saw that she was flushing and looking very miserable. Joseph jumped to his feet. "I suppose I've done it wrong. Now I'm confused, but I got it out first. And now I'll go, Miss McGreggor. I'll come back after we've stopped being embarrassed." He hurried out without saying good-bye, leaped on his horse and galloped away into the night.

There was a burn of shame and of exultance in his throat. When he came to the wooded river bottom he pulled up his horse, rose in his stirrups and shouted to ease the burn, and the echo blatted back at him. The night was very black and a high mist dulled the sharpness of the stars and muffled the night noises. His cry had blasted a thick silence and frightened him. For a moment he sat dumbly in his saddle and felt the swell and fall of his panting horse.

"This night is too still," he said, "too unimpressed. I must do something." He felt that the time required a sign, an act to give it point. Somehow an act of his must identify him with the moment that was passing or it would slip away, taking no part of him with it. He whipped off his hat and flung it away into the dark. But this was not enough. He felt for his quirt where it hung from the saddle-horn, and plucking it off, lashed his own leg viciously to make a moment of pain. The horse plunged aside, away from the whistle of the blow, and then reared. Joseph threw his quirt away into the brush, controlled the horse with a powerful pressure of his knees, and when it was quieted, trotted the nervous animal toward the ranch. Joseph opened his mouth to let the cool air into his throat.

Elizabeth watched the door close behind him. "There is too big a crack under that door," she thought. "When the wind blows, a draft will come in under the door. I wonder if I should move to another house." She spread her skirt tightly down, and then drew her finger up the center so that the cloth adhered to her legs and defined their shape. She inspected her fingers carefully.

"Now I am ready," she went on. "Now I am all ready to punish him. He is a bumpkin, a blundering fool. He has no manners. He doesn't know how to do things politely. He wouldn't know manners if he saw them. I don't like his beard. He stares too much. And his suit is pitiful." She thought over the punishment and nodded her head slowly. "He said he didn't know how to fence. And he wants to marry me. I'd have to bear those eyes all my life. His beard is probably coarse, but I don't think so. No, I don't think so. What a fine thing to go straight to a point. And his suit—and he would put his hand on my side." Her mind bolted away. "I wonder what I will do." The person who must act in the future was a stranger whose reactions Elizabeth did not quite understand. She walked up the stairs to her bedroom and slowly took off her clothes. "I must look at his palm next time. That will tell." She nodded gravely, and then threw herself face-downward on the bed and cried. Her crying was as satisfying and as luxurious as a morning's yawn. After a while she got up and blew out her lamp and dragged a little velvet-seated rocking chair to the window. Resting her elbows on the window-sill, she looked out into the night. There was a heavy misty dampness in the air now; a lighted window down the rutted street was fringed with light.

Elizabeth heard a stealthy movement in the yard below and leaned out to look. There was a pounce, a hissing, rasping cry, and then the crunch of bone. Her eyes pierced the grey darkness and made out a long, low, shadowy cat creeping away with some little creature in its mouth. A nervous bat circled her head, gritting as it looked about. "Now I wonder where he is," she thought. "He'll be riding now, and his beard will be blowing. When he gets home he'll be very tired. And I'm here, resting, doing nothing. It serves him right." She heard a concertina playing, coming nearer, from the other end of the village, where the saloon was. As it drew close, a voice joined, a voice as sweet and hopeless as a tired sigh.

"Maxwellton's braes are bonnie—"

Two lurching figures were passing by. "Stop! You're not playing the right tune. Keep your damn Mexican tunes out of this. Now—*Maxwellton's braes are bonnie*—wrong again!" The men paused. "I wish I could play the blasted squeeze-organ."

"You can try, señor."

"Try, Hell. I have tried. It only belches when I try." He paused.

"Shall we try again, señor, this Maxwellton?" One of the men moved close to the fence. Elizabeth could see him looking up at her window.

"Come down," he pleaded. "Please come down." Elizabeth sat very still, afraid to move. "I'll send the cholo along home."

"Señor, no 'cholos' to me!"

"I'll send the gentleman along home if you'll come down. I am lonely."

"No," she said, and her voice startled her.

"I'll sing to you if you'll come down. Listen how I can sing. Play, Pancho, play *Sobre las Olas*." His voice filled the air like vaporized gold, and his voice was filled with delicious sorrow. The song finished so softly that she leaned forward to hear. "Now will you come down? I'm waiting for you."

She shuddered violently and reaching up, pulled the window down, but even through the glass she could hear the voice. "She won't, Pancho. How about the next house?"

"Old people, señor; eighty, nearly."

"And the next house?"

"Well, maybe—a little girl, thirteen."

"We'll try the little girl thirteen, then. Now—*Maxwellton's braes are bonnie*—"

Elizabeth had pulled the covers over her head, and she was shivering with fright. "I would have gone," she said miserably. "I'm afraid I would have gone if he had asked again."

8

JOSEPH allowed two weeks to pass before he went again to call on Elizabeth. The fall was coming hazily, greying the sky with high mist. Huge puffy cotton clouds sailed in from the ocean every day and sat on the hilltops for a while, and then retired to the sea again like reconnoitering navies of the sky. The red-wing blackbirds massed their squadrons and practiced at maneuvering over the fields. The doves, unseen in the spring and summer, came from their hiding and sat in clusters on fences and dead trees. The sun, in its rising and setting, was red behind the autumn veil of air-borne dust.

Burton had taken his wife and gone to a camp meeting in Pacific Grove. Thomas said, wryly, "He's eating God the way a bear eats meat against the winter."

Thomas was sad with the coming winter. He seemed to fear the wet and windy time when he could find no cave to crawl into.

The children on the ranch began to consider Christmas as not too far buried in the future for anticipation. They addressed guarded questions to Rama concerning the kind of conduct most admired by the saints of the solstice, and Rama made the most of their apprehension.

Benjy was lazily ill. His young wife tried to understand why no one paid much attention.

There was little to be done on the ranch. The tall dry grass on the foothills was thick enough to feed the stock all winter. The barns were full of hay for the horses. Joseph spent a great deal of time sitting under the oak tree thinking of Elizabeth. He could remember how she sat, with her feet close together and her head held high, as though it was only restrained from flying upward by being attached to her body. Juanito came and sat beside him and looked secretly at Joseph's face to read his temper and to imitate it.

"I might be having a wife before the spring, Juanito," Joseph said. "Right in my house here, living here. She'd ring a little bell when it came dinnertime—not a cowbell. I would buy a little silver bell. I guess you'd like to hear a little bell like that, Juanito, ringing at dinnertime."

And Juanito, flattered at the confidence, uncovered his own secret. "I, too, señor."

"A wife, Juanito? You, too?"

"Yes, señor, Alice Garcia. They have a paper to prove their grandfather was Castillian."

"Why I'm glad of that, Juanito. We'll help you to build a house here, and then you won't be a rider any more. You'll live here."

Juanito giggled with happiness. "I'll have a bell, señor, hanging beside the porch; but a cowbell, me. It wouldn't be good to hear your bell and come for my dinner."

Joseph tilted back his head and smiled up at the twisted branches of the tree. Several times he had thought of whispering about Elizabeth, but a shame at doing a thing so silly had forbidden it. "I'm going to drive to town day after tomorrow, Juanito. I guess you'll want to go with me."

"Oh yes, señor. I'll sit in the buckboard and you can say, 'He is my driver. He is good with horses. Of course I never drive myself.'"

Joseph laughed at the rider. "I guess you'd like me to do the same for you."

"Oh no, señor, not I."

"We'll go in early, Juanito. You should have a new suit for a time like this."

Juanito stared at him incredulously. "A suit, señor? Not overalls? A suit with a coat?"

"Why, a coat and a vest, and for a wedding present a watch-chain for the vest."

It was too much. "Señor," Juanito said, "I have a broken cincha to fix," and he walked away toward the barn, for it would be necessary to think a good deal about a suit and a watch-chain. His manner of wearing such a costume would require consideration and some practice.

Joseph leaned back against the tree, and the smile slowly left his eyes. He looked again into the branches. A colony of hornets had made a button on a limb above his head and around this nucleus they were beginning to construct their papery nest. To Joseph's mind there leaped the memory of the round glade among the pines. He remembered every detail of the place, the curious moss-covered rock, the dark cave with its fringe of ferns and the silent clear water flowing out and hurrying stealthily away. He saw how the cress grew in the water and how it moved its leaves in the current. Suddenly Joseph wanted to go to that place, to sit by the rock and to stroke the soft moss.

"It would be a place to run to, away from pain or sorrow or disappointment or fear," he thought. "But I have no such need now. I have none of these things to run from. I must remember this place, though. If ever there's need to lose some plaguing thing, that will be the place to go." And he remembered how the tall trunks grew up and how peacefulness was almost a touchable thing in the glade. "I must look inside the cave some time to see where the spring is," he thought.

Juanito spent the whole next day working on the harness, the two bay driving-horses and the buckboard. He washed and polished, curried and brushed. And then, fearing he had missed some potential brightness, he went through the whole process again. The brass knob on the pole glittered fiercely; every buckle was silver; the harness shone like patent-leather. A bow of red ribbon fluttered from the middle of the whip.

Before noon on the great day he had the equipage out, to listen for squeaks in the newly-greased wagon. At length he slipped the bridle and tied the horses in the shade before he went in to lunch with Joseph. Neither of them ate very much, a slice or two of bread torn in pieces and dropped in milk. They finished, nodded at each other and rose from the table. In the buckboard, patiently waiting for them was Benjy. Joseph grew angry. "You shouldn't go, Benjy. You've been sick."

"I'm well again," said Benjy.

"I'm taking Juanito. There won't be room for you."

Benjy smiled disarmingly. "I'll sit in the box," he said, and he climbed over the seat and half reclined on the boards.

They started off over the rough wheel-tracks, and their spirits were a little damped by Benjy's presence. Joseph leaned back over the seat. "You mustn't drink anything, Benjy. You've been sick."

"Oh no, I'm going in to get a new clock."

"Remember what I say, Benjy. I don't want you to drink."

"I wouldn't swallow a drop, Joe, not even if it was in my mouth."

Joseph gave him up. He knew that Benjy would be drunk within an hour of his arrival, and there was nothing he could do to prevent it.

The sycamores along the creek were beginning to drop their leaves on the ground. The road was deep in the crisp brown fragments. Joseph lifted the lines and the horses broke into a trot, and their hoofs crashed softly in the leaves.

Elizabeth heard Joseph's voice on the porch and hurried upstairs so she could come down again. She was afraid of Joseph Wayne. Since his last visit she had thought of him nearly all the time. How could she refuse to marry him even though she hated him? Some terrible thing might happen if she should refuse—he might die; or perhaps he might strike her with his fist. In her room, before she went down to the parlor, she brought out all her knowledge to protect her— her algebra and when Caesar landed in England and the Nicene council and the verb *être*. Joseph didn't know things like that. Probably the only date he knew was 1776. An ignorant man, really. Her mouth pinched at the corners with contempt. Her eyes grew stern. She would put him in his place as she would a smart-alec boy in school. Elizabeth ran her fingers around her waist, inside her skirt, to make sure that her shirt-waist was tucked in. She patted her hair, rubbed her lips harshly with her knuckles to bring the blood to the surface, and last, blew out the lamp. She came majestically into the parlor where Joseph stood.

"Good evening," she said. "I was reading when they told me you were here. *Pippa Passes*, Browning. Do you like Browning, Mr. Wayne?"

He raked a nervous hand through his hair and destroyed the careful part. "Have you decided yet?" he demanded. "I must ask you that first. I don't know who Browning is." He was staring at her with eyes so hungry, so beseeching, that her superiority dropped away from her and her facts crawled back into their cells.

Her hands made a helpless gesture. "I—I don't know," she said.

"I'll go away again. You aren't ready now. That is, unless you'd like to talk about Browning. Or maybe you might like to go for a drive. I came in the buckboard."

Elizabeth stared downward at the green carpet with its brown footpath where the pile had been worn through, and her eyes moved to Joseph's boots, glittering with daubed polish which was not black but irridescent, green and blue and purple. Elizabeth's mind fastened on the shoes and felt safe for a moment. "The polish was old," she thought. "He probably had the bottle for a long time and left the cork out. That always makes the colors in it. Black ink does the same thing when it's left open. He doesn't know that, I guess, and I won't tell him. If I told him, I wouldn't have any privacy any more." And she wondered why he didn't move his feet.

"We could drive down by the river," Joseph said. "The river is fine, but it's very dangerous to cross on foot. The stones are slippery, you see. You must not cross on foot. But we could drive down there." He wanted to tell her how the wheels would sound, crushing the crisp leaves, and how a long blue spark with a head like a serpent's tongue, would leap from the crash of iron and stone now and then. He wanted to say how the sky was low this night, so low that one bathed one's head in it. There seemed no way to say such things. "I'd like you to go," he said. He took a short step toward her, and destroyed the safety her mind had found.

Elizabeth had a quick impulse to be gay. She put her hand timidly on his arm and then patted his sleeve. "I'll go," she said, hearing an unnecessary loudness in her voice. "I think I'll like to go. Teaching is a strain. I need to be out in the air." She ran upstairs for her coat, humming under her breath, and at the top of the stairs she pointed her toe twice, as little girls do in a Maypole dance. "Now I am committing myself," she thought. "People will see us driving alone at night, and that will mean we are engaged."

Joseph stood at the bottom of the stairs and looked upward, waiting for her to reappear. He felt a desire to open his body for her inspection, so that she could see all the hidden things in him, even the things he did not know were there.

"That would be right," he thought. "Then she would

know the kind of man I am; and if she knew that she would be a part of me."

She paused on the landing and smiled down on him. Over her shoulders she wore a long blue cape, and some of her hair was loose from its puff and caught in the nap of the blue wool. A rush of tenderness came over Joseph for the loose hairs. He laughed sharply. "Come quickly before the horses fade," he said, "or the moment goes. Oh, of course I mean the polish Juanito put on the harness."

He opened the door for her, and when they reached the buckboard he helped her to the near seat before he untied the horses and fastened the ivory loops of their check reins. The horses danced a little, and Joseph was glad of that.

"Are you warm?" he asked.

"Yes, warm."

The horses broke into a trot. Joseph saw how he could make a gesture with his arms and hands, that would sweep in and indicate and symbolize the ripe stars and the whole cup of the sky, the land, eddied with black trees, and the crested waves that were the mountains, an earth storm, frozen in the peak of its rushing, or stone breakers moving eastward with infinite slowness. Joseph wondered whether there were any words to say these things.

He said, "I like the night. It's more strong than day."

From the first moment of her association with him, Elizabeth had been tensed to repel his attack upon her boundaried and fortified self, but now a strange and sudden thing had happened. Perhaps the tone, the rhythm, perhaps some personal implication in his words had done it, had swept her walls cleanly away. She touched his arm with her fingertips, and trembled with delight and drew away. Her throat tightened above her breathing. She thought, "He will hear me panting, like a horse. This is disgraceful," and she laughed nervously under her breath, knowing she didn't care. Those thoughts she had kept weak and pale and hidden in the recesses of her brain, just out of thinking vision, came out into the open, and she saw that they were not foul and loathesome like slugs, as she had always believed, but somehow light and gay and holy. "If he should put his lips upon my breast I would be glad," she thought. "The pressure of gladness in me would be more than I could stand. I would hold my breast to his lips with both hands." She saw herself doing it and she knew how she would feel, pouring the hot fluid of herself toward his lips.

The horses snorted loudly and swung to one side of the road, for a dark figure stood in front of them. Juanito walked quickly beside the wagon to talk to Joseph.

"Are you going home, señor? I was waiting."

"No, Juanito, not for some time."

"I'll wait again, señor. Benjy is drunk."

Joseph twisted nervously in his seat. "I guess I knew he would be."

"He is out on this road, señor. I heard him sing a little while ago. Willie Romas is drunk too. Willie is happy. Willie will kill someone tonight, maybe."

Joseph's hands were white in the starlight, holding the lines taut, jerking forward a little when the horses flung their heads against the bits.

"Find Benjy," Joseph said bitterly. "I'll be ready to go in a couple of hours." The horses leaped forward and Juanito sank away into the darkness.

Now that her wall was down, Elizabeth could feel that Joseph was unhappy. "He will tell me, and then I will help him."

Joseph sat rigid, and the horses, feeling the uncompromising weight of his clenched hands on the lines, slowed their trot to a careful, picking walk. They were nearing the ragged black barrier of the river trees when suddenly the voice of Benjy sounded from the cover of the brush.

"Estando bebiendo de vino,

"Pedro, Rodarte y Simon —"

Joseph tore the whip from its socket and lashed the horses ferociously, and then he had to put all his force on the lines to check their leaping. Elizabeth was crying miserably because of the voice of Benjy. Joseph pulled up the horses until the crashing of their hoofs on the hard road subsided to the intricate rhythm of a trot.

"I have not told you my brother is a drunkard. You'll have to know the kind of family I have. My brother is a drunkard.

I do not mean he goes out and gets drunk now and then the way any man will. Benjy has the disease in his body. Now you know." He stared ahead of him. "That was my brother singing there." He felt her body jerking against his side as she wept. "Do you want me to take you home now?"

"Yes."

"Do you want me to stay away?" When she made no reply, he turned the horses sharply and started them back. "Do you want me to stay away from you?" he demanded.

"No," she said. "I'm being silly. I want to go home and go to bed. I want to try to know what it is I'm feeling. That is an honesty."

Joseph felt an exultance rising again in his throat. He leaned toward her and kissed her on the cheek and then touched up the horses again. At the gate he helped her down and walked to the door with her.

"I will go now to try to find my brother. In a few days I will come back. Good-night."

Elizabeth didn't wait to see him go. She was in bed almost before the sound of the wheels died out. Her heart pounded so that it shook her head against the pillow. It was hard to listen over the pounding of her heart, but at last she made out the sound she was waiting for. It came slowly toward her house, the drunken beautiful voice. Elizabeth gathered her spirit to resist the flaming pain that was coming with the voice.

She whispered to herself, "He is useless, I know! A drunken, useless fool. I have something to do, almost a magic thing." She waited until the voice came in front of the house. "Now I must do this. It is the only chance." She put her head under her pillow and whispered, "I love this singing man, useless as he is, I love him. I have never seen his face and I love him more than anything. Lord Jesus help me to my desire. Help me to have this man."

Then she lay quietly, listening for the response, for the answer to her magic. It came after a last splash of pain. A hatred for Benjy drove out the pain, a hatred so powerful that her jaws tightened and her lips drew snarlingly back from her teeth. She could feel how her skin tingled with the hatred and how her nails ached to attack him. And then the hatred floated off and away. She heard without interest the voice of Benjy growing fainter in the distance. Elizabeth lay on her back and rested her head on crossed wrists.

"Now I will be married soon," she said quietly.

9

THE YEAR had darkened to winter and the spring had come, and another fall, before the marriage took place. There was term-end to think of, and after that, in the heat of the summer, when the white oaks sagged under the sun and the river shrank to a stream, Elizabeth had dealings with dressmakers. The hills were rich with heavy-seeded grain; the cattle came out of the brush at night to eat, and when the sun was up, retired into the sage-scented shade to chew sleepily through the day. In the barn the men were piling the sweet wild hay higher than the rafters.

Once a week during the year Joseph went in to Nuestra Señora and sat in the parlor with Elizabeth or took her driving in the buckboard. And he asked, "When will we be married, Elizabeth?"

"Why, I must serve out my year," she said; "there are a thousand things that must be done. I should go home to Monterey for a little. Of course my father will want to see me once more before I am married."

"That is true," said Joseph soberly. "You might be changed afterwards."

"I know." She clasped her hands around his wrist and regarded her clasped fingers. "Look, Joseph, how hard it is to move the finger you want to move. You lose track of which is which." He smiled at the way her mind caught at things to escape thinking. "I am afraid to change," she said. "I want to, and I am afraid. Will I get stout, do you think? All in a moment will I be another person, remembering Elizabeth as an acquaintance who's dead?"

"I don't know," he said, edging his finger into a pleat at the shoulder of her shirtwaist. "Perhaps there isn't any change, ever, in anything. Perhaps unchangeable things only pass."

One day she went to the ranch and he led her about, boasting a little by implication. "Here is the house. I built it first. And at first there wasn't a building within miles, just the house under the oak tree."

Elizabeth leaned against the tree and stroked its trunk.

"There could be a seat up in the tree, you see, Joseph, where those limbs start out from the trunk. Will you mind if I climb the tree, Joseph?" She looked up into his face and found that he was staring at her with a strange intensity. His hair had blown forward over his eyes. Elizabeth thought suddenly, "If only he had the body of a horse I might love him more."

Joseph moved quickly toward her and held out his hand. "You must climb the tree, Elizabeth. I want you to. Here, I'll help you." He cupped his hands for her foot and steadied her until she sat in the crotch from which the great limbs grew. And when he saw how she fitted in the hollow and how the grey arms guarded her, "I'm glad, Elizabeth," he cried.

"Glad, Joseph? You look glad! Your eyes are shining. Why are you so glad?"

He lowered his eyes and laughed to himself. "Strange things one is glad of. I am glad that you are sitting in my tree. A moment back I thought I saw that my tree loved you."

"Stand away a little," she called. "I'm going up to the next limb so I can see beyond the barn." He moved aside because her skirts were full. "Joseph, I wonder why I hadn't noticed the pines on the ridge. Now I can feel at home. I was born among the pines in Monterey. You'll see them, Joseph, when we go there to be married."

"They are strange pines; I'll take you there some time after we are married."

Elizabeth climbed carefully down from the tree and stood beside him again. She pinned her hair and patted it with dexterous fingers that went inquisitively about searching for loose strands and shaping them to their old course. "When I am homesick, Joseph, I can go up to those pines and it will be like going home."

IO

THE WEDDING was in Monterey, a sombre boding ceremony in a little Protestant chapel. The church had so
often seen two ripe bodies die by the process of marriage that
it seemed to celebrate a mystic double death with its ritual.
Both Joseph and Elizabeth felt the sullenness of the sentence.
"You must endure," said the church; and its music was a sun-
less prophecy.

Elizabeth looked at her bent father, where he glared at the
furniture of Christianity because it insulted what he was calling his intelligence. There was no blessing in the leather fingers of her father. She glanced quickly at the man beside her
who was becoming her husband second by second. Joseph's
face was set and hard. She could see how his jaw muscles
quivered tensely. And suddenly Elizabeth was sorry for Joseph. She thought with a little frantic sadness, "If my mother
were here, she could say to him, 'Here is Elizabeth and she is
a good girl because I love her, Joseph. And she will be a good
wife when she learns how to be. I hope you will get outside
the hard husk you're wearing, Joseph, so you may feel tenderly for Elizabeth. That's all she wants and it's not an impossible thing.'"

Elizabeth's eyes glittered suddenly with bright tears. "I
will," she said aloud, and, silently, "I must pray a little. Lord
Jesus, make things easy for me because I am afraid. In all the
time I've had to learn about myself, I have learned nothing.
Be kind to me, Lord Jesus, at least until I learn what kind of
thing I am." She wished there were a crucifix some place in
the church, but it was a Protestant church, and when she
drew a picture of the Christ in her mind, He had the face, the
youthful beard, the piercing puzzled eyes of Joseph, who
stood beside her.

Joseph's brain was tight with a curious fear. "There's a foulness here," he thought. "Why must we go through this to
find our marriage? Here in the church I've thought there lay a
beauty if a man could find it, but this is only a doddering kind
of devil worship." He was disappointed for himself and for

Elizabeth. He was embarrassed that Elizabeth must witness the maculate entrance to the marriage.

Elizabeth tugged at his arm and whispered, "It's over now. We must walk out. Turn toward me slowly." She helped him to turn, and as they took the first step down the aisle, the bells broke forth in the belfry above them. Joseph sighed shudderingly. "Here's God come late to the wedding. Here's the iron god at last." He felt that he would pray if he knew some powerful way to do it. "This ties in. This is the marriage—the good iron voice!" And he thought, "This is my own thing and I know it. Beloved bells, pounding your bodies with your frantic hearts! It is the sun sticks, striking the bell of the sky in the morning; and it's the hollow beating of rain on the earth's full belly—of course, I know—the thing that whips the tortured air with lightning. And sometimes the hot sweet wind plucks at the treetops in a yellow afternoon."

He looked sidewise and down and whispered, "The bells are good, Elizabeth. The bells are holy."

She started and peered up at him in wonder, for her vision had not changed; the Christ's face was still the face of Joseph. She laughed uneasily and confessed to herself, "I'm praying to my own husband."

McGreggor, the saddler, was wistful when they went away. He kissed Elizabeth clumsily on the forehead. "Don't forget your father," he said. "But it wouldn't be an unusual thing if you did. It's almost a custom in these days."

"You'll come to the ranch to see us, won't you, father?"

"I visit no one," he replied angrily. "A man takes only weakness and a little pleasure from an obligation."

"We'll be glad to see you if you come," said Joseph.

"Well, you'll wait a long time, you and your thousand acre ranches. I'd see you both in Hell before I'd visit you."

After a time he drew Joseph aside, out of hearing of Elizabeth, and he said plaintively, "It's because you're stronger than I am that I hate you. Here I'm wanting to like you, and I can't because I'm a weak man. And it's the same about Elizabeth and about her crazy mother. Both of them knew I was a weak man, and I hated both of them."

Joseph smiled on the saddler and felt pity and love for him. "It's not a weak thing you're doing now," he observed.

"No," McGreggor cried, "it's a good strong thing. Oh, I know in my head how to be strong, but I can't learn to do it."

Joseph patted him roughly on the arm. "We'll be glad to see you when you come to visit." And instantly McGreggor's lip stiffened in anger.

They went by train from Monterey and down the long Salinas Valley, a grey-and-gold lane between two muscular mountain lines. From the train they could see how the wind blew down the valley, toward the sea, how its dry force bent the grain against the ground until it lay like the coat of a sleek-haired dog, how it drove the herds of rolling tumbleweeds toward the valley mouth and how it blew the trees lopsided and streaming until they grew that way. At the little stations, Chualar, Gonzales and Greenfield, they saw the grain teams standing in the road, waiting to store their fat sacks in the warehouses. The train moved beside the dry Salinas river with its broad yellow bed where blue herons stalked disconsolately over the hot sand, searching for water to fish in, and where now and then a grey coyote trotted nervously away, looking back apprehensively at the train; and the mountains continued on with them on either side like huge rough outer tracks for a tremendous juggernaut.

In King City, a small railroad town, Joseph and Elizabeth left the train and walked to the livery barn where Joseph's horses had been stabled while they were gone. They felt new and shiny and curiously young as they drove out of King City on the road to the valley of Our Lady. New clothes were in the traveling baskets in the wagon box. Over their clothes they wore long linen dusters to protect them from the road dirt, and Elizabeth's face was covered with a dark blue veil, behind which her eyes darted about, collecting data for memory. Joseph and Elizabeth were embarrassed, sitting shoulder to shoulder and looking ahead at the tan road, for it seemed a presumptuous game they were playing. The horses, four days rested and full of fat barley, flung their heads and tried to run, but Joseph tightened the brake a little and held them down, saying, "Steady, Blue. Steady, Pigeon. You'll be tired enough before we get home."

A few miles ahead they could see the willow boundary of their own home stream where it strode out to meet the broad

Salinas river. The willows were yellow in this season, and the poison-oak that climbed into the branches had turned scarlet and menacing. Where the rivers joined, Joseph pulled up to watch how the glittering water from Nuestra Señora sank tiredly and disappeared into the white sand of its new bed. It was said the river ran pure and sweet under the ground, and this could be proved by digging a few feet into the sand. Even within sight of the juncture there were broad holes dug in the river bed so the cattle might drink.

Joseph unbuttoned his duster, for the afternoon was very hot, and he loosened the neckerchief designed to keep his collar free from dust, and removing his black hat he wiped the leather head-band with a bandana. "Would you like to get down, Elizabeth?" he asked. "You could bathe your wrists in the water and that would make you cool."

But Elizabeth shook her head. It was strange to see the swathed head shake. "No, I am comfortable, dear. It will be very late when we get home. I am anxious to go on."

He slapped the flat lines on the horses' buttocks and they moved on beside the river. The tall willows along the road whipped at their heads and sometimes drew a long pliant switch caressingly over their shoulders. The crickets in the hot brush sang their head-piercing notes, and flying grasshoppers leaped up with a flash of white or yellow wings, rattled a moment through the air and dropped to safety in the dry grass. Now and then some little blue brush rabbit skittered in panic off the road, and once safe, perched on its haunches and peeked at the wagon. There was a smell of toasting grass-stems in the air, and the bitter of willow bark, and the perfume of river bay trees.

Joseph and Elizabeth leaned loosely back against the leather seat, caught in the rhythm of the day and drowsed by the pounding hoofs. Their backs and shoulders supply absorbed the vibrations of the buckboard. Theirs was a state close to sleep but more withdrawn to thoughtlessness, more profound than sleep. The road and the river pointed straight at the mountains now. The dark sage covered the higher ridges like a coarse fur, except in the water scars, which were grey and bare like healed saddle sores on a horse's back. The sun was quartering to the westward and the road and the river pointed

the place of its setting. For the two riding behind the plodding horses, clock time dissolved into the inconstant interval
between thought and thought. The hills and the river pass
swept toward them grandly, and then the road began to as-
cend and the horses hunched along stiffly, pounding the air
with heads that swung up and down like hammers. Up a long
slope they went. The wheels grated on shattered flakes of
limestone, of which the hills were made. The iron tires
ground harshly on the rock.

Joseph leaned forward and shook his head to be rid of the
spell, as a dog shakes water from its ears. "Elizabeth," he said,
"we're coming to the pass."

She untied her veil and laid it back over her hat. Her eyes
came slowly to life. "I must have been asleep," she said.

"I too. My eyes were open and I was asleep. But here is the
pass."

The mountain was split. Two naked shoulders of smooth
limestone dropped cleanly down, verging a little together,
and at the bottom there was only room for the river bed. The
road itself was blasted out of the cliffside, ten feet above the
surface of the water. Midway in the pass where the constrained river flowed swift and deep and silently, a rough
monolith rose out of the water, cutting and mangling the current like a boat prow driving speedily upstream, making an
angry swirling whisper. The sun was behind the mountain
now, but through the pass they could see the trembling light
of it falling on the valley of Our Lady. The wagon had driven
into the chill blue shade of the white cliffs. The horses, having
reached the top of the long foothill slope, walked easily
enough, but they stretched their necks and snorted at the
river far below them, under the road.

Joseph took a shorter grip on the lines and his right foot
moved out and rested lightly on the brake. He looked down
on the serene water and he felt a gush of pure warm pleasure
in anticipation of the valley he would see in a moment. He
turned to look at Elizabeth, for he wanted to tell her of the
pleasure. He saw that her face had gone haggard and that her
eyes were horrified.

She cried, "I want to stop, dear. I'm afraid." She was staring through the cleft into the sunlit valley.

Joseph pulled up the horses and set the brake. He looked at her questioningly. "I didn't know. Is it the narrow road and the stream below?"

"No, it is not."

He stepped to the ground, then, and held out a hand to her; but when he tried to lead her toward the pass she pulled her hand away from him and stood shivering in the shade. And he thought, "I must try to tell her. I've never tried to tell her things like this. It's seemed too difficult a thing, but now I'll have to try to tell her," and he practiced in his mind the thing he must try to say. "Elizabeth," he cried in his mind, "can you hear me? I am cold with a thing to say, and prayerful for a way to say it." His eyes widened and he was entranced. "I have thought without words," he said in his mind. "A man told me once that was not possible, but I have thought—Elizabeth, listen to me. Christ nailed up might be more than a symbol of all pain. He might in very truth contain all pain. And a man standing on a hilltop with his arms outstretched, a symbol of the symbol, he too might be a reservoir of all the pain that ever was."

For a moment she broke into his thinking, crying, "Joseph, I'm afraid."

And then his thought went on, "Listen, Elizabeth. Do not be afraid. I tell you I have thought without words. Now let me grope a moment among the words, tasting them, trying them. This is a space between the real and the clean, unwavering real, undistorted by the senses. Here is a boundary. Yesterday we were married and it was no marriage. This is our marriage—through the pass—entering the passage like sperm and egg that have become a single unit of pregnancy. This is a symbol of the undistorted real. I have a moment in my heart, different in shape, in texture, in duration from any other moment. Why, Elizabeth, this is all marriage that has ever been, contained in our moment." And he said in his mind, "Christ in his little time on the nails carried within his body all the suffering that ever was, and in him it was undistorted."

He had been upon a star, and now the hills rushed back and robbed him of his aloneness and of his naked thinking. His arms and hands felt heavy and dead, hanging like weights

on thick cords from the shoulders that were tired of supporting them.

Elizabeth saw how his mouth had gone loose with hopelessness and how his eyes had lost the red gleaming of a moment before. She cried, "Joseph, what is it you want? What
are you asking me to do?"

Twice he tried to answer, but a thickness in his throat pro-
hibited speech. He coughed the passage free. "I want to go
through the pass," he said hoarsely.

"I'm afraid, Joseph. I don't know why, but I'm terribly
afraid."

He broke his lethargy then and coiled one of the swinging
weights about her waist. "There's nothing to be afraid of,
dear. This is nothing. I have been far too much alone. It
seems to mean something to me to go through the pass with
you."

She shivered against him and looked fearfully at the dismal
blue shadow of the pass. "I'll go, Joseph," she said miserably.
"I'll have to go, but I'll be leaving myself behind. I'll think of
myself standing here looking through at the new one who
will be on the other side."

She remembered sharply how she had served cambric tea in
tiny tin cups to three little girls, how they had reminded each
other, "We're ladies now. Ladies always hold their hands like
this." And she remembered how she had tried to catch her
doll's dream in a handkerchief.

"Joseph," she said. "It's a bitter thing to be a woman. I'm
afraid to be. Everything I've been or thought of will stay outside the pass. I'll be a grown woman on the other side. I
thought it might come gradually. This is too quick." And she
remembered how her mother said, 'When you're big, Elizabeth, you'll know hurt, but it won't be the kind of hurt you
think. It'll be a hurt that can't be reached with a curing kiss.'

"I'll go now, Joseph," she said quietly. "I've been foolish.
You'll have to expect so much foolishness from me."

The weight left Joseph then. His arm tightened about her
waist and he urged her forward tenderly. She knew, although
her head was bent, how he gazed down on her and how his
eyes were gentle. They walked slowly through the pass, in the
blue shade of it. Joseph laughed softly. "There may be pains

more sharp than delight, Elizabeth, like sucking a hot pepper-mint that burns your tongue. The bitterness of being a woman may be an ecstasy."

His voice ceased and their footsteps rang on the stone road and clashed back and forth between the cliffs. Elizabeth closed her eyes, relying on Joseph's arm to guide her. She tried to close her mind, to plunge it into darkness, but she heard the angry whisper of the monolith in the river, and she felt the stone chill in the air.

And then the air grew warm; there was no longer rock under her feet. Her eyelids turned black-red and then yellow-red over her eyes. Joseph stopped and drew her tightly against his side. "Now we are through, Elizabeth. Now it is done."

She opened her eyes and looked about on the closed valley. The land was dancing in the shimmer of the sun and the trees, clannish little families of white oaks, stirred slightly under the wind that brought excitement to a sloping afternoon. The village of Our Lady was before them, houses brown with weathering and green with rose vines, picket fences burning with a soft fire of nasturtiums. Elizabeth cried out sharply with relief, "I've been having a bad dream. I've been asleep. I'll forget the dream now. It wasn't real."

Joseph's eyes were radiant. "It's not so bitter, then, to be a woman?" he asked.

"It isn't any different. Nothing seems changed. I hadn't realized how beautiful the valley is."

"Wait here," he said. "I'll go back and bring the horses through."

But when he was gone, Elizabeth cried sadly, for she had a vision of a child in short starched skirts and with pigtails down her back, who stood outside the pass and looked anxiously in, stood on one foot and then on the other, hopped nervously and kicked a stone into the stream. For a moment the vision waited as Elizabeth remembered waiting on a street corner for her father, and then the child turned miserably away and walked slowly toward Monterey. Elizabeth was sorry for her, "For it's a bitter thing to be a child," she thought. "There are so many clean new surfaces to scratch."

II

THE TEAM came through the pass, the horses lifting their feet high, moving diagonally, cocking their heads at the stream while Joseph held tight reins on them and set the brake to shrieking. Once off the narrow place, the horses settled down and their long journey reasserted itself. Joseph pulled up and helped Elizabeth to her seat. She settled herself primly, drew her duster about her knees and dropped the veil over her face.

"We'll be going right through town," she said. "Everyone will see us."

Joseph clucked to the horses and relaxed the lines. "Will you mind that?"

"Of course I won't mind. I'll like it. I'll feel proud, as though I had done an unusual thing. But I must be sitting right and looking right when they see me."

Joseph chuckled. "Maybe no one will look."

"They'll look, all right. I'll make them look."

They drove down the one long street of Our Lady, where the houses clung to the side of the road as though for warmth. As they went, the women came from their houses, shamelessly to stare, to wave fat hands and to say the new title gently because it was a new word. *"Buenas tardes, señora,"* and over their shoulders they called into the houses, *"Ven aca, mira! mira! La nueva señora Wayne viene."* Elizabeth waved back happily and tried to look dignified. Farther along the street they had to stop for gifts. Old Mrs. Gutierrez stood in the middle of the road, waving a chicken by the legs while she shrieked the advantages of this particular chicken. But when the bird lay croaking in the wagon box, Mrs. Gutierrez was overcome with self-consciousness. She fixed her hair and nursed her hands, and finally scuttled back to her yard waving her arms and crying, *"No le hace."*

Before they got through the street the wagon box was loaded with trussed livestock: two little pigs, a lamb, an evil-eyed nanny goat with udders suspiciously shrunken, four hens and a gamecock. The saloon belched forth its customers as the wagon went by, and the men raised their glasses. For a little while they were surrounded by cries of welcome, and then the last house was gone and the river road was before them.

Elizabeth settled back in the seat and relaxed her primness. Her hand crept through the crook of Joseph's arm and pressed for a moment and then remained in quiet there. "It was like a circus," she said. "It was like being the parade."

Joseph took off his hat and laid it on his lap. His hair was tangled and damp, and his eyes tired. "They are good people," he said. "I'll be glad to get home, won't you?"

"Yes, I'll be glad." And she said suddenly, "There are some times, Joseph, when the love for people is strong and warm like a sorrow."

He looked quickly at her in astonishment at her statement of his own thought. "How did you think that, dear?"

"I don't know. Why?"

"Because I was thinking it at that moment—and there are times when the people and the hills and the earth, all, everything except the stars, are one, and the love of them all is strong like a sadness."

"Not the stars, then?"

"No, never the stars. The stars are always strangers—sometimes evil, but always strangers. Smell the sage, Elizabeth. It's good to be getting home."

She raised her veil as high as her nose and sniffed long and hungrily. The sycamores were yellowing and already the ground was thick with the first fallen leaves. The team entered the long road that hid the river, and the sun was low over the seaward mountains.

"It'll be 'way in the middle of the night when we get home," he said. The light in the wood was golden-blue, and the stream rattled among the round rocks.

With evening the air grew clear with moisture, so that the mountains were as hard and sharp as crystal. After the sun was gone, there was a hypnotic time when Joseph and Elizabeth stared ahead at the clear hills and could not take their eyes away. The pounding hoofs and the muttering of water deepened the trance. Joseph looked unblinkingly at the string of light along the western mountain rim. His thoughts grew sluggish, but with their slowness they became pictures, and the figures arranged themselves on the mountain tops. A black cloud sailed in from the ocean and rested on the ridge, and Joseph's thought made it a black goat's head. He could see the yellow, slanting eyes, wise and ironic, and the curved horns. He thought, "I know that it is really there, the goat resting his chin on a mountain range and staring in on the valley. He should be there. Something I've read or something I've been told makes it a fitting thing that a goat should come out of the ocean." He was endowed with the power to create things as substantial as the earth. "If I will admit the goat is there, it will be there. And I will have made it. This goat is important," he thought.

A flight of birds rolled and twisted high overhead, and they caught the last light on their flickering wings, and twinkled like little stars. A hunting owl drifted over and shrieked his cry, designed to make small groundling creatures start uneasily and betray themselves against the grass. The valley filled quickly with dark, and the black cloud, as though it had seen enough, withdrew to the sea again. Joseph thought, "I must maintain to myself that it was the goat. I must never betray the goat by disbelieving it."

Elizabeth shivered slightly and he turned around to her. "Are you cold, dear? I'll get the horseblanket to go over your knees." She shivered again, not quite so well, because she was trying to.

"I'm not cold," she said, "but it's a queer time. I wish you'd talk to me. It's a dangerous time."

He thought of the goat. "What do you mean, dangerous?" He took her clasped hands and laid them on his knee.

"I mean there's a danger of being lost. It's the light that's going. I thought I suddenly felt myself spreading and dissipating like a cloud, mixing with everything around me. It was a good feeling, Joseph. And then the owl went over, and I was afraid that if I mixed too much with the hills I might never be able to collapse into Elizabeth again."

"It's only the time of day," he reassured her. "It seems to affect all living things. Have you ever noticed the animals and the birds when it's evening?"

"No," she said, turning eagerly toward him, for it seemed to her that she had discovered a communication. "I don't think I've ever noticed anything very closely in my life," she said. "Just now it seems to me that the lenses of my eyes have been wiped clean. What do the animals do at evening?" Her voice had grown sharp and had broken through his reverie.

"I don't know," he said sullenly. "I mean—I know, but I'll have to think. These things aren't always ready to hand, you know," he apologized. And he fell silent and looked into the gathering darkness. "Yes," he said at last, "it's like that—why all the animals stand still when it comes dark evening. They don't blink their eyes at all and they go dreaming." He fell silent again.

"I remember a thing," Elizabeth said. "I don't know when I noticed it, but just now—you said yourself it's the time of day, and this picture is important in this time of day."

"What?" he asked.

"Cats' tails lie flat and straight and motionless when they're eating."

"Yes," he nodded, "yes, I know."

"And that's the only time they're ever straight, and that's the only time they're ever still." She laughed gaily. Now that the foolish thing was said, she realized it might be taken as a satire on Joseph's dreaming animals, and she was glad it might. She felt rather clever to have said it.

He did not notice what construction might be put on the cats' tails. He said, "Over a hill and then down to the river wood again, and then out across the long plain and we'll be home. We should see the lights from the hilltop." It was very dark by now, a thick night and silent. The wagon moved up the hill in the darkness, a stranger to the hushed night.

Elizabeth pressed her body against Joseph. "The horses know the road," she said. "Do they smell it?"

"They see it, dear. It is only dark to us. To them it is a deep twilight. We'll be on top of the hill in a little, and then we may see the lights. It's too quiet," he complained. "I don't like this night. Nothing is stirring about." It seemed an hour before they breasted the hill and Joseph stopped the team to rest from its climb. The horses sank their heads low and panted rhythmically. "See," Joseph said, "there are the lights. Late as it is, my brothers are expecting us. I didn't tell them when we would come, but they must have guessed. Look, some of the lights are moving. That's a lantern in the yard, I guess. Tom has been out to the barn to see the horses."

The night was thick on them again. Ahead, they could hear a heavy sigh, and then it rode up to them—a warm wind out of the valley. It whisked gently in the dry grass. Joseph muttered uneasily, "There's an enemy out tonight. The air's unfriendly."

"What do you say, dear?"

"I say there's a change of weather coming. The storms will be here soon."

The wind strengthened and bore to them the long deep howling of a dog. Joseph sat forward angrily. "Benjy has gone to town. I told him not to go while I was gone. That's his dog howling. It howls all night every time he goes away." He lifted the lines and clucked the horses up. For a moment they plodded, but then their necks arched and their ears pivoted forward. Joseph and Elizabeth could hear it now, the even clattering of a galloping horse. "Someone coming," Joseph said. "Maybe it's Benjy on his way to town. I'll head him off if I can."

The running horse came near, and suddenly its rider pulled it down almost to its haunches. A shrill voice cried, "Señor, is it you, Don Joseph?"

"Yes, Juanito, what's the matter? What do you want?"

The saddled horse was passing now, and the shrill voice cried, "You will want me in a little while, my friend. I'll be waiting for you at the rock in the pines. I did not know, señor. I swear I did not know."

They could hear the thud as the spurs drove in. The horse coughed and leaped ahead. They heard it running wildly over the hill. Joseph took the whip from its socket and flicked the horses to a trot.

Elizabeth tried to see into his face. "What's the matter, dear? What did he mean?"

His hands were rising and falling as he kept tight rein on the horses and yet urged them on. The tires cried on the rocks. "I don't know what it is," Joseph said. "I knew this night was bad."

Now they were in the level plain and the horses tried to slow to a walk, but Joseph whipped them sharply until they broke into a ragged run. The wagon lurched and pitched over the uneven road so that Elizabeth braced her feet and grasped the arm handle with both her hands.

They could see the buildings now. A lantern was standing on the manure pile and its light reflected outward from the new whitewash on the barn. Two of the houses were lighted, and as the wagon drew near, Joseph could see people moving about restlessly behind the windows. Thomas came out and stood by the lantern as they drove up. He took the horses by the bits and rubbed their necks with his palm. He wore a set smile that did not change. "You've been coming fast," he said.

Joseph jumped down from the wagon. "What has happened here? I met Juanito on the road."

Thomas unhooked the check reins and went back to loosen the tugs. "Why we knew it would happen some time. We spoke about it once."

Out of the darkness Rama appeared beside the wagon. "Elizabeth, I think you'd better come with me."

"What's the matter?" Elizabeth cried.

"Come with me, dear, I'll tell you."

Elizabeth looked questioningly at Joseph. "Yes, go with her," he said. "Go to the house with her."

The pole dropped and Thomas skinned the harness from the horses' wet backs. "I'll leave them here for a little," he apologized, and he threw the harness over the corral fence. "Now come with me."

Joseph had been staring woodenly at the lantern. He picked it up and turned. "It's Benjy, of course," he said. "Is he badly hurt?"

"He's dead," said Thomas. "He's been dead a good two hours."

They went into Benjy's little house, through the dark living-room and into the bedroom, where a lamp was burning. Joseph looked down into Benjy's twisted face, caught in a moment of ecstatic pain. The lips grinned off the teeth, the nose was flared and spread. Half-dollars lying on his eyes shone dully.

"His face will settle some after a while," Thomas said.

Joseph's eyes wandered slowly to a blood-stained knife which lay on a table beside the bed. He seemed to be looking down from a high place, and he was filled with a strange powerful calmness, and with a curious sense of omniscience. "Juanito did this?" he said with a half-question.

Thomas picked up the knife and held it to his brother. And when Joseph refused to take it, he set it back on the table. "In the back," Thomas said. "Juanito rode to Nuestra Señora to borrow a dehorner for that long-horned bull that's been raising so much Hell. And Juanito made the trip too quickly."

Joseph looked up from the bed. "Let's cover him up. Let's spread something over him. I met Juanito on the road. He said he didn't know."

Thomas laughed brutally. "How could he know? He couldn't see his face. He just saw, and stabbed. He wanted to give himself up, but I told him to wait for you. Why," Thomas said, "the only punishment of a trial would be on us."

Joseph turned away. "Do you suppose we'll have to have a coroner out? Have you changed anything, Tom?

"Well, we brought him home. And we pulled up his pants."

Joseph's hand rose to his beard and he stroked it down and turned the ends under. "Where is Jennie now?" he asked.

"Oh, Burton took her home with him. Burton's praying with her. She was crying when she left. She must be nearly hysterical by now."

"We'll send her home to the East," Joseph said. "She'll never do, out here." He turned to the door. "You'll have to ride in and report it, Tom. Make it an accident. Maybe they'll never question. And it was an accident." He turned quickly back to the bed and patted Benjy's hand before he went out of the house.

He walked slowly across the yard toward where he could see the black tree against the sky. When he was come to it, he leaned his back against the trunk and looked upward, where a few pale misty stars glittered among the branches. His hands caressed the bark. "Benjamin is dead," he reported softly. For a moment he breathed deeply, and then turning, he climbed into the tree and sat between the great arms and laid his cheek against the cool rough bark. He knew his thought would be heard when he said in his mind, "Now I know what the blessing was. I know what I've taken upon me. Thomas and

Burton are allowed their likes and dislikes, only I am cut off. I am cut off. I can have neither good luck nor bad luck. I can have no knowledge of any good or bad. Even a pure true feeling of the difference between pleasure and pain is denied me. All things are one, and all a part of me." He looked toward the house from which he had come. The light from the window alternately flashed and was cut off. Benjy's dog howled again, and in the distance the coyotes heard the howl and took it up with their maniac giggling. Joseph put his arms around the tree and hugged it tight against him. "Benjy is dead, and I am neither glad nor sorry. There is no reason for it to me. It is just so. I know now, my father, what you were—lonely beyond feeling loneliness, calm because you had no contact." He climbed down from the tree and once more reported, "Benjamin is dead, sir. I wouldn't have stopped it if I could. Nothing is required in satisfaction."

And he walked toward the barn, for he must saddle a horse to ride toward the great rock where Juanito was awaiting him.

Rama took Elizabeth by the hand and led her across the farm yard. "No crying, now," she said. "There's no call for it. You didn't know the man that's dead, so you can't miss him. And I'll promise you won't ever see him, so there's no call for fear." She led the way up the steps and into her comfortable sitting-room where rocking-chairs were fitted with quilted pads and where the Rochester lamps wore china shades with roses painted on them. Even the braided rag rugs on the floor were made of the brightest underskirts.

"You have a comfortable place," Elizabeth said, and she looked up at the wide face of Rama, a full span between the cheekbones; the black brows nearly met over the nose; the heavy hair grew far down on her forehead in a widow's peak.

"I make it comfortable," Rama said. "I hope you can do as well."

Rama had dressed for the occasion in a tight-bodiced, full-skirted black taffeta which whispered sharply when she moved. Around her neck, upon a silver chain, she wore an amulet of ivory brought by some sailor ancestor from an island in the Indian Ocean. She seated herself in a rocking-chair of which the seat and back were covered with little flowers in petit point. Rama stretched her white strong fingers on her knees like a pianist sounding a practice chord. "Sit down," she said. "You'll have a time to wait."

Elizabeth felt the strength of Rama and knew she should resent it, but it was a safe pleasant thing to have this sure woman by her side. She seated herself daintily and crossed her hands in her lap. "You haven't told me yet what has happened."

Rama smiled grimly. "Poor child, you are come at a bad time. Any time would have been bad, but this is a shameful time." She stiffened her fingers on her lap again. "Benjamin Wayne was stabbed in the back tonight," she said. "He died in ten minutes. In two days he'll be buried." She looked up at Elizabeth and smiled mirthlessly, as though she had known all this would happen, even to the smallest detail. "Now you know," she continued. "Ask anything you want tonight.

There's a strain on us and we are not ourselves. A thing like this breaks down our natures for a time. Ask anything you wish tonight. Tomorrow we may be ashamed. When we have buried him, we'll never mention Benjy any more. In a year we will forget he ever lived."

Elizabeth sat forward in her chair. This was so different from her picture of homecoming, in which she received the homage of the clan and made herself gracious to them. The room was swimming in a power beyond her control. She sat on the edge of a deep black pool and saw huge pale fishes moving mysteriously in its depth.

"Why was he stabbed?" she asked. "I heard Juanito did it."

A little smile of affection grew on Rama's lips. "Why Benjy was a thief," she said. "He didn't want the things he stole very much. He stole the precious little decency of girls. Why, he drank to steal a particle of death—and now he has it all. This had to happen, Elizabeth. If you throw a great handful of beans at an upturned thimble, one is pretty sure to go in. Now do you see?

"Juanito came home and found the little thief at work.

"We all loved Benjy," Rama said. "There's not a frightful span between contempt and love."

Elizabeth felt lonely and shut out and very weak before Rama's strength. "I've come such a long way," she explained. "And I've had no dinner. I haven't even washed my face." Her lips began to tremble as she remembered, one by one, the things she was suffering. Rama's eyes softened and looked at her, seeing the bride Elizabeth now. "And where's Joseph?" Elizabeth complained. "It's our first night at home and he's gone. I haven't even had a drink of water."

Rama stood up then, and smoothed down her whispering skirt. "Poor child, I'm sorry; I didn't think. Come into the kitchen and wash yourself. I'll make some tea and slice some bread and meat for you."

The teakettle breathed huskily in the kitchen. Rama cut pieces of roast beef and bread and poured a cup of scalding yellow tea.

"Now come back to the sitting-room, Elizabeth. You can have your supper there where it's more comfortable."

Elizabeth made thick sandwiches and ate them hungrily,

but it was the hot tea, strong and bitter, that rested her and removed her complaints. Rama had gone back to her chair again. She sat stiffly upright, watching Elizabeth fill her cheeks too full of bread and meat.

"You're pretty," Rama said critically. "I wouldn't have thought Joseph could pick a pretty wife."

Elizabeth blushed. "What do you mean?" she asked. There were streams of feeling here she couldn't identify, methods of thinking that wouldn't enter the categories of her experience or learning. It frightened her and so she smiled amusedly. "Of course he knows that. Why he told me."

Rama laughed quietly. "I didn't know him as well as I thought I did. I thought he'd pick a wife as he'd pick a cow—to be a good cow, perfect in the activity of cows—to be a good wife and very like a cow. Perhaps he is more human than I thought." There was a little bitterness in her voice. Her strong white fingers brushed her hair down on each side of the sharp part. "I think I'll have a cup of tea. I'll put more water in. It must be poisonously strong."

"Of course he's human," Elizabeth said. "I don't see why you seem to say he isn't. He is self-conscious. He's embarrassed, that is all." And her mind reverted suddenly to the pass in the hills and the swirling river. She was frightened and put the thought away from her.

Rama smiled pityingly. "No, he isn't self-conscious," she explained. "In all the world I think there isn't a man less self-conscious, Elizabeth." And then she said compassionately, "You don't know this man. I'll tell you about him, not to frighten you, but so you won't be frightened when you come to know him."

Her eyes filled with thoughts and her mind ranged for a way to say them. "I can see," she said, "that you are making excuses already—why—excuses like bushes to hide behind, so you need not face the thoughts you have." Her hands had lost their sureness; they crawled about like the searching tentacles of a hungry sea creature. " 'He is a child,' you say to yourself. 'He dreams.' " Her voice turned sharp and cruel. "He is no child," she said, "and if he dreams, you will never know his dreams."

Elizabeth flared angrily. "What are you telling me? He

married me. You are trying to make a stranger of him." Her voice faltered uncertainly. "Why of course I know him. Do you think I would marry a man I didn't know?"

But Rama only smiled at her. "Don't be afraid, Elizabeth. You've seen things already. There's no cruelty in him, Elizabeth, I think. You can worship him without fear of being sacrificed."

The picture of her marriage flashed into Elizabeth's mind, when, as the service was going on, and the air was filled with its monotone, she had confused her husband with the Christ. "I don't know what you mean," she cried. "Why do you say 'worship'? I'm tired, you know; I've been riding all day. Words have meanings that change as I change. What do you mean by 'worship'?"

Rama drew her chair forward so that she could put her hands on Elizabeth's knee. "This is a strange time," she said softly. "I told you at the beginning that a door is open tonight. It's like an All Souls' Eve, when the ghosts are loose. Tonight, because our brother has died, a door is open in me, and partly open in you. Thoughts that hide deep in the brain, in the dark, underneath the bone can come out tonight. I will tell you what I've thought and held secret. Sometimes in the eyes of other people I've seen the same thought, like a shadow in the water." She patted softly on Elizabeth's knee as she spoke, patted out a rhythm to her words, and her eyes shone with intensity until there were red lights in them. "I know men," she continued. "Thomas I know so well that I feel his thought as it is born. And I know his impulse before it is strong enough to set his limbs in motion. Burton I know to the bottom of his meager soul, and Benjy—I knew the sweetness and the laziness of Benjy. I knew how sorry he was to be Benjy, and how he couldn't help it." She smiled in reminiscence. "Benjy came in one night when Thomas was not here. He was so lost and sad. I held him in my arms until nearly morning." Her fingers doubled under, making a loose fist. "I knew them all," she said hoarsely. "My instinct was never wrong. But Joseph I do not know. I did not know his father."

Elizabeth was nodding slowly, caught in the rhythm.

Rama continued: "I do not know whether there are men born outside humanity, or whether some men are so human as to make others seem unreal. Perhaps a godling lives on earth now and then. Joseph has strength beyond vision of shattering, he has the calm of mountains, and his emotion is as wild and fierce and sharp as the lightning and just as reasonless as far as I can see or know. When you are away from him, try thinking of him and you'll see what I mean. His figure will grow huge, until it tops the mountains, and his force will be like the irresistible plunging of the wind. Benjy is dead. You cannot think of Joseph dying. He is eternal. His father died, and it was not a death." Her mouth moved helplessly, searching for words. She cried as though in pain, "I tell you this man is not a man, unless he is all men. The strength, the resistance, the long and stumbling thinking of all men, and all the joy and suffering, too, cancelling each other out and yet remaining in the contents. He is all these, a repository for a little piece of each man's soul, and more than that, a symbol of the earth's soul."

Her eyes dropped and her hand withdrew. "I said a door was open."

Elizabeth rubbed the place on her knee where the rhythm had been. Her eyes were wet and shining. "I'm so tired," she said. "We drove through the heat, and the grass was brown. I wonder if they took the live chickens and the little lamb and the nanny goat out of the wagon. They should be turned loose, else their legs might swell." She took a handkerchief out of her bosom and blew her nose and wiped it harshly and made it red. She would not look at Rama. "You love my husband," she said in a small, accusing voice. "You love him and you are afraid."

Rama looked slowly up and her eyes moved over Elizabeth's face and then dropped again. "I do not love him. There is no chance of a return. I worship him, and there's no need of a return in that. And you will worship him, too, with no return. Now you know, and you needn't be afraid."

For a moment more she stared at her lap, and then her head jerked up and she brushed down the hair on each side of the part. "It's closed now," she said. "It's all over. Only remember it for a time of need. And when that time comes, I'll be here to help you. I'll make some new tea now, and maybe you'll tell me about Monterey."

13

JOSEPH went into the dark barn and walked down the long gallery behind the stalls, toward the lantern hanging on its wire. As he passed behind the horses, they stopped their rhythmic chewing and looked over their shoulders at him, and one or two of the more lively ones stamped their feet to draw his attention. Thomas was in the stall opposite the lantern, saddling a mare. He paused in cinching and looked over the saddle at Joseph. "I thought I'd take Ronny," he said. "She's soft. A good fast go will harden her up. She's surest footed in the dark, too."

"Make up a story," Joseph said. "Say he slipped and fell on a knife. Try to get through with it without having a coroner out. We'll bury Benjy tomorrow if we can." He smiled wearily. "The first grave. Now we're getting someplace. Houses and children and graves, that's home, Tom. Those are the things to hold a man down. What's in the box-stall, Tom?"

"Only Patch," Thomas said. "I turned the other saddle-horses out yesterday to get some grass and to stretch their legs. They weren't being worked enough. Why, are you riding out tonight?"

"Yes, I'm riding out."

"You're riding after Juanito? You'll never catch him in these hills. He knows the roots of every blade of grass and every hole even a snake might hide in."

Joseph threw back cinch and stirrup over a saddle on the rack, and lifted it down by horn and cantle. "Juanito is waiting for me in the pines," he said.

"But Joe, don't go tonight. Wait until tomorrow when it's light. And take a gun with you."

"Why a gun?"

"Because you don't know what he'll do. These Indians are strange people. There's no telling what he'll do."

"He won't shoot me," Joseph reassured him. "It would be too easy, and I wouldn't care enough. That's better than a gun."

Thomas untied his halter rope and backed the sleepy mare

out of the stall. "Anyway, wait until tomorrow. Juanito will keep."

"No, he's waiting for me now. I won't keep him waiting."

Thomas moved on out of the barn, leading his horse. "I still think you'd better take a gun," he said over his shoulder.

Joseph heard him mount and trot his horse away, and immediately there was a panting rush. Two young coyotes and a hound dashed out to follow him.

Joseph saddled big Patch and led him out into the night and mounted. When his eyes cleared from the lantern light he saw that the night was sharper. The mountain flanks, rounded and flesh-like, stood out softly in shallow perspective and a deep purple essence hung on their outlines. All of the night, the hills, the black hummocks of the trees were as soft and friendly as an embrace. But straight ahead, the black arrow-headed pines cut into the sky.

The night was aging toward dawn, and all the leaves and grasses whispered and sighed under the fresh morning wind. Whistle of ducks' wings sounded overhead, where an invisible squadron started over-early for the south. And the great owls swung restlessly through the air at the last of the night's hunting. The wind brought a pine smell down from the hills, and the penetrating odor of tarweed and the pleasant bouquet of a skunk's anger, smelling, since it was far away, like azaleas. Joseph nearly forgot his mission, for the hills reached out tender arms to him and the mountains were as gentle and insistent as a loving woman who is half asleep. He could feel the ground's warmth as he rode up the slope. Patch flung up his big head and snorted out of stretched nostrils and shook his mane, lifted his tail and danced, kicked a few times and threw his feet high like a racehorse.

Because the mountains were womanly, Joseph thought of Elizabeth and wondered what she was doing. He had not thought of her since he saw Thomas standing by the lantern, waiting for him. "But Rama will take care of her," he thought.

The long slope was past now, and a harder, steeper climb began. Patch ceased his foolishness and bent his head over his climbing legs. And as they moved on, the sharp pines lengthened and pierced higher and higher into the sky. Beside the track there was a hissing of a little water, rushing downward toward the valley, and then the pine grove blocked the way. The black bulk of it walled up the path. Joseph turned right and tried to remember how far it was to the broad trail that led to the grove's center. Now Patch nickered shrilly and stamped and shook his head. When Joseph tried to head into the grove path, the horse refused to take it and spurs only made him rear and thresh his front feet, and the quirt sent him whirling down the hill. When Joseph dismounted and tried to lead him into the path, he set his hoofs and refused to stir. Joseph walked to his head and felt the quivering muscles of the neck.

"All right," he said. "I'll tie you out here. I don't know what you're afraid of, but Thomas fears it too, and Thomas knows you better than I could." He took the tie rope from the horn and threw two half-hitches around a sapling.

The pathway through the pines was black. Even the sky was lost behind the interlacing boughs, and Joseph, as he walked along, took careful, feeling steps and stretched his arms ahead to keep from striking a tree trunk. There was no sound except the muttering of a tiny stream somewhere beside the track. Then ahead, a little patch of grey appeared. Joseph dropped his arms and walked quickly toward it. The pine limbs whirred under a wind that could not penetrate down into the forest, but with the wind a restlessness came into the grove—not sound exactly, and not vibration, but a curious half-way between these two. Joseph moved more cautiously, for there was a breath of fear in the slumbering grove. His feet made no sound on the needles, and he came at last to the open circle in the forest. It was a grey place, filled with particles of light and roofed with the dull slaty mirror of the sky. Above, the winds had freshened so that the tall pine-tops moved sedately, and their needles hissed. The great rock in the center of the glade was black, blacker even than the tree trunks, and on its side a glow-worm shed its pale blue luminance.

When Joseph tried to approach the rock he was filled with foreboding and suspicion, as a little boy is who enters an empty church and cuts a wide path around the altar and keeps his eyes upon it for fear some saint may move his hand or the bloody Christ groan on the cross. So Joseph circled widely, keeping his head turned toward the rock. The glow-worm disappeared behind a corner and was lost.

The rustling increased. The whole round space became surcharged with life, saturated with furtive movement. Joseph's hair bristled on his head. "There's evil here tonight," he thought. "I know now what the horse feared." He moved back into the shadow of the trees and seated himself and leaned back against a pine trunk. And as he sat, he could feel a dull vibration on the ground. Then a soft voice spoke beside him. "I am here, señor."

Joseph half leaped to his feet. "You startled me, Juanito."

"I know, señor. It is so quiet. It is always quiet here. You can hear noises, but they're always on the outside, shut out and trying to get in."

They were silent for a moment. Joseph could only see a blacker shadow against the black before him. "You asked me to come," he said.

"Yes, señor, my friend, I would have no one do it but you."

"Do what, Juanito? What do you want me to do?"

"What you must, señor. Did you bring a knife?"

"No," Joseph said wonderingly. "I have no knife."

"Then I will give you my pocket knife. It is the one I used on the calves. The blade is short, but in the right place it will do. I will show you where."

"What are you talking about, Juanito?"

"Strike with the blade flat, my friend. Then it will go between the ribs, and I will show you where, so the blade will reach."

Joseph stood up. "You mean I am to stab you, Juanito."

"You must, my friend."

Joseph moved closer to him and tried to see his face, and could not. "Why should I kill you, Juanito?" he asked.

"I killed your brother, señor. And you are my friend. Now you must be my enemy."

"No," Joseph said. "There's something wrong here." He paused uneasily, for the wind had died out of the trees, and silence, like a thick fog, had settled into the glade so that his voice seemed to fill up the air with unwanted sound. He was uncertain. His voice went on so softly that part of the words were whispered, and even then the glade was disturbed by his speaking. "There's something wrong. You did not know it was my brother."

"I should have looked, señor."

"No, even if you had known, it would make no difference. This thing was natural. You did what your nature demanded. It is natural and—it is finished." Still he could not see Juanito's face, although a little grey of dawn was dropping into the glade.

"I do not understand this, señor," Juanito said brokenly. "It is worse than the knife. There would be a pain like fire for a moment, and then it would be gone. I would be right, and you would be right, too. I do not understand this way. It is like prison all my life." The trees stood out now with a little light between them, and they were like black witnesses.

Joseph looked to the rock for strength and understanding. He could see the roughness of it now, and he could see the straight line of silver light where the little stream cut across the glade.

"It is not punishment," he said at last. "I have no power to punish. Perhaps you must punish yourself if you find that among your instincts. You will act the course of your breed, as a young bird dog does when it comes to point where the birds are hidden, because that is in its breed. I have no punishment for you."

Juanito ran to the rock, then, and scooped up water and drank it from his hands. And he walked quickly back. "This water is good, señor. The Indians take it away with them, to drink when they are sick. They say it comes out of the center of the world." He wiped his mouth on his sleeve. Joseph could see the outline of his face, and the little caves where his eyes were.

"What will you do now?" Joseph asked.

"I will do what you say, señor."

Joseph cried angrily, "You put too much on me. Do what you wish!"

"But I wished you to kill me, my friend."

"Will you come back to work?"

"No," Juanito answered slowly. "It is too near the grave of an unrevenged man. I can't do that until the bones are clean. I will go away for a while, señor. And when the bones are clean I will come back. Memory of the knife will be gone when the flesh is gone."

Joseph was suddenly so filled with sorrow that it hurt his chest to contain it. "Where will you go, Juanito?"

"I know. I will take Willie. We will go together. Where there are horses we will be all right. If I am with Willie, helping him to fight off the dreams of the lonely place and the men who came out of the holes to tear him, then the punishment will not be so hard." He turned suddenly in among the pines and disappeared, and his voice came back from behind the wall of trees, "My horse is here, señor. I will come back when the bones are clean." A moment later Joseph heard the complaint of stirrup leather, and then the pounding of hoofs on pine needles.

The sky was bright now, and high over the center of the glade one little fragment of fiery cloud hung, but the glade was dark and grey yet, and the great rock brooded in its center.

Joseph walked to the rock and drew his hand over the heavy fur of moss. "Out of the center of the world," he thought, and he remembered the poles of a battery. "Out of the heart of the world." He walked away slowly, hating to turn his back on the rock, and as he rode down the slope the sun arose behind him and he could see it flashing on the windows of the farm houses below. The yellow grass glittered with dew. But now the hillsides were getting thin and worn and ready for the winter. A little band of steers watched him go by, turning slowly to keep their heads toward him.

Joseph felt very glad now, for within him there was arising the knowledge that his nature and the nature of the land were the same. He lifted his horse to a trot, for he remembered suddenly that Thomas was gone to Nuestra Señora and there was no one but himself to build a coffin for his brother. For a moment, while the horse hurried on, Joseph tried to think what Benjy had been like, but soon he gave it up, for he couldn't remember very well.

A column of smoke was drifting out of the chimney of Thomas' house as he rode into the corral. He turned Patch loose and hung up the saddle. "Elizabeth will be with Rama," he thought. And he walked eagerly in to see his new wife.

14

THE WINTER came in early that year. Three weeks before Thanksgiving the evenings were red on the mountain tops toward the sea, and the bristling, officious wind raked the valley and sang around the house corners at night and flapped the window shades, and the little whirlwinds took columns of dust and leaves down the road like reeling soldiers. The blackbirds swarmed and flew away in twinkling clouds and doves sat mourning on the fences for a while and then disappeared during a night. All day the flocks of ducks and geese were in the sky, aiming their arrows unerringly at the south, and in the dusk they cried tiredly, and looked for the shine of water where they could rest the night. The frost came into the valley of Our Lady one night and burned the willows yellow and the dogwood red.

There was a scurrying preparation in the sky and on the ground. The squirrels worked frantically in the fields, storing ten times the food they needed in the community rooms under the ground, while in the hole-mouths the grey grandfathers squeaked shrilly and directed the harvest. The horses and cows lost their shiny coats and grew rough with new winter hair, and the dogs dug shallow holes to sleep in against the ground winds. And in spite of the activity, throughout the whole valley sadness hung like the blue smoky mist on the hills. The sage was purple-black. The live oaks dropped leaves like rain and still were clad with leaves. Every night the sky burned over the sea and the clouds massed and deployed, charged and retreated in practice for the winter.

On the Wayne ranch there was preparation, too. The grass was in and the barns piled high with hay. The crosscut saws were working on oak wood and the splitting mauls were breaking up the sticks. Joseph supervised the work, and his brothers labored under him. Thomas built a shed for the tools and oiled the plow shares and the harrow points. And Burton saw to the roofs and cleaned all the harness and saddles. The community woodpile rose up as high as a house.

Jennie saw her husband buried on a sidehill a quarter-mile

away. Burton made a cross and Thomas built a little white paling fence around the grave, with a gate on iron hinges. Every day for a while Jennie took some green thing to put on the grave, but in a short time even she could not remember Benjy very well, and she grew homesick for her own people. She thought of the dances and the rides in the snow, and she thought how her parents were getting old. The more she thought about them, the greater their need seemed. And besides, she was afraid of this new country now that she had no husband. And so one day Joseph drove away with her, and the other Waynes watched them go. All her possessions were in a traveling-basket along with Benjy's watch and chain and the wedding pictures.

In King City Joseph stood with Jennie at the railway station, and Jennie cried softly, partly because she was leaving, but more because she was frightened at the long train trip. She said, "You'll all come home to visit, won't you."

And Joseph, anxious to be back on the ranch for fear the rain might come and he not there to see it, answered, "Yes, of course. Some time we'll go back to visit."

Juanito's wife, Alice, mourned much more deeply than Jennie did. She did not cry at all, but only sat on her doorstep sometimes and rocked her body back and forth. She was carrying a child, and besides, she loved Juanito very much, and pitied him. She sat too many hours there, rocking and humming softly to herself and never crying, and at last Elizabeth brought her to Joseph's house and put her to work in the kitchen. Alice was happier then. She chattered a little sometimes, while she washed the dishes, standing far out from the sink to keep from hurting the baby.

"He is not dead," she explained very often to Elizabeth. "Some time he will come back, and after a night, it'll be just as it always was. I will forget he ever went away. You know," she said proudly, "my father wants me to go home, but I will not. I will wait here for Juanito. Here is where he will come." And she questioned Joseph over and over about Juanito's plans. "Do you think he will come back? You are sure you think that?"

Joseph always seriously answered, "He said he would."

"But when, when do you think it will be?"

"In a year, perhaps, or maybe two years. He has to wait."

And she went back to Elizabeth, "The baby can walk, perhaps, when he comes back."

Elizabeth took on the new life and changed to meet it. For two weeks she went about her new house frowning, peering into everything, and making a list of furniture and utensils to be ordered from Monterey. The work of the house quickly drove away the memory of the evening with Rama. Only at night, sometimes, she awakened cold and fearful, feeling that a marble image lay in bed with her, and she touched Joseph's arm to be sure that it was warm. Rama had been right. A door was open on that night, and now it was closed. Rama never spoke in such a mood again. She was a teacher, Rama, and a tactful woman, for she could show Elizabeth methods of doing things about the house without seeming to criticize Elizabeth's method.

When the walnut furniture arrived, and all the graniteware kettles, and when everything had been arranged or hung up—the hatrack with diamond mirrors, and the little rocking-chairs; the broad maple bed, and the high bureau, then the shining airtight stove was set up in the living room, with a coat of stove black on its sides and nickel polish on the silver parts. When it was all done, the worried look went out of Elizabeth's eyes, and the frown left her brows. She sang, then, Spanish songs she had learned in Monterey. When Alice came to work with her they sang the songs together.

Every morning Rama came to talk, always in secrets, for Rama was full of secrets. She explained things about marriage that Elizabeth, having no mother, had not learned. She told how to have boy children and how to have girl children—not sure methods, true enough; sometimes they failed, but it did no harm to try them; Rama knew a hundred cases where they had succeeded. Alice listened too, and sometimes she said, "That is not right. In this country we do it another way." And Alice told how to keep a chicken from flopping when its head is cut off.

"Draw a cross on the ground first," Alice explained. "And when the head is off, lay the chicken gently on the cross, and it will never flop, because the sign is holy." Rama tried it later and found it true, and ever after that she had more tolerance for Catholics than she had before.

These were good times, filled with mystery and with ritual. Elizabeth watched Rama seasoning a stew. She tasted, smacking her lips and with a stern question in her eyes, "Is this just right? No, not quite." Nothing Rama ever cooked was as good as it should have been.

On Wednesdays, Rama came with a big mending basket on her arm, and behind her trooped those children who had been good. Alice and Rama and Elizabeth sat at three corners of a triangle, and the darning-eggs went searching in and out of socks.

In the center of the triangle the good children sat. (The bad ones were at home doing nothing, for Rama knew how idleness is a punishment to a child.) Rama told stories then, and after a while Alice grew brave and explained a good many miraculous things. Her father had seen a fiery goat crossing the Carmel Valley one night at dusk. Alice knew at least fifty ghost-stories, too; things not far away, but here in Nuestra Señora. She told how the Valdez family was visited All Souls' Eve by a great-great grandmother with a cough in her chest, and how Lieutenant-Colonel Murphy, killed by a troop of sad Yaquis on their way home to Mexico, rode through the valley holding his breast open to show he had no heart. The Yaquis had eaten it, Alice thought. These things were true and could be proved. Her eyes grew wide and frightened when she told the things. And at night the children had only to say, "He had no heart," or "The old lady coughed" to set themselves squealing with fear.

Elizabeth told some stories she had from her mother, tales of the Scotch fairies with their everlasting preoccupation with gold or at least some useful handicraft. They were good stories, but they hadn't the effect of Rama's stories, or Alice's, for they had happened long ago and in a far country which itself had little more reality than the fairies. You could go down the road and see the very place where Lieutenant-Colonel Murphy rode every three months, and Alice could promise to take you to a canyon where every night swinging lanterns plodded along with no one carrying them.

These were good times, and Elizabeth was very happy.

Joseph didn't talk much, but she never passed him that his hand wasn't outstretched to caress her, and she never looked at him and failed to receive a slow calm smile that made her warm and happy. He seemed never to sleep completely, for no matter what time she awakened in the night and stretched an exploring hand toward him, he took her immediately in his arms. Her breasts filled out in these few months, and her eyes grew deep with mystery. It was an exciting time, for Alice was going to have a baby, and the winter was coming.

Benjy's house was vacant now. Two new Mexican riders moved out of the barn and occupied it. Thomas had caught a grizzly-bear cub in the hills and he was trying to tame it with very little success. "It's more like a man than an animal," Thomas said. "It doesn't want to learn." And although it bit him as often as he came near it, he was pleased to have the little bear, because everyone said there were no more grizzlies in the Coast Range mountains.

Burton was busy with inner preparation, for he was planning to go to the camp-meeting town of Pacific Grove and to spend the following summer. He rejoiced in advance at the good emotions to be found there. And he found within himself an exultation when he thought of the time when he would find Christ again and recite sins before a gathering of people.

"You can go to the common house in the evening," he told his wife. "Every evening the people will sing in the common house and eat ice-cream. We'll take a tent and stay a month, or maybe two." And he saw in advance how he would praise the preachers for the message.

15

IT WAS early in November when the rain came. Every day in the morning Joseph searched the sky, studying the bulky rearing clouds, and again at evening he watched the sinking sun reddening the sky. And he thought of those prophetic nursery rhymes:

> "Red sky at morning,
> "Sailors take warning.
> "Red sky at night,
> "Sailors' delight."

and the other way around:

> "Red sky at morning,
> "Rain before dawning.
> "Red sky at night,
> "Clear days in sight."

He looked at the barometer more often than the clock, and when the needle swung down and down he was very happy. He went into the yard and whispered to the tree, "Rain in a few days now. It'll wash the dust off the leaves."

One day he shot a chicken hawk and hung it head downward high in the branches of the oak tree. And he took to watching the horses and the chickens closely.

Thomas laughed at him. "You won't bring it any quicker. You're watching the kettle, Joe. You may keep the rain away if you're too anxious." And Thomas said, "I'm going to kill a pig in the morning."

"I'll hang a cross-bar in the oak tree by my house to hang him on," said Joseph. "Rama will make the sausage, won't she?"

Elizabeth hid her head under a pillow while the pig was screaming, but Rama stood by and caught the throatblood in a milk bucket. And they weren't too soon, for the sides and hams were hardly in the new little stone smoke house before the rain came. There was no maneuvering this time. The wind blew fiercely for a morning, out of the southwest and the ocean, and the clouds rolled in and spread and dropped low until the mountain tops were hidden, and then the fat drops fell. The children stood in Rama's house and watched from the window. Burton gave thanks and helped his wife to give thanks, too, although she wasn't well. Thomas went to the barn and sat on a manger and listened to the rain on the barn roof. The piled hay was still warm with the sun of the summer slopes. The horses moved their feet restlessly and, twisting their heads against the halter ropes, tried to sniff the outside air through the little manure windows.

Joseph was standing under the oak tree when the rain started. The pig's blood he had dabbled on the bark was black and shiny. Elizabeth called to him from the porch, "It's coming now. You'll get wet," and he turned a laughing face to her.

"My skin is dry," he called. "I want to get wet." He saw the first big drops fall, thudding up dust in little spurts, then the ground was peppered with black drops. The rain thickened and a fresh wind slanted it. The sharp smell of dampened dust rose into the air, and then the first winter storm really began, raking through the air and drumming the roofs and knocking the weak leaves from the trees. The ground darkened; little rivulets started to edge out across the yard. Joseph stood with his head uplifted while the rain beat on his cheeks and on his eyelids and the water coursed into his beard and dripped into his open shirt collar, and his clothes hung heavily against him. He stood in the rain a long time to make sure it was not a little piddling shower.

Elizabeth called again: "Joseph, you'll take cold."

"No cold in this," he said. "This is healthy."

"You'll sprout weeds, then, out of your hair. Joseph, come in, there's a good fire going. Come in and change your clothes."

But still he stood in the rain, and only when the streaks of water were running down the oak trunk did he go in. "It will be a good year," he said. "The canyon streams will be flowing before Thanksgiving."

Elizabeth sat in the big leather chair; she had put a stew to simmering on the airtight stove. She laughed when he came in, there was such a feeling of joy in the air. "Why, you're dripping water on the floor, all over the clean floor."

"I know," he said. And he felt such a love for the land and for Elizabeth that he strode across the room and rested his wet hand on her hair in a kind of benediction.

"Joseph, you're dripping water down my neck!"

"I know," he said.

"Joseph, your hand is cold. When I was confirmed, the bishop laid his hand on my head as you are doing, and his hand was cold. It ran shivers down my back. I thought it was the Holy Spirit." She smiled happily up at him. "We talked about it afterwards and all the other girls said it was the Holy Spirit. It was a long time ago, Joseph." She thought back to it, and in the middle of her long narrow picture of time lay the white pass in the mountains, and even it was a long way back in the picture of time.

He leaned over quickly and kissed her on the cheek. "The grass will be up in two weeks," he said.

"Joseph, there's nothing in the world as unpleasant as a wet beard. Your dry clothes are laid out on the bed, dear."

During the evening he sat in his rocking-chair beside the window. Elizabeth stole glances at his face, saw him frown with apprehension when the rain's drumming lightened, and smile slightly with reassurance when it continued again, harder than ever. Late in the evening Thomas came in, kicking and scraping his feet on the front porch.

"Well, it came all right," Joseph said.

"Yes, it came. Tomorrow we'll have to dig some ditches. The corral is under water. We'll have to drain it."

"There's good manure in that water, Tom. We'll run it down over the vegetable-flat."

The rain continued for a week, sometimes thinning to a mist and then pouring again. The drops bent down the old dead grass, and in a few days the tiny new spears came out. The river rumbled out of the western hills and rose over its banks, combing the willows down into the water and growling among the boulders. Every little canyon and crease in the hills sent out a freshet to join the river. The water-cuts deepened and spread in all the gullies.

The children, playing in the houses and in the barn, grew heartily sick of it before it was done; they plagued Rama for methods of amusement. The women had begun to complain about damp clothes hung up in their kitchens.

Joseph dressed in an oilskin and spent his days walking about the farm, now twisting a post-hole digger into the earth to see how deep the wet had gone, now strolling by the riverbank, watching the brush and logs and limbs go bobbing by. At night he slept lightly, listening to the rain or dozing, only to awaken when its force diminished.

And then one morning the sky was clean and the sun shone warmly. The washed air was sweet and clear, and all the leaves on the live oaks glittered with polish. And the grass was coming; anyone could see it, a richness in the color of the farther hills, a shade of blue in the near distance, and right at hand, the tiny green needles poking through the soil.

The children broke out of their cages like animals and played so furiously that they became feverish and had to go to bed.

Joseph brought out a plow and turned over the soil of the vegetable flat, and Thomas harrowed it and Burton rolled it. It was like a procession, each man eager to get his claws into the soil. Even the children begged a bit of dirt for radishes and carrots. Radishes were quickest, but carrots made the finest looking garden, if only they could wait that long. And all the time the grass pushed up and up. Needles became blades, and each blade sprang apart and made two blades. The ridges and flanks of the hills grew soft and smooth and voluptuous again, and the sage lost its dour darkness. In all the country, only the pine grove on the eastern ridge kept to its brooding.

Thanksgiving came with a great feast, and well before Christmas the grass was ankle-high.

One afternoon an old Mexican peddler walked into the farmyard, and he had good things in his pack; needles and pins and thread and little lumps of beeswax and holy pictures and a box of gum and harmonicas and rolls of red and green crêpe paper. He was an old bent man and carried only little things. He opened his pack on Elizabeth's front porch and then stood back, smiling apologetically, now and then turning over a card of pins to make it show to better advantage or prodding the gum gently with his forefinger to gain the attention of the gathered women. Joseph, from the barn door, saw the little crowd and sauntered over. Only then did the old man take off his tattered hat. "Buenas tardes, señor," he said.

"—Tardes," said Joseph.

The peddler grinned in extreme embarrassment. "You do not remember me, señor?"

Joseph searched the dark, lined face. "I guess I don't."

"One day," the old man said, "you rode by on the way from Nuestra Señora. I thought you were going hunting and I begged a piece of venison."

"Yes," Joseph said slowly. "I remember now. You are Old Juan."

The peddler tipped his head like an aged bird. "And then, señor—and then we spoke of a fiesta. I have been way down the country, below San Luis Obispo. Did you make that fiesta, señor?"

Joseph's eyes opened delightedly. "No, I did not, but I will. What would be a good time, Old Juan?"

The peddler spread his hands and pulled his neck between his shoulders at having so much honor put on him. "Why, señor—why in this country any time is good. But some days are better. There is Christmas, the Natividad."

"No," Joseph said. "It's too soon. There won't be time."

"Then there is the New Year, señor. That is the best time, because then everyone is happy and people go about looking for a fiesta."

"That's it!" Joseph cried. "On New Year's Day we'll have it."

"My son-in-law plays the guitar, señor."

"He shall come too. Who shall I invite, Old Juan?"

"Invite?" The old man's eyes filled with astonishment. "You do not 'invite,' señor. When I go back to Nuestra Señora I will tell that you make a fiesta on the New Year, and the people will come. Maybe the priest will come, with his altar in the saddle-bags, and hold the mass. That would be beautiful."

Joseph laughed up into the oak tree. "The grass will be so high by then," he said.

16

THE DAY after Christmas, Martha, Rama's oldest girl, gave the other children a bad fright. "It will rain for the fiesta," she said, and because she was older than the others, a serious child who used her age and seriousness as a whip on the other children, they believed her and felt very badly about it.

The grass was deep. A spell of warm weather had sent it shooting up, and there were millions of mushrooms in the field, and puff-balls and toadstools too. The children brought buckets of mushrooms in, which Rama fried in a pan containing a silver spoon to test them for poison. She said that silver would turn black if a toadstool was present.

Two days before New Year, Old Juan appeared along the road, and his son-in-law, a smiling shiftless Mexican boy, walked directly behind him, for the son-in-law, Manuel, did not even like to take the responsibility of keeping out of ditches. The two of them stood smiling in front of Joseph's porch, caressing their hats against their chests. Manuel did everything Old Juan did, as a puppy imitates a grown dog.

"He plays the guitar," Old Juan said, and in proof, Manuel shifted the battered instrument around from his back and displayed it while he grinned agonizingly. "I told about the fiesta," Old Juan continued. "The people will come—four more guitars, señor, and father Angelo will come," (Here was the fine successful thing) "and he will hold mass right here! And I," he said proudly, "I am to build the altar. Father Angelo said so."

Burton's eyes grew sullen then. "Joseph, you won't have that, will you? Not on our ranch, not with the name we've always had."

But Joseph was smiling joyfully. "They are our neighbors, Burton, and I don't want to convert them."

"I won't stay to see it," Burton cried angrily. "I'll give no sanction to the Pope on this land."

Thomas chuckled. "You stay in the house, then, Burton. Joe and I aren't afraid of being converted, so we'll watch it."

There were a thousand things to be done. Thomas drove a wagon to Nuestra Señora and bought a barrel of red wine and a keg of whiskey. The vaqueros butchered three steers and hung the meat in the trees, and Manuel sat under the trees to keep the vermin off. Old Juan built an altar of boards under the great oak, and Joseph leveled and swept a dancing place in the farmyard. Old Juan was every place, showing the women how to make a tub of *salsa pura*. They had to use preserved tomatoes and chili and green peppers and some dried herbs that Old Juan carried in his pocket. He directed the digging of the cooking pits and carried the seasoned oak wood to the edges. Under the meat trees Manuel sat tiredly plucking the strings of his guitar, now and then breaking into a feverish melody. The children inspected everything, and were good, for Rama had let it be known that a bad child would stay in the house and see the fiesta from a window, a punishment so staggering that the children carried wood to the barbecue pits and offered to help Manuel watch the meat.

The guitars arrived at nine o'clock on New Year's Eve, four lank brown men with black straight hair and beautiful hands. They could ride forty miles, play their guitars for a day and a night and ride forty miles home again. They staggered with exhaustion after fifteen minutes behind a plow. With their arrival, Manuel came to life. He helped them to hang their precious saddle-bags out of harm and he spread their blankets for them in the hay, but they didn't sleep long; at three o'clock in the night, Old Juan built the fires in the pits, and then the guitars came out carrying their saddle-bags. They set four posts around the dancing place and took the fine things out of the saddle-bags: red and blue bunting and paper lanterns and ribbons. They worked in the leaping light from the barbecue pits, and well before day had built a pavilion.

Before daylight Father Angelo arrived on a mule, followed by a hugely packed horse and two sleepy altar boys riding together on a burro. Father Angelo went directly to work. He spread the service on Old Juan's altar, set up the candles, slapped the altar boys and set them running about. He laid the vestments out in the tool-shed and, last of all, brought out his figures. They were wonderful things, a crucifix and a mother and child. Father Angelo had carved and painted them himself and he had invented their peculiarities. They folded in the middle on hinges so carefully hidden that when they were set up the crack could not be seen; their heads screwed on, and the Child fitted into the Mother's arms with a peg that went into a slot. Father Angelo loved his figures, and they were very famous. Although they were three feet high, when folded both could fit into a saddle-bag. Besides being interesting mechanically, they were blessed and had the complete sanction of the archbishop. Old Juan had made separate stands for them, and he himself had brought a thick candle for the altar.

Before sunup the guests began to arrive, some of the richer families in surreys with swaying top fringes, the others in carts, buggies, wagons and on horseback. The poor whites came down from their scrabble ranch on King's Mountain on a sled half filled with straw and completely filled with children. The children arrived in droves and for a time stood about and stared at each other. The Indians walked up quietly and stood apart with stolid incurious faces, watching everything and never taking part in anything.

Father Angelo was a stern man where the church was concerned, but once out of the church, and with the matters of the church out of the way, he was a tender and a humorous man. Let him get a mouthful of meat, and a cup of wine in his hand, and there were no eyes that could twinkle more brightly than his. Promptly at eight o'clock he lighted the candles, drove out the altar boys and began the mass. His big voice rumbled beautifully.

Burton, true to his promise, remained in his house and held prayer with his wife, but even though he raised his voice he could not drown out the penetrating Latin.

As soon as the mass was done, people gathered close to watch Father Angelo fold up the Christ and the Mary. He did it well, genuflecting before each one before he took it down and unscrewed its head.

The pits were rosy with coals by now and the pit-sides glowed under the heat. Thomas, with more help than he needed, rolled the wine barrel up on a cradle and set a spiggot in its end and knocked the bung out. The huge pieces of meat hung over the fire and dripped their juices, and the coals jet-ted up white fire. This was prime beef, killed on the range and hung. Three men brought the tub of salsa out and went back for a wash boiler full of beans. The women carried sour bread like armloads of wood and stacked the golden loaves on a table. The Indians on the outskirts edged in closer, and the children, playing by now but still diffident, became a little insane with hunger when the meat smells began to fill the air.

To start the fiesta Joseph did a ceremonial thing Old Juan had told him about, a thing so ancient and so natural that Joseph seemed to remember it. He took a tin cup from the table and went to the wine cask. The red wine sang and sparkled into it. When it was full, he raised the cup level with his eyes and then poured it on the ground. Again he filled the cup, and this time drank it, in four thirsty gulps. Father Angelo nodded his head and smiled at the fine way in which the thing was done. When his ceremony was finished, Joseph walked to the tree and poured a little wine on its bark, and he heard the priest's voice speaking softly beside him: "This is not a good thing to do, my son."

Joseph whirled on him. "What do you mean?—There was a fly in the cup!"

But Father Angelo smiled wisely and a little sadly at him. "Be careful of the groves, my son. Jesus is a better saviour than a hamadryad." And his smile became tender, for Father Angelo was a wise as well as a learned man.

Joseph started to turn rudely away but then, uncertainly, he swung back. "Do you understand everything, Father?"

"No, my son," the priest said. "I understand very little, but the Church understands everything. Perplexing things become simple in the Church, and I understand this thing you do," Father Angelo continued gently. "It is this way: The Devil has owned this country for many thousands of years, Christ for a very few. And as in a newly conquered nation, the old customs are practiced a long time, sometimes secretly and sometimes changing slightly to comply with the tenor of the new rule, so here, my son, some of the old habits persist, even under the dominion of Christ."

Joseph said, "Thank you. The meat is ready now, I think."

At the pits the helpers were turning chunks of beef with pitchforks, and the guests, holding tin cups in their hands, had formed a line to the wine cask. First to be served were the guitars, and they drank whiskey, for the sun was high and their work was to be done. They wolfed their food, and while the other people were still eating, the guitars sat on boxes in a half-circle and played softly, bringing their rhythms together, feeling for a mood, so that when the dancing started they might be one passionate instrument. Old Juan, knowing the temper of music, kept their cups full of whiskey.

Now two couples entered the dancing place and stepped sedately through a formal dance, all bowings and slow turnings. The guitars ran trilling melodies into the throb of the beat. The line to the wine barrel formed again, and more couples entered the dancing space, these not so clever as the first few. The guitars sensed the change and took more heavily to the bass strings, and the rhythm grew stout and pounding. The space was filling now with guests who took little care to dance, but, standing arm in arm, thudded their feet on the earth. At the pits the Indians moved up and thanklessly took the bread and meat that was offered. They moved closer to the dancers, then, and gnawed the meat and tore at the hard bread with their teeth. As the rhythm grew heavy and insistent, the Indians shuffled their feet in time and their faces remained blank.

The music did not stop. On it went, and on, pounding and unchanging. Now and then one of the players plucked the unstopped strings while his left hand sought his whiskey cup. Now and then a dancer left the space to move to the wine barrel, toss off a cup and hurry back. There was no dancing in couples any more. Arms were outstretched to embrace everyone within reach, and knees were bent and feet pounded the earth to the slow beating of the guitars. The dancers began in low humming, one note struck deep in the throat, and in off-beat. A quarter-tone came in. More and more voices took up the beat and the quarter-tone. Whole sections of the packed dancing space were bobbing to the rhythm. The humming grew savage and deep and vibrant where at first there had been laughter and shouted jokes. One man had been notable for his heighth, another for the deepness of his voice; one woman had been beautiful, another ugly and fat, but that was changing. The dancers lost identity. Faces grew rapt, shoulders fell slightly forward, each person became a part of the dancing body, and the soul of the body was the rhythm.

The guitars sat like demons, slitted eyes glittering, conscious of their power yet dreaming of a greater power. And the strings rang on together. Manuel, who had grinned and smirked from embarrassment in the morning, threw back his head and howled a high shrill minor bar with meaningless words. The dancers chanted a deep refrain. The next player added his segment and the chant answered him.

The sun wheeled past meridian and slanted toward the hills, and a high wind soughed out of the west. The dancers, one by one, went back for meat and wine.

Joseph, with glowing eyes, stood apart. His feet moved slightly with the throbbing, and he felt tied to the dancing body, but he did not join it. He thought exultantly: "We have found something here, all of us. In some way we've come closer to the earth for a moment." He was strong with a pleasure as deep as the pounding bass strings, and he began to feel a strange faith arising in him. "Something will come of this. It's a kind of powerful prayer." When he looked at the western hills and saw a black cloud-head, high and ominous, coming over from the sea, he knew what was to come. "Of course," he said, "it will bring the rain. Something must happen when such a charge of prayer is let loose." He watched with confidence while the towering cloud grew over the mountains and stalked upward toward the sun.

Thomas had gone into the barn when the dancing started, for he was afraid of the wild emotion as an animal is afraid of thunder. The rhythm came into the barn to him now, and he stroked a horse's neck to soothe himself. After a time he heard a soft sobbing near him and, walking toward it, found Burton kneeling in a stall, whimpering and praying. Then Thomas laughed and caught himself back from fear. "What's the matter, Burton, don't you like the fiesta?"

Burton cried angrily, "It's devil-worship, I tell you! It's horrible! On our own place! First the devil-worshiping priest and his wooden idols, and then this!"

"What does it remind you of, Burton?" Thomas asked innocently.

"Remind me of? It reminds me of witchcraft and the Black

Sabbath. It reminds me of all the devilish heathen practices in the world."

Thomas said, "Go on with your praying, Burton. Do you know what it puts me in mind of? Why only listen with your ears half open. It's like a camp meeting. It's like a great evangelist enlightening the people."

"It's devil-worship," Burton cried again. "It's unclean devil-worship, I tell you. If I had known, I would have gone away."

Thomas laughed harshly and went back to sit on his manger, and he listened to Burton's praying. It pleased Thomas to hear how Burton's supplication fell into the rhythm of the guitars.

As Joseph watched the swollen black cloud it seemed not to move, and yet it was eating up the sky, and all suddenly it caught and ate the sun. And so thick and powerful was the cloud that the day went to dusk and the mountains radiated a metallic light, hard and sharp. A moment after the sun had gone, a golden lance of lightning shot from the cloud, and the thunder ran, stumbling and falling, over the mountain tops— another quiver of light and a plunge of thunder.

The music and the dancing stopped instantly. The dancers looked upward with sleepy startled eyes, like children awakened and frightened by the grind of an earthquake. They stared uncomprehendingly for a moment, half-awake and wondering, before their reason came back. And then they scurried to the tied horses and began hooking up the surreys, fastening traces and tugs, backing their teams around the poles. The guitars stripped down the buntings and the unused lanterns and slipped them into the saddle-bags out of danger of the wet.

In the barn Burton arose to his feet and shouted triumphantly, "It's God's voice in anger!"

And Thomas answered him, "Listen again, Burton. It's a thunderstorm."

The glancing fires fell like rain from the great cloud now, and the air shook with the impact of thunder. In a few minutes the conveyances were moving out, a line of them toward the village of Our Lady and a few toward the hill ranches. Canvases were up against the coming rain. The horses snorted at the battering of the air and tried to run.

Since the beginning of the dance the Wayne women had sat on Joseph's porch holding a little aloof from the guests, as hostesses should. Alice had been unable to resist, and she had gone down to the dancing flat. But Elizabeth and Rama sat in rocking-chairs and watched the fiesta.

Now that the cloud had put a cap over the sky, Rama stood up from her chair and prepared to go. "It was a curious thing," Rama said. "You've been quiet today, Elizabeth. Be sure you don't take cold."

"I'm all right, Rama. I've felt a little dull today, with the excitement and the sadness. Ever since I can remember, parties have made me sad." All afternoon she had been watching Joseph where he had stood apart from the dancers. She had seen him looking at the sky. "Now he feels the rain." And when the thunder rolled over, "Joseph will like that. Storms make him glad." Now that the people were gone and the thunder had walked on over their heads, she continued to watch furtively the lonely figure of her husband.

The vaqueros were hustling the utensils and the remaining food under cover. Joseph watched until the first rain began to fall, and then he sauntered to the porch and sat on the top step, in front of Elizabeth; his shoulders slumped forward and his elbows rested on his knees. "Did you like the fiesta, Elizabeth?" he asked.

"Yes."

"Did you ever see one before?"

"I've seen fiestas before," she said, "but never one quite like this. Do you think all the electricity in the air might have made the people wild?"

He turned about and looked into her face. "More likely the wine in their stomachs, dear." His eyes narrowed seriously. "You don't look well, Elizabeth. Are you feeling well?" He stood up and leaned over her anxiously. "Come inside, Elizabeth, it's getting too cold to sit out here."

He went in ahead of her and lighted the lamp hung from a chain in the center of the room, and then he built up a fire in the stove and opened the draft until it roared softly up the chimney. The rain swished gustily on the roof, like a rough broom sweeping. In the kitchen Alice was humming softly in memory of the dance. Elizabeth sat down heavily in a rocking-chair by the stove. "We'll have a little, late supper, dear."

Joseph knelt on the floor beside her. "You look so tired," he said.

"It was the excitement; all the people. And the music was—well, it was strenuous." She paused, trying to think what the music and the dancing meant. "It was such an odd day," she said. "There was the outwardness, the people coming and the mass and the feasting and then the dance, and last of all the storm. Am I being silly, Joseph, or was there a meaning, right under the surface? It seemed like those pictures of simple landscapes they sell in the cities. When you look closely, you see all kinds of figures hidden in the lines. Do you know the kind of pictures I mean? A rock becomes a sleeping wolf, a little cloud is a skull, and the line of trees marching soldiers when you look closely. Did the day seem like that to you, Joseph, full of hidden meanings, not quite understandable?"

He was still kneeling, bending close to her in the low light of the lamp. He watched her lips intently, as though he could not hear. His hands stroked his beard roughly, and he nodded again and again. "You see closely, Elizabeth," he said sharply. "You look too deeply into things."

"And Joseph, you did feel it, didn't you? The meanings seemed to me to be a warning. Oh—I don't know how to say it."

He dropped back and sat on his heels and stared at the specks of light that came from the cracks in the stove. His left hand still caressed his beard, but his right moved up and rested on her knee. The wind cried shrilly in the oak tree over the house, and the stove ticked evenly as the fire died down a little.

Alice sang, *"Corono ale de flores que es cosa mia—"*

Joseph said softly, "You see, Elizabeth; it should make me less lonely that you can see under the covering, but it doesn't. I want to tell you, and I can't. I don't think these are warnings to us, but only indications how the world fares. A cloud is not a sign set up for men to see and to know that it will rain. Today was no warning, but you are right. I think there were things hidden in today." He licked his lips carefully.

Elizabeth put out her hand to stroke his head. "The dance was timeless," Joseph said, "do you know?—a thing eternal, breaking through to vision for a day." He fell silent again, and tried to back his mind out of the heavy and vague meanings that rolled about it like grey coils of fog. "The people enjoyed it," he said, "everyone but Burton. Burton was miserable and afraid. I can never tell when Burton will be afraid."

She watched how his lips curved up for a moment in faint amusement. "Will you be hungry soon, dear? You can have your supper any time—just cold things, tonight." These were words to keep a secret in, she knew, but the secret came sneaking out before she could stop it.

"Joseph—I was sick this morning."

He looked at her compassionately. "You worked too hard at the preparation."

"Yes—maybe," she said. "No, Joseph, it isn't that. I didn't mean to tell you yet, but Rama says—do you think Rama knows? Rama says she is never wrong, and Rama should know. She's seen enough, and she says she can tell."

Joseph chuckled, "What does Rama know? You'll choke yourself on words in a moment."

"Well, Rama says I'm going to have a baby."

Her words fell into a curious silence. Joseph had settled back and he was staring at the stove again. The rain had stopped for a moment, and Alice was not singing.

Elizabeth gently, timorously broke into the silence. "Are you glad, dear?"

Joseph's breath broke heavily out. "More glad than I ever have been."—then, in a whisper, "and more afraid."

"What did you say dear? What was that last? I didn't hear."

He stood up and bent down over her. "You must take care," he said sharply. "I'll get a robe to go about your knees. Take care against cold, care against falling." He tucked a blanket about her waist.

She was smiling, proud and glad of his sudden worry. "I'll know what to do, dear, don't fear for me. I'll know. Why," she said confidently, "a whole plane of knowledge opens when a woman is carrying a child. Rama told me."

"See you take care then," he repeated.

She laughed happily. "Is the child so precious to you already?"

He studied the floor and frowned. "Yes—the child is precious, but not so precious as the bearing of it. That is as real as a mountain. That is a tie to the earth." He stopped, thinking of words for the feeling. "It is a proof that we belong here, dear, my dear. The only proof that we are not strangers." He looked suddenly at the ceiling. "The rain has stopped. I'll go to see how the horses are."

Elizabeth laughed at him. "Some place I've read or heard of a strange custom, maybe it's in Norway or Russia, I don't know, but wherever it is, they say the cattle must be told. When anything happens in a family, a birth or a death, the father goes to the barn and tells the horses and cows about it. Is that why you are going, Joseph?"

"No," he said. "I want to see that all the halter ropes are short."

"Don't go," she begged. "Thomas will look after the stock. He always does. Stay with me tonight. I'll be lonely if you go out tonight. Alice," she called, "will you set the supper now? I want you to sit beside me, Joseph."

She hugged his whole forearm against her breast. "When I was little a doll was given me, and when I saw it on the Christmas-tree an indescribable heat came into my heart. Before I ever took up the doll I was afraid for it, and filled with sorrow. I remember it so well! I was sorry the doll was mine, I don't know why. It seemed too precious, too agonizingly precious to be mine. It had real hair for eyebrows and real hair for lashes. Christmas has been like that every time since then, and this is a time like that. If this thing I have told you is true, it is too precious, and I am afraid. Sit with me, dear. Don't go walking in the hills tonight."

He saw that there were tears in her eyes. "Surely I'll stay," he comforted her. "You are too tired; and you must go to bed early from now on."

He sat with her all evening, and went to bed with her, but when her breathing was even he crept out and slipped on his clothes. She heard him going and lay still, pretending to be asleep. "He has some business with the night," she thought, and her mind reverted to what Rama had said. 'If he dreams you'll never know his dreams.' She went cold with loneliness, and shivered, and began to cry softly.

Joseph stepped quietly down from the porch. The sky had cleared, and the night sharpened with frost, but the trees still dripped water, and from the roof a tiny stream fell to the ground. Joseph walked straight to the great oak and stood beneath it. He spoke very softly, so no one could hear.

"There is to be a baby, sir. I promise that I will put it in your arms when it is born." He felt the cold wet bark, drew his fingertips slowly downward. "The priest knows," he thought. "He knows part of it, and he doesn't believe. Or maybe he believes and is fearful."

"There's a storm coming," he said to the tree. "I know I can't escape it. But you, sir, you might know how to protect us from the storm."

For a long time he stood, moving his fingers nervously on the black bark. "This thing is growing strong," he thought. "I began it because it comforted me when my father was dead, and now it is grown so strong that it overtops nearly everything. And still it comforts me."

He walked to the barbecue pit and brought back a piece of meat that remained on the grate. "There," he said, and reaching high up, laid the meat in the crotch of the tree. "Protect us if you can," he begged. "The thing that's coming may destroy us all." He was startled by footsteps near to him.

Burton's voice said, "Joseph, is it you?"

"Yes. It's late. What do you want?"

Burton advanced and stood close. "I want to talk to you, Joseph. I want to warn you."

"This is no time," Joseph said sullenly. "Talk to me tomorrow. I've been out to look at the horses."

Burton did not move. "You are lying, Joseph. You think you have been secret, but I have watched you. I've seen you make offerings to the tree. I've seen the pagan growth in you, and I come to warn you." Burton was excited and his breath came quick. "You saw the wrath of God this afternoon warning the idolators. It was only a warning, Joseph. The lightning will strike next time. I've seen you creeping out to the tree, Joseph, and I've remembered Isaiah's words. You have left God, and his wrath will strike you down." He paused, breathless from the torrent of emotion, and the anger died out of him. "Joseph," he begged, "come to the barn and pray with me. Christ will receive you back. Let us cut down the tree."

But Joseph swung away from him and shook off the hand that was put out to restrain him. "Save yourself, Burton," he laughed shortly. "You're too serious, Burton. Now go to bed. Don't interfere with my games. Keep to your own." He left his brother standing there, and crept back into the house.

17

THE SPRING came richly, and the hills lay deep in grass—emerald green, the rank thick grass; the slopes were sleek and fat with it. Under the constant rains the river ran sturdily on, and its sheltering trees bowed under the weight of leaves and joined their branches over the river so that it ran for miles in a dim cavern. The farm buildings took a deep weathering in the wet winter; the pale moss started on the northerly roofs; the manure piles were crowned with forced grass.

The stock, sensing a great quantity of food shooting up on the sidehills, increased the bearing of young. Rarely did so many cows have two calves as during that spring. The pigs littered and there were no runts. In the barn only a few horses were tied, for the grass was too sweet to waste.

When April came, and warm grass-scented days, the flowers burdened the hills with color, the poppies gold and the lupins blue, in spreads and comforters. Each variety kept to itself and splashed the land with its color. And still the rain fell often, until the earth was spongy with moisture. Every depression in the ground became a spring, and every hole a well. The sleek little calves grew fat and were hardly weaned before their mothers received the bulls again.

Alice went home to Nuestra Señora and bore her son and brought it back to the ranch with her.

In May the steady summer breeze blew in from the sea, with salt and the faint smell of kelp. It was a springtime of work for the men. All the flat lands about the houses grew black under the plows, and the orderly, domestic seed sprouted the barley and the wheat. The vegetable-flat bore so copiously that only the finest fattest vegetables were taken for the kitchens; the pigs received every turnip of questionable shape and every imperfect carrot. The ground squirrels came out to squeak in their doorways, and they were fatter in the spring than fall usually found them. Out on the hills the foals tried practice leaps and fought among themselves while their dams looked on amusedly. When the warm rains fell, the horses and cows no longer sought the protection of the trees, but continued eating while the water streamed down their sides and made them as glossy as lacquer.

In Joseph's house there was a quiet preparation for the birth. Elizabeth worked on the layette for her baby, and the other women, well-knowing that this would be the chief child of the ranch and the inheritor of power, came to sit with her and to help. They lined a wash basket with quilted satin, and Joseph set it on rockers. They hemmed more rough diapers than one child could ever use. They made long baby-dresses and embroidered them. They told Elizabeth that she was having an easy time, for she was rarely ill; in fact, she grew more robust and happy as the time went by. Rama taught her how to quilt the cover for the lying-in bed, and Elizabeth made it as carefully as though it were to last her life, instead of being burned immediately after the child was born. Because this was Joseph's child, Rama added an unheard-of elegance. She made a thick velvet rope, with a loop on either end, to slip over the bed-posts. No other woman had pulled on anything but a twisted sheet during the bearing pains.

When warm weather came the women sat on the porch in the warm sun and went on with the sewing. They prepared everything months too soon. The heavy piece of unbleached muslin that was to bind Elizabeth's hips was made, and fringed and laid away. The small pillows stuffed with duck feathers and all the quilted coverlets were ready by the first of June.

And there was endless talk of babies—how they were born, and all the accidents that might occur, and how the memory of the pain fades from a woman's mind, and how boys differ from girls in their earliest habits. There was endless anecdote. Rama could recount stories of children born with tails, with extra limbs, with mouths in the middle of their backs; but these were not frightening because Rama knew why such things were. Some were the results of drink, and some of disease, but the worst, the very worst monstrosities came of conception during a menstrual period.

Joseph walked in sometimes with grass-blades in the laces of his shoes and green grass stains on the knees of his jeans and sweat still shining on his forehead. He stood stroking his beard and listening to the talk. Rama appealed to him occasionally for corroboration.

Joseph was working tremendously in the prodigal spring. He cut the bull calves, moved rocks out of the flowers' way, and went out with his new branding-iron to burn his "JW" into the skins of the stock. Thomas and Joseph worked silently together, stringing the barbed-wire fences out around the land, for it was easy to dig post-holes in a wet spring. Two more vaqueros were hired to take care of the increasing stock.

In June the first heat struck heavily and the grass responded and added a foot to its growth. But with the breathless days, Elizabeth grew sick and irritable. She made a list of things needed for the birth and gave it to Joseph. One morning before the sun was up he drove away in the buckboard to buy the things for her in San Luis Obispo. The trip and return required three days of traveling.

The moment he was gone, fears began to fall upon Elizabeth: Maybe he would be killed. The most unreasonable things seemed to possess verity. He might meet another woman and run off with her. The wagon might overturn in the white pass and throw him into the river.

She had not got up to see him off, but when the sun was up she dressed and went to sit on the porch. Everything irritated her, the noise of grasshoppers ticking as they flew, the pieces of rusty baling wire lying on the ground. The smell of ammonia from the barns nearly nauseated her. When she had seen and hated all the things close to her, she raised her eyes to the hills for more prey, and the first thing she saw was the pine grove on the ridge. Immediately a sharp nostalgia for Monterey assailed her, a homesickness for the dark trees of the peninsula, and for the little sunny streets and for the white houses and for the blue bay with colored fishing boats; but more than anything for the pines. The resinous odor of the needles seemed the most delicious thing in the world. She longed to smell it until her body ached with desire. And all the time she looked at the black pine grove on the ridge.

Gradually the desire changed until she wanted only the trees. They called down to her from their ridge, called for her to come in among the trunks, out of the sun, and to know the peace that lay in a pine forest. She could see herself, and even feel herself lying on a pine needle bed, looking up at the sky between the boughs, and she could hear how the wind would swish softly in the tops of the trees, and go flying away, laden with the pine scent.

Elizabeth stood up from the steps and walked slowly toward the barn. Someone was in there, for she could see forkfuls of manure come bursting through the windows. She walked into the dark sweet barn and approached Thomas. "I want to go for a little ride," she said. "Would you mind hitching up a buggy for me?"

He leaned on the manure-fork. "Will you wait half an hour? When I finish this I will drive you."

She was angry at his interference. "I want to drive myself, I want to be alone," she said shortly.

He regarded her quietly. "I don't know whether Joseph would like you to go out alone."

"But Joseph isn't here. I want to go."

He leaned his fork against the wall then. "All right, I'll hitch up old Moonlight. She's gentle. Don't go off the road, though, you might get stuck in the mud. It's still pretty deep in some of the hollows."

He helped her into the buggy and stood apprehensively watching her as she drove away.

Instinctively Elizabeth knew he didn't want her to go to the pines. She drove a good distance from the house before she turned the old white mare's head up the hill and went bumping over the uneven ground. The sun was very hot and the valley windless. She had driven a long way up the hill before a deep water-cut stopped her progress. In both directions the crevass extended, too far to go around, and the pines were only a short distance away. Elizabeth climbed from the buggy, snapped the tie-strap around a root and unhooked the check-rein. Then she clambered down into the cut and up the other side, and walked slowly toward the pine grove. In a moment she came upon a little twinkling stream that ran from the forest and flowed quietly because there were no stones to bar its way. She stooped and pulled a sprig of cress out of the water and nibbled it as she sauntered upward beside the stream.

All of her irritation was gone now; she went happily forward and entered the forest. The deep needle beds muffled her footsteps and the forest swallowed every other sound except the whispering of the needles in the tree-tops. For a few moments she walked on, unimpeded, and then the screen of vines and brambles barred her way. She turned her shoulder to them and forced a passage through, and sometimes she crawled through an opening on her hands and knees. There was a demand upon her that she penetrate deep into the forest.

Her hands were scratched and her hair pulled down when she came at last through the bramble wall and straightened up. Her eyes grew wide with wonder at the circle of trees and the clear flat place. And then her eyes swept to the huge, misshapen green rock.

She whispered to herself, "I think I knew it was here. Something in my breast told me it was here, this dear good thing." There was no sound at all in the place except the high whispering of the trees, and it was shut out, which only made the silence deeper, more impenetrable. The green moss covering of the rock was as thick as fur, and the long ferns hung down over the little cavern in its side like a green curtain. Elizabeth seated herself beside the tiny stream, slipping secretly away across the glade, and disappearing into the underbrush. Her eyes centered upon the rock and her mind wrestled with its suggestive shape. "Some place I've seen this thing," she thought. "I must have known it was here, else why did I come straight to it?" Her eyes widened as she watched the rock, and her mind lost all sharp thought and became thronged with slowly turning memories, untroubled, meaningless and vague. She saw herself starting out for Sunday School in Monterey, and then she saw a slow procession of white-dressed Portuguese children marching in honor of the Holy Ghost, with a crowned queen leading them. Vaguely she saw the waves driving in from seven different directions to meet and to convulse at Point Joe near Monterey. And then as she gazed at the rock she saw her own child curled headdownward in her womb, and she saw it stir slightly, and felt its movement at the same time.

Always the whispering went on over her head and she

could see out of the corners of her eyes how the black trees
crowded in and in on her. It came upon her as she sat there
that she was alone in all the world; every other person had
gone away and left her and she didn't care. And then it came
upon her that she could have anything she wished, and in the
train of this thought there came the fear that she most wished
for death, and after that, for a knowledge of her husband.

Her hand moved slowly from her lap and fell into the cold
water of the spring, and instantly the trees rushed back and
the low sky flew upward. The sun had leaped forward as she
sat there. There was a rustling in the forest now, not soft but
sharp and malicious. She looked quickly at the rock and saw
that its shape was as evil as a crouched animal and as gross as
a shaggy goat. A stealthy cold had crept into the glade. Elizabeth sprang to her feet in panic, and her hands rose up and
held her breasts. A vibration of horror was sweeping through
the glade. The black trees cut off escape. There was the great
rock crouching to spring. She backed away, fearing to take
her eyes from it. When she had reached the entrance of the
broad trail, she thought she saw a shaggy creature stir within
the cave. The whole glade was alive with fear. She turned and
ran down the trail, too frightened to scream, and she came,
after a great time, to the open, where the warm sun shone.

The forest closed behind her and left her free.

She sat down, exhausted, by the little stream; her heart
throbbed painfully and her breath came in gasps. She saw
how the stream gently moved the cress that grew in its water,
and she saw the mica specks glittering in the sand at the bottom. Then, turning for protection, she looked down on the
clustered farm buildings where they were drenched with sun,
and on the yellowing grass that bowed in long, flat silver
waves before the afternoon wind. These were safe things; she
was grateful for having seen them.

Before her fear was gone, she scrambled up to her knees to
pray. She tried to think what had happened in the glade, but
the memory of it was fading. "It was an old thing, so old that
I have nearly forgotten it." She recollected her posture, "It
was an unlawful thing." And she prayed, "Our Father which
art in Heaven, hallowed be Thy name—" And she prayed,
"Lord Jesus protect me from these forbidden things, and keep

me in the way of light and tenderness. Do not let this thing pass through me into my child, Lord Jesus. Guard me against the ancient things in my blood." She remembered how her father said his ancestors a thousand years ago followed the Druidic way.

When the prayer was done, she felt better. A clear light entered her mind again and drove out the fear, and with it, a memory of the fear. "It's my condition," she said. "I should have known. Nothing was in that place except my imagination. Rama has told me often enough what kind of things to expect."

She stood up then, reassured and comforted. And as she strolled down the hill she picked an armful of the late flowers to decorate the house against Joseph's return.

18

T HE SUMMER HEAT was very great. Every day the sun beat down on the valley, sucking the moisture from the earth, drying the grass and causing every living thing to seek the deep shade of the sage thickets on the hills. All day the horses and cattle lay there, waiting for the night so they might come out for their feeding. The ranch dogs sprawled on the ground, with their quivering dripping tongues falling out of the sides of their mouths and their chests pumping like bellows. Even the noisy insects let the middle of the day be silent. At the meridian there was only a faint whine of rocks and earth, too fiercely scorched. The river receded until it was only a little stream, and when August came, even that disappeared.

Thomas was cutting the hay and shocking it to cure, while Joseph picked out the cattle for sale and drove them into the new corral. Burton prepared for his trip to Pacific Grove to attend the camp-meetings. He piled a tent, utensils, bedding and food in the buckboard, and one morning he and his wife set out behind two good horses to drive the ninety miles to the camp-ground. Rama had agreed to take care of his children for the three weeks of his absence.

Elizabeth came out to wave him off, and she was glowing with health again. After her little spell of illness, she had grown beautiful and well. Her cheeks were red with coursing blood and her eyes shone with a mysterious happiness. Often Joseph, watching her, wondered what she knew or what she thought to make her seem always on the verge of laughter. "She knows something," he said to himself. "Women in this condition have a strong warmth of God in them. They must know things no one else knows. And they must feel a joy beyond any other joy. In some way they take up the nerve-ends of the earth in their hands." Joseph regarded her narrowly, and stroked his beard as slowly as an old man would.

With her coming time, Elizabeth grew increasingly possessive of her husband. She wanted him to sit with her all day and all evening, and she complained a little when he told her of the work to be done. "I'm idle here," she said. "Idleness loves company."

And he replied, "No, you're working." He could see in his mind how she was doing it. Her helpless hands lay crossed in her lap, but her bones were casting bones and her blood was distilling blood and her flesh was moulding flesh. He laughed shortly at the thought that she was idle.

In the evenings when she demanded that he sit with her, she put out her arm to be stroked. "I'm afraid you'll go away," she said. "You might go out by that door and never come back, and then there'd be no father for the baby."

One day when they were sitting on the porch she asked abruptly, "Why do you love the tree so much, Joseph? Remember how you made me sit in it the first time I ever came out here?" She looked up to the high crotch where she had sat.

"Why, it's a fine big tree," he explained slowly. "I like it because it's a perfect tree, I guess."

She caught him up, then. "Joseph, there's more than that. One night I heard you speak to it as though it were a person. You called it 'sir', I heard you."

He looked fixedly at the tree before he answered, and then after a while he told her how his father had died wanting to come West, and he told her about the morning when the letter came. "It's a kind of a game, you see," he said. "It gives me a feeling that I have my father yet."

She turned her wide-set eyes on him, eyes full of the wisdom of child bearing. "It isn't a game, Joseph," she said gently. "You couldn't play a game if you wanted to. No, it isn't a game, but it's a good practice." And for the first time she saw into her husband's mind; all in a second she saw the shapes of his thoughts, and he knew that she saw them. The emotion rushed to his throat. He leaned to kiss her, but instead, his forehead fell upon her knees, and his chest filled to breaking.

She stroked his hair and smiled her wise smile. "You should have let me see before." And then she said, "But likely I hadn't proper eyes before."

When he lay with her at night and she rested her head on his arm for a little time before they went to sleep, she begged night after night to be reassured. "When my time comes,

Joseph, you'll stay with me? I'm afraid I'll be afraid. I'm afraid I'll call and you won't be near. You won't be far away, will you? And if I call, you'll come?"

And he assured her, a little grimly, "I'll be with you, Elizabeth. Don't be worried about that."

"But not in the same room, Joseph. I wouldn't like you to see it. I don't know why. If you could be sitting in the other room and listening in case I should call, then I don't think I'd be afraid at all."

Sometimes in these nights in bed she told him of the things she knew, how the Persians invaded Greece and were beaten, and how Orestes came to the tripod for protection, and the Furies sat waiting for him to get hungry and let go his hold. She told them laughingly, all her little bits of knowledge that were designed to make her superior. All of her knowledge seemed very silly to her now.

She began to count the weeks until her time—three weeks from Thursday; and then two weeks and one day; and then, just ten days off. "This is Friday. Why, Joseph, it will be on a Sunday. I hope it will. Rama has listened. She says she can even hear the heartbeats. Would you believe that?"

One night she said, "It'll be just about a week now. I get little shivers when I think about it."

Joseph slept very lightly. When Elizabeth sighed in her sleep, his eyes opened and he listened uneasily.

One morning he awakened when the chorus of young roosters crowed on their perches. It was still dark, but the air was alive with the coming dawn and with the freshness of the morning. He heard the older cocks crowing with full rounded notes as though reproving the younger ones for their cracked thin voices. Joseph lay with his eyes open and saw the myriad points of light come in and make the air dark grey. Gradually the furniture began to appear. Elizabeth was breathing shortly in her sleep. A slight catch was in her breath. Joseph prepared to slip out of the bed, to dress and to go out to the horses, when suddenly Elizabeth sprang upright beside him. Her breath stopped and then her legs stiffened and she screamed with pain.

"What is it?" he cried. "What's the matter, dear?"

When she didn't answer he jumped up and lighted the lamp

and bent over her. Her eyes were bulging and her mouth had dropped open and her whole body quivered tensely. Then she screamed hoarsely again. He fell to rubbing her hands, until, after a moment, she dropped back on the pillow.

"There's a pain in my back, Joseph," she moaned. "Something's wrong. I'm going to die."

He said, "Just a moment, dear. I'm going for Rama," and he ran out of the room.

Rama, aroused from sleep, smiled gravely. "Go back to her," she commanded. "I'll be right over. It's a little sooner than I thought. She'll be all right for a while now."

"But hurry," he demanded.

"There's no hurry. You'll start walking her right away. I'll get Alice to help now."

The dawn was flushing when the two women came across the yard, their arms full of clean rags. Rama took charge immediately. Elizabeth, still shocked by the sharpness of the pain, looked helplessly at her.

"It's all right," Rama reassured her. "It's just as it should be." She sent Alice to the kitchen to build a fire and to heat a wash-boiler of water. "Now Joseph, help her to her feet, help her to walk." And while he walked her back and forth across the room, Rama slipped the covers from the bed and put the quilted birth pad down and hooked the loops of the velvet rope over the foot posts. When the blighting pain struck again, they let her sit in a straight chair until it was over. Elizabeth tried not to scream, until Rama leaned over her and said, "Don't hold it in. There's no need. Everything you feel like doing is needful now."

Joseph, with his arm around her waist, walked her back and forth across the room, supporting her when she stumbled. He had lost his fear. There was a fierce glad light in his eyes. The pains came closer and closer together. Rama brought the big Seth Thomas clock in from the sitting-room and hung it on the wall, and she looked at it every time the pains came. And the pains grew closer and closer together. The hours passed.

It was nearly noon when Rama nodded her head sharply. "Now let her lie down. You can go out now, Joseph. I'll be getting my hands ready."

He looked at her with half-closed eyes. He seemed entranced. "What do you mean, 'getting your hands ready'?" he demanded.

"Why washing and washing in hot water and soap, and cutting the nails close."

"I'll do it," he said.

"It's time for you to go, Joseph. The time is short."

"No," he said sullenly. "I'll take my own child. You tell me what to do."

"You can't, Joseph. It's not a thing for a man to do."

He looked gravely at her, and her will gave away before his calm. "It's a thing for me to do," he said.

As soon as the sun had risen the children congregated outside the bedroom window, where they stood listening to Elizabeth's weak screaming, and shivering with interest. Martha took charge from the first. "Sometimes they die," she said.

Although the morning sun beat fiercely upon them, they did not leave their post. Martha laid down the rules. "First one that hears the baby cry says, 'I hear it!' and that one gets a present, and that one gets the first baby. Mother told me." The others were very much excited. They cried in unison, "I hear it," every time a new series of screams began. Martha made them help her to climb up where she could peek quickly into the window. "Uncle Joseph is walking with her," she reported. And later, "Now she's lying on the bed and she's holding the red rope that mother made."

The screams grew ever closer together. The other children helped Martha to look again, and she came down a little pale and choking at what she had seen. They gathered close about her for the report. "I saw—Uncle Joseph—and he was leaning over—" She paused to get her breath. "And—and his hands were *red*." She fell silent and all the children stared at her in amazement. There wasn't any more talking or whispering. They simply stood and listened. The screams were so weak by now that they could barely hear them.

Martha wore a secret look. She cautioned the others to silence in a whisper. They heard three faint smacks, and instantly Martha cried, "I hear it." And even a little after, they all heard the baby cry. They stood in awe, looking at Martha.

"How did you know when to say it?"

Martha was tantalizing. "I'm the oldest, and I've been good for a long time. And mother told me how to listen."

"How?" they demanded. "How did you listen?"

"For the spank!" she said in triumph. "They always spank the baby to make it cry. I won, and I want a hair-doll for a present."

A little later Joseph came out on the porch and leaned over the porch-rail. The children moved over and stood in front of him and looked up. They were disappointed that his hands were not still red. His face was so drawn and haggard and his eyes so listless that they hated to speak to him.

Martha began, lamely, "I heard the first cry," she said. "I want a hair-doll for a present."

He looked down on them and smiled slightly. "I'll get it for you," he said. "I'll have presents for all of you when I go to town."

Martha asked politely, "Is it a boy-baby, or a girl-baby?"

"A boy," Joseph said. "Maybe you can see it after a while." His hands were clenched tightly over the porch-rail, and his stomach still racked with the pains he had received from Elizabeth. He took a deep breath of the hot midday air and went back into the house.

Rama was washing out the baby's toothless mouth with warm water while Alice set the safety pins in the strip of muslin that would bind Elizabeth's hips after the placenta came. "Only a little while yet," Rama said. "It will be over in an hour."

Joseph sat heavily in a chair and watched the women, and he watched the dull, pained eyes of Elizabeth, filled with suffering. The baby lay in its basket-crib, dressed in a gown twice as long as itself.

When the birth was all over, Joseph lifted Elizabeth and held her in his lap while the women took up the foul birth pad and made the bed again. Alice took out all the rags and burned them in the kitchen stove, and Rama pinned the bandage around Elizabeth's hips as tightly as she could pull it.

Elizabeth lay wanly in the clean bed after the women had gone. She put out her hand for Joseph to take. "I've been dreaming," she said weakly. "Here's a whole day gone and I've been dreaming."

He caressed her fingers, one at a time. "Would you like me to bring the baby to you?"

Her forehead wrinkled in a tired frown. "Not yet," she said. "I still hate it for making so much pain. Wait until I've rested a while." Soon after that she fell asleep.

Late in the afternoon Joseph walked out to the barn. He barely looked at the tree as he passed it. "You are the cycle," he said to himself, "and the cycle is too cruel." He found the barn carefully cleaned, and every stall deep with new straw. Thomas was sitting in his usual place, on the manger of Blue's stall. He nodded shortly to Joseph.

"My coyote bitch has a tick in her ear," he observed. "Devil of a place to get it out."

Joseph walked into the stall and sat down beside his brother. He rested his chin heavily in his cupped hands.

"What luck?" Thomas asked gently.

Joseph stared at a sun-sheet cutting the air from a crack in the barn wall. The flies blazed through it like meteors plunging into the earth's air. "It is a boy," he said absently. "I cut the cord myself. Rama told me how. I cut it with a pair of scissors and I tied a knot, and I bound it up against his chest with a bandage."

"Was it a hard birth?" Thomas asked. "I came out here to keep from going in to help."

"Yes, it was hard, and Rama said it was easy. God, how the little things fight against life!"

Thomas plucked a straw from the rack behind him and stripped it with his bared teeth. "I never saw a human baby born. Rama would never let me. I've helped many a cow when she couldn't help herself."

Joseph moved restlessly down from the manger and walked to one of the little windows. He said over his shoulder, "It's been a hot day. The air's dancing over the hills yet." The sun, sinking behind the hills, was melting out of shape. "Thomas, we've never been over the ridge to the coast. Let's go when we have time. I'd like to see the ocean over there."

"I've been to the ridge and looked down," Thomas said. "It's wild over there, redwoods taller than anything you ever saw, and thick undergrowth, and you can see a thousand miles out on the ocean. I saw a little ship going by, half-way up the ocean."

The evening was setting quickly toward night. Rama called, "Joseph, where are you?"

He walked quickly to the barn door. "I'm here. What is it?"

"Elizabeth is awake again. She wants you to sit with her a while. Thomas, your dinner will be ready in a little."

Joseph sat beside Elizabeth's bed in the half-dark, and again she put out her hand to him. "You wanted me?" he asked.

"Yes, dear. I haven't slept enough, but I want to talk to you before I go to sleep again. I might forget what it is I want to say. You must remember for me."

It was getting dark in the room. Joseph lifted her hand to his lips and she wriggled her fingers slightly against his mouth.

"What is it, Elizabeth?"

"Well, when you were away, I drove up to the pine grove on the ridge. And I found a clear place inside, and a green rock in the place."

He sat forward tensely. "Why did you go?" he demanded.

"I don't know. I wanted to. The green rock frightened me, and later I dreamed of it. And Joseph, when I am well, I want to go back and look at the rock again. When I am well it won't frighten me any more, and I won't dream about it any more. Will you remember, dear? You're hurting my fingers, Joseph."

"I know the place," he said. "It's a strange place."

"And you won't forget to take me there?"

"No," he said after a pause. "I won't forget. I'll have to think whether you should go."

"Then sit for a while, I'll go to sleep in a few moments," she said.

19

THE SUMMER dragged wearily on, and even when the autumn months came the heat did not grow less. Burton came back exalted from the camp-meeting town of Pacific Grove. He described with enthusiasm the lovely peninsula and the blue bay, and he told how the preachers had given the word to the people. "Some time," he said to Joseph, "I'll go up there and build a little house, and I'll live there all the year around. A number of people are settling there. It will be a fine town some day."

He was pleased with the baby. "It's our stock," he said, "just a little changed." And he boasted to Elizabeth, "Ours is a strong stock. It comes out every time. For nearly two hundred years now the boys have had those eyes."

"They aren't far from the color of my eyes," Elizabeth protested. "And besides, babies' eyes change color as they get older."

"It's the expression," Burton explained. "There's always the Wayne expression in the eyes. When will you have him baptized?"

"Oh, I don't know. Maybe we'll be going to San Luis Obispo before very long, and of course I'd like to go home to Monterey for a visit some time."

The day's heat came early over the mountains and drove the chickens from their morning talking on manure piles. By eleven it was unpleasant to be out in the sun, but before eleven, Joseph and Elizabeth often took chairs out of the house and sat under the shading limbs of the great oak. Elizabeth engaged in the morning nursing then, for Joseph liked to watch the baby sucking at the breast.

"It doesn't grow as fast as I thought it would," he complained.

"You're too used to the cattle," she reminded him. "They grow so much more quickly, and they don't live very long."

Joseph silently contemplated his wife. "She's grown so wise," he thought. "Without any study she has learned so many things." It puzzled him. "Do you feel very much different from the girl who came to teach school in Nuestra Señora?" he asked.

She laughed. "Do I seem different, Joseph?"

"Why, of course."

"Then I suppose I am." She changed the breast and shifted the baby to the other knee, and he struck hungrily at the nipple, like a trout at a bait. "I'm split up," Elizabeth went on. "I hadn't really thought of it. I used to think in terms of things I had read. I never do now. I don't think at all. I just do things that occur to me. What will his name be, Joseph?"

"Why," he said, "I guess it will be John. There has always been either a Joseph or a John. John has always been the son of Joseph, and Joseph the son of John. It has always been that way."

She nodded, and her eyes looked far away. "Yes, it's a good name. It won't ever give him any trouble or make him embarrassed. It hasn't even much meaning. There have been so many Johns—all kinds of men, good and bad." She took the breast away and buttoned her dress, and then turned the baby to pat the air bubbles out of him. "Have you noticed, Joseph, Johns are either good or bad, never neutral? If a neutral boy has that name, he doesn't keep it. He becomes Jack." She turned the baby around, to look in its face, and it squinted its eyes like a little pig. "Your name is John, do you hear?" she said playfully. "Do you hear that? I hope it never gets to be Jack. I'd rather you were very bad than Jack."

Joseph smiled amusedly at her. "He has never sat in the tree, dear. Don't you think it's about time?"

"Always your tree!" she said. "You think everything moves by order of your tree."

He leaned back to look up into the great tender branches. "I know it now, you see," he said softly. "I know it now so well that I can look at the leaves and tell what kind of a day it will be. I'll make a seat for the baby up in the crotch. When he's a little older I may cut steps in the bark for him to climb on."

"But he might fall and hurt himself."

"Not from that tree. It wouldn't let him fall."

She looked penetratingly at him. "Still playing the game that isn't a game, Joseph?"

"Yes," he said, "still playing. Give the baby to me now. I'll put him in the arms." The leaves had lost their shine under a coat of summer dust. The bark was pale gray and dry.

"He might fall, Joseph," she warned him. "You forget he can't sit up by himself."

Burton strolled up from the vegetable-patch and stood with them, wiping his wet forehead with a bandana. "The melons are ripe," he said. "The 'coons are getting at them, too. We'd better set some traps."

Joseph leaned toward Elizabeth with his hands out-stretched.

"But he might fall," she protested.

"I'll hold him. I won't let him fall."

"What are you going to do with him?" Burton asked.

"Joseph wants to sit him in the tree."

Instantly Burton's face grew hard, and his eyes sullen. "Don't do it, Joseph," he said harshly. "You must not do it."

"I won't let him fall. I'll hold him all the time."

The perspiration stood in large drops on Burton's forehead. Into his eyes there came a look of horror and of pleading. He stepped forward and put a restraining hand on Joseph's shoulder. "Please don't do it," he begged.

"But I won't let him fall, I tell you."

"It isn't that. You know what I mean. Swear to me that you won't ever do it."

Joseph turned on him irritably. "I'll swear nothing," he said. "Why should I swear? I see nothing wrong in what I do."

Burton said quietly, "Joseph, you have never heard me beg for anything. It isn't the manner of our family to beg. But now I am begging you to give up this thing. If I am willing to do that, you must see how important it is." His eyes were wet with emotion.

Joseph's face softened. "If it bothers you so much, I won't do it," he said.

"And will you swear never to do it?"

"No, I won't swear. I won't give up my thing to your thing. Why should I?"

"Because you're letting evil in," Burton cried passionately. "Because you are opening the door to evil. A thing like this will not go unpunished."

Joseph laughed. "Then let me take the punishment," he said.

"But don't you see, Joseph, it isn't only you! All of us will be in the ruin."

"You're protecting yourself, then, Burton?"

"No I'm trying to protect all of us. I'm thinking of the baby, and of Elizabeth here."

Elizabeth had been staring from one to the other of them. She stood up and held the baby against her breast. "What are you two arguing about?" she demanded. "There's something in this I don't know about."

"I'll tell her," Burton threatened.

"Tell her what? What is there to tell?"

Burton sighed deeply. "On your head, then. Elizabeth, my brother is denying Christ. He is worshipping as the old pagans did. He is losing his soul and letting in the evil."

"I'm denying no Christ," Joseph said sharply. "I'm doing a simple thing that pleases me."

"Then the hanging of sacrifices, the pouring of blood, the offering of every good thing to this tree is a simple thing? I've seen you sneak out of the house at night, and I've heard you talk to this tree. Is that a simple thing?"

"Yes, a simple thing," Joseph said. "There's no hurt in it."

"And the offering of your own first-born child to the tree—is that a simple thing, too?"

"Yes, a little game."

Burton turned away and looked out over the land, where the heat waves were so intense that they were blue in color and their twisting made the hills seem to writhe and shudder. "I've tried to help you," he said sadly. "I've tried harder than Scripture tells us to." He swung back fiercely. "You won't swear, then?"

"No," Joseph replied. "I won't swear to anything that limits me, that cuts down my activity. Surely I won't swear."

"Then I cast you out." Burton's hands hid in his pockets. "Then I won't stay to be involved."

"Is what he says true?" Elizabeth asked. "Have you been doing what he says?"

Joseph gazed moodily at the ground. "I don't know." His hand arose to caress his beard. "I don't think so. It doesn't sound like the thing I have been doing."

"I've seen him," Burton cut in. "Night after night I've seen him come out into the dark under the tree. I've done what I can. Now I am going away from this wrong."

"Where will you go, Burton?" Joseph asked.

"Harriet has three thousand dollars. We'll go to Pacific Grove and build a house there. I'll sell my part of the ranch. Maybe I'll open a little store. That town will grow, I tell you."

Joseph stepped forward, as though to intercept his resolve. "I'll be sorry to think I've driven you away," he said.

Burton stood over Elizabeth and looked down at the child. "It isn't only you, Joseph. The rot was in our father, and it was not dug out. It grew until it possessed him. His dying words showed how far he had gone. I saw the thing even before you ever started for the West. If you had gone among people who knew the Word and were strong in the Word, the thing might have died—but you came here." His hands swept out to indicate the country. "The mountains are too high," he cried. "The place is too savage. And all the people carry the seed of this evil thing in them. I've seen them, and I know. I saw the fiesta, and I know. I can only pray that your son will not inherit the rot."

Joseph resolved quickly. "I will swear if you will stay. I don't know how I'll keep it, but I'll swear. Sometimes, you see, I might forget and think in the old way."

"No, Joseph, you love the earth too much. You give no thought to the hereafter. The force of an oath is not strong in you." He moved away toward his house.

"Don't go at least until we talk this over," Joseph called, but Burton did not turn nor answer him.

Joseph looked after him for a minute before he turned back to Elizabeth. She was smiling with a kind of contemptuous amusement. "I think he wants to go," she said.

"Yes, that's partly it. And he really is afraid of my sins, too."

"Are you sinning, Joseph?" she asked.

He scowled in thought. "No," he said at last. "I'm not sinning. If Burton were doing what I am, it would be sin. I only want my son to love the tree." He stretched out his hands for the baby, and Elizabeth put the swathed little body in his hands. Burton looked back as he was entering his house, and he saw that Joseph was holding the baby within the crotch of the tree, and he saw how the gnarled limbs curved up protectingly about it.

20

BURTON did not stay long on the ranch after his mind was made up. Within a week he had his things packed and ready. On the night before his departure he worked late, nailing the last of the boxes. Joseph heard him walking about in the night, chopping and hammering, and before daylight he was up again. Joseph found him in the barn, currying the horses he was to take, while Thomas sat nearby on a pile of hay and offered some short advice.

"That Bill will tire soon. Let him rest every little while until he gets well warm. This team has never been through the pass. You may have to lead them through—but maybe not, now that the water is so low."

Joseph strolled in and leaned against the wall, under the lantern. "I'm sorry you're going, Burton," he said.

Burton arrested his curry-comb on the horse's broad rump. "There are a good many reasons for going. Harriet will be happier in a little town where she can have friends to drop in on. We were too cut off out here. Harriet has been lonely."

"I know," Joseph said gently, "but we'll miss you, Burton. It will cut the strength of the family."

Burton dropped his eyes uneasily and went back to currying. "I've never wanted to be a farmer," he said lamely. "Even at home I thought of opening a little store in town." His hands stopped working. He said passionately, "I've tried to lead an acceptable life. What I have done I have done because it seemed to me to be right. There is only one law. I have tried to live in that law. What I have done seems right to me, Joseph. Remember that. I want you to remember that."

Joseph smiled affectionately at him. "I'm not trying to keep you here if you want to go, Burton. This is a wild country. If you do not love it, there's only hatred left. You've had no church to go to. I don't blame you for wanting to be among people who carry your own thoughts."

Burton moved to the next stall. "It's turning light," he said nervously. "Harriet is getting breakfast. I want to start as soon after daylight as I can."

The families and the riders came out into the dawn to watch Burton start away.

"You'll come to see us," Harriet called sadly. "It's nice up there. You must come to visit us."

Burton took up the lines, but before he clucked to the horses, he turned to Joseph. "Good-bye. I've done right. When you come to see it, you'll know it was right. It was the only way. Remember that, Joseph. When you come to see it, you'll thank me."

Joseph moved close to the wagon and patted his brother's shoulder. "I offered to swear, and I would have tried to keep the oath."

Burton raised the lines and clucked. The horses strained into the collars. The children, sitting on the load, waved their hands, and those who were to stay ran behind and hung to the tail-board and dragged their feet.

Rama stood waving a handkerchief, but she said aside to Elizabeth, "They wear out more shoes that way than by all the walking in the world."

Still the family stood in the morning sunlight and watched the departing wagon. It disappeared into the river wood, and after a while it came in sight again, and they saw it mount a little hill and finally drop from sight over the ridge.

When it was gone a listlessness came over the families. They stood silently, wondering what they should do now. They were conscious that a period was over, that a phase was past. At length the children moved slowly away.

Martha said, "Our dog had puppies last night," and they all ran to see the dog, which hadn't had puppies at all.

Joseph turned away at last, and Thomas walked with him. "I'm going to bring in some horses, Joe," he said. "I'm going to level part of the vegetable-flat so the water won't all run off."

Joseph walked slowly, with his head down. "You know I'm responsible for Burton's going."

"No you aren't. He wanted to go."

"It was because of the tree," Joseph went on. "He said I worshipped it." Joseph's eyes raised to the tree, and suddenly he stood still, startled. "Thomas, look at the tree!"

"I see it. What's the matter?"

Joseph walked hurriedly to the trunk and looked up at the branches. "Why, it seems all right." He paused and ran his hand over the bark. "That was funny. When I looked at it, I thought something was wrong with it. It was just a feeling, I guess." And he continued, "I didn't want Burton to go away. It splits the family."

Elizabeth passed behind them, toward the house. "Still at the game, Joseph?" she called mockingly.

He jerked his hand from the bark and turned to follow her. "We'll try to get along without another hand," he told Thomas. "If the work gets too much for us, I'll hire another Mexican." He went into the house and stood idly in the sitting-room.

Elizabeth came out of the bedroom, brushing her hair back with her fingertips. "I hardly had time to dress," she explained. She looked quickly at Joseph. "Are you feeling badly about having Burton go?"

"I think I am," he said uncertainly. "I'm worried about something, and I don't know what it is."

"Why don't you ride? Haven't you anything to do?"

He shook his head impatiently. "I have fruit trees coming to Nuestra Señora. I should go in for them."

"Why don't you go, then?"

He walked to the front door and looked out at the tree. "I don't know," he said. "I'm afraid to go. There's something wrong."

Elizabeth stood beside him. "Don't play your game too hard, Joseph. Don't let the game take you in."

He shrugged his shoulders. "That's what I'm doing, I guess. I told you once I could tell weather by the tree. It's a kind of ambassador between the land and me. Look at the tree, Elizabeth! Does it seem all right to you?"

"You're overwrought," she said. "The tree is all right. Go in and get the fruit trees. It won't do them any good to be standing out of ground."

But it was with a powerful reluctance to leave the ranch that he hitched up the buckboard and drove to town.

It was the time of flies, when they became active before the winter death. They cut dazzling slashes in the sunlight, landed on the horses' ears and sat in circles around their eyes. Although the morning had been cool with the sharpness of autumn, the Indian-summer sun still burned the land. The river had disappeared underground, while in the few deep pools that remained, the black eels swam sluggishly and big trout mouthed the surface without fear.

Joseph drove his team at a trot over the crisp sycamore leaves. A foreboding followed him and enveloped him. "Maybe Burton was right," he thought. "Maybe I've been doing wrong without knowing it. There's an evil hanging over the land." And he thought, "I hope the rain comes early and starts the river again."

The dry river was a sad thing to him. To defeat the sadness he thought of the barn, piled to the rooftrees with hay, and of the haystacks by the corral, all thatched against the winter. And then he wondered whether the little stream in the pine grove still ran from its cave. "I'll go up and see pretty soon," he thought. He drove quickly, and hurried back to the ranch, but it was late at night when he arrived. The tired horses hung down their heads when the check-reins were loosened.

Thomas was waiting at the stable entrance. "You drove too fast," he said. "I didn't expect you back for a couple of hours."

"Put up the horses, will you?" Joseph asked. "I'll pump some water on these little trees." He carried an armload of the switches to the tank and saturated their burlap root-coverings with water. And then he went quickly toward the oak tree. "There *is* something wrong with it," he thought fearfully. "There's no life in it." He felt the bark again, picked off a leaf, crumpled and smelled it, and nothing appeared wrong.

Elizabeth had his supper ready almost as soon as he went into the house. "You look tired, dear. Go to bed early."

But he looked over his shoulder with worried eyes. "I want to talk to Thomas after supper," he said.

And when he had done eating, he walked out past the barn and up on the hillside. He felt with his palms the dry earth, still warm from the day's sun. And he walked to a copse of little live oaks and rested his hands on the bark and crushed and smelled a leaf of each. Everywhere he went, inquiring with his fingers after the earth's health. The cold was coming in over the mountains, chilling the grasses, and on this night Joseph heard the first flight of wild geese.

The earth told him nothing. It was dry but alive, needing only the rain to make it shoot its spears of green. At last, satisfied, he walked back to the house and stood under his own tree. "I was afraid, sir," he said. "Something in the air made me afraid." And as he stroked the bark, suddenly he felt cold and lonely. "This tree is dead," his mind cried. "There's no life in my tree." The sense of loss staggered him, and all the sorrow he should have felt when his father died rolled in on him. The black mountains surrounded him, and the cold grey sky and the unfriendly stars shut him down, and the land stretched out from the center where he stood. It was all hostile, not ready to attack but aloof and silent and cold. Joseph sat at the foot of the tree, and not even the hard bark held any comfort for him. It was as hostile as the rest of the earth, as frigid and contemptuous as the corpse of a friend.

"Now what will I do?" he thought. "Where will I go now?" A white meteor flared into the air and burned up. "Perhaps I'm wrong," Joseph thought. "The tree may be all right after all." He stood up and went into the house; and that night, because of his loneliness, he held Elizabeth so fiercely in his arms that she cried out in pain and was very glad.

"Why are you so lonely, dear?" she asked. "Why do you hurt me tonight?"

"I didn't know I was hurting you, I am sorry," he said. "I think my tree is dead."

"How could it be dead? Trees don't die so quickly, Joseph."

"I don't know how. I think it is dead."

She lay quietly after a while, pretending to be asleep. And she knew he was not sleeping.

When the dawn came he slipped out of bed and went outside. The oak leaves were a little shriveled and some of their glossiness was gone.

Thomas, on his way to the stable, saw Joseph and walked over. "By George, there is something wrong with that tree," he said. Joseph watched anxiously while he inspected the bark and the limbs. "Nothing to kill it here," Thomas said. He picked up a hoe and dug into the soft earth at the base of the trunk. Only two stokes he made, and then stepped back. "There it is, Joseph."

Joseph knelt down beside the hole and saw a chopped path on the trunk. "What did it?" he demanded angrily.

Thomas laughed brutally. "Why, Burton girdled your tree! He's keeping the devil out."

Joseph frantically dug around with his fingers until the whole path of the girdle was exposed. "Can't we do something, Thomas? Wouldn't tar help it?"

Thomas shook his head. "The veins are cut. There's nothing to do," he paused,—"except beat Hell out of Burton."

Joseph sat back on his heels. Now that it was done, the muffling calm settled over him, the blind inability to judge. "That was what he was talking about, then, about being right?"

"I guess it was. I'd like to beat Hell out of him. That was a fine tree."

Joseph spoke very slowly, as though he pulled each word out of a swirling mist. "He wasn't sure he was right. No, he wasn't sure. It wasn't quite his nature to do this thing. And so he will suffer for it."

"Won't you do anything at all to him?" Thomas demanded.

"No." The calm and the sorrow were so great that they bore down on his chest, and the loneliness was complete, a circle impenetrable. "He will punish himself. I have no punishments." His eyes went to the tree, still green, but dead. After a long time he turned his head and looked up to the pine grove on the ridge, and he thought, "I must go there soon. I'll be needing the sweetness and the strength of that place."

21

THE COLD of late autumn came into the valley, and the high brindled clouds hung in the air for days at a time. Elizabeth felt the golden sadness of the approaching winter, but there was missing the excitement of the storms. She went often to the porch to look at the oak tree. The leaves were all pale tan by now, waiting only the buffeting of rain to fall to the ground. Joseph did not look at the tree any more. When its life was gone, no remnant of his feeling for it remained. He walked often in the brittle grass of the side-hills. He went bareheaded, wearing jeans and a shirt and a black vest. Often he looked up at the grey clouds and sniffed at the air and found nothing in the air to reassure him. "There's no rain in these clouds," he told Thomas. "This is a high fog from the ocean."

Thomas had caught two baby hawks in the spring and he was making hoods for them and preparing to fly them against the wild ducks that whistled down the sky. "It isn't time, Joseph," he said. "Last year the rains came early, I know, but I've heard it isn't usual in this country to get much rain before Christmas."

Joseph stooped and picked up a handful of ash-dry dust and let it trickle through his fingers. "It'll take a lot of rain to do any good," he complained. "The summer drank the water out deep down. Have you noticed how low the water is in the well? Even the potholes in the river are dry now."

"I've smelled the dead eels," Thomas said. "Look! This little leather cap goes on the hawk's head to keep him blind until I'm ready to start him. It's better than shooting ducks." The hawk gashed at his thick gloves while he fitted the leather hood on its head.

When November came and went without rain, Joseph grew quiet with worry. He rode to the springs and found them dried up, and he drove his post-hole digger deep into the ground without finding damp soil. The hills were turning grey as the covering of grass wore off, and the white flints stuck out and caught the light. When December was half gone, the clouds broke and scattered. The sun grew warm and an apparition of summer came to the valley.

Elizabeth saw how the worry was making Joseph thin, how his eyes were strained and almost white. She tried to find tasks to keep him busy. She needed new cupboard space, new clothes lines; it was time a high-chair was made ready for the baby. Joseph went about the tasks and finished them before Elizabeth could think of new ones. She sent him to town for supplies, and he returned on a wet and panting horse.

"Why do you rush back?" she demanded.

"I don't know. I'm afraid to go away. Something might happen." Slowly in his mind there was arising the fear that the dry years had come. The dusty air and the high barometer did not reassure him. Head colds broke out among the people on the ranch. The children sniffled all day long. Elizabeth developed a hard cough, and even Thomas, who was never sick, wore a cold compress made of a black stocking on his throat at night. But Joseph grew leaner and harder. The muscles of his neck and jaws stood out under a thin covering of brown skin. His hands grew restless, went to playing with pieces of stick, or with a pocket-knife, or worked interminably at his beard, smoothing it down and turning the ends under.

He looked about his land and it seemed to be dying. The pale hills and fields, the dust-grey sage, the naked stones frightened him. On the hills only the black pine grove did not change. It brooded darkly, as always, on the ridge top.

Elizabeth was very busy in the house. Alice had gone home to Nuestra Señora to take up her rightful position as a sad woman whose husband would return some day. She carried the affair with dignity, and her mother received compliments upon Alice's fine restraint and decent mourning. Alice began every day as though Juanito would return by evening.

The loss of her helper made more work for Elizabeth. Caring for her child, washing and cooking filled her days. She remembered the time before her marriage only hazily, and with a good deal of contempt. In the evenings, when she sat with Joseph, she tried to reestablish the fine contact she had made before the baby was born. She liked to tell him things that had happened when she was a little girl in Monterey, although the things didn't seem real to her any more. While Joseph stared moodily at the spots of fire that showed through the little windows of the stove, she talked to him.

"I had a dog," she said. "His name was Camille. I used to think that was the loveliest name in the world. I knew a little girl who was named Camille, and the name fitted her. She had a skin with the softness of camellias, so I named my dog after her, and she was very angry." Elizabeth told how Tarpey shot a squatter and was hanged to the limb of a tree on the fish flats; and she told of the lean stern woman who kept the lighthouse at Point Joe. Joseph liked to hear her soft voice, and he didn't usually listen to her words, but he took her hand and explored it all over with his fingertips.

Sometimes she tried to argue him out of his fear. "Don't worry about the rain. It will come. Even if there isn't much water this year, there will be in another year. I know this country, dear."

"But it would take so much rain. There won't be time if it doesn't start pretty soon. The rain will get behind in the year."

One evening she said, "I think I'd like to ride again. Rama says it won't hurt me now. Will you ride with me, dear?"

"Of course," he said. "Begin a little at a time. Then it won't hurt you."

"I'd like to have you ride up to the pines with me. The smell of pines would be good."

He looked slowly over at her. "I've thought of going there, too. There's a spring in the grove, and I want to see if it is dried up like all the rest." His eyes grew more animated as he thought of the circle in the pines. The rock had been so green when he saw it last. "That must be a deep spring, I don't see how it could dry up," he said.

"Oh I have more reasons than that for wanting to go," she said laughing. "I think I told you something about it. When I was carrying the baby I deceived Thomas one day and drove up to the pines. And I went into that central place where the big rock is, and where the spring is." She frowned, trying to remember the thing exactly. "Of course," she said, "my condition was responsible for what happened. I was over-sensitive."

She glanced up to find Joseph eagerly looking at her. "Yes?" he said. "Tell me."

"Well, as I say, it was my condition. When I was carrying the child, little things grew huge. I didn't find the path, going in. I broke my way through the underbrush, and then I came into the circle. It was quiet, Joseph, more quiet than anything I've ever known. I sat in front of the rock because that place seemed saturated with peace. It seemed to be giving me something I needed." In speaking of it, the feeling came back to her. She brushed her hair over her ears, and the wide-set eyes looked far off. "And I loved the rock. It's hard to describe. I loved the rock more than you or the baby or myself. And this is harder to say: While I sat there I went into the rock. The little stream was flowing out of me and I was the rock, and the rock was—I don't know—the rock was the strongest dearest thing in the world." She looked nervously about the room. Her fingers picked at her skirt. The thing she had intended to tell as a joke was forcing itself back upon her.

Joseph took up her nervous hand and held the fingers still. "Tell me," he insisted gently.

"Well, I must have stayed there quite a while, because the sun moved, but it seemed only a moment to me. And then the feeling of the place changed. Something evil came into it." Her voice grew husky with the memory. "Something malicious was in the glade, something that wanted to destroy me. I ran away. I thought it was after me, that great crouched rock, and when I got outside, I prayed. Oh, I prayed a long time."

Joseph's light eyes were piercing. "Why do you want to go back there?" he demanded.

"Why don't you see?" she replied eagerly. "The whole thing was my condition. But I've dreamed about it several times and it comes often to my mind. Now that I'm all well again, I want to go back, and see that it is just an old moss-covered rock in a clearing. Then I won't dream about it any more. Then it won't threaten me any more. I want to touch it. I want to insult it because it frightened me." She released her fingers from Joseph's grip and rubbed them to ease the pain in them. "You've hurt my hand, dear. Are you afraid of the place, too?"

"No," he said. "I'm not afraid. I'll take you up there." He fell silent, wondering whether he should tell her what Juanito had said about the pregnant Indian women who went to sit in front of the rock, and about the old ones who lived in the forest. "It might frighten her," he thought. "It is better that she should lose her fear of the place." He opened the stove and threw in an armful of wood and turned the damper straight, to set the flame roaring. "When would you like to go?" he asked.

"Why, any time. If the day is warm tomorrow, I'll pack a lunch into a saddle bag. Rama will take care of the baby. We'll have a picnic." She spoke eagerly. "We haven't had a picnic since I've been here. I don't know anything I love more. At home," she said, "we took our lunches to Huckleberry Hill, and after we'd eaten, mother and I picked buckets of berries."

"We'll go there tomorrow," he agreed. "I'm going to look in at the barn now, dear."

As she watched him leave the room, she knew that he was concealing something from her. "Probably it's only his worry about the rain," she thought, and from habit she turned her eyes to the barometer and saw that the needle was high.

Joseph stepped down from the porch. He moved close to the oak tree before he realized that it was dead. "If only it were alive," he thought, "I would know what to do. I have no counsel any more." He walked on into the barn, expecting to find Thomas there, but the barn was dark and the horses snorted at him as he walked behind them. "There's plenty of hay for the stock this year," he thought. The knowledge comforted him.

The sky was misty clear when he went back across the yard. He thought he could see a pale ring around the moon, but it was so faint that he could not be sure.

Before sunup the next morning Joseph went to the barn, curried two horses and brushed them, and, as a last elegance, painted their hoofs black and rubbed their coats with oil.

Thomas came in while he was at work. "You're making considerable fuss," he said. "Going to town?"

Joseph rubbed the oil in until the skins shone like dull metal. "I'm taking Elizabeth to ride," he announced. "She hasn't been on a horse for a long time."

Thomas rubbed his hand down one of the shining rumps. "I wish I could go with you, but I've work to do. I'm taking the men down to the river-bed to dig a hole. We may have trouble finding water for the cattle pretty soon."

Joseph stopped his work and looked worriedly at Thomas. "I know it. But there must be water under the river-bed. You should strike it a few feet down."

"It'll rain pretty soon, Joseph. I hope it will. I'm getting sick of a dusty throat."

The sun came up behind a high thin film of cloud that sucked the warmth and paled the light. Over the hills there came a cold steady wind that blew the dust to ripples and made little drifts of yellow fallen leaves. It was a lonely wind, scudding along the ground, flowing evenly, with very little sound.

After breakfast Joseph led out the saddle-horses, and Elizabeth, in her divided skirt and high-heeled boots, came out of the house carrying a bag of lunch.

"Take a warm coat," Joseph warned her.

She lifted her face to the sky. "It's winter at last, isn't it, Joseph? The sun has lost its heat."

He helped her on her horse and she laughed because of the good feeling of the saddle, and she patted the flat horn-top affectionately. "It's good to be able to ride again," she said. "Where shall we go first?"

Joseph pointed to a little peak on the eastern ridge above the pines. "If we go to the top of that we can look through the pass of the Puerto Suelo and see the ocean," he said. "And we can see the tops of the redwoods."

"It's good to feel the horse moving," she repeated. "I've been missing it, and I didn't know."

The flashing hoofs kicked up a fine white dust which stayed in the air after they had passed, and made a path behind them like the smoke of a train. They rode up the gentle slope through the thin spare grass, and at the water cuts they went down and up again with a quick jerk.

"Remember how the cuts raced with water last year?" she reminded him. "Pretty soon it'll be that way again."

Far off on a hillside they saw a dead cow, almost covered by slow gluttonous buzzards. "I hope we don't get to windward of that, Joseph."

He looked away from the feast. "They don't give meat a chance to spoil," he said. "I've seen them standing in a circle around a dying animal, waiting for the moment of death. They know that moment."

The hill grew steeper, and they entered the crackling sage, dark and dry and leafless now. The twigs were so brittle that they seemed dead. In an hour they came to the peak, and from there, sure enough, they saw the triangle of ocean through the pass. The ocean was not blue, it was steel-grey, and on the horizon the dark fog banks rose in heavy ramparts.

"Tie up the horses, Joseph," she said. "Let's sit a while. I haven't seen the ocean for so long. Sometimes I wake up in the night and listen for the waves and for the foghorn of the lighthouse, and the bell buoy off China Point. And sometimes I can hear them, Joseph. They must be very deeply fixed in me. Sometimes I can hear them. In the mornings, early, when the air was still, I remember how I could hear the fishing boats pounding out and the voices of the men calling back and forth from boat to boat."

He turned away from her. "I haven't that to miss," he said. These things of hers seemed like a little heresy to him.

She sighed deeply. "When I hear those things in my head I get homesick, Joseph. This valley traps me and I have the feeling that I can never escape from it and that I'll never really hear the waves again, nor the bell buoy, nor see the gulls sliding on the wind."

"You can go back to visit any time," he said gently. "I'll take you back."

But she shook her head. "It wouldn't ever be the same. I can remember how excited I was at Christmas, but I couldn't be again."

He lifted his head and sniffed the wind. "I can smell the salt," he said. "I shouldn't have brought you here, Elizabeth, to make you sad."

"But it's a good full sadness, dear. It's a luxurious sadness. I can remember how the pools were in the early morning at low tide, glistening and damp, the crabs scrambling over the rocks, and the little eels under the round stones. Joseph," she asked, "can't we eat lunch now?"

"It isn't nearly noon yet. Are you hungry already?"

"I'm always hungry at a picnic," she said smiling. "When mother and I went up to Huckleberry Hill we sometimes started to eat lunch before we were out of sight of the house. I'd like to eat while I'm up here."

He walked to the horses and loosened their cinches and brought back the saddle bags, and he and Elizabeth munched the thick sandwiches and stared off at the pass and at the angry ocean beyond.

"The clouds seem to be moving in," she observed. "Maybe there'll be rain tonight."

"It's only fog, Elizabeth. It's always fog this year. The earth is turning white. Do you see? The brown is going out of it."

She chewed her sandwich and gazed always at the little patch of sea. "I remember so many things," she said. "They pop up in my mind suddenly, like ducks in a shooting gallery. I just thought then how the Italians go out on the rocks at low tide with big slabs of bread in their hands. They crack open the sea urchins and spread part of them on the bread. The males are sweet and the females sour—the urchins, not the Italians, of course." She scrunched up the papers from the lunch and wadded them back into the saddle bag. "We'd better ride on now, dear. It won't do to stay out very long."

Although there had been no movement of the clouds, the haze was thickening about the sun and the wind grew colder. Joseph and Elizabeth walked their horses down the slope. "You still want to go to the pine grove?" he asked.

"Why of course. That's the main reason for the trip. I'm going to scotch the rock." As she spoke a hawk shot from the air with doubled fists. They heard the shock of flesh, and in a second the hawk flew up again, bearing a screaming rabbit in its claws. Elizabeth dropped her reins and covered her ears until the sound was out of hearing. Her lip trembled. "It's all right; I know it is. I hate to see it, though."

"He missed his stroke," Joseph said. "He should have broken its neck with the first blow, but he missed." They watched the hawk fly to the cover of the pine grove and disappear among the trees.

They had not far to go, down a long slope and then along the ridge until they came at last to the outpost trees. Joseph pulled up. "We'll tie the horses here and walk in," he said. When they were afoot, he hurried ahead to the little stream. "It isn't dry," he called. "It isn't down a bit."

Elizabeth walked over and stood beside him. "Does that make you feel better, Joseph?"

He glanced quickly at her, feeling a little mockery in her words, but he could see none in her face. "It's the first running water I've seen for a long time," he said. "It's as though the country were not dead while this stream is running. This is like a vein still pumping blood."

"Silly," she said, "you come from a country where it rains often. See how the sky is darkening, Joseph. I wouldn't be surprised if it should rain."

He glanced upward. "Only fog," he said. "But it will be cold soon. Come, let's go in."

The glade was silent, as always, and the rock was still green. Elizabeth spoke loudly to break the silence. "You see, I knew it was only my condition that made me afraid of it."

"It must be a deep spring to be still running," Joseph said. "And the rock must be porous to suck up water for the moss."

Elizabeth leaned down and looked into the dark cave from which the stream flowed. "Nothing in there," she said. "Just a deep hole in the rock, and the smell of wet ground." She stood up again and patted the shaggy sides of the rock. "It's lovely moss, Joseph. See how deep." She pulled out a handful and held up the damp black roots for him to see. "I'll never dream of you any more," she said to the rock. The sky was dark grey by now, and the sun had gone.

Joseph shivered and turned away. "Let's start for home, dear. The cold's coming." He strolled toward the path.

Elizabeth still stood beside the rock. "You think I'm silly, don't you, Joseph," she called. "I'll climb up on its back and tame it." She dug her heel into the steep side of the mossy rock, and made a step and pulled herself up, and then another.

Joseph turned around. "Be careful you don't slip," he called.

Her heel dug for a third step. And then the moss stripped off a little. Her hands gripped the moss and tore it out.

Joseph saw her head describe a little arc and strike the ground. As he ran toward her, she turned slowly on her side. Her whole body shuddered violently for a second, and then relaxed. He stood over her for an instant before he ran to the spring and filled his hands with water. But when he came back to her, he let the water fall to the ground, for he saw the position of her neck, and the grey that was stealing into her cheeks. He sat stolidly on the ground beside her, and mechanically picked up her hand and opened the fingers clenched full of pine needles. He felt for her pulse and found none there. Joseph put her hand gently down as though he feared to awaken her. He said aloud, "I don't know what it is." The icy chill was creeping inward upon him. "I should turn her over," he thought. "I should take her home." He looked at the black scars on the rock where her heels had dug a moment before. "It was too simple, too easy, too quick," he said aloud. "It was too quick." He knew that his mind could not grasp what had happened. He tried to make himself realize it. "All the stories, all the incidents that made the life were stopped in a second—opinions stopped, and the ability to feel, all stopped without any meaning." He wanted to make himself know what happened, for he could feel the beginning of the calm settling upon him. He wanted to cry out once in personal pain before he was cut off and unable to feel sorrow or resentment. There were little stinging drops of cold on his head. He looked up and saw that it was raining gently. The drops fell on Elizabeth's cheeks and flashed in her hair. The calm was settling on Joseph. He said, "Good-bye, Elizabeth," and before the words were completely out he was cut off and aloof. He removed his coat and laid it over her head. "It was the one chance to communicate," he said. "Now it is gone."

The pattering rain was kicking up little explosions of dust in the glade. He heard the faint whisper of the stream as it stole across the flat and disappeared into the brush. And still he sat by the body of Elizabeth, loathe to move, muffled in the calm. Once he stood up and touched the rock timidly, and looked up at its flat top. In the rain a vibration of life came into the place. Joseph lifted his head as though he were listening, and then he stroked the rock tenderly. "Now you are two, and you are here. Now I will know where I must come."

His face and beard were wet. The rain dripped into his open shirt. He stooped and picked up the body in his arms and supported the sagging head against his shoulder. He marched down the trail and into the open.

There was a dull rainbow in the east, fastened by its ends to the hills. Joseph turned the extra horse loose to follow. He slung his burden to one shoulder while he mounted his horse, and then settled the loose bundle on the saddle in front of him. The sun broke through and flashed on the windows of the farm buildings below him. The rain had stopped now; the clouds withdrew toward the ocean again. Joseph thought of the Italians on the rocks, cracking sea urchins to eat on their bread. And then his mind went back to a thing Elizabeth had said ages before. "Homer is thought to have lived nine hundred years before Christ." He said it over and over, "before Christ, before Christ. Dear earth, dear land! Rama will be sorry. She can't know. The forces gather and center and become one and strong. Even I will join the center." He shifted the bundle to rest his arm. And he knew how he loved the rock, and hated it. The lids drew halfway down over his eyes with fatigue. "Yes, Rama will be sorry. She will have to help me with the baby."

Thomas came into the yard to meet Joseph. He started to ask a question, and then, seeing how tight and grey Joseph's face was, he advanced quietly and held up his arms to take the body. Joseph dismounted wearily, caught the free horse and tied it to the corral fence. Thomas still stood mutely, holding the body in his arms.

"She slipped and fell," Joseph explained woodenly. "It was only a little fall. I guess her neck is broken." He reached out to take the burden again. "She tried to climb the rock in the pines," he went on. "The moss skinned off. Just a little fall. You wouldn't believe it. I thought at first she had only fainted. I brought water before I saw."

"Be still!" Thomas said sharply. "Don't talk about it now." And Thomas withheld the body from him. "Go away, Joseph, I'll take care of this. Take your horse and ride. Go into Nuestra Señora and get drunk."

Joseph received the orders and accepted them. "I'll go to

walk along the river," he said. "Did you find any water to-day?"

"No."

Thomas turned away and walked toward his own house, carrying the body of Elizabeth. For the first time that he could remember, Thomas was crying. Joseph watched him until he climbed the steps, and then he walked away at a quick pace, nearly a run. He came to the dry river and hurried up it, over the round smooth stones. The sun was going down in the mouth of the Puerto Suelo, and the clouds that had rained a little towered in the east like red walls and threw back a red light on the land and made the leafless trees purple. Joseph hurried on up the river. "There was a deep pool," he thought. "It couldn't be all dry, it was too deep." For at least a mile he went up the stream bed, and at last he found the pool, deep and brown and ill-smelling. In the dusk-light he could see the big black eels moving about in slow convolutions. The pool was surrounded on two sides by round, smooth boulders. In better times a little waterfall plunged into it. The third side gave on a sandy beach, cut and trampled with the tracks of animals; the dainty spear-heads of deer and the pads of lions and the little hands of racoons, and over everything the miring spread of wild pigs' hoofs. Joseph climbed to the top of one of the water-worn boulders and sat down, clasping one knee in his arms. He shivered a little with the cold, although he did not feel it. As he stared down into the pool, the whole day passed before him, not as a day, but as an epoch. He remembered little gestures he had not known he saw. Elizabeth's words came back to him, so true in into-nation, so complete in emphasis that he thought he really heard them again. The words sounded in his ears.

"This is the storm," he thought. "This is the beginning of the thing I knew. There is some cycle here, steady and quick and unchangeable as a fly-wheel." And the tired thought came to him that if he gazed into the pool and cleaned his mind of every cluttering picture he might come to know the cycle.

There came a sharp grunting from the brush. Joseph lost his thought and looked toward the beach. Five lean wild pigs and one great curved-tusked boar came into the open and approached the water. They drank cautiously, and then wading noisily into the water they began to catch the eels and to eat them while the slimy fish slapped and struggled in their mouths. Two pigs caught one eel and squalling angrily tore it in two, and each chewed up its portion. The night was almost down before they waded back to the beach and drank once more. Suddenly there came a flash of yellow light. One of the pigs fell under the furious ray. There was a crunch of bone and a shrill screaming, and then the ray arched its back as the lean and sleek lion looked around and leaped back from the charging boar. The boar snorted at its dead and then whirled and led the four others into the brush. Joseph stood up and the lion watched him, lashing its tail. "If I could only shoot you," Joseph said aloud, "there would be an end and a new beginning. But I have no gun. Go on with your dinner." He climbed down from the rock and walked away, through the trees. "When that pool is gone the beasts will die," he thought, "or maybe they'll move over the ridge." He walked slowly back to the ranch, reluctant to go, and yet fearing a little to be out in the night. He thought how a new bond tied him to the earth, and how this land of his was closer now.

A lantern shone in the shed behind the barn, and there came a sound of hammering. Joseph went to the door and saw Thomas working on the box, and entered. "It hardly looks large enough," he said.

Thomas did not look up. "I measured. It will be right."

"I saw a lion, Thomas; saw it kill a wild pig. Some time soon you'd better take some dogs and kill it. The calves will suffer, else." He hurried on, "Tom, we talked when Benjy died. We said it takes graves to make a place one's own. That is a true thing. That makes us a part of the place. There's some enormous truth in this."

Thomas nodded over his work. "I know. Jose and Manuel will dig in the morning. I don't want to dig for our own dead."

Joseph turned away, trying to leave the shed. "You are sure it's big enough?"

"Sure, I measured."

"And, Tom, don't put a little fence around. I want it to sink and be lost as soon as it can." He went, then, quickly. In the yard he heard the warned children whispering.

"There he goes," and Martha, "You're not to say anything to him."

He went to his own dark house and lighted the lamps and set fire in the stove. The clock wound by Elizabeth still ticked, storing in its spring the pressure of her hand, and the wool socks she had hung to dry over the stove screen were still damp. These were vital parts of Elizabeth that were not dead yet. Joseph pondered slowly over it—Life cannot be cut off quickly. One cannot be dead until the things he changed are dead. His effect is the only evidence of his life. While there remains even a plaintive memory, a person cannot be cut off, dead. And he thought, "It's a long slow process for a human to die. We kill a cow, and it is dead as soon as the meat is eaten, but a man's life dies as a commotion in a still pool dies, in little waves, spreading and growing back toward stillness." He leaned back in his chair and turned the lamp wick down until only a little blue light came from it. And then he sat relaxed and tried to shepherd his thoughts again, but they had spread out, feeding in a hundred different places, so that his attention was lost. And he thought in tones, in currents of movement, in color, and in a slow plodding rhythm. He looked down at his slouched body, at his curved arms and hands resting in his lap.

Size changed.

A mountain range extended in a long curve and on its end were five little ranges, stretching out with narrow valleys between them. If one looked carefully, there seemed to be towns in the valleys. The long curved range was clad in black sage, and the valleys ended on a flat of dark tillable earth, miles in length, which dropped off at last to an abyss. Good fields were there, and the houses and the people were so small they could be seen only a little. High up on a tremendous peak, towering over the ranges and the valleys, the brain of the world was set, and the eyes that looked down on the earth's body. The brain could not understand the life on its body. It lay inert, knowing vaguely that it could shake off the life, the towns, the little houses of the fields with earthquake fury. But the brain was drowsed and the mountains lay still, and the fields were peaceful on their rounded cliff that went down to the abyss. And thus it stood a million years, unchanging and quiet, and the world-brain in its peak lay close to sleep. The world-brain sorrowed a little, for it knew that some time it would have to move, and then the life would be shaken and destroyed and the long work of tillage would be gone, and the houses in the valleys would crumble. The brain was sorry, but it could change nothing. It thought, "I will endure even a little discomfort to preserve this order which has come to exist by accident. It will be a shame to destroy this order." But the towering earth was tired of sitting in one position. It moved, suddenly, and the houses crumbled, the mountains heaved horribly, and all the work of a million years was lost.

And size changed, and time changed.

There were light footsteps on the porch. The door opened and Rama came in, her dark eyes wide and glittering with sorrow. "You are sitting in the dark, almost, Joseph," she said.

His hands rose to stroke his black beard. "I turned down the lamp."

She stepped over and turned up the wick a little. "It is a hard time, Joseph. I want to see how you look at this time. Yes," she said. "There is no change. That makes me strong again. I was afraid there might have been a break. Are you thinking about Elizabeth?"

He wondered how to answer. There was an impulse in him to tell the thing as truly as he could. "Yes, somewhat," he said slowly and uncertainly, "of Elizabeth and of all the things that die. Everything seems to work with a recurring rhythm except life. There is only one birth and only one death. Nothing else is like that."

Rama moved close and sat down beside him. "You loved Elizabeth."

"Yes," he said, "I did."

"But you didn't know her as a person. You never have known a person. You aren't aware of persons, Joseph; only people. You can't see units, Joseph, only the whole." She shrugged her shoulders and sat up straight. "You aren't even listening to me. I came over to see if you had had anything to eat."

"I don't want to eat," he said.

"Well, I can understand that. I have the baby, you know. Do you want me to keep it over at my house?"

"I'll get someone to take care of it as soon as I can," he said.

She stood up, preparing to go. "You are tired, Joseph. Go to bed and get some sleep if you can. And if you can't, at least lie down. In the morning you'll be hungry, and then you can come to breakfast."

"Yes," he said absently, "in the morning I'll be hungry."

"And you'll go to bed now?"

He agreed, hardly knowing what she had said. "Yes, I'll go to bed." And when she went out he obeyed her automatically. He took off his clothes and stood in front of the stove, looking down at his lean hard stomach and legs. Rama's voice kept repeating in his head, "You must lie down and rest." He took the lamp from its hanging ring and walked into the bedroom and got into bed, leaving the light on the table. Since he had entered the house his senses had been boxed up in his thoughts, but now, as his body stretched and relaxed, sounds of the night became available to his ears, so that he heard the murmuring of the wind and the harsh whisper of the dry leaves in the dead oak tree. And he heard the far-off moaning of a cow. Life flowed back into the land, and the movement that had been deadened by thought started up again. He considered turning off the lamp, but his reluctant body refused the task.

A furtive step sounded on the porch. He heard the front door open quietly. A rustling sound came from the sitting-room. Joseph lay still and listened, and wondered idly who was there, but he did not call out. And then the bedroom door opened, and he turned his head to look. Rama stood naked in the doorway, and the lamplight fell upon her. Joseph saw the full breasts, ending in dark hard nipples, and the broad round belly and the powerful legs, and the triangle of crisp black hair. Rama's breath came panting, as though she had been running.

"This is a need," she whispered hoarsely.

In Joseph's throat and chest a grinding started, like hot gravel, and it moved downward.

Rama blew out the light and flung herself into the bed. Their bodies met furiously, thighs pounding and beating, her thewed legs clenched over him. Their breath sobbed in their throats. Joseph could feel the hard nipples against his breast; then Rama groaned harshly, and her broad hips drummed against him, and her body quivered until the pressure of her straining arms crushed the breath from his chest, and her hungry limbs drew irresistibly the agonizing seed of his body.

She relaxed, breathing heavily. The strong muscles grew soft; they lay together in exhaustion.

"It was a need to you," she whispered. "It was a hunger in me, but a need to you. The long deep river of sorrow is diverted and sucked into me, and the sorrow which is only a warm wan pleasure is drawn out in a moment. Do you think that, Joseph?"

"Yes," he said. "The need was there." He arose from her and turned on his back and lay beside her.

She spoke sleepily: "It's in my memory now. Once in my life — once in my life! My whole life approaching it, and after, my whole life backing away hungrily. It was not for you. It seems enough now, perhaps it is, but I am afraid it will bear litters of desires, and each one will grow larger than its mother." She sat up and kissed his forehead, and for a moment her hair fell about his face. "Is there a candle on the table, Joseph? I'll need a little light."

"Yes, on the table, in a tin candle-stick, and matches in the tray."

She got up and put flame to the candle. She looked down at herself and with her finger explored the dark-red bruises on her breast. "I've thought of this," she said. "Often I've thought of it. And in my thought we lay together after we had joined, and I asked you a great many questions. Always in my thought that was the way it was." As though a modesty crept upon her, she shielded the candle-light from her body with her hand. "I think I've asked my questions and you have answered them."

Joseph supported himself on one elbow. "Rama, what do you want of me?" he demanded.

She turned, then, to the door and opened it slowly. "I want nothing now. You are complete again. I wanted to be a part of you, and perhaps I am. But—I do not think so." Her voice changed then. "Go to sleep now. And in the morning come to breakfast." She closed the door after her. He heard the rustling of her dressing, but sleep fell so quickly upon him that he did not hear her leave the house.

22

In January there was a time of shrill cold winds and mornings when the frost lay on the ground like a light snow. The cattle and horses ranged the hillsides, picking up forgotten wisps of grass, reaching up to nibble the live oak leaves, and finally they moved in and stood all day about the fenced haystacks. Morning and night Joseph and Thomas pitched hay over the fence to them and filled the troughs with water. And when the stock had eaten and drunk, they stood about waiting for the next feeding. The hills were picked clean.

The earth grew more grey and lifeless every week and the haystacks dwindled. One was finished and another started, and it melted, too, under the appetites of the hungry cows. In February an inch of rain fell and the grass started up, grew a few inches and turned yellow. Joseph walked moodily about with his hands knotted and thrust into his pockets.

The children played quietly. They played "Aunt Elizabeth's Funeral" for weeks, burying a cartridge box over and over. And later in the year they played at gardening, dug tiny plots of ground and planted wheat and watched the long thin blades shoot up under poured water. Rama still cared for Joseph's baby. She gave more time to it than she had devoted to her own.

But it was Thomas who really grew afraid. When he saw that the cattle could find no more feed in the hills the terror of starvation began to arise in him. When the second haystack was half gone, he came nervously to Joseph.

"What will we do when the other two stacks run out?" he demanded.

"I don't know. I'll think what to do."

"But Joseph, we can't buy hay."

"I don't know. I'll have to think what to do."

There were showers in March, and a little stand of feed started up and wildflowers began to grow. The cattle moved out from the stacks and nibbled hungrily all day long at the short grass to get their stomachs full. April dried out the ground again, and the hope of the country was gone. The cattle were thin and laced with ribs. Hip-bones stood out. There were few calves born. Two sows died with a mysterious illness before they littered. Some of the cows took a harsh cough from the dusty air. The game was going away from the hills. The quail came no longer to the house to sing in the evenings. And the nights when the coyotes jibbered were rare. It was an odd thing to see a rabbit.

"The wild things are going away," Thomas explained. "Everything that can move is going over the range to the coast. We'll go there soon, Joseph, just to see it."

In May the wind blew for three days from the sea, but it had done that so often that no one believed it. There was a day of massed clouds, and then the rain fell in torrents. Both Joseph and Thomas walked about, getting wet, gloating a little in the water, although they knew it was too late. Almost overnight the grass sprang up again and clothed the hills and grew furiously. The cattle spread a little fat on their ribs. And then one morning there was a burn in the sunlight, and at noon the weather was hot. The summer had come early. Within a week the grass withered and drooped, and within two weeks the dust was in the air again.

Joseph saddled a horse one morning in June and rode to Nuestra Señora and found the teamster Romas. Romas came out into his chicken yard and sat on a wagon-tongue, and he played with a bull whip while he talked.

"These are the dry years?" Joseph asked sullenly.

"It looks that way, Mr. Wayne."

"Then these are the years you talked about."

"This is one of the worst I ever saw, Mr. Wayne. Another like this and there will be trouble in the family."

Joseph was scowling. "I have one stack of hay left. When that is gone, what do I feed the cattle?" He took off his hat and wiped the sweat out with a handkerchief.

Romas snapped his bull-whip, and the popper spat up the dirt like an explosion. And then he hung the whip over his knee and took tobacco and papers from his vest and rolled a cigarette. "If you can keep your cows until next winter, you may save them. If you haven't enough hay for that, you'll have to move them or they'll starve. This sun won't leave a straw."

"Can't I buy hay?" Joseph asked.

Romas chuckled. "In three months a bale of hay will be worth a cow."

Joseph sat down on the wagon-tongue beside him and looked at the ground, and picked up a handful of the hot dust. "Where do you people drive the stock?" he asked finally.

Romas smiled. "That's a good time for me. I drive the cattle. I'll tell you, Mr. Wayne, this year has hit not only this valley but the Salinas valley, beyond. We won't find grass this side of the San Joaquin river."

"But that's over a hundred miles away."

Romas picked up the bull-whip from his lap again. "Yes, over a hundred miles," he said. "And if you haven't much hay left, you'd better start the herd pretty soon, while they have the guts to go."

Joseph stood up and walked toward his horse. And Romas walked beside him.

"I remember when you came," Romas said quietly. "I remember when I hauled the lumber to your place. You said the drought would never come again. All of us who live here and were born here know it will come again."

"Suppose I sell all my stock and wait for the good years?"

Romas laughed loudly at that. "Man, you aren't thinking. What does your stock look like?"

"It's pretty poor," Joseph admitted.

"Fat beef is cheap enough, Mr. Wayne. You couldn't sell Nuestra Señora beef this year."

Joseph untied his lead rope and slowly mounted. "I see. Drive the cows then, or lose them—"

"Looks that way, Mr. Wayne."

"And if I drive, how many do I lose?"

Romas scratched his head and pretended to be thinking. "Sometimes half, sometimes two-thirds, and sometimes all of them."

Joseph's mouth tightened as though he had been struck. He lifted his reins and moved his spurred boot in toward the horse's belly.

"Do you remember my boy Willie?" Romas asked. "He drove one of the teams when we brought the lumber."

"Yes, I remember. How is he?"

"He's dead," said Romas. And then, in a shamed voice, "He hung himself."

"Why, I hadn't heard. I'm sorry. Why did he do that?"

Romas shook his head bewilderedly. "I don't know, Mr. Wayne. He never was very strong in the head." He smiled up at Joseph. "That's a Hell of a way for a father to talk." And then, as though he spoke to more than one person, he looked at a spot beside Joseph, "I'm sorry I said a thing like that. Willie was a good boy. He never was very well, Mr. Wayne."

"I'm sorry, Romas," Joseph said, and then he continued, "I may be needing you to drive stock for me." The spur lightly touched the horse and Joseph trotted off toward the ranch.

He rode slowly home along the banks of the dead river. The dusty trees, ragged from the sun's flaying, cast very little shade on the ground. Joseph remembered how he had ridden out in a dark night and flung his hat and quirt away to save a good moment out of a tide of moments. And he remembered how thick and green the brush had been under the trees, and how the grass of the hills bowed under its weight of seed; how the hills were heavy-coated as a fox's back. The hills were gaunt now; here was a colony from the southern desert come to try out the land for a future spreading of the desert's empire.

The horse panted in the heat, and the sweat dripped from the cowlick in the center of its belly. It was a long trip and there was no water on the way. Joseph didn't want to go home, for he was feeling a little guilty at the news he carried. This would break up the ranch and leave it abandoned to the sun and to the desert's outposts. He passed a dead cow with pitifully barred sides, and with a stomach swelled to bursting with the gas of putrefaction. Joseph pulled his hat down and bent his head so that he might not see the picked carcass of the land.

It was late afternoon when he arrived. Thomas had just ridden in from the range. He walked excitedly to Joseph, his red face drawn.

"I found ten dead cows," he said. "I don't know what killed them. The buzzards are working on them." He grasped Joseph's arm and shook it fiercely. "They're over the ridge there. In the morning there will be only a little plot of bones."

Joseph looked away from him in shame. "I'm failing to protect the land," he thought sadly. "The duty of keeping life in my land is beyond my power."

"Thomas," he said. "I rode to town today for news of the country."

"Is it all this way?" Thomas demanded. "The water in the well is low."

"Yes; all this way. We'll have to move the cows—over a hundred miles. There's pasturage along the San Joaquin."

"Christ, let's get moving, then!" Thomas cried. "Let's get out of this bastard valley, this double-crossing son-of-a-bitch. I don't want to come back to it! I can't trust it any more!"

Joseph shook his head slowly. "I keep hoping something may happen. I know there's no chance. A heavy rain wouldn't help now. We'll start the cows next week."

"Why wait for next week? Let's get 'em ready tomorrow!"

Joseph tried to soothe him. "This is a week of heat. It may be a little cooler next week. We'll have to feed them up so they can make the trip. Tell the men to pitch out more hay."

Thomas nodded. "I hadn't thought about the hay." Suddenly his eyes brightened. "Joseph, we'll go over the range to the coast while the men are feeding up the cows. We'll get a look at some water before we start riding in the dust."

Joseph nodded. "Yes, we can do that. We can go tomorrow."

They started in the night, to get ahead of the sun. They headed their horses toward the dark west, and let the horses find the trail. The earth still radiated heat from the day before, and the hillsides were quiet. The ringing of hoofs on the rocky trail splashed uneasy sounds in the quietness. Once, when the dawn was coming, they stopped to rest their horses, and they thought they heard a little bell tinkling in front of them.

"Did you hear it?" Thomas asked.

"It might be a belled animal," said Joseph. "It isn't a cowbell. It sounds more like a sheep bell. We'll listen for it when the daylight comes."

The day's heat started when the sun appeared. There was no cool dawn. A few grasshoppers rattled and snapped through the air. The cooked bay trees spiced the air and drops of sweet heavy juice boiled out of the greasewood. As the men rode up the steep slope, the trail grew more rocky and the earth more desolate. Everywhere the bones of the earth stuck through and flung the dazzling light away. A snake rattled viciously in the path ahead. Both horses stopped stiffly in their tracks and backed away. Thomas reached down and slipped a carbine from the saddle scabbard under his leg. The gun crashed and the thick snake's body rotated slowly around its crushed head. The horses turned downhill to rest, and closed their eyes against the cutting light. A faint whining came from the earth, as though it protested against the intolerable sun.

"It makes me sad," Joseph said. "I wish I could be less sad about it."

Thomas threw a leg around his saddle horn. "You know what the whole damn country looks like?" he asked. "It looks like a smoking heap of ashes with cinders sticking out." They heard the faint tinkling of the bell again. "Let's see what it is," Thomas said. They turned the horses back uphill. The slope was strewn with great boulders, ruins of perfect mountains that once were, and the trail twisted about among the rocks. "I think I heard that bell go by the house in the night," Thomas said. "I thought it was a dream then, but I remember it now that I hear it again. We're nearly to the top now."

The trail went into a pass of shattered granite, and the next moment the two men looked down on a new fresh world. The downward slope was covered with tremendous redwood trees, and among the great columned trunks there grew a wild tangle of berry vines, of gooseberry, of swordferns as tall as a man. The hill slipped quickly down, and the sea rose up level with the hilltops. The two men stopped their horses and stared hungrily at the green underbrush. The hills stirred with life. Quail skittered and rabbits hopped away from the path. While the men looked, a little deer walked into an open place, caught their scent and bounced away. Thomas wiped his eyes on his sleeve. "All the game from our side is here," he said. "I wish we could bring our cattle over, but there isn't a flat place for a cow to stand." He turned about to face his brother. "Joseph, wouldn't you like to crawl under the brush, into a damp cool hollow there, and curl up and go to sleep?"

Joseph had been staring at the up-ended sea. "I wonder where the moisture comes from." He pointed to the long barren sweeps that dropped to the ocean far below. "No grass is there, but here in the creases it's as green as a jungle." And he said, "I've seen the fog heads looking over into our valley. Every night the cool grey fog must lie in these creases in the mountains and leave some of its moisture. And in the daytime it goes back to the sea, and at night it comes again, so that this forest is never kept waiting, never. Our land is dry, and there's no help for it. But here—I resent this place, Thomas."

"I want to get down to the water," Thomas said. "Come on, let's move." They started down the steep slope on the trail that wound among the columns of the redwoods, and the brambles scratched at their faces. Part of the way down, they came to a clearing, and in it two packed burros stood with drooped heads, and an old, white-bearded man sat on the ground in front of them. His hat was in his lap and his damp white hair lay plastered against his head. He looked up at the two with sharp shiny black eyes. He held one nostril shut and blew out of the other, and then reversed and blew again.

"I heard you coming a long way back," he said. And he laughed without making a sound. "I guess you heard my burro bell. It's a real silver bell my burro wears. Sometimes I let one wear it, and sometimes the other." He put on his hat with dignity and lifted his beaked nose like a sparrow. "Where are you going, down the hill?"

Thomas had to answer, for Joseph was staring at the little man in curious recognition. "We're going to camp on the coast," Thomas explained. "We'll catch some fish, and we'll swim if the sea is calm."

"We heard your bell a long way back," said Joseph. "I've seen you somewhere before." He stopped suddenly in embarrassment, for he knew he had never really seen the old man before at all.

"I live over to the right, on a flat," the old man said. "My house is five hundred feet above the beach." He nodded at them impressively. "You shall come to stay with me. You will see how high it is." He paused, and a secret hesitant mist settled over his eyes. He looked at Thomas, and then looked long at Joseph. "I guess I can tell you," he said. "Do you know why I live out there on the cliff? I've only told the reason to a few. I'll tell you, because you're coming to stay with me." He stood up, the better to deliver his secret. "I am the last man in the western world to see the sun. After it is gone to everyone else, I see it for a little while. I've seen it every night for twenty years. Except when the fog was in or the rain was falling, I've seen the sun set." He looked from one to the other, smiling proudly. "Sometimes," he went on, "I go to town for salt and pepper and thyme and tobacco. I go fast. I start after the sun has set, and I'm back before it sets again. You shall see tonight how it is." He looked anxiously at the sky. "It's time to be going. You follow after me. Why, I'll kill a little pig, and we'll roast it for dinner. Come, follow after me." He started at a half run down the trail, and the burros trotted after him, and the silver bell jingled sharply.

"Come," Joseph said. "Let's go with him."

But Thomas hung back. "The man is crazy. Let him go on."

"I want to go with him, Thomas," Joseph said eagerly. "He isn't crazy, not violently crazy. I want to go with him."

Thomas had the animals' fear of insanity. "I'd rather not. If we do go with him, I'll take my blankets off into the brush."

"Come on, then, or we'll lose him." They clucked up their horses and started down the hill, through the underbrush and in and out among the straight red pillars of the trees. So fast had the old man gone that they were nearly down before they took sight of him. He waved his hand and beckoned to them. The trail left the crease where the redwoods grew and led over a bare ridge to a long narrow flat. The mountains sat with their feet in the sea, and the old man's house was on the knees. All over the flat was tall sagebrush. A man riding the trail could not be seen above the scrub. The brush stopped a hundred feet from the cliff, and on the edge of the abyss was a pole cabin, hairy with stuffed moss and thatched with a great pile of grass. Beside the house there was a tight pigpen of poles, and a little shed, and a vegetable garden, and a patch of growing corn. The old man spread his arms possessively.

"Here is my house." He looked at the lowering sun. "There's over an hour yet. See, that hill is blue," he said,

pointing. "That's a mountain of copper." He started to un-
pack the mules, laying his boxes of supplies on the ground.
Joseph slipped his saddle and hobbled his horse, and Thomas
reluctantly did the same. The burros trotted away into the
brush, and the horses hopped after them.

"We'll find them by the bell," said Joseph. "The horses will
never leave the burros."

The old man led them to the pigpen, where a dozen lean
wild pigs eyed them suspiciously and tried to force their way
through the farther fence. "I trap them." He smiled proudly. "I
have my traps all over. Come, I'll show you." He walked to the
low, thatched shed and, leaning down, pointed to twenty little
cages, woven and plaited with willows. In the cages were grey
rabbits and quail and thrushes and squirrels, sitting in the
straw behind their wooden bars and peering out. "I catch all
of them in my box-traps. I keep them until I need them."

Thomas turned away. "I'm going for a walk," he said
sharply. "I'm going down the cliff to the ocean."

The old man stared after him as he strode away. "Why does
that man hate me?" he demanded of Joseph. "Why is he afraid
of me?"

Joseph looked affectionately after Thomas. "He has his life
as you have, and as I have. He doesn't like things caged. He
puts himself in the place of the beasts, and can feel how
frightened they are. He doesn't like fear. He catches it too
easily." Joseph smoothed down his beard. "Let him alone.
He'll come back after a while."

The old man was sad. "I should have told him. I am gentle
with the little creatures. I don't let them be afraid. When I kill
them, they never know. You shall see." They strolled around
the house, toward the cliff. Joseph pointed to three little
crosses stuck in the ground close to the cliff's edge.

"What are those?" he asked. "It's a strange place for
them."

His companion faced him eagerly. "You like them. I can see
you like them. We know each other. I know things you don't
know. You will learn them. I'll tell you about the crosses.
There was a storm. For a week the ocean down there was
wild and grey. The wind blew in from the center of the sea.
Then it was over. I looked down the cliff to the beach. Three

little figures were there. I went down my own trail that I built
with my hands. I found three sailors washed up on the beach.
Two were dark men, and one was light. The light one wore a
saint's medallion on a string around his neck. Then I carried
them up here. That was work. And I buried them on the cliff.
I put the crosses there because of the medallion. You like the
crosses, don't you?" His bright black eyes watched Joseph's
face for any new expression.

And Joseph nodded. "Yes, I like the crosses. It was a good
thing to do."

"Then come to see the sunset place. You'll like that, too."
He half ran around his house in his eagerness. A little platform was built on the cliff's edge, with a wooden railing in
front and a bench a few feet back. In front of the bench was a
large stone slab, resting on four blocks of wood, and the
smooth surface of the stone was scoured and clean. The two
men stood at the railing and looked off at the sea, blue and
calm, and so far below that the rollers sliding in seemed no
larger than ripples, and the pounding of the surf on the beach
sounded like soft beating on a wet drum-head. The old man
pointed to the horizon, where a rim of black fog hung. "It'll
be a good one," he cried. "It'll be a red one in the fog. This is
a good night for the pig."

The sun was growing larger as it slipped down the sky.
"You sit here every day?" Joseph asked. "You never miss?"

"I never miss except when the clouds cover. I am the last
man to see it. Look at a map and you'll see how that is. It is
gone to everyone but me." He cried, "I'm talking while I
should be getting ready. Sit on the bench there and wait."

He ran around the house. Joseph heard the angry squealing
of the pig, and then the old man reappeared, carrying the
struggling animal in his arms. He had trussed its legs all together. He laid it on the stone slab and stroked it with his
fingers, until it ceased its struggling and settled down, grunting contentedly.

"You see," the old man said, "it must not cry. It doesn't
know. The time is nearly here, now." He took a thick short-
bladed knife from his pocket and tried its edge on his palm,
and then his left hand stroked the pig's side and he turned to
face the sun. It was rushing downward toward the far-off rim

of fog, and it seemed to roll in a sac of lymph. "I was just in time," the old man said. "I like to be a little early."

"What is this," Joseph demanded. "What are you doing with the pig?"

The old man put his finger to his lips. "Hush! I'll tell you later. Hush now."

"Is it a sacrifice? Are you sacrificing the pig?" Joseph asked. "Do you kill a pig every night?"

"Oh no. I have no use for it. Every night I kill some little thing, a bird, a rabbit or a squirrel. Yes, every night some creature. Now, it's nearly time." The sun's edge touched the fog. The sun changed its shape; it was an arrowhead, an hour glass, a top. The sea turned red, and the wave-tops became long blades of crimson light. The old man turned quickly to the table. "Now!" he said, and cut the pig's throat. The red light bathed the mountains and the house. "Don't cry, little brother." He held down the struggling body. "Don't cry. If I have done it right, you will be dead when the sun is dead." The struggling grew weaker. The sun was a flat cap of red light on the fog wall, and then it disappeared, and the pig was dead.

Joseph had been sitting tensely on his bench, watching the sacrifice. "What has this man found?" he thought. "Out of his experience he has picked out the thing that makes him happy." He saw the old man's joyful eyes, saw how in the moment of the death he became straight and dignified and large. "This man has discovered a secret," Joseph said to himself. "He must tell me if he can."

His companion sat on the bench beside him now, and looked out to the edge of the sea, where the sun had gone. And the sea was dark and the wind was whipping it to white caps. "Why do you do this?" Joseph asked quietly.

The old man jerked his head around. "Why?" he asked excitedly. And then he grew more calm. "No, you aren't trying to trap me. Your brother thinks I'm crazy. I know. That's why he went to walk. But you don't think that. You're too wise to think that." He looked out on the darkening sea again. "You really want to know why I watch the sun—why I kill some little creature as it disappears." He paused and ran his lean fingers through his hair. "I don't know," he said quietly. "I have made up reasons, but they aren't true. I have said to myself, 'The sun is life. I give life to life'—'I make a symbol of the sun's death.' When I made these reasons I knew they weren't true." He looked around for corroboration.

Joseph broke in, "These were words to clothe a naked thing, and the thing is ridiculous in clothes."

"You see it. I gave up reasons. I do this because it makes me glad. I do it because I like to."

Joseph nodded eagerly. "You would be uneasy if it were not done. You would feel that something was left unfinished."

"Yes," the old man cried loudly. "You understand it. I tried to tell it once before. My listener couldn't see it. I do it for myself. I can't tell that it does not help the sun. But it is for me. In the moment, I am the sun. Do you see? I, through the beast, am the sun. I burn in the death." His eyes glittered with excitement. "Now you know."

"Yes," Joseph said. "I know now. I know for you. For me there is a difference that I don't dare think about yet, but I will think about it."

"The thing did not come quickly," the old man said. "Now it is nearly perfect." He leaned over and put his hands on Joseph's knees. "Some time it will be perfect. The sky will be right. The sea will be right. My life will reach a calm level place. The mountains back there will tell me when it is time. Then will be the perfect time, and it will be the last." He nodded gravely at the slab where the dead pig lay. "When it comes, I, myself, will go over the edge of the world with the sun. Now you know. In every man this thing is hidden. It tries to get out, but a man's fears distort it. He chokes it back. What does get out is changed—blood on the hands of a statue, emotion over the story of an ancient torture—the giving or drawing of blood in copulation. Why," he said, "I've told the creatures in the cages how it is. They are not afraid. Do you think I am crazy?" he demanded.

Joseph smiled. "Yes, you're crazy. Thomas says you are. Burton would say you are. It is not thought safe to open a clear path to your soul for the free, undistorted passage of the things that are there. You do well to preach to the beasts in the cage, else you might be in a cage yourself."

The old man stood up and picked up the pig and carried it

away. He brought water and scrubbed the blood off the slab and dusted the ground under it with fresh gravel.

It was almost dark when he had finished cleaning the little pig. A great pale moon looked over the mountains, and its light caught the white-caps as they rose and disappeared. The pounding of the waves on the beach grew louder. Joseph sat in the little cave-like hut and the old man turned pieces of the pig on a spit in the fireplace. He talked quietly about the country.

"The tall sage hides my house," he said. "There are little cleared places in the sage. I've found some of them. In autumn the bucks fight there. I can hear the clashing of their horns at night. In the spring the does bring their spotted fawns to those same places to teach them. They must know many things if they are to live at all—what noises to run from; what the odors mean, how to kill snakes with their front hoofs." And he said, "The mountains are made of metal; a little layer of rock and then black iron and red copper. It must be so."

There were footsteps outside the house. Thomas called, "Joseph, where are you?"

Joseph got up from the floor of the hut and went out. "The dinner is waiting. Come in and eat," he said.

But Thomas protested, "I don't like to be with this man. I have abalones here. Come down to the beach. We'll build a fire and eat down there. The moon lights up the trail."

"But the supper is ready," Joseph said. "Come in and eat, at least."

Thomas entered the low house warily, as though he expected some evil beast to pounce upon him out of a dark corner. There was no light except from the fireplace. The old man tore at his meat with his teeth and threw the bones into the fire, and when he was finished, he stared sleepily into the blaze.

Joseph sat beside him. "Where did you come from?" Joseph asked. "What made you come here?"

"What do you say?"

"I say, why did you come here to live alone?"

The sleepy eyes cleared for a moment and then drooped

sullenly. "I don't remember," he said. "I don't want to re-member. I would have to think back, looking for what you want. If I do that, I'll stumble against other things in the past that I don't want to meddle with. Let it alone."

Thomas stood up. "I'll take my blanket out on the cliff to sleep," he said.

Joseph followed him out of the house, calling "Good-night," over his shoulder. The brothers walked in silence to-ward the cliff and laid their blankets side by side on the ground.

"Let's ride up the coast tomorrow," Thomas begged. "I don't like it here."

Joseph sat on his blankets and watched the faint far move-ment of the moonlit sea. "I'm going back tomorrow, Tom," he said. "I can't stay away. I must be there in case anything happens."

"Yes, but we'd planned to stay three days," Thomas ob-jected. "I'll need a rest from the dust if I'm to drive the cows a hundred miles, and so will you."

Joseph sat silent for a long time. "Thomas," he asked. "Are you asleep yet?"

"No."

"I'm not going with you, Thomas. You take the cows. I'll stay with the ranch."

Thomas rolled up on his elbow. "What are you talking about? Nothing will hurt the ranch. It's the cows we have to save."

"You take the cows," Joseph repeated. "I can't go away. I've thought of going, I've put my mind to the act of going, and I can't. Why, it'd be like leaving a sick person."

Thomas grunted, "Like leaving a dead body! And there's no harm in that."

"It isn't dead," Joseph protested. "The rain will come next winter, and in the spring the grass will be up and the river will be flowing. You'll see, Tom. There was some kind of ac-cident that made this. Next spring the ground will be full of water again."

Thomas jeered: "And you'll get another wife, and there won't ever be another drought."

"It might be so," Joseph said gently.

"Then come with us to the San Joaquin and help us with the cows."

Joseph saw lights of a ship passing far out on the ocean, and he watched the lights and held up his finger to see how fast they moved. "I can't go away," he said. "This is my land. I don't know why it's mine, what makes it mine, but I cannot leave it. In the spring when the grass is up you'll see. Don't you remember how the grass was green all over the hills, even in the cracks of the rocks, and how the mustard was yellow? The redwing blackbirds built nests in the mustard stems."

"I remember it," Thomas said truculently, "and I remember how it was this morning, burned to a cinder and picked clean. Sure, and I remember the circle of dead cows. I can't get out too quickly. It's a treacherous place." He turned on his side. "We'll go back tomorrow if you say so. I hope you won't stay on the damn place."

"I'll have to stay," Joseph said. "If I went with you, I'd be wanting to start back every moment to see if the rain had fallen yet, or if there was any water in the river. I might as well not go away."

23

T HEY AWAKENED to a world swaddled in grey fog. The house and the sheds were dark shadows in the mist, and from below the cliff the surf sounded muffled and hollow. Their blankets were damp. The moisture clung in fine drops to their faces and hair. Joseph found the old man sitting beside a smouldering fire in his hut, and he said, "We must start back as soon as we can find our horses."

The old man seemed sad at their going. "I hoped you would stay a little while. I've told you my knowledge. I thought you might give me yours."

Joseph laughed bitterly. "I have none to give. My knowledge has failed. How can we find our horses in the mist?"

"Oh, I'll get them for you." He went to the door and whistled shrilly, and in a moment the silver bell began to ring. The burros came trotting in, and the two horses after them.

Joseph and Thomas saddled their horses and tied the blankets on them, and then Joseph turned to say good-bye to the old man, but he had disappeared into the mist, and he didn't answer when Joseph called.

"He's crazy," Thomas said. "Come on, let's go." They turned the horses into the trail and let them have their heads, for the fog was too thick for a man to find his way. They came to the crease where the violent growth and the redwoods were. Every leaf dripped moisture, and the shreds of the mist clung to the tree trunks like tattered flags. The men were half way to the pass before the fog began to thin and break and whirl about like a legion of ghosts caught by the daylight. At last the trail climbed above the mist level and, looking back, Joseph and Thomas saw the tumbling sea of fog extending to the horizon, covering from sight the sea and the mountain slopes. And in a little they reached the pass and looked over at their own dry dead valley, burning under the vicious sun, smoking with heat waves. They paused in the pass and looked back at the green growth in the canyon they had come from, and at the grey sea of fog.

"I hate to leave it," Thomas said. "If there were only feed for the cattle I would move over."

Joseph looked back only for a moment, and then he started ahead over the pass. "It isn't ours, Thomas," he said. "It's like a beautiful woman, and she isn't ours." He urged his horse over the hot broken rock. "The old man knew a secret, Tom. He told me some straight clean things."

"He was crazy," Thomas insisted. "In any other place he would be locked up. What did he have all of those caged creatures for?"

Joseph thought of explaining. He tried to think how he would begin. "Oh, he—keeps them to eat," he said. "It isn't easy to shoot game, and so he traps the things and keeps them until he needs them."

"But that's all right," Thomas said more easily. "I thought there was something else. If that's all it is, I don't mind. His craziness hasn't to do with the animals and birds then."

"Not at all," said Joseph.

"If I'd known that, I wouldn't have walked away. I was afraid there was some ceremony."

"You are afraid of every kind of ritual, Thomas. Do you know why?" Joseph slowed his horse so that Thomas could come closer.

"No, I don't know why," Thomas admitted slowly, "it seems a trap, a kind of little trap."

"Perhaps it is," Joseph said. "I hadn't thought of it."

When they had got down the slope to the river source with its dry and brittle moss and its black ferns, they drew up under a bay tree. "Let's go over the ridge and drive in any cattle we can see," Thomas said. They left the river and followed the shoulder of the ridge, and the dust clouded up and clung about them. Suddenly Thomas pulled up his horse and pointed down the slope. "There, look there." Fifteen or twenty little piles of picked bones lay on the sidehill, and grey coyotes were slinking away toward the brush, and vultures roosted on the ribs and pulled off the last strips of flesh.

Thomas' face was pinched. "That's what I saw before. That's why I hate the country. I'll never come back," he cried. "Come on, I want to get to the ranch. I want to start away tomorrow if I can." He swung his horse down the hill and spurred it to a trot, and he fled from the acre of bones.

Joseph kept him in sight, but he did not try to follow him. Joseph's heart was filled with sorrow and with defeat. "Something has failed," he thought. "I was appointed to care for the land, and I have failed." He was disappointed in himself and in the land. But he said, "I won't leave it. I'll stay here with it. Maybe it isn't dead." He thought of the rock in the pines, and excitement arose in him. "I wonder if the little stream is gone. If that still flows, the land is not dead. I'll go to see, pretty soon." He rode over the ridge top in time to see Thomas gallop up to the houses. The fences were down around the last stacks of hay, and the voracious cattle were eating holes in it. As Joseph came close, he saw how lean they were, and poor, and how their hips stuck out. He rode to where Thomas talked with the rider Manuel.

"How many?" he demanded.

"Four hundred and sixteen," Manuel said. "Over a hundred gone."

"Over a hundred!" Thomas walked quickly away. Joseph, looking after him, saw him go into the barn. He turned back to the rider.

"Will these others make it to the San Joaquin, Manuel?"

Manuel shrugged slightly. "We go slow. Maybe we find a little grass. Maybe we get some over there. But we lose some cows, too. Your brother hates to lose the cows. He likes the cows."

"Let them eat all the hay," Joseph ordered. "When the hay is gone, we will start."

"The hay will be gone tomorrow," Manuel said.

They were loading the wagons in the yard, mattresses and chicken coops and cooking utensils, piled high and carefully. Romas came in with another rider to help with the herds. Rama would drive a buckboard, Thomas, a Studebaker wagon with grain for the horses and two barrels of water. There were folded tents on the wagons, supplies of food, three live pigs and a couple of geese. They were taking everything to last until winter.

In the evening Joseph sat on his porch, watching the last of the preparation, and Rama left her work and came to him and sat on the step. "Why do you stay?" she asked.

"Someone must take care of the ranch, Rama."

"But what remains to be taken care of? Thomas is right, Joseph; there's nothing left."

His eyes sought the ridge where the dark pines were. "There's something left, Rama. I'll stay with the ranch."

She sighed deeply. "I suppose you want me to take the baby."

"Yes. I wouldn't know how to care for it."

"You know it won't be a very good life for him in a tent."

"Don't you want to take him, Rama?" he asked.

"Yes, I want him. I want him for my own."

Joseph turned away and looked up at the pine forest again. The last of the sun was sinking over the Puerto Suelo. Joseph thought of the old man and of his sacrifice. "Why do you want the child?" he asked softly.

"Because he is part of you."

"Do you love me, Rama? Is that it?"

Her breath caught harshly in her throat. "No," she cried, "I am very near to hating you."

"Then take the child," he said quickly. "This child is yours. I swear it now. He is yours forever. I have no more claim on him." And he looked quickly back to the pine ridge, as though for an answer.

"How can I be sure?" Rama fretted. "When I have made my mind over so the baby is my own, when he has come to think of me as his mother, how can I be sure you will not come and take him away?"

He smiled at her, and the calm he knew came upon him. He pointed to the dead and naked tree beside the porch. "Look, Rama! That was my tree. It was the center of the land, a kind of father of the land. And Burton killed it." He stopped and stroked his beard and turned the ends under, as his father had done. His eyes drooped with pain and tightened with resistance to the pain. "Look on the ridge where the pines are, Rama," he said. "There's a circle in the grove, and a great rock in the circle. The rock killed Elizabeth. And on the hill over there are the graves of Benjy and Elizabeth." She stared at him uncomprehendingly. "The land is struck," he went on. "The land is not dead, but it is sinking under a force too strong for it. And I am staying to protect the land."

"What does all this mean to me?" she asked, "to me or to the child?"

"Why," he said, "I don't know. It might help, to give the child to you. It seems to me a thing that might help the land."

She brushed her hair back nervously, smoothed it beside the part. "Do you mean you're sacrificing the child? Is that it, Joseph?"

"I don't know what name to give it," he said. "I am trying to help the land, and so there's no danger that I shall take the child again."

She stood up then, and backed away from him slowly. "Good-bye to you, Joseph," she said. "I am going in the morning, and I am glad, for I shall always be afraid of you now. I shall always be afraid." Her lips trembled, and her eyes filled with tears. "Poor lonely man!" She hurried away toward her house, but Joseph smiled gravely up at the pine grove.

"Now we are one," he thought, "and now we are alone; we will be working together." A wind blew down from the hills and raised a choking cloud of dust into the air.

The cattle munched at the hay all night.

The wagons set out well before daylight. For two hours the lanterns moved about. Rama got breakfast for the children and saw them to their high secure seat on top of the load. She put the baby in its basket on the floor of the wagon, in front of her. At last they were ready, and the horses hitched in. Rama climbed to her seat, and Thomas stood beside her. Joseph strode up. They stood in the dark, and all three unconsciously sniffed the air. The children were very quiet. Rama put her foot out on the brake. Thomas sighed deeply. "I'll write you how we get through," he said.

"I'll be waiting to hear," Joseph replied.

"Well, we may as well get started."

"You'll stop in the hot part of the day?"

"If we can find a tree to stop under. Well, good-bye," Thomas said. "It's a long trip." One of the horses bowed its neck against the check-rein and stamped.

"Good-bye, Thomas. Good-bye, Rama."

"I'll have Thomas write you how the baby is," Rama said.

Still Thomas stood waiting. But suddenly he turned and walked away without another word. His brake whispered for a moment, and the axles creaked under the load. Rama started her horses and the teams moved off. Martha, on top of the load, cried bitterly because no one could see her waving a handkerchief. The other children had gone to sleep, but Martha awakened them. "We're going to a bad place," she said quietly, "but I'm glad we're going because this place will burn up in a week or two."

Joseph could hear the creaking wheels after the teams disappeared. He strolled to the house that had been Juanito's, where the drovers were finishing their coffee and fried meat. As the first dawn appeared, they emptied their cups and rose heavily to their feet. Romas walked out to the corral with Joseph.

"Take them slowly," Joseph said.

"Sure, I will. It's a good bunch of riders, Mr. Wayne. I know all of them."

The men were wearily saddling their horses. A pack of six long-haired ranch dogs got up out of the dust and walked tiredly out to go to work, serious dogs. The red dawn broke. The dogs lined out. Then the corral gate swung open and the herd started, three dogs on each side to keep them in the road, and the riders fanned out behind. With the first steps the dust billowed into the air. The riders raised their handkerchiefs and tied them over the bridges of their noses. In a hundred yards the herd had almost disappeared in the dust cloud. Then the sun started up and turned the cloud to red. Joseph stood by the corral and watched the line of dust that crawled like a worm over the land, spreading in the rear like a yellow mist.

The thick cloud moved over the hill at last, but the dust hung in the air for hours.

Joseph felt the weariness of the long journey. The heat of the early sun burned him and the dust stung his nose. For a long time he did not move away from his place, but stood and watched the dust-laden air where the herd had passed. He was filled with sorrow. "The cattle are gone for good," he thought. "Most of them were born here, and now they're gone." He thought how they had been fresh-coated calves, sleek and shiny with the licking of their mothers; how they had flattened little beds in the grass at night. He remembered the mournful bellowing of the cows when the calves got lost; and now there were no cows left. He turned away at last to the dead houses, the dead barn and the great dead tree. It was quieter than anything should be. The barn door swung open on its hinges. Rama's house was open, too. He could see the chairs inside, and the polished stove. He picked up a piece of loose baling wire from the ground, rolled it up and hung it on the fence. He walked into the barn, empty of hay. Hard black clods were on the floor, on the packed straw. Only one horse was left. Joseph walked down the long line of empty stalls, and his mind made history of his memories. "This is the stall where Thomas sat when the loft was full of hay." He looked up and tried to imagine how it had been. The air was laced with flashing yellow streaks of sun. The three barn-owls sat, faces inward, in their dark corners under the eaves. Joseph walked to the feed-room and brought an extra measure of rolled barley and poured it in the horse's barley box, and he carried out another measure and scattered it on the ground outside the door. He sauntered slowly across the yard.

It would be about now that Rama came out with a basket of washed clothes and hung them on the lines, red aprons and jeans, pale blue with so much soaking, and the little blue frocks and red knitted petticoats of the girls. And it would be about now that the horses were turned out of the barn to stretch their necks over the watering trough and to snort bubbles into the water. Joseph had never felt the need for work as he did now. He went through all the houses and locked the doors and the windows and nailed up the doors of the sheds. In Rama's house he picked up a damp drying cloth from the floor and hung it over the back of a chair. Rama was a neat woman; the bureau drawers were closed and the floor was swept, the broom and dustpan stood in their corner, and the turkey wing had been used on the stove that morning. Joseph lifted the stove lid and saw the last coals darkening. When he locked the door of Rama's house he felt a guilt such as one feels when the lid of a coffin is closed for the last time, and the body is deserted and left alone.

He went back to his own house, spread up his bed, and

carried in wood for the night's cooking. He swept his house and polished the stove and wound the clock. And everything was done before noon. When he had finished everything, he went to sit on the front porch. The sun beat down on the yard and glittered on bits of broken glass. The air was still and hot, but a few birds hopped about, picking up the grain Joseph had scattered. And, led on by the news that the ranch was deserted, a squirrel trotted fearlessly across the yard, and a brown weasel ran at him and missed, and the two rolled about in the dust. A horned toad came out of the dust and waddled to the bottom step of the porch, and settled to catch flies. Joseph heard his horse stamping the floor, and he felt friendly toward the horse for making a sound. He was rendered stupid by the quiet. Time had slowed down and every thought waddled as slowly through his brain as the horned toad had when he came out of the fine dust. Joseph looked up at the dry, white hills and squinted his eyes against their reflection of the glaring sun. His eyes followed the water scars up the hill to the dry springs and over the unfleshed mountains. And, as always, his eyes came at last to the pine grove on the ridge. For a long time he stared at it, and then he stood up and walked down the steps. And he walked toward the pine grove—walked slowly up on the gentle slope. Once, from the foothills, he looked back on the dry houses, huddled together under the sun. His shirt turned dark with perspiration. His own little dust cloud followed him, and he walked on and on toward the black trees.

At last he came to the gulch where the grove stream flowed. There was a trickle of water in it, and the green grass grew on the edges. A little watercress still floated on the water. Joseph dug a hole in the bed under the tiny stream, and when the water had cleared, he knelt and drank from it, and he felt the cool water on his face. Then he walked on, and the stream grew a little wider and the streak of green grass broadened. Where it ran close under the bank of the gully, a few ferns grew in the black and mossy earth, out of reach of the sun. Some of the desolation left Joseph then. "I knew it would still be here," he said. "It couldn't fail. Not from that place." He took off his hat and walked quickly on. He entered the glade bareheaded and stood looking at the rock.

The thick moss was turning yellow and brittle, and the ferns around the cave had wilted. The stream still stole out of the hole in the rock, but it was not a quarter as large as it had been. Joseph walked to the rock apprehensively and pulled out some of the moss. It was not dead. He dug a hole in the stream bed, a deep hole, and when it was full he took up water in his hat and threw it over the rock and saw it go sucking into the dying moss. The hole filled slowly. It took a great many hatfuls of water to dampen the moss, and the moss drank thirstily, and showed no sign that it had been dampened. He threw water on the scars where Elizabeth's feet had slipped. He said, "Tomorrow I'll bring a bucket and a shovel. Then it will be easier." As he worked, he knew the rock no longer as a thing separated from him. He had no more feeling of affection for it than he had for his own body. He protected it against death as he would have saved his own life.

When he had finished throwing water, he sat down beside the pool and washed his face and neck in the cold water and drank from his hat. After a while he leaned back against the rock and looked across at the protecting ring of black trees. He thought of the country outside the ring, the hard burned hills, the grey and dusty sage. "Here it is safe," he thought. "Here is the seed that will stay alive until the rain comes again. This is the heart of the land, and the heart is still beating." He felt the dampness of the watered moss soaking through his shirt, and his thought went on, "I wonder why the land seems vindictive, now it is dead." He thought of the hills, like blind snakes with frayed and peeling skins, lying in wait about this stronghold where the water still flowed. He remembered how the land sucked down his little stream before it had run a hundred yards. "The land is savage," he thought, "like a dog far gone in hunger." And he smiled at the thought because he nearly believed it. "The land would come in and blot this stream and drink my blood if it could. It is crazy with thirst." He looked down at the little stream stealing across the glade. "Here is the seed of the land's life. We must guard against the land gone crazy. We must use the water to protect the heart, else the little taste of water may drive the land to attack us."

The afternoon was waning now; the shadow of the tree-line crossed the rock and closed on the other side of the circle. It was peaceful in the glade. "I came in time," Joseph said to the rock and to himself. "We will wait here, barricaded against the drought." His head nodded forward after a while, and he slept.

The sun slipped behind the hills and the dust withdrew, and the night came before he awakened. The hunting owls were coasting in front of the stars and the breeze that always follows the night was slipping along the hills. Joseph awakened and looked into the black sky. In a moment his brain reeled up from sleep and he knew the place. "But some strange thing has happened," he thought. "I live here now." The farmhouses down in the valley were not his home any more. He would go creeping down the hill and hurry back to the protection of the glade. He stood up and kicked his sleeping muscles awake, and then he walked quietly away from the rock, and when he reached the outside he walked secretly, as though he feared to awaken the land.

There were no lights in the houses to guide him this time. He walked in the direction of his memory. The houses were close before he saw them. And then he saddled his horse and tied blankets and a sack of grain and bacons and three hams and a great bag of coffee to the saddle. At last he crept away again, leading the packed horse. The houses were sleeping; the land rustled in the night wind. Once he heard some heavy animal walking in the brush and his hair pricked with fear, and he waited until the steps had died away before he went on.

He arrived back at the glade in the false dawn. This time the horse did not refuse the path. Joseph tied it to a tree and fed it from the bag of rolled barley; then he went back to the rock and spread his blankets beside the little pool he had built. The light was coming when he lay down to sleep in safety beside the rock. A little tattered fragment of cloud, high in the air, caught fire from the hidden sun, and Joseph fell asleep while he watched it.

24

ALTHOUGH the year turned into autumn and the weeks built months, the summer's heat continued on, and at length withdrew so gradually that no change of season was perceptible. The doves, which flocked near water, were gone long ago, and the wild ducks flying over looked for their resting ponds in the evening and flew tiredly on, while the weaklings landed in dry fields and joined some new flock in the morning. It was November before the air cooled and the winter seemed really coming in, and by then the earth was tinder-dry. Even dry lichens had scaled off the rocks.

The hot weeks drew on, and Joseph lived in the circle of the pines and waited for the winter. His new life had built its habits. Each morning he carried water from the deep wide pool he had dug and flooded the mossy rock with it, and in the evening he watered it again. The moss had responded; it was sleek and thick and green. And in the whole land there was no other green thing. Joseph watched it closely to see that there was no sign of dryness. The stream decreased little by little, but winter was coming, and there was still plenty of water to keep the rock dripping with moisture.

Every two weeks Joseph rode through the parched hills to Nuestra Señora for his food supply. Early in the fall he found a letter waiting for him there.

Thomas wrote only information: "There is grass here. We lost three hundred head of stock on the way over. What's left is fat. Rama is well, and the children. The pasture rent is too high because of the dry years. The children swim in the river."

Joseph found Romas in town, and Romas told dully of the trip over the mountains. He told how the cows dropped, one by one, and did not get up under the goad, but only looked tiredly at the sky. Romas could tell their condition to an ounce of strength. He looked at their eyes, and then he shot the tired beasts, and the weary eyes set and glazed, but did not change. Little feed and little water—the moving herds filled the road and the farmers along the road were hostile. They patrolled their fence lines and shot any stock that broke through. The roads were lined with dust-covered carcasses and the path of travel stank from end to end with rotting flesh. Rama, afraid the children might sicken with the smell, kept their faces covered with wet handkerchiefs. The miles covered daily grew fewer and fewer, and the tired stock rested all night, and did not search for food. A rider was sent back, and then another, as the herd dwindled, but Romas stayed, and the two home men, until the little band came stiffly to the river and rested on their knees to eat all night. Romas smiled as he told it, and his voice had no inflection. When the account was finished he walked quickly away, calling over his shoulder, "Your brother paid me," and he went into the saloon, out of sight.

While Joseph listened to the report a hollow pain came into his stomach, and he was glad when Romas went away. He bought his supplies and rode back to the barricade. For once he did not see the dry earth, cracked in long lightning lines. He did not feel the feeble tugging of the brittle brush as he rode through. His mind was a dusty road, and the weary cattle died in his brain. He was sorry he had heard, for now this new enemy would crowd up against the protecting pines.

The underbrush of the grove was dead by now, but the straight trunks still guarded the rock. The drought crept along the ground first, and killed all the low vines and the shrubs, but the pine roots pierced to bedrock and still drank a little water, and the needles were still black-green. Joseph rode back to the glade and he felt the rock to be sure it was moist, and he studied the little stream of water. This was the first time he set markers on the water's edge to determine how quickly it diminished.

In December the black frost struck the country. The sun rose and set redly and the north wind surged through the country every day, filling the air with dust, and tattering the dry leaves. Joseph went down to the houses and brought up a tent to sleep in. While he was among the quiet houses, he started the windmill and listened for a moment while it sucked air through the pipes, and then he turned the little crank that stopped the blades. He did not look back on the houses as he rode up the slope. He cut a wide path around the graves on the sidehill.

That afternoon he saw the fog heads on the western range. "I might go back to the old man," he thought. "There may be more things he could tell me." But his thought was play. He knew he couldn't leave the rock, for fear the moss would wilt. He went back into the silent glade and spread his tent. He picked the bucket from his gear and walked over to throw water on the rock. Something had happened. The stream had receded from his marking pegs a good two inches. Somewhere under the earth the drought had attacked the spring. Joseph filled his bucket at the pool and threw water on the rock, and then filled again. And soon the pool was empty—he had to wait half an hour for the dying stream to fill it again. For the first time a panic fell upon him. He crawled into the little cave and looked at the fissure from which the water slowly trickled, and he crawled out again, covered with the moisture of the cave. He sat beside the stream and watched it flow into the pool. And he thought he could see it decrease while he looked. The wind ruffled the pine branches nervously.

"It will win," Joseph said aloud. "The drought will get in at us." He was frightened.

In the evening he walked out the path and watched the sun setting in the Puerto Suelo. The fog came out of the hidden sea and swallowed the sun. In the chill winter evening Joseph gathered an armful of dead pine twigs and a bag of cones for his evening's fire. He built his fire close to the pool this night, so that its light fell on the tiny stream. When his meager supper was finished, he leaned back against his saddle and watched the water, slipping noiselessly into the pool. The wind had fallen, and the pines were quiet. All around the grove Joseph could hear the drought creeping, slipping on dry scales over the ground, circling and exploring the edges of the grove. And he heard the dry frightened whisper of the earth as the drought passed over it. He stood up now and put his bucket in the pool, under the stream, and each time it filled he poured it over the rock and sat down to wait for the bucket to fill again. It seemed to take a longer time with each bucketful. The owls flew ceaselessly about in the air, for there were few little creatures to catch. Then Joseph heard a faint slow pounding on the earth. He stopped breathing to listen.

"It's coming up the hill now. It will get in tonight."

He took a new breath and listened again for the rhythmic pounding, and he whispered, "When it gets here, the land will be dead, and the stream will stop." The sound came steadily up the hill, and Joseph, trapped with the rock, listened to it coming. Then his horse lifted its head and bickered, and an answering bicker came back from the hillside below the grove. Joseph started up and stood by his little fire, waiting with his shoulders set and his head forward to resist the blow. In the dim night light he saw a horseman ride into the glade and pull up his horse. The horseman looked taller than the pines, and a pale blue light seemed to frame his head. But then his voice called softly, "Señor Wayne."

Joseph sighed, and his muscles relaxed. "It is you, Juanito," he said tiredly. "I know your voice."

Juanito dismounted and tied his horse and then he strode to the little fire. "I came first to Nuestra Señora. They told me there that you were alone. I went to the ranch, then, and the houses were deserted."

"How did you know to look for me here?" Joseph asked.

Juanito knelt by the fire and warmed his hands, throwing on twigs to make a fresh blaze. "I remembered what you told your brother once, señor. You said, 'This place is like cool water.' I came over the dry hills, and I knew where you'd be." Now that the blaze was leaping, he looked into Joseph's face. "You are not well, señor. You are thin and sick."

"I am well, Juanito."

"You look dry and feverish. You should see a doctor tomorrow."

"No, I am well. Why did you come back, Juanito?"

Juanito smiled at a remembered pain. "The thing that made me go was gone, señor. I knew when it was gone, and I wanted to come back. I have a little son, señor. I just saw him tonight. He looks like me, with blue eyes, and he talks a little. His grandfather calls him Chango, and he says it is a little *piojo*, and he laughs. That Garcia is a happy man." His face had grown bright with all this gladness, but he grew sad again. "You, señor. They told me about you and the poor lady. There are candles burning for her."

Joseph shook his head a little against the memory. "There

was this thing coming, Juanito. I felt it coming. I felt it creeping in on us. And now it is nearly through, just this little island left."

"What do you mean, señor?"

"Listen, Juanito, first there was the land, and then I came to watch over the land; and now the land is nearly dead. Only this rock and I remain. I am the land." His eyes grew sad. "Elizabeth told me once of a man who ran away from the old Fates. He clung to an altar where he was safe." Joseph smiled in recollection. "Elizabeth had stories for everything that happened, stories that ran alongside things that happened and pointed the way they'd end."

A silence fell upon them. Joseph broke up more sticks and threw them on the fire. Joseph asked, "Where did you go, Juanito, when you went away?"

"I went to Nuestra Señora. I found Willie and took him away with me." He looked hard at Joseph. "It was the dream, señor. You remember the dream. He told me often. He dreamed he was on a hard dusty land which shone. There were holes in the ground. The men who came out of the holes pulled him to pieces like a fly. It was a dream. I took him with me, that poor Willie. We went to Santa Cruz and worked on a ranch nearby, in the mountains. Willie liked the big trees on the hills. The country was so different from that place in the dreams, you see." Juanito stopped and looked up into the sky at a half moon that showed its face over the treetops.

"One moment," Joseph said, and he lifted the full bucket from the hole and flung the water on the rock.

Juanito watched him and made no comment. "I do not like the moon any more," Juanito continued. "We worked there on the mountain, herding cattle among the trees, and Willie was glad. Sometimes he had the dream, but I was always there to help him. And after each time he dreamed, we went to Santa Cruz and drank whiskey and saw a girl." Juanito pulled his hat down to keep the moonlight from his face. "One night Willie had his dream, and the next night we went to town. There is a beach in Santa Cruz, and amusements, tents, and little cars to ride on. Willie liked those things. We walked along in the evening by the beach, and there was a man with a telescope, to see the moon. Five cents, it cost. I looked first, and then Willie looked." Juanito turned away from Joseph. "Willie was very sick," he said. "I carried him in front of me on my saddle and led his horse. But Willie couldn't stand it, and he hanged himself from a tree limb with a riata that night. It had been all right when he thought it was a dream, but when he saw the place was really there, and not a dream, he couldn't stand it to live. Those holes, señor, and that dry dead place. It was really there, you see. He saw it in the telescope." He broke some twigs and threw them in the fire. "I found him hanging in the morning."

Joseph jerked upright. "Make up the fire, Juanito. I'll put some coffee to cook. It's cold tonight."

Juanito broke more twigs and kicked a dry limb to pieces with his boot heel. "I wanted to come back, señor. I was lonely. Is the old thing gone from you?"

"Yes, gone. It was never in me. There's nothing here for you. Only I am here."

Juanito put out a hand as though to touch Joseph's arm, but then he drew it back. "Why do you stay? They say the cattle are gone, and all your family. Come with me out of this country, señor." Juanito watched Joseph's face in the firelight and saw the eyes harden.

"There is only the rock and the stream. I know how it will be. The stream is going down. In a little while it will be gone and the moss will turn yellow, and then it will turn brown, and it will crumble in your hand. Then only I will be left. And I will stay." His eyes were feverish. "I will stay until I am dead. And when that happens, nothing will be left."

"I will stay with you," Juanito said. "The rains will come. I'll wait here with you for the rains."

But Joseph's head sank down. "I don't want you here," he said miserably. "That would make too much time to wait. Now there is only night and day and dark and light. If you should stay, there would be a thousand other intervals to stretch out the time, intervals between words, and the long time between striding steps. Is Christmas nearly here?" he demanded suddenly.

"Christmas is past," Juanito said. "It will be the New Year in two days."

"Ah." Joseph sighed and sank back against his saddle. He caressed his beard jealously. "A new year," he said softly. "Did you see any clouds as you rode up, Juanito?"

"No clouds, señor. I thought there was a little mist, but see, the moon has no fringe."

"There might be clouds in the morning," Joseph said. "It's so close to the new year, there might be clouds." He lifted his bucket again and threw the water over the rock.

They sat silently before the fire, feeding it with twigs now and then, while the moon slipped over the circle of sky. The frost settled down, and Joseph gave Juanito one of his blankets to wrap about his body, and they waited for the bucket to be slowly filled. Juanito asked no questions about the rock, but once Joseph explained, "I can't let any of the water go to waste. There isn't enough."

Juanito roused himself. "You are not well, señor."

"Of course I'm well. I do not work, and I eat little, but I am well."

"Have you thought to see Father Angelo," Juanito asked suddenly.

"The priest? No. Why should I see him?"

Juanito spread his hands, as though to deprecate the idea. "I don't know why. He is a wise man and a priest. He is close to God."

"What could he do?" Joseph demanded.

"I don't know, señor, but he is a wise man and a priest. Before I rode away, after that other thing, I went to him and confessed. He is a wise man. He said you were a wise man, too. He said, 'One time that man will come knocking at my door.' That is what Father Angelo said. 'One time he will come,' he said. 'It may be in the night. In his wisdom he will need strength.' He is a strange man, señor. He hears confession and puts the penance and then sometimes he talks, and the people do not understand. He looks over their heads and doesn't care whether they understand or not. Some of the people do not like it. They are afraid."

Joseph was leaning forward with interest. "What could I want from him?" he demanded. "What could he give me that I need now?"

"I don't know," Juanito said. "He might pray for you."

"And would that be good, Juanito? Can he get what he prays for?"

"Yes," Juanito said. "His prayer is through the Virgin. He can get what he prays for."

Joseph leaned back against his saddle again, and suddenly he chuckled. "I will go," he said. "I will take every means. Look, Juanito. You know this place, and your ancestors knew this place. Why did none of your people come here when the drought started. This was the place to come."

"The old ones are dead," Juanito said soberly. "The young ones may have forgotten. I only remember because I came here with my mother. The moon is going down. Won't you sleep, señor?"

"Sleep? No, I won't sleep. I can't waste the water."

"I will watch it for you while you sleep. Not a drop will get away."

"No, I won't sleep," Joseph said. "Sometimes I sleep a little in the daytime when the bucket is filling. That's enough. I'm not working." He stood up to get the bucket, and suddenly he bent over exclaiming, "Look, Juanito!" He lighted a match and held it close to the stream. "It is so. The water is increasing. Your coming brought it. Look, it flows around the pegs. It's up half an inch." He moved excitedly to the rock and leaned into the cave, and lighted another match to look at the spring. "It's coming faster," he cried. "Build up a fire, Juanito."

"The moon is down," Juanito said. "Go to sleep, señor. I will watch the water. You will be needing sleep."

"No, build up the fire for light. I want to watch the water." And he said, "Maybe something good has happened where the water comes from. Maybe the stream will grow, and we shall move outward from here and take back the land. A ring of green grass, and then a bigger ring." His eyes glittered. "Down the hillsides and into the flat from this center—Look, Juanito, it is more than half an inch above the peg! It is an inch!"

"You must sleep," Juanito insisted. "You need the sleep. I see how the water is coming up. It will be safe with me." He patted Joseph's arm and soothed him. "Come, you must sleep."

And Joseph let himself be covered with the blankets, and in relief at the rising stream, he fell into a heavy sleep.

Juanito sat in the dark and faithfully emptied the water on the rock when the bucket was filled. This was the first unbroken rest that Joseph had taken for a long time. Juanito conserved his little flame of twigs and warmed his hands, while the frost that had been in the air all night settled a white gauze on the ground. Juanito gazed at Joseph sleeping. He saw how lean and dry he had grown and how his hair was turning grey. The terse Indian stories his mother had told him came into his mind, stories of the great misty Spirit, and the jokes he played on man and on other gods. And then, while he looked at Joseph's face, Juanito thought of the old church in Nuestra Señora, with its thick adobe walls and mud floors. There was an open space at the eaves, and the birds flew in sometimes, during the mass. Often there were bird droppings on Saint Joseph's head, and on the blue mantle of Our Lady. The reason for his thought came slowly out of the picture. He saw the crucified Christ hanging on his cross, dead and stained with blood. There was no pain in his face, now he was dead, but only disappointment and perplexity, and over these, an infinite weariness. Jesus was dead and the Life was finished. Juanito built a tall blaze to see Joseph's face clearly, and the same things were there, the disappointment and the weariness. But Joseph was not dead. Even in his sleep his jaw was resistingly set. Juanito crossed himself and walked to the bed and pulled up the covers around the sleeping man. And he stroked the hard shoulder. Juanito loved Joseph achingly. He watched on while the dawn came, and he tossed the water on the rock again and again.

The water had increased a little during the night. It washed around the peg Joseph had set and made a little swirl. The cold sun came up at last and shone through the forest. Joseph awakened and sat up. "How is the water?" he demanded.

Juanito laughed with pleasure at his message. "The stream is bigger," he said. "It grew while you slept."

Joseph kicked off the blankets and went to look. "It is," he said. "There's a change somewhere." He felt the mossy rock with his hand. "You've kept it well wet, Juanito. Thank you. Does it seem greener to you this morning?"

"I could not see the color in the night," Juanito said.

They cooked their breakfast then, and sat beside the fire drinking their coffee. Juanito said, "We will go to Father Angelo today."

Joseph shook his head slowly. "It would be too much water lost. Besides, there's no need to go. The stream is coming up."

Juanito answered without looking up, for he didn't want to see Joseph's eyes. "It will be good to see the priest," he insisted. "You come away from the priest feeling good. Even if it is only a little thing confessed, you feel good."

"I don't belong to that church, Juanito. I couldn't confess."

Juanito puzzled over that. "Anyone can see Father Angelo," he said at last. "Men who have not been to church since they were little children come back at last to Father Angelo, like wild pigeons to the water holes in the evening."

Joseph looked back at the rock. "But the water is coming up," he said. "There is no need to go now."

Because Juanito thought the church might help Joseph, he struck slyly. "I have been in this country since I was born, señor, and you have lived here only a little while. There are things you do not know."

"What things?" Joseph asked.

Juanito looked him full in the eyes then. "I have seen it many times, señor," he said in compassion. "Before a spring goes dry it grows a little."

Joseph looked quickly at the stream. "This is a sign of the end, then?"

"Yes, señor. Unless God interferes, the spring will stop."

Joseph sat in silence for several minutes, pondering. At last he stood up and lifted his saddle by the horn. "Let's go to see the priest," he said harshly.

"Maybe he can't help," Juanito said.

Joseph was carrying the saddle to the tethered horse. "I can't let any chance go by," he cried.

When the horses were saddled, Joseph threw one more bucket of water over the rock. "I'll be back before it can get dry," he said. They cut a straight path across the hills and joined the road far on their way. A dust cloud hung over their trotting horses. The air was chilly and stinging with frost. When they were half way to Nuestra Señora, the wind came up and filled the whole valley with the dust cloud, and spread the dirt in the air until it was a pale yellow mist that obscured the sun. Juanito turned in his saddle and looked to the west, from whence the wind came.

"The fog is on the coast," he said.

Joseph did not look. "It's always there. The coast has no danger as long as the ocean lasts."

Juanito said hopefully, "The wind is from the west, señor."

But Joseph laughed bitterly. "In any other year we would thatch the stacks and cover the woodpiles. The wind has often been in the west this year."

"But some time it must rain, señor."

"Why must it?" The desolate land was harping on Joseph's temper. He was angry with the bony hills and stripped trees. Only the oaks lived, and they were hiding their life under a sheet of dust.

Joseph and Juanito rode at last into the quiet street of Nuestra Señora. Half the people had gone away, had gone to visit relatives in luckier fields, leaving their houses and their burned yards and their empty chickenpens. Romas came to his door and waved without speaking, and Mrs. Gutierrez peered at them from her window. There were no customers in front of the saloon. When they rode up the street to the squat mud church, the evening of the short winter day was approaching. Two black little boys were playing in the ankle-deep dust of the road. The horsemen tied their beasts to an ancient olive tree.

"I will go into the church to burn a candle," Juanito said. "Father Angelo's house is behind. When you are ready to go back, I will be waiting at the house of my father-in-law." He turned into the church, but Joseph called him back.

"Listen, Juanito. You must not go back with me."

"I want to go, señor. I am your friend."

"No," Joseph said finally. "I do not want you there. I want to be alone."

Juanito's eyes dulled with rebellion and hurt. "Yes, my friend," he said softly, and he went into the open door of the church.

Father Angelo's little whitewashed house stood directly behind the church. Joseph climbed the steps and knocked at the door, and in a moment Father Angelo opened it. He was dressed in an old cassock over a pair of overalls. His face was paler than it had been, and his eyes were bloodshot with reading. He smiled a greeting. "Come in," he said.

Joseph stood in a tiny room decorated with a few bright holy pictures. The corners of the room were piled with thick books, bound in sheepskin, old books, from the missions. "My man, Juanito, told me to come," Joseph said. He felt a tenderness emanating from the priest, and the soft voice soothed him.

"I thought you might come some time," Father Angelo said. "Sit down. Did the tree fail you, finally?"

Joseph was puzzled. "You spoke about the tree before. What did you know about the tree?"

Father Angelo laughed. "I'm priest enough to recognize a priest. Hadn't you better call me Father? That's what all the people do."

Joseph felt the power of the man before him. "Juanito told me to come, Father."

"Of course he did, but did the tree fail you at last?"

"My brother killed the tree," Joseph said sullenly.

Father Angelo looked concerned. "That was bad. That was a stupid thing. It might have made the tree more strong."

"The tree died," Joseph said. "The tree is standing dead."

"And you've come to the Church at last?"

Joseph smiled in amusement at his mission. "No, Father," he said. "I've come to ask you to pray for rain. I am from Vermont, Father. They told us things about your church."

The priest nodded. "Yes, I know the things."

"But the land is dying," Joseph cried suddenly. "Pray for rain, Father! Have you prayed for rain?"

Father Angelo lost some of his confidence, then. "I will help you to pray for your soul, my son. The rain will come. We have held mass. The rain will come. God brings the rain and withholds it of his knowledge."

"How do you know the rain will come?" Joseph demanded. "I tell you the land's dying."

"The land does not die," the priest said sharply.

But Joseph looked angrily at him. "How do you know? The deserts were once alive. Because a man is sick often, and each time gets well, is that proof that he will never die?"

Father Angelo got out of his chair and stood over Joseph. "You are ill, my son," he said. "Your body is ill, and your soul is ill. Will you come to the church to make your soul well? Will you believe in Christ and pray help for your soul?"

Joseph leaped up and stood furiously before him. "My soul? To Hell with my soul! I tell you the land is dying. Pray for the land!"

The priest looked into his glaring eyes and felt the frantic fluid of his emotion. "The principal business of God has to do with men," he said, "and their progress toward heaven, and their punishment in Hell."

Joseph's anger left him suddenly. "I will go now, Father," he said wearily. "I should have known. I'll go back to the rock now, and wait."

He moved toward the door, and Father Angelo followed him. "I'll pray for your soul, my son. There's too much pain in you."

"Good-bye, Father, and thank you," and Joseph strode away into the dark.

When he had gone, Father Angelo went back to his chair. He was shaken by the force of the man. He looked up at one of his pictures, a descent from the cross, and he thought, "Thank God this man has no message. Thank God he has no will to be remembered, to be believed in." And, in sudden heresy, "else there might be a new Christ here in the West." Father Angelo got up then, and went into the church. And he prayed for Joseph's soul before the high altar, and he prayed forgiveness for his own heresy, and then, before he went away, he prayed that the rain might come quickly and save the dying land.

25

JOSEPH tightened his cinch and untied the hair rope from the old olive tree. And then he mounted his horse and turned him in the direction of the ranch. The night had fallen while he was in the priest's house. It was very dark before the moonrise. Along the street of Our Lady a few lights shone from the windows, blurred by the moisture on the insides of the glass. Before Joseph had gone a hundred feet into the cold night, Juanito rode up beside him.

"I want to go with you, señor," he said firmly.

Joseph sighed. "No, Juanito. I told you before."

"You've had nothing to eat. Alice has supper for you, waiting and hot."

"No, thank you," Joseph said. "I'll be riding on."

"But the night is cold," insisted Juanito. "Come in and have a drink, anyway."

Joseph looked at the dull light shining through the windows of the saloon. "I will have a drink," he said. They tied their horses to the hitching post and went through the swinging doors. No one was there but the bartender sitting on a high stool behind the bar. He looked up as the two entered, and climbed from his stool and polished a spot on the bar.

"Mr. Wayne," he said in greeting. "I haven't seen you for a long time."

"I don't get in to town often. Whiskey."

"And whiskey for me," Juanito said.

"I heard you saved some of your cows, Mr. Wayne."

"Yes, a few."

"You're better off than some. My brother-in-law lost every single head." And he told how the ranches were deserted and the cattle all dead, and he told how the people had gone away from the town of Our Lady. "No business now," he said. "I don't sell a dozen drinks a day. Sometimes a man comes in for a bottle. People don't like to drink together now," he said. "They take a bottle home, and drink alone."

Joseph tasted his empty glass and set it down. "Fill it," he said. "I guess we'll be having a desert from now on. Have one yourself."

The bartender filled his glass. "When the rain comes, they'll all be back. I'd set a barrel of whiskey in the road, free, if the rain would come tomorrow."

Joseph drank his whiskey and stared at the bartender questioningly. "If the rain doesn't come at all, what then?" he demanded.

"I don't know, Mr. Wayne, and I won't know. If it doesn't come pretty soon, I'll have to go too. I'd put a whole barrel of whiskey out on the porch, free for everyone, if the storms would come."

Joseph put down his glass. "Good-night," he said. "I hope you get your wish."

Juanito followed him closely. "Alice has the dinner hot for you," he said.

Joseph stopped in the road and lifted his head to look at the misty stars. "The drink has made me hungry. I'll go."

Alice met them at the door of her father's house. "I'm glad you came," she said. "The dinner is nothing but it will be a change. My father and mother have gone visiting to San Luis Obispo since Juanito is back." She was excited at the importance of her guest. In the kitchen she seated the two men at a snow-white table and served them with red beans and red wine, and thin tortillas and fluffy rice. "You haven't eaten my beans, Mr. Wayne, since—oh, for a long time."

Joseph smiled. "They are good. Elizabeth said they were the best in the world."

Alice caught her breath. "I am glad you speak of her." Her eyes filled with tears.

"Why should I not speak of her?"

"I thought it might give you too much pain."

"Be silent, Alice," Juanito said gently. "Our guest is here to eat."

Joseph ate his plate of beans and wiped up the juice with a tortilla, and accepted another helping.

"He will see the baby?" Alice asked timidly. "His grandfather calls him Chango, but that is not his name."

"He is asleep," Juanito said. "Wake him and bring him here."

She carried out the sleepy child and stood him in front of

Joseph. "See," she said. "His eyes will be grey. That's blue for Juanito and black for me."

Joseph looked at the child searchingly. "He is strong and handsome. I am glad of that."

"He knows the names of ten trees, and Juanito is going to get him a pony when the good years come."

Juanito nodded with pleasure. "He is a Chango," he said self-consciously.

Joseph stood up from the table. "What is his name?"

Alice blushed, and then she took up the sleepy baby. "He is your namesake," she said. "His name is Joseph. Will you give him a blessing?"

Joseph looked at her incredulously. "A blessing? From me? Yes," he said quickly. "I will." He took the little boy in his arms and brushed back the black hair from the forehead. And he kissed the forehead. "Grow strong," he said. "Grow big and strong."

Alice took the baby back as though he were not quite her own any more. "I'll put him to bed, and then we will go to the sitting-room."

But Joseph strode quickly to the door. "I must go now," he said. "Thank you for dinner. Thank you for my namesake."

And when Alice started to protest, Juanito silenced her. He followed Joseph to the yard and felt the cinch for him and put the bit in the horse's mouth. "I am afraid to have you go, señor," Juanito protested.

"Why should you be afraid? See, the moon is coming up."

Juanito looked and cried excitedly, "Look, there's a ring around the moon!"

Joseph laughed harshly and climbed into the saddle. "There is a saying in this country, I learned it long ago: 'In a dry year all signs fail.' Good-night, Juanito."

Juanito walked a moment beside the horse. "Good-bye, señor. See you take care." He patted the horse and stepped back. And he looked after Joseph until he had disappeared into the dim moonlit night.

Joseph turned his back on the moon and rode away from it, into the west. The land was unsubstantial under the misty, strained light; the dry trees seemed shapes of thicker mist. He left the town and took the river road, and his contact with the town dropped behind him. He smelled the peppery dust that arose under the horse's hoofs, but he couldn't see it. Away in the dark north there was a faint flicker of aurora borealis, rarely seen so far south. The cold stony moon rose high and followed him. The mountains seemed edged with phosphorus, and a pale cold light like a glow-worm's light seemed to shine through the skin of the land. The night had a quality of memory. Joseph remembered how his father had given him the blessing. Now he thought of it, he wished he had given the same blessing to his namesake. And he remembered that there had been a time when the land was drenched with his father's spirit so that every rock and bush was close and dear. He remembered how damp earth felt and smelled, and how the grass roots wove a fabric just under the surface. The horse plodded steadily on, head down, resting some of his head's weight on the bridle. Joseph's mind went wearily among the days of the past, and every event was colored like the night. He was aloof from the land now. He thought, "Some change is beginning. It will not be long before some new thing is on the way." And as he thought it, the wind began to blow. He heard it coming out of the west, heard it whisking a long time before it struck him, a sharp steady wind, carrying the refuse of dead trees and bushes along the ground. It was acrid with dust. The tiny rocks it carried stung Joseph's eyes. As he rode, the wind increased and long veils of dust swept down the moonlit hills. Ahead, a coyote barked a staccato question, and another answered from the other side of the road. Then the two voices drew together into a high shrieking giggle that rode down the wind. A third sharp question, from a third direction, and all three giggled. Joseph shivered a little. "They're hungry," he thought, "there's so little carrion left to eat." Then he heard a calf moan in the high brush beside the road, and he turned his horse and spurred it up and broke through the brittle bushes. In a moment he came to a little clearing in the brush. A dead cow lay on its side and a skinny calf butted frantically to find a teat. The coyotes laughed again, and went away to wait. Joseph dismounted and walked to the dead cow. Its hip was a mountain peak, and its ribs were like the long water-scars on the hillsides. It had died, finally, when bits of dry brush would not support it any more.

The calf tried to get away, but it was too weak with hunger. It stumbled and fell heavily and floundered on the ground, trying to get up again. Joseph untied his riata and roped the skinny legs together. Then he lifted the calf in front of the saddle and mounted behind it. "Now come for your dinner," he called to the coyotes. "Eat the cow. Pretty soon there will be no more to eat." He glanced over his shoulder at the bone-white moon, sailing and hovering in the blown dust. "In a little while," he said, "it will fly down and eat the world." As he rode on, his hand explored the lean calf, his fingers followed the sharp ribs and felt the bony legs. The calf tried to rest its head against the horse's shoulder, and its head bobbed weakly with the movement. At last they topped the rise and Joseph saw the houses of the ranch, bleached and huddled. The blades of the windmill shone faintly in the moonlight. It was a view half obscured, for the white dust filled the air, and the wind drove fiercely down the valley. Joseph turned up the hill to avoid the houses, and as he went up toward the black grove, the moon sank over the western hills and the land was blotted out of sight. The wind howled down from the slopes and cried in the dry branches of the trees. The horse lowered its head against the wind. Joseph could make out the pine grove darkly as he approached it, for a streak of dawn was coming over the hills. He could hear the tossing branches and the swish of the needles combing the wind, and the moan of limbs rubbing together. The black branches tossed against the dawn. The horse walked wearily in among the trees and the wind stayed outside. It seemed quiet in the grey place; more so because of the noise around it. Joseph climbed down and lifted the calf to the ground. And he unsaddled the horse and put a double measure of rolled barley in the feed-box. At last he turned reluctantly to the rock.

The light had come secretly in, and the sky and the trees and the rock were grey. Joseph walked slowly across the glade and knelt by the little stream.

And the stream was gone. He sat quietly down and put his hand in the bed. The gravel was still damp, but no water moved out of the little cave any more.

Joseph was very tired. The wind howling around the grove

and the stealthy drought were too much to fight. He thought, "Now it is over. I think I knew it would be."

The dawn brightened. Pale streaks of sunlight shone on the dust-clouds that filled the air. Joseph stood up and went to the rock and stroked it. The moss was growing brittle already, and the green had begun to fade out of it. "I might climb up on top and sleep a little," he thought, and then the sun shone over the hills, and the shaft of its light cut through the pine trunks and threw a blinding spot on the ground. Joseph heard a little struggle behind him where the calf tried to loosen its legs from the riata loops. Suddenly Joseph thought of the old man on the cliff-top. His eyes shone with excitement. "This might be the way," he cried. He carried the calf to the stream-side, held its head out over the dry bed and cut its throat with his pocket-knife, and its blood ran down the stream bed and reddened the gravel and fell into the bucket. It was over too soon. "So little," Joseph thought sadly. "Poor, starved creature, it had so little blood." He watched the red stream stop running and sink into the gravel. And while he watched, it lost its brightness and turned dark. He sat beside the dead calf and thought again of the old man. "His secret was for him," he said. "It won't work for me."

The sun lost its brilliance and sheathed itself in thin clouds. Joseph regarded the dying moss and the circle of trees. "This is gone now. I am all alone." And then a panic fell upon him. "Why should I stay in this dead place?" He thought of the green canyon over the Puerto Suelo. Now that he was no longer supported by the rock and the stream, he was horribly afraid of the creeping drought. "I'll go!" he cried suddenly. He picked up his saddle and ran across the glade with it. The horse raised its head and snorted with fear. Joseph lifted the heavy saddle, and as the tapadero struck the horse's side, it reared, plunged away and broke its tether. The saddle was flung back on Joseph's chest. He stood smiling a little while he watched the horse run out of the glade and away. And now the calm redescended upon him, and his fear was gone. "I'll climb up on the rock and sleep a while," he said. He felt a little pain on his wrist and lifted his arm to look. A saddle buckle had cut him; his wrist and palm were bloody. As he looked at the little wound, the calm grew more secure about him, and the aloofness cut him off from the grove and from all the world. "Of course," he said, "I'll climb up on the rock." He worked his way carefully up its steep sides until at last he lay in the deep soft moss on the rock's top. When he had rested a few minutes, he took out his knife again and carefully, gently opened the vessels of his wrist. The pain was sharp at first, but in a moment its sharpness dulled. He watched the bright blood cascading over the moss, and he heard the shouting of the wind around the grove. The sky was growing grey. And time passed and Joseph grew grey too. He lay on his side with his wrist outstretched and looked down the long black mountain range of his body. Then his body grew huge and light. It arose into the sky, and out of it came the streaking rain. "I should have known," he whispered. "I am the rain." And yet he looked dully down the mountains of his body where the hills fell to an abyss. He felt the driving rain, and heard it whipping down, pattering on the ground. He saw his hills grow dark with moisture. Then a lancing pain shot through the heart of the world. "I am the land," he said, "and I am the rain. The grass will grow out of me in a little while."

And the storm thickened, and covered the world with darkness, and with the rush of waters.

26

THE RAIN swept through the valley. In a few hours the little streams were boiling down from the hillsides and falling into the river of Our Lady. The earth turned black and drank the water until it could hold no more. The river itself churned among the boulders and raced for the pass in the hills.

Father Angelo was in his little house, sitting among the parchment books and the holy pictures, when the rain started. He was reading *La Vida del San Bartolomeo*. But when the pattering on the roof began, he laid the book down. Through the hours he heard the roaring of the water over the valley and the shouting of the river. Now and then he went to his door and looked out. All the first night he stayed awake and listened happily to the commotion of the rain. And he was glad when he remembered how he had prayed for it.

At dusk of the second night, the storm was unabated. Father Angelo went into his church and replaced the candles before the Virgin, and did his duties to her. And then he stood in the dark doorway of the church and looked out on the sodden land. He saw Manuel Gomez hurry past carrying a wet coyote pelt. And soon afterward, Jose Alvarez trotted by with a deer's horns in his hands. Father Angelo covered himself with the shadow of the doorway. Mrs. Gutierrez splashed through the puddles holding an old moth-eaten bear skin in her arms. The priest knew what would take place in this rainy night. A hot anger flared up in him. "Only let them start it, and I'll stop them," he said.

He went back into the church and took a heavy crucifix from a cupboard and retired with it to his house. Once in his sitting-room he coated the crucifix with phosphorus so that it might be better seen in the dark, and then he sat down and listened for the expected sounds. It was difficult to hear them over the splash and the battering of the rain, but at last he made them out—the throb of the bass strings of the guitars, pounding and pounding. Still Father Angelo sat and listened, and a strange reluctance to interfere came over him. A low chanting of many voices joined the rhythm of the strings, rising and falling. The priest could see in his mind how the people were dancing, beating the soft earth to slush with their bare feet. He knew how they would be wearing the skins of animals, although they didn't know why they wore them. The pounding rhythm grew louder and more insistent, and the chanting voices shrill and hysterical. "They'll be taking off their clothes," the priest whispered, "and they'll roll in the mud. They'll be rutting like pigs in the mud."

He put on a heavy cloak and took up his crucifix and opened the door. The rain was roaring on the ground, and in the distance, the river crashed on its stones. The guitars throbbed feverishly and the chant had become a bestial snarling. Father Angelo thought he could hear the bodies splashing in the mud.

Slowly he closed the door again, and took off his cloak and laid down his phosphorescent cross. "I couldn't see them in the dark," he said. "They'd all get away in the dark." And then he confessed to himself: "They wanted the rain so, poor children. I'll preach against them on Sunday. I'll give everybody a little penance."

He went back to his chair and sat listening to the rush of the waters. He thought of Joseph Wayne, and he saw the pale eyes suffering because of the land's want. "That man must be very happy now," Father Angelo said to himself.

TORTILLA FLAT

Chapter Headings

Preface

THIS is the story of Danny and of Danny's friends and of Danny's house. It is a story of how these three became one thing, so that in Tortilla Flat if you speak of Danny's house you do not mean a structure of wood flaked with old whitewash, overgrown with an ancient untrimmed rose of Castile. No, when you speak of Danny's house you are understood to mean a unit of which the parts are men, from which came sweetness and joy, philanthropy and, in the end, a mystic sorrow. For Danny's house was not unlike the Round Table, and Danny's friends were not unlike the knights of it. And this is the story of how that group came into being, of how it flourished and grew to be an organization beautiful and wise. This story deals with the adventuring of Danny's friends, with the good they did, with their thoughts and their endeavors. In the end, this story tells how the talisman was lost and how the group disintegrated.

In Monterey, that old city on the coast of California, these things are well known, and they are repeated and sometimes elaborated. It is well that this cycle be put down on paper so that in a future time scholars, hearing the legends, may not say as they say of Arthur and of Roland and of Robin Hood—"There was no Danny nor any group of Danny's friends, nor any house. Danny is a nature god and his friends primitive symbols of the wind, the sky, the sun." This history is designed now and ever to keep the sneers from the lips of sour scholars.

Monterey sits on the slope of a hill, with a blue bay below it and with a forest of tall dark pine trees at its back. The lower parts of the town are inhabited by Americans, Italians, catchers and canners of fish. But on the hill where the forest and the town intermingle, where the streets are innocent of asphalt and the corners free of street lights, the old inhabitants of Monterey are embattled as the Ancient Britons are embattled in Wales. These are the paisanos.

They live in old wooden houses set in weedy yards, and the

pine trees from the forest are about the houses. The paisanos are clean of commercialism, free of the complicated systems of American business, and, having nothing that can be stolen, exploited or mortgaged, that system has not attacked them very vigorously.

What is a paisano? He is a mixture of Spanish, Indian, Mexican and assorted Caucasian bloods. His ancestors have lived in California for a hundred or two years. He speaks English with a paisano accent and Spanish with a paisano accent. When questioned concerning his race, he indignantly claims pure Spanish blood and rolls up his sleeve to show that the soft inside of his arm is nearly white. His color, like that of a well-browned meerschaum pipe, he ascribes to sunburn. He is a paisano, and he lives in that uphill district above the town of Monterey called Tortilla Flat, although it isn't a flat at all.

Danny was a paisano, and he grew up in Tortilla Flat and every one liked him, but he did not stand out particularly from the screeching children of Tortilla Flat. He was related to nearly every one in the Flat by blood or romance. His grandfather was an important man who owned two small houses in Tortilla Flat and was respected for his wealth. If the growing Danny preferred to sleep in the forest, to work on ranches and to wrest his food and wine from an unwilling world, it was not because he did not have influential relatives. Danny was small and dark and intent. At twenty-five his legs were bent to the exact curves of a horse's sides.

Now when Danny was twenty-five years old, the war with Germany was declared. Danny and his friend Pilon (Pilon, by the way, is something thrown in when a trade is concluded—a boot) had two gallons of wine when they heard about the war. Big Joe Portagee saw the glitter of the bottles among the pines and he joined Danny and Pilon.

As the wine went down in the bottles, patriotism arose in the three men. And when the wine was gone they went down the hill arm in arm for comradeship and safety, and they walked into Monterey. In front of an enlistment station they cheered loudly for America and dared Germany to do her worst. They howled menaces at the German Empire until the enlistment sergeant awakened and put on his uniform and came into the street to silence them. He remained to enlist them.

The sergeant lined them up in front of his desk. They passed everything but the sobriety test and then the sergeant began his questions with Pilon.

"What branch do you want to go in?"

"I don' give a god-dam," said Pilon jauntily.

"I guess we need men like you in the infantry." And Pilon was written so.

He turned then to Big Joe, and the Portagee was getting sober. "Where do you want to go?"

"I want to go home," Big Joe said miserably.

The sergeant put him in the infantry too. Finally he confronted Danny, who was sleeping on his feet. "Where do you want to go?"

"Huh?"

"I say, what branch?"

"What you mean, 'branch'?"

"What can you do?"

"Me? I can do anything."

"What did you do before?"

"Me? I'm a mule skinner."

"Oh, you are? How many mules can you drive?"

Danny leaned forward, vaguely and professionally. "How many you got?"

"About thirty thousand," said the sergeant.

Danny waved his hand. "String 'em up!" he said.

And so Danny went to Texas and broke mules for the duration of the war. And Pilon marched about Oregon with the infantry, and Big Joe, as shall be later made clear, went to jail.

I

*How Danny, home from the wars, found himself an heir,
and how he swore to protect the helpless.*

WHEN Danny came home from the army he learned that
he was an heir and an owner of property. The viejo,
that is the grandfather, had died leaving Danny the two small
houses on Tortilla Flat.

When Danny heard about it he was a little weighed down
with the responsibility of ownership. Before he ever went to
look at his property he bought a gallon of red wine and drank
most of it himself. The weight of responsibility left him then,
and his very worst nature came to the surface. He shouted, he
broke a few chairs in a poolroom on Alvarado Street; he had
two short but glorious fights. No one paid much attention to
Danny. At last his wavering bow-legs took him toward the
wharf where, at this early hour in the morning, the Italian
fishermen were walking down in rubber boots to go out to
sea.

Race antipathy overcame Danny's good sense. He menaced
the fishermen. "Sicilian bastards," he called them, and "Scum
from the prison island," and "Dogs of dogs of dogs." He
cried, *"Chinga tu madre, Piojo."* He thumbed his nose and
made obscene gestures below his waist. The fishermen only
grinned and shifted their oars and said, "Hello, Danny.
When'd you get home? Come around to-night. We got new
wine."

Danny was outraged. He screamed, *"Pon un condo a la
cabeza."*

They called, "Good-by, Danny. See you to-night." And
they climbed into their little boats and rowed out to the lam-
para launches and started their engines and chugged away.

Danny was insulted. He walked back up Alvarado Street,
breaking windows as he went, and in the second block a policeman took him in hand. Danny's great respect for the law
caused him to go quietly. If he had not just been discharged
from the army after the victory over Germany, he would have

been sentenced to six months. As it was, the judge gave him only thirty days.

And so for one month Danny sat on his cot in the Monterey city jail. Sometimes he drew obscene pictures on the walls, and sometimes he thought over his army career. Time hung heavy on Danny's hands there in his cell in the city jail. Now and then a drunk was put in for the night, but for the most part crime in Monterey was stagnant, and Danny was lonely. The bedbugs bothered him a little at first, but as they got used to the taste of him and he grew accustomed to their bites, they got along peacefully.

He started playing a satiric game. He caught a bedbug, squashed it against the wall, drew a circle around it with a pencil and named it "Mayor Clough." Then he caught others and named them after the City Council. In a little while he had one wall decorated with squashed bedbugs, each named for a local dignitary. He drew ears and tails on them, gave them big noses and mustaches. Tito Ralph, the jailer, was scandalized; but he made no complaint because Danny had not included either the justice of the peace who had sentenced him, nor any of the police force. He had a vast respect for the law.

One night when the jail was lonely, Tito Ralph came into Danny's cell bearing two bottles of wine. An hour later he went out for more wine, and Danny went with him. It was cheerless in the jail. They stayed at Torrelli's, where they bought the wine, until Torrelli threw them out. After that Danny went up among the pines and fell asleep, while Tito Ralph staggered back and reported his escape.

When the brilliant sun awakened Danny about noon, he determined to hide all day to escape pursuit. He ran and dodged behind bushes. He peered out of the undergrowth like a hunted fox. And, at evening, the rules having been satisfied, he came out and went about his business.

Danny's business was fairly direct. He went to the back door of a restaurant. "Got any old bread I can give my dog?" he asked the cook. And while that gullible man was wrapping up the food, Danny stole two slices of ham, four eggs, a lamb chop and a fly swatter.

"I will pay you sometime," he said.

"No need to pay for scraps. I throw them away if you don't take them."

Danny felt better about the theft then. If that was the way they felt, on the surface he was guiltless. He went back to Torrelli's, traded the four eggs, the lamb chop and the fly swatter for a water glass of grappa and retired toward the woods to cook his supper.

The night was dark and damp. The fog hung like limp gauze among the black pines that guard the landward limits of Monterey. Danny put his head down and hurried for the shelter of the woods. Ahead of him he made out another hurrying figure; and as he narrowed the distance, he recognized the scuttling walk of his old friend Pilon. Danny was a generous man, but he recalled that he had sold all his food except the two slices of ham and the bag of stale bread.

"I will pass Pilon by," he decided. "He walks like a man who is full of roast turkey and things like that."

Then suddenly Danny noticed that Pilon clutched his coat lovingly across his bosom.

"Ai, Pilon, *amigo*!" Danny cried.

Pilon scuttled on faster. Danny broke into a trot. "Pilon, my little friend! Where goest thou so fast?"

Pilon resigned himself to the inevitable and waited. Danny approached warily, but his tone was enthusiastic. "I looked for thee, dearest of little angelic friends, for see, I have here two great steaks from God's own pig, and a sack of sweet white bread. Share my bounty, Pilon, little dumpling."

Pilon shrugged his shoulders. "As you say," he muttered savagely. They walked on together into the woods. Pilon was puzzled. At length he stopped and faced his friend. "Danny," he asked sadly, "how knewest thou I had a bottle of brandy under my coat?"

"Brandy?" Danny cried. "Thou hast brandy? Perhaps it is for some sick old mother," he said naïvely. "Perhaps thou keepest it for Our Lord Jesus when He comes again. Who am I, thy friend, to judge the destination of this brandy? I am not even sure thou hast it. Besides I am not thirsty. I would not touch this brandy. Thou art welcome to this big roast of pork I have, but as for thy brandy, that is thine own."

Pilon answered him sternly. "Danny, I do not mind sharing

my brandy with you, half and half. It is my duty to see you do not drink it all."

Danny dropped the subject then. "Here in the clearing I will cook this pig, and you will toast the sugar cakes in this bag here. Put thy brandy here, Pilon. It is better here, where we can see it, and each other."

They built a fire and broiled the ham and ate the stale bread. The brandy receded quickly down the bottle. After they had eaten, they huddled near the fire and sipped delicately at the bottle like effete bees. And the fog came down upon them and grayed their coats with moisture. The wind sighed sadly in the pines about them.

And after a time, a loneliness fell upon Danny and Pilon. Danny thought of his lost friends.

"Where is Arthur Morales?" Danny asked, turning his palms up and thrusting his arms forward. "Dead in France," he answered himself, turning the palms down and dropping his arms in despair. "Dead for his country. Dead in a foreign land. Strangers walk near his grave and they do not know Arthur Morales lies there." He raised his hands palms upward again. "Where is Pablo, that good man?"

"In jail," said Pilon. "Pablo stole a goose and hid in the brush; and that goose bit Pablo and Pablo cried out and so was caught. Now he lies in jail for six months."

Danny sighed and changed the subject, for he realized that he had prodigally used up the only acquaintance in any way fit for oratory. But the loneliness was still on him and demanded an outlet. "Here we sit," he began at last.

"—broken hearted," Pilon added rhythmically.

"No, this is not a poem," Danny said. "Here we sit, homeless. We gave our lives for our country, and now we have no roof over our head."

"We never did have," Pilon added helpfully.

Danny drank dreamily until Pilon touched his elbow and took the bottle. "That reminds me," Danny said, "of a story of a man who owned two whore houses——" His mouth dropped open. "Pilon!" he cried. "Pilon! my little fat duck of a baby friend. I had forgotten! I am an heir! I own two houses."

"Whore houses?" Pilon asked hopefully. "Thou art a drunken liar," he continued.

"No, Pilon. I tell the truth. The viejo died. I am the heir. I, the favorite grandson."

"Thou art the only grandson," said the realist, Pilon. "Where are these houses?"

"You know the viejo's house on Tortilla Flat, Pilon?"

"Here in Monterey?"

"Yes, here in Tortilla Flat."

"Are they any good, these houses?"

Danny sank back, exhausted with emotion. "I do not know. I forgot I owned them."

Pilon sat silent and absorbed. His face grew mournful. He threw a handful of pine needles on the fire, watched the flames climb frantically among them and die. For a long time he looked into Danny's face with deep anxiety, and then Pilon sighed noisily, and again he sighed. "Now it is over," he said sadly. "Now the great times are done. Thy friends will mourn, but nothing will come of their mourning."

Danny put down the bottle, and Pilon picked it up and set it in his own lap.

"Now what is over?" Danny demanded. "What do you mean?"

"It is not the first time," Pilon went on. "When one is poor, one thinks, 'If I had money I would share it with my good friends.' But let that money come and charity flies away. So it is with thee, my once-friend. Thou art lifted above thy friends. Thou art a man of property. Thou wilt forget thy friends who shared everything with thee, even their brandy."

His words upset Danny. "Not I," he cried. "I will never forget thee, Pilon."

"So you think now," said Pilon coldly. "But when you have two houses to sleep in, then you will see. Pilon will be a poor paisano, while you eat with the mayor."

Danny arose unsteadily and held himself upright against a tree. "Pilon, I swear, what I have is thine. While I have a house, thou hast a house. Give me a drink."

"I must see this to believe it," Pilon said in a discouraged voice. "It would be a world wonder if it were so. Men would come a thousand miles to look upon it. And besides, the bottle is empty."

II

*How Pilon was lured by greed of position to forsake
Danny's hospitality.*

THE LAWYER left them at the gate of the second house and climbed into his Ford and stuttered down the hill into Monterey.

Danny and Pilon stood in front of the paintless picket fence and looked with admiration at the property, a low house streaked with old whitewash, uncurtained windows blank and blind. But a great pink rose of Castile was on the porch, and grandfather geraniums grew among the weeds in the front yard.

"This is the best of the two," said Pilon. "It is bigger than the other."

Danny held a new skeleton key in his hand. He tip-toed over the rickety porch and unlocked the front door. The main room was just as it had been when the viejo had lived there. The red rose calendar for 1906, the silk banner on the wall, with Fighting Bob Evans looking between the super-structures of a battleship, the bunch of red paper roses tacked up, the strings of dusty red peppers and garlic, the air-tight stove, the battered rocking chairs.

Pilon looked in the door. "Three rooms," he said breathlessly, "and a bed and a stove. We will be happy here, Danny."

Danny moved cautiously into the house. He had bitter memories of the viejo. Pilon darted ahead of him, and into the kitchen. "A sink with a faucet," he cried. He turned the handle. "No water. Danny, you must have the company turn on the water."

They stood and smiled at each other. Pilon noticed that the worry of property was settling on Danny's face. No more in life would that face be free of care. No more would Danny break windows now that he had windows of his own to break. Pilon had been right—he had been raised among his fellows. His shoulders had straightened to withstand the complexity of life. But one cry of pain escaped him before he left for all time his old and simple existence.

"Pilon," he said sadly, "I wish you owned it and I could come to live with you."

While Danny went to Monterey to have the water turned on, Pilon wandered into the weed-tangled back yard. Fruit trees were there, bony and black with age, and gnarled and broken from neglect. A few tent-like chicken coops lay among the weeds, a pile of rusty barrel hoops, a heap of ashes and a sodden mattress. Pilon looked over the fence into Mrs. Morales' chicken yard, and after a moment of consideration he opened a few small holes in the fence for the hens. "They will like to make nests in the tall weeds," he thought kindly. He considered how he could make a figure-four trap in case the roosters came in too and bothered the hens and kept them from the nests. "We will live happily," he thought again.

Danny came back indignant from Monterey. "That company wants a deposit," he said.

"Deposit?"

"Yes. They want three dollars before they will turn on the water."

"Three dollars," Pilon said severely, "is three gallons of wine. And when that is gone, we will borrow a bucket of water from Mrs. Morales, next door."

"But we haven't three dollars for wine."

"I know," Pilon said. "Maybe we can borrow a little wine from Mrs. Morales."

The afternoon passed. "To-morrow we will settle down," Danny announced. "To-morrow we will clean and scrub. And you, Pilon, will cut the weeds and throw the trash in the gulch."

"The weeds?" Pilon cried in horror. "Not *those* weeds." He explained his theory of Mrs. Morales' chickens.

Danny agreed immediately. "My friend," he said, "I am glad you have come to live with me. Now, while I collect a little wood, you must get something for dinner."

Pilon, remembering his brandy, thought this unfair. "I am getting in debt to him," he thought bitterly. "My freedom will be cut off. Soon I shall be a slave because of this Jew's house." But he did go out to look for some dinner.

Two blocks away, near the edge of the pine wood, he came upon a half-grown Plymouth Rock rooster scratching in the road. It had come to that adolescent age when its voice cracked, when its legs and neck and breast were naked. Perhaps because he had been thinking of Mrs. Morales' hens in a charitable vein, this little rooster engaged Pilon's sympathy. He walked slowly on toward the dark pine woods, and the chicken ran ahead of him.

Pilon mused, "Poor little bare fowl. How cold it must be for you in the early morning, when the dew falls and the air grows cold with the dawn. The good God is not always so good to little beasts." And he thought, "Here you play in the street, little chicken. Some day an automobile will run over you; and if it kills you, that will be the best that can happen. It may only break your leg or your wing. Then all of your life you will drag along in misery. Life is too hard for you, little bird."

He moved slowly and cautiously. Now and then the chicken tried to double back, but always there was Pilon in the place it chose to go. At last it disappeared into the pine forest, and Pilon sauntered after it.

To the glory of his soul be it said that no cry of pain came from that thicket. That chicken, which Pilon had prophesied might live painfully, died peacefully, or at least quietly. And this is no little tribute to Pilon's technique.

Ten minutes later he emerged from the woods and walked back toward Danny's house. The little rooster, picked and dismembered, was distributed in his pockets. If there was one rule of conduct more strong than any other to Pilon, it was this: Never under any circumstances bring feathers, head or feet home, for without these a chicken cannot be identified.

In the evening they had a fire of cones in the air-tight stove. The flames growled in the chimney. Danny and Pilon, well-fed, warm and happy, sat in the rocking chairs and gently teetered back and forth. At dinner they had used a piece of candle, but now only the light from the stove cracks dispelled the darkness of the room. To make it perfect, rain began to patter on the roof. Only a little leaked through, and that in places where no one wanted to sit anyway.

"It is good, this," Pilon said. "Think of the nights when we slept in the cold. This is the way to live."

"Yes, and it is strange," Danny said. "For years I had no house. Now I have two. I cannot sleep in two houses."

Pilon hated waste. "This very thing has been bothering me. Why don't you rent the other house?" he suggested.

Danny's feet crashed down on the floor. "Pilon," he cried. "Why didn't I think of it!" The idea grew more familiar. "But who will rent it, Pilon?"

"I will rent it," said Pilon. "I will pay ten dollars a month in rent."

"Fifteen," Danny insisted. "It's a good house. It is worth fifteen."

Pilon agreed grumbling. But he would have agreed to much more, for he saw the elevation that came to a man who lived in his own house; and Pilon longed to feel that elevation.

"It is agreed, then," Danny concluded. "You will rent my house. Oh, I will be a good landlord, Pilon. I will not bother you."

Pilon, except for his year in the army, had never possessed fifteen dollars in his life. But, he thought, it would be a month before the rent was due, and who could tell what might happen in a month.

They teetered contentedly by the fire. After a while Danny went out for a few moments and returned with some apples. "The rain would have spoiled them anyway," he apologized.

Pilon, not to be outdone, got up and lighted the candle; he went into the bedroom and in a moment returned with a wash bowl and pitcher, two red glass vases and a bouquet of ostrich plumes. "It is not good to have so many breakable things around," he said. "When they are broken you become sad. It is much better never to have had them." He picked the paper roses from the wall. "A compliment for Señora Tor-relli," he explained as he went out the door.

Shortly afterward he returned, wet through from the rain, but triumphant in manner, for he had a gallon jug of red wine in his hand.

They argued bitterly later, but neither cared who won, for they were tired with the excitements of the day. The wine made them drowsy, and they went to sleep on the floor. The fire died down; the stove cricked as it cooled. The candle tipped over and expired in its own grease, with little blue, protesting flares. The house was dark and quiet and peaceful.

III

*How the poison of possessions wrought with Pilon and how
evil temporarily triumphed in him.*

THE NEXT DAY Pilon went to live in the other house. It
was exactly like Danny's house, only smaller. It had its
pink rose of Castile over the porch, its weed-grown yard, its
ancient, barren fruit trees, its red geraniums—and Mrs.
Soto's chicken yard was next door.

Danny became a great man, having a house to rent, and
Pilon went up the social scale by renting a house.

It is impossible to say whether Danny expected any rent, or
whether Pilon expected to pay any. If they did, both were
disappointed. Danny never asked for it, and Pilon never offered it.

The two friends were often together. Let Pilon come by a
jug of wine or a piece of meat and Danny was sure to drop in
to visit. And, if Danny were lucky or astute in the same way,
Pilon spent a riotous night with him. Poor Pilon would have
paid the money if he ever had any, but he never did have—
not long enough to locate Danny. Pilon was an honest man.
It worried him sometimes to think of Danny's goodness and
his own poverty.

One night he had a dollar, acquired in a manner so astounding that he tried to forget it immediately for fear the
memory might make him mad. A man in front of the San
Carlos hotel had put the dollar in his hand, saying, "Run
down and get four bottles of ginger-ale. The hotel is out."
Such things were almost miracles, Pilon thought. One should
take them on faith, not worry and question them. He took
the dollar up the road to give to Danny, but on the way he
bought a gallon of wine, and with the wine he lured two
plump girls into his house.

Danny, walking by, heard the noise and joyfully went in.
Pilon fell into his arms and placed everything at Danny's disposal. And later, after Danny had helped to dispose of one of
the girls and half of the wine, there was a really fine fight.

387

Danny lost a tooth, and Pilon had his shirt torn off. The girls stood shrieking by, and kicked whichever man happened to be down. At last Danny got up off the floor and butted one of the girls in the stomach, and she went out the door croaking like a frog. The other girl stole two cooking pots and followed her.

For a little while, Danny and Pilon wept over the perfidy of women.

"Thou knowest not what bitches women are," Danny said wisely.

"I do know," said Pilon.

"Thou knowest not."

"I do know."

"Liar."

There was another fight, but not a very good one.

After that, Pilon felt better about the unpaid rent. Had he not been host to his landlord?

A number of months passed. Pilon began again to worry about the rent. And as time went by, the worry grew intolerable. At last in desperation he worked a whole day cleaning squids for Chin Kee and made two dollars. In the evening he tied his red handkerchief around his neck, put on his father's revered hat and started up the hill to pay Danny the two dollars on account.

But on the way he bought two gallons of wine. "It is better so," he thought. "If I give him hard money, it does not express how warmly I feel toward my friend. But a present, now. And I will tell him the two gallons cost five dollars." This was silly, and Pilon knew it, but he indulged himself. No one in Monterey better knew the price of wine than Danny.

Pilon was proceeding happily. His mind was made up; his nose pointed straight toward Danny's house. His feet moved, not quickly, but steadily, in the proper direction. Under each arm he carried a paper bag, and a gallon of wine was in each bag.

It was purple dusk, that sweet time when the day's sleeping is over, and the evening of pleasure and conversation has not begun. The pine trees were very black against the sky, and all objects on the ground were obscured with dark; but the sky was as mournfully bright as memory. The gulls flew lazily home to the sea rocks after a day's visit to the fish canneries of Monterey.

Pilon was a lover of beauty and a mystic. He raised his face into the sky and his soul arose out of him into the sun's afterglow. That not too perfect Pilon, who plotted and fought, who drank and cursed, trudged slowly on; but a wistful and shining Pilon went up to the sea gulls where they bathed on sensitive wings in the evening. That Pilon was beautiful, and his thoughts were unstained with selfishness and lust. And his thoughts are good to know.

"Our Father is in the evening," he thought. "These birds are flying across the forehead of the Father. Dear birds, dear sea gulls, how I love you all. Your slow wings stroke my heart as the hand of a gentle master strokes the full stomach of a sleeping dog, as the hand of Christ stroked the heads of little children. Dear birds," he thought, "fly to our Lady of Sweet Sorrows with my open heart." And then he said the loveliest words he knew, "Ave Maria, gratia plena——"

The feet of the bad Pilon had stopped moving. In truth the bad Pilon for the moment had ceased to exist. (Hear this, recording angel!) There was, nor is, nor ever has been a purer soul than Pilon's at that moment. Galvez' bad bulldog came to Pilon's deserted legs standing alone in the dark. And Galvez' bulldog sniffed and went away without biting the legs.

A soul washed and saved is a soul doubly in danger, for everything in the world conspires against such a soul. "Even the straws under my knees," says Saint Augustine, "shout to distract me from prayer."

Pilon's soul was not even proof against his own memories; for, as he watched the birds, he remembered that Mrs. Pastano used sea gulls sometimes in her tamales, and that memory made him hungry, and hunger tumbled his soul out of the sky. Pilon moved on, once more a cunning mixture of good and evil. Galvez' bad bulldog turned snarling and stalked back, sorry now that he had let go such a perfect chance at Pilon's legs.

Pilon hunched his arms to ease the weight of the bottles.

It is a fact verified and recorded in many histories that the soul capable of the greatest good is also capable of the greatest evil. Who is there more impious than a backsliding priest? Who more carnal than a recent virgin? This, however, may be a matter of appearance.

Pilon, just back from Heaven, was, although he did not know it, singularly receptive of every bitter wind, toward every evil influence that crowded the night about him. True, his feet still moved toward Danny's house, but there was neither intention nor conviction in them. They awaited the littlest signal to turn about. Already Pilon was thinking how stupendously drunk he could get on two gallons of wine, and more, how long he could stay drunk.

It was almost dark now. The dirt road was no longer visible, nor the ditches on either side. No moral conclusion is drawn from the fact that at this moment, when Pilon's impulses were balanced as precariously as a feather, between generosity and selfishness, at this very moment Pablo Sanchez happened to be sitting in the ditch at the side of the road wishing he had a cigarette and a glass of wine.

Ah, the prayers of the millions, how they must fight and destroy each other on their way to the throne of God.

Pablo first heard footsteps, then saw a blurred figure, and then recognized Pilon. "Ai, *amigo*," he called enthusiastically. "What great burden is it thou carriest?"

Pilon stopped dead and faced the ditch. "I thought you were in jail," he said severely. "I heard about a goose."

"So I was, Pilon," Pablo said jocularly. "But I was not well received. The judge said the sentence did me no good, and the police said I ate more than the allowance for three men. And so," he finished proudly, "I am on parole."

Pilon was saved from selfishness. True, he did not take the wine to Danny's house, but instantly he invited Pablo to share it at the rented house. If two generous paths branch from the highroad of life and only one can be followed, who is to judge which is best?

Pilon and Pablo entered the little house joyfully. Pilon lighted a candle and produced two fruit jars for glasses.

"Health!" said Pablo.

"*Salud!*" said Pilon.

And in a few moments, "*Salud!*" said Pablo.

"Mud in your eye!" said Pilon.

They rested a little while. *"Su servidor,"* said Pilon.

"Down the rat-hole," said Pablo.

Two gallons is a great deal of wine, even for two paisanos. Spiritually the jugs may be graduated thus: Just below the shoulder of the first bottle, serious and concentrated conversation. Two inches farther down, sweetly sad memory. Three inches more, thoughts of old and satisfactory loves. An inch, thoughts of old and bitter loves. Bottom of the first jug, general and undirected sadness. Shoulder of the second jug, black, unholy despondency. Two fingers down, a song of death or longing. A thumb, every other song each one knows. The graduations stop here, for the trail splits and there is no certainty. From this point on anything can happen.

But let us go back to the first mark, which says serious and concentrated conversation, for it was at that place that Pilon made his coup.

"Pablo," he said, "dost thou never get tired of sleeping in ditches, wet and homeless, friendless and alone?"

"No," said Pablo.

Pilon mellowed his voice persuasively. "So *I* thought, my friend, when I was a dirty gutter-dog, I too, was content, for I did not know how sweet a little house is, and a roof, and a garden. Ah, Pablo, this is indeed living."

"It's pretty nice," Pablo agreed.

Pilon pounced. "See, Pablo, how would you like to rent part of my house? There would never be the cold ground for you any more. Never the hard sand under the wharf with crabs getting in your shoes. How would you like to live here with me?"

"Sure," said Pablo.

"Look, you will pay only fifteen dollars a month! And you may use all the house except my bed, and all the garden. Think of it, Pablo! And if some one should write you a letter, he will have some place to send it to."

"Sure," said Pablo. "That's swell."

Pilon sighed with relief. He had not realized how the debt to Danny rode on his shoulders. The fact that he was fairly sure Pablo would never pay any rent did not mitigate his triumph. If Danny should ever ask for money, Pilon could say, "I will pay when Pablo pays."

They moved on to the next graduation, and Pilon remembered how happy he had been when he was a little boy. "No
care then, Pablo. I knew not sin. I was very happy."

"We have never been happy since," Pablo agreed sadly.

IV

How Jesus Maria Corcoran, a good man, became an unwilling vehicle of evil.

LIFE passed smoothly on for Pilon and Pablo. In the morning when the sun was up clear of the pine trees, when the blue bay rippled and sparkled below them, they arose slowly and thoughtfully from their beds.

It is a time of quiet joy, the sunny morning. When the glittery dew is on the mallow weeds, each leaf holds a jewel which is beautiful if not valuable. This is no time for hurry or for bustle. Thoughts are slow and deep and golden in the morning.

Pablo and Pilon in their blue jeans and blue shirts walked in comradeship into the gulch behind the house, and after a little time they returned to sit in the sun on the front porch, to listen to the fish horns on the streets of Monterey, to discuss in wandering, sleepy tones the doings of Tortilla Flat; for there are a thousand climaxes on Tortilla Flat for every day the world wheels through.

They were at peace there on the porch. Only their toes wriggled on the warm boards when the flies landed on them.

"If all the dew were diamonds," Pablo said, "we would be very rich. We would be drunk all our lives."

But Pilon, on whom the curse of realism lay uneasily, added, "Everybody would have too many diamonds. There would be no price for them, but wine always costs money. If only it would rain wine for a day, now, and we had a tank to catch it in."

"But good wine," interjected Pablo. "Not rotgut swill like the last you got."

"I didn't pay for it," said Pilon. "Some one hid it in the grass by the dance hall. What can you expect of wine you find?"

They sat and waved their hands listlessly at the flies. "Cornelia Ruiz cut up the black Mexican yesterday," Pilon observed.

Pablo raised his eyes in mild interest. "Fight?" he asked.

"Oh no, the black one did not know Cornelia got a new man yesterday, and he tried to come in. So Cornelia cut him."

"He should have known," Pablo said virtuously.

"Well, he was down in the town when Cornelia got her new man. The black one just tried to go in through the window when she locked the door."

"The black one is a fool," said Pablo. "Is he dead?"

"Oh, no. She just cut him up a little bit on the arms. Cornelia was not angry. She just didn't want the black one to come in."

"Cornelia is not a very steady woman," said Pablo. "But still she has masses sung for her father, ten years dead."

"He will need them," Pilon observed. "He was a bad man and never went to jail for it, and he never went to confession. When old Ruiz was dying, the priest came to give him solace, and Ruiz confessed. Cornelia says that priest was white as buckskin when he came out of the sickroom. But afterwards that priest said he didn't believe half what Ruiz confessed."

Pablo, with a cat-like stroke, killed a fly that landed on his knee. "Ruiz was always a liar," he said. "That soul will need plenty of masses. But do you think a mass has virtue when the money for that mass comes out of men's pockets while they sleep in wine at Cornelia's house?"

"A mass is a mass," said Pilon. "Where you get two-bits is no interest to the man who sells you a glass of wine. And where a mass comes from is of no interest to God. He just likes them, the same as you like wine. Father Murphy used to go fishing all the time, and for months the Holy Sacrament tasted like mackerel, but that did not make it less holy. These things are for priests to explain. They are nothing for us to worry about. I wonder where we could get some eggs to eat. It would be good to eat an egg now."

Pablo tilted his hat down over his eyes to keep the sun from bothering him. "Charlie Meeler told me that Danny is with Rosa Martin, that Portagee girl."

Pilon sat upright in alarm. "Maybe that girl will want to marry Danny. Those Portagees always want to marry, and they love money. Maybe when they are married Danny will bother us about the rent. That Rosa will want new dresses. All women do. I know them."

Pablo, too, looked annoyed. "Maybe if we went and talked to Danny——" he suggested.

"Maybe Danny has some eggs," said Pilon. "Those chickens of Mrs. Morales are good layers."

They put on their shoes and walked slowly toward Danny's house.

Pilon stooped and picked up a beer bottle cap and cursed and threw it down. "Some evil man has left it there to deceive people," he said.

"I tried it last night," said Pablo. He looked into a yard where the green corn was ripe, and made a mental note of its ripeness.

They found Danny sitting on his front porch, behind the rose bush, wriggling his toes to keep the flies off.

"Ai, *amigos*," he greeted them listlessly.

They sat down beside him and took off their hats and their shoes. Danny took out a sack of tobacco and some papers and passed them to Pilon. Pilon looked mildly shocked, but made no comment.

"Cornelia Ruiz cut up the black Mexican," he said.

"I heard about it," said Danny.

Pablo spoke acidly. "These women, there is no virtue in them any more."

"It is dangerous to lie with them," said Pilon. "I have heard that there is one young Portagee girl here on the Flat who can give a man something to remember her by, if he goes to the trouble to get it."

Pablo made disapproving clucking noises with his tongue. He spread his hands in front of him. "What is a man to do?" he asked. "Is there no one to trust?"

They watched Danny's face, and saw no alarm appear there.

"This girl's name is Rosa," said Pilon. "I would not say her last name."

"Oh, you mean Rosa Martin," Danny observed with very little interest. "Well, what can you expect of a Portagee?"

Pablo and Pilon sighed with relief.

"How are Mrs. Morales' chickens getting along?" Pilon asked casually.

Danny shook his head sadly. "Every one of those chickens is dead. Mrs. Morales put up some string-beans in jars, and the jars blew up, and she fed the beans to the chickens, and those chickens all died, every one."

"Where are those chickens now?" Pablo demanded.

Danny waved two fingers back and forth in negation. "Some one told Mrs. Morales not to eat those chickens or she would be sick, but we scraped the insides good and sold them to the butcher."

"Has anybody died?" Pablo asked.

"No. I guess those chickens would have been all right."

"Perhaps you bought a little wine with the money from those chickens?" Pilon suggested.

Danny smiled cynically at him. "Mrs. Morales did, and I went to her house last night. That is a pretty woman in some lights, and not so old, either."

The alarm came back to Pablo and Pilon.

"My cousin Weelie says she is fifty years old," Pilon said excitedly.

Danny spread his hands. "What is it how old in years she is?" he observed philosophically. "She is lively, that one. She owns her house and has two hundred dollars in the bank." Then Danny became a little embarrassed. "I would like to make a present to Mrs. Morales."

Pilon and Pablo regarded their feet, and tried by strenuous mental effort to ward off what was coming. But their effort had no value.

"If I had a little money," said Danny, "I would buy her a box of big candy." He looked meaningly at his tenants, but neither one answered him. "I would need only a dollar or two," he suggested.

"Chin Kee is drying squids," Pilon observed. "Perhaps you could cut squids for half a day."

Danny spoke pointedly. "It would not look well for a man who owns two houses to cut squids. But perhaps if a little rent were ever paid——"

Pilon arose angrily. "Always the rent," he cried. "You would force us into the streets—into the gutters, while you sleep in your soft bed. Come, Pablo," Pilon said angrily, "we will get money for this miser, this Jew."

The two of them stalked off.

"Where will we get money?" Pablo asked.

"I don't know," said Pilon. "Maybe he won't ask again." But the inhuman demand had cut deep into their mental peace. "We will call him 'Old Jew' when we see him," said Pilon. "We have been his friends for years. When he was in need, we fed him. When he was cold, we clothed him."

"When was that?" Pablo asked.

"Well, we would have, if he needed anything and we had it. That is the kind of friends we were to him. And now he crushes our friendship into the ground for a box of big candy to give to an old fat woman."

"Candy is not good for people," said Pablo.

So much emotion had exhausted Pilon. He sat down in the ditch beside the road and put his chin in his hands and was disconsolate.

Pablo sat down too, but he only did it to rest, for his friendship with Danny was not as old and beautiful as Pilon's was.

The bottom of the ditch was choked with dry grass and bushes. Pilon, staring downward in his sorrow and resentment, saw a human arm sticking out from under a bush. And then, beside the arm, a half-full gallon bottle of wine. He clutched Pablo's arm and pointed.

Pablo stared. "Maybe he is dead, Pilon."

Pilon had got his breath and his fine clear vision again. "If he is dead, the wine will do him no good. He can't be buried with it."

The arm stirred, swept back the bushes, and disclosed the frowsy face and red stubble beard of Jesus Maria Corcoran. "Ai, Pilon. Ai, Pablo," he said hazily. *"Que tomas?"*

Pilon leaped down the bank on him. *"Amigo,* Jesus Maria! you are not well!"

Jesus Maria smiled sweetly. "Just drunk," he murmured. He rose to his knees. "Come have a drink, my friends. Drink deep. There is plenty more."

Pilon tilted the bottle over his elbow. He swallowed four times and over a pint left the jug. Then Pablo took the bottle from him, and Pablo played with it as a cat plays with a feather. He polished the mouth with his sleeve. He smelled the wine. He took three or four preliminary sips and let a few drops run all around his mouth, to tantalize himself. At last, "Madre de Dios, *que vino!*" he said. He raised the jug and the red wine gurgled happily down his throat.

Pilon's hand was out long before Pablo had to breathe again. Pilon turned a soft and admiring countenance to his friend Jesus Maria. "Hast thou discovered a treasure in the woods?" he asked. "Has some great man died and named thee in his will, my little friend?"

Jesus Maria was a humanitarian, and kindness was always in him. He cleared his throat and spat. "Give me a drink," he said. "My throat is dry. I will tell you how it was." He drank dreamily, like a man who has so much wine that he can take his time in drinking it, can even spill a little without remorse. "I was sleeping on the beach two nights ago," he said. "Out on the beach near Seaside. In the night the little waves washed a rowboat to the shore. Oh, a nice little rowboat, and the oars were there. I got in and rowed it down to Monterey. It was easily worth twenty dollars, but trade was slow, and I only got seven."

"Thou hast money left?" Pilon put in excitedly.

"I am telling you how it was," Jesus Maria said with some dignity. "I bought two gallons of wine and brought them up here to the woods, and then I went to walk with Arabella Gross. For her I bought one pair of silk drawers in Monterey. She liked them—so soft they were, and so pink. And then I bought a pint of whisky for Arabella, and then after a while we met some soldiers and she went away with them."

"Oh, the thief of a good man's money!" Pilon cried in horror.

"No," said Jesus Maria dreamily. "It was time she went anyway. And then I came here and went to sleep."

"Then thou hast no more money?"

"I don't know," said Jesus Maria. "I will see." He fished in his pocket and brought out three crumpled dollar bills and a dime. "To-night," he said, "I will buy for Arabella Gross one of those little things that goes around higher up."

"You mean the little silk pockets on a string?"

"Yes," said Jesus Maria, "and not so little as you might think, either." He coughed to clear his throat.

Instantly Pilon was filled with solicitude. "It is the night air," he said. "It is not good to sleep out in the open. Come, Pablo, we will take him to our house and cure this cold of his. The malady of the lungs has a good start, but we will cure it."

"What are you talking about?" said Jesus Maria. "I'm all right."

"So you think," said Pilon. "So Rudolfo Keeling thought. And you yourself went to his funeral a month ago. So Angelina Vasquez thought. She died last week."

Jesus Maria was frightened. "What do you think is the matter?"

"It is sleeping in this night air," Pilon said sagely. "Your lungs will not stand it."

Pablo wrapped the wine jug in a big weed, so disguising it that any one passing would have been consumed with curiosity until he knew what that weed contained.

Pilon walked beside Jesus Maria, touching him now and then under the elbow to remind him that he was not a well man. They took him to their house and laid him on a cot, and although the day was warm, they covered him with an old comforter. Pablo spoke movingly of those poor ones who writhed and suffered with tuberculosis. And then Pilon pitched his voice to sweetness. He spoke with reverence of the joy of living in a little house. When the night was far gone, and all the talk and wine were gone, and outside the deadly mists clung to the ground like the ghosts of giant leeches, then one did not go out to lie in the sickly damp of a gulch. No, one got into a deep, soft, warm bed and slept like a little child.

Jesus Maria went to sleep at this point. Pilon and Pablo had to wake him up and give him a drink. Then Pilon spoke movingly of the mornings when one lay in one's warm nest until the sun was high enough to be of some use. One did not go shivering about in the dawn, beating one's hands to keep them from freezing.

At last Pilon and Pablo moved in on Jesus Maria as two silent hunting Airedales converge on their prey. They rented the use of their house to Jesus for fifteen dollars a month. He accepted happily. They shook hands all around. The jug came out of its weed. Pilon drank deeply, for he knew his hardest task was before him. He said it very gently and casually, while Jesus Maria was drinking out of the bottle.

"And you will pay only three dollars on account now."

Jesus Maria put down the bottle and looked at him in horror. "No," he exploded. "I made a promise to Arabella Gross to buy one of those little things. I will pay the rent when it is time."

Pilon knew he had blundered. "When you lay on that beach at Seaside, God floated the little rowboat to you. Do you think the good God did it so you could buy silk drawers for a cannery slut? No! God did it so you would not die from sleeping on the ground in the cold. Do you think God is interested in Arabella's breasts? And besides, we will take a two dollar deposit," he went on. "For one dollar you can get one of those things big enough to hold the udders of a cow."

Still Jesus Maria protested.

"I will tell you," Pilon went on, "unless we pay Danny two dollars we shall all be turned into the street, and it will be your fault. You will have it on your soul that we sleep in ditches."

Under so many shots, coming from so many directions, Jesus Maria Corcoran succumbed. He passed two of the crumpled bills to Pilon.

And now the tense feeling went out of the room, and peace and quiet and a warm deep comradeship took its place. Pilon relaxed. Pablo took the comforter back to his own bed, and conversation sprang up.

"We must take this money to Danny."

Their first appetite over, they were sipping the wine out of fruit jars now.

"What is this great need Danny has for two dollars?" Jesus Maria asked.

Pilon grew confidential. His hands came into play like twin moths, restrained only by his wrists and arms from flying out the door. "Danny, our friend, is taking up with Mrs. Morales. Oh, don't think Danny is a fool. Mrs. Morales has two hundred dollars in the bank. Danny wants to buy a box of big candy for Mrs. Morales."

"Candy is not good for people," Pablo observed. "It makes their teeth ache."

"That is up to Danny," said Jesus Maria. "If he wants to ache Mrs. Morales' teeth, that is his business. What do we care for Mrs. Morales' teeth?"

A cloud of anxiety had settled on Pilon's face. "But," he interposed sternly, "if our friend Danny takes big candy to Mrs. Morales, he will eat some too. So it is the teeth of our friend that will ache."

Pablo shook his head anxiously. "It would be a bad thing if Danny's friends, on whom he depends, should bring about the aching of his teeth."

"What shall we do, then?" asked Jesus Maria, although he and every one else knew exactly what they would do. They waited politely, each one for another, to make the inevitable suggestion. The silence ran on. Pilon and Pablo felt that the suggestion should not come from them, since, by some lines of reasoning, they might be considered interested parties. Jesus Maria kept silence in duty to his hosts, but when their silence made him aware of what was required of him, he came instantly into the breach.

"A gallon of wine makes a nice present for a lady," he suggested in a musing tone.

Pilon and Pablo were astonished at his brilliance. "We can tell Danny it would be better for his teeth to get wine."

"But maybe Danny will pay no heed to our warning. If you give money to that Danny, you can't tell what he will do with it. He might buy candy anyway, and then all our time and worry are wasted."

They had made of Jesus Maria their feeder of lines, their opener of uneasy situations. "Maybe if we buy the wine ourselves and then give it to Danny there is no danger," he suggested.

"That is the thing," cried Pilon. "Now you have it."

Jesus Maria smiled modestly at being given credit for this. He felt that sooner or later this principle would have been promulgated by some one in the room.

Pablo poured the last little bit of wine into the fruit jars and they drank tiredly after their effort. It was a matter of pride to them that the idea had been arrived at so logically, and in such a philanthropic cause.

"Now I am hungry," said Pablo.

Pilon got up and went to the door and looked at the sun. "It is after noon," he said. "Pablo and I will go to Torrelli's to get the wine, while you, Jesus Maria, go into Monterey for something to eat. Maybe Mrs. Bruno, on the wharf, will give you a fish. Maybe you can get a little bread some place."

"I would rather go with you," said Jesus Maria, for he suspected that another sequence, just as logical, and just as inevitable, was beginning to grow in the heads of his friends.

"No, Jesus Maria," they said firmly. "It is now two o'clock, or about that. In an hour it will be three o'clock. Then we will meet you here and have something to eat. And maybe a little glass of wine to go with it."

Jesus Maria started for Monterey very reluctantly, but Pablo and Pilon walked happily down the hill toward Torrelli's house.

V

*How St. Francis turned the tide and put a gentle
punishment on Pilon and Pablo and Jesus Maria.*

THE AFTERNOON came down as imperceptibly as age comes to a happy man. A little gold entered into the sunlight. The bay became bluer and dimpled with shore-wind ripples. Those lonely fishermen who believe that the fish bite at high tide left their rocks, and their places were taken by others, who were convinced that the fish bite at low tide.

At three o'clock the wind veered around and blew softly in from the bay, bringing all manner of fine kelp odors. The menders of nets in the vacant lots of Monterey put down their spindles and rolled cigarettes. Through the streets of the town, fat ladies, in whose eyes lay the weariness and the wisdom one sees so often in the eyes of pigs, were trundled in overpowered motor cars toward tea and gin fizzes at the Hotel Del Monte. On Alvarado Street, Hugo Machado, the tailor, put a sign in his shop door, "Back in Five Minutes," and went home for the day. The pines waved slowly and voluptuously. The hens in a hundred hen yards complained in placid voices of their evil lot.

Pilon and Pablo sat under a pink rose of Castile in Torrelli's yard, and quietly drank wine and let the afternoon grow on them as gradually as hair grows.

"It is just as well that we do not take two gallons of wine to Danny," said Pilon. "He is a man who knows little restraint in drinking."

Pablo agreed. "Danny looks healthy," he said, "but it is just such people that you hear of dying every day. Look at Rudolfo Kelling. Look at Angelina Vasquez."

Pilon's realism arose mildly to the surface. "Rudolfo fell into the quarry above Pacific Grove," he observed in mild reproof. "Angelina ate a bad can of fish. But," he continued kindly, "I know what you mean. And there are plenty of people who die through abuse of wine."

*   *   *

All Monterey began to make gradual instinctive preparations against the night. Mrs. Guttierez cut little chiles into her
enchilada sauce. Rupert Hogan, the seller of spirits, added
water to his gin and put it away to be served after midnight.
And he shook a little pepper into his early evening whisky. At
El Paseo dancing pavilion, Bullet Rosendale opened a carton
of pretzels and arranged them like coarse brown lace on the
big courtesy plates. The Palace Drug Company wound up its
awnings. A little group of men who had spent the afternoon
in front of the post office, greeting their friends, moved toward the station to see the Del Monte Express from San
Francisco come in. The sea gulls arose glutted from the fish
cannery beaches and flew toward the sea rocks. Lines of peli-
cans pounded doggedly over the water wherever they go to
spend the night. On the purse-seine fishing boats the Italian
men folded their nets over the big rollers. Little Miss Alma
Alvarez, who was ninety years old, took her daily bouquet of
pink geraniums to the Virgin on the outer wall of the church
of San Carlos. In the neighboring and Methodist village of
Pacific Grove the W.C.T.U. met for tea and discussion, listened while a little lady described the vice and prostitution of
Monterey with energy and color. She thought a committee
should visit these resorts to see exactly how terrible conditions really were. They had gone over the situation so often,
and they needed new facts.

The sun went westering and took on an orange blush.
Under the rose bush in Torrelli's yard Pablo and Pilon finished the first gallon of wine. Torrelli came out of his house
and passed out of the yard without seeing his erstwhile customers. They waited until he was out of sight on the way to
Monterey; whereupon Pablo and Pilon went into the house,
and with a conscious knowledge of their art, cozened their
supper out of Mrs. Torrelli. They slapped her on the buttocks and called her a "Butter Duck" and took little courteous liberties with her person, and finally left her, flattered
and slightly tousled.

Now it was evening in Monterey, and the lights went on.
The windows glowed softly. The Monterey Theater began to
spell "Children of Hell—Children of Hell" over and over

with its lights. A small but fanatic group of men who believe that the fish bite in the evening took their places on the cold sea rocks. A little fog drifted through the streets and hung about the chimneys, and a fine smell of burning pine wood filled the air.

Pablo and Pilon went back to their rose bush and sat on the ground, but they were not as contented as they had been. "It is cool here," said Pilon, and he took a drink of wine to warm himself.

"We should go to our own house where it is warm," said Pablo.

"But there is no wood for the stove."

"Well," said Pablo, "if you will take the wine, I will meet you at the corner of the street." And he did, in about half an hour.

Pilon waited patiently, for he knew there are some things even one's friends cannot help with. While he waited, Pilon kept a watchful eye aimed down the street in the direction Torrelli had taken, for Torrelli was a forceful man to whom explanations, no matter how carefully considered nor how beautifully phrased, were as chaff. Moreover, Torrelli had, Pilon knew, the Italians' exaggerated and wholly quixotic ideal of marital relations. But Pilon watched in vain. No Torrelli came brutally home. In a little while Pablo joined him, and Pilon noticed with admiration and satisfaction that he carried an armful of pine sticks from Torrelli's wood pile.

Pablo made no comment on his recent adventure until they arrived at their house. Then he echoed Danny's words, "A lively one, that Butter Duck."

Pilon nodded his head in the dark and spoke with a quiet philosophy. "It is seldom that one finds all things at one market—wine, food, love and fire wood. We must remember Torrelli, Pablo, my friend. There is a man to know. We must take him a little present sometime."

Pilon built a roaring fire in the cast-iron stove. The two friends drew their chairs close and held their fruit jars to the heat to warm the wine a little. This night the light was holy, for Pablo had bought a candle to burn for San Francisco. Something had distracted his attention before that sacred plan had consummated. Now the little wax taper burned beautifully in an abalone shell, and it threw the shadows of Pablo and Pilon on the wall and made them dance.

"I wonder where that Jesus Maria has gone," Pilon observed.

"He promised he would come back long ago," said Pablo. "I do not know whether that is a man to trust or not."

"Perhaps some little thing happened to detain him, Pablo. Jesus Maria, with that red beard and that kind heart is nearly always in some kind of trouble with ladies."

"His is a grasshopper brain," said Pablo. "He sings and plays and jumps. There is no seriousness in him."

They had no great time to wait. They had barely started their second fruit jar of wine when Jesus Maria staggered in. He held each side of the door to steady himself. His shirt was torn and his face was bloody. One eye showed dark and ominous in the dancing candlelight.

Pablo and Pilon rushed to him. "Our friend! He is hurt. He has fallen from a cliff. He has been run over by a train!" There was not the slightest tone of satire, but Jesus Maria knew it for the most deadly kind of satire. He glared at them out of the eye which still had some volition in such matters.

"Both thy mothers were udderless cows," he remarked.

They fell back from him in horror at the vulgarity of the curse. "Our friend is wandering in his mind."

"The bone of his head has been broken."

"Pour him a little wine, Pablo."

Jesus Maria sat morosely by the fire and caressed his fruit jar, while his friends waited patiently for an explanation of the tragedy. But Jesus Maria seemed content to leave his friends in ignorance of the mishap. Although Pilon cleared his throat several times, and although Pablo looked at Jesus Maria with eyes which offered sympathy and understanding, Jesus Maria sat sullenly and glared at the stove and at the wine and at the blessed candle, until at length his discourteous reticence drove Pilon to an equal discourtesy. Afterwards he did not see how he could have done it.

"Those soldiers again?" he asked.

"Yes," Jesus Maria growled. "This time they came too soon."

"There must have been twenty of them to have used thee

so," Pablo observed, for the good of his friend's spirit. "Every one knows thou art a bad man in a fight."

And Jesus Maria did look a little happier then.

"They were four," he said. "Arabella Gross helped, too. She hit me on the head with a rock."

Pilon felt a wave of moral resentment rising within him. "I would not remind thee," he said severely, "how thy friends warned thee against this cannery slob." He wondered whether he had warned Jesus Maria, and seemed to remember that he had.

"These cheap white girls are vicious, my friend," Pablo broke in. "But did you give her that little thing that goes around?"

Jesus Maria reached into his pocket and brought out a crumpled pink rayon brassiere. "The time had not come," he said. "I was just getting to that point; and besides, we had not come into the woods yet."

Pilon sniffed the air and shook his head, but not without a certain sad tolerance. "Thou hast been drinking whisky."

Jesus Maria nodded.

"Where did this whisky come from?"

"From those soldiers," said Jesus Maria. "They had it under a culvert. Arabella knew it was there, and she told me. But those soldiers saw us with the bottle."

The story was gradually taking shape. Pilon liked it this way. It ruined a story to have it all come out quickly. The good story lay in half-told things which must be filled in out of the hearer's own experience. He took the pink brassiere from Jesus Maria's lap and ran his fingers over it, and his eyes went to musing. But in a moment they shone with a joyous light.

"I know," he cried. "We'll give this thing to Danny as a gift to Mrs. Morales."

Every one except Jesus Maria applauded the idea, and he felt himself hopelessly outnumbered. Pablo, with a delicate understanding of the defeat, filled up Jesus Maria's fruit jar.

When a little time had passed, all three men began to smile. Pilon told a very funny story of a thing that had happened to his father. Good spirits returned to the company. They sang. Jesus Maria did a shuffling dance to prove he was not badly hurt. The wine went down and down in the jug, but before it was gone the three friends grew sleepy. Pilon and Pablo staggered off to bed, and Jesus Maria lay comfortably on the floor, beside the stove.

The fire died down. The house was filled with the deep sounds of slumber. In the front room only one thing moved. The blessed candle darted its little spear-pointed flame up and down with incredible rapidity.

Later, this little candle gave Pilon and Pablo and Jesus Maria some ethical things to think about. Simple small rod of wax with a string through it: Such a thing, you would say, is answerable to certain physical laws, and to none other. Its conduct, you would think, was guaranteed by certain principles of heat and combustion. You light the wick; the wax is caught and drawn up the wick; the candle burns a number of hours, goes out, and that is all. The incident is finished. In a little while the candle is forgotten, and then, of course, it has never existed.

Have you forgotten that this candle was blessed? That in a moment of conscience or perhaps pure religious exaltation, it was designed by Pablo for San Francisco? Here is the principle which takes the waxen rod outside the jurisdiction of physics.

The candle aimed its spear of light at heaven, like an artist who consumes himself to become divine. The candle grew shorter and shorter. A wind sprang up outside and sifted through the cracks in the wall. The candle sagged sideways. A silken calendar, bearing the face of a lovely girl looking out of the heart of an American Beauty rose, floated out a little distance from the wall. It came into the spear of flame. The fire licked up the silk and raced toward the ceiling. A loose piece of wallpaper caught fire and fell flaming into a bundle of newspapers.

In the sky, saints and martyrs looked on with set and unforgiving faces. The candle was blessed. It belonged to Saint Francis. Saint Francis will have a big candle in its place tonight.

If it were possible to judge depth of sleep, it could be said with justice that Pablo, whose culpable action was responsible for the fire, slept even more soundly than his two friends. But since there is no gauge, it can only be said that he slept very very soundly.

The flames ran up the walls and found little holes in the roof, and leaked through into the night. The house filled with the roar of fire. Jesus Maria turned over uneasily and began, in his sleep, to take off his coat. Then a flaming shingle dropped in his face. He leaped up with a cry, and stood shocked at the fire that raged about him.

"Pilon!" he shrieked. "Pablo!" He ran into the other room, pulled his friends out of bed and pushed them out of the house. Pilon still grasped the pink brassiere in his fingers.

They stood outside the burning house, and looked in the open fire-curtained door. They could see the jug standing on the table with a good two inches of wine in it.

Pilon sensed the savage incipient heroism of Jesus Maria. "Do not do it," he shouted. "It must be lost in the fire as a punishment on us for leaving it."

The cry of sirens came to them, and the roar of trucks climbing the hill in second gear from the fire house in Monterey. The big red fire vehicles drew near and their searchlights played among the pine trunks.

Pilon turned hastily to Jesus Maria. "Run and tell Danny his house is burning. Run quickly, Jesus Maria."

"Why don't you go?"

"Listen," said Pilon. "Danny does not know you are one who rents his house. He may be a little bit angry with Pablo and me."

Jesus Maria grasped this logic and raced toward Danny's house. The house was dark. "Danny," Jesus Maria cried. "Danny, your house is on fire!" There was no answer. "Danny!" he cried again.

A window went up in Mrs. Morales' house next door. Danny sounded irritable. "What the hell do you want?"

"Your other house is on fire, the one Pablo and Pilon live in."

For a moment Danny did not answer. Then he demanded, "Is the fire department there?"

"Yes," cried Jesus Maria.

The whole sky was lighted up by now. The crackling of burning timbers could be heard. "Well," said Danny, "if the fire department can't do anything about it, what does Pilon expect me to do?"

Jesus Maria heard the window bang shut, and he turned and trotted back toward the fire. It was a bad time to call Danny, he knew, but then how could one tell? If Danny had missed the fire, he might have been angry. Jesus Maria was glad he had told him about it anyway. Now the responsibility lay on Mrs. Morales.

It was a little house, there was plenty of draft, the walls were perfectly dry. Perhaps not since old Chinatown had burned had there been such a quick and thorough fire. The men of the fire department took a look at the blazing walls and then began wetting the brush and the trees and the neighboring houses. In less than an hour the house was completely gone. Only then did the hoses play on the heap of ashes to put out the coals and the sparks.

Pilon and Pablo and Jesus Maria stood shoulder to shoulder and watched the whole thing. Half the population of Monterey and all the population of Tortilla Flat except Danny and Mrs. Morales stood happily about and watched the fire. At last, when it was all over, when only a cloud of steam arose from the black heap, Pilon turned silently away.

"Where goest thou?" Pablo called.

"I go," said Pilon, "to the woods to have out my sleep. I counsel you to come too. It will be well if Danny does not see us for a little while." They nodded gravely and followed him into the pine forest. "It is a lesson to us," said Pilon. "By this we learn never to leave wine in a house overnight."

"Next time," Pablo said hopelessly, "you will take it outside and some one will steal it."

VI

How three sinful men, through contrition, attained peace.
How Danny's Friends swore comradeship.

WHEN the sun was clear of the pines, and the ground was warm, and the night's dew was drying on the geranium leaves, Danny came out on his porch to sit in the sunshine and to muse warmly of certain happenings. He slipped off his shoes and wriggled his toes on the sun-warmed boards of the porch. He had walked down earlier in the morning and viewed the square black ashes and twisted plumbing which had been his other house. He had indulged in a little conventional anger against careless friends, had mourned for a moment over that transitory quality of earthly property which made spiritual property so much more valuable. He had thought over the ruin of his status as a man with a house to rent; and, all this clutter of necessary and decent emotion having been satisfied and swept away, he had finally slipped into his true emotion, one of relief that at least one of his burdens was removed.

"If it were still there, I would be covetous of the rent," he thought. "My friends have been cool toward me because they owed me money. Now we can be free and happy again."

But Danny knew he must discipline his friends a little, or they would consider him soft. Therefore, as he sat on his porch, warding off flies with a moving hand which conveyed more warning than threat to the flies, he went over the things he must say to his friends before he allowed them back into the corral of his affection. He must show them that he was not a man to be imposed upon. But he yearned to get it over and to be once more that Danny whom every one loved, that Danny whom people sought out when they had a gallon of wine or a piece of meat. As the owner of two houses he had been considered rich, and he had missed a great many tidbits.

Pilon and Pablo and Jesus Maria Corcoran slept a long time on the pine needles in the forest. It had been a night of terrible excitement, and they were tired. But at length the sun shone into their faces with noonday ardor and the ants walked on them, and two blue jays stood on the ground nearby, calling them all manner of sharp names.

What finished their sleep, though, was a picnic party which settled just on the other side of the bush from them and opened a big lunch basket from which moving smells drifted to Pilon and Pablo and Jesus Maria. They awakened; they sat up; and then the enormity of their situation burst upon them.

"How did the fire start?" asked Pablo plaintively, and no one knew.

"Perhaps," said Jesus Maria, "we had better go to another town for a while—to Watsonville or to Salinas; those are nice towns."

Pilon pulled the brassiere from his pocket and ran his fingers over its pink smoothness. And he held it to the sunlight and looked through it.

"That would only delay matters," he decided. "I think it would be better to go to Danny and confess our fault, like little children to a father. Then he can't say anything without being sorry. And besides, have we not this present for Mrs. Morales?"

His friends nodded agreement. Pilon's eyes strayed through the thick brush to the picnic party, and particularly to that huge lunch basket from which came the penetrating odors of deviled eggs. Pilon's nose wrinkled a little, like a rabbit's. He smiled in a quiet reverie. "I am going to walk, my friends. In a little while I will meet you at the quarry. Do not bring the basket if you can help it."

They watched sadly as Pilon got up and walked away, through the trees, in a direction at right angles to the picnic and the basket. Pablo and Jesus Maria were not surprised a few moments later, to hear a dog bark, a rooster crow, high shrill laughter, the snarl of a wild cat, a little short scream and a cry for help; but the picnic party was surprised and fascinated. The two men and two women left their basket and trotted away toward these versatile sounds.

Pablo and Jesus Maria obeyed Pilon. They did not take the basket, but always afterwards their hats and their shirts were stained with deviled eggs.

At about three o'clock in the afternoon the three penitents

walked slowly toward Danny's house. Their arms were loaded with offerings of reconciliation: oranges and apples and bananas, bottles of olives and pickles, sandwiches of pressed ham, egg sandwiches, bottles of soda pop, a paper carton of potato salad and a copy of the Saturday Evening Post.

Danny saw them coming, and he stood up and tried to remember the things he had to say. They lined up in front of him and hung their heads.

"Dogs of dogs," Danny called them, and "thieves of decent folks' other house," and "spawn of cuttlefish." He named their mothers cows and their fathers ancient sheep.

Pilon opened the bag he held and exposed the ham sandwiches. And Danny said he had no more trust in friends, that his faith had been frostbitten and his friendship trampled upon. And then he began to have a little trouble remembering, for Pablo had taken two deviled eggs out of his bosom. But Danny went back to the grand generation and criticized the virtue of its women and the potency of its men.

Pilon pulled the pink brassiere from his pocket and let it dangle listlessly from his fingers.

Danny forgot everything, then. He sat down on the porch and his friends sat down, and the packages came open. They ate to a point of discomfort. It was an hour later, when they reclined at ease on the porch, giving attention to little besides digestion, when Danny asked casually, as about some far-off object, "How did the fire start?"

"We don't know," Pilon explained. "We went to sleep, and then it started. Perhaps we have enemies."

"Perhaps," said Pablo devoutly, "perhaps God had a finger in it."

"Who can say what makes the good God act the way He does?" added Jesus Maria.

When Pilon handed over the brassiere and explained how it was a present for Mrs. Morales, Danny was reticent. He eyed the brassiere with some skepticism. His friends, he felt, were flattering Mrs. Morales. "That is not a woman to give presents to," he said finally. "Too often we are tied to women by the silk stockings we give them." He could not explain to his friends the coolness that had come to his relationship with

Mrs. Morales since he was the owner of only one house; nor could he, in courtesy to Mrs. Morales, describe his own pleasure at that coolness. "I will put this little thing away," he said. "Some day it may be of use to some one."

When the evening came, and it was dark, they went into the house and built a fire of cones in the air-tight stove. Danny, in proof of his forgiveness, brought out a quart of grappa and shared its fire with his friends.

They settled easily into the new life. "It is too bad Mrs. Morales' chickens are all dead," Pilon observed.

But even here was no bar to happiness. "She is going to buy two dozen new ones on Monday," said Danny.

Pilon smiled contentedly. "Those hens of Mrs. Soto's were no good," he said. "I told Mrs. Soto they needed oyster shells, but she paid no attention to me."

They drank the quart of grappa, and there was just enough to promote the sweetness of comradeship.

"It is good to have friends," said Danny. "How lonely it is in the world if there are no friends to sit with one and to share one's grappa."

"Or one's sandwiches," Pilon added quickly.

Pablo was not quite over his remorse, for he suspected the true state of celestial politics which had caused the burning of the house. "In all the world there are few friends like thee, Danny. It is not given to many to have such solace."

Before Danny sank completely under the waves of his friends, he sounded one warning. "I want all of you to keep out of my bed," he ordered. "That is one thing I must have to myself."

Although no one had mentioned it, each of the four knew they were all going to live in Danny's house.

Pilon sighed with pleasure. Gone was the worry of the rent; gone the responsibility of owing money. No longer was he a tenant, but a guest. In his mind he gave thanks for the burning of the other house.

"We will all be happy here, Danny," he said. "In the evenings we will sit by the fire and our friends will come in to visit. And sometimes maybe we will have a glass of wine to drink for friendship's sake."

Then Jesus Maria, in a frenzy of gratefulness, made a rash

promise. It was the grappa that did it, and the night of the fire, and all the deviled eggs. He felt that he had received great gifts, and he wanted to distribute a gift. "It shall be our burden and our duty to see that there is always food in the house for Danny," he declaimed. "Never shall our friend go hungry."

Pilon and Pablo looked up in alarm, but the thing was said; a beautiful and generous thing. No man could with impunity destroy it. Even Jesus Maria understood, after it was said, the magnitude of his statement. They could only hope that Danny would forget it.

"For," Pilon mused to himself, "if this promise were enforced, it would be worse than rent. It would be slavery."

"We swear it, Danny!" he said.

They sat about the stove with tears in their eyes, and their love for one another was almost unbearable.

Pablo wiped his wet eyes with the back of his hand, and he echoed Pilon's remark. "We shall be very happy living here," he said.

VII

How Danny's Friends became a force for Good. How they succored the poor Pirate.

A GREAT many people saw the Pirate every day, and some laughed at him, and some pitied him; but no one knew him very well, and no one interfered with him. He was a huge, broad man, with a tremendous black and bushy beard. He wore jeans and a blue shirt, and he had no hat. In town he wore shoes. There was a shrinking in the Pirate's eyes when he confronted any grown person, the secret look of an animal that would like to run away if it dared turn its back long enough. Because of this expression, the paisanos of Monterey knew that his head had not grown up with the rest of his body. They called him The Pirate because of his beard. Every day people saw him wheeling his barrow of pitchwood about the streets until he sold the load. And always in a cluster at his heels walked his five dogs.

Enrique was rather houndish in appearance, although his tail was bushy. Pajarito was brown and curly, and these were the only two things you could see about him. Rudolph was a dog of whom passers-by said, "He is an American dog." Fluff was a Pug and Señor Alec Thompson seemed to be a kind of an Airedale. They walked in a squad behind the Pirate, very respectful toward him, and very solicitous for his happiness. When he sat down to rest from wheeling his barrow, they all tried to sit in his lap and have their ears scratched.

Some people had seen the Pirate early in the morning on Alvarado Street; some had seen him cutting pitchwood; some knew he sold kindling; but no one except Pilon knew everything the Pirate did. Pilon knew everybody and everything about everybody.

The Pirate lived in a deserted chicken house in the yard of a deserted house on Tortilla Flat. He would have thought it presumptuous to live in the house itself. The dogs lived around and on top of him, and the Pirate liked this, for his dogs kept him warm on the coldest nights. If his feet were cold, he had only to put them against the warm belly of Señor Alec Thompson. The chicken house was so low that the Pirate had to crawl in on his hands and knees.

Early every morning, well before daylight, the Pirate crawled out of his chicken house, and the dogs followed him, roughing their coats and sneezing in the cold air. Then the party went down to Monterey and worked along an alley. Four or five restaurants had their back doors on this alley. The Pirate entered each one, into a restaurant kitchen, warm and smelling of food. Grumbling cooks put packages of scraps in his hands at each place. They didn't know why they did it.

When the Pirate had visited each back door and had his arms full of parcels, he walked back up the hill to Munroe Street and entered a vacant lot, and the dogs excitedly swarmed about him. Then he opened the parcels and fed the dogs. For himself he took bread or a piece of meat out of each package, but he did not pick the best for himself. The dogs sat down about him, licking their lips nervously, and shifting their feet while they waited for food. They never fought over it, and that was a surprising thing. The Pirate's dogs never fought each other, but they fought everything else that wandered the streets of Monterey on four legs. It was a fine thing to see the pack of five, hunting fox-terriers and Pomeranians like rabbits.

Daylight had come by the time the meal was over. The Pirate sat on the ground and watched the sky turn blue with the morning. Below him he saw the schooners put out to sea with deckloads of lumber. He heard the bell buoy ringing sweetly off China Point. The dogs sat about him and gnawed at the bones. The Pirate seemed to be listening to the day rather than seeing it, for while his eyes did not move about, there was an air of attentiveness in him. His big hands strayed to the dogs and his fingers worked soothingly in the coarse hair. After about half an hour, the Pirate went to the corner of the vacant lot, threw the covering of sacks from his wheel-barrow and dug up his ax out of the ground where he buried it every evening. Then up the hill he pushed the barrow, and into the woods, until he found a dead tree, full of pitch. By noon he had a load of fine kindling; and then, still followed by his dogs, he walked the streets until he had sold the load for twenty-five cents.

It was possible to observe all this, but what he did with the quarter, no one could tell. He never spent it. In the night, guarded from danger by his dogs, he went into the woods and hid the day's quarter with hundreds of others. Somewhere he had a great hoard of money.

Pilon, that acute man, from whom no details of the life of his fellows escaped, and who was doubly delighted to come upon those secrets that nestled deep in the brains of his acquaintances, discovered the Pirate's hoard by a logical process. Pilon reasoned thus: "Every day that Pirate has a quarter. If it is two dimes and a nickel, he takes it to a store and gets a twenty-five cent piece. He never spends any money at all. Therefore, he must be hiding it."

Pilon tried to compute the amount of the treasure. For years the Pirate had been living in this way. Six days a week he cut pitchwood, and on Sundays he went to church. His clothes he got from the back doors of houses, his food at the back doors of restaurants. Pilon puzzled with the great numbers for a while, and then gave it up. "The Pirate must have at least a hundred dollars," he thought.

For a long time Pilon had considered these things. But it was only after the foolish and enthusiastic promise to feed Danny that the thought of the Pirate's hoard gained any personal significance to Pilon.

Before he approached the subject at all, Pilon put his mind through a long and stunning preparation. He felt very sorry for the Pirate. "Poor little half-formed one," he said to himself. "God did not give him all the brain he should have. That poor little Pirate cannot look after himself. For see, he lives in filth in an old chicken house. He feeds upon scraps fit only for his dogs. His clothes are thin and ragged. And because his brain is not a good one, he hides his money."

Now, with his groundwork of pity laid, Pilon moved on to his solution. "Would it not be a thing of merit," he thought, "to do those things for him which he cannot do for himself? To buy him warm clothes, to feed him food fit for a human? But," he reminded himself, "I have no money to do these things, although they lie squirming in my heart. How can these charitable things be accomplished?"

Now he was getting somewhere. Like the cat, which during a long hour closes in on a sparrow, Pilon was ready for his pounce. "I have it!" his brain cried. "It is like this: The Pirate has money, but he has not the brain to use it. I have the brain! I will offer my brain to his use. I will give freely of my mind. That shall be my charity toward this poor little half-made man."

It was one of the finest structures Pilon had ever built. The urge of the artist to show his work to an audience came upon him. "I will tell it to Pablo," he thought. But he wondered whether he would dare do such a thing. Was Pablo strictly honest? Would he not want to divert some of this money to his own ends? Pilon decided not to take the chance, right then, anyway.

It is astounding to find that the belly of every black and evil thing is as white as snow. And it is saddening to discover how the concealed parts of angels are leprous. Honor and peace to Pilon, for he had discovered how to uncover and to disclose to the world the good that lay in every evil thing. Nor was he blind, as so many saints are, to the evil of good things. It must be admitted with sadness that Pilon had neither the stupidity, the self-righteousness nor the greediness for re-ward ever to become a saint. Enough for Pilon to do good and to be rewarded by the glow of human brotherhood accomplished.

That very night he paid a visit to the chicken house where the Pirate lived with his dogs. Danny, Pablo and Jesus Maria, sitting by the stove, saw him go and said nothing. For, they thought delicately, either a vapor of love had been wafted to Pilon or else he knew where he could get a little wine. In either case it was none of their business until he told them about it.

It was well after dark, but Pilon had a candle in his pocket, for it might be a good thing to watch the expression on the Pirate's face while he talked. And Pilon had a big round sugar cookie in a bag, that Susie Francisco, who worked in a bakery, had given him in return for a formula for getting the love of

Charlie Guzman. Charlie was a Postal Telegraph messenger and rode a motorcycle; and Susie had a man's cap to put on backward in case Charlie should ever ask her to ride with him. Pilon thought the Pirate might like the sugar cookie.

The night was very dark. Pilon picked his way along a narrow street bordered with vacant lots and with weed-grown, neglected gardens.

Galvez' bad bulldog came snarling out of Galvez' yard, and Pilon spoke soothing compliments to him. "Nice dog," he said gently, and "Pretty dog," both of them palpable lies. They impressed the bulldog, however, for he retired into Galvez' yard.

Pilon came at last to the vacant property where the Pirate lived. And now he knew he must be careful, for the Pirate's dogs, if they suspected ill of any one toward their master, were known to become defending furies. As Pilon stepped into the yard, he heard deep and threatening growls from the chicken house.

"Pirate," he called. "It is thy good friend Pilon, come to talk with thee."

There was silence. The dogs stopped growling.

"Pirate, it is only Pilon."

A deep surly voice answered him, "Go away. I am sleeping now. The dogs are sleeping. It is dark, Pilon. Go to bed."

"I have a candle in my pocket," Pilon called. "It will make a light as bright as day in thy dark house. I have a big sugar cookie for thee, too."

A faint scuffling sounded in the chicken house. "Come then," the Pirate said. "I will tell the dogs it is all right."

As he advanced through the weeds, Pilon could hear the Pirate talking softly to his dogs, explaining to them that it was only Pilon, who would do no harm. Pilon bent over in front of the dark doorway and scratched a match and lighted his candle.

The Pirate was seated on the dirt floor, and his dogs were all about him. Enrique growled, and had to be reassured again. "That one is not so wise as the others," the Pirate said pleasantly. His eyes were the pleased eyes of an amused child. When he smiled his big white teeth glistened in the candle-light.

Pilon held out the bag. "It is a fine cake for you," he said.

The Pirate took the bag and looked into it; then he smiled delightedly, and brought out the cookie. The dogs all grinned and faced him, and moved their feet and licked their lips. The Pirate broke his cookie into seven pieces. The first he gave to Pilon, who was his guest. "Now, Enrique," he said. "Now Fluff. Now Señor Alec Thompson." Each dog received his piece and gulped it and looked for more. Last, the Pirate ate his and held up his hands to the dogs. "No more, you see," he told them. Immediately the dogs lay down about him.

Pilon sat on the floor and stood the candle on the ground in front of him. The Pirate questioned him self-consciously with his eyes. Pilon sat silently, to let many questions pass through the Pirate's head. At length he said, "Thou art a worry to thy friends."

The Pirate's eyes filled with astonishment. "I? To my friends? What friends?"

Pilon softened his voice. "Thou hast many friends who think of thee. They do not come to see thee because thou art proud. They think it might hurt thy pride to have them see thee living in this chicken house, clothed in rags, eating garbage with thy dogs. But these friends of thine worry for fear the bad life may make thee ill."

The Pirate was following his words with breathless astonishment, and his brain tried to realize these new things he was hearing. It did not occur to him to doubt them, since Pilon was saying them. "I have all these friends?" he said in wonder. "And I did not know it. And I am a worry to those friends. I did not know, Pilon. I would not have worried them if I had known." He swallowed to clear his throat of emotion. "You see, Pilon, the dogs like it here. And I like it because of them. I did not think I was a worry to my friends." Tears came into the Pirate's eyes.

"Nevertheless," Pilon said, "thy mode of living keeps all thy friends uneasy."

The Pirate looked down at the ground and tried to think clearly, but as always, when he attempted to cope with a problem, his brain grew gray and no help came from it, but only a feeling of helplessness. He looked to his dogs for protection, but they had gone back to sleep, for it was none of their business. And then he looked earnestly into Pilon's eyes. "You must tell me what to do, Pilon. I did not know these things."

It was too easy. Pilon was a little ashamed that it should be so easy. He hesitated; nearly gave it up; but then he knew he would be angry with himself if he did. "Thy friends are poor," he said. "They would like to help thee, but they have no money. If thou hast money hidden, bring it out into the open. Buy thyself some clothes. Eat food that is not cast out by other people. Bring thy money out of its hiding place, Pirate."

Pilon had been looking closely at the Pirate's face while he spoke. He saw the eyes droop with suspicion and then with sullenness. In a moment Pilon knew two things certainly; first, that the Pirate had money hidden; and second, that it was not going to be easy to get at it. He was pleased at the latter fact. The Pirate had become a problem in tactics such as Pilon enjoyed.

Now the Pirate was looking at him again, and in his eyes was cunning, and on top of that, a studied ingenuousness. "I have no money anywhere," he said.

"But every day, my friend, I have seen thee get a quarter for thy wood, and never have I seen thee spend it."

This time the Pirate's brain came to his rescue. "I give it to a poor old woman," he said. "I have no money anywhere." And with his tone he closed a door tightly on the subject.

"So it must be guile," Pilon thought. So those gifts, that in him were so sharpened, must be called into play. He stood up and lifted his candle. "I only thought to tell thee how thy friends worry," he said critically. "If thou wilt not try to help, I can do nothing for thee."

The sweetness came back into the Pirate's eyes. "Tell them I am healthy," he begged. "Tell my friends to come and see me. I will not be too proud. I will be glad to see them any time. Wilt thou tell them for me, Pilon?"

"I will tell them," Pilon said ungraciously. "But thy friends will not be pleased when they see thou dost nothing to relieve their minds." Pilon blew out his candle and went away into the darkness. He knew that the Pirate would never tell where his hoard was. It must be found by stealth, taken by force and then all the good things given to the Pirate. It was the only way.

And so Pilon set himself to watch the Pirate. He followed him into the forest when he went to cut kindlings. He lay in wait outside the chicken house at night. He talked to him long and earnestly, and nothing came of it. The treasure was as far from discovery as ever. Either it lay buried in the chicken house or it was hidden deep in the forest, and was only visited at night.

The long and fruitless vigils wore out the patience of Pilon. He knew he must have help and advice. And who could better give it than those comrades, Danny, Pablo and Jesus Maria? Who could be so stealthy, so guileful? Who could melt to kindness with more ease?

Pilon took them into his confidence; but first he prepared them, as he had prepared himself: The Pirate's poverty, his helplessness, and finally—the solution. When he came to the solution, his friends were in a philanthropic frenzy. They applauded him. Their faces shone with kindness. Pablo thought there might be well over a hundred dollars in the hoard.

When their joy had settled to a working enthusiasm, they came to plans.

"We must watch him," Pablo said.

"But I have watched him," Pilon argued. "It must be that he creeps off in the night, and then one cannot follow too close, for his dogs guard him like devils. It is not going to be so easy."

"You've used every argument?" Danny asked.

"Yes. Every one."

In the end it was Jesus Maria, that humane man, who found the way out. "It is difficult while he lives in that chicken house," he said. "But suppose he lived here, with us? Either his silence would break under our kindness, or else it would be easier to know when he goes out at night."

The friends gave a good deal of thought to this suggestion. "Sometimes the things he gets out of restaurants are nearly new," mused Pablo. "I have seen him with a steak out of which only a little was missing."

"It might be as much as two hundred dollars," said Pilon.

Danny offered an objection. "But those dogs—he would bring his dogs with him."

"They are good dogs," said Pilon. "They obey him exactly. You may draw a line around a corner and say, 'Keep thy dogs within this line.' He will tell them, and those dogs will stay."

"I saw the Pirate one morning, and he had nearly half a cake, just a little bit damp with coffee," said Pablo.

The question settled itself. The house resolved itself into a committee, and the committee visited the Pirate.

It was a crowded place, that chicken house, when they all got inside. The Pirate tried to disguise his happiness with a gruff tone.

"The weather has been bad," he said socially. And, "You wouldn't believe, maybe, that I found a tick as big as a pigeon's egg on Rudolph's neck." And he spoke disparagingly of his home, as a host should. "It is too small," he said. "It is not a fit place for one's friends to come. But it is warm and snug, especially for the dogs."

Then Pilon spoke. He told the Pirate that worry was killing his friends; but if he would go to live with them, then they could sleep again, with their minds at ease.

It was a very great shock to the Pirate. He looked at his hands. And he looked to his dogs for comfort, but they would not meet his glance. At last he wiped the happiness from his eyes with the back of his hand, and he wiped his hand on his big black beard.

"And the dogs?" he asked softly. "You want the dogs, too? Are you friends of the dogs?"

Pilon nodded. "Yes, the dogs, too. There will be a whole corner set aside for the dogs."

The Pirate had a great deal of pride. He was afraid he might not conduct himself well. "Go away now," he said pleadingly. "Go home now. To-morrow I will come."

His friends knew how he felt. They crawled out of the door and left him alone.

"He will be happy with us, that one," said Jesus Maria.

"Poor little lonely man," Danny added. "If I had known, I would have asked him long ago, even if he had no treasure."

A flame of joy burned in all of them.

They settled soon into the new relationship. Danny, with a

piece of blue chalk, drew a segment of a circle, enclosing a corner of the living room, and that was where the dogs must stay when they were in the house. The Pirate slept in that corner too, with the dogs.

The house was beginning to be a little crowded, with five men and five dogs; but from the first, Danny and his friends realized that their invitation to the Pirate had been inspired by that weary and anxious angel who guarded their destinies and protected them from evil.

Every morning, long before his friends were awake, the Pirate arose from his corner and, followed by his dogs, he made the rounds of the restaurants and the wharves. He was one of those for whom every one feels a kindliness. His packages grew larger. The paisanos received his bounty and made use of it; fresh fish, half pies, untouched loaves of stale bread, meat that required only a little soda to take the green out. They began really to live.

And their acceptance of his gifts touched the Pirate more deeply than anything they could have done for him. There was a light of worship in his eyes as he watched them eat the food he brought.

In the evening, when they sat about the stove and discussed the doings of Tortilla Flat with the lazy voices of fed gods, the Pirate's eyes darted from mouth to mouth, and his own lips moved, whispering again the words his friends said. The dogs pressed in about him jealously.

These were his friends, he told himself in the night, when the house was dark, when the dogs snuggled close to him so that all might be warm. These men loved him so much that it worried them to have him live alone. The Pirate had often to repeat this to himself, for it was an astounding thing, an unbelievable thing. His wheelbarrow stood in Danny's yard now, and every day he cut his pitchwood and sold it. But so afraid was the Pirate that he might miss some word his friends said in the evening, might not be there to absorb some stream of the warm companionship, that he had not visited his hoard for several days to put the new coins there.

His friends were kind to him. They treated him with a sweet courtesy; but always there was some eye open and upon him. When he wheeled his barrow into the woods, one of the friends walked with him, and sat on a log while he worked. When he went into the gulch, the last thing at night, Danny or Pablo or Pilon or Jesus Maria kept him company. And in the night he must have been very quiet to have crept out without a shadow behind him.

For a week, the friends merely watched the Pirate. But at last the inactivity tired them. Direct action was out of the question, they knew. And so one evening the subject of the desirability of hiding one's money came up for discussion.

Pilon began it. "I had an uncle, a regular miser, and he hid his gold in the woods. And one time he went to look at it, and it was gone. Some one had found it and stolen it. He was an old man, then, and all his money was gone, and he hanged himself." Pilon noticed with some satisfaction, the look of apprehension that came upon the Pirate's face.

Danny noticed it, too; and he continued, "The viejo, my grandfather, who owned this house, also buried money. I do not know how much, but he was reputed a rich man, so there must have been three or four hundred dollars. The viejo dug a deep hole and put his money in it, and then he covered it up, and then he strewed pine needles over the ground until he thought no one could see that anything had been done there. But when he went back, the hole was open, and the money was gone."

The Pirate's lips followed the words. A look of terror had come into his face. His fingers picked among the neck hairs of Señor Alec Thompson. The friends exchanged a glance and dropped the subject for the time-being. They turned to the love life of Cornelia Ruiz.

In the night the Pirate crept out of the house, and the dogs crept after him; and Pilon crept after all of them. The Pirate went swiftly into the forest, leaping with sure feet over logs and brush. Pilon floundered behind him. But when they had gone at least two miles, Pilon was winded, and torn by vines. He paused to rest a moment; and then he realized that all sounds ahead of him had ceased. He waited and listened and crept about, but the Pirate had disappeared.

After two hours, Pilon went back again, slowly and tiredly. There was the Pirate in the house, fast asleep among his dogs.

The dogs lifted their heads when Pilon entered, and Pilon thought they smiled satirically at him for a moment.

A conference took place in the gulch the next morning.

"It is not possible to follow him," Pilon reported. "He vanished. He sees in the dark. He knows every tree in the forest. We must find some other way."

"Perhaps one is not enough," Pablo suggested. "If all of us should follow him, then one might not lose track of him."

"We will talk again to-night," said Jesus Maria, "only worse. A lady I know is going to give me a little wine," he added modestly. "Maybe if the Pirate has a little wine in him, he will not disappear so easily." So it was left.

Jesus Maria's lady gave him a whole gallon of wine. What could compare with the Pirate's delight that evening when a fruit jar of wine was put into his hand, when he sat with his friends and sipped his wine and listened to the talk? Such joy had come rarely into the Pirate's life. He wished he might clasp these dear people to his breast and tell them how much he loved them. But that was not a thing he could do, for they might think he was drunk. He wished he could do some tremendous thing to show them his love.

"We spoke last night of burying money," said Pilon. "To-day I remembered a cousin of mine, a clever man. If any one in the world could hide money where it would never be found, he could do it. So he took his money and hid it. Perhaps you have seen him, that poor little one who crawls about the wharf and begs fish heads to make soup of. That is my cousin. Some one stole his buried money."

The worry came back into the Pirate's face.

Story topped story, and in each one all manner of evil dogged the footsteps of those who hid their money.

"It is better to keep one's money close, to spend some now and then, to give a little to one's friends," Danny finished.

They had been watching the Pirate narrowly, and in the middle of the worst story they had seen the worry go from his face, and a smile of relief take its place. Now he sipped his wine and his eyes glittered with joy.

The friends were in despair. All their plans had failed. They were sick at heart. After all their goodness and their charity, this had happened. The Pirate had in some way escaped the good they had intended to confer upon him. They finished their wine and went moodily to bed.

Few things could happen in the night without Pilon's knowledge. His ears remained open while the rest of him slept. He heard the stealthy exit of the Pirate and his dogs from the house. He leaped to awaken his friends; and in a moment the four were following the Pirate in the direction of the forest. It was very dark when they entered the pine forest. The four friends ran into trees, tripped on berry vines; but for a long time they could hear the Pirate marching on ahead of them. They followed as far as Pilon had followed the night before, and then, suddenly, silence, and the whispering forest and the vague night wind. They combed the woods and the brush patches, but the Pirate had disappeared again.

At last, cold and disconsolate, they came together and trudged wearily back toward Monterey. The dawn came before they got back. The sun was already shining on the bay. The smoke of the morning fires arose to them out of Monterey.

The Pirate walked out on the porch to greet them, and his face was happy. They passed him sullenly, and filed into the living room. There on the table lay a large canvas bag.

The Pirate followed them in. "I lied to thee, Pilon," he said. "I told thee I had no money, for I was afraid. I did not know about my friends, then. You have told how hidden money is so often stolen, and I am afraid again. Only last night did a way out come to me. My money will be safe with my friends. No one can steal it if my friends guard it for me."

The four men stared at him in horror. "Take thy money back to the woods and hide it," Danny said savagely. "We do not want to watch it."

"No," said the Pirate. "I would not feel safe to hide it. But I will be happy knowing my friends guard it for me. You would not believe it, but the last two nights some one followed me into the forest to steal my money."

Terrible as the blow was, Pilon, that clever man, tried to escape it. "Before this money is put into our hands, maybe you would like to take some out," he suggested smoothly.

The Pirate shook his head. "No. I cannot do that. It is promised. I have nearly a thousand two-bitses. When I have a thousand I will buy a gold candle-stick for San Francisco de Assisi.

"Once I had a nice dog, and that dog was sick; and I promised a gold candle-stick of one thousand days if that dog would get well. And," he spread his great hands, "that dog got well."

"Is it one of these dogs?" Pilon demanded.

"No," said the Pirate. "A truck ran over him a little later."

So it was over, all hope of diverting the money. Danny and Pablo morosely lifted the heavy bag of silver quarters, took it in the other room and put it under the pillow of Danny's bed. In time they would take a certain pleasure in the knowledge that this money lay under the pillow, but now their defeat was bitter. There was nothing in the world they could do about it. Their chance had come, and it had gone.

The Pirate stood before them, and there were tears of happiness in his eyes, for he had proved his love for his friends.

"To think," he said, "all those years I lay in that chicken house, and I did not know any pleasure. But now," he added, "oh, now I am very happy."

VIII

How Danny's Friends sought mystic treasure on
St. Andrew's Eve. How Pilon found it and later how
a pair of serge pants changed ownership twice.

IF HE had been a hero, the Portagee would have spent a miserable time in the army. The fact that he was Big Joe Portagee, with a decent training in the Monterey jail, not only saved him the misery of patriotism thwarted, but solidified his conviction that as a man's days are rightly devoted half to sleeping and half to waking, so a man's years are rightly spent half in jail and half out. Of the duration of the war, Joe Portagee spent considerably more time in jail than out.

In civilian life, one is punished for things one does; but army codes add a new principle to this—they punish a man for things he does not do. Joe Portagee never did figure this out. He didn't clean his rifle; he didn't shave; and once or twice, on leave, he didn't come back. Coupled with these shortcomings was a propensity Big Joe had for genial argument when he was taken to task.

Ordinarily, he spent half his time in jail; of two years in the army, he spent eighteen months in jail. And he was far from satisfied with prison life in the army. In the Monterey jail he was accustomed to ease and companionship. In the army, he found only work. In Monterey, only one charge was ever brought against him: Drunk and Disorderly Conduct. The charges in the army bewildered him so completely that the effect on his mind was probably permanent.

When the war was over, and all the troops were disbanded, Big Joe still had six months' sentence to serve. The charge had been: "Being drunk on duty. Striking a sergeant with a kerosene can. Denying his identity (he couldn't remember it, so he denied everything). Stealing two gallons of cooked beans, and going A.W.O.L. on the Major's horse."

If the Armistice had not already been signed, Big Joe would probably have been shot. He came home to Monterey long after the other veterans had arrived and had eaten up all the sweets of victory.

When Big Joe swung down from the train, he was dressed in an army overcoat and tunic and a pair of blue serge trousers.

The town hadn't changed much, except for prohibition; and prohibition hadn't changed Torrelli's. Joe traded his overcoat for a gallon of wine and went out to find his friends.

True friends he found none that night, but in Monterey he found no lack of those vile and false harpies and pimps who are ever ready to lead men into the pit. Joe, who was not very moral, had no revulsion for the pit; he liked it.

Before very many hours had passed, his wine was gone, and he had no money; and then the harpies tried to get Joe out of the pit, and he wouldn't go. He was comfortable there.

When they tried to eject him by force, Big Joe, with a just and terrible resentment, broke all the furniture and all the windows, sent half-clothed girls screaming into the night; and then, as an afterthought, set fire to the house. It was not a safe thing to lead Joe into temptation; he had no resistance to it at all.

A policeman finally interfered and took him in hand. The Portagee sighed happily. He was home again.

After a short and juryless trial, in which he was sentenced to thirty days, Joe lay luxuriously on his leather cot and slept heavily for one tenth of his sentence.

The Portagee liked the Monterey jail. It was a place to meet people. If he stayed there long enough, all his friends were in and out. The time passed quickly. He was a little sad when he had to go, but his sadness was tempered with the knowledge that it was very easy to get back again.

He would have liked to go into the pit again, but he had no money and no wine. He combed the streets for his old friends, Pilon and Danny and Pablo, and could not find them. The police sergeant said he hadn't booked them for a long time.

"They must be dead," said the Portagee.

He wandered sadly to Torrelli's, but Torrelli was not friendly toward men who had neither money nor barterable property, and he gave Big Joe little solace; but Torrelli did say that

Danny had inherited a house on Tortilla Flat, and that all his friends lived there with him.

Affection and a desire to see his friends came to Big Joe. In the evening he wandered up toward Tortilla Flat to find Danny and Pilon. It was dusk as he walked up the street, and on the way he met Pilon, hurrying by in a businesslike way.

"Ai, Pilon. I was just coming to see you."

"Hello, Joe Portagee," Pilon was brusque. "Where you been?"

"In the army," said Joe.

Pilon's mind was not on the meeting. "I have to go on."

"I will go with you," said Joe.

Pilon stopped and surveyed him. "Don't you remember what night it is?" he asked.

"No. What is it?"

"It is St. Andrew's Eve."

Then the Portagee knew; for this was the night when every paisano who wasn't in jail wandered restlessly through the forest. This was the night when all buried treasure sent up a faint phosphorescent glow through the ground. There was plenty of treasure in the woods, too. Monterey had been invaded many times in two hundred years, and each time valuables had been hidden in the earth.

The night was clear. Pilon had emerged from his hard daily shell, as he did now and then. He was the idealist to-night, the giver of gifts. This night he was engaged in a mission of kindness.

"You may come with me, Big Joe Portagee, but if we find any treasure I must decide what to do with it. If you do not agree, you can go by yourself and look for your own treasure."

Big Joe was not an expert at directing his own efforts. "I will go with you, Pilon," he said. "I don't care about the treasure."

The night came down as they walked into the forest. Their feet found the pine-needle beds. Now Pilon knew it for a perfect night. A high fog covered the sky, and behind it, the moon shone so that the forest was filled with a gauze-like light. There was none of the sharp outline we think of as reality. The tree trunks were not black columns of wood, but soft and unsubstantial shadows. The patches of brush were formless and shifting in the queer light. Ghosts could walk freely to-night, without fear of the disbelief of men; for this night was haunted, and it would be an insensitive man who did not know it.

Now and then Pilon and Big Joe passed other searchers who wandered restlessly, zig-zagging among the pines. Their heads were down and they moved silently and passed no greeting. Who could say whether all of them were really living men? Joe and Pilon knew that some were shades of those old folk who had buried the treasures; and who, on Saint Andrew's Eve, wandered back to the earth to see that their gold was undisturbed. Pilon wore his saint's medallion, hung around his neck, outside his clothes; so he had no fear of the spirits. Big Joe walked with his fingers crossed in the Holy Sign. Although they might be frightened, they knew they had protection more than adequate to cope with the unearthly night.

The wind arose as they walked, and drove the fog across the pale moon like a thin wash of gray water color. The moving fog gave shifting form to the forest, so that every tree crept stealthily along and the bushes moved soundlessly, like great dark cats. The tree-tops in the wind talked huskily, told fortunes and foretold deaths. Pilon knew it was not good to listen to the talking of the trees. No good ever came of knowing the future; and besides, this whispering was unholy. He turned the attention of his ears from the trees' talking.

He began a zig-zag path through the forest, and Big Joe walked beside him like a great alert dog. Lone silent men passed them, and went on without a greeting; and the dead passed them noiselessly, and went on without a greeting.

The fog siren began its screaming on the Point, far below them; and it wailed its sorrow for all the good ships that had drowned on the iron reef, and for all those others that would sometime die there.

Pilon shuddered and felt cold, although the night was warm. He whispered a Hail Mary under his breath.

They passed a gray man who walked with his head down, and who gave them no greeting.

An hour went by, and still Pilon and Big Joe wandered as restlessly as the dead who crowded the night.

Suddenly Pilon stopped. His hand found Big Joe's arm. "Do you see?" he whispered.

"Where?"

"Right ahead there."

"Ye-s—I think so."

It seemed to Pilon that he could see a soft pillar of blue light that shone out of the ground ten yards ahead of him.

"Big Joe," he whispered, "find two sticks about three or four feet long. I do not want to look away. I might lose it."

He stood like a pointing dog while Big Joe scurried off to find the sticks. Pilon heard him break two small dead limbs from a pine tree. And he heard the snaps as Big Joe broke the twigs from his sticks. And still Pilon stared at the pale shaft of nebulous light. So faint it was that sometimes it seemed to disappear altogether. Sometimes he was not sure he saw it at all. He did not move his eyes when Big Joe put the sticks in his hands. Pilon crossed the sticks at right angles and advanced slowly, holding the cross in front of him. As he came close, the light seemed to fade away, but he saw where it had come from, a perfectly round depression in the pine needles.

Pilon laid his cross over the depression, and he said, "All that lies here is mine by discovery. Go away, all evil spirits. Go away, spirits of men who buried this treasure, *In Nomen Patris et Filius et Spiritu Sancti*," and then he heaved a great sigh and sat down on the ground.

"We have found it, oh my friend, Big Joe," he cried. "For many years I have looked, and now I have found it."

"Let's dig," said Big Joe.

But Pilon shook his head impatiently. "When all the spirits are free? When even to be here is dangerous? You are a fool, Big Joe. We will sit here until morning; and then we will mark the place, and to-morrow night we will dig. No one else can see the light now that we have covered it with the cross. To-morrow night there will be no danger."

The night seemed more fearful now that they sat in the pine needles, but the cross sent out a warmth of holiness and safety, like a little bonfire on the ground. Like a fire, however, it only warmed the front of them. Their backs were to the cold and evil things that wandered about in the forest.

Pilon got up and drew a big circle around the whole place, and he was inside when he closed the circle. "Let no evil thing cross this line, in the Name of the Most Holy Jesus," he chanted. Then he sat down again. Both he and Big Joe felt better. They could hear the muffled footsteps of the weary wandering ghosts; they could see the little lights that glowed from the transparent forms as they walked by; but their protecting line was impregnable. Nothing bad from this world or from any other world could cross into the circle.

"What are you going to do with the money?" Big Joe asked.

Pilon looked at him with contempt. "You have never looked for treasure, Big Joe Portagee, for you do not know how to go about it. I cannot keep this treasure for myself. If I go after it intending to keep it, then the treasure will dig itself down and down like a clam in the sand, and I shall never find it. No, that is not the way. I am digging this treasure for Danny."

All the idealism in Pilon came out then. He told Big Joe how good Danny was to his friends.

"And we do nothing for him," he said. "We pay no rent. Sometimes we get drunk and break the furniture. We fight with Danny when we are angry with him, and we call him names. Oh, we are very bad, Big Joe. And so all of us, Pablo and Jesus Maria and the Pirate and I talked and planned. We are all in the woods, to-night, looking for treasure. And the treasure is to be for Danny. He is so good, Big Joe. He is so kind; and we are so bad. But if we take a great sack of treasure to him, then he will be glad. It is because my heart is clean of selfishness that I can find this treasure."

"Won't you keep any of it?" Big Joe asked, incredulous. "Not even for a gallon of wine?"

Pilon had no speck of the Bad Pilon in him this night. "No, not one scrap of gold! Not one little brown penny! It is all for Danny, every bit."

Joe was disappointed. "I walked all this way, and I won't even get a glass of wine for it," he mourned.

"When Danny has the money," Pilon said delicately, "it

may be that he will buy a little wine. Of course I shall not suggest it, for this treasure is Danny's. But I think maybe he might buy a little wine. And then if you were good to him, you might get a glass."

Big Joe was comforted, for he had known Danny a long time. He thought it possible that Danny might buy a great deal of wine.

The night passed on over them. The moon went down and left the forest in muffled darkness. The fog siren screamed and screamed. During the whole night Pilon remained unspotted. He preached a little to Big Joe as recent converts are likely to do.

"It is worth while to be kind and generous," he said. "Not only do such actions pile up a house of joy in Heaven; but there is, too, a quick reward here on earth. One feels a golden warmth glowing like a hot enchilada in one's stomach. The Spirit of God clothes one in a coat as soft as camel's hair. I have not always been a good man, Big Joe Portagee. I confess it freely."

Big Joe knew it perfectly well.

"I have been bad," Pilon continued ecstatically. He was enjoying himself thoroughly. "I have lied and stolen. I have been lecherous. I have committed adultery and taken God's name in vain."

"Me too," said Big Joe happily.

"And what was the result, Big Joe Portagee? I have had a mean feeling. I have known I would go to Hell. But now I see that the sinner is never so bad that he cannot be forgiven. Although I have not yet been to confession, I can feel that the change in me is pleasing to God, for His grace is upon me. If you, too, would change your ways, Big Joe, if you would give up drunkenness and fighting and those girls down at Dora Williams' House, you too might feel as I do."

But Big Joe had gone to sleep. He never stayed awake very long when he was not moving about.

The grace was not quite so sharp to Pilon when he could not tell Big Joe about it, but he sat and watched the treasure place while the sky grayed and the dawn came behind the fog. He saw the pine trees take shape and emerge out of obscurity.

The wind died down and the little blue rabbits came out of the brush and hopped about on the pine needles. Pilon was heavy-eyed but happy.

When it was light he stirred Big Joe Portagee with his foot. "It is time to go to Danny's house. The day has come." Pilon threw the cross away, for it was no longer needed, and he erased the circle. "Now," he said, "we must make no mark, but we must remember this by trees and rocks."

"Why don't we dig now?" Big Joe asked.

"And everybody in Tortilla Flat would come to help us," Pilon said sarcastically.

They looked hard at the surroundings, saying, "Now there are three trees together on the right, and two on the left. That patch of brush is down there, and here is a rock." At last they walked away from the treasure, memorizing the way as they went.

At Danny's house they found tired friends. "Did you find any?" the friends demanded.

"No," said Pilon quickly, to forestall Joe's confession.

"Well, Pablo thought he saw the light, but it disappeared before he got to it. And the Pirate saw the ghost of an old woman, and she had his dog with her."

The Pirate broke into a smile. "That old woman told me my dog was happy now," he said.

"Here is Big Joe Portagee, back from the army," announced Pilon.

"Hello, Joe."

"You got a nice place here," said the Portagee, and let himself down easily into a chair.

"You keep out of my bed," said Danny, for he knew that Joe Portagee had come to stay. The way he sat in a chair and crossed his knees had an appearance of permanence.

The Pirate went out, and took his wheelbarrow and started into the forest to cut his kindlings; but the other five men lay down in the sunshine that broke through the fog, and in a little while they were asleep.

It was mid-afternoon before any of them awakened. At last they stretched their arms and sat up and looked listlessly down at the bay below, where a brown oil tanker moved slowly out to sea. The Pirate had left the bags on the table, and the friends opened them and brought out the food the Pirate had collected.

Big Joe walked down the path toward the sagging gate. "See you later," he called to Pilon.

Pilon anxiously watched him until he saw that Big Joe was headed down the hill to Monterey, not up toward the pine forest. The four friends sat down and dreamily watched the evening come.

At dusk Joe Portagee returned. He and Pilon conferred in the yard, out of earshot of the house.

"We will borrow tools from Mrs. Morales," Pilon said. "A shovel and a pick-ax stand by her chicken house."

When it was quite dark they started. "We go to see some girls, friends of Joe Portagee's," Pilon explained. They crept into Mrs. Morales' yard and borrowed the tools. And then, from the weeds beside the road, Big Joe lifted out a gallon jug of wine.

"Thou hast sold the treasure," Pilon cried fiercely. "Thou art a traitor, oh dog of a dog."

Big Joe quieted him firmly. "I did not tell where the treasure was," he said with some dignity. "I told like this, 'We found a treasure,' I said, 'But it is for Danny. When Danny has it, I will borrow a dollar and pay for the wine.' "

Pilon was overwhelmed. "And they believed, and let you take the wine?" he demanded.

"Well—" Big Joe hesitated. "I left something to prove I would bring the dollar."

Pilon turned like lightning and took him by the throat. "What did you leave?"

"Only one little blanket, Pilon," Joe Portagee wailed. "Only one."

Pilon shook at him, but Big Joe was so heavy that Pilon only succeeded in shaking himself. "What blanket," he cried. "Say what blanket it was you stole."

Big Joe blubbered. "Only one of Danny's. Only one. He has two. I took only the little tiny one. Do not hurt me, Pilon. The other one was bigger. Danny will get it back when we find the treasure."

Pilon whirled him around and kicked him with accuracy

and fire. "Pig," he said, "dirty thieving cow. You will get the blanket back or I will beat you to ribbons."

Big Joe tried to placate him. "I thought how we are working for Danny," he whispered. "I thought, 'Danny will be so glad, he can buy a hundred new blankets.' "

"Be still," said Pilon. "You will get that same blanket back or I will beat you with a rock." He took up the jug and uncorked it and drank a little to soothe his frayed sensibilities; moreover he drove the cork back and refused the Portagee even a drop. "For this theft you must do all the digging. Pick up those tools and come with me."

Big Joe whined like a puppy, and obeyed. He could not stand against the righteous fury of Pilon.

They tried to find the treasure for a long time. It was late when Pilon pointed to three trees in a row. "There!" he said.

They searched about until they found the depression in the ground. There was a little moonlight to guide them, for this night the sky was free of fog.

Now that he was not going to dig, Pilon developed a new theory for uncovering treasure. "Sometimes the money is in sacks," he said, "and the sacks are rotted. If you dig straight down you might lose some." He drew a generous circle around the hollow. "Now, dig a deep trench around, and then we will come *up* on the treasure."

"Aren't you going to dig?" Big Joe asked.

Pilon broke into fury. "Am I a thief of blankets?" he cried. "Do I steal from the bed of my friend who shelters me?"

"Well, I ain't going to do all the digging," Big Joe said.

Pilon picked up one of the pine limbs that only the night before had served as part of the cross. He advanced ominously toward Big Joe Portagee. "Thief," he snarled. "Dirty pig of an untrue friend. Take up that shovel."

Big Joe's courage flowed away, and he stooped for the shovel on the ground. If Joe Portagee's conscience had not been bad, he might have remonstrated; but his fear of Pilon, armed with a righteous cause and a stick of pine wood, was great.

Big Joe abhorred the whole principle of shoveling. The line of the moving shovel was unattractive. The end to be gained, that of taking dirt from one place and putting it in another, was, to one who held the larger vision, silly and gainless. A whole lifetime of shoveling could accomplish practically nothing. Big Joe's reaction was a little more simple than this. He didn't like to shovel. He had joined the army to fight, and had done nothing but dig.

But Pilon stood over him, and the trench stretched around the treasure place. It did no good to profess sickness, hunger or weakness. Pilon was inexorable, and Joe's crime of the blanket was held against him. Although he whined, complained, held up his hands to show how they were hurt, Pilon stood over him and forced the digging.

Midnight came, and the trench was three feet down. The roosters of Monterey crowed. The moon sank behind the trees. At last Pilon gave the word to move in on the treasure. The bursts of dirt came slowly now; Big Joe was exhausted. Just before daylight, his shovel struck something hard.

"Ai," he cried. "We have it, Pilon."

The find was large and square. Frantically they dug at it in the dark, and they could not see it.

"Careful," Pilon cautioned. "Do not hurt it."

The daylight came before they had it out. Pilon felt metal and leaned down in the gray light to see. It was a good-sized square of concrete. On the top was a round brown plate. Pilon spelled out the words on it:

> "United States Geodetic Survey + 1915 + Elevation
> 600 Feet."

Pilon sat down in the pit and his shoulders sagged in defeat.

"No treasure?" Big Joe asked plaintively.

Pilon did not answer him. The Portagee inspected the cement post and his brow wrinkled with thought. He turned to the sorrowing Pilon. "Maybe we can take this good piece of metal and sell it."

Pilon peered up out of his dejection. "Johnny Pom-pom found one," he said with a quietness of great disappointment. "Johnny Pom-pom took the metal piece and tried to sell it. It is a year in jail to dig one of these up," Pilon mourned. "A year in jail and two thousand dollar fine." In his pain, Pilon wanted only to get away from this tragic place. He stood up, found a weed in which to wrap the wine bottle, and started down the hill.

Big Joe trotted after him solicitously. "Where are we going?" he asked.

"I don't know," said Pilon.

The day was bright when they arrived at the beach; but even there Pilon did not stop. He trudged along the hard sand by the water's edge until Monterey was far behind and only the sand dunes of Seaside and the rippling waves of the bay were there to see his sorrow. At last he sat in the dry sand, with the sun warming him. Big Joe sat beside him, and he felt that in some way he was responsible for Pilon's silent pain.

Pilon took the jug out of its weed and uncorked it and drank deeply, and because sorrow is the mother of a general compassion, he passed Joe's wine to the miscreant Joe.

"How we build," Pilon cried. "How our dreams lead us. I had thought how we would carry bags of gold to Danny. I could see how his face would look. He would be surprised. For a long time he would not believe it." He took the bottle from Joe Portagee and drank colossally. "All this is gone, blown away in the night."

The sun was warming the beach now. In spite of his disappointment, Pilon felt a traitorous comfort stealing over him, a treacherous impulse to discover some good points in the situation.

Big Joe, in his quiet way, was drinking more than his share of the wine. Pilon took it indignantly and drank again and again.

"But after all," he said philosophically, "maybe if we had found gold, it might not have been good for Danny. He has always been a poor man. Riches might make him crazy."

Big Joe nodded solemnly. The wine went down and down in the bottle.

"Happiness is better than riches," said Pilon. "If we try to make Danny happy, it will be a better thing than to give him money."

Big Joe nodded again and took off his shoes. "Make him happy. That's the stuff."

Pilon turned sadly upon him. "You are only a pig, and not

fit to live with men," he said gently. "You who stole Danny's blanket should be kept in a sty and fed potato peelings."

They were getting very sleepy in the warm sun. The little waves whispered along the beach. Pilon took off his shoes.

"Even Stephen," said Big Joe, and they drained the jug to the last drop.

The beach was swaying gently, heaving and falling with a movement like a ground-swell.

"You aren't a bad man," Pilon said. But Big Joe Portagee was already asleep. Pilon took off his coat and laid it over his face. In a few moments, he too was sleeping sweetly.

The sun wheeled over the sky. The tide spread up the beach, and then retreated. A squad of scampering kildeers inspected the sleeping men. A wandering dog sniffed them. Two elderly ladies, collecting seashells, saw the bodies and hurried past lest these men should awaken in passion, pursue and criminally assault them. It was a shame, they agreed, that the police did nothing to control such matters. "They are drunk," one said.

And the other stared back up the beach at the sleeping men. "Drunken beasts," she agreed.

When at last the sun went behind the pines of the hill in back of Monterey, Pilon awakened. His mouth was as dry as alum; his head ached and he was stiff from the hard sand. Big Joe snored on.

"Joe," Pilon cried, but the Portagee was beyond call. Pilon rested on his elbow and stared out to sea. "A little wine would be good for my dry mouth," he thought. He tipped up the jug and got not a single drop to soothe his dry tongue. Then he turned out his pockets in the hope that while he slept some miracle had taken place there; but none had. There was a broken pocket knife for which he had been refused a glass of wine at least twenty times. There was a fish-hook in a cork, a piece of dirty string, a dog's tooth and several keys that fit nothing Pilon knew of. In the whole lot was not a thing Torrelli would consider as worth having, even in a moment of insanity.

Pilon looked speculatively at Big Joe. "Poor fellow," he thought. "When Joe Portagee wakes up, he will feel as dry as I do. He will like it if I have a little wine for him." He pushed

Big Joe roughly several times; and when the Portagee only mumbled, and then snored again, Pilon looked through his pockets. He found a brass pants button, a little metal disk which said "Good Eats at the Dutchman," four or five head-less matches and a little piece of chewing tobacco.

Pilon sat back on his heels. So it was no use. He must wither here on the beach while his throat called lustily for wine.

He noticed the serge trousers the Portagee was wearing, and stroked them with his fingers. "Nice cloth," he thought. "Why should this dirty Portagee wear such good cloth when all his friends go about in jeans?" Then he remembered how badly the pants fit Big Joe, how tight the waist was even with two fly-buttons undone, how the cuffs missed the shoe tops by inches. "Some one of a decent size would be happy in those pants."

Pilon remembered Big Joe's crime against Danny, and he became an avenging angel. How did this big black Portagee dare to insult Danny so! "When he wakes up I will beat him! But," the more subtle Pilon argued, "his crime was theft. Would it not teach him a lesson to know how it feels to have something stolen? What good is punishment unless some-thing is learned?" It was a triumphant position for Pilon. If, with one action, he could avenge Danny, discipline Big Joe, teach an ethical lesson and get a little wine, who in the world could criticize him?

He pushed the Portagee vigorously, and Big Joe brushed at him as though he were a fly. Pilon deftly removed the trousers, rolled them up and sauntered away into the sand dunes.

Torrelli was out, but Mrs. Torrelli opened the door to Pi-lon. He was mysterious in his manner, but at last he held up the pants for her inspection.

She shook her head decisively.

"But look," said Pilon. "You are seeing only the spots and the dirt. Look at this fine cloth underneath. Think, señora! You have cleaned the spots off and pressed the trousers! Tor-relli comes in! He is silent; he is glum. And then you bring him these fine pants! See how his eyes grow bright! See how happy he is! He takes you on his lap! Look how he smiles at you, señora! Is so much happiness too high at one gallon of red wine?"

"The seat of the pants is thin," she said.

He held them up to the light. "Can you see through them? No! The stiffness, the discomfort is taken out of them. They are in prime condition."

"No," she said firmly.

"You are cruel to your husband, señora. You deny him happiness. I should not be surprised to see him going to other women, who are not so heartless. For a quart, then?"

Finally her resistance was beaten down and she gave him the quart. Pilon drank it off immediately. "You try to break down the price of pleasure," he warned her. "I should have half a gallon."

Mrs. Torrelli was hard as stone. Not a drop more could Pilon get. He sat there brooding in the kitchen. "Jewess, that's what she is. She cheats me out of Big Joe's pants."

Pilon thought sadly of his friend out there on the beach. What could he do? If he came into town he would be arrested. And what had this harpy done to deserve the pants? She had tried to buy Pilon's friend's pants for a miserable quart of miserable wine. Pilon felt himself dissolving into anger at her.

"I am going away in a moment," he told Mrs. Torrelli. The pants were hung in a little alcove off the kitchen.

"Good-by," said Mrs. Torrelli over her shoulder. She went into her little pantry to prepare dinner.

On his way out Pilon passed the alcove and lifted down not only the pants, but Danny's blanket.

Pilon walked back down the beach, toward the place where he had left Big Joe. He could see a bonfire burning brightly on the sand, and as he drew nearer, a number of small dark figures passed in front of the flame. It was very dark now; he guided himself by the fire. As he came close, he saw that it was a Girl Scout wienie bake. He approached warily.

For a while he could not see Big Joe, but at last he discovered him, lying half covered with sand, speechless with cold and agony. Pilon walked firmly up to him and held up the pants.

"Take them, Big Joe, and be glad you have them back."

Joe's teeth were chattering. "Who stole my pants, Pilon? I have been lying here for hours, and I could not go away because of those girls."

Pilon obligingly stood between Big Joe and the little girls who were running about the bonfire. The Portagee brushed the cold damp sand from his legs and put on his pants. They walked side by side along the dark beach toward Monterey, where the lights hung, necklace above necklace against the hill. The sand dunes crouched along the back of the beach like tired hounds, resting; and the waves gently practiced at striking, and hissed a little. The night was cold and aloof, and its warm life was withdrawn, so that it was full of bitter warnings to man that he is alone in the world, and alone among his fellows; that he has no comfort owing him from anywhere.

Pilon was still brooding, and Joe Portagee sensed the depth of his feeling. At last Pilon turned his head toward his friend. "We learn by this that it is great foolishness to trust a woman," he said.

"Did some woman take my pants?" Big Joe demanded excitedly. "Who was it? I'll kick the hell out of her!"

But Pilon shook his head as sadly as old Jehovah, who, resting on the seventh day, sees that his world is tiresome. "She is punished," Pilon said. "You might say she punished herself, and that is the best way. She had thy pants; she bought them with greed; and now she has them not."

These things were beyond Big Joe. They were mysteries it was better to let alone; and this was as Pilon wished it. Big Joe said humbly, "Thanks for getting my pants back, Pilon." But Pilon was so sunk in philosophy that even thanks were valueless.

"It was nothing," he said. "In the whole matter only the lesson we learn has any value."

They climbed up from the beach and passed the great silver tower of the gas works.

Big Joe Portagee was happy to be with Pilon. "Here is one who takes care of his friends," he thought. "Even when they sleep he is alert to see that no harm comes to them." He resolved to do something nice for Pilon sometime.

IX

DOLORES ENGRACIA RAMIREZ lived in her own little
house on the upper edge of Tortilla Flat. She did house-
work for some of the ladies in Monterey, and she belonged to
the Native Daughters of the Golden West. She was not pretty,
this lean-faced paisana, but there was in her figure a certain
voluptuousness of movement; there was in her voice a throat-
iness some men found indicative. Her eyes could burn behind
a mist with a sleepy passion which those men, to whom the
flesh is important, found attractive and downright inviting.

In her brusque moments she was not desirable, but an amorous combination came about within her often enough so
that she was called Sweets Ramirez on Tortilla Flat.

It was a pleasant thing to see her when the beast in her was
prowling. How she leaned over her front gate! How her voice
purred drowsily! How her hips moved gently about, now
pressing against the fence, now swelling back like a summer
beach-wave, and then pressing the fence again! Who in the
world could put so much husky meaning into "Ai, amigo.
A'onde vas?"

It is true that ordinarily her voice was shrill, her face hard
and sharp as a hatchet, her figure lumpy and her intentions
selfish. The softer self came into possession only once or twice
a week, and then, ordinarily, in the evening.

When Sweets heard that Danny was an heir, she was glad
for him. She dreamed of being his lady, as did every other
female on Tortilla Flat. In the evenings she leaned over the
front gate waiting for the time when he would pass by and
fall into her trap. But for a long time her baited trap caught
nothing but poor Indians and paisanos who owned no
houses, and whose clothes were sometimes fugitive from
better wardrobes.

Sweets was not content. Her house was up the hill from
Danny's house, in a direction he did not often take. Sweets

could not go looking for him. She was a lady, and her conduct was governed by very strict rules of propriety. If Danny should walk by, now, if they should talk, like the old friends they were, if he should come in for a social glass of wine; and then, if nature proved too strong, and her feminine resistance too weak, there was no grave breach of propriety. But it was unthinkable to leave her web on the front gate.

For many months of evenings she waited in vain, and took such gifts as walked by in jeans. But there are only a limited number of pathways on Tortilla Flat. It was inevitable that Danny should, sooner or later, pass the gate of Dolores Engracia Ramirez; and so he did.

In all the time they had known each other, there had never been an occasion when it was more to Sweets' advantage to have him walk by; for Danny had only that morning found a keg of copper shingle nails, lost by the Central Supply Company. He had judged them jetsam because no member of the company was anywhere near. Danny removed the copper nails from the keg and put them in a sack. Then, borrowing the Pirate's wheelbarrow, and the Pirate to push it, he took his salvage to the Western Supply Company, where he sold the copper for three dollars. The keg he gave to the Pirate.

"You can keep things in it," he said. That made the Pirate very happy.

And now Danny came down the hill, aimed with a fine accuracy toward the house of Torrelli, and the three dollars were in his pocket.

Dolores' voice sounded as huskily sweet as the drone of a bumble-bee. "Ai, amigo, a'onde vas?"

Danny stopped. A revolution took place in his plans. "How are you, Sweets?"

"What difference is it how I am? None of my friends are interested," she said archly. And her hips floated in a graceful and circular undulation.

"What do you mean?" he demanded.

"Well, does my friend Danny ever come to see me?"

"I am here to see thee now," he said gallantly.

She opened the gate a little. "Wilt thou come in for a tiny glass of wine in friendship's name?" Danny went into her house. "What hast thou been doing in the forest?" she cooed.

Then he made an error. He told vaingloriously of his transaction up the hill, and he boasted of his three dollars.

"Of course I have only enough wine to fill two thimbles," she said.

They sat in Sweets' kitchen and drank a glass of wine. In a little while Danny assaulted her virtue with true gallantry and vigor. He found to his amazement, a resistance out of all proportion to her size and reputation. The ugly beast of lust was awakened in him. He was angry. Only when he was leaving was the way made clear to him.

The husky voice said, "Maybe you would like to come and see me this evening, Danny." Sweets' eyes swam in a mist of drowsy invitation. "One has neighbors," she suggested with delicacy.

Then he understood. "I will come back," he promised.

It was mid-afternoon. Danny walked down the street, re-aimed at Torrelli's; and the beast in him had changed. From a savage and snarling wolf it had become a great, shaggy, sentimental bear. "I will take wine to that nice Sweets," he thought.

On the way down, whom should he meet but Pablo, and Pablo had two sticks of gum. He gave one to Danny and fell into step. "Where goest thou?"

"It is no time for friendship," Danny said tartly. "First I go to buy a little wine to take to a lady. You may come with me, and have one glass only. I am tired of buying wine for ladies, only to have my friends drink it all up."

Pablo agreed that such a practice was unendurable. For himself, he didn't want Danny's wine, but only his companionship.

They went to Torrelli's. They had a glass of wine out of the new bought gallon. Danny confessed that it was shabby treatment to give his friend only one little glass. Over Pablo's passionate protest they had another. "Ladies," Danny thought, "should not drink too much wine. They were apt to become silly; and besides, it dulled some of those senses one liked to find alert in a lady." They had a few more glasses. Half a gallon of wine was a bountiful present, especially as Danny was about to go down to buy another present. They measured down half a gallon, and drank what was over. Then Danny hid the jug in the weeds in a ditch.

"I would like you to come with me to buy the present, Pablo," he said.

Pablo knew the reason for the invitation. Half of it was a desire for Pablo's company, and half was fear of leaving the wine while Pablo was at large. They walked with studied dignity and straightness down the hill to Monterey.

Mr. Simon, of Simon's Investment, Jewelry and Loan Company, welcomed them into his store. The name of the store defined the outward limits of the merchandise the company sold; for there were saxophones, radios, rifles, knives, fishing-rods and old coins on the counter; all second-hand, but all really better than new because they were just well broken-in.

"Something you would like to see?" Mr. Simon asked.

"Yes," said Danny.

The proprietor named over a tentative list, and then stopped in the middle of a word, for he saw that Danny was looking at a large aluminum vacuum-cleaner. The dust-bag was blue and yellow checks. The electric cord was long and black and slick. Mr. Simon went to it and rubbed it with his hand, and stood off and admired it. "Something in a vacuum-cleaner?" he asked.

"How much?"

"For this one, fourteen dollars." It was not a price so much as an endeavor to find out how much Danny had. And Danny wanted it, for it was large and shiny. No woman of Tortilla Flat had one. In this moment he forgot there was no electricity on Tortilla Flat. He laid his two dollars on the counter and waited while the explosion took place; the fury, the rage, the sadness, the poverty, the ruin, the cheating. The polish was invoked, the color of the bag, the extra long cord, the value of the metal alone. And when it was all over, Danny went out carrying the vacuum-cleaner.

Often as a pasatiempo in the afternoon, Sweets brought out the vacuum-cleaner and leaned it against a chair. While her friends looked on, she pushed it back and forth to show how easily it rolled. And she made a humming with her voice to imitate a motor.

"My friend is a rich man," she said. "I think pretty soon there will be wires full of electricity coming right into the house, and then zip and zip and zip! And you have the house clean!"

Her friends tried to belittle the present, saying, "It is too bad you can't run this machine." And, "I have always held that a broom and dust-pan, *properly* used, are more thorough."

But their envy could do nothing against the vacuum. Through its possession, Sweets climbed to the peak of the social scale of Tortilla Flat. People who did not remember her name referred to her as "that one with the sweeping-machine." Often when her enemies passed the house, Sweets could be seen through the window, pushing the cleaner back and forth, while a loud humming came from her throat. Indeed, after she had swept her house every day, she pushed the cleaner about on the theory that of course it would clean better with electricity, but one could not have everything.

She excited envy in many houses. Her manner became dignified and gracious, and she held her chin high as befitted one who had a sweeping-machine. In her conversation she included it. "Ramon passed this morning, while I was pushing the sweeping-machine." "Louise Meater cut her hand this morning, not three hours after I had been pushing the sweeping-machine."

But in her elevation she did not neglect Danny. Her voice growled with emotion when he was about. She swayed like a pine tree in the wind. And he spent every evening at the house of Sweets.

At first his friends ignored his absence, for it is the right of every man to have these little affairs. But as the weeks went on, and as a rather violent domestic life began to make Danny listless and pale, his friends became convinced that Sweets' gratitude for the sweeping-machine was not to Danny's best physical interests. They were jealous of a situation that was holding his attention so long.

Pilon and Pablo and Jesus Maria Corcoran in turn assaulted the nest of his affections during his absence; but Sweets, while she was sensible of the compliment, remained true to the man who had raised her position to such a gratifying level. She tried to keep their friendship for a future time of need, for she knew how fickle fortune is; but she stoutly refused to share with Danny's friends that which was dedicated for the time being to Danny.

Wherefore the friends, in despair, organized a group, formed for and dedicated to her destruction.

It may be that Danny, deep in his soul, was beginning to tire of Sweets' affection and the duty of attendance it demanded. If such a change were taking place, he did not admit it to himself.

At three o'clock one afternoon, Pilon and Pablo and Jesus Maria, followed vaguely by Big Joe Portagee, returned triumphant from three-quarters of a day of strenuous effort. Their campaign had called into play and taxed to the limit the pitiless logic of Pilon, the artistic ingenuousness of Pablo and the gentleness and humanity of Jesus Maria Corcoran. Big Joe had contributed nothing.

But now, like four hunters, they returned from the chase more happy because their victory had been a difficult one. And in Monterey, a poor puzzled Italian came gradually to the conviction that he had been swindled.

Pilon carried a gallon jug of wine concealed in a bundle of ivy. They marched joyfully into Danny's house and Pilon set the gallon on the table.

Danny, awakened out of a sound sleep, smiled quietly, got up from bed and laid out the fruit jars. He poured the wine. His four friends fell into chairs, for it had been an exhausting day.

They drank quietly in the late afternoon, that time of curious intermission. Nearly every one in Tortilla Flat stops then and considers those things that have taken place in the day just past, and thinks over the possibilities of the evening. There are many things to discuss in an afternoon.

"Cornelia Ruiz got a new man this morning," Pilon observed. "He has a bald head. His name is Kilpatrick. Cornelia says her other man didn't come home three nights last week. She didn't like that."

"Cornelia is a woman who changes her mind too quickly," said Danny. He thought complacently of his own sure establishment, built on the rock of the vacuum-cleaner.

"Cornelia's father was worse," said Pablo. "He could not tell the truth. Once he borrowed a dollar from me. I have told Cornelia about it, and she does nothing."

"Two of one blood. 'Know the breed and know the dog,'" Pilon quoted virtuously.

Danny poured the jars full of wine again, and the gallon was exhausted. He looked ruefully at it.

Jesus Maria, that lover of the humanities, spoke up quietly. "I saw Susie Francisco, Pilon. She said the recipe worked fine. She has been out riding with Charlie Guzman on his motorcycle three times. The first two times she gave him the love medicine it made him sick. She thought it was no good. But now Susie says you can have some cookies any time."

"What was in that potion?" Pablo asked.

Pilon became secretive. "I cannot tell all of it. I guess it must have been the poison oak in it that made Charlie Guzman sick."

The gallon of wine had gone too quickly. Each of the six friends was conscious of a thirst so sharp that it was a pain of desire. Pilon looked at his friends with drooped eyes, and they looked back at him. The conspiracy was ready.

Pilon cleared his throat. "What hast thou done, Danny, to set the whole town laughing at thee?"

Danny looked worried. "What do you mean?"

Pilon chuckled. "It is said by many that you bought a sweeping-machine for a lady, and that machine will not work unless wires are put into the house. Those wires cost a great deal of money. Some people find this present very funny."

Danny grew uncomfortable. "That lady likes the sweeping-machine," he said defensively.

"Why not?" Pablo agreed. "She has told some people that you have promised to put wires into her house so the sweeping-machine will work."

Danny looked even more perturbed. "Did she say that?"

"So I was told."

"Well, I will not," Danny cried.

"If I did not think it funny, I should be angry to hear my friend laughed at," Pilon observed.

"What will you do when she asks for those wires?" Jesus Maria asked.

"I will tell her no," said Danny.

Pilon laughed. "I wish I could be there. It is not such a simple thing to tell that lady 'no.' "

Danny felt that his friends were turning against him. "What shall I do?" he asked helplessly.

Pilon gave the matter his grave consideration and brought his realism to bear on the subject. "If that lady did not have the sweeping-machine, she would not want those wires," he said.

The friends nodded in agreement.

"Therefore," Pilon continued, "the thing to do is to re-move the sweeping-machine."

"Oh, she wouldn't let me take it," Danny protested.

"Then we will help you," said Pilon. "I will take the ma-chine, and in return you can take the lady a present of a gal-lon of wine. She will not even know where the sweeping-machine has gone."

"Some neighbor will see you take it."

"Oh, no," said Pilon. "You stay here, Danny. I will get the machine."

Danny sighed with relief that his problem was assumed by his good friends.

There were few things going on in Tortilla Flat that Pilon did not know. His mind made sharp little notes of everything that his eyes saw or his ears heard. He knew that Sweets went to the store at four-thirty every afternoon. He depended upon this almost invariable habit to put his plan into effect.

"It is better that you do not know anything about it," he told Danny.

In the yard Pilon had a gunny sack in readiness. With his knife he cut a generous branch from the rose bush and pushed it into the sack.

At Sweets' house, he found her absent, as he had expected and hoped she would be. "It is really Danny's machine," he told himself.

It was a moment's work to enter the house, to put the vacuum-cleaner in the sack and to arrange the rose branch artistically in the sack's mouth.

As he came out of the yard, he met Sweets. Pilon took off his hat politely. "I stepped in to pass the time," he said.

"Will you stop now, Pilon?"

"No. I have business down in Monterey. It is late."

"Where do you go with this rose bush?"

"A man in Monterey is to buy it. A very fine rose bush. See how strong it is."

"Stop in some other time, Pilon."

He heard no cry of anger as he walked sedately down the street. "Perhaps she will not miss it for a while," he thought.

Half the problem was solved, but half was yet to be approached. "What can Danny do with this sweeping-machine?" Pilon asked himself. "If he has it, Sweets will know he has taken it. Can I throw it away? No, for it is valuable. The thing to do would be to get rid of it, and still to reap the benefit of its value."

Now the whole problem was solved. Pilon headed down the hill toward Torrelli's house.

It was a large and shining vacuum-cleaner. When Pilon came again up the hill, he had a gallon of wine in each hand.

The friends received him in silence when he entered Danny's house. He set one jug on the table and the other on the floor.

"I have brought you a present to take to the lady," he told Danny. "And here is a little wine for us."

They gathered happily, for their thirst was a raging fire. When the first gallon was far gone, Pilon held his glass to the candle-light and looked through it. "Things that happen are of no importance," he said. "But from everything that happens, there is a lesson to be learned. By this we learn that a present, especially to a lady, should have no quality that will require a further present. Also we learn that it is sinful to give presents of too great value, for they may excite greed."

The first gallon was gone. The friends looked at Danny to see how he felt about it. He had been very quiet, but now he saw that his friends were waiting on him.

"That lady was lively," he said judiciously. "That lady had a very sympathetic nature. But God damn it!" he said, "I'm sick of it!" He went to the second jug and drew the cork.

The Pirate, sitting in the corner among his dogs, smiled to himself and whispered in admiration, " 'God damn it, I'm sick of it.' " That, thought the Pirate, was very fine.

They had not more than half finished the second jug, indeed they had sung only two songs, when young Johnny Pom-pom came in. "I was at Torrelli's," Johnny said. "Oh, that Torrelli is mad! He is shouting! He is beating on the table with his fists."

The friends looked up with mild interest. "Something has happened. It is probable Torrelli deserves it."

"Often he has refused his good customers a little glass of wine."

"What is the matter with Torrelli?" Pablo asked.

Johnny Pom-pom accepted a jar of wine. "Torrelli says he bought a sweeping-machine from Pilon, and when he hooked it up to his light wire, it would not work. So he looked on the inside, and it had no motor. He says he will kill Pilon."

Pilon looked shocked. "I did not know this machine was at fault," he said. "But did I not say Torrelli deserved what was the matter with him. That machine was worth three or four gallons of wine, but that miser Torrelli would give no more than two."

Danny still felt a glow of gratitude toward Pilon. He smacked his lips on his wine. "This stuff of Torrelli's is getting worse and worse," he said. "At its best, it is swill the pigs leave, but lately it is so bad that Charlie Marsh even would not drink it."

They all felt a little bit revenged on Torrelli then.

"I think," said Danny, "that we will buy our wine some place else, if Torrelli does not look out."

X

How the Friends solaced a Corporal and in return received a lesson in paternal ethics.

JESUS MARIA CORCORAN was a pathway for the humanities. Suffering he tried to relieve; sorrow he tried to assuage; happiness he shared. No hard nor haunted Jesus Maria existed. His heart was free for the use of any one who had a use for it. His resources and wits were at the disposal of any one who had less of either than had Jesus Maria.

He it was who carried José de la Nariz four miles when José's leg was broken. When Mrs. Palochico lost the goat of her heart, the good goat of milk and cheese, it was Jesus Maria who tracked that goat to Big Joe Portagee and halted the murder and made Big Joe give it back. It was Jesus Maria who once picked Charlie Marsh out of a ditch where he lay in his own filth, a deed which required not only a warm heart, but a strong stomach.

Together with his capacity for doing good, Jesus Maria had a gift for coming in contact with situations where good wanted doing.

Such was his reputation that Pilon had once said, "If that Jesus Maria had gone into the Church, Monterey would have had a saint for the calendar, I tell you."

Out of some deep pouch in his soul, Jesus Maria drew kindness that renewed itself by withdrawal.

It was Jesus Maria's practice to go to the post office every day, first because there he could see many people whom he knew, and second because on that windy post office corner he could look at the legs of a great many girls. It must not be supposed that in this latter interest there was any vulgarity. As soon criticize a man who goes to art galleries or to concerts. Jesus Maria liked to look at girls' legs.

One day when he had leaned against the post office for two hours with very little success, he was witness to a pitiful scene. A policeman came along the sidewalk leading a young boy of about sixteen, and the boy carried a little baby, wrapped in a piece of gray blanket.

The policeman was saying, "I don't care if I can't understand you. You can't sit in the gutter all day. We'll find out about you."

And the boy, in Spanish, with a peculiar inflection, said, "But señor, I do nothing wrong. Why do you take me away?"

The policeman saw Jesus Maria. "Hey paisano," he called. "What's this cholo talking about?"

Jesus Maria stepped out and addressed the boy. "Can I be of service to you?"

The boy broke into a relieved flood. "I came here to work. Some Mexican men said there would be work here, and there was none. I was sitting down resting when this man came to me and dragged me away."

Jesus Maria nodded and turned back to the policeman. "Has he done some crime, this little one?"

"No, but he's been sitting in the gutter on Alvarado Street for about three hours."

"He is a friend of mine," Jesus Maria said. "I will take care of him."

"Well, keep him out of the gutter."

Jesus Maria and his new friend walked up the hill. "I will take you to the house where I live. There you will have something to eat. What baby is this?"

"It is my baby," said the boy. "I am a caporál, and he is my baby. He is sick now; but when he grows up, he is going to be a generál."

"What is he sick from, Señor Caporál?"

"I don't know. He is just sick." He showed the baby's face, and it looked very ill indeed.

The sympathies of Jesus Maria mounted. "The house where I live is owned by my friend Danny, and there is a good man, Señor Caporál. There is one to appeal to when trouble is upon one. Look, we will go there, and that Danny will give us shelter. My friend Mrs. Palochico has a goat. We will borrow a little milk for the baby."

The corporal's face for the first time wore a smile of comfort. "It is good to have friends," he said. "In Torreón I have many friends who would make themselves beggars to help me." He boasted a little to Jesus Maria. "I have rich friends, but of course they do not know my need."

Pilon pushed open the gate of Danny's yard, and they entered together. Danny and Pablo and Big Joe were sitting in the living room, waiting for the daily miracle of food. Jesus Maria pushed the boy into the room.

"Here is a young soldier, a caporál," he explained. "He has a baby here with him, and that baby is sick."

The friends arose with alacrity. The corporal threw back the gray blanket from the baby's face.

"He is sick, all right," Danny said. "Maybe we should get a doctor."

But the soldier shook his head. "No doctors. I do not like doctors. This baby does not cry, and he will not eat much. Maybe when he rests, then he will be well again."

At this moment Pilon entered and inspected the child. "This baby is sick," he said.

Pilon immediately took control. Jesus Maria he sent to Mrs. Palochico's house to borrow goat milk; Big Joe and Pablo to get an apple box, pad it with dry grass and line it with a sheepskin coat. Danny offered his bed, but it was refused. The corporal stood in the living room and smiled gently on these good people. At last the baby lay in its box, but its eyes were listless and it refused the milk.

The Pirate came in, bearing a bag of mackerels. The friends cooked the fish and had their dinner. The baby would not even eat mackerel. Every now and then one of the friends jumped up and ran to look at the baby. When supper was over, they sat about the stove and prepared for a quiet evening.

The corporal had been silent, had given no account of himself. The friends were a little hurt at this, but they knew he would tell them in time. Pilon, to whom knowledge was as gold to be mined, made a few tentative drills into the corporal's reticence.

"It is not often that one sees a young soldier with a baby," he suggested delicately.

The corporal grinned with pride.

Pablo added, "This baby was probably found in the garden

of love. And that is the best kind of babies, for only good things are in it."

"We too have been soldiers," said Danny. "When we die, we will go to the grave on a gun carriage, and a firing squad will shoot over us."

They waited to see whether the corporal would improve upon the opportunity they had offered. The corporal looked his appreciation. "You have been good to me," he said. "You have been as good and kind as my friends in Torreón would be. This is my baby, the baby of my wife."

"And where is your wife?" Pilon asked.

The corporal lost his smile. "She is in Mexico," he said. Then he grew vivacious again. "I met a man, and he told me a curious thing. He said we can make of babies what we will. He said, 'You tell the baby often what you want him to do, and when he grows up he will do that.' Over and over I tell this baby, 'You will be a generál.' Do you think it will be so?"

The friends nodded politely. "It may be," said Pilon. "I have not heard of this practice."

"I say twenty times a day, 'Manuel, you will be a generál some day. You will have big epaulets and a sash. Your sword will be gold. You will ride a palamino horse. What a life for you, Manuel!' The man said he surely will be a generál if I say it so."

Danny got up and went to the apple box. "You will be a generál," he said to the baby. "When you grow up you will be a great generál."

The others trooped over to see whether the formula had had any effect.

The Pirate whispered, "You will be a generál," and he wondered whether the same method would work on a dog.

"This baby is sick all right," Danny said. "We must keep him warm."

They went back to their seats.

"Your wife is in Mexico—" Pilon suggested.

The corporal wrinkled his brows and thought for a while, and then he smiled brilliantly. "I will tell you. It is not a thing to tell to strangers, but you are my friends. I was a soldier in Chihuahua, and I was diligent and clean and kept oil in my rifle, so that I became a caporál. And then I was married to a beautiful girl. I do not say that it was not because of the chevrons that she married me. But she was very beautiful and young. Her eyes were bright, she had good white teeth and her hair was long and shining. So pretty soon this baby was born."

"That is good," said Danny. "I should like to be you. There is nothing so good as a baby."

"Yes," said the corporal, "I was glad. And we went in to the baptism, and I wore a sash, although the book of the army did not mention it. And when we came out of that church, a capitán with epaulets and a sash and a silver sword saw my wife. Pretty soon my wife went away. Then I went to that capitán and I said, 'Give me back my wife,' and he said, 'You do not value your life, to talk this way to your superior.'" The corporal spread his hands and lifted his shoulders in a gesture of caged resignation.

"Oh, that thief!" cried Jesus Maria.

"You gathered your friends. You killed that capitán," Pablo anticipated.

The corporal looked self-conscious. "No. There was nothing to do. The first night, some one shot at me through the window. The second day a field gun went off by mistake and it came so close to me that the wind knocked me down. So, I went away from there, and I took the baby with me."

There was fierceness in the faces of the friends, and their eyes were dangerous. The Pirate, in his corner, snarled, and all the dogs growled.

"We should have been there," Pilon cried. "We would have made that capitán wish he had never lived. My grandfather suffered at the hands of a priest, and he tied that priest naked to a post in a corral and turned a little calf in with him. Oh, there are ways."

"I was only a caporál," said the boy. "I had to run away." Tears of shame were in his eyes. "There is no help for a caporál when a capitán is against him; so I ran away, with the baby Manuel. In Fresno I met this wise man, and he told me I could make Manuel be what I wished. I tell that baby twenty times every day, 'You will be a generál. You will wear epaulets and carry a golden sword.'"

Here was drama that made the experiments of Cornelia

Ruiz seem uninteresting and vain. Here was a situation which demanded the action of the friends. But its scene was so remote that action was impossible. They looked in admiration at the corporal. He was so young to have had such an adventure!

"I wish," Danny said wickedly, "that we were in Torreón now. Pilon would make a plan for us. It is too bad we cannot go there."

Big Joe Portagee had stayed awake, a tribute to the fascination of the corporal's story. He went to the apple box and looked in. "You going to be a general," he said. And then, "Look! This baby is moving funny." The friends crowded around. The spasm had already started. The little feet kicked down and then drew up. The hands clawed about helplessly, and then the baby scrabbled and shuddered.

"A doctor," Danny cried. "We must have a doctor." But he and every one knew it was no use. Approaching death wears a cloak no one ever mistakes. While they watched, the baby stiffened and the struggle ended. The mouth dropped open, and the baby was dead. In kindness, Danny covered the apple box with a piece of blanket. The corporal stood very straight and stared before him, so shocked that he could not speak nor think.

Jesus Maria laid a hand on his shoulder and led him to a chair. "You are so young," he said. "You will have many more babies."

The corporal moaned, "Now he is dead. Now he will never be a generál with that sash and that sword."

There were tears in the eyes of the friends. In the corner, all the dogs whined miserably. The Pirate buried his big head in the fur of Señor Alec Thompson.

In a soft tone, almost a benediction, Pilon said, "Now you yourself must kill the capitán. We honor you for a noble plan of revenge; but that is over and you must take your own vengeance, and we will help you, if we can."

The corporal turned dulled eyes to him. "Revenge?" he asked. "Kill the capitán? What do you mean?"

"Why, it was plain what your plan was," Pilon said. "This baby would grow up, and he would be a generál; and in time he would find that capitán, and he would kill him slowly. It was a good plan. The long waiting, and then the stroke. We, your friends, honor you for it."

The corporal was looking bewilderedly at Pilon. "What is this?" he demanded. "I have nothing to do with this capitán. He is the capitán."

The friends sat forward.

Pilon cried, "Then what was this plan to make the baby be a generál? Why was that?"

The corporal was a little embarrassed then. "It is the duty of a father to do well by his child. I wanted Manuel to have more good things than I had."

"Is that all?" Danny cried.

"Well," said the corporal, "my wife was so pretty, and she was not any *puta*, either. She was a good woman, and that capitán took her. He had little epaulets, and a little sash, and his sword was only of a silver color. Consider," said the corporal; and he spread out his hands, "if that capitán, with the little epaulets and the little sash could take my wife, imagine what a generál with a big sash and a gold sword could take!"

There was a long silence while Danny and Pilon and Pablo and Jesus Maria and the Pirate and Big Joe Portagee digested the principle. And when it was digested, they waited for Danny to speak.

"It is to be pitied," said Danny at last, "that so few parents have the well-being of their children at heart. Now we are more sorry than ever that the baby is gone, for with such a father, what a happy life he has missed."

All of the friends nodded solemnly.

"What will you do now?" asked Jesus Maria, the discoverer.

"I will go back to Mexico," said the corporal. "I am a soldier in my heart. It may be, if I keep oiling my rifle, I myself may be an officer some day. Who can tell?"

The six friends looked at him admiringly. They were proud to have known such a man.

XI

How, under the most adverse circumstances, love came to Big Joe Portagee.

FOR Big Joe Portagee, to feel love was to do something about it. And this is the history of one of his love affairs.

It had been raining in Monterey; from the tall pines the water dripped all day. The paisanos of Tortilla Flat did not come out of their houses, but from every chimney a blue column of pine wood smoke drifted so that the air smelled clean and fresh and perfumed.

At five o'clock in the afternoon, the rain stopped for a few moments and Big Joe Portagee, who had been under a rowboat on the beach most of the day, came out and started up the hill toward Danny's house. He was cold and hungry.

When he came to the very edge of Tortilla Flat, the skies opened and the rain poured down. In an instant Big Joe was soaked through. He ran into the nearest house to get out of the rain, and that house was inhabited by Tia Ignacia.

The lady was about forty-five, a widow of long standing and some success. Ordinarily she was taciturn and harsh, for there was in her veins more Indian blood than is considered decent in Tortilla Flat.

When Big Joe entered, she had just opened a gallon of red wine and was preparing to pour out a glass for her stomach's sake. Her attempt to push the jug under a chair was unsuccessful. Big Joe stood in her doorway dripping water on the floor.

"Come in and get dry," said Tia Ignacia. Big Joe, watching the bottle as a terrier watches a bug, entered the room. The rain roared down on the roof. Tia Ignacia poked up a blaze in her air-tight stove.

"Would you care for a glass of wine?"

"Yes," said Big Joe. Before he had finished his first glass, Big Joe's eyes had refastened themselves on the jug. He drank three glasses before he consented to say a word, and before the wolfishness went out of his eyes.

Tia Ignacia had given her new jug of wine up for lost. She drank with him as the only means to preserve a little of it to her own use. It was only when the fourth glass of wine was in his hand that Big Joe relaxed and began to enjoy himself.

"This is not Torrelli's wine," he said.

"No, I get it from an Italian lady who is my friend." She poured out another glass.

The early evening came. Tia Ignacia lighted a kerosene lamp and put some wood in the fire. As long as the wine must go, it must go, she thought. Her eyes dwelt on the huge frame of Big Joe Portagee with critical appraisal. A little flush warmed her chest.

"You have been working out in the rain, poor man," she said. "Here, take off your coat and let it dry."

Big Joe rarely told a lie. His mind didn't work quickly enough. "I been on the beach under a rowboat, asleep," he said.

"But you are all wet, poor fellow." She inspected him for some response to her kindness, but on Big Joe's face nothing showed except gratification at being out of the rain and drinking wine. He put out his glass to be filled again. Having eaten nothing all day, the wine was having a profound effect on him.

Tia Ignacia addressed herself anew to the problem. "It is not good to sit in a wet coat. You will be ill with cold. Come, let me help you to take off your coat."

Big Joe wedged himself comfortably into his chair. "I'm all right," he said stubbornly.

Tia Ignacia poured herself another glass. The fire made a rushing sound to counteract with comfort the drumming of water on the roof.

Big Joe made absolutely no move to be friendly, to be gallant, even to recognize the presence of his hostess. He drank his wine in big swallows. He smiled stupidly at the stove. He rocked himself a little in the chair.

Anger and despair arose in Tia Ignacia. "This pig," she thought, "this big and dirty animal. It would be better for me if I brought some cow in the house out of the rain. Another man would say some little friendly word, at least."

Big Joe stuck out his glass to be filled again.

Now Tia Ignacia strove heroically. "In a little warm house there is happiness on such a night," she said, "when the rain is dripping and the stove burns sweetly, then is a time for people to feel friendly. Don't you feel friendly?"

"Sure," said Big Joe.

"Perhaps the light is too bright in your eyes," she said coyly. "Would you like me to blow out the light?"

"It don't bother me none," said Big Joe, "if you want to save oil, go ahead."

She blew down the lamp chimney, and the room leaped to darkness. Then she went back to her chair and waited for his gallantry to awaken. She could hear the gentle rocking of his chair. A little light came from the cracks of the stove and struck the shiny corners of the furniture. The room was nearly luminous with warmth. Tia Ignacia heard his chair stop rocking and braced herself to repel him. Nothing happened.

"To think," she said, "you might be out in this storm, shivering in a shed or lying on the cold sand under a boat. But no; you are sitting in a good chair, drinking good wine, in the company of a lady who is your friend."

There was no answer from Big Joe. She could neither hear him nor see him. Tia Ignacia drank off her glass. She threw virtue to the winds. "My friend Cornelia Ruiz has told me that some of her best friends came to her out of the rain and cold. She comforted them, and they were her good friends."

The sound of a little crash came from the direction of Big Joe. She knew he had dropped his glass, but no movement followed the crash. "Perhaps he is ill," she thought. "Maybe he has fainted." She jumped up, lighted a match and set it to the lamp wick. And then she turned to her guest.

Big Joe was mountainously asleep. His feet stuck out ahead of him. His head was back and his mouth wide open. While she looked, amazed and shocked, a tremendous rattling snore came from his mouth. Big Joe simply could not be warm and comfortable without going to sleep.

It was a moment before Tia Ignacia could move all her crowding emotions into line. She inherited a great deal of Indian blood. She did not cry out. No, shivering with rage although she was, she walked to her wood basket, picked out a likely stick, weighed it, put it down and picked out another

one. And then she turned slowly on Big Joe Portagee. The
first blow caught him on the shoulder and knocked him out
of the chair.

"Pig!" Tia Ignacia screamed. "Big dirty garbage! Out in the
mud with you!"

Joe rolled over on the floor. The next blow made a muddy
identation on the seat of his pants. Big Joe was waking up
rapidly now.

"Huh?" he said. "What's the matter? What you doing?"

"I'll show you," she screamed. She flung open her door and
ran back to him. Big Joe staggered to his feet under the beating. The stick hammered at his back and shoulders and head.
He ran out of the door, protecting his head with his hands.

"Don't," he pleaded. "Now don't do that. What's the
matter?"

The fury followed him like a hornet, down the garden path
and into the muddy street. Her rage was terrible. She followed him along the street, still beating him.

"Hey," he cried. "Now don't." He grabbed her and held
her while her arms struggled violently to be free to continue
the beating.

"Oh, great garbage pig!" she cried. "Oh, cow!"

He could not let her go without more beating, so he held
her tightly; and as he stood there, love came to Big Joe Por-
tage. It sang in his head; it roared through his body like a
great freshet; it shook him as a tropical storm shakes a forest
of palms. He held her tightly for a moment, until her anger
relaxed.

In the night, in Monterey, a policeman patrols the streets
on a motorcycle to see that good things come to no evil.
Jake Lake rode about now, his slicker shining dully, like ba-
salt. He was unhappy and uncomfortable. It was not so bad
on the paved streets, but part of his route lay through the
mud paths of Tortilla Flat, and there the yellow mud
splashed nastily. His little light flashed about. The motor
coughed with effort.

All of a sudden Jake Lake cried out in astonishment and
stopped his motor. "What the devil! Say, what the hell is
this?"

Big Joe twisted his neck. "Oh, is that you, Jake? Say, Jake, as long as you're going to take us to jail anyway, can't you just wait a minute?"

The policeman turned his motor around. "You get out of the street," he said. "Somebody'll come along and run over you."

His motor roared in the mud, and the flicker of his little headlight disappeared around the corner. The rain pattered gently among the trees of Tortilla Flat.

XII

*How Danny's Friends assisted the Pirate to keep a vow,
and how as a reward for merit the Pirate's dogs saw
an holy vision.*

E VERY afternoon the Pirate pushed his empty wheelbarrow
up the hill and into Danny's yard. He leaned it against
the fence and covered it with a sack; then he buried his ax in
the ground, for, as every one knows, it makes steel much
harder to be buried. Last, he went into the house, reached
into a Bull Durham bag which hung around his neck on a
string, took out the day's quarter dollar and gave it to Danny.
Then Danny and the Pirate and any other of the friends who
happened to be in the house went solemnly into the bedroom, stepping over the bedding that littered the floor. While
the paisanos looked on, Danny reached under his pillow,
brought out the canvas bag and deposited the new quarter.
This practice had continued for a long time.

The bag of money had become the symbolic center of the
friendship, the point of trust about which the fraternity re-
volved. They were proud of the money, proud that they had
never tampered with it. About the guardianship of the Pirate's money there had grown a structure of self-respect and
not a little complacency. It is a fine thing for a man to be
trusted. This money had long ceased, in the minds of the
friends, to be currency. It is true that for a time they had
dreamed of how much wine it would buy, but after a while
they lost the conception of it as legal tender. The hoard was
aimed at a gold candlestick, and this potential candlestick was
the property of San Francisco de Assisi. It is far worse to
defraud a saint than it is to take liberties with the law.

One evening, by that quick and accurate telegraph no one
understands, news came in that a coast guard cutter had gone
on the rocks near Carmel. Big Joe Portagee was away on business of his own, but Danny and Pablo and Pilon and Jesus
Maria and the Pirate and his dogs joyfully started over the
ridge; for if there was anything they loved, it was to pick up

useable articles on the beach. This they thought the most exciting thing in the world. Although they arrived a little late, they made up for lost time. All night the friends scurried about the beach, and they accumulated a good pile of flotsam, a five-pound can of butter, several cases of canned goods, a water-soaked Bowditch, two pea jackets, a water barrel from a life boat and a machine gun. When daylight came, they had a goodly pile under guard.

They accepted a lump sum of five dollars for the lot from one of the spectators, for it was out of the question to carry all those heavy things over six miles of steep hillside to Tortilla Flat.

Because he had not cut his day's wood, the Pirate received a quarter from Danny, and he put it in his Bull Durham bag. Then they started tiredly, but with a warm and expectant happiness, straight over the hills to Monterey.

It was afternoon when they got back to Danny's house. The Pirate ritualistically opened his bag and gave the quarter to Danny. The whole squad trooped into the other room. Danny reached under the pillow—and his hand came out empty. He threw the pillow back, threw the mattress back, and then he turned slowly to his friends, and his eyes had become as fierce as a tiger's eyes. He looked from face to face, and on every one saw horror and indignation that could not be simulated.

"Well," he said, "—well." The Pirate began to cry. Danny put his arm around his shoulder. "Do not cry, little friend," he said ominously. "Thou wilt have thy money again."

The paisanos went silently out of the room. Danny walked out into the yard and found a heavy pine stick three feet long, and swung it experimentally. Pablo went into the kitchen and returned bearing an ancient can-opener with a vicious blade. Jesus Maria from under the house pulled out a broken pick handle. The Pirate watched them bewilderedly. They all came back to the house and sat quietly down.

The Pirate aimed down the hill with his thumb. "Him?" he asked.

Danny nodded slowly. His eyes were veiled and deadly. His chin stuck out, and, as he sat in the chair, his whole body weaved a little, like a rattlesnake aiming to strike.

The Pirate went into the yard and dug up his ax.

For a long time they sat in the house. No words were spoken, but a wave of cold fury washed and crouched in the room. The feeling in the house was the feeling of a rock when the fuse is burning in toward the dynamite.

The afternoon waned; the sun went behind the hill. The whole of Tortilla Flat seemed hushed and expectant.

They heard his footsteps on the street and their hands tightened on their sticks. Joe Portagee walked uncertainly up on the porch and in at the front door. He had a gallon of wine in his hand. His eyes went uneasily from face to face, but the friends sat still and did not look directly at him.

"Hello," said Big Joe.

"Hello," said Danny. He stood up and stretched lazily. He did not look at Big Joe; he did not walk directly toward him, but at an angle, as though to pass him. When he was abreast, he struck with the speed of a striking snake. Fair on the back of Big Joe's head the stick crashed, and Big Joe went down, completely out.

Danny thoughtfully took a string of rawhide from his pocket and tied the Portagee's thumbs together. "Now water," he said.

Pablo threw a bucket of water in Big Joe's face. He turned his head and stretched his neck like a chicken, and then he opened his eyes and looked dazedly at his friends. They did not speak to him at all. Danny measured his distance carefully, like a golfer addressing the ball. His stick smashed on Big Joe's shoulder; then the friends went about the business in a cold and methodical manner. Jesus Maria took the legs, Danny the shoulders and chest. Big Joe howled and rolled on the floor. They covered his body from the neck down. Each blow found a new space and welted it. The shrieks were deafening. The Pirate stood helplessly by, holding his ax.

At last, when the whole front of the body was one bruise, they stopped. Pablo knelt at Big Joe's head with his canopener. Pilon took off the Portagee's shoes and picked up his stick again.

Then Big Joe squalled with fear. "It's buried out by the front gate," he cried. "For the love of Christ don't kill me!"

Danny and Pilon went out the front door and in a few

minutes they came back, carrying the canvas bag. "How much did you take out?" Danny asked. There was no inflection in his voice at all.

"Only four, Honest to God. I only took four, and I'll work and put them back."

Danny leaned down, took him by the shoulder and rolled him over on his face. Then the friends went over his back with the same deadly precision. The cries grew weaker, but the work only stopped when Big Joe was beaten into unconsciousness. Then Pilon tore off the blue shirt and exposed the pulpy raw back. With the can-opener he cross-hatched the skin so deftly that a little blood ran from each line. Pablo brought the salt to him and helped him to rub it in all over the torn back. At last Danny threw a blanket over the unconscious man.

"I think he will be honest now," said Danny.

"We should count the money," Pilon observed. "We have not counted it for a long time." They opened Big Joe's gallon of wine and poured the fruit jars full, for they were tired from their work, and their emotions were exhausted.

Then they counted the quarters out in piles of ten, and excitedly counted again. "Pirate," Danny cried, "there are seven over a thousand! Thy time is done! The day is come for thee to buy thy candlestick for San Francisco!"

The day had been too full for the Pirate. He went into the corner with his dogs, and he put his head down on Fluff and burst into hysterical sobs. The dogs moved uneasily about, and they licked his ears and pushed at his head with their noses; but Fluff, sensible of the honor of being chosen, lay quietly and nuzzled the thick hair on the Pirate's neck.

Danny put all the money back in the bag, and the bag under his pillow again.

Now Big Joe came to and groaned, for the salt was working into his back. The paisanos paid no attention to him until at last Jesus Maria, that prey to the humanities, untied Big Joe's thumbs and gave him a jar of wine. "Even the enemies of our Saviour gave him a little comfort," he excused himself.

That action broke up the punishment. The friends gathered tenderly about Big Joe. They laid him on Danny's bed and washed the salt out of his wounds. They put cold cloths on his head and kept his jar full of wine. Big Joe moaned whenever they touched him. His morals were probably untouched, but it would have been safe to prophesy that never again would he steal from the paisanos of Danny's house.

The Pirate's hysteria was over. He drank his wine and his face shone with pleasure while he listened to Danny make plans for him.

"If we take all this money into town, to the bank, they will think we have stolen it from a slot machine. We must take this money to Father Ramon and tell him about it. Then he will buy the gold candlestick, and he will bless it, and the Pirate will go into the church. Maybe Father Ramon will say a word about him on Sunday. The Pirate must be there to hear."

Pilon looked distastefully at the Pirate's dirty, ragged clothes. "To-morrow," he said sternly, "you must take the seven extra two-bitses and buy some decent clothes. For ordinary times these may be all right, but on such an occasion as this you cannot go into the church looking like such a gutter rat. It will not be a compliment to your friends."

The Pirate beamed at him. "To-morrow I will do it," he promised.

The next morning, true to his promise, he went down to Monterey. He shopped carefully, and bargained with an astuteness that seemed to belie the fact that he had bought nothing in over two years. He came back to Danny's house in triumph, bearing a huge silk handkerchief in purple and green and also a broad belt studded profusely with colored glass jewels. His friends admired his purchases.

"But what are you going to wear?" Danny asked despairingly. "Two toes are out of your shoes where you cut holes to ease your bunions. You have only ragged overalls and no hat."

"We will have to lend him clothes," said Jesus Maria. "I have a coat and vest. Pilon has his father's good hat. You, Danny, have a shirt and Big Joe has those fine blue pants."

"But then we can't go," Pilon protested.

"It is not our candlestick," said Jesus Maria. "Father Ramon is not likely to say anything nice about us."

That afternoon they convoyed the treasure to the priest's house. He listened to the story of the sick dog, and his eyes softened. "—and then, Father," said the Pirate, "there was that good little dog, and his nose was dry, and his eyes were like the glass of bottles out of the sea, and he groaned because he hurt inside. And then, Father, I promised the gold candle-stick of one thousand days to San Francisco. He is really my patron, Father. And then there was a miracle! For that dog wagged his tail three times, and right away he started to get well. It was a miracle from San Francisco, Father, wasn't it?"

The priest nodded his head gravely. "Yes," he said. "It was a miracle sent by our good Saint Francis. I will buy the candlestick for thee."

The Pirate was very glad, for it is no little thing to have one's prayer answered with a true miracle. If it were noised about, the Pirate would have a higher station on Tortilla Flat. Already his friends looked at him with a new respect. They thought no more of his intelligence than they had before, but they knew now that his meager wits were supplemented with all the power of Heaven and all the strength of the saints.

They walked back up to Danny's house, and the dogs walked behind them. The Pirate felt that he had been washed in a golden fluid of beatitude. Little chills and fevers of plea-sure chased one another through his body. The paisanos were glad they had guarded his money, for even they took a little holiness from the act. Pilon was relieved that he had not sto-len the money in the first place. What terrible things might not have happened if he had taken the two-bitses belonging to a saint! All of the friends were as subdued as though they were in church.

The five dollars from the salvage had lain like fire in Danny's pocket, but now he knew what to do with it. He and Pilon went to the market and bought seven pounds of ham-burger and a bag of onions and bread and a big paper of candy. Pablo and Jesus Maria went to Torrelli's for two gallons of wine, and not a drop did they drink on the way home, either.

That night when the fire was lighted and two candles burned on the table, the friends feasted themselves to reple-tion. It was a party in the Pirate's honor. He behaved himself with a great deal of dignity. He smiled and smiled when he should have been grave, though. But he couldn't help that.

After they had eaten enormously, they sat back and sipped

wine out of the fruit jars. "Our little friend," they called the Pirate.

Jesus Maria asked, "How did you feel when it happened? When you promised the candlestick and the dog began to get well, how did you feel? Did you see any holy vision?"

The Pirate tried to remember. "I don't think so— Maybe I saw a little vision—maybe I saw San Francisco in the air and he was shining like the sun——"

"Wouldn't you remember that?" Pilon demanded.

"Yes—I think I remember—San Francisco looked on me—and he smiled, like the good saint he is. Then I knew the miracle was done. He said, 'Be good to little doggies, you dirty man.'"

"He called you that?"

"Well, I was, and he is not a saint to be telling lies."

"I don't think you remember that at all," said Pablo.

"Well—maybe not. I think I do, though," The Pirate was drunk with happiness from the honor and the attention.

"My grandmother saw the Holy Virgin," said Jesus Maria. "She was sick to death, and I myself heard her cry out. She said, 'Ohee. I see the Mother of God. Ohee. My dear Mary, full of grace.'"

"It is given to some to see these things," said Danny. "My father was not a very good man, but he sometimes saw saints, and sometimes he saw bad things. It depended on whether he was good or bad when he saw them. Have you ever seen any other visions, Pirate?"

"No," said the Pirate. "I would be afraid to see any more."

It was a decorous party for a long time. The friends knew that they were not alone this night. Through the walls and the windows and the roof they could feel the eyes of the holy saints looking down upon them.

"On Sunday your candlestick will be there," said Pilon. "We cannot go, for you will be wearing our clothes. I do not say Father Ramon will mention you by name, but maybe he will say something about the candlestick. You must try to remember what he says, Pirate, so you can tell us."

Then Pilon grew stern. "To-day, my little friend, there were dogs all over Father Ramon's house. That was all right for to-day, but you must remember not to take them to the church on Sunday. It is not fitting that dogs should be in the church. Leave the dogs at home."

The Pirate looked disappointed. "They want to go," he cried. "How can I leave them? Where can I leave them?"

Pablo was shocked. "In this affair so far thou hast conducted thyself with merit, little Pirate. Right at the last do you wish to commit sacrilege?"

"No," said the Pirate humbly.

"Then leave thy dogs here, and we will take care of them. It will be a sacrilege to take them into the church."

It was curious how soberly they drank that night. It was three hours before they sang even an obscene song. And it was late before their thoughts strayed to light women. And by the time their minds turned to fighting they were almost too sleepy to fight. This evening was a great good marker in their lives.

On Sunday morning the preparation was violent. They washed the Pirate and inspected his ears and his nostrils. Big Joe, wrapped in a blanket, watched the Pirate put on his blue serge trousers. Pilon brought out his father's hat. They persuaded the Pirate not to wear his jewel-studded belt outside his coat, and showed him how he could leave his coat open so that the jewels flashed now and then. The item of shoes gave the most trouble. Big Joe had the only shoes big enough for the Pirate, and his were worse even than the Pirate's. The difficulty lay in the holes cut for the comfort of bunions, where the toes showed through. Pilon solved it finally with a little soot from the inside of the stove. Well rubbed into the skin, the soot made it quite difficult to see the bunion holes.

At last he was ready; Pilon's father's hat rakishly on his head, Danny's shirt, Big Joe's pants, the huge handkerchief around his neck, and at intervals, the flashing of the jeweled belt. He walked, for the friends to inspect him, and they looked on critically.

"Pick up your feet, Pirate."

"Don't drag your heels."

"Stop picking at your handkerchief."

"Those people who see you will think you are not in the habit of good clothes."

At last the Pirate turned to his friends. "If those dogs could only come with me," he complained. "I would tell them they must not come in the church."

But the paisanos were firm. "No," said Danny. "They might get in some way. We will keep them here in the house for you."

"They won't like it," said the Pirate helplessly. "They will be lonely, maybe." He turned to the dogs in the corner. "You must stay here," he said. "It would not be good for you to go to church. Stay with my friends until I come back again." And then he slipped out and closed the door behind him. Instantly a wild clamor of barking and howling broke out in the house. Only his faith in the judgment of his friends prevented the Pirate's relenting.

As he walked down the street, he felt naked and unprotected without his dogs. It was as though one of his senses were gone. He was frightened to be out alone. Any one might attack him. But he walked bravely on, through the town and out to the Church of San Carlos.

Now, before the service began, the swinging doors were open. The Pirate dipped Holy Water out of the marble font, crossed himself, genuflected before the Virgin, went into the church, did his duty to the altar and sat down. The long church was rather dark, but the high altar was on fire with candles. And in front of the images at the sides, the votive lights were burning. The old and sweet incense perfumed the church.

For a time the Pirate sat looking at the altar, but it was too remote, too holy to think about very much, too unapproachable by a poor man. His eyes sought something warmer, something that would not frighten him. And there, in front of the figure of Saint Francis, was a beautiful golden candlestick, and in it a tall candle was burning.

The Pirate sighed with excitement. And although the people came in, and the swinging doors were shut and the service began and the Pirate went through the form, he could not stop looking at his saint and at the candlestick. It was so beautiful. He could not believe that he, the Pirate, had given it. He searched the face of the saint to see whether St. Francis liked the candlestick. He was sure the image smiled a little now and then, the recurring smile of one who thinks of pleasant things.

CHAPTER XII 477

At last the sermon began. "There is a new beauty in the church," Father Ramon said. "One of the children of the church has given a golden candlestick to the glory of Saint Francis." He told the story of the dog, then, told it rather baldly on purpose. His eyes searched the faces of the parishioners until he saw little smiles appear there. "It is not a thing to be considered funny," he said. "Saint Francis loved the beasts so much that he preached to them." Then Father Ramon told the story of the bad wolf of Gubbio and he told of the wild turtledoves and of the sister larks. The Pirate looked at him in wonder as the sermon went on.

Suddenly a rushing sound came from the door. A furious barking and scratching broke out. The doors swung wildly and in rushed Fluff and Rudolph, Enrique, Pajarito and Señor Alec Thompson. They raised their noses, and then darted in a struggling squad to the Pirate. They leaped upon him with little cries and whinings. They swarmed over him.

The priest stopped talking and looked sternly down toward the commotion. The Pirate looked back helplessly, in agony. So it was in vain, and the sacrilege was committed.

Then Father Ramon laughed, and the congregation laughed. "Take the dogs outside," he said. "Let them wait until we are through."

The Pirate, with embarrassed, apologetic gestures, conducted his dogs outside. "It is wrong," he said to them. "I am angry with you. Oh, I am ashamed of you." The dogs cringed to the ground and whined piteously. "I know what you did," said the Pirate. "You bit my friends, you broke a window, and you came. Now stay here and wait, oh, wicked dogs; oh, dogs of sacrilege."

He left them stricken with grief and repentance and went back into the church. The people, still laughing, turned and looked at him, until he sank into his seat and tried to efface himself.

"Do not be ashamed," Father Ramon said. "It is no sin to be loved by your dogs, and no sin to love them. See how Saint Francis loved the beasts." Then he told more stories of that good saint.

The embarrassment left the Pirate. His lips moved. "Oh," he thought, "if the dogs could only hear this. They would be glad if they could know all this." When the sermon was over, his ears still rang with the stories. Automatically he followed the ritual, but he did not hear the service. And when it was over, he rushed for the door. He was first out of the church. The dogs, still sad and diffident, crowded about him.

"Come," he cried. "I have some things to tell you."

He started at a trot up the hill toward the pine forest, and the dogs galloped and bounced about him. He came at last to the shelter of the woods, and still he went on, until he found a long aisle among the pines, where the branches met over-head, where the tree trunks were near together. For a mo-ment he looked helplessly about.

"I want it to be the way it was," he said. "If only you could have been there, and heard the father say it." He laid one big stone on top of another. "Now here is the image," he told the dogs. He stuck a little stick in the ground. "Right here is the candlestick, with a candle in it."

It was dusky in the glade, and the air was sweet with pine resin. The trees whispered softly in the breeze. The Pirate said with authority, "Now, Enrique, you sit here. And you, Ru-dolph, here. I want Fluff here because he is the littlest. Paja-rito, thou great fool, sit here and make no trouble. Señor Alec Thompson, you may *not* lie down."

Thus he arranged them in two rows, two in the front line and three in the back.

"I want to tell you how it was," he said. "You are forgiven for breaking into the church. Father Ramon said it was no sacrilege this time. Now, attention. I have things to tell."

The dogs sat in their places and watched him earnestly. Señor Alec Thompson flapped his tail, until the Pirate turned to him. "Here is no place for that," he said. "Saint Francis would not mind, but I do not like you to wag your tail while you listen. Now, I am going to tell you about Saint Francis."

That day his memory was inspired. The sun found inter-stices in the foliage and threw brilliant patterns on the pine-needle carpet. The dogs sat patiently, their eyes on the Pirate's lips. He told everything the priest had told, all the stories, all the observations. Hardly a word was out of its place.

When he was done, he regarded the dogs solemnly. "Saint Francis did all that," he said.

The trees hushed their whispering. The forest was silent and enchanted.

Suddenly there was a tiny sound behind the Pirate. All the dogs looked up. The Pirate was afraid to turn his head. A long moment passed.

And then the moment was over. The dogs lowered their eyes. The tree-tops stirred to life again and the sunlight patterns moved bewilderingly.

The Pirate was so happy that his heart pained him. "Did you see him?" he cried. "Was it San Francisco? Oh! What good dogs you must be to see a vision."

The dogs leaped up at his tone. Their mouths opened and their tails threshed joyfully.

XIII

How Danny's Friends threw themselves to the aid of a distressed lady.

S EÑORA TERESINA CORTEZ and her eight children and her ancient mother lived in a pleasant cottage on the edge of the deep gulch that defines the southern frontier of Tortilla Flat. Teresina was a good figure of a mature woman, nearing thirty. Her mother, that ancient, dried, toothless one, relict of a past generation, was nearly fifty. It was long since any one had remembered that her name was Angelica.

During the week work was ready to this vieja's hand, for it was her duty to feed, punish, cajole, dress and bed down seven of the eight children. Teresina was busy with the eighth, and with making certain preparations for the ninth.

On Sunday, however, the vieja, clad in black satin more ancient even than she, hatted in a grim and durable affair of black straw, on which were fastened two true cherries of enameled plaster, threw duty to the wind and went firmly to church, where she sat as motionless as the saints in their niches. Once a month, in the afternoon, she went to confession. It would be interesting to know what sins she confessed, and where she found the time to commit them, for in Teresina's house there were creepers, crawlers, tumblers, shriekers, cat-killers, fallers-out-of-trees; and each one of these charges could be trusted to be ravenous every two hours.

Is it any wonder that the vieja had a remote soul and nerves of steel? Any other kind would have gone screaming out of her body like little skyrockets.

Teresina was a mildly puzzled woman, as far as her mind was concerned. Her body was one of those perfect retorts for the distillation of children. The first baby, conceived when she was fourteen, had been a shock to her; such a shock, that she delivered it in the ball park at night, wrapped it in newspaper and left it for the night watchman to find. This is a secret. Even now Teresina might get into trouble if it were known.

When she was sixteen, Mr. Alfred Cortez married her and

gave her his name and the two foundations of her family, Alfredo and Ernie. Mr. Cortez gave her that name gladly. He was only using it temporarily anyway. His name, before he came to Monterey and after he left, was Guggliemo. He went away after Ernie was born. Perhaps he foresaw that being married to Teresina was not going to be a quiet life.

The regularity with which she became a mother always astonished Teresina. It occurred sometimes that she could not remember who the father of the impending baby was; and occasionally she almost grew convinced that no lover was necessary. In the time when she had been under quarantine as a diphtheria carrier she conceived just the same. However, when a question became too complicated for her mind to unravel, she usually laid that problem in the arms of the Mother of Jesus, who, she knew, had more knowledge of, interest in and time for such things than she.

Teresina went often to confession. She was the despair of Father Ramon. Indeed he had seen that while her knees, her hands and her lips did penance for an old sin, her modest and provocative eyes, flashing under drawn lashes, laid the foundations for a new one.

During the time I have been telling this, Teresina's ninth child was born, and for the moment she was unengaged. The vieja received another charge; Alfredo entered his third year in the first grade, Ernie his second, and Panchito went to school for the first time.

At about this time in California it became the stylish thing for school nurses to visit the classes and to catechize the children on intimate details of their home life. In the first grade, Alfredo was called to the principal's office, for it was thought that he looked thin.

The visiting nurse, trained in child psychology, said kindly, "Freddie, do you get enough to eat?"

"Sure," said Alfredo.

"Well, now. Tell me what you have for breakfast."

"Tortillas and beans," said Alfredo.

The nurse nodded her head dismally to the principal. "What do you have when you go home for lunch?"

"I don't go home."

"Don't you eat at noon?"

"Sure. I bring some beans wrapped up in a tortilla."

Actual alarm showed in the nurse's eyes, but she controlled herself. "At night what do you have to eat?"

"Tortillas and beans."

Her psychology deserted her. "Do you mean to stand there and tell me you eat nothing but tortillas and beans?"

Alfredo was astonished. "Jesus Christ," he said, "what more do you want?"

In due course the school doctor listened to the nurse's horrified report. One day he drove up to Teresina's house to look into the matter. As he walked through the yard the creepers, the crawlers and the stumblers were shrieking one terrible symphony. The doctor stood in the open kitchen door. With his own eyes he saw the vieja go to the stove, dip a great spoon into a kettle and sow the floor with boiled beans. Instantly the noise ceased. Creepers, crawlers and stumblers went to work with silent industry, moving from bean to bean, pausing only to eat them. The vieja went back to her chair for a few moments of peace. Under the bed, under the chairs, under the stove the children crawled with the intentness of little bugs. The doctor stayed two hours, for his scientific interest was piqued. He went away shaking his head.

He shook his head incredulously while he made his report. "I gave them every test I know of," he said, "teeth, skin, blood, skeleton, eyes, co-ordination. Gentlemen, they are living on what constitutes a slow poison, and they have from birth. Gentlemen, I tell you I have never seen healthier children in my life!" His emotion overcame him. "The little beasts," he cried. "I never saw such teeth in my life. I *never* saw such teeth!"

You will wonder how Teresina procured food for her family. When the bean threshers have passed, you will see, where they have stopped, big piles of bean chaff. If you will spread a blanket on the ground, and, on a windy afternoon, toss the chaff in the air over the blanket, you will understand that the threshers are not infallible. For an afternoon of work you may collect twenty or more pounds of beans.

In the autumn the vieja and those children who could walk went into the fields and winnowed the chaff. The landowners did not mind, for she did no harm. It was a bad year when the vieja did not collect three or four hundred pounds of beans.

When you have four hundred pounds of beans in the house, you need have no fear of starvation. Other things, delicacies such as sugar, tomatoes, peppers, coffee, fish or meat may come sometimes miraculously, through the intercession of the Virgin, sometimes through industry or cleverness; but your beans are there, and you are safe. Beans are a roof over your stomach. Beans are a warm cloak against economic cold.

Only one thing could threaten the lives and happiness of the family of the Señora Teresina Cortez; that was a failure of the bean crop.

When the beans are ripe, the little bushes are pulled and gathered into piles, to dry crisp for the threshers. Then is the time to pray that the rain may hold off. When the little piles of beans lie in lines, yellow against the dark fields, you will see the farmers watching the sky, scowling with dread at every cloud that sails over; for if a rain comes, the bean piles must be turned over to dry again. And if more rain falls before they are dry, they must be turned again. If a third shower falls, mildew and rot set in, and the crop is lost.

When the beans were drying, it was the vieja's custom to burn a candle to the Virgin.

In the year of which I speak, the beans were piled and the candle had been burned. At Teresina's house, the gunny sacks were laid out in readiness.

The threshing machines were oiled and cleaned.

A shower fell.

Extra hands rushed to the fields and turned the sodden hummocks of beans. The vieja burned another candle.

More rain fell.

Then the vieja bought two candles with a little gold piece she had kept for many years. The field hands turned over the beans to the sun again; and then came a downpour of cold streaking rain. Not a bean was harvested in all Monterey County. The soggy lumps were turned under by the plows.

Oh, then distress entered the house of Señora Teresina Cortez. The staff of life was broken; the little roof destroyed. Gone was that eternal verity, beans. At night the children cried with terror at the approaching starvation. They were not told, but they knew. The vieja sat in church, as always, but her lips drew back in a sneer when she looked at the Virgin. "You took my candles," she thought. "Ohee, yes. Greedy you are for candles. Oh, thoughtless one." And sullenly she transferred her allegiance to Santa Clara. She told Santa Clara of the injustice that had been done. She permitted herself a little malicious thought at the Virgin birth. "You know, sometimes Teresina can't remember either," she told Santa Clara viciously.

It has been said that Jesus Maria Corcoran was a greathearted man. He had also that gift some humanitarians possess of being inevitably drawn toward those spheres where his instinct was needed. How many times had he not come upon young ladies when they needed comforting. Toward any pain or sorrow he was irresistibly drawn. He had not been to Teresina's house for many months. If there is no mystical attraction between pain and humanitarianism, how did it happen that he went there to call on the very day when the last of the old year's beans was put in the pot?

He sat in Teresina's kitchen, gently brushing children off his legs. And he looked at Teresina with polite and pained eyes while she told of the calamity. He watched, fascinated, when she turned the last bean sack inside out to show that not one single bean was left. He nodded sympathetically when she pointed out the children, so soon to be skeletons, so soon to die of starvation.

Then the vieja told bitterly how she had been tricked by the Virgin. But upon this point, Jesus Maria was not sympathetic. "What do you know, old one?" he said sternly. "Maybe the Blessed Virgin had business some place else."

"But four candles I burned," the vieja insisted shrilly.

Jesus Maria regarded her coldly. "What are four candles to Her?" he said. "I have seen one church where She had hundreds. She is no miser of candles."

But his mind burned with Teresina's trouble. That evening he talked mightily and piteously to the friends at Danny's house. Out of his great heart he drew a compelling oratory, a passionate plea for those little children who had no beans. And so telling was his speech that the fire in his heart ignited the hearts of his friends. They leaped up. Their eyes glowed.

"The children shall not starve," they cried. "It shall be our trust!"

"We live in luxury," Pilon said.

"We shall give of our substance," Danny agreed. "And if they needed a house, they could live here."

"To-morrow we shall start," Pablo exclaimed. "No more laziness! To work! There are things to be done!"

Jesus Maria felt the gratification of a leader with followers.

Theirs was no idle boast. Fish they collected. The vegetable patch of the Hotel Del Monte they raided. It was a glorious game. Theft robbed of the stigma of theft, crime altruistically committed— What is more gratifying?

The Pirate raised the price of kindlings to thirty cents and went to three new restaurants every morning. Big Joe stole Mrs. Palochico's goat over and over again, and each time it went home.

Now food began to accumulate in the house of Teresina. Boxes of lettuce lay on her porch, spoiled mackerel filled the neighborhood with a strong odor. And still the flame of charity burned in the friends.

If you could see the complaint book at the Monterey Police Department, you would notice that during this time there was a minor crime wave in Monterey. The police car hurried from place to place. Here a chicken was taken, there a whole patch of pumpkins. Paladini Company reported the loss of two one-hundred-pound cases of abalone steaks.

Teresina's house was growing crowded. The kitchen was stacked high with food. The back porch overflowed with vegetables. Odors like those of a packing house permeated Tortilla Flat. Breathlessly the friends dashed about at their larcenies, and long they talked and planned with Teresina.

At first Teresina was maddened with joy at so much food, and her head was turned by the compliment. After a week of it, she was not so sure. The baby was down with colic, Ernie had some kind of bowel trouble, Alfredo's face was flushed. The creepers and crawlers cried all the time. Teresina was ashamed to tell the friends what she must tell them. It took her several days to get her courage up; and during that time there arrived fifty pounds of celery and a crate of cantaloupes. At last she had to tell them. The neighbors were beginning to look at her with lifted brows.

She asked all of Danny's friends into her kitchen, and then she informed them of the trouble, modestly and carefully, that their feelings might not be hurt.

"Green things and fruit are not good for children," she explained. "Milk is constipating to a baby after it is weaned." She pointed to the flushed and irritable children. See, they were all sick. They were not getting the proper food.

"What is the proper food?" Pilon demanded.

"Beans," she said. "There you have something to trust, something that will not go right through you."

The friends went silently away. They pretended to themselves to be disheartened, but they knew that the first fire of their enthusiasm had been lacking for several days.

At Danny's house they held a conference.

This must not be told in some circles, for the charge might be serious.

Long after midnight, four dark forms who shall be nameless, moved like shadows through the town. Four indistinct shapes crept up on the Western Warehouse Company platform. The watchman said, afterward, that he heard sounds, investigated and saw nothing. He could not say how the thing was done, how a lock was broken and the door forced. Only four men know that the watchman was sound asleep, and they will never tell on him.

A little later the four shadows left the warehouse, and now they were bent under tremendous loads. Pantings and snortings came from the shadows.

At three o'clock in the morning Teresina was awakened by hearing her back door open. "Who is there?" she cried.

There was no answer, but she heard four great thumps that shook the house. She lighted a candle and went to the kitchen in her bare feet. There, against the wall, stood four one-hundred-pound sacks of pink beans.

Teresina rushed in and awakened the vieja. "A miracle!" she cried. "Come look in the kitchen."

The vieja regarded with shame the plump full sacks. "Oh, miserable dirty sinner am I," she moaned. "Oh, Holy Mother, look with pity on an old fool. Every month thou shalt have a candle, as long as I live."

At Danny's house, four friends were lying happily in their blankets. What pillow can one have like a good conscience? They slept well into the afternoon, for their work was done.

And Teresina discovered, by a method she had found to be infallible, that she was going to have a baby. As she poured a quart of the new beans into the kettle, she wondered idly which one of Danny's friends was responsible.

XIV

*Of the good life at Danny's House, of a gift pig,
of the pain of Tall Bob, and of the thwarted love of
the Viejo Ravanno.*

C LOCKS and watches were not used by the paisanos of
Tortilla Flat. Now and then one of the friends acquired
a watch in some extraordinary manner, but he kept it only
long enough to trade it for something he really wanted.
Watches were in good repute at Danny's house, but only as
media of exchange. For practical purposes, there was the great
golden watch of the sun. It was better than a watch, and safer,
for there was no way of diverting it to Torrelli.

In the summer, when the hands of a clock point to seven, it
is a nice time to get up, but in winter the same time is of no
value whatever. How much better is the sun! When he clears
the pine tops and clings to the front porch, be it summer
or winter, that is the sensible time to get up. That is a time
when one's hands do not quiver nor one's belly quake with
emptiness.

The Pirate and his dogs slept in the living room, secure and
warm in their corner. Pilon and Pablo and Jesus Maria and
Danny and Big Joe Portagee slept in the bedroom. For all his
kindness, his generosity, Danny never allowed his bed to be
occupied by any one but himself. Big Joe tried it twice, and
was smacked across the soles of the feet with a stick; so that
even he learned the inviolable quality of Danny's bed.

The friends slept on the floor, and their bedding was unusual. Pablo had three sheepskins stitched together. Jesus
Maria retired by putting his arms through the sleeves of one
old overcoat, and his legs through the sleeves of another. Pilon wrapped himself in a big strip of carpet. Most of the time
Big Joe simply curled up like a dog, and slept in his clothes.
Big Joe, while he had no ability to keep any possession for
very long, had a well-developed genius for trading everything
that came into his hands for some little measure of wine.
Thus they slept, noisily sometimes, but always comfortably.

On one cold night, Big Joe tried to borrow a dog for his feet, and got well bitten, for the Pirate's dogs were not lendable.

No curtains covered the windows, but a generous Nature had obscured the glass with cobwebs, with dust and with the neat marks of raindrops.

"It would be nice to clean that window with soap and water," Danny said one time.

Pilon's sharp mind leaped to the problem with energy, but it was too easy for him. It did not require a decent quota of his powers. "More light would get in," he said. "We would not spend so much time out in the air if it were light in here. And at night, when the air is poisonous, we have no need for light."

Danny retired from the field, for if one little mention brought such clear and quick refutation of his project, what crushing logic would insistence bring forth? The window remained as it was; and as time passed, as fly after fly went to feed the spider family with his blood and left his huskish body in the webs against the glass, as dust adhered to dust, the bedroom took on a pleasant obscurity which made it possible to sleep in a dusky light even at noonday.

They slept peacefully, the friends; but when the sun struck the window in the morning and, failing to get in, turned the dust to silver and shone on the iridescence of the blue-bottle flies, then the friends awakened and stretched and looked about for their shoes. They knew the front porch was warm when the sun was on the window.

They did not awaken quickly, nor fling about nor shock their systems with any sudden movement. No, they arose from slumber as gently as a soap bubble floats out from its pipe. Down into the gulch they trudged, still only half awake. Gradually their wills coagulated. They built a fire and boiled some tea and drank it from the fruit jars, and at last they settled in the sun on the front porch. The flaming flies made halos about their heads. Life took shape about them, the shape of yesterday and of to-morrow.

Discussion began slowly, for each man treasured the little sleep he still possessed. From this time until well after noon, intellectual comradeship came into being. Then roofs were lifted, houses peered into, motives inspected, adventures recounted. Ordinarily their thoughts went first to Cornelia Ruiz, for it was a rare day and night during which Cornelia had not some curious and interesting adventure. And it was an unusual adventure from which no moral lesson could be drawn.

The sun glistened in the pine needles. The earth smelled dry and good. The rose of Castile perfumed the world with its flowers. This was one of the best of times for the friends of Danny. The struggle for existence was remote. They sat in judgment on their fellows, judging not for morals, but for interest. Any one having a good thing to tell saved it for recounting at this time. The big brown butterflies came to the rose and sat on the flowers and waved their wings slowly, as though they pumped honey out by wing power.

"I saw Albert Rasmussen," said Danny. "He came from Cornelia's house. What trouble that Cornelia has. Every day some trouble."

"It is her way of life," said Pablo. "I am not one to cast stones, but sometimes I think Cornelia is a little too lively. Two things only occur to Cornelia, love and fighting."

"Well," said Pilon. "What do you want?"

"She never has any peace," Jesus Maria said sadly.

"She doesn't want any," said Pilon. "Give peace to that Cornelia, and she will die. Love and fighting. That is good, what you said, Pablo. Love and fighting, and a little wine. Then you are always young, always happy. What happened to Cornelia yesterday?"

Danny looked in triumph at Pilon. It was an unusual thing for Pilon not to know everything that happened. And now Danny could tell by the hurt and piqued look on Pilon's face that he did not know this one.

"All of you know Cornelia," he began. "Sometimes men take presents to Cornelia, a chicken or a rabbit or a cabbage. Just little things, and Cornelia likes those things. Well, yesterday Emilio Murietta took to Cornelia a little pig, only so long; a nice little pink pig. Emilio found that pig in the gulch. The sow chased him when he picked it up, but he ran fast, and he came to Cornelia's house with that pig.

"This Emilio is a great talker. He said to Cornelia, 'There is nothing nicer to have than a pig. He will eat anything. He is a nice pet. You get to love that little pig. But then that pig grows up and his character changes. That pig becomes mean and evil-tempered, so that you do not love him any more. Then one day that pig bites you, and you are angry. And so you kill that pig and eat him.' "

The friends nodded gravely, and Pilon said, "In some ways Emilio is not a dull man. See how many satisfactions he has made with his pig—affection, love, revenge and food. I must go to talk with Emilio sometime." But the friends could see that Pilon was jealous of a rival logician.

"Go on with this pig," said Pablo.

"Well," said Danny, "Cornelia took that little pig, and she was nice to Emilio. She said that when the time came, and she was angry at that pig, Emilio could have some of it to eat. Well, then Emilio went away. Cornelia made a little box for that pig to sleep in, by the stove.

"Some ladies came in to see her, then, and Cornelia let them hold the little pig and pet it. After a while Sweets Ramirez stepped on that pig's tail. Oh! It squealed like a steam whistle. The front door was open. That big sow she came in for her little pig again. All the tables and all the dishes were smashed. All the chairs, they were broken. And that big sow bit Sweets Ramirez, and pulled off Cornelia's skirt, and then, when those ladies were in the kitchen and the door locked, the sow went away, and that little pig went too. Now Cornelia is furious. She says she will beat Emilio."

"There it is," said Pablo. "That is the way life goes, never the way you planned. It was that way when Tall Bob Smoke went to kill himself."

The faces of the friends swung appreciatively toward Pablo.

"You will know Bob Smoke," Pablo began. "He looks the way a vaquero should look, long legs, thin body; but he cannot ride very well. At the rodeo he is often in the dust. Now this Bob is one who wants to be admired. When there is a parade he likes to carry the flag. When there is a fight he wants to be referee. At the show he is always the first one to say 'Down in front!' Yes, there is a man who wants to be a great man, and to have people see him, and admire him. And something you do not know, perhaps, he wants people to love him, too.

"Poor unfortunate one, he is a man born to be laughed at. Some people pity him, but most of them just laugh at him. And laughter stabs that Tall Bob Smoke.

"Maybe you remember that time in the parade when he carried the flag. Very straight Bob sat, on a big white horse. Right in front of the place where the judges sat, that big stupid horse fainted from the heat. Bob went flying right over that horse's head, and the flag sailed through the air like a spear and stuck in the ground, upside down.

"That is how it is with him. Whenever he tries to be a great man, something happens and everybody laughs. You remember when he was poundmaster he tried all afternoon to lasso a dog. Everybody in town came to see. He threw the rope and the dog squatted down and the rope slipped off and the dog ran away. Oh, the people laughed. Bob was so ashamed that he thought, 'I will kill myself, and then people will be sad. They will be sorry they laughed.' And then he thought, 'But I will be dead. I will not know how sorry they are.' So he made this plan, 'I will wait until I hear some one coming to my room. I will point a pistol at my head. Then that friend will argue with me. He will make me promise not to shoot myself. The people will be sorry then that they drove me to kill myself.' That is the way he thought it.

"So he walked home to his little house, and everybody he passed called out, 'Did you catch the dog, Bob?' He was very sad when he got home. He took a pistol and put cartridges in it, and then he sat down and waited for some one to come.

"He planned how it would be, and he practiced it with a pistol. The friend would say, 'Ai, what you doing? Don't shoot yourself, poor fellow.' Then Bob would say how he didn't want to live any more because every one was so mean.

"He thought about it over and over, but no one came. And the next day he waited, and no one came. But that next night Charlie Meeler came. Bob heard him on the porch and put the pistol to his head. And he cocked it to make it look more real. 'Now he will argue with me, and I will let him persuade me,' Bob thought.

"Charlie Meeler opened the door. He saw Bob holding that pistol to his head. But he did not shout; no, Charlie Meeler jumped and grabbed that gun and that gun went off and shot away the end of Bob's nose. And then the people laughed even more. There were pieces in the paper about it. The whole town laughed.

"You have all seen Bob's nose, with the end shot off. The people laughed; but it was a hard kind of laughing, and they felt bad to laugh. And ever since then, they let Tall Bob carry the flag in every parade there is. And the city bought him a net to catch dogs with.

"But he is not a happy man, with his nose like that." Pablo fell silent and picked up a stick from the porch and whipped his leg a little.

"I remember his nose, how it was," said Danny. "He is not a bad one, that Bob. The Pirate can tell you, when he gets back. Sometimes the Pirate puts all his dogs in Bob's wagon and then the people think Bob has caught them, and the people say, 'There is a poundman for you.' It is not so easy to catch dogs when it is your business to catch dogs."

Jesus Maria had been brooding, with his head back against the wall. He observed, "It is worse than whipping to be laughed at. Old Tomas, the rag sucker, was laughed right into his grave. And afterwards the people were sorry they laughed.

"And," said Jesus Maria, "there is another kind of laughing, too. That story of Tall Bob is funny; but when you open your mouth to laugh, something like a hand squeezes your heart. I know about old Mr. Ravanno who hanged himself last year. And there is a funny story too, but it is not pleasant to laugh at."

"I heard something about it," said Pilon, "but I do not know that story."

"Well," said Jesus Maria. "I will tell you that story, and you will see if you can laugh. When I was a little boy, I played games with Petey Ravanno. A good quick little boy, that Petey, but always in trouble. He had two brothers and four sisters, and there was his father, Old Pete. All that family is gone now. One brother is in San Quentin, the other was killed by a Japanese gardener for stealing a wagonload of watermelons. And the girls, well, you know how girls are; they went away. Susy is in Old Jenny's house in Salinas right now.

"So there was only Petey and the old man left. Petey grew up, and always he was in trouble. He went to reform school for a while, and then he came back. Every Saturday he was drunk, and every time he went to jail until Monday. His father was a kind of a friendly man. He got drunk every week with Petey. Nearly always they were in jail together. Old man Ravanno was lonely when Petey was not there with him. He liked that boy Petey. Whatever Petey did, that old man did, even when he was sixty years old.

"Maybe you remember that Gracie Montez?" Jesus Maria asked. "She was not a very good girl. When she was only twelve years old, the fleet came to Monterey, and Gracie had her first baby, so young as that. She was pretty, you see, and quick, and her tongue was sharp. Always she seemed to run away from men, and men ran fast after her. And sometimes they caught her. But you could not get close to her. Always that Gracie seemed to have something nice that she did not give to you, something in back of her eyes that said, 'If I really wanted to, I would be different to you from any woman you ever knew.'

"I know about that," said Jesus Maria, "for I ran after Gracie, too. And Petey ran after her. Only Petey was different." Jesus Maria looked sharply into his friends' eyes to emphasize his point.

"Petey wanted what Gracie had so much that he grew thin, and his eyes were as wide and pained as the eyes of one who smokes marihuana. Petey could not eat, and he was sick. Old Man Ravanno went over and talked to Gracie. He said, 'If you are not nice to Petey, he will die.' But she only laughed. She was not a very good one. And then her little sister 'Tonia came into the room. 'Tonia was fourteen years old. The old man looked at her and his breath stopped. 'Tonia was like Gracie, with that funny thing that she kept away from men. Old Man Ravanno could not help it. He said, 'Come to me, little girl.' But 'Tonia was not a little girl. She knew. So she laughed and ran out of the room.

"Old Man Ravanno went home then. Petey said, 'Something is the matter with thee, my father.'

" 'No, Petey,' the old man said, 'only I worry that you do not get this Gracie, so you can be well again.'

"Hot blooded, all those Ravannos were!

"And then what do you think?" Jesus Maria continued.

"Petey went to cut squids for Chin Kee, and he made presents to Gracie, big bottles of Agua Florida and ribbons and garters. He paid to have her picture taken, with colors on the picture, too.

"Gracie took all the presents and she ran away from him, and laughed. You should have heard how she laughed. It made you want to choke her and pet her at the same time. It made you want to cut her open and get that thing that was inside of her. I know how it was. I ran after her, and Petey told me, too. But it made Petey crazy. He could not sleep any more. He said to me, 'If that Gracie will marry me in the church, then she will not dare to run away any more, because she will be married, and it will be a sin to run away.' So he asked her. She laughed that high laugh that made you want to choke her.

"Oh! Petey was crazy. He went home and put a rope over a rafter and he stood on a box and put the rope around his neck and then he kicked out the box. Well, Petey's father came in then. He cut the rope and called the doctor. But it was two hours before Petey opened his eyes, and it was four days before he could talk."

Jesus Maria paused. He saw with pride that his friends were leaning in toward the story. "That was the way of it," he said.

"But Gracie Montez married that Petey Ravanno," Pilon cried excitedly. "I know her. She is a good woman. She never misses mass, and she goes once a month to confession."

"So it is now," Jesus Maria agreed. "Old man Ravanno was angry. He ran to Gracie's house, and he cried, 'See how you murder my boy with your foolishness. He tried to kill himself for you, dung-heap chicken.'

"Gracie was afraid, but she was pleased, too, because it is not many women who can make a man go so far. She went to see Petey where he was in bed with a crooked neck. After a little while they were married.

"It turned out the way Petey thought it would, too. When the church told her to be a good wife, she was a good wife. She didn't laugh to men any more. And she didn't run away so they chased her. Petey went on cutting squids, and pretty soon Chin Kee let him empty the squid boxes. And not long after that he was the mayordomo of the squid yard. You see," said Jesus Maria, "there is a good story. It would be a story for a priest to tell, if it stopped there."

"Oh, yes," said Pilon gravely. "There are things to be learned in this story."

The friends nodded appreciatively, for they liked a story with a meaning.

"I knew a girl in Texas like that," said Danny. "Only she didn't change. They called her the wife of the second platoon. 'Mrs. Second Platoon,' they said."

Pablo held up his hand. "There is more to this story," he said. "Let Jesus Maria tell the rest."

"Yes, there is more. And it is not such a good story, in the ending. There was the viejo, over sixty. And Petey and Gracie went to live in another house. The Viejo Ravanno was lonely, for he had always been with Petey. He didn't know how to take up his time. He just sat and looked sad, until one day he saw 'Tonia again. 'Tonia was fifteen, and she was prettier, even, than Gracie. Half the soldiers from the Presidio followed her around like little dogs.

"Now as it had been with Petey, so it was with the old man. His desire made him ache all over. He could not eat or sleep. His cheeks sunk in, and his eyes stared like the eyes of a marihuana smoker. He carried candy to 'Tonia, and she grabbed the candy out of his hands and laughed at him. He said, 'Come to me, little dear one, for I am thy friend.' She laughed again.

"Then the viejo told Petey about it. And Petey laughed too. 'You old fool,' Petey said. 'You've had enough women in your life. Don't run after babies.' But it did no good. Old Man Ravanno grew sick with longing. They are hot-blooded, those Ravannos. He hid in the grass and watched her pass by. His heart ached in his breast.

"He needed money to buy presents, so he got a job in the Standard Service Station. He raked the gravel and watered the flowers at that station. He put water in the radiators and cleaned the windshields. With every cent he bought presents for 'Tonia, candy and ribbons and dresses. He paid to have her picture taken with colors.

"She only laughed more, and the viejo was nearly crazy. So he thought, 'If marriage in the church made Gracie a good woman, it will make 'Tonia a good woman, too.' He asked her to marry him. Then she laughed more than ever. She flung up her skirts at him to worry him. Oh, she was a devil, that 'Tonia."

"He was a fool," said Pilon smugly. "Old men should not run after babies. They should sit in the sun."

Jesus Maria went on irritably, "Those Ravannos are different," he said, "so hot-blooded."

"Well, it was not a decent thing," said Pilon. "It was a shame on Petey."

Pablo turned to him. "Let Jesus Maria go on. It is his story, Pilon, not thine. Sometime we will listen to thee."

Jesus Maria looked gratefully to Pablo. "I was telling.

"The viejo could not stand it any more. But he was not a man to invent anything. He was not like Pilon. He could not think of anything new. The Viejo Ravanno thought like this: 'Gracie married Petey because he hanged himself. I will hang myself, and maybe 'Tonia will marry me.' And then he thought, 'If no one finds me soon enough, I will be dead. Some one must find me.'

"You must know," said Jesus Maria, "at that service station there is a tool house. Early in the morning, the viejo went down and unlocked the tool house and raked the gravel and watered the flowers before the station opened. The other men came to work at eight o'clock. So, one morning, the viejo went into the tool house and put up a rope. Then he waited until it was eight o'clock. He saw the men coming. He put the rope around his neck and stepped off a work bench. And just when he did that, the door of the tool shed blew shut."

Broad smiles broke out on the faces of the friends. Sometimes, they thought, life was very, very humorous.

"Those men did not miss him right away," Jesus Maria went on. "They said, 'He is probably drunk, that old one.' It was an hour later when they opened the door of that tool shed." He looked around.

The smiles were still on the faces of the friends, but they were changed smiles. "You see," Jesus Maria said, "it is funny. But it squeezes in you, too."

"What did 'Tonia say?" Pilon demanded. "Did she read a lesson and change her living?"

"No. She did not. Petey told her, and she laughed. Petey laughed too. But he was ashamed. 'Tonia said, 'What an old fool he was,' and 'Tonia looked at Petey that way she had.

"Then Petey said, 'It is good to have a little sister like thee. Some night I will walk in the woods with thee.' Then 'Tonia laughed again, and ran away a little. And she said, 'Do you think I am as pretty as Gracie?' So Petey followed her into the house."

Pilon complained, "It is not a good story. There are too many meanings and too many lessons in it. Some of those lessons are opposite. There is not a story to take into your head. It proves nothing."

"I like it," said Pablo. "I like it because it hasn't any meaning you can see, and still it does seem to mean something, I can't tell what."

The sun had turned across noon, and the air was hot.

"I wonder what the Pirate will bring to eat," said Danny.

"There is a mackerel run in the bay," Pablo observed.

Pilon's eyes brightened. "I have a plan that I thought out," he said. "When I was a little boy, we lived by the railroad. Every day when the train went by, my brothers and I threw rocks at the engine, and the fireman threw coal at us. Sometimes we picked up a big bucketful of coal, and took it in to our mother. Now I thought maybe we could take rocks down on the pier. When the boats come near, we will call names, we will throw rocks. How can those fishermen get back at us? Can they throw oars, or nets? No. They can only throw mackerel."

Danny stood up joyfully. "Now there is a plan!" he cried. "How this little Pilon of ours is our friend! What would we do without our Pilon? Come, I know where there is a great pile of rocks."

"I like mackerel better than any other fish," said Pablo.

XV

How Danny brooded and became mad. How the devil in the shape of Torrelli assaulted Danny's House.

THERE is a changeless quality about Monterey. Nearly every day in the morning the sun shines in the windows on the west sides of the streets; and, in the afternoons, on the east sides of the streets. Every day the red bus clangs back and forth between Monterey and Pacific Grove. Every day the canneries send a stink of reducing fish into the air. Every afternoon the wind blows in from the bay and sways the pines on the hills. The rock fishermen sit on the rocks holding their poles, and their faces are graven with patience and with cynicism.

On Tortilla Flat, above Monterey, the routine is changeless, too; for there are only a given number of adventures that Cornelia Ruiz can have with her slowly changing procession of sweethearts. She has been known to take again a man long since discarded.

In Danny's house there was even less change. The friends had sunk into a routine which might have been monotonous for any one but a paisano—up in the morning, to sit in the sun and wonder what the Pirate would bring. The Pirate still cut pitchwood and sold it in the streets of Monterey, but now he bought food with the quarter he earned every day. Occasionally the friends procured some wine, and then there was singing and fighting.

Time is more complex near the sea than in any other place, for in addition to the circling of the sun and the turning of the seasons, the waves beat out the passage of time on the rocks and the tides rise and fall as a great clepsydra.

Danny began to feel the beating of time. He looked at his friends, and saw how with them every day was the same. When he got out of his bed in the night and stepped over the sleeping paisanos, he was angry with them for being there. Gradually, sitting on the front porch, in the sun, Danny began to dream of the days of his freedom. He had slept in the woods in summer, and in the warm hay of barns when the winter cold was in. The weight of property was not upon him. He remembered that the name of Danny was a name of storm. Oh, the fights! The flights through the woods with an outraged chicken under his arm! The hiding places in the gulch when an outraged husband proclaimed feud! Storm and violence, sweet violence! When Danny thought of the old lost time, he could taste again how good the stolen food was, and he longed for that old time again. Since his inheritance had lifted him, he had not fought often. He had been drunk, but not adventurously so. Always the weight of the house was upon him; always the responsibility to his friends.

Danny began to mope on the front porch, so that his friends thought him ill.

"Tea made from yerba buena will be good," Pilon suggested. "If you will go to bed, Danny, we will put hot rocks to your feet."

It was not coddling Danny wanted, it was freedom. For a month he brooded, stared at the ground, looked with sullen eyes at his ubiquitous friends, kicked the friendly dogs out of his way.

In the end he gave up to his longing. One night he ran away. He went into the pine woods and disappeared.

When in the morning the friends awakened and found him missing, Pilon said, "It is some lady. He is in love."

They left it there, for every man has a right to love. The friends went on living as they had. But when a week passed with no sign of Danny, they began to worry. In a body they went to the woods to look for him.

"Love is nice," said Pilon. "We cannot blame any man for following a girl, but a week is a week. It must be a lively girl to keep Danny away for a week."

Pablo said, "A little love is like a little wine. Too much of either will make a man sick. Maybe Danny is already sick. Maybe this girl is too lively."

Jesus Maria was worried, too. "Is it not like the Danny we know to be gone so long. Some bad thing has happened."

The Pirate took his dogs into the woods. The friends advised the dogs, "Find Danny. He may be sick. Somewhere he may be dead, that good Danny who lets you sleep in his house."

The Pirate whispered to them, "Oh, evil, ungrateful dogs, find our friend." But the dogs waved their tails happily and sought out a rabbit and went kyoodling after it.

The paisanos ranged all day through the woods, calling Danny's name, looking in places they themselves might have chosen to sleep in, the good hollows between the roots of trees, the thick needle beds, encircled by bushes. They knew where a man would sleep, but they found no sign of Danny.

"Perhaps he is mad," Pilon suggested. "Some secret worry may have turned his wit."

In the evening they went back to Danny's house and opened the door and went in. Instantly they became intense. A thief had been busy. Danny's blankets were gone. All the food was stolen. Two pots were missing.

Pilon looked quickly at Big Joe Portagee, and then he shook his head. "No, you were with us. You didn't do it."

"Danny did it," Pablo said excitedly. "Truly he is mad. He is running through the woods like an animal."

Great care and worry settled on Danny's house. "We must find him," the friends assured one another. "Some harm will fall upon our friend in his craziness. We must search through the whole world until we find him."

They threw off their laziness. Every day they looked for him, and they began to hear curious rumors. "Yes, Danny was here last night. Oh, that drunk one! Oh, that thief! For see, Danny knocked down the viejo with a fence picket and he stole a bottle of grappa. What kind of friends are these who let their friend do such things?"

"Yes, we saw Danny. His eye was closed, and he was singing, 'Come into the woods and we will dance, little girls,' but we would not go. We were afraid. That Danny did not look very quiet."

At the wharf they found more evidence of their friend. "He was here," the fishermen said. "He wanted to fight everybody. Benito broke an oar on Danny's head. Then Danny broke some windows, and then a policeman took him to jail."

Hot on the path of their wayward friend, they continued. "McNear brought him in last night," the sergeant said. "Some way he got loose before morning. When we catch him, we'll give him six months."

The friends were tired of the chase. They went home, and to their horror, they found that the new sack of potatoes that Pilon had found only that morning was gone.

"Now it is too much," Pilon cried. "Danny is crazy, and he is in danger. Some terrible thing will happen to him if we do not save him."

"We will search," said Jesus Maria.

"We will look behind every tree and every shed," Pablo guaranteed.

"Under the boats on the beach," Big Joe suggested.

"The dogs will help," the Pirate said.

Pilon shook his head. "That is not the way. Every time we come to a place after Danny has gone. We must wait in some place where he will come. We must act as wise men, not as fools."

"But where will he come?"

The light struck all of them at once. "Torrelli's! Sooner or later, Danny will go to Torrelli's. We must go there to catch him, to restrain him in the madness that has fallen upon him."

"Yes," they agreed. "We must save Danny."

In a body they visited Torrelli, and Torrelli would not let them in. "Ask me," he cried through the door, "have I seen Danny? Danny brought three blankets and two cooking pots, and I gave him a gallon of wine. What did that devil do then? My wife he insulted and me he called bad names. My baby he spanked, my dog he kicked! He stole the hammock from my porch." Torrelli gasped with emotion. "I chased him to get my hammock back, and when I returned, he was with my wife! Seducer, thief, drunkard! That is your friend Danny! I myself will see that he goes to penitentiary."

The eyes of the friends glinted. "Oh, Corsican pig," Pilon said evenly. "You speak of our friend. Our friend is not well."

Torrelli locked the door. They could hear the bolt slide, but Pilon continued to speak through the door. "Oh, Jew," he said. "If thou wert a little more charitable with thy wine, these things would not happen. See that thou keepest that cold frog which is thy tongue from dirtying our friend. See thou treatest him gently, for his friends are many. We will tear thy stomach out if thou art not nice to him."

Torrelli made no sound inside the locked house, but he trembled with rage and fear at the ferocity of the tones. He was relieved when he heard the footsteps of the friends receding up the path.

That night, after the friends had gone to bed, they heard a stealthy step in the kitchen. They knew it was Danny, but he escaped before they could catch him. They wandered about in the dark, calling disconsolately, "Come, Danny, our little sugar friend, we need thee with us."

There was no reply, but a thrown rock struck Big Joe in the stomach and doubled him up on the ground. Oh, how the friends were dismayed, and how their hearts were heavy!

"Danny is running to his death," they said sadly. "Our little friend is in need, and we cannot help him."

It was difficult to keep house now, for Danny had stolen nearly everything in it. A chair turned up at a bootlegger's. All the food was taken, and once, when they were searching for Danny in the woods, he stole the air-tight stove; but it was heavy, he abandoned it in the gulch. Money there was none, for Danny stole the Pirate's wheelbarrow and traded it to Joe Ortiz for a bottle of whisky. Now all peace had gone from Danny's house, and there was only worry and sadness.

"Where is our happiness gone?" Pablo mourned. "Somewhere we have sinned. It is a judgment. We should go to confession."

No more did they discuss the marital parade of Cornelia Ruiz. Gone were the moralities, lost were the humanities. Truly the good life lay in ruins. And into the desolation came the rumors.

"Danny committed partial rape last night."

"Danny has been milking Mrs. Palochico's goat."

"Danny was in a fight with some soldiers the night before last."

Sad as they were at his moral decay, the friends were not a little jealous of the good time Danny was having.

"If he is not crazy, he will be punished," said Pilon. "Be sure of that. Danny is sinning in a way which, sin for sin, beats any record I ever heard of. Oh, the penances when he wants to be decent again! In a few weeks Danny has piled up more sins than Old Ruiz did in a lifetime."

That night Danny, unhindered by the friendly dogs, crept into the house as silently as the moving shadow of a limb under a street light, and wantonly he stole Pilon's shoes. In the morning it did not take Pilon long to understand what had happened. He went firmly to the porch and sat down in the sun and regarded his feet.

"Now he has gone too far," Pilon said. "Pranks he has played, and we were patient. But now he turns to crime. This is not the Danny we know. This is another man, a bad man. We must capture this bad man."

Pablo looked complacently down at his shoes. "Maybe this is only a prank too," he suggested.

"No," Pilon said severely. "This is crime. They were not very good shoes, but it is a crime against friendship to take them. And that is the worst kind of crime. If Danny will steal the shoes of his friends, there is no crime he will stop at."

The friends nodded in agreement. "Yes, we must catch him," said Jesus Maria of the humanities. "We know he is sick. We will tie him to his bed and try to cure him of the sickness. We must try to wipe the darkness from his brain."

"But now," said Pablo, "before we catch him, we must remember to put our shoes under our pillows when we sleep."

The house was in a state of siege. All about it raged Danny, and Danny was having a wonderful time.

Seldom did the face of Torrelli show any emotions but suspicion and anger. In his capacity as bootlegger, and in his dealings with the people of Tortilla Flat, those two emotions were often called into his heart, and their line was written on his face. Moreover, Torrelli had never visited any one. He had only to stay at home to have every one visit him. Consequently, when Torrelli walked up the road toward Danny's house in the morning, his face suffused with a ferocious smile of pleasure and anticipation, the children ran into their yards and peeked through the pickets at him; the dogs caressed their stomachs with their tails and fled with backward, fearful looks; men meeting him, stepped out of his path, and clenched their fists to repel a madman.

This morning the fog covered the sky. The sun, after a number of unsuccessful skirmishes, gave up and retired behind the gray folds. The pine trees dripped dusty dew on the ground; and in the faces of the few people who were about, the day was reflected with sombre looks and gray skins. There were no hearty greetings. There was none of that human idealism which blandly hopes this day will be better than all other days.

Old Roca, seeing Torrelli smiling, went home and told his wife, "That one has just killed and eaten his children. You will see!"

Torrelli was happy, for in his pocket there was a folded, precious paper. His fingers sought his coat again and again, and pressed until a little crackling sound assured Torrelli that the paper was still there. As he walked through the gray morning, he muttered to himself.

"Nest of snakes," he said. "I will wipe out this pestilence of Danny's friends. No more will I give wine for goods, and have the goods stolen again. Each man alone is not so bad, but the nest of them! Madonna, look down how I will cast them out into the street! The toads, the lice, the stinging flies! When they sleep in the woods again, they will not be so proud.

"I would have them know that Torrelli has triumphed. They thought to cheat me, to despoil my house of furniture and my wife of virtue! They will see that Torrelli, the great sufferer, can strike back. Oh, yes, they will see!"

Thus he muttered as he walked, and his fingers crackled the paper in his pocket. The trees dripped mournful drops into the dust. The seagulls circled in the air, screaming tragically. Torrelli moved like gray Fate on Danny's house.

In Danny's house there was gloom. The friends could not sit on the porch in the sunshine, for there was no sunshine. No one can produce a better reason for gloom. They had brought back the stolen stove from the gulch and set it up. They clustered to it now, and Johnny Pom-pom, who had come to call, told the news he had.

"Tito Ralph," he said, "is no longer the jailer down at the city jail. No, this morning the police judge sent him away."

"I liked Tito Ralph," said Pilon. "When a man was in jail,

Tito Ralph would bring him a little wine. And he knew more stories than a hundred other men. Why did he lose his job, Johnny Pom-pom?"

"That is what I came to tell. Tito Ralph, you know, was often in jail, and he was a good prisoner. He knew how a jail should be run. After a while he knew more about the jail than any one. Then Daddy Marks, the old jailer, died, and Tito Ralph took his place. Never has there been such a good jailer as Tito Ralph. Everything he did just right. But he has one little fault. When he drinks wine, he forgets he is the jailer. He escapes, and they have to catch him."

The friends nodded. "I know," said Pablo. "I have heard he is hard to catch, too. He hides."

"Yes," continued Johnny Pom-pom, "except for that, he is the best jailer they ever had. Well, this is the thing that I came to tell. Last night Danny had enough wine for ten men, and he drank it. Then he drew pictures on windows. He was very rich; he bought eggs to throw at a Chinaman. And one of those eggs missed the Chinaman and hit a policeman. So, Danny was in jail.

"But he was rich. He sent Tito Ralph out to get some wine, and then some more wine. There were four men in the jail. They all drank wine. And at last that fault of Tito Ralph's came out. So he escaped, and all the others escaped with him. They caught Tito Ralph this morning and told him he could not be jailer any more. He was so sad that he broke a window, and now he is in jail again."

"But Danny," Pilon cried. "What about Danny?"

"Oh, Danny," said Johnny Pom-pom, "he escaped too. They did not catch him."

The friends sighed in dismay.

"Danny is getting bad," Pilon said seriously. "He will not come to a good end. I wonder where he got the money."

It was at this moment that the triumphant Torrelli opened the gate and strode up the path. The Pirate's dogs got up nervously from their corner and moved toward the door, snarling. The friends looked up and questioned one another with their eyes. Big Joe picked up the pick-handle that had so lately been used on him. The heavy confident step of Torrelli pounded on the porch. The door flew open, and there stood

Torrelli, smiling. He did not bluster at them. No, he approached as delicately as a house cat. He patted them kindly, as a house cat pats a cockroach.

"Ah, my friends," he said gently, at their looks of alarm. "My dear good friends and customers. My heart is torn that I must be a carrier of bad news to those whom I love."

Pilon leaped up. "It is Danny. He is sick, he is hurt. Tell us."

Torrelli shook his head daintily. "No, my little ones, it is not Danny. My heart bleeds, but I must tell you that you cannot live here any more." His eyes gloated at the amazement his words wrought. Every mouth dropped open, every eye went blank with astonishment.

"That is foolish," Pablo cried. "Why can't we live here any more?"

Torrelli's hand went lovingly into his breast pocket, and his fingers brought out the precious paper and waved it in the air. "Imagine my suffering," Torrelli went on. "Danny does not own this house any more."

"What!" they cried. "What do you mean? How does not Danny own his house any more? Speak, oh, Corsican pig."

Torrelli giggled, a thing so terrible that the paisanos stepped back from him. "Because," he said, "the house belongs to me. Danny came to me and sold me his house for twenty-five dollars last night." Fiendishly he watched the thoughts crowd on their faces.

"It is a lie," their faces said. "Danny would not do such a thing." And then, "But Danny has been doing many bad things lately. He has been stealing from us. Maybe he has sold the house over our heads."

"It is a lie," Pilon cried aloud. "It is a dirty wop lie."

Torrelli smiled on and waved the paper. "Here I have proof," he said. "Here is the paper Danny signed. It is what we of business call a bill of sale."

Pablo came to him furiously. "You got him drunk. He did not know what he did."

Torrelli opened the paper a little bit. "The law will not be interested in that," he said. "And so, my dear little friends, it is my terrible duty to tell you that you must leave my house. I have plans for it." His face lost its smile, then, and all the cruelty came back into it. "If you are not out by noon, I will send a policeman."

Pilon moved gently toward him. Oh, beware, Torrelli, when Pilon moves smiling on you! Run, hide yourself in some iron room and weld up the door. "I do not understand these things," Pilon said gently. "Of course I am sad that Danny should do a thing like this."

Torrelli giggled again.

"I never had a house to sell," Pilon continued. "Danny signed this paper, is that it?"

"Yes," Torrelli mimicked him, "Danny signed this paper. That is it."

Pilon blundered on, stupidly. "That is the thing that proves you own this house?"

"Yes, oh, little fool. This is the paper that proves it."

Pilon looked puzzled. "I thought you must take it down and have some record made."

Torrelli laughed scornfully. Oh, beware, Torrelli! Do you not see how quietly these snakes are moving? There is Jesus Maria in front of the door. There is Pablo by the kitchen door. See Big Joe's knuckles white on the pick-handle.

Torrelli said, "You know nothing of business, little hoboes and tramps. When I leave here I shall take this paper down and——"

It happened so quickly that the last words belched out explosively. His feet flew up in the air. He landed with a great thump on the floor and clawed at the air with his fat hands. He heard the stove-lid clang.

"Thieves," he screamed. The blood pressed up his neck and into his face. "Thieves, oh, rats and dogs, give me my paper."

Pilon, standing in front of him, looked amazed.

"Paper?" he asked politely. "What is this paper you speak of so passionately?"

"My bill of sale, my ownership. Oh, the police will hear of this!"

"I do not recall a paper," said Pilon. "Pablo, do you know what is this paper he talks about?"

"Paper?" said Pablo. "Does he mean a newspaper or a cigarette paper?"

Pilon continued with the roll. "Johnny Pom-pom?"

"He is dreaming, maybe, that one," said Johnny Pom-pom. "Jesus Maria? Do you know of a paper?"

"I think he is drunk," Jesus Maria said in a scandalized voice. "It is too early in the morning to be drunk."

"Joe Portagee?"

"I wasn't here," Joe insisted. "I just came in now."

"Pirate?"

"He don't have no paper," the Pirate turned to his dogs, "do he?"

Pilon turned back to the apoplectic Torrelli. "You are mistaken, my friend. It is possible that I might have been wrong about this paper, but you can see for yourself that no one but you saw this paper. Do you blame me when I think that maybe there was no paper? Maybe you should go to bed and rest a little."

Torrelli was too stunned to shout any more. They turned him about and helped him out of the door and sped him on his way, sunk in the awfulness of his defeat.

And then they looked at the sky, and were glad; for the sun had fought again, and this time won a pathway through the fog. The friends did not go back into the house. They sat happily down on the front porch.

"Twenty-five dollars," said Pilon. "I wonder what he did with the money."

The sun, once its first skirmish was won, drove the fog headlong from the sky. The porch boards warmed up, and the flies sang in the light. Exhaustion had settled on the friends.

"It was a close thing," Pablo said wearily. "Danny should not do such things."

"We will get all our wine from Torrelli to make it up to him," said Jesus Maria.

A bird hopped into the rose bush and flirted its tail. Mrs. Morales' new chickens sang a casual hymn to the sun. The dogs, in the front yard, thoughtfully scratched all over and gnawed their tails.

At the sound of footsteps from the road, the friends looked up, and then stood up with welcoming smiles. Danny and Tito Ralph walked in the gate, and each of them carried two heavy bags. Jesus Maria darted into the house and brought out the fruit jars. The friends noticed that Danny looked a little tired when he set his jugs on the porch.

"It is hot climbing that hill," Danny said.

"Tito Ralph," cried Johnny Pom-pom, "I heard you were put in jail."

"I escaped again," Tito Ralph said wanly. "I still had the keys."

The fruit jars gurgled full. A great sigh escaped from the men, a sigh of relief that everything was over.

Pilon took a big drink. "Danny," he said, "that pig, Torrelli, came up here this morning with lies. He had a paper he said you signed."

Danny looked startled. "Where is that paper?" he demanded.

"Well," Pilon continued. "We knew it was a lie, so we burned that paper. You didn't sign it, did you?"

"No," said Danny, and he drained his jar.

"It would be nice to have something to eat," observed Jesus Maria.

Danny smiled sweetly. "I forgot. In one of those bags are three chickens and some bread."

So great was Pilon's pleasure and relief that he stood up and made a little speech. "Where is there a friend like our friend?" he declaimed. "He takes us into his house out of the cold. He shares his good food with us, and his wine. Ohee, the good man, the dear friend."

Danny was embarrassed. He looked at the floor. "It is nothing," he murmured. "It has no merit."

But Pilon's joy was so great that it encompassed the world, and even the evil things of the world. "We must do something nice some time for Torrelli," he said.

XVI

Of the sadness of Danny. How through sacrifice Danny's Friends gave a party. How Danny was Translated.

WHEN Danny came back to his house and to his friends after his amok, he was not conscience stricken, but he was very tired. The rough fingers of violent experience had harped upon his soul. He began to live listlessly, arising from bed only to sit on the porch, under the rose of Castile; arising from the porch only to eat; arising from the table only to go to bed. The talk flowed about him and he listened, but he did not care. Cornelia Ruiz had a quick and superb run of husbands, and no emotion was aroused in Danny. When Big Joe got in his bed one evening, so apathetic was Danny that Pilon and Pablo had to beat Big Joe for him. When Sammy Rasper, celebrating a belated New Year with a shotgun and a gallon of whisky, killed a cow and went to jail, Danny could not even be drawn into a discussion of the ethics of the case, although the arguments raged about him and although his judgment was passionately appealed to.

After a while it came about that the friends began to worry about Danny. "He is changed," said Pilon. "He is old."

Jesus Maria suggested, "This Danny has crowded the good times of a life into a little three weeks. He is sick of fun."

In vain the friends tried to draw him from the cavern of his apathy. In the mornings, on the porch, they told their funniest stories. They reported details of the love life of Tortilla Flat so penetrating that they would have been of interest to a dissection class. Pilon winnowed the Flat for news, and brought home every seedling of interest to Danny; but there was age in Danny's eyes and weariness.

"Thou art not well," Jesus Maria insisted in vain. "There is some bitter secret in thine heart."

"No," said Danny.

It was noticed that he let flies crawl on his feet a long time, and that when he did slap them off there was no art in his stroke. Gradually the high spirits, the ready laughter went out of Danny's house and tumbled into the dark pool of Danny's quietness.

Oh, it was a pity to see him, that Danny who had fought for lost causes, or any other kind; that Danny who could drink glass for glass with any man in the world; that Danny who responded to the look of love like an aroused tiger. Now he sat on his front porch in the sunlight, his blue-jeaned knees drawn up against his chest, his arms hanging over, his hands dangling from limp wrists, his head bent forward as though by a heavy black thought. His eyes had no light of desire nor displeasure nor joy nor pain.

Poor Danny, how has life left thee! Here thou sittest like the first man before the world grew up around him; and like the last man, after the world has eroded away. But see, Danny! Thou art not alone. Thy friends are caught in this state of thine. They look at thee from their eye-corners. They wait like expectant little dogs for the first waking movement of their master. One joyful word from thee, Danny, one joyful look, and they will bark and chase their tails. Thy life is not thine own to govern, Danny, for it controls other lives. See how thy friends suffer! Spring to life, Danny, that thy friends may live again!

This, in effect, although not in words so beautiful, was what Pilon said. Pilon held out a jar of wine to Danny. "Come on," he said. "Get up off your can."

Danny took the jar and drained it. And then he settled back and tried to find again his emotional Nirvana.

"Do you hurt any place?" Pilon asked.

"No," said Danny.

Pilon poured him another jar of wine and watched his face while the wine disappeared. The eyes lost their lack-lustre. Somewhere in the depths, the old Danny stirred to life for a moment. He killed a fly with a stroke that would have done justice to a master.

Slowly a smile spread over Pilon's face. And later he gathered all the friends, Pablo and Jesus Maria and Big Joe and the Pirate and Johnny Pom-pom and Tito Ralph.

Pilon led them all into the gulch behind the house. "I gave Danny the last of the wine, and it did him good. What Danny needs is lots of wine, and maybe a party. Where can we get wine?"

Their minds combed the possibilities of Monterey like rat terriers in a barn, but there were no rats. These friends were urged on by altruism more pure than most men can conceive. They loved Danny.

Jesus Maria said, finally, "Chin Kee is packing squids."

Their minds bolted, turned with curiosity and looked at the thing, crept stealthily back and sniffed it. It was several moments before their shocked imaginations could become used to the thing. "But after all, why not?" they argued silently. "One day would not be so bad—only one day."

Their faces showed the progress of the battle, and how they were defeating their fears in the interest of Danny's welfare.

"We will do it," Pilon said. "To-morrow we will all go down and cut squid, and to-morrow night we will give a party for Danny."

When Danny awakened the next morning, the house was deserted. He got up from his bed and looked through the silent rooms. But Danny was not a man to brood very long. He gave it up as a problem, and then as a thought. He went to the front porch and listlessly sat down.

Is it premonition, Danny? Do you fear the fate that is closing in on you? Are there no pleasures left? No. Danny is as sunk in himself as he had been for a week.

Not so Tortilla Flat. Early the rumor flew about, "Danny's friends are cutting squids for Chin Kee." It was a portent, like the overthrow of government, or even of the solar system. It was spoken of in the street, called over back fences to ladies who were just then hurrying to tell it. "All of Danny's friends are down cutting squids."

The morning was electric with the news. There must be some reason, some secret. Mothers instructed their children and sent them running toward Chin Kee's squid yard. Young matrons waited anxiously behind their curtains for later news. And news came.

"Pablo has cut his hand with a squid knife."

"Chin Kee has kicked the Pirate's dogs."

Riot.

"The dogs are back."

"Pilon looks grim."

A few small bets were laid. For months nothing so exciting had happened. During one whole morning not a single person spoke of Cornelia Ruiz. It was not until the noon hour that the real news leaked out, but then it came with a rush.

"They are going to give a big party for Danny."

"Every one is going."

Instructions began to emerge from the squid yard. Mrs. Morales dusted her phonograph and picked out her loudest records. Some spark flared, and Tortilla Flat was tinder. Seven friends, indeed, to give a party for Danny! It is as though to say Danny had only seven friends! Mrs. Soto descended upon her chicken yard with a cleaver. Mrs. Palochico poured a bag of sugar into her largest cooking pot to make dulces. A delegation of girls went into the Woolworth store in Monterey and bought the complete stock of colored crepe paper. Guitars and accordions cried experimentally through the Flat.

News! More news from the squid yard. They are going to make it. They are firm. They will have at least fourteen dollars. See that fourteen gallons of wine are ready.

Torrelli was overwhelmed with business. Every one wanted to buy a gallon to take to Danny's house. Torrelli himself, caught in the fury of the movement, said to his wife, "Maybe we will go to Danny's house. I will take a few gallons for my friends."

As the afternoon passed, waves of excitement poured over the flat. Dresses unworn in a lifetime were unpacked and hung to air. Shawls the moths had yearned for during two hundred years hung from porch railings and exuded the odor of moth balls.

And Danny? He sat like a half-melted man. He moved only when the sun moved. If he realized that every inhabitant of Tortilla Flat had passed his gate that afternoon, he gave no sign. Poor Danny! At least two dozen pairs of eyes watched his front gate. At about four o'clock he stood up, stretched and sauntered out of his yard, toward Monterey.

Why, they hardly waited until he was out of sight. Oh, the

twisting and stringing of green and yellow and red crepe paper! Oh, the candles shaved, and the shavings thrown on the floor! Oh, the mad children who skated the wax in evenly.

Food appeared. Basins of rice, pots of steaming chicken, dumplings to startle you! And the wine came, gallons and gallons of it. Martinez dug up a keg of potato whisky from his manure pile and carried it to Danny's house.

At five-thirty the friends marched up the hill, tired and bloody, but triumphant. So must the Old Guard have looked when they returned to Paris after Austerlitz. They saw the house, bristling with color. They laughed, and their weariness fell from them. They were so happy that tears came into their eyes.

Mama Chipo walked into the yard followed by her two sons who carried a washtub of salsa pura between them. Paulito, that rich scamp, rushed the fire under a big kettle of beans and chili. Shouts, songs broken off, shrieks of women, the general turmoil of excited children.

A carful of apprehensive policemen drove up from Monterey. "Oh, it is only a party. Sure, we'll have a glass of wine. Don't kill anybody."

Where is Danny? Lonely as smoke on a clear cold night, he drifts through Monterey in the evening. To the post-office he goes, to the station, to the pool rooms on Alvarado Street, to the wharf where the black water mourns among the piles. What is it, Danny? What makes you feel this way? Danny didn't know. There was an ache in his heart like the farewell to a dear woman; there was vague sorrow in him like the despair of autumn. He walked past the restaurants he used to smell with interest, and no appetite was aroused in him. He walked by Madam Zuca's great establishment, and exchanged no obscene jests with the girls in the windows. Back to the wharf he went. He leaned over the rail and looked into the deep, deep water. Do you know, Danny, how the wine of your life is pouring into the fruit jars of the gods? Do you see the procession of your days in the oily water among the piles? He remained motionless, staring down.

They were worried about him at Danny's house, when it began to get dark. The friends left the party and trotted down the hill into Monterey. They asked, "Have you seen Danny?"

"Yes, Danny walked by here an hour ago. He walked slow."

Pilon and Pablo hunted together. They traced their friend over the route he had followed, and at last they saw him, on the end of the dark pier. He was lighted by a dim electric wharf light. They hurried out to him.

Pablo did not mention it then, but ever afterwards it was his custom, when Danny was mentioned, to describe what he saw as he and Pilon walked out on the wharf toward Danny. "There he stood," Pablo always said. "I could just see him, leaning on the rail. I looked at him, and then I saw something else. At first it looked like a black cloud in the air over Danny's head. And then I saw it was a big black bird, as big as a man. It hung in the air like a hawk over a rabbit hole. I crossed myself and said two Hail Marys. The bird was gone when we came to Danny."

Pilon did not see it. Moreover, Pilon did not remember Pablo crossing himself and saying the Hail Marys. But he never interfered with the story, for it was Pablo's story.

They walked rapidly toward Danny; the wharf boards drummed hollowly under their feet. Danny did not turn. They took him by the arms and turned him about.

"Danny! What is wrong?"

"Nothing. I'm all right."

"Are you sick, Danny?"

"No."

"Then what is it that makes you so sad?"

"I don't know," said Danny. "I just feel this way. I don't want to do anything."

"Maybe a doctor could do something for you, Danny."

"I tell you I am not sick."

"Then look," Pilon cried. "We are having a party for you at your house. Everybody in Tortilla Flat is there, and music and wine and chicken! There are maybe twenty or thirty gallons of wine. And bright paper hanging up. Don't you want to come?"

Danny breathed deeply. For a moment he turned back to the deep black water. Perhaps he whispered to the gods a promise or a defiance.

He swung around again to his friends. His eyes were feverish.

"You're goddamn right I want to go. Hurry up. I am thirsty. Any girls there?"

"Lots of girls. All the girls."

"Come on, then. Hurry up."

He led them, running up the hill. Long before they arrived they could hear the sweetness of the music through the pines, and the shrill notes of excited happy voices. The three belated ones arrived at a dead run. Danny lifted his head and howled like a coyote. Jars of wine were held out to him. He took a gulp from each one.

That was a party for you! Always afterward when a man spoke of a party with enthusiasm, some one was sure to say with reverence, "Did you go to that party at Danny's house?" And, unless the first speaker were a newcomer, he had been there. That was a party for you! No one ever tried to give a better one. Such a thing was unthinkable; for within two days Danny's party was lifted out of possible comparison with all other parties that ever were. What man came out of that night without some glorious cuts and bruises? Never had there been so many fights; not fights between two men, but roaring battles that raged through whole clots of men, each one for himself.

Oh, the laughter of women! Thin and high and brittle as spun glass. Oh, the lady-like shrieks of protest from the gulch. Father Ramon was absolutely astounded and incredulous at the confessions the next week. The whole happy soul of Tortilla Flat tore itself from restraint and arose into the air, one ecstatic unit. They danced so hard that the floor gave way in one corner. The accordions played so loudly that always afterwards they were windbroken, like foundered horses.

And Danny—just as this party knew no comparison, so Danny defied emulation as a celebrant. In the future let some squirt say with excitement, "Did you see me? Did you see me ask that nigger wenches for a dance? Did you seen us go 'round and 'round like a tom-cats?" and some old, wise and baleful eye would be turned on him. Some voice, sated with having known the limit of possibilities, would ask quietly, "Did you see Danny the night of the party?"

Some time a historian may write a cold, dry, fungus-like history of The Party. He may refer to the moment when

Danny defied and attacked the whole party, men, women and children, with a table-leg. He may conclude, "A dying organism is often observed to be capable of extraordinary endurance and strength." Referring to Danny's super-human amorous activity that night, this same historian may write with unshaking hand: "When any living organism is attacked, its whole function seems to aim toward reproduction."

But I say, and the people of Tortilla Flat would say, "To hell with it. That Danny was a man for you!" No one kept actual count, and afterwards, naturally, no lady would willingly admit that she had been ignored; so that the reputed prowess of Danny may be somewhat overstated. One tenth of it would be an overstatement for any one in the world.

Where Danny went, a magnificent madness followed. It is passionately averred in Tortilla Flat that Danny alone drank three gallons of wine. It must be remembered, however, that Danny is now a god. In a few years it may be thirty gallons. In twenty years it may be plainly remembered that the clouds flamed and spelled DANNY in tremendous letters; that the moon dripped blood; that the wolf of the world bayed prophetically from the mountains of the Milky Way.

Gradually a few of those whose stuff was less stern than Danny's began to wilt, to sag, to creep out from under foot. Those who were left, feeling the lack, shouted the louder, fought the more viciously, danced the harder. In Monterey the motors of the fire trucks were kept running and the firemen, in their red tin hats and raincoats silently sat in their places and waited.

The night passed quickly, and still Danny roared through the party.

What happened is attested by many witnesses, both men and women. And although their value as witnesses is sometimes attacked on the ground that they had drunk thirty gallons of wine and a keg of potato whisky, those people are sullenly sure of the major points. It took some weeks to get the story into line, some said one thing, some another. But gradually the account clarified into the reasonable form it now has and always will have.

Danny, say the people of Tortilla Flat, had been rapidly changing his form. He had grown huge and terrible. His eyes flared like the headlights of an automobile. There was something fearsome about him. There he stood, in the room of his own house. He held the pine table-leg in his right hand, and even it had grown. Danny challenged the world.

"Who will fight?" he cried. "Is there no one left in the world who is not afraid?" The people were afraid; that table-leg, so hideous and so alive, had become a terror to them all. Danny swung it back and forth. The accordions wheezed to silence. The dancing stopped. The room grew chill and a silence seemed to roar in the air like an ocean.

"No one?" Danny cried again. "Am I alone in the world? Will no one fight with me?" The men shuddered before his terrible eyes, and watched fascinated the slashing path of the table-leg through the air. And no one answered the challenge.

Danny drew himself up. It is said that his head just missed touching the ceiling. "Then I will go out to The One who can fight. I will find The Enemy who is worthy of Danny!" He stalked to the door, staggering a little as he went. The terrified people made a broad path for him. He bent to get out of the door. The people stood still and listened.

Outside the house they heard his roaring challenge. They heard the table-leg whistle like a meteor through the air. They heard his footsteps charging down the yard. And then, behind the house, in the gulch, they heard an answering challenge so fearful and so chill that their spines wilted like nasturtium stems under frost. Even now, when the people speak of Danny's Opponent, they lower their voices and look furtively about. They heard Danny charge to the fray. They heard his last shrill cry of defiance, and then a thump. And then silence.

For a long moment the people waited, holding their breaths lest the harsh rush of air from their lungs should obscure some sound. But they listened in vain. The night was hushed, and the gray dawn was coming.

Pilon broke the silence. "Something is wrong," he said. And Pilon it was who first rushed out of the door. Brave man, no terror could restrain him. The people followed him. Back of the house they went, where Danny's footsteps had sounded, and there was no Danny. They came to the edge of the gulch, where a sharp zig-zag path led down to the bottom of that ancient watercourse wherein no stream had flowed for many generations. The following people saw Pilon dart down the path. They went after him, slowly. And they found Pilon at the bottom of the gulch, leaning over a broken and twisted Danny. He had fallen forty feet. Pilon lighted a match. "I think he is alive," he shrieked. "Run for a doctor. Run for Father Ramon."

The people scattered. Within fifteen minutes four doctors were awakened, dragged from their beds by frantic paisanos. They were not allowed that slow deliberateness by which doctors love to show that they are no slaves to emotion. No! They were hustled, rushed, pushed, their instrument cases were shoved into their hands by men hopelessly incapable of saying what they wanted. Father Ramon, dragged from his bed, came panting up the hill, uncertain whether it was a devil to drive out, a newborn baby to baptize before it died or a lynching to attend. Meanwhile Pilon and Pablo and Jesus Maria carried Danny up the hill and laid him on his bed. They stood candles all about him. Danny was breathing heavily.

First the doctors arrived. They glanced suspiciously at one another, considered precedence; but the moment of delay brought threatening looks into the eyes of the people. It did not take long to look Danny over. They were all through by the time Father Ramon arrived.

I shall not go into the bedroom with Father Ramon, for Pilon and Pablo and Jesus Maria and Big Joe and Johnny Pompom and Tito Ralph and the Pirate and the dogs were there; and they were Danny's family. The door was, and is, closed. For after all there is pride in men, and some things cannot decently be pried into.

But in the big room, crowded to suffocation with the people of Tortilla Flat, there was tenseness and a waiting silence. Priests and doctors have developed a subtle means of communication. When Father Ramon came out of the bedroom his face had not changed, but at sight of him the women broke into a high and terrible wail. The men shifted their feet like horses in a box-stall, and then went outside into the dawning. And the bedroom door remained closed.

XVII

*How Danny's sorrowing Friends defied the conventions.
How the Talismanic Bond was burned. How each
Friend departed alone.*

D EATH is a personal matter, arousing sorrow, despair, fervor or dry-hearted philosophy. Funerals, on the other hand, are social functions. Imagine going to a funeral without first polishing the automobile. Imagine standing at a graveside not dressed in your best dark suit and your best black shoes, polished delightfully. Imagine sending flowers to a funeral with no attached card to prove you had done the correct thing. In no social institution is the codified ritual of behavior more rigid than in funerals. Imagine the indignation if the minister altered his sermon or experimented with facial expression. Consider the shock if, at the funeral parlors, any chairs were used but those little folding yellow torture chairs with the hard seats. No, dying, a man may be loved, hated, mourned, missed; but once dead he becomes the chief ornament of a complicated and formal social celebration.

Danny was dead, two days dead; and already he had ceased to be Danny. Although the faces of the people were decently and mournfully veiled with gloom, there was excitement in their hearts. The government has promised a military funeral to all of its ex-soldier sons who wish it. Danny was the first of Tortilla Flat to go, and Tortilla Flat was ready critically to test the government promises. Already news had been sent to the Presidio and Danny's body had been embalmed at government expense. Already a caisson was newly painted and waiting in the artillery shed with a neat new flag folded on top of it. Already orders of the day for Friday were made out:

"Ten to eleven A.M., funeral. Escort, Squadron A, 11th Cavalry, 11th Cavalry Band and Firing Squad."

Were these not things to set every woman in Tortilla Flat window shopping at the National Dollar Store in Monterey? During the day dark children walked the streets of Monterey begging flowers from the gardens for Danny's funeral. And at night the same children visited the same gardens to augment their bouquets.

At the party, the finest clothes had been worn. During the two-day interval, those clothes had to be cleaned, washed, starched, mended and ironed. The activity was frantic. The excitement was decently intense.

On the evening of the second day, Danny's friends were gathered in Danny's house. The shock and the wine had worn off; and now they were horror-stricken, for in all Tortilla Flat they, who had loved Danny most, who had received the most from his hands, they, the paisanos, were the only ones who could not attend Danny's funeral. Through the murk of the headaches they had been conscious of this appalling tragedy, but only on this evening had the situation become so concrete that it must be faced. Ordinarily, their clothes were unspeakable. The party had aged their jeans and blue shirts by years. Where was the trouser knee unburst? Where the shirt unripped? If any one else had died, they could have borrowed clothes; but there was no person in Tortilla Flat who was not going to wear his good clothes to the funeral. Only Cocky Riordan was not going, but Cocky was in quarantine for smallpox, and so were his clothes. Money might be begged or stolen to buy one good suit, but money for six suits was simply impossible to get.

You may say, did they not love Danny enough to go to his funeral in rags? Would you go in rags when your neighbors were dressed in finery? Would not the disrespect to Danny be more if they went in rags than if they did not go at all?

The despair that lay on their hearts was incalculable. They cursed their fate. Through the front door they could see Galvez parading by. Galvez had bought a new suit for the funeral, and he had it on twenty-four hours in advance. The friends sat, chin in hand, crushed by their ill fortune. Every possibility had been discussed.

Pilon, for once in his life, descended to absurdity. "We might go out to-night and each one steal a suit," he suggested. He knew that was silly, for every suit would be laid on a chair beside a bed that night. It would be death to steal a suit.

"The Salvation Army sometimes gives suits," said Jesus Maria.

"I have been there," Pablo said. "They have fourteen dresses this time, but no suits."

On every side Fate was against them. Tito Ralph came in with his new green handkerchief sticking out of his breast pocket, but the hostility he aroused made him back apologetically out of the room.

"If we had a week, we could cut squids," Pilon said heroically. "The funeral is tomorrow. We must look in the eye at this thing. Of course we can go to the funeral all right."

"How?" the friends demanded.

"We can go on the sidewalk, while the band and the people march in the street. It is all grass around the cemetery fence. We can lie there in the grass and see everything."

The friends looked at Pilon gratefully. They knew how his sharp wits had been digging over possibilities. But it was only half, less than half, to see the funeral. Being seen at the funeral was the more important half. This was the best that could be done.

"In this we learn a lesson," said Pilon. "We must take it to heart that we should always have a good suit of clothes laid by. We can never tell what may happen."

There they left it, but they felt that they had failed. All through the night they wandered in the town. What yard then was not plundered of its finest blooms? What flowering tree remained standing? In the morning the hole in the cemetery that was to receive Danny's body was almost hidden by a mound of the finest flowers from the best gardens in Monterey.

It is not always that Nature arranges her effects with good taste. Truly, it rained before Waterloo; forty feet of snow fell in the path of the Donner Party. But Friday turned out a nice day. The sun arose as though this were a day for a picnic. The gulls flew in across a smiling bay to the sardine canneries. The rock fishermen took their places on the rocks for the ebbing tide. The Palace Drug Company ran down its awnings to protect the red hot-water bottles in its windows from the chemical action of the sun. Mr. Machado, the tailor, put a sign in his window, Back In Ten Minutes, and went home to dress for the funeral. Three purse seiners came in, loaded with sardines. Louie Duarte painted his boat, and changed its name from Lolita to The Three Cousins. Jake Lake, the cop, arrested a roadster from Del Monte and turned it loose and bought a cigar.

It is a puzzle. How can life go on its stupid course on such a day? How can Mamie Jackson hose off her front sidewalk? How can George W. Merk write his fourth and angriest letter to the water company? How can Charlie Marsh be as dirtily drunk as usual? It is sacrilege. It is outrage.

Danny's friends awakened sadly, and got up off the floor. Danny's bed was empty. It was like the riderless charger of an officer which follows its master to his grave. Even Big Joe Portagee had cast no covetous glance at Danny's bed. The sun shone enthusiastically through the window and cast the delicate shadows of spider webs on the floor.

"Danny was glad on mornings like this," said Pilon.

After their trip to the gulch, the friends sat for a while on the front porch and celebrated the memory of their friend. Loyally they remembered and proclaimed Danny's virtues. Loyally they forgot his faults.

"And strong," said Pablo. "He was as strong as a mule! He could lift a bale of hay."

They told little stories of Danny, of his goodness, his courage, his piety.

All too soon it was time to go to the church, to stand across the street in their ragged clothes. They blushed inwardly when luckier people went into the church, dressed so beautifully, smelling so prodigally of Agua Florida. The friends could hear the music and the shrill drone of the service. From their vantage point they saw the cavalry arrive, and the band with muffled drums, and the firing squad, and the caisson with its three pairs of horses, and a cavalryman on the near horse of each pair. The mournful clop-clop of shod horses on asphalt put despair in the hearts of the friends. Helplessly they watched the casket carried out and laid on the caisson, and the flag draped over it. The officer blew his whistle, raised his hand and threw it forward. The squadron moved, the firing squad dropped its rifles. The drums thundered their heart-breaking, slow rhythm. The band played its sodden march. The caisson moved. The people walked majestically behind, men straight and stern, women daintily holding their skirts up out of the indelible trail of the cavalry. Every one was there, Cornelia Ruiz, Mrs. Morales, Galvez, Torrelli and his plump wife, Mrs. Palochico, Tito Ralph the traitor, Sweets Ramirez, Mr. Machado, every one who amounted to anything on Tortilla Flat, and every one else, was there.

Is it any wonder that the friends could not stand the shame and misery of it? For a little while they slunk along the sidewalk, bolstered with heroism.

Jesus Maria broke down first. He sobbed with shame, for his father had been a rich and respected prize-fighter. Jesus Maria put down his head and bolted; and the five other friends followed, and the five dogs bounded behind them.

Before the procession was in sight, Danny's friends were lying in the tall grass that edged the cemetery. The service was short and military. The casket was lowered; the rifles cracked; the bugle sang taps, and at the sound Enrique and Fluff, Pajarito and Rudolph and Señor Alec Thompson laid back their heads and howled. The Pirate was proud of them then!

It was over too soon; the friends walked hurriedly away so that the people would not see them.

They had to pass Torrelli's deserted house anyway, on the way home. Pilon went in through a window and brought out two gallons of wine. And then they walked slowly back to Danny's quiet house. Ceremoniously they filled the fruit jars and drank.

"Danny liked wine," they said. "Danny was happy when he had a little wine."

The afternoon passed, and the evening came. Each man, as he sipped his wine, roved through the past. At seven o'clock a shamed Tito Ralph came in with a box of cigars he had won on a punch board. The friends lighted the cigars and spat, and opened the second gallon. Pablo tried a few notes of the song "Tuli Pan," to see whether his voice was gone for good.

"Cornelia Ruiz was alone to-day," Pilon said speculatively.

"Maybe it would be all right to sing a few sad songs," said Jesus Maria.

"But Danny did not like sad songs," Pablo insisted. "He liked the quick ones, about lively women."

They all nodded gravely. "Yes, Danny was a great one for women."

Pablo tried the second verse to "Tuli Pan," and Pilon helped a little, and the others joined in toward the end.

When the song was done, Pilon puffed at his cigar, but it had gone out. "Tito Ralph," he said, "why don't you get your guitar so we can sing a little better?" He lighted his cigar and flipped the match.

The little burning stick landed on an old newspaper against the wall. Each man started up to stamp it out; and each man was struck with a celestial thought, and settled back. They found one another's eyes and smiled the wise smiles of the deathless and hopeless ones. In a reverie they watched the flame flicker and nearly die, and sprout to life again. They saw it bloom on the paper. Thus do the gods speak with tiny causes. And the men smiled on as the paper burned and the dry wooden wall caught.

Thus must it be, oh, wise friends of Danny. The cord that bound you together is cut. The magnet that drew you has lost its virtue. Some stranger will own the house, some joyless relative of Danny's. Better that this symbol of holy friendship, this good house of parties and fights, of love and comfort, should die as Danny died, in one last glorious hopeless assault on the gods.

They sat and smiled. And the flame climbed like a snake to the ceiling and broke through the roof and roared. Only then did the friends get up from their chairs and walk like dreaming men out of the door.

Pilon, who profited by every lesson, took what was left of the wine with him.

The sirens screamed from Monterey. The trucks roared up the hill in second gear. The searchlights played among the trees. When the Department arrived, the house was one great blunt spear of flame. The hoses wet the trees and brush to keep the flames from spreading.

Among the crowding people of Tortilla Flat Danny's

friends stood entranced and watched until at last the house was a mound of black, steaming cinders. Then the fire trucks turned and coasted away down the hill.

The people of the Flat melted into the darkness. Danny's friends still stood looking at the smoking ruin. They looked at one another strangely, and then back to the burned house. And after a while they turned and walked slowly away, and no two walked together.

IN DUBIOUS BATTLE

Innumerable force of Spirits armed,
That durst dislike his reign, and, me preferring,
His utmost power with adverse power opposed
In dubious battle on the plains of Heaven
And shook his throne. What though the field be lost?
All is not lost—the unconquerable will,
And study of revenge, immortal hate,
And courage never to submit or yield:
And what is else not to be overcome?

PARADISE LOST

The Persons and Places in This Book
Are Fictitious

I

At last it was evening. The lights in the street outside came on, and the Neon restaurant sign on the corner jerked on and off, exploding its hard red light in the air. Into Jim Nolan's room the sign threw a soft red light. For two hours Jim had been sitting in a small, hard rocking-chair, his feet up on the white bedspread. Now that it was quite dark, he brought his feet down to the floor and slapped the sleeping legs. For a moment he sat quietly while waves of itching rolled up and down his calves; then he stood up and reached for the unshaded light. The furnished room lighted up—the big white bed with its chalk-white spread, the golden-oak bureau, the clean red carpet worn through to a brown warp.

Jim stepped to the washstand in the corner and washed his hands and combed water through his hair with his fingers. Looking into the mirror fastened across the corner of the room above the washstand, he peered into his own small grey eyes for a moment. From an inside pocket he took a comb fitted with a pocket clip and combed his straight brown hair, and parted it neatly on the side. He wore a dark suit and a grey flannel shirt, open at the throat. With a towel he dried the soap and dropped the thin bar into a paper bag that stood open on the bed. A Gillette razor was in the bag, four pairs of new socks and another grey flannel shirt. He glanced about the room and then twisted the mouth of the bag closed. For a moment more he looked casually into the mirror, then turned off the light and went out the door.

He walked down narrow, uncarpeted stairs and knocked at a door beside the front entrance. It opened a little. A woman looked at him and then opened the door wider—a large blonde woman with a dark mole beside her mouth.

She smiled at him. "*Mis*-ter Nolan," she said.

"I'm going away," said Jim.

"But you'll be back, you'll want me to hold your room?"

"No. I've got to go away for good. I got a letter telling me."

"You didn't get no letters here," said the woman suspiciously.

"No, where I work. I won't be back. I'm paid a week in advance."

Her smile faded slowly. Her expression seemed to slip toward anger without any great change. "You should of give me a week's notice," she said sharply. "That's the rule. I got to keep that advance because you didn't give me no notice."

"I know," Jim said. "That's all right. I didn't know how long I could stay."

The smile was back on the landlady's face. "You been a good quiet roomer," she said, "even if you ain't been here long. If you're ever around again, come right straight here. I'll find a place for you. I got sailors that come to me every time they're in port. And I find room for them. They wouldn't go no place else."

"I'll remember, Mrs. Meer. I left the key in the door."

"Light turned out?"

"Yes."

"Well, I won't go up till tomorrow morning. Will you come in and have a little nip?"

"No, thank you. I've got to be going."

Her eyes narrowed wisely. "You ain't in trouble? I could maybe help you."

"No," Jim said. "Nobody's after me. I'm just taking a new job. Well, good night, Mrs. Meer."

She held out a powdered hand. Jim shifted his paper bag and took her hand for a moment, and felt the soft flesh give under his fingers.

"Don't forget," she said. "I can always find room. People come back to me year after year, sailors and drummers."

"I'll remember. Good night."

She looked after him until he was out the front door and down the cement steps to the sidewalk.

He walked to the corner and looked at the clock in a jeweller's window—seven-thirty. He set out walking rapidly eastward, through a district of department stores and specialty shops, and then through the wholesale produce district, quiet now in the evening, the narrow streets deserted, the depot entrances closed with wooden bars and wire netting. He came at last to an old street of three-storey brick buildings. Pawn-shops and second-hand tool dealers occupied the ground floors, while failing dentists and lawyers had offices in the upper two flights. Jim looked at each doorway until he found the number he wanted. He went in a dark entrance and climbed the narrow stairs, rubber-treaded, the edges guarded with strips of brass. A little night light burned at the head of the steps, but only one door in the long hall showed a light through its frosted glass. Jim walked to it, looked at the "Sixteen" on the glass, and knocked.

A sharp voice called, "Come in."

Jim opened the door and stepped into a small, bare office containing a desk, a metal filing cabinet, an army cot and two straight chairs. On the desk sat an electric cooking plate, on which a little tin coffee-pot bubbled and steamed. A man looked solemnly over the desk at Jim. He glanced at a card in front of him. "Jim Nolan?" he asked.

"Yes." Jim looked closely at him, a small man, neatly dressed in a dark suit. His thick hair was combed straight down on each side from the top in a vain attempt to cover a white scar half an inch wide that lay horizontally over the right ear. The eyes were sharp and black, quick nervous eyes that moved constantly about—from Jim to the card, and up to a wall calendar, and to an alarm clock, and back to Jim. The nose was large, thick at the bridge and narrow at the point. The mouth might at one time have been full and soft, but habitual muscular tension had drawn it close and made a deep line on each lip. Although the man could not have been over forty, his face bore heavy parenthetical lines of resistance to attack. His hands were as nervous as his eyes, large hands, almost too big for his body, long fingers with spatulate ends and flat, thick nails. The hands moved about on the desk like the exploring hands of a blind man, feeling the edges of paper, following the corner of the desk, touching in turn each button on his vest. The right hand went to the electric plate and pulled out the plug.

Jim closed the door quietly and stepped to the desk. "I was told to come here," he said.

Suddenly the man stood up and pushed his right hand across. "I'm Harry Nilson. I have your application here." Jim shook hands. "Sit down, Jim." The nervous voice was soft, but made soft by an effort.

Jim pulled the extra chair close and sat down by the desk. Harry opened a desk drawer, took out an open can of milk, the holes plugged with matches, a cup of sugar and two thick mugs. "Will you have a cup of coffee?"

"Sure," said Jim.

Nilson poured the black coffee into the mugs. He said, "Now here's the way we work on applications, Jim. Your card went in to the membership committee. I have to talk to you and make a report. The committee passes on the report and then the membership votes on you. So you see, if I question you pretty deep, I just have to." He poured milk into his coffee, and then he looked up, and his eyes smiled for a second.

"Sure, I know," said Jim. "I've heard you're more select than the Union League Club."

"By God, we have to be!" He shoved the sugar bowl at Jim, then suddenly, "Why do you want to join the Party?"

Jim stirred his coffee. His face wrinkled up in concentration. He looked down into his lap. "Well—I could give you a lot of little reasons. Mainly, it's this: My whole family has been ruined by this system. My old man, my father, was slugged so much in labor trouble that he went punch-drunk. He got an idea that he'd like to dynamite a slaughter-house where he used to work. Well, he caught a charge of buckshot in the chest from a riot gun."

Harry interrupted, "Was your father Roy Nolan?"

"Yeah. Killed three years ago."

"Jesus!" Harry said. "He had a reputation for being the toughest mug in the country. I've heard he could lick five cops with his bare hands."

Jim grinned. "I guess he could, but every time he went out he met six. He always got the hell beat out of him. He used to come home all covered with blood. He'd sit beside the cook stove. We had to let him alone then. Couldn't even speak to him or he'd cry. When my mother washed him later, he'd whine like a dog." He paused. "You know he was a sticker in the slaughter-house. Used to drink warm blood to keep up his strength."

Nilson looked quickly at him, and then away. He bent the corner of the application card and creased it down with his thumb nail. "Your mother is alive?" he asked softly.

Jim's eyes narrowed. "She died a month ago," he said. "I was in jail. Thirty days for vagrancy. Word came in she was dying. They let me go home with a cop. There wasn't anything the matter with her. She wouldn't talk at all. She was a Catholic, only my old man wouldn't let her go to church. He hated churches. She just stared at me. I asked her if she wanted a priest, but she didn't answer me, just stared. 'Bout four o'clock in the morning she died. Didn't seem like dying at all. I didn't go to the funeral. I guess they would've let me. I didn't want to. I guess she just didn't want to live. I guess she didn't care if she went to hell, either."

Harry started nervously. "Drink your coffee and have some more. You act half asleep. You don't take anything, do you?"

"You mean dope? No, I don't even drink."

Nilson pulled out a piece of paper and made a few notes on it. "How'd you happen to get vagged?"

Jim said fiercely, "I worked in Tulman's Department Store. Head of the wrapping department. I was out to a picture show one night, and coming home I saw a crowd in Lincoln Square. I stopped to see what it was all about. There was a guy in the middle of the park talking. I climbed up on the pedestal of that statue of Senator Morgan so I could see better. And then I heard the sirens. I was watching the riot squad come in from the other side. Well, a squad came up from behind, too. Cop slugged me from behind, right in the back of the neck. When I came to I was already booked for vagrancy. I was rum-dum for a long time. Got hit right here." Jim put his fingers on the back of his neck at the base of his skull. "Well, I told 'em I wasn't a vagrant and had a job, and told 'em to call up Mr. Webb, he's manager at Tulman's. So they did. Webb asked where I was picked up, and the sergeant said 'at a radical meeting,' and then Webb said he never heard of me. So I got the rap."

Nilson plugged in the hot plate again. The coffee started rumbling in the pot. "You look half drunk, Jim. What's the matter with you?"

"I don't know. I feel dead. Everything in the past is gone. I checked out of my rooming house before I came here. I still had a week paid for. I don't want to go back to any of it again. I want to be finished with it."

Nilson poured the coffee cups full. "Look, Jim, I want to give you a picture of what it's like to be a Party member. You'll get a chance to vote on every decision, but once the vote's in, you'll have to obey. When we have money we try to give field workers twenty dollars a month to eat on. I don't remember a time when we ever had the money. Now listen to the work: In the field you'll have to work alongside the men, and you'll have to do the Party work after that, sometimes sixteen, eighteen hours a day. You'll have to get your food where you can. Do you think you could do that?"

"Yes."

Nilson touched the desk here and there with his fingertips. "Even the people you're trying to help will hate you most of the time. Do you know that?"

"Yes."

"Well, why do you want to join, then?"

Jim's grey eyes half closed in perplexity. At last he said, "In the jail there were some Party men. They talked to me. Everything's been a mess, all my life. Their lives weren't messes. They were working toward something. I want to work toward something. I feel dead. I thought I might get alive again."

Nilson nodded. "I see. You're God-damn right I see. How long did you go to school?"

"Second year in high-school. Then I went to work."

"But you talk as though you had more school than that."

Jim smiled. "I've read a lot. My old man didn't want me to read. He said I'd desert my own people. But I read anyway. One day I met a man in the park. He made lists of things for me to read. Oh, I've read a hell of a lot. He made lists like Plato's Republic, and the Utopia, and Bellamy, and like Herodotus and Gibbon and Macaulay and Carlyle and Prescott, and like Spinoza and Hegel and Kant and Nietzsche and Schopenhauer. He even made me read *Das Kapital*. He was a crank, he said. He said he wanted to know things without believing them. He liked to group books that all aimed in the same direction."

Harry Nilson was quiet for a while. Then he said, "You see why we have to be so careful. We only have two punishments, reprimand and expulsion. You've got to want to belong to the Party pretty badly. I'm going to recommend you, 'cause I think you're a good man; you might get voted down, though."

"Thanks," said Jim.

"Now listen, have you any relatives who might suffer if you use your right name?"

"I've an uncle, Theodore Nolan. He's a mechanic. Nolan's an awful common name."

"Yeah, I guess it is common. Have you any money?"

"About three dollars. I had some, but I spent it for the funeral."

"Well, where you going to stay?"

"I don't know. I cut off from everything. I wanted to start new. I didn't want to have anything hanging over."

Nilson looked around at the cot. "I live in this office," he said. "I eat and sleep and work here. If you want to sleep on the floor, you can stay here for a few days."

Jim smiled with pleasure. "I'd like that. The bunks in jail weren't any softer than your floor."

"Well, have you had any dinner?"

"No. I forgot it."

Nilson spoke irritably. "If you think I'm chiseling, go ahead," he said. "I haven't any money. You have three dollars."

Jim laughed. "Come on, we'll get dried herrings and cheese and bread. And we'll get stuff for a stew tomorrow. I can make a pretty good stew."

Harry Nilson poured the last of the coffee into the mugs. "You're waking up, Jim. You're looking better. But you don't know what you're getting into. I can tell you about it, but it won't mean anything until you go through it."

Jim looked evenly at him. "Did you ever work at a job where, when you got enough skill to get a raise in pay, you were fired and a new man put in? Did you ever work in a place where they talked about loyalty to the firm, and loyalty meant spying on the people around you? Hell, I've got nothing to lose."

"Nothing except hatred," Harry said quietly. "You're going to be surprised when you see that you stop hating people. I don't know why it is, but that's what usually happens."

Aʟʟ during the day Jim had been restive. Harry Nilson, working on a long report, had turned on him several times in exasperation. "Look," he said finally, "you can go down to the spot alone if you want. There's no reason why you can't. But in an hour I'll go down with you. I've got to finish this thing."

"I wonder if I ought to change my name," said Jim. "I wonder if changing your name would have any effect on you."

Nilson turned back to his report. "You get some tough assignments and go to jail enough and change your name a few times, and a name won't mean any more to you than a number."

Jim stood by the window and looked out. A brick wall was opposite, bounding the other side of a narrow vacant lot between two buildings. A crowd of boys played handball against the building. Their yells came faintly through the closed window.

"I used to play in lots when I was a kid," Jim said. "Seems to me we fought most of the time. I wonder if the kids fight as much as they used to."

Harry did not pause in his writing. "Sure they do," he said. "I look out and see 'em down there. Sure they fight."

"I used to have a sister," Jim went on. "She could lick nearly everybody in the lot. She was the best marble shot I ever saw. Honest, Harry, I've seen her split an agate at ten feet, with her knuckles down, too."

Harry looked up. "I didn't know you had a sister. What happened to her?"

"I don't know," said Jim.

"You don't know?"

"No. It was funny—I don't mean funny. It was one of those things that happen."

"What do you mean, you don't know what happened to her?" Harry laid his pencil down.

"Well, I can tell you about it," said Jim. "Her name was

May. She was a year older than I was. We always slept in the kitchen. Each had a cot. When May was about fourteen and I was thirteen, she hung a sheet across the corner to make a kind of a little closet to dress and undress behind. She got giggly, too. Used to sit on the steps downstairs with a lot of other girls, and giggle when boys went by. She had yellow hair. She was kind of pretty, I guess. Well, one evening I came home from playing ball over on Twenty-third and Fulton— used to be a vacant lot, there's a bank there now. I climbed up to our flat. My mother said, 'Did you see May down on the steps?' I said I hadn't. Pretty soon my old man came home from work. He said, 'Where's May?' My mother said, 'She hasn't come in yet.'

"It's funny how this whole thing stands out, Harry. I remember every bit of it, what everybody said, and how everybody looked.

"We waited dinner a while, but pretty soon my old man stuck out his chin and got mad. 'Put on the food,' he said. 'May's getting too smart. She thinks she's too big to get licked.'

"My mother had light blue eyes. I remember they looked like white stones. Well, after dinner my old man sat in his chair by the stove. And he got madder and madder. My mother sat beside him. I went to bed. I could see my mother turn her head from my father and move her lips. I guess she was praying. She was a Catholic, but my father hated churches. Every little while he'd growl out what he'd do to May when she did come home.

"About eleven o'clock both of 'em went into the bedroom, but they left the light burning in the kitchen. I could hear them talking for a long time. Two or three times in the night I woke up and saw my mother looking out from the bedroom. Her eyes looked just like white stones."

Jim turned from the window and sat down on the cot. Harry was digging his pencil into the desk top. Jim said, "When I woke up the next morning it was sunshiny outside, and that light was still burning. It gives you a funny, lonely feeling to see a light burning in the daytime. Pretty soon my mother came out of the bedroom and started a fire in the stove. Her face was stiff, and her eyes didn't move much.

Then my father came out. He acted just as though he'd been hit between the eyes—slugged. He couldn't get a word out. Just before he went to work, he said, 'I think I'll stop in at the precinct station. She might of got run over.'

"Well, I went to school, and right after school I came home. My mother told me to ask all the girls if they'd seen May. By that time the news had got around that May was gone. They said they hadn't seen May at all. They were all shivery about it. Then my father came home. He'd been to the police station on the way home, too. He said, 'The cops took a description. They said they'd keep their eyes peeled.'

"That night was just like the one before. My old man and my mother sitting side by side, only my father didn't do any talking that second night. They left the light on all night again. The next day my old man went back to the station house. Well, the cops sent a dick to question the kids on the block, and a cop came and talked to my mother. Finally they said they'd keep their eyes open. And that was all. We never heard of her again, ever."

Harry stabbed the desk and broke his pencil point. "Was she going around with any older boys she might've run off with?"

"I don't know. The girls said not, and they would have known."

"But haven't you an idea of what might have happened to her?"

"No. She just disappeared one day, just dropped out of sight. The same thing happened to Bertha Riley two years later—just dropped out."

Jim felt with his hand along the line of his jaw. "It might have been my imagination, but it seemed to me that my mother was quieter even than before. She moved kind of like a machine, and she hardly ever said anything. Her eyes got a kind of a dead look, too. But it made my old man mad. He had to fight everything with his fists. He went to work and beat hell out of the foreman at the Monel packing house. Then he did ninety days for assault."

Harry stared out the window. Suddenly he put down his pencil and stood up. "Come on!" he said. "I'm going to take you down to the house and get rid of you. I've got to get that report out. I'll do it when I get back."

Jim walked to the radiator and picked off two pairs of damp socks. He rolled them up and put them in his paper bag. "I'll dry them down at the other place," he said.

Harry put on his hat, and folded the report and put it in his pocket. "Every once in a while the cops go through this place," he explained. "I don't leave anything around." He locked the office door as he went out.

They walked through the business center of the city, and past blocks of apartment houses. At last they came to a district of old houses, each in its own yard. Harry turned into a driveway. "Here we are. It's in back of this house." They followed the gravelled drive, and in back came to a tiny cottage, newly painted. Harry walked to the door and opened it, and motioned Jim inside.

The cottage contained one large room and a kitchenette. In the big room there were six steel cots, made up with army blankets. Three men were in the room, two lying on cots and one large man, with the face of a scholarly prize-fighter, pecking slowly at a typewriter.

He looked up quickly when Harry opened the door, and then stood up and came forward smiling. "Hello, Harry," he said. "What's on your mind?"

"This is Jim Nolan," Harry explained. "Remember? His name came up the other night. Jim, this is Mac. He knows more about field work than anybody in the state."

Mac grinned. "Glad to see you, Jim," he said.

Harry, turning to go, said, "Take care of him, Mac. Put him to work. I've got to get out a report." He waved to the two who were lying down. " 'Bye, boys."

When the door was closed, Jim looked about the room. The wallboarded walls were bare. Only one chair was in the room, and that stood in front of the typewriter. From the kitchenette came an odor of boiling corned beef. He looked back at Mac, at his broad shoulders and long arms, at his face, wide between the cheek-bones with flat planes under the eyes like those of a Swede. Mac's lips were dry and cracked. He looked at Jim as closely as he was being inspected.

Suddenly he said, "Too bad we're not dogs, we could get

that all over with. We'd either be friends or fighting by now. Harry said you were O.K., and Harry knows. Come on, meet the boys. This pale one here is Dick, a bedroom radical. We get many a cake because of Dick."

The pale, dark-haired boy on the bed grinned and held out his hand.

Mac went on, "See how beautiful he is? We call him the Decoy. He tells ladies about the working classes, and we get cakes with pink frosting, huh, Dick?"

"Go to hell," said Dick pleasantly.

Mac, guiding Jim by his arm, turned him toward the man on the other cot. It was impossible to tell how old he was. His face was wizened and battered, his nose crushed flat against his face; his heavy jaw sagged sideways. "This is Joy," said Mac. "Joy is a veteran, aren't you, Joy?"

"Damn right," said Joy. His eyes flared up, then almost instantly the light went out of them again. His head twitched several times. He opened his mouth to speak, but he only repeated, "Damn right," very solemnly, as though it finished off an argument. He caressed one hand with the other. Jim saw that they were crushed and scarred.

Mac explained, "Joy won't shake hands with anybody. Bones are all broken. It hurts Joy to shake hands."

The light flared in Joy's eyes again. "Why is it?" he cried shrilly. " 'Cause I've been beat, that's why! I been handcuffed to a bar and beat over the head. I been stepped on by horses." He shouted, "I been beat to hell, ain't I, Mac?"

"That's right, Joy."

"And did I ever crawl, Mac? Didn't I keep on calling 'em sons-of-bitches till they knocked me cold?"

"That's right, Joy. And if you'd kept your trap shut, they wouldn't have knocked you cold."

Joy's voice rose to a frenzy. "But they was sons-of-bitches. I told 'em, too. Let 'em beat me over the head with my hands in 'cuffs. Let 'em ride over me! See that hand? That was rode over with a horse. But I told 'em, didn't I, Mac?"

Mac leaned over and patted him. "You sure did, Joy. Nobody's going to make you keep quiet."

"Damn right," said Joy, and the light went out of his eyes again.

Mac said, "Come on over here, Jim." He led him to the other end of the room, where the typewriter stood on a little table. "Know how to type?"

"A little," said Jim.

"Thank God! You can get right to work." Mac lowered his voice. "Don't mind Joy. He's slug-nutty. He's been smacked over the head too much. We take care of him and try to keep him out of trouble."

"My old man was like that," said Jim. "One time I found him in the street. He was walking in big circles off to the left. I had to steer him straight. A scab had smashed him under the ear with a pair of brass knuckles. Seemed to affect his sense of direction."

"Now look here," said Mac. "Here's a general letter. I've got four carbons in the typewriter. We've got to have twenty copies. You want to get to it while I fix some supper?"

"Sure," said Jim.

"Well, hit the keys hard. Those carbon sheets aren't much good." Mac went into the kitchen calling, "Dick, come out and peel some onions if you can stand the horrible smell."

Dick got up from the couch; after rolling the sleeves of his white shirt neatly above his elbows, he followed Mac into the kitchen.

Jim had just started his heavy, deliberate typing when Joy eased himself off the couch and walked over. "Who produces the goods?" Joy demanded.

"Why—the workers," said Jim.

A foxy look came on Joy's face, a very wise and secret look. "And who takes the profits?"

"The people with invested capital."

Joy shouted, "But they don't produce nothing. What right they got to the profits?"

Mac looked in through the kitchen door. He walked quickly over, a stirring spoon in his hand. "Now listen to me, Joy," he said. "Stop trying to convert our own people. Jesus Christ, it seems to me our guys spend most of their time converting each other. Now you go back and rest, Joy. You're tired. Jim here's got work to do. After he finishes, I'll maybe let you address some of the letters, Joy."

"Will you, Mac? Well, I sure told 'em, didn't I, Mac? Even when they was smackin' me, I told 'em."

Mac took him gently by the elbow and led him back to his cot. "Here's a copy of *New Masses*. You just look at the pictures till I get dinner ready."

Jim pounded away at the letter. He wrote it four times and laid the twenty copies beside the typewriter. He called into the kitchen, "Here they are, all ready, Mac."

Mac came in and looked at some of the copies. "Why, you type fine, Jim. You don't cross out hardly anything. Now here's some envelopes. Put these letters in. We'll address 'em after we eat."

Mac filled the plates with corned beef and carrots and potatoes and raw sliced onions. Each man retired to his cot to eat. The daylight was dim in the room until Mac turned on a powerful unshaded light that hung from the center of the ceiling.

When they had finished, Mac went into the kitchen again and returned with a platter of cup cakes. "Here's some more of Dick's work," he said. "That Dick uses the bedroom for political purposes. Gentlemen, I give you the DuBarry of the Party!"

"You go to hell," said Dick.

Mac picked up the sealed envelopes from Jim's bed. "Here's twenty letters. That's five for each one of us to address." He pushed the plates aside on the table, and from a drawer brought out a pen and a bottle of ink. Then, drawing a list from his pocket, he carefully addressed five of the envelopes. "Your turn, Jim. You do these five."

"What's it for?" Jim asked.

"Well, I guess it don't make much difference, but it might make it a little harder. We're getting our mail opened pretty regular. I just thought it might make it a little harder for the dicks if all these addresses were in different writing. We'll put one of each in a mail box, you see. No good looking for trouble."

While the other two men were writing their addresses, Jim picked up the dishes, carried them into the kitchen and stacked them on the sinkboard.

Mac was stamping the letters and putting them into his pocket when Jim came back. Mac sajd, "Dick, you and Joy wash the dishes tonight. I did 'em alone last night. I'm going out to mail these letters. Want to walk with me, Jim?"

"Sure," said Jim. "I've got a dollar. I'll get some coffee, and we'll have some when we get back."

Mac held out his hand. "We've got some coffee. We'll get a dollar's worth of stamps."

Jim handed him the dollar. "That cleans me," he said. "It's the last cent I have." He followed Mac out into the evening. They walked along the street looking for mail-boxes. "Is Joy really nuts?" Jim asked.

"Pretty nuts, all right. You see the last thing that happened to him was the worst. Joy was speaking at a barber shop. The barber put in a call and the cops raided the meeting. Well, Joy's a pretty tough fighter. They had to break his jaw with a night stick to stop him; then they threw him in the can. Well, I don't know how Joy did much talking with a busted jaw, but he must have worked on the doctor in the jail some, 'cause the doctor said he wouldn't treat a God-damn red, and Joy lay there three full days with a broken jaw. He's been screwy ever since. I expect he'll be put away pretty soon. He's just taken it on the conk too often."

"Poor devil," said Jim.

Mac drew his bundle of envelopes from his pocket and collected five in different handwritings. "Well, Joy just never learned to keep his mouth shut. Look at Dick. Not a mark on him. And that pretty Dick's just as tough as Joy is when there's some good in it. But just as soon as Dick gets picked up he starts calling the cops 'sir,' and they got him sitting in their laps before he gets through with them. Joy's got no more sense than a bulldog."

They found the last of four mail boxes on the edge of Lincoln Square, and after Mac had deposited his letters the two of them strolled slowly up the brick walk. The maples were beginning to drop leaves on the path. Only a few of the benches along the walks were occupied. The high-hung park lights were on now, casting black patterns of the trees on the ground. Not far from the center of the square stood a statue of a bearded man in a frock coat. Jim pointed to it. "I was standing up on that pedestal," he said. "I was trying to see what was going on. A cop must've reached up and swatted me the way a man swats a fly. I knew a little how Joy feels. It was four or five days before I could think straight. Little pictures went flying through my head, and I couldn't quite catch them. Right in the back of the neck I got it."

Mac turned to a bench and sat down. "I know," he said. "I read Harry's report. Is that the only reason you wanted to join the Party?"

"No," said Jim. "When I got in jail, there were five other men in the same cell, picked up at the same time—a Mexican and a Negro and a Jew and a couple of plain mongrel Americans like me. 'Course they talked to me, but it wasn't that. I'd read more than they knew." He picked up a maple leaf from the ground and began carefully stripping the covering from the hand-like skeleton. "Look," he said. "All the time at home we were fighting, fighting something—hunger mostly. My old man was fighting the bosses. I was fighting the school. But always we lost. And after a long time I guess it got to be part of our mind-stuff that we always would lose. My old man was fighting just like a cat in a corner with a pack of dogs around. Sooner or later a dog was sure to kill him; but he fought anyway. Can you see the hopelessness in that? I grew up in that hopelessness."

"Sure, I can see," Mac said. "There's millions of people with just that."

Jim waved the stripped leaf in front of him, and spun it between his thumb and forefinger. "There was more than that to it," he said. "The house where we lived was always filled with anger. Anger hung in the house like smoke; that beaten, vicious anger against the boss, against the superintendent, against the groceryman when he cut off credit. It was an anger that made you sick to your stomach, but you couldn't help it."

"Go on," said Mac. "I don't see where you're getting, but maybe you do."

Jim jumped up and stood in front of the bench and whipped the leaf skeleton across his palm. "I'm getting to this: In that cell were five men all raised in about the same condition. Some of them worse, even. And while there was anger in them, it wasn't the same kind of anger. They didn't hate a boss or a butcher. They hated the whole system of bosses, but that was a different thing. It wasn't the same kind of anger. And there was something else, Mac. The hopelessness wasn't in them. They were quiet, and they were working; but in the back of every mind there was conviction that sooner or later they would win their way out of the system they hated. I tell you, there was a kind of peacefulness about those men."

"Are you trying to convert me?" Mac asked sarcastically.

"No, I'm trying to tell you. I'd never known any hope or peacefulness, and I was hungry for it. I probably knew more about so-called radical movements than any of those men. I'd read more, but they had the thing I wanted, and they'd got it by working."

Mac said sharply, "Well, you typed a few letters tonight. Do you feel any better?"

Jim sat down again. "I liked doing it, Mac," he said softly. "I don't know why. It seemed a good thing to be doing. It seemed to have some meaning. Nothing I ever did before had any meaning. It was all just a mess. I don't think I resented the fact that someone profited from the mess, but I did hate being in the rat-cage."

Mac thrust his legs out straight before him and put his hands in his pockets. "Well," he said, "if work will keep you happy, you've got a pretty jolly time ahead of you. If you'll learn to cut stencils and run a mimeograph I can almost guarantee you twenty hours a day. And if you hate the profit system, I can promise you, Jim, you won't get a damn cent for it." His voice was genial.

Jim said, "Mac, you're the boss in the joint back there, aren't you?"

"Me? No, I tell 'em what to do, but they don't have to do it. I can't issue any orders. The only orders that really stick are the ones that come down after a vote."

"Well, anyway, you've got some say, Mac. What I'd really like to do is get into the field. I'd like to get into the action."

Mac laughed softly. "You want punishment, don't you? Well, I don't know but what the committee'll think a hell of a lot more of a good typist. You'll have to put romance off for a

while—the noble Party assaulted by the beast of Capitalism."
Suddenly his tone changed and he turned on Jim. "It's all
work," he said. "In the field it's hard work and dangerous
work. But don't think it's so soft at the joint, either. You
don't know what night a bunch of American Legioners all full
of whisky and drum corps music may come down and beat
hell out of you. I've been through it, I tell you. There's no
veteran like the man who got drafted into the army and
served six months in a training camp punching a bayonet into
a sack of sawdust. The men who were in the trenches are
mostly different; but for pure incendiarism and brass knuckle
patriotism, give me twenty training camp ex-soldiers. Why
twenty of 'em will protect their country from five kids any
dark night when they can get a little whisky. Most of 'em got
their wound stripes because they were too drunk to go to a
prophylaxis station."

Jim chuckled. "You don't like soldiers much, do you, Mac?"

"I don't like the ex-soldiers with the gold hats. I was in
France. They were good, honest, stupid cattle. They didn't
like it, but they were nice guys." His voice sobered down. Jim
saw him grin quickly in embarrassment. "I got hot, didn't I,
Jim? I'll tell you why. Ten of the brave bastards licked me one
night. And after they'd licked me unconscious they jumped
on me and broke my right arm. And then they set fire to my
mother's house. My mother pulled me out in the front yard."

"What happened?" Jim asked. "What were you doing?"

The sarcasm came back into Mac's voice. "Me? I was sub-
verting the government. I'd made a speech saying there were
some people starving." He stood up. "Let's go back, Jim.
They ought to have the dishes washed up by now. I didn't
mean to get bitter, but somehow that busted arm still makes
me mad."

They walked slowly back down the path. A few men on the
benches pulled in their legs to let them by.

Jim said, "If you can ever put in a word, Mac, so I can get
out in the field to work, I'll be glad."

"O.K. But you'd better learn to cut stencils and run a mimeograph. You're a good kid; I'm glad to have you with us."

3

JIM sat under the hard white light typewriting letters. Occasionally he stopped and listened, his ears turned toward the door. Except for a kettle simmering huskily in the kitchen, the house was still. The soft roar of streetcars on distant streets, the slap of feet on the pavement in front only made the inside seem more quiet. He looked up at the alarm clock hanging to a nail on the wall. He got up and went into the kitchen and stirred the stew, and turned down the gas until each jet held a tiny blue globe.

As he went back to the typewriter he heard quick steps on the gravelled path. Dick came bursting into the house. "Mac's not here yet?"

"No," said Jim. "He hasn't got here. Neither has Joy. Collect any money today?"

"Twenty dollars," said Dick.

"Boy, you sure do it, I don't know how. We could eat for a month on that; but Mac'll probably spend it all on stamps. Lord, how he goes through stamps."

"Listen," Dick cried. "I think I hear Mac now."

"Or Joy."

"No, it's not Joy."

The door opened and Mac entered. "Hello, Jim. Hello, Dick. Get any money out of the sympathizers today?"

"Twenty dollars."

"Good boy!"

"Say, Mac, Joy did it this afternoon."

"Did what?"

"Well, he started a crazy speech on a street corner and a cop picked him up, and Joy stuck the cop in the shoulder with a pocket knife. They got him locked up, and they got felonious assault on the book. He's sitting in a cell right now, yelling 'son-of-a-bitch' at the top of his lungs."

"I thought he was screwier than usual this morning. Now listen, Dick. I've got to get out of here tomorrow morning, and I've got things to do now. You run to a public phone and call George Camp, Ottman 4211. Tell him the works, and tell him Joy's nuts. Tell him to get down there if he can and say he's Joy's attorney. Joy's got a sweet record if they put it on him—about six incites to riot, twenty or thirty vagrancies, and about a dozen resists and simple assaults. They'll give him the works if George doesn't get busy. Tell George to try to spring him for a drunk." He paused. "Jesus! If a sanity board ever gets hold of that poor devil, he's in for life. Tell George to try to get Joy to keep his mouth shut. And when you do that, Dick, you make the rounds and try to pick up some bail money—in case."

"Can't I eat first?" Dick asked.

"Hell, no. Get George down there. Here, give me ten of the twenty. Jim and I are going down to the Torgas Valley tomorrow. After you call George, come back and eat. And then start rounding up the sympathizers for bail. I hope to God George can get out a writ and get bail set sometime tonight."

Dick said, "O.K.," and hurried out.

Mac turned to Jim. "I guess they'll have to lock poor Joy up pretty soon, for good. He's a long way gone. This is the first time he ever used a knife."

Jim pointed to a pile of finished letters on the desk. "There they are, Mac. Three more to do, that's all. Where'd you say we're going?"

"Down the Torgas Valley. There're thousands of acres of apples ready to pick down there. Be damn near two thousand fruit tramps. Well, the Growers' Association just announced a pay cut to the pickers. They'll be sore as hell. If we can get a good ruckus going down there we might be able to spread it over to the cotton fields in Tandale. And then we *would* have something. That'd be a fuss!" He sniffed the air. "Say, that stew smells swell. Is it ready?"

"I'll dish it up," said Jim. He brought in two bowls half full of soup, out of which arose a mound of meat squares, potatoes and carrots, pale turnips and steaming whole onions.

Mac put his bowl on the table and tasted it. "Christ! Let it cool. It's like this, Jim, I always said we shouldn't send green men into trouble areas. They make too many mistakes. You can read all the tactics you want and it won't help much. Well, I remembered what you said in the park that night when you first came, so when I got this assignment, and it's a nice assignment, I asked if I could take you along as a kind of understudy. I've been out, see? I'll train you, and then you can train new men. Kind of like teaching hunting dogs by running them with the old boys, see? You can learn more by getting into it than by reading all you like. Ever been in the Torgas Valley, Jim?"

Jim blew on a hot potato. "I don't even know where it is," he said. "I've only been out of town four or five times in my life. Thanks for taking me, Mac." His small grey eyes were ashine with excitement.

"You'll probably cuss hell out of me before we're through if we get in a mess down there. It's going to be no picnic. I hear the Growers' Association is pretty well organized."

Jim gave up trying to eat the hot stew. "How we going to go about it, Mac? What do we do first?"

Mac looked over at him and saw his excitement, and laughed. "I don't know, Jim. That's the trouble with reading, you see. We just have to use any material we can pick up. That's why all the tactics in the world won't do it. No two are exactly alike." For a while he ate in silence, finished off his stew, and when he exhaled, steam came out of his mouth. "Enough for another helping, Jim? I'm hungry."

Jim went to the kitchen and filled his bowl again.

Mac said, "Here's the layout. Torgas is a little valley, and it's mostly apple orchards. Most of it's owned by a few men. Of course there's some little places, but there's not very many of them. Now when the apples are ripe the crop tramps come in and pick them. And from there they go on over the ridge and south, and pick the cotton. If we can start the fun in the apples, maybe it will just naturally spread over into the cotton. Now these few guys that own most of the Torgas Valley waited until most of the crop tramps were already there. They spent most of their money getting there, of course. They always do. And then the owners announced their price cut. Suppose the tramps are mad? What can they do? They've got to work picking apples to get out even."

Jim's dinner was neglected. With his spoon he stirred the meat and potatoes around and around. He leaned forward. "So then we try to get the men to strike? Is that it?"

"Sure. Maybe it's all ready to bust and we just give it a little tiny push. We organize the men, and then we picket the orchards."

Jim said, "Suppose the owners raise the wages to get their apples picked?"

Mac pushed away his finished second bowl. "Well, we'd find another job to do somewhere else soon enough. Hell, we don't want only temporary pay raises, even though we're glad to see a few poor bastards better off. We got to take the long view. A strike that's settled too quickly won't teach the men how to organize, how to work together. A tough strike is good. We want the men to find out how strong they are when they work together."

"Well, suppose," Jim insisted, "suppose the owners do meet the demands?"

"I don't think they will. There's the bulk of power in the hands of a few men. That always makes 'em cocky. Now we start our strike, and Torgas County gets itself an ordinance that makes congregation unlawful. Now what happens? We congregate the men. A bunch of sheriff's men try to push them around, and that starts a fight. There's nothing like a fight to cement the men together. Well, then the owners start a vigilantes committee, bunch of fool shoe clerks, or my friends the American Legion boys trying to pretend they aren't middle-aged, cinching in their belts to hide their pot-bellies—there I go again. Well, the vigilantes start shooting. If they knock over some of the tramps we have a public funeral; and after that, we get some real action. Maybe they have to call out the troops." He was breathing hard in excitement. "Jesus, man! The troops win, all right! But every time a guardsman jabs a fruit tramp with a bayonet a thousand men all over the country come on our side. Christ Almighty! If we can only get the troops called out." He settled back on his cot. "Aw, I'm looking ahead too much. Our job's just to push along our little baby strike, if we can. But God damn it, Jim, if we could get the National Guard called out, now with the crops coming ready, we'd have the whole district organized by spring."

Jim had been crouching on his bed, his eyes shining and his jaws set. Now and then his fingers went nervously to his throat. Mac continued, "The damn fools think they can settle strikes with soldiers." He laughed. "Here I go again—talking like a soap-boxer. I get all worked up, and that's not so good. We got to think good. Oh say, Jim, have you got some blue jeans?"

"No. This suit's all the clothes I own."

"Well, we'll have to go out and buy you some in a second-hand store, then. You're going to pick apples, boy. And you're going to sleep in jungles. And you're going to do Party work after you've done ten hours in the orchard. Here's the work you wanted."

Jim said, "Thanks, Mac. My old man always had to fight alone. He got licked every time."

Mac came and stood over him. "Get those three letters finished, Jim, and then we'll go out and buy you some jeans."

4

THE SUN was just clearing the buildings of the city when Jim and Mac came to the railroad yards, where the shining metals converged and separated and spread out into the great gridiron of storage tracks where line after line of cars stood.

Mac said, "There's a freight train supposed to go out at seven-thirty, empties. Let's go down the track a way." He hurried through the yard toward the end, where the many tracks drew together into the main line.

"Do we have to get it on the move?" Jim asked.

"Oh, it won't be going fast. I forgot, you never caught a freight, did you?"

Jim spread his stride in an attempt to walk on every other tie, and found he couldn't quite make it. "Seems to me I never did much of anything," he admitted. "Everything's new to me."

"Well, it's easy now. The company lets guys ride. In the old days it was tough. Train crews used to throw the stiffs off a moving train when they could catch them."

A great black water tower stood beside the track, its gooseneck spout raised up against its side. The multitude of tracks was behind them, and only one line of worn and mirror-polished rails extended ahead. "Might as well sit down and wait," said Mac. "She'll be along pretty soon now."

The long, lonely howl of a train whistle and the slow crash of escaping steam sounded at the end of his words. And at the signal, men began to stand up out of the ditch beside the track and to stretch their arms lazily in the cool morning sun.

"We're going to have company," Mac observed.

The long freight of empties came slowly down the yard, red box-cars and yellow refrigerator cars, black iron gondolas and round tank cars. The engine went by at little more pace than a man could walk, and the engineer waved a black, shiny glove at the men in the ditch. He yelled, "Going to the picnic?" and playfully released a spurt of white steam from between the wheels.

Mac said, "We want a box-car. There, that one. The door's open a little." Trotting beside the car he pushed at the door. "Give a hand," he called. Jim put his hand to the iron handle and threw his weight against it. The big sliding door screeched rustily open a few feet. Mac put his hands on the sill, vaulted, turned in the air and landed in a sitting position in the doorway. Quickly he stood up out of the way while Jim imitated him. The floor of the car was littered with lining paper, torn down from the walls. Mac kicked a pile of the paper together and forced it against the wall. "Get yourself some," he shouted. "It makes a nice cushion."

Before Jim had piled up his paper, a new head appeared in the doorway. A man flung himself in and two more followed him. The first man looked quickly about the car floor and then stood over Mac. "Got just about all of it, didn't you?"

"Got what?" Mac asked innocently.

"The paper. You done a good clean job."

Mac smiled disarmingly. "We didn't know there was guests coming." He stood up. "Here, take some of it."

The man gaped at Mac for a moment, and then he leaned over and picked up the whole cushion of papers.

Mac touched him gently on the shoulder. "All right, punk," he said in a monotone. "Put it all down. If you're going to be a hog you don't get none."

The man dropped the paper. "You going to make me?" he asked.

Mac dropped daintily back, balancing on the balls of his feet. His hands hung open and loose at his sides. "Do you ever go to the Rosanna Fight Stadium?" he asked.

"Yeah, and what of it?"

"You're a God-damn liar," Mac said. "If you went there, you'd know who I am, and you'd take better care of yourself."

A look of doubt came over the man's face. He glanced uneasily at the two men who had come with him. One stood by the doorway, looking out at the moving country. The other one elaborately cleaned his nostrils with a bandana and inspected his findings. The first man looked at Mac again. "I don't want no trouble," he said. "I just wanted a little bit of paper to sit on."

Mac dropped on his heels. "O.K.," he said. "Take some. But leave some, too." The man approached the pile and picked up a small handful. "Oh, you can have more than that."

"We ain't goin' far," said the man. He settled down beside the door and clasped his legs with his arms, and rested his chin on his knees.

The blocks were passed now, and the train gathered speed. The wooden car roared like a sounding-box. Jim stood up and pushed the door wide open to let in the morning sunlight. He sat down in the doorway and hung his legs over. For a while he looked down, until the flashing ground made him dizzy. And then he raised his eyes to the yellow stubble fields beside the track. The air was keen and pleasantly flavored with smoke from the engine.

In a moment Mac joined him. "Look you don't fall out," he shouted. "I knew a guy once that got dizzy looking at the ground and fell right out on his face."   ·

Jim pointed to a white farmhouse and a red barn, half hidden behind a row of young eucalyptus trees. "Is the country we're going to as pretty as this?"

"Prettier," said Mac. "It's all apple trees, miles of 'em. They'll be covered with apples this season, just covered with 'em. The limbs just sagging down with apples you pay a nickel apiece for in town."

"Mac, I don't know why I didn't come into the country oftener. It's funny how you want to do a thing and never do it. Once when I was a kid one of those lodges took about five hundred of us on a picnic, took us in trucks. We walked around and around. There were big trees. I remember I climbed up in the top of a tree and sat there most of the afternoon. I thought I'd go back there every time I could. But I never did."

Mac said, "Stand up, Jim. Let's close this door. We're coming to Wilson. No good irritating the railroad cops."

Together they pulled the door shut, and suddenly the car was dark and warm, and it throbbed like the body of a bass viol. The beat of wheels on the rail-ends grew less rapid as the freight slowed to go through the town. The three men stood up. "We get out here," the leader said. He pushed open the door a foot. His two followers swung out. He turned to Mac. "I hope you don't hold no grudge, pardner."

"No, 'course not."

"Well, so long." He swung out. "You dirty son-of-a-bitch," he yelled as he hit the ground.

Mac laughed and pulled the door nearly shut. For a few moments the train rolled slowly. And the rail-end tempo increased. Mac threw the door wide again and sat down in the sun. "There was a beauty," he said.

Jim asked, "Are you really a prize-fighter, Mac?"

"Hell no. He was the easiest kind of a sucker. He figured I was scared of him when I offered him some of my paper. You can't make a general rule of it, because sometimes it flops, but mostly a guy that tries to scare you is a guy that can be scared." He turned his heavy, good-natured face to Jim. "I don't know why it is, but every time I talk to you I either end up soap-boxing or giving a lecture."

"Well, hell, Mac, I like to listen."

"I guess that's it. We've got to get off at Weaver and catch an east-bound freight. That's about a hundred miles down. If we're lucky, we ought to get to Torgas in the middle of the night." He pulled out a sack of tobacco and rolled a cigarette, holding the paper in out of the rushing air. "Smoke, Jim?"

"No, thanks."

"You got no vices, have you. And you're not a Christer either. Don't you even go out with girls?"

"No," said Jim. "Used to be, when I got riled up I'd go to a cat-house. You wouldn't believe it, Mac, but ever since I started to grow up I been scared of girls. I guess I was scared I'd get caught."

"Too attractive, huh?"

"No, you see all the guys I used to run around with went through the mill. They used to try to make girls behind billboards and down in the lumber yard. Well, sooner or later some girl'd get knocked higher than a kite, and then—well, hell, Mac, I was scared I'd get caught like my mother and my old man—two room flat and a wood stove. Christ knows I don't want luxury, but I don't want to get batted around the way all the kids I knew got it. Lunch pail in the morning with a piece of soggy pie and a thermos bottle of stale coffee."

Mac said, "You've picked a hell of a fine life if you don't want to get batted around. Wait till we finish this job, you'll get batted plenty."

"That's different," Jim protested. "I don't mind getting smacked on the chin. I just don't want to get nibbled to death. There's a difference."

Mac yawned. "It's not a difference that's going to keep me awake. Cat-houses aren't much fun." He got up and went back to the pile of papers, and he spread them out and lay down and went to sleep.

For a long time Jim sat in the doorway, watching the farms go by. There were big market vegetable gardens with rows of round lettuces and rows of fern-like carrots, and red beet leaves, with glistening water running between the rows. The train went by fields of alfalfa, and by great white dairy barns from which the wind brought the rich, healthy smell of manure and ammonia. And then the freight entered a pass in the hills, and the sun was cut off. Ferns and green live oaks grew on the steep sides of the right-of-way. The roaring rhythm of the train beat on Jim's senses and made him drowsy. He fought off sleep so that he might see more of the country, shook his head violently to jar himself awake; but at last he stood up, ran the door nearly closed, and retired to his own pile of papers. His sleep was a shouting, echoing black cave, and it extended into eternity.

Mac shook him several times before he could wake up. "It's nearly time to get off," Mac shouted.

Jim sat up. "Good God, have we gone a hundred miles?"

"Pretty near. Noise kind of drugs you, don't it. I can't ever stay awake in a box-car. Pull yourself together. We're going to slow down in a couple of minutes."

Jim held his dull head between his hands for a moment. "I do feel slugged," he said.

Mac threw open the door. He called, "Jump the way we're going, and land running." He leaped out, and Jim followed him.

Jim looked at the sun, almost straight overhead. In front of him he could see the clustered houses and the shade trees of a little town. The freight pulled on and left them standing.

Mac explained, "The railroad branches here. The line we

want cuts over that way toward the Torgas Valley. We won't go through town at all. Let's jump across the fields and catch the line over there."

Jim followed him over a barbed-wire fence and across a stubble field, and into a dirt road. They skirted the edge of the little town, and in half a mile came upon another railroad right-of-way.

Mac sat down on the embankment and called Jim to sit beside him. "Here's a good place. There's lots of cars moving. I don't know how long we'll have to wait." He rolled a brown cigarette. "Jim," he said. "You ought to take up smoking. It's a nice social habit. You'll have to talk to a lot of strangers in your time. I don't know any quicker way to soften a stranger down than to offer him a smoke, or even to ask him for one. And lots of guys feel insulted if they offer you a cigarette and you don't take it. You better start."

"I guess I will," said Jim. "I used to smoke with the kids. I wonder if it'd make me sick now."

"Try it. Here, I'll roll one for you."

Jim took the cigarette and lighted it. "It tastes pretty good," he said. "I'd almost forgotten what it tasted like."

"Well, even if you don't like it, it's a good thing to do in our work. It's the one little social thing guys in our condition have. Listen, there's a train coming." He stood up. "It looks like a freight, too."

The train came slowly down the track. "Well, for Christ' sake!" Mac cried. "Eighty-seven! It's our own train. They told me in town that train went on south. It must of just dropped off a few cars and then come right out."

"Let's get our old car back," said Jim. "I liked that car."

As it came abreast, they hopped aboard the box-car again. Mac settled into his pile of papers. "We might just as well have stayed asleep."

Jim sat in the doorway again, while the train crept into the round brown hills, and through two short tunnels. He could still taste the tobacco in his mouth, and it tasted good. Suddenly he dug in the pocket of his blue denim coat. "Mac," he cried.

"Yeah? What?"

"Here's a couple of chocolate bars I got last night."

Mac took one of the bars and lazily unwrapped it. "I can see you're going to be an asset in any man's revolution," he said.

In about an hour the drowsiness came upon Jim again. Reluctantly he closed the door of the car and curled up in his papers. Almost instantly he was in the black, roaring cave again, and the sound made dreams of water pouring over him. Vaguely he could see debris and broken bits of wood in the water. And the water bore him down and down into the dark place below dreaming.

He awakened when Mac shook him. "I bet you'd sleep a week if I'd let you. You've put in over twelve hours today."

Jim rubbed his eyes hard. "I feel slugged again."

"Well, get yourself together. We're coming into Torgas."

"Good God, what time is it?"

"Somewhere about midnight, I guess. Here we come; you ready to hop?"

"Sure."

"O.K. Come on."

The train pulled slowly on away from them. The station of Torgas was only a little way ahead, with its red light on and glancing along the blade of the semaphore. The brakeman was swinging a lantern back and forth. Over to the right the lonely, cold street lights of the town burned and put a pale glow in the sky. The air was cold now. A sharp, soundless wind blew.

"I'm hungry," Jim said. "Got any ideas about eating, Mac?"

"Wait till we get to a light. I think I've got a good prospect on my list." He hurried away into the darkness, and Jim trotted after him. They came immediately into the edge of the town, and on a corner, under one of the lights, Mac stopped and pulled out a sheet of paper. "We got a nice town here, Jim," he said. "Nearly fifty active sympathizers. Guys you can rely on to give you a lift. Here's the guy I want. Alfred Anderson, Townsend, between Fourth and Fifth, Al's Lunch Wagon. What do you think of that?"

"What's that paper?" Jim asked.

"Why, it's a list of all the people in town we know to be sympathizers. With this list we can get anything from knitted wristlets to a box of shotgun shells. But Al's Lunch Wagon—

lunch wagons generally stay open all night, Jim. Townsend, that'll be one of the main streets. Come on, but let me work this."

They turned soon into the main street, and walked down its length until, near the end, where stores were vacant and lots occurred between buildings, they found Al's Lunch Wagon, a cozy looking little car with red stained-glass in the windows, and a sliding door. Through the window they could see that two customers sat on the stools, and that a fat young man with heavy, white, bare arms hovered behind the counter.

"Pie and coffee guys," Mac said. "Let's wait till they finish."

While they loitered, a policeman approached, and eyed them. Mac said loudly, "I don't want to go home till I get a piece of pie."

Jim reacted quickly. "Come on home," he said. "I'm too sleepy to eat."

The policeman passed them. He seemed almost to sniff at them as he went by. Mac said quietly, "He thinks we're trying to get up our nerve to stick up the wagon." The policeman turned and walked back toward them. Mac said, "Well, go home then, if you want. I'm going to get a piece of pie." He climbed the three steps and slid open the door of the lunch wagon.

The proprietor smiled at them. " 'Evening, gents," he said. "Turning on cold, ain't it?"

"Sure is," said Mac. He walked to the end of the counter farthest from the other two customers and sat down. A shadow of annoyance crossed Al's face.

"Now listen, you guys," he said. "If you got no money you can have a cup of coffee and a couple of sinkers. But don't eat up a dinner on me and then tell me to call a cop. Jesus, I'm being busted by pan-handlers."

Mac laughed shortly. "Coffee and sinkers will be just elegant, Alfred," he said.

The proprietor glanced suspiciously at him and took off his high white cook's hat, and scratched his head.

The customers drained their cups together. One of them asked, "Do you always feed bums, Al?"

"Well, Jesus, what can you do? If a guy wants a cup of coffee on a cold night, you can't let him down because he hasn't got a lousy nickel."

The customer chuckled. "Well, twenty cups of coffee is a dollar, Al. You'll fold up if you go about it that way. Coming, Will?" The two got up and paid their checks and walked out.

Al came around the corner and followed them to the door and slid it more tightly closed. Then he walked back down the counter and leaned over toward Mac. "Who are you guys?" he demanded. He had fat, comfortable white arms, bare to the elbows. He carried a damp cloth with which he wiped and wiped at the counter, with little circular movements. His manner of leaning close when he spoke made every speech seem secret.

Mac winked solemnly, like a conspirator. "We're sent down from the city on business," he said.

A red flush of excitement bloomed on Al's fat cheeks. "Oho-o. That's just what I thought when you come in. How'd you know to come to me?"

Mac explained. "You been good to our people, and we don't forget things like that."

Al beamed importantly, as though he were receiving a gift instead of being bummed for a meal. "Here, wait," he said. "You guys probably ain't ate today. I'll sling on a couple of hamburg steaks."

"That'll be swell," Mac agreed enthusiastically. "We're just about starved."

Al went to his ice-box and dug out two handfuls of ground meat. He patted them thin between his hands, painted the gas plate with a little brush and tossed down the steaks. He put chopped onions on top and around the meat. A delicious odor filled the room instantly.

"Lord," said Mac. "I'd like to crawl right over this counter and nest in that hamburger."

The meat hissed loudly and the onions began to turn brown. Al leaned over the counter again. "What you guys got on down here?"

"Well, you got a lot of nice apples," said Mac.

Al pushed himself upright and leaned against the fat buttresses of his arms. His little eyes grew very wise and secret. "Oho," he said. "O-ho-o, I get you."

"Better turn over that meat, then," said Mac.

Al flipped the steaks and pressed them down with his spatula. And he gathered in the vagrant onions and heaped them on top of the meat, and pressed them in. Very deliberate he was in his motions, as inwardly-thoughtful-looking as a ruminating cow. At last he came back and planted himself in front of Mac. "My old man's got a little orchard and a piece of land," he said. "You guys wouldn't hurt him none, would you? I been good to you."

"Sure you been good," said Mac. "The little farmers don't suffer from us. You tell your father we won't hurt him; and if he gives us a break, we'll see his fruit gets picked."

"Thanks," said Al. "I'll tell him." He took up the steaks, spooned mashed potatoes on the plates from the steam table, made a hollow in each potato mountain and filled the white craters with light brown gravy.

Mac and Jim ate voraciously and drank the mugs of coffee Al set for them. And they wiped their plates with bread and ate the bread while Al filled up their coffee cups again. "That was swell, Al," Jim said. "I was starved."

Mac added, "It sure was. You're a good guy, Al."

"I'd be along with you," Al explained, "if I didn't have a business, and if my old man didn't own land. I guess I'd get this joint wrecked if anybody ever found out."

"They'll never find out from us, Al."

"Sure, I know that."

"Listen, Al, are there many working stiffs in yet for the harvest?"

"Yeah, big bunch of them. Good many eat here. I set up a pretty nice dinner for a quarter—soup, meat, two vegetables, bread and butter, pie and two cups of coffee for a quarter. I take a little profit and sell more."

"Good work," said Mac. "Listen, Al, did you hear any of the stiffs talking about a leader?"

"Leader?"

"Sure, I mean some guy that kind of tells 'em where to put their feet."

"I see what you mean," said Al. "No, I don't rightly recall nothing about it."

"Well, where are the guys hanging out?"

Al rubbed his soft chin. "Well, there's two bunches I know of. One's out on Palo Road, alongside the county highway, and then there's a bunch jungled up by the river. There's a regular old jungle down there in the willows."

"That's the stuff. How do we get there?"

Al pointed a thick finger. "You take that cross street and stay on it till you get to the edge of town, and there's the river and the bridge. Then you'll find a path through the willows, off to the left. Follow that about a quarter mile, and there you are. I don't know how many guys is there."

Mac stood up and put on his hat. "You're a good guy, Al. We'll get along now. Thanks for the feed."

Al said, "My old man's got a shed with a cot in it, if you'd like to stay out there."

"Can't do it, Al. If we're going to work, we got to get out among them."

"Well, if you want a bite now and then, come on in," said Al. "Only pick it like tonight when there's nobody here, won't you?"

"Sure, Al. We get you. Thanks again."

Mac let Jim precede him through the door and then slid it closed behind him. They walked down the steps and took the street Al had pointed out. At the corner the policeman stepped out of a doorway. "What's on your mind?" he asked harshly.

Jim jumped back at the sudden appearance, but Mac stood quietly. "Couple of workin' stiffs, mister," he said. "We figure to pick a few apples."

"What you doing on the street this time of night?"

"Hell, we just got off that freight that went through an hour ago!"

"Where you going now?"

"Thought we'd jungle up with the boys down by the river."

The policeman maintained his position in front of them. "Got any money?"

"You saw us buy a meal, didn't you? We got enough to keep out of jail on a vag charge."

The policeman stood aside then. "Well, get going, and keep off the streets at night."

"O.K., mister."

They walked quickly on. Jim said, "You sure talked to him pretty, Mac."

"Why not? That's the first lesson. Never argue with a cop, particularly at night. It'd be swell if we got thirty days for vagrancy right now, wouldn't it?"

They hugged their denim clothes against their chests and hurried along the street, and the lights grew more infrequent.

"How are you going to go about getting started?" Jim asked.

"I don't know. We've got to use everything. Look, we start out with a general plan, but the details have to be worked out with any materials we can find. We use everything we can get hold of. That's the only thing we can do. We'll just look over the situation."

Jim lengthened his stride with a drive of energy. "Well, let me do things, won't you, Mac? I don't want to be a stooge all my life."

Mac laughed. "You'll get used, all right. You'll get used till you'll wish you was back in town with an eight-hour job."

"No, I don't think I will, Mac. I never felt so good before. I'm all swelled up with a good feeling. Do you feel that way?"

"Sometimes," said Mac. "Mostly I'm too damn busy to know how I feel."

The buildings along the street were more dilapidated as they went. Welding works and used car lots and the great trash piles of auto-wrecking yards. The street lights shone on the blank, dead windows of old and neglected houses, and made shadows under shrubs that had gone to brush. The men walked quickly in the cool night air. "I think I see the bridge lights now," Jim said. "See those three lights on each side?"

"I see 'em. Didn't he say turn left?"

"Yeah, left."

It was a two-span concrete bridge over a narrow river that was reduced at this season to a sluggish little creek in the middle of a sandy bed. Jim and Mac went to the left of the bridge ramp, and near the edge of the river bed they found the opening of a trail into the willows. Mac took the lead. In a moment they were out of range of the bridge lights, and the thick willow scrub was all about them. They could see the branches against the lighter sky, and, to the right, on the edge of the river bed, a dark wall of large cottonwoods.

"I can't see this path," Mac said. "I'll just have to feel it with my feet." He moved carefully, slowly. "Hold up your arms to protect your face, Jim."

"I am. I got switched right across the mouth a minute ago." For a while they felt their way along the hard, used trail. "I smell smoke," Jim said. "It can't be far now."

Suddenly Mac stopped. "There's lights ahead. Listen, Jim, the same thing goes as back there. Let me do the talking."

"O.K."

The trail came abruptly into a large clearing, flickeringly lighted by a little bonfire. Along the farther side were three dirty white tents; and in one of them a light burned and huge black figures moved on the canvas. In the clearing itself there were perhaps fifty men, some sleeping on the ground in sausage rolls of blankets, while a number sat around the little fire in the middle of the flat cleared place. As Jim and Mac stepped clear of the willows they heard a short, sharp cry, quickly checked, which came from the lighted tent. Immediately the great shadows moved nervously on the canvas.

"Somebody's sick," Mac said softly. "We didn't hear it yet. It pays to appear to mind your own business."

They moved toward the fire, where a ring of men sat clasping their knees. "Can a guy join this club?" Mac asked, "or does he got to be elected?"

The faces of the men were turned up at him, unshaven faces with eyes in which the firelight glowed. One of the men moved sideways to make room. "Ground's free, mister."

Mac chuckled. "Not where I come from."

A lean, lighted face across the fire spoke. "You come to a good place, fella. Everything's free here, food, liquor, automobiles, houses. Just move in and set down to a turkey dinner."

Mac squatted and motioned Jim to sit beside him. He pulled out his sack of tobacco and made a careful, excellent cigarette; then, as an afterthought, "Would any of you capital-ists like a smoke?"

Several hands thrust out. The bag went from man to man. "Just get in?" the lean face asked.

"Just. Figure to pick a few apples and retire on my income."

Lean-face burst out angrily. "Know what they're payin', fella? Fifteen cents, *fifteen lousy cents!*"

"Well, what do you want?" Mac demanded. "Jesus Christ, man! You ain't got the nerve to say you want to eat? You can eat an apple while you're workin'. All them nice apples!" His tone grew hard. "S'pose we don't pick them apples?"

Lean-face cried, "We got to pick 'em. Spent every God-damn cent gettin' here."

Mac repeated softly, "All them nice apples. If we don't pick 'em, they'll rot."

"If we don't pick 'em, somebody else will."

"S'pose we didn't let nobody else pick?" Mac said.

The men about the fire grew tense. "You mean—strike?" Lean-face asked.

Mac laughed. "I don't mean nothin'."

A short man who rested his chin between his knees said, "When London found out what they was payin' he damn near had a stroke." He turned to the man next to him. "You seen him, Joe. Didn't he damn near have a stroke?"

"Turned green," said Joe. "Just stood there and turned green. Picked up a stick and bust it to splinters in his hands."

The bag of tobacco came back to its starting place, but there was not much left in it. Mac felt it with his fingers and then put it in his pocket. "Who's London?" he asked.

Lean-face answered him. "London's a good guy—a big guy. We travel with him. He's a big guy."

"The boss, huh?"

"Well, no, he ain't a boss, but he's a good guy. We kind of travel with him. You ought to hear him talk to a cop. He——"

The cry came from the tent again, more prolonged this time. The men turned their heads toward it, and then looked apathetically back at the fire.

"Somebody sick?" Mac asked.

"London's daughter'n-law. She's havin' a kid."

Mac said, "This ain't no place t'have a kid. They got a doctor?"

"Hell no! Where'd they get a doctor?"

"Why'n't they take her to the county hospital?"

Lean-face scoffed. "They won't have no crop tramps in the county hospital. Don't you know that? They got no room. Always full-up."

"I know it," said Mac. "I just wondered if you did."

Jim shivered and picked up a little willow stick and thrust the end into the coals until it flared into flame. Mac's hand came stealing out of the darkness and took his arm for a moment, and gripped it.

Mac asked, "They got anybody that knows anything about it?"

"Got an old woman," Lean-face said. His eyes turned suspicious under the questioning. "Say, what's it to you?"

"I had some training," Mac explained casually. "I know something about it. Thought I might help out."

"Well, go see London." Lean-face shucked off responsibility. "It ain't none of our business to answer questions about him."

Mac ignored the suspicion. "Guess I will." He stood up. "Come on, Jim. Is London in that tent with the light?"

"Yeah, that's him."

A circle of lighted faces watched Jim and Mac walk away, and then the heads swung back to the fire again. The two men picked their way across the clearing, avoiding the bundles of cloth that were sleeping men.

Mac whispered, "What a break! If I can pull it off, we're started."

"What do you mean? Mac, I didn't know you had medical training."

"A whole slough of people don't know it," said Mac. They approached the tent, where dark figures moved about on the canvas. Mac stepped close and called, "London."

Almost instantly the tent-flap bellied and a large man stepped out. His shoulders were immense. Stiff dark hair grew in a tonsure, leaving the top of the head perfectly bald. His face was corded with muscular wrinkles and his dark eyes were as fierce and red as those of a gorilla. A power of authority

was about the man. It could be felt that he led men as naturally as he breathed. With one big hand he held the tent-flap
closed behind him. "What you want?" he demanded.

"We just got in," Mac explained. "Some guys over by the
fire says there was a girl havin' a baby."

"Well, what of it?"

"I thought I might help out as long as you got no doctor."

London opened the flap and let a streak of light fall on
Mac's face. "What you think you can do?"

"I worked in hospitals," Mac said. "I done this before. It
don't pay to take no chances, London."

The big man's voice dropped. "Come on in," he said. "We
got an old woman here, but I think she's nuts. Come in and
take a look." He held up the tent-flap for them to enter.

Inside it was crowded and very hot. A candle burned in a
saucer. In the middle of the tent stood a stove made of a
kerosene can, and beside it sat an old and wrinkled woman. A
white-faced boy stood in one corner of the tent. Along the
rear wall an old mattress was laid on the ground, and on this
lay a young girl, her face pale and streaked with brown dirt,
her hair matted. The eyes of all three turned to Mac and Jim.
The old woman looked up for a moment and then dropped
her eyes to the red-hot stove. She scratched the back of one
hand with the nails of the other.

London walked over to the mattress and kneeled down beside it. The girl pulled her frightened eyes from Mac and
looked at London. He said, "We got a doctor here now. You
don't need to be scared no more."

Mac looked down at her and winked. Her face was stiff
with fright. The boy came over from his corner and pawed
Mac's shoulder. "She gonna be all right, Doc?"

"Sure, she's O.K."

Mac turned to the old woman. "You a midwife?"

She scratched the backs of her wrinkled hands and looked
vacantly up at him, but she didn't answer. "I asked if you was
a midwife?" he cried.

"No—but I've took one or two babies in my life."

Mac reached down and picked up one of her hands and
held the lighted candle close to it. The nails were long and
broken and dirty, and the hands were bluish-grey. "You've

took some dead ones, then," he said. "What was you goin' to use for cloths?"

The old woman pointed to a pile of newspapers. "Lisa ain't had but two pains," she whined. "We got papers to catch the mess."

London leaned forward, his mouth slightly open with attention, his eyes searching Mac's eyes. The tonsure shone in the candle-light. He corroborated the old woman. "Lisa had two pains, just finished one."

Mac made a little gesture toward the outside with his head. He went out through the tent-flap and London and Jim followed him. "Listen," he said to London, "you seen them hands. The kid might live if he's grabbed with hands like that, but the girl don't stand a hell of a chance. You better kick that old girl out."

"You do the job then?" London demanded.

Mac was silent for a moment. "Sure I'll do it. Jim, here'll help me some; but I got to have more help, a whole hell of a lot more help."

"Well, I'll give you a hand," London said.

"That ain't enough. Will any of the guys out there give a hand?"

London laughed shortly. "You damn right they will if I tell 'em."

"Well, you tell 'em, then," Mac said. "Tell 'em now." He led the way to the little fire, around which the circle of men still sat. They looked up as the three approached.

Lean-face said, "Hello, London."

London spoke loudly. "I want you guys should listen to Doc, here." A few other men strolled up and stood waiting. They were listless and apathetic, but they came to the voice of authority.

Mac cleared his throat. "London's got a daughter'n-law, and she's goin' to have a baby. He tried to get her in the county hospital, but they wouldn't take her. They're full up, and besides we're a bunch of lousy crop tramps. O.K. They won't help us. We got to do it ourselves."

The men seemed to stiffen a little, to draw together. The apathy began to drop from them. They hunched closer to the fire. Mac went on, "Now I worked in hospitals, so I can help, but I need you guys to help too. Christ, we got to stand by our own people. Nobody else will."

Lean-face boosted himself up. "All right, fella," he said. "What do you want us to do?"

In the firelight Mac's face broke into a smile of pleasure and of triumph. "Swell!" he said. "You guys know how to work together. Now first we got to have water boiling. When it's boiling, we got to get white cloth into it, and boil the cloth. I don't care where you get the cloth, or how you get it." He pointed out three men. "Now you, and you and you get a big fire going. And you get a couple of big kettles. There ought to be some five-gallon cans around. The rest of you gather up cloth; get anything, handkerchiefs, old shirts—anything, as long as it's white. When you get the water boiling, put the cloth in and keep it boiling for half an hour. I want a little pot of hot water as quick as I can get it." The men were beginning to get restive. Mac said, "Wait. One more thing. I want a lamp, a good one. Some of you guys get me one. If nobody'll give you one, steal it. I got to have light."

A change was in the air. The apathy was gone from the men. Sleepers were awakened and told, and added themselves to the group. A current of excitement filled the jungle, but a kind of joyful excitement. Fires were built up. Four big cans of water were put on to boil; and then cloth began to appear. Every man seemed to have something to add to the pile. One took off his undershirt and threw it into the water and then put on his shirt again. The men seemed suddenly happy. They laughed together as they broke dead cottonwood branches for the fire.

Jim stood beside Mac, watching the activity. "What do you want me to do?" he asked.

"Come in with me. You can help me in the tent." At that moment a cry came from the tent. Mac said quickly, "Bring me a can of hot water as quick as you can, Jim. Here," he held out a little bottle. "Put about four of these tablets in each of those big cans. Bring the bottle back to me when you bring the water." He hurried away toward the tent.

Jim counted the tablets into the cans, and then he scooped a large bucketful of water from one of them and followed Mac into the tent. The old woman was crouched in a corner, out of the way. She scratched her hands and peered out suspiciously while Mac dropped two of the tablets into the warm water and dipped his hands into it. "We can anyway get our hands clean," he said.

"What's the bottle?"

"Bichloride of mercury. I always take it with me. Here, you wash your hands, Jim, and then get some fresh water."

A voice outside the tent called, "Here's your lamps, Doc."

Mac went to the flap and brought them back, a round-wick Rochester lamp and a powerful gasoline lantern. "Some poor devil's going to do his milking in the dark," he said to Jim. He pumped up pressure in the gasoline lamp, and when he lighted it the mantles glared, a hard, white light, and the lantern's hiss filled the tent. The crack of breaking wood and the sound of voices came in from outside.

Mac set his lantern down beside the mattress. "Going to be all right, Lisa," he said. Gently he tried to lift the dirty quilt which covered her. London and the white-faced boy looked on. In a panic of modesty Lisa held the quilt down about her. "Come on, Lisa, I've got to get you ready," Mac said persuasively. Still she clutched at the quilt.

London stepped over. "Lisa," he said. "You do it." Her frightened eyes swung to London, and then reluctantly she let go her hold on the quilt. Mac folded it back over her breast and unbuttoned her cotton underwear. "Jim," he called. "Go out and fish me a piece of cloth and get me some soap."

When Jim had brought him a steaming cloth and a thin, hard piece of soap, Mac washed the legs and thighs and stomach. He worked so gently that some of the fear left Lisa's face.

The men brought in the boiled cloths.

The pains came quicker and quicker.

It was dawn when the birth started. Once the tent shook violently. Mac looked over his shoulder. "London, your kid's fainted," he said. "Better take him out in the air." With a look of profound embarrassment London slung the frail boy over his shoulder and carried him out.

The baby's head appeared. Mac supported it with his hands, and while Lisa squealed weakly, the birth was completed. Mac cut the cord with a sterilized pocket-knife.

The sun shone on the canvas and the lantern hissed on. Jim

wrung out the warm cloths and handed them to Mac when he washed the shrunken little baby. And Jim washed and scrubbed the hands of the old woman before Mac let her take the baby. An hour later the placenta came, and Mac carefully washed Lisa again. "Now get all this mess out," he told London. "Burn all these rags."

London asked, "Even the cloths you didn't use?"

"Yep. Burn it all. It's no good." His eyes were tired. He took a last look around the tent. The old woman held the wrapped baby in her arms. Lisa's eyes were closed and she breathed quietly on her mattress. "Come on, Jim. Let's get some sleep."

In the clearing the men were sleeping again. The sun shone on the tops of the willows. Mac and Jim crawled into a little cave in the undergrowth and lay down together.

Jim said, "My eyes feel sandy. I'm tired. I never knew you worked in a hospital, Mac."

Mac crossed his hands behind his head. "I never did."

"Well, where did you learn about births?"

"I never learned till now. I never saw one before. The only thing I knew was that it was a good idea to be clean. God, I was lucky it came through all right. If anything'd happened, we'd've been sunk. That old woman knew lots more than I did. I think she knew it, too."

"You acted sure enough," Jim said.

"Well, Christ Almighty, I had to! We've got to use whatever material comes to us. That was a lucky break. We simply had to take it. 'Course it was nice to help the girl, but hell, even if it killed her—we've got to use anything." He turned on his side and pillowed his head on his arm. "I'm all in, but I feel good. With one night's work we've got the confidence of the men and the confidence of London. And more than that, we made the men work for themselves, in their own defense, as a group. That's what we're out here for anyway, to teach them to fight in a bunch. Raising wages isn't all we're after. You know all that."

"Yes," Jim said. "I knew that, but I didn't know how you were going to go about it."

"Well, there's just one rule—use whatever material you've

got. We've got no machine guns and troops. Tonight was good; the material was ready, and we were ready. London's with us. He's the natural leader. We'll teach him where to lead. Got to go awful easy, though. Leadership has to come from the men. We can teach them method, but they've got to do the job themselves. Pretty soon we'll start teaching method to London, and he can teach it to the men under him. You watch," Mac said, "the story of last night will be all over the district by tonight. We got our oar in already, and it's better than I hoped. We might go to the can later for practicing medicine without a license, but that would only tie the men closer to us."

Jim asked, "How did it happen? You didn't say much, but they started working like a clock, and they liked it. They felt fine."

"Sure they liked it. Men always like to work together. There's a hunger in men to work together. Do you know that ten men can lift nearly twelve times as big a load as one man can? It only takes a little spark to get them going. Most of the time they're suspicious, because every time someone gets 'em working in a group the profit of their work is taken away from them; but wait till they get working for themselves. To-night the work concerned them, it was their job; and see how well they did it."

Jim said, "You didn't need all that cloth. Why did you tell London to burn it?"

"Look, Jim. Don't you see? Every man who gave part of his clothes felt that the work was his own. They all feel responsible for that baby. It's theirs, because something from them went to it. To give back the cloth would cut them out. There's no better way to make men part of a movement than to have them give something to it. I bet they all feel fine right now."

"Are we going to work today?" Jim asked.

"No, we'll let the story of last night go the rounds. It'll be a hell of a big story by tomorrow. No, we'll go to work later. We need sleep now. But Jesus, what a swell set-up it is for us so far."

The willows stirred over their heads, and a few leaves fell

down on the men. Jim said, "I don't know when I ever was so tired, but I do feel fine."

Mac opened his eyes for a moment. "You're doing all right, kid. I think you'll make a good worker. I'm glad you came down with me. You helped a lot last night. Now try to shut your God-damned eyes and mouth and get some sleep."

5

THE AFTERNOON SUN glanced on the tops of the apple trees and then broke into stripes and layers of slanting light beneath the heavy branches, and threw blots of sunshine on the ground. The wide aisles between the trees stretched away until the rows seemed to meet in a visual infinity. The great orchard crawled with activity. Long ladders leaned among the branches and piles of new yellow boxes stood in the aisles. From far away came the rumble of the sorting machines and the tap of the boxers' hammers. The men, with their big buckets slung to baldrics, ran up the ladders and twisted the big green pippins free and filled the buckets until they could hold no more, and then they ran down the ladders to empty the buckets into the boxes. Between the rows came the trucks to load the picked apples and take them to the sorting and packing plant. A checker stood beside the boxes and marked with a pencil in his little book as the bucket men came up. The orchard was alive. The branches of the trees shook under the ladders. The over-ripes dropped with dull plops to the ground underneath the trees. Somewhere, hidden in a tree-top, a whistling virtuoso trilled.

Jim hurried down his ladder and carried his bucket to the box pile and emptied the load. The checker, a blond young man in washed white corduroys, made a mark in his book and nodded his head. "Don't dump 'em in so hard, buddy," he warned. "You'll bruise 'em."

"O.K.," said Jim. He walked back to his ladder, drumming on the bucket with his knee as he went. Up the ladder he climbed, and he hooked the wire of the bale-hook over a limb. And then in the tree he saw another man, who had stepped off the ladder and stood on a big limb. He reached high over his head for a cluster of apples. He felt the tree shudder under Jim's weight and looked down.

"Hello, kid. I didn't know this was your tree."

Jim stared up at him, a lean old man with black eyes and a sparse, chewed beard. The veins stood out heavy and blue on his hands. His legs seemed as thin and straight as sticks, too thin for the big feet with great heavy-soled shoes.

Jim said, "I don't give a damn about the tree. Aren't you too old to be climbing around like a monkey, Dad?"

The old man spat and watched the big white drop hit the ground. His bleak eyes grew fierce. "That's what you think," he said. "Lots of young punks think I'm too old. I can out-work you any day in the week, and don't you forget it, nei-ther." He put an artificial springiness in his knees as he spoke. He reached up and picked the whole cluster of apples, twig and all, skinned the apples into his bucket and contemptu-ously dropped the twig on the ground.

The voice of the checker called, "Careful of those trees, over there."

The old man grinned maliciously, showing two upper and two lower yellow teeth, long and sloped outward, like a go-pher's teeth. "Busy bastard, ain't he," he remarked to Jim.

"College boy," said Jim. "Every place you go you run into 'em."

The old man squatted down on his limb. "And what do they know?" he demanded. "They go to them colleges, and they don't learn a God damn thing. That smart guy with the little book couldn't keep his ass dry in a barn." He spat again.

"They get pretty smart, all right," Jim agreed.

"Now you and me," the old man went on, "we know—not much, maybe, but what we know we know good."

Jim was silent for a moment, and then he lanced at the old man's pride as he had heard Mac do to other men. "You don't know enough to keep out of a tree when you're seventy. I don't know enough to wear white cords and make pencil marks in a little book."

The old man snarled, "We got no pull, that's what. You got to have pull to get an easy job. We just get rode over because we got no pull."

"Well, what you going to do about it?"

The question seemed to let air out of the old man. His anger disappeared. His eyes grew puzzled and a little fright-ened. "Christ only knows," he said. "We just take it, that's all. We move about the country like a bunch of hogs and get beat on the ass by a college boy."

"It's not his fault," said Jim. "He's just got a job. If he's going to keep the job, he's got to do it."

The old man reached for another cluster of apples, picked them with little twisting lifts and put each one carefully into his bucket. "When I was a young man, I used to think somethin' could be done," he said, "but I'm seventy-one." His voice was tired.

A truck went by, carrying off the filled boxes. The old man continued, "I was in the north woods when the Wobblies was raising hell. I'm a top-faller, a damn good one. Maybe you noticed how I take to a tree at my age. Well, I had hopes then. 'Course the Wobblies done some good, used to be there was no crappers but a hole in the ground, and no place to take a bath. The meat used to spoil. Well, them Wobblies made 'em put in toilets and showers; but, hell, it all went to pieces." His hand went up automatically for more apples. "I joined unions," he said. "We'd elect a president and first thing we knowed, he'd be kissing the ass of the superintendent, and then he'd sell us out. We'd pay dues, and the treasurer'd run out on us. I don' know. Maybe you young squirts can figure something out. We done what we could."

"You all ready to give up?" Jim asked, glancing at him again.

The old man squatted down on his limb and held himself there with one big skinny hand. "I got feelings in my skin," he said. "You may think I'm a crazy old coot; them other things was planned; nothing come of 'em; but I got feelings in my skin."

"What kind of feelings?"

"It's hard to say, kid. You know quite a bit before water boils, it gets to heavin' around? That's the kind of feeling I got. I been with workin' stiffs all my life. There ain't a plan in this at all. It's just like that water heavin' before it boils." His eyes were dim, seeing nothing. His head rose up so that two strings of skin tautened between his chin and his throat. "Maybe there's been too much goin' hungry; maybe too many bosses've kicked hell out of the men. I dunno. I just feel it in my skin."

"Well, what is it?" Jim asked.

"It's anger," the old man cried. "That's what it is. You

know when you're about to get fightin', crazy mad, you get a hot, sick, weak feelin' in your guts? Well, that's what it is. Only it ain't just in one man. It's like the whole bunch, millions and millions was one man, and he's been beat and starved, and he's gettin' that sick feelin' in his guts. The stiffs don't know what's happenin', but when the big guy gets mad, they'll all be there; and by Christ, I hate to think of it. They'll be bitin' out throats with their teeth, and clawin' off lips. It's anger, that's what it is." He swayed on his limb, and tightened his arms to steady himself. "I feel it in my skin," he said. "Ever' place I go, it's like water just before it gets to boilin'."

Jim trembled with excitement. "There's got to be a plan," he said. "When the thing busts, there's got to be a plan all ready to direct it, so it'll do some good."

The old man seemed tired after his outburst. "When that big guy busts loose, there won't be no plan that can hold him. That big guy'll run like a mad dog, and bite anything that moves. He's been hungry too long, and he's been hurt too much; and worst thing of all, he's had his feelings hurt too much."

"But if enough men expected it and had a plan——" Jim insisted.

The old man shook his head. "I hope I'm dead before it happens. They'll be bitin' out throats with their teeth. They'll kill each other off an' after they're all wore out or dead, it'll be the same thing over again. I want to die and get shut of it. You young squirts got hopes." He lifted his full bucket down. "I got no hope. Get out of the way, I'm comin' down the ladder. We can't make no money talkin': that's for college boys."

Jim stood aside on a limb and let him down the ladder. The old man emptied his bucket and then went to another tree. Although Jim waited for him, he did not come back. The sorting belt rumbled on its rollers in the packing-house, and the hammers tapped. Along the highway the big transport trucks roared by. Jim picked his bucket full and took it to the box pile. The checker made a mark in his book.

"You're going to owe us money if you don't get off your dime," the checker said.

Jim's face went red and his shoulders dropped. "You keep to your God-damn book," he said.

"Tough guy, huh?"

Then Jim caught himself and grinned in embarrassment. "I'm tired," he apologized. "It's a new kind of work to me."

The blond checker smiled. "I know how it is," he said. "You get pretty touchy when you're tired. Why don't you get up in a tree and have a smoke?"

"I guess I will." Jim went back to his tree. He hooked his bucket over a limb and went to picking again. He said aloud to himself. "Even me, like a mad dog. Can't do that. My old man did that." He did not work quickly, but he reduced his movements to a machine-like perfection. The sun went low, until it left the ground entirely and remained only on the tops of the trees. Far away, in the town, a whistle blew. But Jim worked steadily on. It was growing dusky when the rumble in the packing-house stopped at last and the checkers called out, "Come on in, you men. It's time to quit."

Jim climbed down the ladder, emptied his bucket and stacked it up with the others. The checker marked in the buckets and then totaled the picking. The men stood about for a few moments, rolling cigarettes, talking softly in the evening. They walked slowly away down a row, toward the county road, where the orchard bunk houses were.

Jim saw the old man ahead of him and speeded up to catch him. The thin legs moved with jointed stiffness. "It's you again," he said as Jim caught up with him.

"Thought I'd walk in with you."

"Well, who's stoppin' you?" Obviously he was pleased.

"You got any folks here?" Jim asked.

"Folks? No."

Jim said, "Well, if you're all alone, why don't you get into some charity racket and make the county take care of you?"

The old man's tone was chilled with contempt. "I'm a top-faller. Listen, punk, if you never been in the woods, that don't mean nothing to you. Damn few top-fallers ever get to be my age. I've had punks like you damn near die of heart failure just *watchin'* me work; and here I'm climbin' a lousy apple tree. Me take charity! I done work in my life that took guts. I been ninety foot up a pole and had the butt split and snap my safety-belt. I worked with guys that got swatted to pulp with a limb. Me take charity! They'd say, 'Dan, come get your soup,' and I'd sop my bread in my soup and suck the soup out of it. By Christ, I'd jump out of an apple tree and break my neck before I'd take charity. I'm a top-faller."

They trudged along between the trees. Jim took off his hat and carried it in his hand. "You didn't get anything out of it," he said. "They just kicked you out when you got too old."

Dan's big hand found Jim's arm just above the elbow, and crushed it until it hurt. "I got things out of it while I was at it," he said. "I'd go up a pole, and I'd know that the boss and the owner of the timber and the president of the company didn't have the guts to do what I was doing. It was *me*. I'd look down on ever'thing from up there. And ever'thing looked small, and the men were little, but I was up there. I was my own size. I got things out of it, all right."

"They took all the profits from your work," Jim said. "They got rich, an' when you couldn't go up any more, they kicked you out."

"Yes," said Dan, "they did that, all right. I guess I must be gettin' pretty old, kid. I don't give a damn if they did—I just don't give a damn."

Ahead they could see the low, whitewashed building the owners set aside for the pickers—a low shed nearly fifty yards long, with a door and a little square window every ten feet. Through some of the open doors lamps and candles could be seen burning. Some men sat in the doorways and looked out at the dusk. In front of the long building stood a faucet where a clot of men and women had gathered. As the turn of each came, he cupped his hands under the stream and threw water on his face and hair and rubbed his hands together for a moment. The women carried cans and cooking pots to fill at the faucet. In and out of the dark doorways children swarmed, restless as rats. A tired, soft conversation arose from the group. Men and women were coming back, men from the orchard, women from the sorting and packing house. So built that it formed a short angle at the north end of the building stood the orchard's store, brightly lighted now. Here food and work clothes were sold on credit against the working sheets. A line of women and men stood waiting to get in, and another line came out carrying canned goods and loaves of bread.

Jim and old Dan walked up to the building. "There's the kennel," Jim said. "It wouldn't be so bad if you had a woman to cook for you."

Dan said, "Guess I'll go over to the store and get me a can of beans. These damn fools pay seventeen cents for a pound of canned beans. Why, they could get four pounds of dried beans for that, and cooked up that'd make nearly eight pounds."

Jim asked, "Why don't you do that, Dan?"

"I ain't got the time. I come in tired an' I want to eat."

"Well, what time have the others got? Women work all day, men work all day; and the owner charges three cents extra for a can of beans because the men are too damn tired to go into town for groceries."

Dan turned his bristly beard to Jim. "You sure worry at the thing, don't you, kid? Just like a puppy with a knuckle-bone. You chew and chew at it, but you don't make no marks on it, and maybe pretty soon you break a tooth."

"If enough guys got to chewing they'd split it."

"Maybe—but I lived seventy-one years with dogs and men, and mostly I seen 'em try to steal the bone from each other. I never seen two dogs help each other break a bone; but I seen 'em chew hell out of each other tryin' to steal it."

Jim said, "You make a guy feel there isn't much use."

Old Dan showed his four long, gopher teeth. "I'm seventy-one," he apologized. "You get on with your bone, and don't mind me. Maybe dogs and men ain't the same as they used to be."

As they drew nearer on the cloddy ground a figure detached itself from the crowd around the faucet and strolled out toward them. "That's my pardner," Jim said. "That's Mac. He's a swell guy."

Old Dan replied ungraciously. "Well, I don't want to talk to nobody. I don't think I'll even heat my beans."

Mac reached them. "Hello, Jim. How'd you make out?"

"Pretty good. This is Dan, Mac. He was in the north woods when the Wobblies were working up there."

"Glad to meet you." Mac put a tone of deference in his voice. "I heard about that time. There was some sabotage."

The tone pleased old Dan. "I wasn't no Wobbly," he said. "I'm a top-faller. Them Wobblies was a bunch of double-crossin' sons-of-bitches, but they done the work. Damn it, they'd burn down a sawmill as quick as they'd look at it."

The tone of respect remained in Mac's voice. "Well, if they got the work done, I guess that's all you can expect."

"They was a tough bunch," said Dan. "A man couldn't take no pleasure talkin' to 'em. They hated ever'thing. Guess I'll go over and get my beans." He turned to the right and walked away from them.

It was almost dark. Jim, looking up at the sky saw a black V flying across. "Mac, look, what's that?"

"Wild ducks. Flying pretty early this year. Didn't you ever see ducks before?"

"I guess not," said Jim. "I guess I've read about them."

"Say, Jim, you won't mind if we just have some sardines and bread, will you? We've got things to do tonight. I don't want to take time to cook anything."

Jim had been walking loosely, tired from the new kind of work. Now his muscles tightened and his head came up. "What you got on, Mac?"

"Well, look. I worked alongside London today. That guy doesn't miss much. He came about two-thirds of the way. Now he says he thinks he can swing this bunch of stiffs. He knows a guy that kind of throws another crowd. They're on the biggest orchard of the lot, four thousand acres of apples. London's so damn mad at this wage drop, he'll do anything. His friend on the Hunter place is called Dakin. We're going over there and talk to Dakin tonight."

"You got it really moving, then?" Jim demanded.

"Looks that way." Mac went into one of the dark doorways and in a moment he emerged with a can of sardines and a loaf of bread. He laid the bread down on the doorstep and turned the key in the sardine can, rolling back the tin. "Did you sound out the men the way I told you, Jim?"

"Didn't have much chance. I talked some to old Dan, there."

Mac paused in opening the can. "What in Christ's name for? What do you want to talk to him for?"

"Well, we were up in the same tree."

"Well, why didn't you get in another tree? Listen, Jim, lots of our people waste their time. Joy would try to convert a litter of kittens. Don't waste your time on old guys like that. He's no good. You'll get yourself converted to hopelessness if you talk to old men. They've had all the kick blasted right out of 'em." He turned the can lid off and laid the open tin in front of him. "Here, put some fish on a slice of bread. London's eating his dinner right now. He'll be ready pretty soon. We'll go in his Ford."

Jim took out his pocket-knife, arranged three sardines on a slice of bread and crushed them down a little. He poured some olive oil from the can over them, and then covered them with another slice of bread. "How's the girl?" he asked.

"What girl?"

"The girl with the baby."

"Oh, she's all right. But you'd think I was God the way London talks. I told him I wasn't a doctor, but he goes right on calling me 'Doc.' London gives me credit for a lot. You know, she'll be a cute little broad when she gets some clothes and some make-up on. Make yourself another sandwich."

It was quite dark by now. Many of the doors were closed, and the dim lights within the little rooms threw square patches of light on the ground outside. Mac chewed his sandwich. "I never saw such a bunch of bags as this crowd," he said. "Only decent one in the camp is thirteen years old. I'll admit she's got an eighteen-year-old can, but I'm doing no fifty years."

Jim said, "You seem to be having trouble keeping your economics out of the bedroom."

"Who the hell wants to keep it out?" Mac demanded. He chuckled. "Every time the sun shines on my back all afternoon I get hot pants. What's wrong with that?"

The bright, hard stars were out, not many of them, but sharp and penetrating in the cold night sky. From the rooms nearby came the rise and fall of many voices talking, with now and then a single voice breaking clear.

Jim turned toward the sound. "What's going on over there, Mac?"

"Crap game. Got it started quick. I don't know what they're using for money. Shooting next week's pay, maybe.

Most of 'em aren't going to have any pay when they settle up with the store. One man tonight in the store got two big jars of mince-meat. Probably eat both jars tonight and be sick to-morrow. They get awful hungry for something nice. Ever notice when you're hungry, Jim, your mind fastens on just one thing? It's always mashed potatoes with me, just slimy with melted butter. I s'pose this guy tonight had been thinking about mince-meat for months."

Along the front of the building a big man moved, and the lights from the windows flashed on him as he passed each one. "Here comes London," Mac said.

He strode up to them, swinging his shoulders. The tonsure showed white against the black rim of hair. "I finished eatin'," London said. "Let's get goin'. My Ford's around back." He turned and walked in the direction from which he had come; Mac and Jim followed him. Behind the building a topless model T Ford touring car stood nosed in against the build-ing. The oilcloth seats were frayed and split, so that the coil spring stuck through, and wads of horsehair hung from the holes. London got in and turned the key. The rasp of the points sounded.

"Crank 'er, Jim," said Mac.

Jim put his weight on the stiff crank. "Spark down? I don't want my head kicked off."

"She's down. Pull out the choke in front there," said London.

The gas wheezed in. Jim spun the crank. The engine choked and the crank kicked viciously backward. "Nearly got me! Keep that spark down!"

"She always kicks a little," said London. "Don't give her no more choke."

Jim spun the crank again. The engine roared. The little dim lights came on. Jim climbed into the back seat among old tubes and tire-irons and gunny sacks.

"Makes a noise, but she still goes," London shouted. He backed around and drove out the rough dirt road through the orchard, and turned right on the concrete state highway. The car chattered and rattled over the road; the cold air whistled in through the broken windshield so that Jim crouched down behind the protection of the front seat. Town lights glowed in the sky behind them. On both sides the road was lined with big dark apple trees, and sometimes the lights of houses shone from behind them. The Ford overtook and passed great transport trucks, gasoline tank trucks, silver milk tanks, outlined with little blue lights. From a small ranch house a shepherd dog ran out, and London swerved sharply to avoid hitting him.

"He won't last long," Mac shouted.

"I hate to hit a dog," said London. "Don't mind cats. I killed three cats on the way here from Radcliffe."

The car rattled on, going about thirty miles an hour. Sometimes two of the cylinders stopped firing, so that the engine jerked along until the missing two went back to work.

When they had gone about five miles, London slowed down. "Road ought to be somewhere in here," he said. A little row of silver mail-boxes showed him where to turn into the dirt road. Over the road was a wooden arch bearing the words, "Hunter Bros. Fruit Co. S Brand Apples." The car stuttered slowly along the road. Suddenly a man stepped into the road and held up his hand. London brought the Ford to a stop.

"You boys working here?" the man asked.

"No, we ain't."

"Well, we don't need any more help. We're all full up."

London said, "We just come to see some friends of ours. We're workin' on the Talbot place."

"Not bringing in liquor to sell?"

"Sure not."

The man flashed a light into the back of the car and looked at the litter of iron and old inner tubes. The light snapped off. "O.K., boys. Don't stay too long."

London pushed down the pedal. "That smart son-of-a-bitch," he growled. "There ain't no nosey cops like private cops. Busy little rat." He swung the car savagely around a turn and brought it to a stop behind a building very like the one from which they had come, a long, low, shed-like structure, partitioned into little rooms. London said, "They're workin' a hell of a big crew here. They got three bunk houses like this one." He walked to the first door and knocked. A grunt came from inside, and heavy steps. The door opened a little. A fat woman with stringy hair looked out. London said gruffly, "Where's Dakin puttin' up?"

The woman reacted instantly to the authority of his voice. "He's the third door down, mister, him and his wife and a couple of kids."

London said, "Thanks," and turned away, leaving the woman with her mouth open to go on talking. She stuck out her head and watched the three men while London knocked on the third door. She didn't go inside until Dakin's door was closed again.

"Who was it?" a man asked from behind her.

"I don't know," she said. "A big guy. He wanted Dakin."

Dakin was a thin-faced man with veiled, watchful eyes and an immobile mouth. His voice was a sharp monotone. "You old son-of-a-bitch," he said. "Come on in. I ain't seen you since we left Radcliffe." He stepped back and let them in.

London said, "This here's Doc and his friend, Dakin. Doc helped Lisa the other night. Maybe you heard about it."

Dakin put out a long, pale hand to Mac. "Sure I heard. Couple of guys working right here was there. You'd think Lisa'd dropped an elephant the way they don't talk about nothing else. This here's the missus, Doc. You might take a look at them two kids, too, they're strong."

His wife stood up, a fine, big-bosomed woman with a full face, with little red spots of rouge on her cheeks, and with a gold upper bridge that flashed in the lamplight. "Glad to meet you boys," she said in a husky voice. "You boys like a spot of coffee or a little shot?"

Dakin's eyes warmed a trifle out of pride in her.

"Well, it was pretty cold coming over," Mac said tentatively.

The gold bridge flashed. "Just what I thought. You'll do with a snort." She set out a bottle of whisky and a jigger. "Pour your own, boys. You can't pour it no higher'n the top."

The bottle and the glass went around. Mrs. Dakin tossed hers off last. She corked the bottle and stood it in a small cupboard.

Three folding canvas chairs were in the room, and two canvas cots for the children. A big patent camp bed stood against the wall. Mac said, "You do yourself pretty nice, Mr. Dakin."

"I got a light truck," said Dakin. "I get some truckin' to do now and then, and besides I can move my stuff. The missus is quick with her hands; in good times she can make money doin' piece work." Mrs. Dakin smiled at the praise.

Suddenly London dropped his social manner. "We want to go somewheres and talk," he said.

"Well, why not here?"

"We want to talk some kind of private stuff."

Dakin turned slowly to his wife. His voice was monotonous. "You and the kids better pay a call to Mrs. Schmidt, Alla."

Her face showed her disappointment. Her lips pouted and closed over the gold. For a moment she looked questioningly at her husband, and he stared back with his cold eyes. His long white hands twitched at his sides. Suddenly Mrs. Dakin smiled widely. "You boys stay right here an' do your talkin'," she said. "I ought to been to see Mrs. Schmidt before. Henry, take your brother's hand." She put on a short jacket of rabbit's fur and pushed at her golden hair. "You boys have a good time." They heard her walk away and knock at a door down the line.

Dakin pulled up his trousers and sat down on the big bed and waved the others to the folding canvas chairs. His eyes were veiled and directionless, like the eyes of a boxer. "What's on your mind, London?"

London scratched his cheek. "How you feel about that pay cut just when we was here already?"

Dakin's tight mouth twitched. "How do you think I feel? I ain't givin' out no cheers."

London moved forward on his chair. "Got any idears what to do?"

The veiled eyes sharpened a little bit. "No. You got any idears?"

"Ever think we might organize and get some action?" London glanced quickly sideways at Mac.

Dakin saw the glance. He motioned with his head to Mac and Jim. "Radicals?" he asked.

Mac laughed explosively. "Anybody that wants a living wage is a radical."

Dakin stared at him for a moment. "I got nothing against

radicals," he said. "But get this straight. I ain't doin' no time for no kind of outfit. If you belong to anythin', I don't want to know about it. I got a wife and kids and a truck. I ain't doin' no stretch because my name's on somebody's books. Now, what's on your mind, London?"

"Apples got to be picked, Dakin. S'pose we organize the men?"

Dakin's eyes showed nothing except a light-grey threat. His toneless voice said, "All right. You organize the stiffs and get 'em all hopped up with a bunch of bull. They vote to call a strike. In twelve hours a train-load of scabs comes rollin' in. Then what?"

London scratched his cheek again. "Then I guess we picket."

Dakin took it up. "So then they pass a supervisors' ordinance—no congregation, and they put a hundred deputies out with shot-guns."

London looked around questioningly at Mac. His eyes asked Mac to answer for him. Mac seemed to be thinking hard. He said, "We just thought we'd see what you thought about it, Mr. Dakin. Suppose there's three thousand men strikin' from a steel mill and they picket? There's a wire fence around the mill. The boss gives the wire a jolt of high voltage. They put guards at the gate. That's soft. But how many deputy sheriffs you think it'll take to guard a whole damn valley?"

Dakin's eyes lighted for a moment, and veiled. "Shot-guns," he said. "S'pose we kick hell out of the scabs, and they start shootin'? This bunch of bindle-stiffs won't stand no fire, and don't think they will. Soon's somebody sounds off with a ten-gauge, they go for the brush like rabbits. How about this picketin'?"

Jim's eyes leaped from speaker to speaker. He broke in, "Most scabs'll come off the job if you just talk to 'em."

"And how about the rest?"

"Well," said Mac, "a bunch of quick-movin' men could fix that. I'm out in the trees pickin', myself. The guys are sore as hell about this cut. And don't forget, apples got to be picked. You can't close down no orchard the way you do a steel mill."

Dakin got up and went to the box-cupboard and poured

himself a short drink. He motioned to the others with the bottle, but all three shook their heads. Dakin said, "They say we got a right to strike in this country, and then they make laws against picketin'. All it amounts to is that we got a right to quit. I don't like to get mixed up in nothing like this. I got a light truck."

Jim said, "Where——," found that his throat was dry, and coughed to clear it. "Where you going when we get the apples picked, Mr. Dakin?"

"Cotton," said Dakin.

"Well, the ranches over there are bigger, even. If we take a cut here, the cotton people will cut deeper."

Mac smiled encouragement and praise. "You know damn well they will," he seconded. "They'll do it every time; cut and cut until the men finally fight."

Dakin set the whisky bottle gently down and walked to the big bed and seated himself. He looked at his long white hands, kept soft with gloves. He looked at the floor between his hands. "I don't want no trouble," he said. "The missus, the kids and me got along fine so far; but damn it, you're right, we'll get a cotton cut sure as hell. Why can't they let things alone?"

Mac said, "I don't see we got anything to do but organize."

Dakin shook himself nervously. "I guess we got to. I don't want to much. What you guys want me to do?"

London said, "Dakin, you can swing this bunch, and I can swing my bunch, maybe."

Mac broke in, "You can't swing nobody that doesn't want to be swung. Dakin and London got to start talkin', that's all. Get the men talkin'. They're mad already, but they ain't talked it out. We got to get talk goin' on all the other places, too. Let 'em talk tomorrow and the next day. Then we'll call a meetin'. It'll spread quick enough, with the guys this mad."

Dakin said, "I just thought of somethin'. S'pose we go out on strike? We can't camp here. They won't let us camp on the county or the state roads. Where we goin' to go?"

"I thought of that," said Mac. "I got an idear, too. If there was a nice piece of private land, it'd be all right."

"Maybe. But you know what they done in Washington. They kicked 'em out because they said it was a danger to public health. An' then they burned down the shacks and tents."

"I know all about that, Mr. Dakin. But s'pose there was a doctor takin' care of all that? They couldn't do much then."

"You a real doctor?" Dakin said suspiciously.

"No, but I got a friend that is, and he'd prob'ly do it. I been thinkin' about it, Mr. Dakin. I've read quite a bit about strikes."

Dakin smiled frostily. "You done a hell of a lot more'n read about 'em," he said. "You know too much. I don't want to hear nothin' about you. I don't know nothin'."

London turned to Mac. "Do you honest think we can lick this bunch, Doc?"

Mac said, "Listen, London, even if we lose we can maybe kick up enough hell so they won't go cuttin' the cotton wages. It'll do that much good even if we lose."

Dakin nodded his head slowly in agreement. "Well, I'll start talkin' the first thing in the morning. You're right about the guys bein' mad; they're sore as hell, but they don't know what to do about it."

"We'll give 'em an idear," said Mac. "Try to contact the other ranches all you can, Mr. Dakin, won't you?" He stood up. "I guess we better move along." He held out his hand. "Glad I met you, Mr. Dakin."

Dakin's stiff lips parted, showing even, white false teeth. He said, "If I owned three thousand acres of apples, d' you know what I'd do? I'd get behind a bush an' when you went by, I'd blow your God damn head off. It'd save lots of trouble. But I don't own nothing but a light truck and some camp stuff."

"Good night, Mr. Dakin. Be seein' you," said Mac.

Jim and Mac went out. They heard London talking to Dakin. "These guys are O.K. They may be reds, but they're good guys." London came out and closed the door. A door down the building a bit opened and let out a square of light. Mrs. Dakin and the two kids walked toward them. "G'night, boys," she said. "I was watchin' to see when you come out."

The Ford rattled and chuckled homeward, and pushed its nose up against the bunk house. Mac and Jim parted from London and went to their dark little room. Jim lay on the floor wrapped in a piece of carpet and a comforter. Mac leaned against the wall, smoking a cigarette. After a while he crushed out the spark. "Jim, you awake?"

"Sure."

"That was a smart thing, Jim. She was beginning to drag when you brought in that thing about that cotton. That was a smart thing."

"I want to help," Jim cried. "God, Mac, this thing is singing all over me. I don't want to sleep. I want to go right on helping."

"You better go to sleep," Mac said. "We're going to do a lot of night work."

6

THE WIND swept down the rows, next morning, swaying the branches of the trees, and the windfalls dropped on the ground with soft thuds. Frost was in the wind, and between the gusts the curious stillness of autumn. The pickers scurried at their work, coats buttoned close over their chests. When the trucks went by between the rows, a wall of dust rolled out and went sailing down the wind.

The checker at the loading station wore a sheepskin coat, and when he was not tallying, thrust hands and book and pencil into his breast pocket and moved his feet restlessly.

Jim carried his bucket to the station. "Cold enough for you?"

"Not as cold as it will be if this wind doesn't change. Freeze the balls off a brass monkey," the checker said.

A sullen looking boy came up and dumped his bucket. His dark brows grew low to his eyes and his dark, stiff hair grew low on his forehead. His eyes were red and hot. He dumped his bucketful of apples into a box.

"Don't bruise those apples," the checker said. "Rot sets in on a bruise."

"Oh, yeah?"

"Yeah, that's what I said." The checker made a slashing mark with his pencil. "That bucket's out. Try again."

The smouldering eyes regarded him with hostility. "You sure got it comin'. An' you're goin' to get it."

The checker reddened with anger. "If you're going to get smart, you'd better pad along out and hit the road."

The boy's mouth spat venomously. "We'll get you; one of the first." He looked knowingly at Jim. "O.K., pal?"

"You'd better get on to work," Jim said quietly. "We can't make wages if we don't work."

The boy pointed down the row. "I'm in that fourth tree, buddy," he said, and moved away.

"What's the gag?" the checker asked. "Everybody's touchy this morning."

"It's the wind, maybe," said Jim. "I guess it's the wind. Makes people nervous when the wind blows."

The checker glanced quickly at him, for his tone had been satiric. "You too?"

"Me too."

"What's in the air, Nolan? Something up?"

"What you mean, 'something'?"

"You know God-damn well what I mean."

Jim knocked his bucket lightly against his leg. He stepped aside as a truck went by, and a dust wall covered him for a moment. "Maybe the little black book keeps you ignorant," he said. "You might turn in the little book, and then see if you can find out."

"So that's it. Organizing for trouble, are you? Well, the air's full of it."

"Air's full of dust," said Jim.

"I've seen that kind of dust before, Nolan."

"Well, then you know all about it." He started to move away.

"Wait a minute, Nolan." Jim stopped and turned. "You're a good man, Nolan, a good worker. What's going on?"

"I can't hear you," said Jim. "I don't know what you're talking about."

"I'll put the black mark on you."

Jim took two fierce steps toward him. "Put down your black mark and be damned," he cried. "I never said a thing. You've built all this up because a kid got smart with you."

The checker glanced away uneasily. "I was just kidding," he said. "Listen, Nolan, they need a checker up on the north end. I thought you might do for the job. You could go to work tomorrow. It would be better pay."

Jim's eyes darkened in anger for a second, and then he smiled and stepped close to the checker again. "What do you want?" he asked softly.

"I'll tell you straight, Nolan. There's something going on. The 'super' told me to try and find out. You get the dope for me and I'll put in a word for you on that checker's job, fifty cents an hour."

Jim seemed to study. "I don't know anything," he said

slowly. "I might try to find out if there was anything in it for me."

"Well, would five bucks say anything?"

"Sure would."

"O.K. You circulate around. I'll check you in on buckets so you won't lose anything today. See what you can dig up for me."

Jim said, "How do I know you won't double-cross me? Maybe I find something out and tell you. If the men ever found I told you, they'd skin me."

"Don't you worry about that, Nolan. If the 'super' can get a good man like you, he won't throw him over. There might be a steady job here for you when the picking's over, running a pump or something."

Jim thought for a moment. "I don't promise anything," he said. "I'll keep my ears open, and if I find anything, I'll let you know."

"Good boy. There's five in it, and a job."

"I'll try that tough kid," Jim said. "He seemed to know something." He walked down the row toward the fourth tree. Just as he reached it the boy came down the ladder with a full bucket.

"Hi," he said. "I'll dump these and be back."

Jim went up the ladder and sat down on a limb. The muttering of a sorting belt at the packing-plant blew clearly on the wind, and the smell of fresh cider came from the presses. From a long way off Jim could hear the hiss and bark of a switch-engine making up a train.

The sullen boy came running up the ladder like a monkey. He said angrily, "When we get down to business I'm gonna get me a nice big rock, and I'm gonna sock that bastard."

Jim used Mac's method. "A nice guy like that? What you want to hurt him for? What do you mean 'when we get down to business'?"

The boy squatted down beside him. "Ain't you heard?"

"Heard what?"

"You ain't a rat?"

"No, I won't rat."

The boy cried, "We're goin' to strike, that's what!"

"Strike? With nice jobs? What you want to strike for?"

" 'Cause we're gettin' screwed, that's why. The bunk houses is full of pants rabbits, and the company's store is takin' five per cent house-cut, and they drop the pay after we get here, that's why! And if we let 'em get by with it, we'll be worse in the cotton. We'll get screwed there, too; and you know it damn well."

"Sounds reasonable," said Jim. "Who's strikin' besides you?"

The boy squinted at him with his hot eyes. "Gettin' smart, ain't you?"

"No. I'm trying to find out something, and you aren't telling me."

"I can't tell you nothing. We can't let nothing out yet. You'll find out when it's time. We got the men all organized. We got ever'thing about ready, and we're gonna raise hell. There's gonna be a meetin' tonight for a few of us, then we'll let the rest of you guys in on it."

"Who's in back of it?" Jim asked.

"I ain't tellin'. Might spoil ever'thing if I was to tell."

"O.K.," said Jim, "if that's the way you feel about it."

"I'd tell you if I could, but I promised not to. You'll know in time. You'll go out with us, won't you?"

"I don't know," said Jim. "I won't if I don't know any more about it than I do now."

"Well, by Christ, we'll kill anybody that scabs on us; I'm tellin' you that now."

"Well, I don't ever like to get killed." Jim hung his bucket on a limb and slowly set about filling it. "What's chances of goin' to that meeting?"

"Not a chance. That's going to be only the big guys."

"You a big guy?"

"I'm on the in," said the boy.

"Well, who are these big guys?"

The sullen eyes peered suspiciously at Jim. "You ask too damn many questions. I ain't tellin' you nothin'. You act to me like a pigeon."

Jim's bucket was full. He lifted it down. "Are the guys talking it up in the trees?"

"*Are they?* Where you been all morning?"

"Working," said Jim. "Making my daily bread. It's a nice job."

The boy blazed at him. "Don't you get pushin' me around unless you'd like to step down on the ground with me."

Jim winked at him the way he'd seen Mac do. "Turn off the heat, kid. I'll be along when the stuff starts."

The boy grinned foolishly. "You catch a guy off balance," he said.

Jim carried his bucket down the row and emptied it gently into a box. "Got the time?"

The checker looked at his watch. "Eleven-thirty. Find out anything?"

"Hell, no. That kid's just shooting off his face. He thinks he's a newspaper. I'll mix around some after dinner and see."

"Well, get the dope as quick as you can. Can you drive a truck?"

"Why not?"

"We might be able to put you on a truck."

"That'd be swell." Jim walked away, down the row. The men in the trees and on the ladders were talking. He went up a heavy-laden tree where two men were.

"Hello, kid. Come on up and join the party."

"Thanks." Jim settled to picking. "Lots of talk this morning," he observed.

"Sure is. We was just doin' some. Ever'body's talkin' strike."

Jim said, "When enough guys talk strike, a strike usually comes off."

The second man, high up in the tree, broke in. "I was just tellin' Jerry, I don't like it. Christ knows we ain't makin' much, but if we strike, we don't make nothin'."

"Not right now we don't," said Jerry. "But later we make more. This damn apple pickin' don't last long, but cotton pickin' lasts longer. The way I figure it out, the cotton people is watchin' this thing. If we take dirt like a bunch of lousy sheep then the cotton people will nick us deeper. That's the way I figure it out, anyway."

Jim smiled. "Sounds reasonable."

The other man said, "Well, I don't like it. I don't like no

trouble if I can get out of it. Lot of men'll get hurt. I can't see no good in it at all. I never yet seen a strike raise wages for long."

Jerry said, "If the guys go out, you goin' to be a scab?"

"No, Jerry, I wouldn't do that. If the men go out, I'll go too. I won't scab, but I don't like it."

Jim asked, "They got any organization going yet?"

"Not that I heard," said Jerry. "Nobody's called a meeting up yet. We'll just sit tight; but the way I got it figured, if the guys go out, I'm goin' out too."

A wheezy whistle tooted at the packing plant. "Noon," said Jerry. "I got some sanriches under that pile of boxes there. Want some?"

"No, thanks," said Jim. "I got to meet the guy I travel with."

He left his bucket at the checker's post and walked toward the packing plant. Through the trees he could see a tall, white-washed building with a loading platform along one side. The sorting belt was still now. As Jim drew near he saw men and women sitting on the platform, hanging their legs over while they ate their lunches. A group of about thirty men had collected at one end of the building. Someone in the center of the crowd was talking excitedly. Jim could hear the rise and fall of his voice, but not his words.

The wind had fallen now, so that the warmth of the sunshine got through. As Jim approached, Mac detached himself from the group and came toward him carrying two paper-wrapped parcels. "Hi, Jim," he said. "Here's lunch, french bread and some sliced ham."

"Swell. I'm hungry."

Mac observed, "More of our men go out with stomach ulcers than with firing squads. How're things out your way?"

"Buzzing," said Jim. "Buzzing to beat hell. I met a kid who knows all about it. There's going to be a meeting of the big guys tonight."

Mac laughed. "That's good. I wondered whether the men with secret knowledge had got working yet. They can do us a lot of good. Men out your way getting mad?"

"They're talking a lot, anyway. Oh, say, Mac, the checker's

going to give me five bucks and a permanent job if I find out what's going on. I told him I'd keep my ears open."

"Nice work," said Mac. "Maybe you can make a little money on the side."

"Well, what do you want me to tell him?"

"Well, let's see—tell him it's just a splash, and it'll blow over. Tell him it's nothing to get excited about." He swung his head. A man had approached quietly, a heavy man dressed in dirty overalls, with a face nearly black with dirt. He came close and glanced about to see that they were alone.

"The committee sent me down," he said softly. "How're things going?"

Mac looked up at him in surprise. "What things you talkin' about, mister?"

"You know what I mean. The committee wants a report."

Mac looked helplessly at Jim. "The man's crazy," he said. "What committee's this?"

"You know what I mean—" the voice sank, "comrade."

Mac stepped stiffly forward, his face black with anger. "Where you get this 'comrade' stuff," he growled. "If you're one of them lousy radicals, I got no use for you. Now you get on your way before I call some of the boys."

The intruder's manner changed. "Watch your step, baby," he said. "We've got the glass on you." He moved slowly away.

Mac sighed. "Well, these apple boys think quick even if they don't think awful good," he said.

"That guy a dick?" Jim asked.

"Hell, yes. A man couldn't get his face that dirty without giving nature a lift. They lined us up quick, though, didn't they? Sit down and have something to eat."

They sat in the dirt and made thick ham sandwiches. "There goes your chance for a bribe," Mac said. He turned a serious face to Jim and quoted, " 'Watch your step, baby,' and that's straight. We can't afford to drop out now. And just remember that a lot of these guys will sell out for five bucks. Make other people talk, but keep pretty quiet yourself."

"How'd they make us, d'you s'pose?" Jim asked.

"I don't know. Some bull from town put the finger on us, I guess. Maybe I better get some help down here in case you or

I go out. This thing's coming off, and it needs direction. It's a pretty good layout, too."

"Will they jail us?" Jim asked.

Mac chewed a thick crust before he answered. "First they'll try to scare us," he said. "Now listen, if any time when I'm not around somebody tells you you're going to be lynched, you just agree to anything. Don't let 'em scare you, but don't go to using Joy's tricks. Jesus, they got moving quick! Oh, well, we'll get moving tomorrow, ourselves. I sent off last night for some posters. They should be here by tomorrow morning if Dick got off his dime. There ought to be some kind of word by mail tonight."

"What do you want me to do?" Jim asked. "All I do is just listen. I want to do something."

Mac looked around at him and grinned. "I'll use you more and more," he said. "I'll use you right down to the bone. This is going to be a nice mess, from the looks of it. That crack of yours about the cotton was swell. I've heard half a dozen guys use it for their own idea this morning."

"Where we going tonight, Mac?"

"Well, you remember Al, the fellow in the lunch wagon? He said his old man had a little orchard. I thought we might go out and see Al's father."

"Is that what you meant about getting a place for the guys when they go out?"

"I'm going to try to work it, anyway," Mac said. "This thing's going to break any time now. It's like blowing up a balloon. You can't tell when it's going to bust. No two of 'em bust just the same."

"You figure the big meeting for tomorrow night?"

"Yeah, that's what I figure; but you can't ever tell. These guys are plenty steamed up. Something might set 'em off before. You can't tell. I want to be ready. If I can get that place for the guys, I'll send for Doc Burton. He's a queer kind of a duck, not a Party man, but he works all the time for the guys. He'll lay out the place and tend to the sanitation, so the Red Cross can't run us off."

Jim lay back in the dirt and put his arms under his head. "What's the big argument over by the packing-house?"

"I don't know. The men just feel like arguing, that's all. By now maybe it's Darwin versus Old Testament. They'd just as soon fight over that. When they get to feeling like this, they'll fight about anything. Be pretty careful for yourself, Jim. Some guy might slug you just because he's feeling nervous."

"I wish it would start," Jim said. "I'm anxious for it to get going. I think I can help more when it once gets going."

"Keep your pants on," said Mac.

They rested in the dirt until the wheezy whistle blew a short toot for one o'clock. As they parted, Mac said, "Come running when we quit. We've got to cover some ground to-night. Maybe Al'll give us a hand-out again."

Jim walked back to the checking station, where his bucket was. The sorting belts began rumbling in the plant. Truck motors roared as they were started. Among the trees the pickers were sullenly going back to work. A number of men were standing around the checking station when Jim got his bucket. The checker did not speak to him then; but when Jim brought in his first full bucket, the question came. "Find out anything, Nolan?"

Jim leaned over the apple box and put his apples in it by hand. "I think it's all going to blow over. Most of the guys don't seem very mad."

"Well, what makes you think that?"

Jim asked, "Did you hear what made 'em mad?"

"No, I didn't. I thought it was the cut."

"Hell, no," said Jim. "A guy over on the Hunter place got a can of fish at the Hunter store that was bad. Made him sick. Well, you know how working stiffs are; they got sore, then the feeling spread over here. But I talked to some of the guys at noon. They're getting over it."

The checker asked, "You pretty sure that's all it is?"

"Sure. How about my five bucks?"

"I'll get it for you tomorrow."

"Well, I want that five, and you said you'd see about a better job."

"I will see about it. Let you know tomorrow."

"I should've got the money first, before I told you," Jim complained.

"Don't worry, you'll get it."

Jim walked off into the orchard. Just as he started to climb a ladder, a voice called from above him, "Look out for that ladder, she's shaky."

Jim saw old Dan standing in the tree. "By God, it's the boy radical," said old Dan.

Jim climbed up carefully. The rungs were loose in the ladder. "How's things, Dan?" he asked as he hung up his bucket.

"Oh, pretty good. I ain't feeling so good. Them cold beans lay like a flatiron in me all night."

"Well, you ought to have a warm supper."

"I was just too tired to build a fire. I'm getting on. I didn't want to get up this morning. It was cold."

"You should try one of the charity rackets," said Jim.

"I don't know. All the men is talkin' strike, and there's goin' to be trouble. I'm tired. I don't want no trouble to come now. What'll I do if the men strike?"

"Why strike with them. Lead them." Jim tried to spur him through pride. "The men would respect an old worker like you. You could lead the pickets."

"I s'pose I could," said Dan. He wiped his nose with a big hand and flicked his fingers. "I just don't want to. It's goin' to get cold early this afternoon. I'd like a little hot soup for supper—hot as hell, with little bits of meat in it, and some hot toast to soak in it. I *love* poached eggs. When I used to come to town out of the woods, with money, sometimes I'd get me half a dozen eggs poached in milk, and let 'em soak into toast. And then I'd mash the eggs up into the toast, and I'd eat 'em. Sometimes eight eggs. I made good pay in the woods. I could just as easy of got two dozen poached eggs. I wish I had. Lots of butter, an' all sprinkled with pepper."

"Not so hard-boiled as you were yesterday, huh, Pop? Yesterday you could out-work anybody on the lot."

The light of reminiscence went out of old Dan's eyes. His scraggly chin thrust forward. "I still can out-work a bunch of lousy punks that spends their time talkin'." He reached indignantly for the apples, fumbling over his head. One big, bony hand clung to a branch.

Jim watched him with amusement. "You're just showing off, Pop."

"Think I am? Well, try an' keep up with me, then."

"What's the use of you an' me racing, and then the orchard owner's the only one that makes anything?"

Old Dan piled apples into his bucket. "You punks got something to learn yet. There's more to work than you ever knew. Like a bunch of horses—you want more hay! Whining around for more hay. Want all the hay there is! You make a good man sick, that's what you do, whining around." His bucket was over-full. When he lifted it clear of the hook, five or six fat apples rolled out and bounced on the limbs and struck the ground under the tree. "Get out o' my way, punk," Dan cried. "Go on, get out o' the way o' that ladder."

"O.K., Pop, but take your time. You won't get a thing for rushing." Jim stepped clear of the ladder-top and climbed out a limb. He hung his bucket and reached for an apple. Behind him he heard a splintering crash and a sullen thump. He looked around. Old Dan lay on his back on the ground under the tree. His open eyes looked stunned. His face was blue pale under the white stubble. Two rungs were stripped out of the ladder.

Jim cried, "That was a fall! Hurt yourself, Pop?"

The old man lay still. His eyes were full of a perplexed question. His mouth writhed, and he licked his lips.

Jim shinnied down the tree and knelt beside him. "Where are you hurt, Pop?"

Dan gasped, "I don't know. I can't move. I think I've bust my hip. It don't hurt none, yet."

Men were running toward them. Jim could see men dropping from the trees all around and running toward them. The checker trotted over from his pile of boxes. The men crowded close. "Where's he hurt?"

"How'd it happen?"

"Did he bust his leg?"

"He's too old to be up a tree."

The ring of men was thrust inward by more arriving. Jim heard the checker cry, "Let me through here." The faces were dull and sullen and quiet.

Jim shouted, "Stand back, can't you. Don't crowd in." The men shifted their feet. A little growl came from the back row. A voice shouted, "Look at that ladder."

All heads went up with one movement, and all eyes looked

to where the old loose rungs had splintered and torn out. Someone said, "That's what they make us work on. Look at it!"

Jim could hear the thudding of feet as more men ran up in groups. He stood up and tried to push the ring apart. "Get back, you bastards. You'll smother him."

Old Dan had closed his eyes. His face was still and white with shock. On the outskirts of the mob the men began to shout, "Look at the ladder! That's what they make us work on!" The growl of the men, and the growl of their anger arose. Their eyes were fierce. In a moment their vague unrest and anger centered and focused.

The checker still cried, "Let me through there."

Suddenly a voice shrill with hysteria shouted, "You get out of here, you son-of-a-bitch." There was a scuffle.

"Look out, Joe. Hold Joe. Don't let him. Grab his feet."

"Now, mister, scram, and go fast."

Jim stood up. "You guys clear away. We got to get this poor fellow out of here." The men seemed to awaken from a sleep. The inner ring pushed violently outward. "Get a couple of sticks. We can make a stretcher out of a pair of coats. There, put the sticks through the arms. Now, button up the fronts." Jim said, "Easy now, with him. I think his hip's busted." He looked down at Dan's quiet, white face. "I guess he's fainted. Now, easy."

They lifted Dan on to the coat stretcher. "You two guys carry him," Jim said. "Some of you clear a way."

At least a hundred men had collected by this time. The men with the stretcher stepped out. Newcomers stood looking at the broken ladder. Over and over the words, "Look what they give us to use."

Jim turned to a man who stood stupidly staring up into the tree. "What happened to the checker?"

"Huh? Oh, Joe Teague slugged him. Tried to kick his brains out. The guys held Joe. Joe went to pieces."

"Damn good thing he didn't kill him," Jim said.

The band of men moved along behind the stretcher, and more were running in from all over the orchard. As they drew near the packing-plant the rumble of the sorting belt stopped. Men and women crowded out of the loading doors. A quiet had settled on the growing mob. The men walked stiffly, as men do at a funeral.

Mac came tearing around the corner of the packing-plant. He saw Jim and ran to him. "What is it? Come over here away from the mob." The crowd of ominous, quiet people moved on after the stretcher. Newcomers were told in low tones, "The ladder. An old ladder." The body of the mob went ahead of Mac and Jim.

"Now what happened? Tell me quick. We've got to move while they're hot."

"It was old Dan. He got smart about how strong he was. Broke a couple of rungs out of a ladder and fell on his back. He thought he broke his hip."

Mac said, "Well, it's happened. I kind of expected it. It doesn't take much when the guys feel this way. They'll grab on anything. The old buzzard was worth something after all."

"Worth something?" Jim asked.

"Sure. He tipped the thing off. We can use him now." They walked quickly after the mob of men. The dust, raised by many feet, filled the air with a slow-blowing brown cloud. From the direction of the town the switch-engine crashed monotonously making up a train. On the outskirts of the mob women ran about, but the men were silent, trudging on after the stretcher, toward the bunk houses.

"Hurry up, Jim," Mac cried. "We've got to rush."

"Where we going?"

"We've got to find London first, and tell him how to work; then we've got to go in and send a telegram; and I want to go and see Al's old man, right away. Look, there's London over there.

"Hi, London." Mac broke into a run, and Jim ran behind him. "It's busted out, London," Mac said breathlessly. "That old guy, Dan, fell out of a tree. It's wide open, now."

"Well, that's what we want, ain't it?" said London. He took off his hat and scratched his tonsure.

"The hell it is," Mac broke in. "These guys'll go nuts if we don't take charge. Look, there goes your long lean buddy. Call him over."

London cupped his hands. "Sam," he yelled.

Jim saw that it was the same man who had sat by the campfire in the jungle. Mac said, "Listen, London, and you, Sam. I'm going to tell you a lot of stuff quick, 'cause I've got to get along. These guys are just as likely to pop in a few minutes. You go over, Sam, and tell 'em they ought to hold a meeting. And then you nominate London, here, for chairman. They'll put him in all right. They'll do almost anything. That's all you got to do, Sam." Mac picked up a handful of dirt and rubbed it between his palms. His feet stirred and kicked at the ground. "Now listen, London, soon's you're chairman, you tell 'em we got to have order. You give 'em a list of guys, about ten, and tell 'em to vote for those guys as a committee to figure things out. Got that?"

"Sure. I get you."

"Now look—here's the way to do it. If you want 'em to vote for something, you say 'do you want to do it?' and if you want to vote down somethin', just say, 'you don't want to do this, do you?' and they'll vote no. Make 'em vote on every-thin', *everythin'*, see? They're all ready for it."

They looked toward the crowd at the bunk house. The men were still quiet, shifting about, never standing very long in a place, moving their arms; their faces were as relaxed as those of sleeping men.

London demanded, "Where you guys going now?"

"We're going to see about that place for the crowd to stay when the thing busts open, that little farm. Oh, one other thing, you pick out a bunch of the craziest of these guys and send 'em over to the other ranches to talk. Get the men that are doin' the most talkin'. You all set now?"

"All set," said London.

"Well, let us use your Ford, will you? We got to cover ground."

"Sure, take it, if you can run it; it's got tricks."

Mac turned to Sam. "All right, get over there. Just stand up on somethin' and yell 'Boys, we ought to hold a meetin',' and then yell, 'I move London for chairman.' Get going, Sam. Come on, Jim."

Sam trotted off toward the bunk houses, and London followed more slowly. Mac and Jim circled the buildings and went to the ancient Ford touring car. "Get in, Jim. You drive the gillopy." A roar of voices came from the other side of the bunk house. Jim turned the key and retarded the spark lever. The coils buzzed like little rattlesnakes. Mac spun the crank and primed, and spun again. A second roar from the mob came over the house. Mac threw his shoulder into the work. The engine caught and its noise drowned the shouting of the men. Mac leaped into the car, yelling, "Well, I guess London's our new chairman. Push 'er along."

Jim backed around and drove out to the highway. The road was deserted. The green, heavy-laden trees threw their shadows' weight sideways under the declining sun. The car rolled along, its pistons battering in the cylinders. "First to a telegraph office, and then to the post office," Mac shouted.

They rolled into the town. Jim drove to the main street and parked in front of a Western Union office. "Post office is just a block up, see?" he said.

"Well, listen, Jim, while I send the wire, you go up and ask for mail for William Dowdy."

In a few moments Jim came back with three letters. Mac was already sitting in the car. He ripped the letters open and read them. "Hot-damn, listen. This one's from Dick. He says Joy broke jail; they don't know where he is. He was bein' taken for a hearing and he smacked a cop and beat it. I just wired for more help, and for Doc Burton to take over the sanitation. Wait, I'll crack 'er up. Let's move along to Al's lunch wagon."

When Jim drew up in front of the lunch wagon, he could see Al through the windows, leaning over his deserted counter, staring out at the sidewalk. Al recognized them as they got out. He raised a fat arm at them.

Mac pushed open the sliding door. "Hi, Al. How's business?"

Al's eyes were bright with interest. "Been just fine," he said. "Whole flock of guys from the orchards come in last night."

"I been tellin' 'em what a swell steak you put out," said Mac.

"Nice of you. Like a bite yourself?"

"Sure," said Mac. "We could even pay for it. Imagine us guys payin' for anything."

"Aw, this is just your cut," said Al. "Kind of a commission

for sending the guys in town." He opened his ice-box and patted out two hamburger steaks and slapped them down on the stove-top; and he arranged a wreath of chopped onions about each one. "How's things coming out your way?" he asked.

Mac leaned confidentially over the counter. "Listen, Al. I know you're a guy I can trust. We got you on the books. You been swell to us."

Al blushed with pleasure at the praise. "Well, I'd be out with you guys if I didn't have a business to keep up. A man sees the way conditions is, and injustice, and things—and if he's got any brains he comes to it."

"Sure," said Mac hurriedly. "A guy with brains don't have to be taught. He sees things for himself."

Al turned away to hide his pleasure. He flipped the steaks and pressed them down with his spatula and gathered up the wilting onions and forced them into the meat. He scraped the grease into the little trough on the side of the stove-top. When he had forced his face back to a proper gravity, he turned around again. "Sure you guys can trust me," he said. "You ought to know it. What you got on?" He filled two cups with coffee and slid them along the counter.

Mac tapped delicately on the counter with a knife-blade. "There may be bulls askin' about me and Jim."

"Sure. I don't know nothin' about you," said Al.

"That's right. Now here's the dope, Al. This valley's about to bust wide open. Already has over on the place where we been working. The others'll probably crack tonight."

Al said softly, "You know, the way the guys was talkin' in here, I thought it wasn't far off. What d'you want me to do?"

"Better take up that meat." Al held two plates fanwise in one hand, put a steak on each, mashed potatoes, carrots and turnips, loaded the plates.

"Gravy, gents?"

"Smear it," said Mac.

Al ladled gravy over the whole pile of food and set the plates before them. "Now go on," he said.

Mac filled his mouth. His speech was muffled and spaced with chewing. "You said your old man had a little ranch."

"He has. Want to hide out there?"

"No." Mac pointed his fork at Al. "There won't be an apple picked in this valley."

"Well, say—mister——"

"Wait. Listen. Any plow land on your old man's place?"

"Yeah, about five acres. Had it in hay. Hay's all out now."

"Here it is," said Mac. "We're goin' to have a thousand or two men with no place to go. They'll kick 'em off the ranches and won't let 'em on the road. Now if they could camp on that five acres, they'd be safe."

Al's face sagged with fear and doubt. "Aw, no, mister. I don't think my old man'd do it."

Mac broke in, "He'd get his apples picked, picked quick, and picked for nothing. Price'll be high with the rest of 'em shut off."

"Well, wouldn't the town guys raise hell with him afterwards?"

"Who?" Mac asked.

"Why, the Legion, and guys like that. They'd sneak out and beat him up."

"No, I don't think they would. He's got a right to have men on his place. I'll have a doctor lay out the camp and see it's kept clean, and your old man'll get his crop picked for nothing."

Al shook his head. "I don't know."

"Well, we can easy find out," said Mac. "Let's go talk to your old man."

"I got to keep this place open. I can't go away."

Jim suddenly saw his neglected food and began to eat. Mac's squinted eyes never left Al's face. He sat and chewed and looked. Al began to get nervous. "You think I'm scared," he began.

"I don't think anything before I see it," said Mac. "I just wondered why a guy can't close up his own joint for an hour, if he wants to."

"Well, the guys that eat early'll be here in an hour."

"You could get back in an hour."

Al fidgeted. "I don't think my old man'll do it. He's got to look out for himself, don't he?"

"Well, he ain't been jumped yet. How do you know what'll

happen?" A chill was creeping into Mac's voice, a vague hostility.

Al picked up a rag and mopped around on the counter. His nervous eyes came to Mac's and darted away and came back. At last he stepped close. "I'll do it," he said. "I'll just pin a little card to the door. I don't think my old man'll do it, but I'll take you out there."

Mac smiled broadly. "Good guy. We won't forget it. Next time I see any stiff with a quarter, I'll send him in to get one of your steaks."

"I give a nice dinner for the money," said Al. He took off his tall cook's hat and rolled down his shirt sleeves, and turned the gas off under the cooking plate.

Mac finished his food. "That was good."

Jim had to bolt his dinner not to be late.

"I got a little car in the lot behind here," said Al. "Maybe you guys could just follow me; then I don't get into no trouble and I'm still some good to you."

Mac drained his cup. "That's right, Al. Don't you get into no bad company."

"You know what I mean."

"Sure, I know. Come on, Jim, let's go."

Al wrote a sign and pinned it inside the door, facing out through the glass. He struggled his chubby arms into his coat and held the door open for Mac and Jim.

Mac cranked the Ford and jumped in, and Jim idled the motor until Al came bumping out of the lot in an old Dodge roadster. Jim followed him down the street to the east, across the concrete bridge over the river and out into the pleasant country. The sun was nearly down by now, red and warm with autumn dust. The massed apple trees along the road were grey with dust.

Mac turned in the seat and looked down the rows as they passed. "I don't see anybody working," he cried to Jim. "I wonder if he took hold already. There's boxes, but nobody working."

The paved road gave way to a dirt road. The Ford leaped and shuddered on the rough road. About a mile further Al's dust-cloud swung off into a yard. Jim followed and came to a stop beside the Dodge. A white tank-house rose into the air, and on its top a windmill thrashed and glittered in the sun, and the pump bonged with a deep, throaty voice. It was a pleasant place. The apple trees grew in close to a small white ranch house. Tame mallards nuzzled the mud in the overflow under the tank. In a wire-bounded kennel against a big barn two rubbery English pointers stood against the screen and yearned out at the men with little yelps. The house itself was surrounded by a low picket fence, behind which geraniums grew big and red, and a Virginia creeper, dropping its red leaves, hung over the porch. Big square Plymouth Rock chickens strolled about, cawing contentedly and cocking their heads at the newcomers.

Al got out of the car. "Look a' them dogs," he said. "Best pointers in the Valley. My old man loves them better'n me."

Mac asked, "Where's the five acres, Al?"

"Down that way, behind the trees, on the other road."

"Good. Let's find your old man. You say he likes his dogs?"

Al laughed shortly. "Just make a pass at one o' them dogs an' see. He'll eat you."

Jim stared at the house, and at the newly whitewashed barn. "This is nice," he said. "Makes a man want to live in a place like this."

Al shook his head. "Takes an awful lot of work to keep it up. My old man works from dawn till after dark, and then he don't keep up with the work."

Mac insisted, "Where is your old man? Let's find him."

"Look," Al said. "That's him coming in from the orchard."

Mac glanced up for a moment, and then he moved back to the kennel. The squirming pointers flung themselves at the wire, moaning with love. Mac stuck his fingers through the mesh and rubbed their muzzles.

Jim said, "Do you like dogs, Mac?"

Mac retorted irritably, "I like anything."

Al's father came walking up. He was totally unlike Al, small and quick as a terrier. The energy seemed to pour out of some inner reservoir into his arms and legs, and into his fingers so that all of him was on the move all of the time. His white hair was coarse, and his eyebrows and mustache bristled. His brown eyes flitted about as restlessly as bees. Because his fingers had nothing else to do while he walked, they snapped at his sides with little rhythmic reports. When he spoke, his words were like the rest of him, quick, nervous, sharp. "What's the matter with your business?" he demanded of Al.

Al went heavily on the defensive. "Well, you see—I thought——"

"You wanted to get off the ranch, wanted to go into town, start a business, town boy, wanted to lounge around. Didn't like to whitewash, never did. What's the matter with your business?" His eyes hovered on each of the men, on their shoes and on their faces.

Mac still looked into the kennel and rubbed the dogs' noses. Al explained, "Well, you see, I brang these guys out, they wanted to see you."

The old man eliminated Al. "Well, they're here. You can get back to your business now."

Al looked at his little father with the hurt eyes of a dog about to be bathed, and then reluctantly he climbed into his car and drove disconsolately away.

Mac said, "I haven't seen such pointers in a long time."

Al's father stepped up beside him. "Man, you never seen such pointers in your life." A warmth was established.

"Do you shoot over 'em much?"

"Every season. And I get birds, too. Lots of fools use setters. Setter's a net dog, nobody nets birds any more. Pointer's a real gun dog."

"I like the looks of that one with the liver saddle."

"Sure, he's good. But he can't hold up to that sweet little bitch. Name's Mary, gentle as Jesus in the pen, but she's jumping hell in the field. Never seen a dog could cover the ground the way she can."

Mac gave the noses a rub. "I see they got holes into the barn. You let 'em run in the barn?"

"No, their beds are tight against the wall. Warmer in there."

"If the bitch ever whelps, I'd like to speak a pup."

The old man snorted. "She'd have to whelp ever' day in the year to supply the people that wants her pups."

Mac turned slowly from the pen and looked into the brown eyes. "My name's McLeod," he said, and held out his hand.

"Anderson's mine. What you want?"

"I want to talk straight to you."

The sun was gone now, and the chickens had disappeared from the yard. The evening chill settled down among the trees. "Selling something, Mr. McLeod? I don't want none."

"Sure, we're selling something, but it's a new product."

His tone seemed to reassure Anderson. "Why'n't you come into the kitchen and have a cup of coffee?"

"I don't mind," said Mac.

The kitchen was like the rest of the place, painted, scrubbed, swept. The nickel trimmings on the stove shone so that it seemed wet.

"You live here alone, Mr. Anderson?"

"My boy Al comes out and sleeps. He's a pretty good boy." From a paper bag the old man took out a handful of carefully cut pine splinters and laid them in the stove, and on top he placed a few little scraps of pitchwood, and on top of those, three round pieces of seasoned apple wood. It was so well and deftly done that the fire flared up when he applied a match. The stove cricked, and a burst of heat came from it. He put on a coffee-pot and measured ground coffee into it. From a bag he took two egg shells and dropped them into the pot.

Mac and Jim sat at a kitchen table covered with new yellow oilcloth. Anderson finished his work at the stove. He came over, sat primly down, put his two hands on the table; they lay still, even as good dogs do when they want to be off. "Now, what is it, McLeod?"

A look of perplexity lay on Mac's muscular face. "Mr. Anderson," he said hesitatingly, "I haven't got a hell of a lot of cards. I ought to play 'em hard and get the value out of 'em. But I don't seem to want to. I think I'll lay 'em down. If they take the pot, O.K. If they don't, there's no more deal."

"Well, lay 'em then, McLeod."

"It's like this. By tomorrow a couple of thousand men will be on strike, and the apple picking will stop."

Anderson's hands seemed to sniff, to stiffen, and then to lie still again.

Mac went on, "The reason for the strike is this pay-cut. Now the owners'll run in scabs, and there'll be trouble. But there's a bunch of men going out, enough to picket the Valley. D'you get the picture?"

"Part of it; but I don't know what you're driving at."

"Well, here's the rest. Damn soon there'll be a supervisors' ordinance against gathering on a road or on any public property. The owners'll kick the strikers off their land for trespassing."

"Well, I'm an owner. What do you want of me?"

"Al says you've got five acres of plow land." Anderson's hands were still and tense as dogs at point. "Your five acres are private property. You can have men on it."

Anderson said cautiously, "You're selling something; you don't say what it is."

"If the Torgas Valley apples don't go on the market, the price'll go up, won't it?"

"Sure it will."

"Well, you'll get your crop picked free."

Anderson relaxed slightly in his chair. The coffee-pot began to breathe gently on the stove. "Men like that'd litter the land up," he said.

"No, they won't. There's a committee to keep order. There won't even be any liquor allowed. A doctor's coming down to look out for the sanitation. We'll lay out a nice neat camp, in streets."

Anderson drew a quick breath. "Look here, young fellow, I own this place. I got to get along with my neighbors. They'd raise hell with me if I did a thing like that."

"You say you own this place," Mac said. "Is it clear? Is there any paper on it?"

"Well, no, it ain't clear."

"And who are your neighbors?" Mac asked quickly. "I'll tell you who they are: Hunter, Gillray, Martin. Who holds your paper? Torgas Finance Company. Who owns Torgas Finance Company? Hunter, Gillray, Martin. Have they been squeezing you? You know God damn well they have. How long you going to last? Maybe one year; and then Torgas Finance takes your place. Is that straight? Now suppose you got a crop out with no labor charges; suppose you sold it on a rising market? Could you clear out your paper?"

Anderson's eyes were bright and beady. Two little spots of anger were on his cheeks. His hands crept under the edge of the table and hid. For a moment he seemed not to breathe. At last he said softly, "You didn't lay 'em down, fellow, you played 'em. If I could get clear—if I could get a knife in——"

"We'll give you two regiments of men to get your knife in."

"Yeah, but my neighbors'd run me out."

"Oh no they won't. If they touch you or your place we won't leave a barn standing in the Valley."

Anderson's lean old jaw was set hard. "What you getting out of it?"

Mac grinned. "I could tell you the other stuff straight. I don't know whether you'd believe the answer to that one or not. Me an' Jim here get a sock in the puss now and then. We get sixty days for vagrancy pretty often."

"You're one of those reds?"

"You win; we're reds, as you call them."

"And what do you figure to do with your strike?"

"Don't get us wrong, Mr. Anderson. We didn't start it. Gillray, Martin and Hunter started it. They told you what to pay the men, didn't they?"

"Well, the Growers' Association did. Torgas Finance Company runs that."

"O.K. We didn't start it. But once it's started, we want to help it win. We want to keep the men from running to hell, teach 'em to work together. You come in with us, and you'll never have labor trouble as long as you live."

Anderson complained, "I don't know whether I can trust a red."

"You never tried; but you've tried trusting Torgas Finance."

Anderson smiled coldly. His hands came up on the table, and played together like puppies. "It'll probably break me, and put me on the road. Christ knows I'm headed for it anyway. Might as well have some fun. I'd give a hell of a lot to stick Chris Hunter." The coffee boiled over and fizzed fiercely on the stove, and the smell of burning coffee filled the air. The electric light glistened on Anderson's white eyebrows, and on his stiff hair. He lifted the coffee-pot and wiped the stove carefully with a newspaper. "I'll pour you out some coffee, Mr. Red."

But Mac sprang to his feet. "Thanks, but we've got to get along. We'll see you get a square deal out of this. Right now we got a million things to do. Be seeing you tomorrow."

They left the old man standing holding the coffee-pot in his hand. Mac forced a trot across the yard. He muttered, "Jesus, that was ticklish. I was scared I'd slip any minute. What a tough old baby he is. I knew a hunting man'd be tough."

"I like him," said Jim.

"Don't you go liking people, Jim. We can't waste time liking people."

"Where'd you get that dope on him about the Finance Company, Mac?"

"Came in the mail tonight. But thank God for those dogs! Jump in, Jim. I'll turn her over."

They rattled through the clear night. The little flaring head-lamps flickered dizzily along the road. Jim looked up at the sky for a moment. "Lord, I'm excited. Look at the stars, Mac. Millions of 'em."

"You look at the road," Mac growled. "Listen, Jim, I just happened to think. That guy this noon means they've got us spotted. From now on you be careful, and don't go away from the crowd very far. If you want to go someplace, see you take about a dozen men with you."

"You mean they'll try to get us?"

"You're damn right! They'll figure they can stop the ruckus with us out of it."

"Well, when're you going to give me something to do, Mac? I'm just following you around like a little dog."

"You're learning plenty, kid. When there's some use for you, I'll get it out, don't you worry. You can take out a flock of pickets in a day or so. Turn off to the left, Jim. We won't be wanting to go through town much from now on."

Jim bumped the car along rutty side-roads. It was an hour before he came finally to the ranch and turned into the dark road among the apple trees. He throttled down the Ford until it was barely able to fire. The headlights jerked and shivered. Without warning a blinding light cut out through the darkness and fell on the men's faces. At the same moment two men, muffled in overcoats, stepped into the road ahead. Jim ground the Ford to a stop.

A voice behind the light called, "These are the guys." One of the overcoated men lounged around the car and leaned on the door. The motor idled unevenly. Because of the light beam, the man leaning on the door was almost invisible. He said, "We want you two out of the Torgas Valley by daylight tomorrow, get it? Out."

Mac's foot crept over and pressed Jim's leg. His voice became a sweet whine. "Wha's the matter 'th us, mister? We never done nothing."

The man answered angrily, "Lay off, buddy. We know who you are, and what you are. We want you *out*."

Mac whined, "If you're the law, we're citizens. We got a right to stand trial. I pay taxes back home."

"Well, go home and pay 'em. This isn't the law: this is a citizens' committee. If you think you God-damned reds can come in here and raise hell, you're crazy. You get out of here in your tin can or you'll go out in a box. Get it?"

Jim felt Mac's foot creep under his legs and find the gear pedal of the Ford. Jim tapped the foot with his toe to show he understood. The old engine staggered around and around. Sometimes one cylinder missed fire, sometimes two. Mac said, "You got us wrong, mister. We're just workin' stiffs. We don't want no trouble."

"I said '*out*.'"

"Well, leave us get our stuff."

"Listen, you're turning right around and getting out."

Mac cried, "You're yellow, that's what you are. You put twenty men hiding along the road. You're yellow as hell."

"Who's yellow? There's just three of us. But if you're not out of the Valley by morning, there'll be fifty."

"*Step on it, Jim!*"

The engine roared. The Ford bucked ahead like a horse. The man on the side spun off into the darkness, and the man in front jumped for his life. The rattling car leaped over the road with a noise of falling andirons.

Mac looked over his shoulder. "The flashlight's gone," he shouted.

Jim ran the car behind the long building. They jumped out and sprinted around the end of the bunk house.

The space in front of the doorways was dense with men standing in groups, talking in low tones. On the doorsteps the women sat, hugging their skirts down around their knees. A droning, monotonous hum of talk came from the groups.

At least five hundred men were there, men from other ranches. The tough kid Jim had spoken to stalked near. "Didn't believe me, huh? Well, how's this look to you?"

Mac asked him, "Seen London?"

"Sure I seen him. We elected him chairman. He's in his room now with the committee. Thought I was nuts, didn't you?" he said to Jim. "I told you I was on the in."

Mac and Jim edged their way among the crowded men and into the hum of voices. London's door was closed, and his window was closed. A press of men stood on tiptoe and looked through the glass into the lighted room. Mac started up the steps. Two men threw themselves in his way. "What the hell do you want?"

"We want to see London."

"Yeah? Does London want to see you?"

"Ask him, why don't you?"

"What's your name?"

"Tell London Doc and Jim want to see him."

"You're the guy that helped the girl have a kid?"

"Sure."

"Well, I'll ask." The man opened the door and stepped inside. A second later he emerged and held the door open. "Go right on in, boys, London's waitin' for you."

London's room had been hurriedly made into an office by bringing in boxes for seats. London sat on his bed, his tonsured head forward. A committee of seven men stood, sat on boxes, smoked cigarettes. They turned their heads when Jim and Mac entered. London looked glad. "Hello, Doc. Hello, Jim. Glad to see you. Heard the news?"

Mac flopped down on a box. "Heard nothing," he said. "Me and Jim been covering ground. What happened?"

"Well, it seems to be all right. Dakin's crowd went out. There's a guy named Burke, chairman on the Gillray place. There's a meetin' of everybody called for tomorrow."

"Fine," said Mac. "Workin' out fine. But we can't do much till we get an executive committee and a general chairman."

London asked, "How'd you come out on that thing you went for? I didn't tell the boys, case it didn't come off."

"Got it." Mac turned to the seven men. "Listen," he said. "A guy's loaned us five acres for the guys to camp on. It's private property, so nobody but the health people can kick us off. We got a doctor coming down to take care of that." The committeemen set up straight, grinning with enthusiasm. Mac continued, "Now I've promised this farmer that the men'd pick his crop for nothing. It won't take 'em long. There's plenty of water. It's a good central location, too."

One of the men stood up excitedly. "Can I go tell the guys outside, London?"

"Sure, go ahead. Where is this place, Doc? We can have our big meetin' there tomorrow."

"It's Anderson's orchard, a little way out of town." Three of the committeemen broke for the door, to tell the news. Outside there was first a silence, and then a roll of voices, not shouting, but talking excitedly; and the roll spread out and grew louder, until the air was full of it.

Jim asked, "What happened to old Dan?"

London raised his head. "They wanted to take him to a hospital. He wouldn't do no good in a hospital. We got a doctor to set his hip. He's down the row a little. Couple of good women takin' care of the poor old bum. He's havin' a fine time. Couldn't get 'im out of here now. He just gives everybody hell, women and all."

Mac asked, "Have you heard from the owners yet?"

"Yeah, 'super' came in. Asked if we was goin' back to work. We says 'no.' He says, 'Get the hell off the place by morning.' Says he'll have a trainload of stiffs in here by mornin'."

"He won't," Mac interrupted. "He can't get 'em in before day after tomorrow. It takes some time to hand-pick a bunch of scabs. And day after tomorrow we'll be ready for 'em. Say, London, some guys that call 'emselves a committee tried to run me and Jim out of the Valley. Better pass the word to the guys not to go out alone. Tell 'em if they want to go any place take some friends along for company."

London nodded at one of his committeemen. "Pass the word, Sam." Sam went out. Again the roll of voices spreading out and rumbling, like a wave over round stones. This time the tone was deep and angry.

Mac slowly rolled a brown cigarette. "I'm tired," he said. "We got so much to do. I guess we can do it tomorrow."

"Go to bed," said London. "You been goin' like a fool."

"Yep, I been goin', all right. Seems kind of hard when you're tired. They got guns. We can't have no guns. They got money. They can buy our boys. Five bucks looks like a hell of a lot of jack to these poor half-starved bastards. Be pretty sure before you tell anythin', London. After all, you can't blame the guys much if they sell out. We got to be clever and mean and quick." His voice had grown sad. "If we don't win, we got to start all over again. It's too bad. We could win so easy, if the guys would only stick together. We could just kick Billy Hell out of the owners. No guns, no money. We got to do it with our hands and our teeth." His head jerked up. London was grinning in sympathy, embarrassed, as men are when one of their number opens his heart.

Mac's heavy face flushed with shame. "I'm tired. You guys carry it while me and Jim get some sleep. Oh, London, in the mail tomorrow there'll be a package for Alex Little. It's hand-bills. Ought to be in by eight o'clock. Send some of the guys down to get it, will you? And see the handbills get around. They ought to do some good. Come on, Jim. Let's sleep."

They lay in their room in the dark. Outside the men sat and waited, and the murmur of their voices penetrated the walls and seemed to penetrate the world. Away, in town, a switch engine crashed back and forth making up a train. The night milk trucks rumbled over the highway beside the orchard. Then oddly, sweetly, someone played a few tunes on a harmonica, and the murmur of voices stopped and the men listened. It was quiet outside, except for the harmonica, so quiet that Jim heard a rooster crowing before he went to sleep.

7

THE DAY was coming in grey and cold when Jim started awake at voices outside the door. He heard a man say, "They're in here, probably asleep yet." The door opened. Mac sat up.

A familiar voice said, "You here, Mac?"

"Dick! How the hell'd you get here this early?"

"Came down with Doc Burton."

"Doc here too?"

"Sure, he's right outside the door."

Mac scratched a match and lighted a candle in a broken saucer. Dick turned to Jim. "Hello, kid. How you makin' it?"

"Fine. What you all dressed up for, Dick? Pants pressed, clean shirt."

Dick smiled self-consciously. "Somebody in this dump's got to look respectable."

Mac said, "Dick'll be infesting every pink parlor in Torgas. Listen, Dick, I got a list of sympathizers right here. We want money of course; but we want tents, pieces of canvas, beds. Remember that—tents. Here's your list. There's lots of names on it. Make the contacts, and we'll send cars for the stuff. Lot of the boys 've got cars."

"O.K., Mac. How's she going?"

"Going like a bat out of hell. We got to work quick to keep up." He tied his shoe. "Where's Doc? Why don't you call him in? Come on in, Doc."

A young man with golden hair stepped into the room. His face was almost girlish in its delicacy, and his large eyes had a soft, sad look like those of a bloodhound. He carried his medical bag and a brief-case in one hand. "How are you, Mac? Dick got your wire and picked me up."

"I'm sure glad you got here quick, Doc. We need you right away. This is Jim Nolan."

Jim stood up, stamping his heels into his shoes. "Glad to know you, Doc."

Mac said, "Better start, Dick. You can bum breakfast at Al's Lunch Wagon, on Townsend. Don't hit 'im up for anything else but breakfast. We already got a ranch off his old man. Shove along, Dick, and remember: tents, canvas, money—and anything else you can get."

"O.K., Mac. All the names on this list good?"

"I don't know. Try 'em. You want me to drive 'em up to you?"

"Go to hell," said Dick. He went out the door and closed it behind him. The candle and the dawn fought each other so that together they seemed to make less light than either would have made alone. The room was cold.

Dr. Burton said, "There wasn't much information in your wire. What's the job?"

"Wait a minute, Doc. Look out the window and see if you can see any coffee cooking outside."

"Well, there's a little fire outside and a pot on it, or rather a can."

Mac said, "Well, wait a minute." He went outside, and in a moment returned carrying a tin can of steaming, unpleasant smelling coffee."

"Jesus, that looks hot," said Jim.

"And lousy," Mac added. "All right, Doc. This is the best set-up I've seen for a long time. I want to work out some ideas. I don't want this ruckus to get out of hand." He gulped some of the coffee. "Sit down on that box. We've got five acres of private property. You'll have all the help you need. Can you lay out a camp, a perfect camp, all straight lines? Dig toilets, take care of sanitation, garbage disposal? Try to figure out some way to take baths? And fill the air so God-damn full of carbolic or chloride of lime that it smells healthy? Make the whole district smell clean—can you do that?"

"Yes. I can do it. Give me enough help and I can." The sad eyes grew sadder. "Give me five gallons of crude carbolic and I'll perfume the country for miles."

"Good. Now, we're moving the men today. You look 'em over as quick as you can. See there's no contagion in any of 'em, will you? The health authorities are going to do plenty of snooping. If they can catch us off base, they'll bounce us. They let us live like pigs in the jungle, but just the minute we start a strike, they get awful concerned about the public health."

"All right, all right."

Mac looked confused. "I busted right into a song, didn't I? Well, you know what's needed. Let's go see London now."

Three men sat on the steps of London's room. They got up and moved aside for Mac. Inside, London was lying down, dozing. He rose up on his elbow. "Chroust! Is it morning?"

"It's Christmas," said Mac. "Mr. London, this here's Doc Burton, Director of Public Health. He wants some men. How many you want, Doc?"

"Well, how many men are we going to handle?"

"Oh—between a thousand and fifteen hundred."

"Better give me fifteen or twenty men, then."

London called, "Hi, out there." One of the sentinels opened the door and looked in. "Try find Sam, will you?"

"Sure."

London said, "We called a meetin' for ten o'clock this mornin'. Great big meetin', I mean. I sent word to the other camps about this Anderson place. They'll start moving' in pretty soon."

The door opened and Sam entered, his lean face sharp with curiosity.

"Sam, this here's Doc Burton. He wants you for his right-hand. Go outside and tell the guys you want volunteers to help the Doc. Get twenty good men."

"O.K., London. When you want 'em?"

Burton said, "Right now. We'll go right over and lay out the camp. I can pile eight or nine in my old car. Get somebody with a car to take the rest."

Sam glanced from London to Burton, and back to London to verify the authority. London nodded his big head. "That's straight, Sam. Anything Doc says."

Burton stood up to go with him. "I'd like to help pick the men."

"Wait," Mac said. "You're all clear in town, aren't you, Doc?"

"What do you mean 'clear'?"

"I mean, is there anything they could hang a malpractice charge on you for?"

"Not that I know of. 'Course they can do anything if they want to bad enough."

"Sure," said Mac. "I know; but it might take 'em some time. 'Bye, Doc. See you later."

When Burton and Sam were gone, Mac turned to London. "He's a good guy. Looks like a pansy with his pretty face, but he's hard-boiled enough. And he's thorough as croton oil. Got anything to eat, London?"

"Loaf of bread and some cheese."

"Well, what are we waitin' for? Jim and me forgot to eat last night."

Jim said, "I woke up in the night and remembered."

London brought a bag from the corner and laid out a loaf of bread and a slab of cheese. There was a stirring outside. The hum of voices that had been still for several hours broke out again. Doors opened and slammed. Men hacked their throats clear of mucous and spat and blew their noses. The clear day had come, and the sun was red through the windows.

Mac, talking around a mouthful of cheese, said, "London, what do you think of Dakin for general chairman of the strike committee and boss-in-chief?"

London looked a little disappointed. "Dakin's a good guy," he said. "I've knowed Dakin for a long time."

Mac went into London's disappointment and dug it out. "I'll be straight with you, London. You'd be a hell of a good chairman, except you'd get mad. Now Dakin don't look like a guy that would ever get mad. If the boss of this mess ever gets mad, we're sunk."

The attempt was successful. London agreed, "I get sore as hell. I get so damn mad it makes me sick. You're straight about Dakin, too; he's a gamblin' kind of a man. Never opens up his eyes wide; never lets his voice get loose. The worse things gets, the quieter Dakin gets."

Mac said, "Then when the meetin' comes off, you throw your weight to Dakin, will you?"

"Sure."

"I don't know about this guy Burke, but I think with our guys and Dakin's guys we could soft-pedal him if he gets rank. We better start the guys movin' pretty soon; it's quite a ways over there."

London asked, "When you think the scabs'll start comin'?"

"Not before tomorrow. I don't think the bosses around

here think we mean it yet. They can't get in any scabs before tomorrow."

"What we goin' to do when they land?"

"Well," said Mac. "We'll meet the train an' give 'em the keys of the city. I ought to have a wire before they start from town. Some of the boys'll kind of be checkin' up on the employment agencies." He lifted his head and looked toward the door. The hum of voices outside had been casual and monotonous, and now it stopped altogether. Suddenly, through the silence, there came a catcall, and then other voices broke into shouts. There was an argument outside.

London stepped over to the door and opened it. The three sentinels stood side by side before the door, and in front of them stood the orchard superintendent in moleskin trousers and field boots. On either side of him stood a man wearing a deputy sheriff's badge, and in each of his hands were shotguns.

The superintendent looked over the heads of the guardians. "I want to talk to you, London."

"You sure come with an olive-branch," said London.

"Well, let me come in. Maybe we can work something out." London looked at Mac, and Mac nodded. The great crowd of men was silent, listening. The 'super' stepped forward, with his deputies beside him. The guards maintained their position. One of them said, "Let him leave his bulls outside, chief."

"That's a good idear," said London. "You don't need no buckshot to talk with."

The 'super' glanced nervously about at the silent, threatening men. "What proof have I that you'll play straight?" he demanded.

"Just about as much as I have that you will."

The 'super' made his decision. "Stay outside and keep order," he said.

Now the guardians stepped aside, letting the one man enter, and then resumed their position. The deputies were nervous. They stood fingering their guns and looking fiercely about them.

London closed the door. "I don't know why you couldn't say it outside, where the guys could hear."

The 'super' saw Mac and Jim. He looked angrily at London. "Put those men out."

"Uh-uh," said London.

"Now look here, London, you don't know what you're doing. I'm offering you the chance to go back to work if you kick those men out."

"What for?" London asked. "They're good guys."

"They're reds. They're getting a lot of good men into trouble. They don't give a *damn* about you men if they can start trouble. Get rid of 'em and you can go back to work."

London said, "S'pose we kick 'em out? Do we get the money we're strikin' for? Do we get what we would of got before the cut?"

"No; but you can go back to work with no more trouble. The owners will overlook everything that's happened."

"Well, what good was the strike, then?"

The 'super' lowered his voice. "I'll tell you what I'm prepared to offer. You get the men back to work and you'll get a steady job here as assistant superintendent at five dollars a day."

"And how about these guys, these friends of mine?"

"Fifty dollars apiece if they get out of the Valley."

Jim looked at the heavy, brooding face of London. Mac was grinning meanly. London went on, "I like to see both sides. S'pose me an' my friends here don't take it, what then?"

"Then we kick you off this place in half an hour. Then we blacklist the whole damn bunch of you. You can't go any place; you can't get a job any place. We'll have five hundred deputy sheriffs if we need 'em. That's the other side. We'll see you can't get a job this side of hell. What's more, we'll jug your pals here, and see they get the limit."

London said, "You can't vag 'em if they've got money."

The 'super' stepped closer, pressing his advantage. "Don't be a fool, London. You know as well as I do what the vagrancy laws are. You know vagrancy's anything the judge doesn't want you to do. And if you *don't* know it, the judge here's named Hunter. Come on, now, London. Bring the men back to work. It's a steady job for you, five dollars a day."

London's eyes fell away. He looked at Mac, asking mutely for instructions. Mac let the silence hang.

"Well, come on, London. How about it? Your red pals here can't help you, and you know it damn well."

Jim, on the outskirts, was shivering. His eyes were wide and quiet. Mac watched London and saw what the 'super' did not see, the shoulders gradually settling and widening, the big, muscled neck dropping down between the shoulders, the arms hooking slowly up, the eyes taking on a dangerous gleam, a flush stealing up the neck and out on the cheeks.

Suddenly Mac cried sharply, "London!" London jerked, and then relaxed a little. Mac said quietly, "I know a way out, London. While this gent is here, let's hold a meetin' of all the men. Let's tell the guys what we've been offered to sell 'em out. We'll take a vote on whether you get that five dollar job and—then—we'll try to keep the guys from lynchin' this gent here."

The 'super' turned red with anger. "This is the last offer," he cried. "Take this, or get out."

"We was just about to get out," Mac said.

"You'll get out of the Torgas Valley. We'll run you out."

"Oh, no you won't. We got a piece of private property we can stay on. The owner invited us."

"That's a lie!"

"Listen, mister," Mac said, "we're goin' to have a little trouble gettin' you and your bodyguard out of here as it is. Don't make it no worse."

"Well, where do you think you're going to stay?"

Mac sat down on a box. His voice grew cold. "Listen, mister, we're goin' to camp on the Anderson place. Now the first thing you babies are goin' to think of is gettin' us off. That's O.K. We'll take our chance. The second thing you weasels are goin' to do is try to get back at Anderson. Now I'm tellin' you this, if any of your boys touch that property or hurt Anderson, if you hurt one single fruit tree, a thousand guys'll start out an' every one of 'em 'll have a box of matches. *Get it, mister?* Take it as a threat if you want to: you touch Anderson's ranch and by Christ we'll burn every fucking house and barn on every ranch in the Valley!" Tears of fury were in Mac's eyes. His chest shuddered as though he were about to cry.

The 'super' snapped his head around to London. "You see

the kind of men you're mixed up with, London? You know how many years you can get for arson?"

London choked. "You better scram on, Mister. I'm goin' to kill you if you don't. You better go now. Make him go now, Mac," he cried. "For Christ's sake, make him *go!*"

The 'super' backed away from the heavy, weaving body of London and reached behind him to find the doorknob. "Threat of murder," he said thickly. The door was open behind him.

"You got no witness to a threat," Mac said.

Outside the deputies tried to see in between the stiff bodies of the guardians. "You're fools, all of you," the 'super' said. "If I need 'em, I'll have a dozen witnesses to anything I want. You've had my last word."

The guardians stepped aside for the 'super.' The deputies ranged up beside him. Not a sound came from the bunched men. A lane opened up for the three and they strode out through it. The silent men followed them with their eyes, and the eyes were puzzled and angry. The three marched stiffly to a big roadster that stood at one end of the building. They climbed in and drove away. And then the crowd looked slowly back at the open door of London's room. London stood leaning against the doorjamb, looking weak and sick.

Mac stepped into the doorway and put his arm around London's shoulders. They were two feet above the heads of the quiet men. Mac cried, "Listen, you guys. We didn't want to tell you before they got away; we was afraid you'd stomp 'em to death. That mug come here to try to get London to sell you out. London was goin' to get a steady job, an' you guys was goin' to get screwed."

A growl started, a snarling growl. Mac held up his hand. "No need to get mad, wait a minute, now. Jus' remember it later; they tried to buy London—an' they couldn't. Now shut up for a minute. We got to get out o' here. We got a ranch to stay on. There's goin' to be order, too. That's the only way we can win this. We all got to take orders. Now the guys that got cars take all the women an' kids an' the truck that can't be carried. The rest'll have to walk. Now be nice. Don't break nothing—yet. An' stay together. While you're gettin' your stuff picked up, London wants to see his committee."

The moment he stopped talking a turbulence broke out. Shouting and laughing, the men eddied. They seemed filled with a terrible joy, a bloody, lustful joy. Their laughter was heavy. Into the rooms they swarmed, and carried out their things and piled them on the ground—pots and kettles, blankets, bundles of clothing. The women rolled out push-carts for the children. Six of the committeemen forced and shouldered their way through the press, and entered London's room.

The sun was clear of the trees now, and the air was warmed by it. Behind the buildings battered old cars began to start with bursts of noise. There were sounds of hammering as possessions were boxed. The place swam with activity, with the commotion of endless trips back and forth, of opinions shouted, of judgments made and overruled.

London let his committee in and shut the door to keep out the noise. The men were silent, dignified, grave and important. They sat on boxes and clasped their knees and bent portentous looks at the walls.

Mac said, "London, d'you mind if I talk to them?"

"Sure, go ahead."

"I don't mean to hog the show, gents," Mac continued. "I had some experience. I been through this before. Maybe I can show you where the thing breaks down, and maybe we can steer clear of some of the things that conk us."

One of the men said, "Go ahead, fella. We'll listen."

"O.K. We got plenty of fire now. That's the trouble with workin' stiffs, though. One minute they're steamed up like a keg of beer, and the next, they're cold as a whore's heart. We got to cut down the steam and warm up the cold. Now I want to make a suggestion. You guys can think it over, an' then you can maybe get the whole bunch to vote on it. Most strikes break down because they got no discipline. Suppose we divide the men in squads, let each squad elect a leader, and then he's responsible for his squad. We can work 'em in groups, then."

One of the men said, "Lot of these guys was in the army. They di'n't like it none."

"Sure they didn't. They was fightin' some other guy's war.

They had officers shoved down their throats. If they elect their officers and fight their own war, it'd be different."

"Most o' these guys don't like *no* officers."

"Well, they got to have 'em. We'll get the pants kicked off us if we got no discipline. If the squad don't like the leader, let 'em vote 'im into the ranks an' elect another leader. That ought to satisfy 'em. Then we ought to have officers over hundreds, an' one chief high-tail boss. Just give it a thought, gents. There's goin' to be a big meetin' in about two hours. We got to have a plan ready."

London scratched his tonsure. "Sounds O.K. to me. I'll talk it over with Dakin soon's I see him."

"All right," said Mac. "Let's get movin'. Jim, you stay close to me."

"Give *me* some work," Jim said.

"No, you stay close. I may need you."

8

THE FIVE ACRES of plow land on the Anderson place was surrounded on three sides by big, dark apple trees; and on the fourth it was bounded by the narrow, dusty county road. The men had arrived in droves, laughing and shouting to one another, and they had found preparations made for them. Stakes were driven into the soft ground defining the streets for the camp. There were five streets running parallel to the county road, and opposite the end of each street a deep hole was dug in the ground as a toilet.

Before the work of building the camp started, they held their general meeting with some order; elected Dakin chairman and assented to his committee. They agreed with enthusiasm to the suggestion of the squads.

Hardly had they begun to assemble when five motorcycle police rode up and parked their motors in the county road. They leaned against the machines and watched the work. Tents were pitched, and shelters laid out. The sad-eyed Dr. Burton was everywhere, ordering the building of the camp. At least a hundred old automobiles lined the road, drawn up like caissons in an artillery park, all facing out toward the road. There were ancient Fords, ravaged in their upholstery; Chevrolets and Dodges with rusty noses, paintless, with loose fenders or no fenders at all. There were worn-out Hudsons that made a noise like machine-guns when they were starting. They stood like aged soldiers at a reunion. At one end of the line of cars stood Dakin's Chevrolet truck, clean and new and shiny. Alone of all the cars it was in good condition; and Dakin, as he walked about the camp, surrounded by members of his committee, rarely got out of sight of his truck. As he talked or listened his cold, secret eyes went again and again to his shining green truck.

When the grey old tents were pitched Burton insisted that the canvas be scrubbed with soap and water. Dakin's truck brought barrels of water from Anderson's tank. The women washed the tents with old brooms.

Anderson walked out and watched with worried eyes while

his five acres was transformed into a camp. By noon it was ready; and nine hundred men went to work in the orchard, picking apples into their cooking kettles, into their hats, into gunny sacks. There were not nearly ladders enough. The men climbed up the trunks into the trees. By dark the crop was picked, the lines of boxes filled, the boxes trucked to Anderson's barn and stored.

Dick had worked quickly. He sent a boy to ask for men and a truck to meet him in town, and the truck came back loaded with tents of all kinds—umbrella tents of pale brown canvas, pup-tents, low and peaked, big troop tents with room in them for ten men. And the truck brought two sacks of rolled oats and sacks of flour, cases of canned goods, sacks of potatoes and onions and a slaughtered cow.

The new tents went up along the streets. Dr. Burton superintended the cooking arrangements. Trucks went out to the city dump and brought back three rusty, discarded stoves. Pieces of tin covered the gaping tops. Cooks were assigned, washtubs filled with water, the cow cut up and potatoes and onions set to cooking in tremendous stews. Buckets of beans were boiled. In the dusk, when the picking was over, the men came in and found tubs of stew waiting for them. They sat on the ground and ate from basins and cups and tin cans.

As darkness fell, the motorcycle police were relieved by five deputy sheriffs armed with rifles. For a time they marched up and down the road in military manner, but finally they sat in the ditch and watched the men. There were few lights in the camp. Here and there a tent was lighted with a lantern. The flares of little fires threw shadows. At one end of the first street, so pitched that it was directly behind his shining green truck, stood Dakin's tent—a large, patented affair with a canvas wall in the middle, making two rooms. His folding table and chairs were set up. A ground cloth lay on the floor, and from the center pole a hissing gasoline lantern hung. Dakin lived in style and traveled in luxury. He had no vices; every cent he or his wife made went to his living, to his truck, to providing new equipment for his camp.

When it was dark, London and Mac and Jim strolled to the tent and went in. With Dakin in the tent sat Burke, a lowering, sullen Irishman, and two short Italian men who looked very much alike. Mrs. Dakin had retired to the other side of the partition. Under the white light of the gasoline lamp Dakin's pink scalp showed through his blond hair. His secret eyes moved restlessly about. "Hello, boys, find some place to sit."

London chose a chair, the only one left. Mac and Jim squatted on the ground; Mac brought out his Durham bag and made a cigarette. "Things seem to be goin' O.K.," he observed.

Dakin's eyes flicked to him, and then away. "Yeah, they seem to be all right."

"They got those cops here quick," said Burke. "I'd like to take a poke at a few of 'em."

Dakin reproved him calmly. "Let cops alone till you can't no more. They ain't hurtin' a thing."

Mac asked, "How the squads shapin'?"

"All right. They all elected their chiefs. Some of 'em kicked out the chief and elected new ones already. Say, that Doc Burton is a swell guy."

"Yeah," Mac said. "He's O.K. Wonder where he's at? You better have one of the squads watch out for him. When we get started, they'll try to get him out of here. If they can get him out, they can clear us out. 'Danger to public health,' they call it."

Dakin turned to Burke. "Fix that up now, will you, Burke? Tell a good bunch to keep care o' Doc. The guys like him." Burke got up and went out of the tent.

London said, "Tell 'im what you told me, Mac."

"Well, the guys think this is a kind of a picnic, Dakin. To-morrow morning the picnic's over. The fun begins."

"Scabs?"

"Yep, a train-load. I got a kid in town. He goes to the telegraph office for me. Got a wire tonight. A freight train-load of scabs is startin' out from the city today. Ought to be in some time in the mornin'."

"Well," said Dakin. "Guess we better meet that train an' have a talk with the new guys. Might do some good, before they all get scattered."

"That's what I thought," said Mac. "I've saw the time

when a whole slough of scabs come over if you just told 'em how things was."

"We'll tell 'em, all right."

"Listen," said Mac. "The cops'll try to head us off. Couldn't we let the guys kind of sneak off through the trees just before daylight, and leave them cops holding the bag here?"

For a second Dakin's cold eyes twinkled. "Think that'd work, you guys?" They laughed delightedly. Dakin went on, "Well, go out an' tell the men about it."

Mac said, "Wait a minute, Dakin. If you tell the guys to-night, it won't be no secret."

"What do you mean?"

"Well, you don't think we ain't got stools in the camp, do you? I bet there's at least five under cover, besides the guys that'd spill anything and hope to get a buck out of it. Hell, it's always that way. Don't tell 'em nothing till you're ready to start."

"Don't trust the guys, huh?"

"Well, if you want to take the chance, go ahead. I bet you find the cops comin' right along with us."

Dakin asked, "What do you guys think?"

"I guess he's right," said one of the little Italian men.

"O.K. Now we got to leave a bunch to take care of the camp."

"At least a hundred," Mac agreed. "If we leave the camp, they'll burn 'er, sure as hell."

"The boys sure got Anderson's crop down quick."

"Yeah," said Dakin. "There's two or three hundred of 'em out in the orchard next door right now. Anderson's goin' to have a bigger crop than he thought."

"I hope they don't cause trouble yet," Mac said. "There'll be plenty later on."

"How many scabs comin'? Did you find out?"

"Somewheres between four and five hundred tomorrow. Be more later, I guess. Be sure an' tell the guys to take plenty of rocks in their pockets."

"I'll tell 'em."

Burke came back in. He said, "The Doc's goin' to sleep in

one of them big army tents. There'll be ten guys sleepin' in the same tent with him."

"Where's Doc at now?" Mac asked.

"He's dug up a couple of ring-worms on a guy. He's fixin' 'im over by the stoves."

At that moment a chorus of yells broke out in the camp, and then a high, angry voice shouting. The six men ran out of the tent. The noise came from a group of men standing in front of the camp street that faced the road. Dakin pushed his way in among the men. "What th' hell's the matter here?"

The angry voice answered, "I'll tell you. Your men started throwin' rocks. I'm tellin' you now if there's any more rocks we're goin' to start shootin', an' we don't care who we hit."

Mac turned to Jim, standing beside him. He said softly, "I wish they would start shooting. This bunch of mugs is going to pieces, maybe, if something dirty doesn't happen pretty soon. They're feeling too good. They'll start fighting themselves."

London walked fiercely into the crowd of men. "You guys get back," he cried. "You got enough to do without no kid tricks. Go on, now, get back where you belong." The authority of the man drove them sullenly back, but they dispersed reluctantly.

The deputy shouted, "You keep those guys in order or we'll do it with Winchesters."

Dakin said coldly, "You can pull in your neck and go back to sleep."

Mac muttered to Jim, "Those cops are scared as hell. That makes 'em dangerous. Just like rattlesnakes when they're scared: they'll shoot at anything."

The crowd had moved away now and the men were scattering to their tents. Mac said, "Let's go have a look at Doc, Jim. Come on over by the stoves." They found Dr. Burton sitting on a box, bandaging a man's arm. A kerosene lantern shed a thin yellow light on his work and illumined a small circle on the ground. He stuck down the bandage with adhesive.

"There you are," he said. "Next time don't let it get so sore. You'll lose an arm some day, if you do."

The man said, "Thanks, Doc," and went away, rolling down his sleeve.

"Hello, Mac. Hello, Jim. I guess I'm finished."

"Was that the ringworm?"

"No, just a little cut, and a nice infection started. They won't learn to take care of cuts."

Mac said, "If Doc could only find a case of small-pox now and set up a quarantine ward, he'd be perfectly happy. What're you going to do now, Doc?"

The sad brown eyes looked tiredly up at Mac. "Well, I think I'm all through. I ought to go and see whether the squad disinfected the toilets the way I told them."

"They smell disinfected," Mac said. "Why don't you get some sleep, Doc? You didn't have any last night."

"Well, I'm tired, but I don't feel sleepy. For the last hour I've thought when I was through I might walk out into the orchard and sit down against a tree and rest."

"Mind company?"

"No. I'd like to have you." Burton stood up. "Wait till I wash my hands." He scrubbed his hands in a pan of warm water and covered them with green soap and rinsed them. "Let's stroll, then," he said.

The three walked slowly away from the tent streets and toward the dark orchard. Their feet crunched softly on the crisp little clods of the plowed ground.

"Mac," Burton said wearily. "You're a mystery to me. You imitate any speech you're taking part in. When you're with London and Dakin you talk the way they do. You're an actor."

"No," said Mac. "I'm not an actor at all. Speech has a kind of a feel about it. I get the feel, and it comes out, perfectly naturally. I don't try to do it. I don't think I could help doing it. You know, Doc, men are suspicious of a man who doesn't talk their way. You can insult a man pretty badly by using a word he doesn't understand. Maybe he won't say anything, but he'll hate you for it. It's not the same thing in your case, Doc. You're supposed to be different. They wouldn't trust you if you weren't."

They entered the arches under the trees, and the leaf clusters and the limbs were dark against the sky. The little murmuring noise of the camp was lost. A barn-owl, screeching overhead with a ripping sound, startled the men.

"That's an owl, Jim," Mac explained. "He's hunting mice." And then to Burton, "Jim's never been in the country much. The things we know are new to him. Let's sit down here."

Mac and the doctor sat on the ground and leaned against the big trunk of an old apple tree. Jim sat in front of them, folding his legs before him. The night was still. Above, the black leaves hung motionless in the quiet air.

Mac spoke softly, for the night seemed to be listening. "You're a mystery to me, too, Doc."

"Me? A mystery?"

"Yes, you. You're not a Party man, but you work with us all the time; you never get anything for it. I don't know whether you believe in what we're doing or not, you never say, you just work. I've been out with you before, and I'm not sure you believe in the cause at all."

Dr. Burton laughed softly. "It would be hard to say. I could tell you some of the things I think; you might not like them. I'm pretty sure you wouldn't like them."

"Well, let's hear them, anyway."

"Well, you say I don't believe in the cause. That's like not believing in the moon. There 've been communes before, and there will be again. But you people have an idea that if you can *establish* the thing, the job'll be done. Nothing stops, Mac. If you were able to put an idea into effect tomorrow, it would start changing right away. Establish a commune, and the same gradual flux will continue."

"Then you don't think the cause is good?"

Burton sighed. "You see? We're going to pile up on that old rock again. That's why I don't like to talk very often. Listen to me, Mac. My senses aren't above reproach, but they're all I have. I want to see the whole picture—as nearly as I can. I don't want to put on the blinders of 'good' and 'bad,' and limit my vision. If I used the term 'good' on a thing I'd lose my license to inspect it, because there might be bad in it. Don't you see? I want to be able to look at the whole thing."

Mac broke in heatedly, "How about social injustice? The profit system? You have to say they're bad."

Dr. Burton threw back his head and looked at the sky. "Mac," he said. "Look at the physiological injustice, the injustice of tetanus, the injustice of syphilis, the gangster methods of amoebic dysentery—that's my field.

"Revolution and communism will cure social injustice."

"Yes, and disinfection and prophylaxis will prevent the others."

"It's different, though; men are doing one, and germs are doing the other."

"I can't see much difference, Mac."

"Well, damn it, Doc, there's lockjaw every place. You can find syphilis in Park Avenue. Why do you hang around with us if you aren't for us?"

"I want to *see*," Burton said. "When you cut your finger, and streptococci get in the wound, there's a swelling and a soreness. That swelling is the fight your body puts up, the pain is the battle. You can't tell which one is going to win, but the wound is the first battleground. If the cells lose the first fight the streptococci invade, and the fight goes on up the arm. Mac, these little strikes are like the infection. Something has got into the men; a little fever had started and the lymphatic glands are shooting in reinforcements. I want to see, so I go to the seat of the wound."

"You figure the strike is a wound?"

"Yes. Group-men are always getting some kind of infection. This seems to be a bad one. I want to *see*, Mac. I want to watch these group-men, for they seem to me to be a new individual, not at all like single men. A man in a group isn't himself at all; he's a cell in an organism that isn't like him any more than the cells in your body are like you. I want to watch the group, and see what it's like. People have said, 'mobs are crazy, you can't tell what they'll do.' Why don't people look at mobs not as men, but as mobs? A mob nearly always seems to act reasonably, for a mob."

"Well, what's this got to do with the cause?"

"It might be like this, Mac: When group-man wants to move, he makes a standard. 'God wills that we re-capture the Holy-Land'; or he says, 'We fight to make the world safe for democracy'; or he says, 'we will wipe out social injustice with communism.' But the group doesn't care about the Holy

Land, or Democracy, or Communism. Maybe the group simply wants to move, to fight, and uses these words simply to reassure the brains of individual men. I say it *might* be like that, Mac."

"Not with the cause, it isn't," Mac cried.

"Maybe not, it's just the way I think of things."

Mac said, "The trouble with you, Doc, is you're too God damn far left to be a communist. You go too far with collectivization. How do you account for people like me, directing things, moving things? That puts your group-man out."

"You might be an effect as well as a cause, Mac. You might be an expression of group-man, a cell endowed with a special function, like an eye cell, drawing your force from group-man, and at the same time directing him, like an eye. Your eye both takes orders from and gives orders to your brain."

"This isn't practical," Mac said disgustedly. "What's all this kind of talk got to do with hungry men, with lay-offs and unemployment?"

"It might have a great deal to do with them. It isn't a very long time since tetanus and lockjaw were not connected. There are still primitives in the world who don't know children are the result of intercourse. Yes, it might be worthwhile to know more about group-man, to know his nature, his ends, his desires. They're not the same as ours. The pleasure we get in scratching an itch causes death to a great number of cells. Maybe group-man gets pleasure when individual men are wiped out in a war. I simply want to see as much as I can, Mac, with the means I have."

Mac stood up and brushed the seat of his pants. "If you see too darn much, you don't get anything done."

Burton stood up too, chuckling softly. "Maybe some day— oh, let it go. I shouldn't have talked so much. But it does clarify a thought to get it spoken, even if no one listens."

They started back over the crisp clods toward the sleeping camp. "We can't look up at anything, Doc," Mac said. "We've got to whip a bunch of scabs in the morning."

"Deus vult," said Burton. "Did you see those pointers of Anderson's? Beautiful dogs; they give me a sensual pleasure, almost sexual."

A light still burned in Dakin's tent. The camp slept. Only a few coals of fire still burned in the streets. The silent line of old cars stood against the road, and in the road itself a clump of sparks waxed and waned, cigarettes of the watchful deputies.

"D'you hear that, Jim? That'll show you what Burton is. Here's a couple of fine dogs, good hunting dogs, but they're not dogs to Doc, they're feelings. They're dogs, to me. And these guys sleeping here are men, with stomachs; but they're not men to Doc, they're a kind of a collective Colossus. If he wasn't a doctor, we couldn't have 'im around. We need his skill, but his brain just gets us into a mess."

Burton laughed apologetically. "I don't know why I go on talking, then. You practical men always lead practical men with stomachs. And something always gets out of hand. Your men get out of hand, they don't follow the rules of common sense, and you practical men either deny that it is so, or refuse to think about it. And when someone wonders what it is that makes a man with a stomach something more than your rule allows, why you howl, 'Dreamer, mystic, metaphysician'. I don't know why I talk about it to a practical man. In all history there are no men who have come to such wild-eyed confusion and bewilderment as practical men leading men with stomachs."

"We've a job to do," Mac insisted. "We've got no time to mess around with high-falutin' ideas."

"Yes, and so you start your work not knowing your medium. And your ignorance trips you up every time."

They were close to the tents now. "If you talked to other people that way," Mac said, "we'd have to kick you out."

A dark figure arose suddenly from the ground. "Who is it?" a voice demanded; and then, "Oh, hello. I didn't know who it was coming in."

"Dakin set out guards?" Mac asked.

"Yeah."

"He's a good man. I knew he was a good man, cool-headed man."

They stopped by a big, peaked troop tent. "Guess I'll turn in," Doc said. "Here's where my bodyguard sleeps."

"Good idea," Mac agreed. "You'll probably have some bandaging to do tomorrow."

When Doc had disappeared inside the tent, Mac turned to Jim. "No reason why you shouldn't get some sleep too."

"What are you going to do, Mac?"

"Me? Oh, I thought I'd take a look around, see if everything's all right."

"I want to go with you. I just follow you around."

"Sh-h, don't talk so loud." Mac walked slowly toward the line of cars. "You do help me, Jim. It may be sloppy as an old woman, but you keep me from being scared."

"I don't do anything but pad around after you," said Jim.

"I know. I guess I'm getting soft. I'm scared something might happen to you. I shouldn't have brought you down, Jim. I'm getting to depend on you."

"Well, what're we going to do now, Mac?"

"I wish you'd go to bed. I'm going to try to have a talk with those cops in the road."

"What for?"

"Listen, Jim, you didn't get bothered by what Doc said, did you?"

"No. I didn't listen."

"Well, it's a bunch of bunk; but here's something that isn't bunk. You win a strike two ways, because the men put up a steady fight, and because public sentiment comes over to your side. Now most of this valley belongs to a few guys. That means the rest of the people don't own much of anything. The few owners either have to pay 'em or lie to 'em. Those cops out in the road are special deputies, just working stiffs with a star and a gun and a two-weeks' job. I thought I'd try and sound 'em out; try and find out how they feel about the strike. I guess how they feel is how the bosses told 'em to feel. But I might get a line on 'em, anyway."

"Well, how about it if they arrest you? Remember what that man said in the road last night."

"They're just deputies, Jim. They won't recognize me the way a regular cop would."

"Well, I want to go with you."

"O.K., but if anything looks funny, you cut for the camp and yell like hell."

In a tent behind them a man started shouting in his sleep. A soft chorus of voices awakened him and stopped his dreaming. Mac and Jim wedged their way silently between two cars and approached the little group of glowing cigarettes. The sparks died down and shifted as they approached.

Mac called, "Hey, you guys, can we come out there?"

From the group a voice, "How many of you?"

"Two."

"Come on, then." As they drew near a flashlight glanced out and touched their faces for a second, and then went off. The deputies stood up. "What do you want?" their spokesman demanded.

Mac replied, "We just couldn't sleep; thought we'd come out and talk."

The man laughed. "We been having lots of company tonight."

In the dark Mac pulled out his Bull Durham bag. "Any of you guys want to smoke?"

"We got smokes. What is it you want?"

"Well, I'll tell you. A lot of the guys want to know how you fellows feel about the strike. They sent us out to ask. They know you're just working men, the same as them. They want to know if you maybe won't help your own kind of guys."

Silence met his words. Mac looked uneasily around.

A voice said softly, "All right, you chickens. Get 'em up. Let out a squawk and we plug you."

"Say, what the hell is this? What's the idea?"

"Get behind 'em, Jack, and you, Ed, get your guns in their backs. If they move, let 'em have it. Now, march!"

The rifles pushed into their backs and punched them along through the darkness. The leader's voice said, "Thought you was God-damn smart, didn't you? You didn't know those day-cops pointed you two guys out." They marched across the road, and in among the trees on the other side. "Thought you was darn smart, getting the men out of here before daylight; thought you'd leave us holding the sack. Hell, we knew that gag ten minutes after you decided it."

"Who told you, mister?"

"Don't you wish you knew?" Their feet pounded along. The rifles jabbed into their backs.

"You takin' us to jail, mister?"

"Jail, hell, we're takin' you God-damn reds to the Vigilance

Committee. If you're lucky they'll beat the crap out of you and dump you over the county line; if you ain't lucky, they'll string you up to a tree. We got no use for radicals in this valley."

"But you guys are cops, you got to take us to jail."

"That what *you* think. There's a nice little house a little ways from here. That's where we're taking you."

Under the orchard trees even the little light from the stars was shut off. "Now be quiet, you guys."

Jim cried, "Go, Mac!" and at the same instant he dropped. His guard toppled over him. Jim rolled around the trunk of a tree, stood up and bolted. At the second row he climbed up into an apple tree, far up, among the leaves. He heard a scuffle and a grunt of pain. The flashlight darted about and then fell to the ground and aimlessly lighted a rotten apple. There came a rip of cloth, and then steady pounding of footsteps. A hand reached down and picked up the flashlight and switched it off. Muffled, arguing voices came from the place of the scuffle.

Jim eased himself gently out of the tree, panting with apprehension every time the leaves quivered. He moved quietly along, came to the road and crossed it. At the line of cars a guard stopped him. "This is the second time tonight, kid. Why'n't you go to bed?"

Jim said, "Listen, did Mac come through?"

"Yeah, goin' like a bat out of hell. He's in Dakin's tent."

Jim hurried on, lifted the brown tent-flap and went in. Dakin and Mac and Burke were there. Mac was talking excitedly. He stopped on a word and stared as Jim came in. "Jesus, I'm glad," he said. "We was just goin' to send out a party to try and get you. What a damn fool I was! What a damn fool! You know, Dakin, they was marchin' us along, had guns right in our backs. I didn't think they'd shoot, but they might of. Jim, what in hell did you do?"

"I just dropped, and the guy fell over me, and his gun dug in the dirt. We used to do that trick in the school yard."

Mac laughed uneasily. "Soon's the guns wasn't touching us, I guess they was afraid they'd kill each other. I jumped sideways and kicked my guy in the stomach."

Burke was standing behind Mac. Jim saw Mac wink at

Dakin. The cold eyes almost disappeared behind pale-lashed lids. Dakin said, "Burke, you'd better make the rounds, and see if the guards are all awake."

Burke hesitated. "I think they're O.K."

"Well, you better see, anyway. We don't want no more raids. What they got in their hands, Burke?"

"They got nice clubs."

"Well, go take a look around."

Burke went out of the tent. Mac stepped close to Dakin. "Tent walls is thin," he said quietly. "I'd like to talk to you alone. Want to take a little walk?"

Dakin nodded his head with two jerks. The three of them strolled out into the darkness, going in the direction Dr. Burton had taken earlier. A guard looked them over as they passed.

Mac said, "Somebody's double-crossin' us already. Them deputies knew we was goin' to shove off before daylight."

Dakin asked coldly, "D'you think it's Burke? He wasn't there, even."

"I don't know who it was. Anybody hanging around could of heard through the tent."

"Well, what are we goin' to do about it? You seem to know all about this stuff." The cold voice went on, "I got an idea you reds ain't goin' to do us no good. A guy come in tonight and says if we kick you out, maybe the bosses 'll talk business."

"And you think they will? They cut the wages before we showed up, don't forget that. Hell, you'd think we started this strike, and you know damn well we didn't. We're just helpin' it to go straight instead of shootin' its wad."

Dakin's monotone cut him off. "What you gettin' out of this?"

Mac retorted hotly, "We ain't gettin' nothin'."

"How do I know that?"

"You don't know it unless you believe it. They ain't no way to prove it."

Dakin's voice became a little warmer. "I don't know that I'd trust you guys if that was so. If a man's gettin' somethin' you know he's only goin' to do one or two things, he's goin' to take orders, or he's goin' to double-cross. But if a guy ain't gettin' nothin', you can't tell what he'll do."

"All right," Mac said irritably. "Let's lay off that junk. When the guys want to kick us out, let 'em take a vote on us. And let us argue our case. But there ain't no good of us fighting each other."

"Well, what we goin' to do, then. No good sneakin' the guys out tomorrow mornin' if the cops know we're goin' to do it."

"Sure not. Let's just march along the road and take our chances. When we see the scabs, and see how they act, we'll know whether we got to fight or talk."

Dakin stopped and moved his foot sideways against the dirt. "What do you want me out here for?"

"I just wanted to tell you we're bein' double-crossed. If you get somethin' you don't want the cops to know, don't tell nobody."

"All right, I got that. Long as everybody's goin' to know, we might as well let 'em know. I'm goin' to bed. You guys see if you can keep out of a mess till morning."

Mac and Jim shared a little pup-tent with no floor cloth. They crawled into the little cave and curled up in their old comforters. Mac whispered, "I think Dakin's straight, but he isn't taking orders."

"You don't think he'll try to get us out of here, do you, Mac?"

"He might. I don't think he will. By tomorrow night enough guys will be bruised up and mad so they'll be meat for us. Jesus, Jim, we can't let this thing peter out. It's too good."

"Mac?"

"Yeah?"

"Why don't the cops just come and take us out of here, you and me?"

"Scared to. They're scared the men might go haywire. It might be like when old Dan fell off the ladder. Cops know pretty well when they've got to leave the stiffs alone. We better go to sleep."

"I just want to ask, Mac, how'd you get loose over in the orchard? You had a battle, didn't you?"

"Sure, but it was so dark they couldn't see who they were socking. I knew I could sock anybody."

Jim lay quiet for a while. "Were you scared, Mac, when they had the guns in our backs?"

"Damn right. I've been up against vigilantes before; so's poor old Joy. Ten or fifteen of 'em gang up on you and beat you to a pulp. Oh, they're brave guys, all right. Mostly they wear masks. Damn right I was scared, weren't you?"

"Sure, I guess so. At first I was. And then they started marching us, and I got cold all over. I could see just what would happen if I dropped. I really saw that guy fall over me, saw it before it happened. I was mostly scared they'd plug you."

Mac said, "It's a funny thing, Jim, how the worse danger you get in, the less it scares you. Once the fuss started, I wasn't scared. I still don't like the way that gun felt."

Jim looked out through the tent opening. The night seemed grey in contrast with the blackness inside the tent. Footsteps went by, crushing the little clods. "D'you think we'll win this strike, Mac?"

"We ought to go to sleep; but you know, Jim, I wouldn't have told you this before tonight: No, I don't think we have a chance to win it. This valley's *organized*. They'll start shooting, and they'll get away with it. We haven't a chance. I figure these guys here'll probably start deserting as soon as much trouble starts. But you don't want to worry about that, Jim. The thing will carry on and on. It'll spread, and some day— it'll work. Some day we'll win. We've got to believe that." He raised up on one elbow. "If we didn't believe that, we wouldn't be here. Doc was right about infection, but that infection is invested capital. We've *got* to believe we can throw it off, before it gets into our hearts and kills us. You never change, Jim. You're always here. You give me strength."

Jim said, "Harry told me right at first what to expect. Everybody hates us, Mac."

"That's the hardest part," Mac agreed. "Everybody hates us; our own side and the enemy. And if we won, Jim, if we put it over, our own side would kill us. I wonder why we do it. Oh, go to sleep!"

9

BEFORE the night had broken at all the voice of awakening men sounded through the camp. There were axe-strokes on wood, and the rattling of the rusty stoves. In a few moments the sweet smell of burning pine and apple wood filled the camp. The cooks' detail was busy. Near the roaring stoves the buckets of coffee were set. The wash boilers of beans began to warm. Out of the tents the people crept, and went to stand near the stoves where they crowded so closely that the cooks had no room to work.

Dakin's truck drove off to Anderson's house and came back with three barrels of water. The word passed, "Dakin wants to see the squad leaders. He wants to talk to 'em right away." The leaders walked importantly toward Dakin's tent.

Now the line of orchard top grew sharp against the eastern sky and the parked cars were greyly visible. The buckets of coffee began to boil, and a rank, nourishing smell came from the bean kettles. The cooks ladled out beans into anything the people brought, pans, jars, cans and tin plates. Many sat on the ground, and with their pocket-knives carved little wooden paddles with which to eat their beans. The coffee was black and bitter, but men and women who had been silent and uncomfortable were warmed by it so that they began to talk, to laugh, to call greetings to one another. The daylight came over the trees and the ground turned greyish-blue. Three great bands of geese flew over, high in the light.

Meanwhile Dakin, flanked by Burke and London, stood in front of his tent. Before Dakin the squad leaders stood and waited, and Mac and Jim stood among them, for Mac had explained to Jim, "We've got to go pretty slow for a while. We don't want the guys to throw us out now."

Dakin had put on a short denim jacket and a tweed cap. His pale eyes darted about over the faces of the men. He said, "I'm goin' to tell you guys what's on, and then you can pull out of it if you want to. I don't want nobody to come that don't want to come. There's a train-load of scabs comin' in. We figure to go in town an' try to stop 'em. We'll talk to 'em some, and then we might have to fight 'em. How's that sound to you?"

A murmur of assent arose.

"All right, then. We'll march in. Keep your guys in hand. Keep 'em quiet, and on the side of the road." He grinned coldly. "If any of 'em want to pick up a few rocks an' shove 'em in their pockets, I can't see no harm in that."

The men laughed appreciatively.

"O.K. If you got that, go talk to your men. I want to get all the kicks in before we start. I'm goin' to leave about a hundred guys to look after the camp. Go get some breakfast."

The men broke and hurried back to the stoves. Mac and Jim moved up to where the leaders stood. London was saying, "I wouldn't trust 'em to put up much of a scrap. They don't look none too mean to me."

"Too early in the morning," Mac assured him. "They ain't had their coffee yet. Guys are different before they've ate."

Dakin demanded, "You guys goin' along?"

"Damn right," said Mac. "But look, Dakin, we got men out gettin' food and supplies together. Fix it so some cars can go in for the stuff when they send the word."

"O.K. We'll need it by tonight, too. Them beans'll be all gone. It takes a hell of a lot to feed a bunch like this."

Burke said, "I'm for startin' a mix soon's the scabs get off the train. Scare hell out of 'em."

"Better talk first," Mac said. "I seen half a trainload of scabs go over to the strike if they was talked to first. You jump on 'em and you'll scare some, and make some mad."

Dakin watched him suspiciously while he talked. "Well, let's be movin'," he said. "I got to pick the guys to stay. Doc and his men can clean up the camp. I'm goin' in my truck; London an' Burke can ride with me. We better leave these damn old cans here."

The sun was just coming up when the long, ragged column started out. The squad leaders kept their men to one side of the road. Jim heard a man say, "Don't bother with clods. Wait till we get to the railroad right-of-way. There's nice granite rocks in the roadbed."

Singing broke out, the tuneless, uneven singing of untrained men. Dakin's green Chevrolet truck led off, idling in low gear. The column of men followed it, and the crowd left in camp with the women howled goodbyes after them.

They had hardly started when ten motorcycle policemen rode up and spaced themselves along the line of march. When they had gone half a mile along the road a big open car, jammed with men, dashed to the head of the column and parked across the road. All of the men carried rifles in their hands, and all wore deputies' badges. The driver stood up on the seat. "You men are going to keep order, and don't forget it," he shouted. "You can march as long as you don't block traffic, but you're not going to interfere with anybody. Get that?" He sat down, moved his car in front of Dakin's truck and led the whole march.

Jim and Mac marched fifty feet behind Dakin's truck. Mac said, "They got a reception committee for us. Ain't that kind of 'em?" The men about him tittered. Mac continued, "They say 'you got a right to strike, but you can't picket,' an' they know a strike won't work without picketin'." There was no laughter this time. The men growled, but there was little anger in the tone. Mac glanced nervously at Jim. "I don't like it," he said softly. "This bunch of bums isn't keyed up. I hope to Christ something happens to make 'em mad before long. This 's going to fizzle out if something don't happen."

The straggling parade moved into town and took to the sidewalks. The men were quiet now, and most of them looked shamefaced. As they came into the town, householders watched through the windows, and children stood on the lawns and looked at them until the parents dragged them into the houses and shut the doors. Very few citizens moved about in the streets. The motorcycles of the police idled along so slowly that the riders had to put out their feet and touch the ground occasionally to keep upright. Led by the sheriff's car, the procession moved along back streets until it came at last to the railroad yard. The men stopped along the edge of the right-of-way, for the line was guarded by twenty men armed with shot-guns and tear gas bombs.

Dakin parked his truck at the curb. The men silently spread out and faced the line of special policemen. Dakin and London walked up and down the dense front, giving instructions.

The men must not start any trouble with the cops if they could help it. There was to be talk first, and that was all.

On the right of way two long lines of refrigerator cars stood idle. Jim said, aside, to Mac, "Maybe they'll stop the freight way up the track and unload the guys. Then we wouldn't get a chance at them."

Mac shook his head. "Later they might, but now I think they want a show-down. They figure they can scare us off. Jesus, I wish the train'd come in. Waiting raises hell with guys like ours. They get scared when they have to wait around."

A number of the men were sitting down on the curb by now. A buzz of quiet talk came from the close-pressed line. They were hemmed in, railroad guards on one side, motor-cycle police and deputy sheriffs on the other. The men looked nervous and self-conscious. The sheriff's deputies carried their rifles in two hands, held across their stomachs.

"The cops are scared, too," Mac said.

London reassured a group of men. "They ain't a goin' to do no shootin'," he said. "They can't afford to do no shootin'."

Someone shouted, "She's in the block!" Far along the track the block arm of the semaphore was up. A line of smoke showed above the trees, and the tracks rumbled under approaching wheels. Now the men stood up from the curb and craned their necks up the track.

London bellowed, "Hold the guys in, now."

They could see the black engine and the freight cars moving slowly in; and in the doorways of the cars they could see the legs of men. The engine crashed slowly in, puffing out bursts of steam from under its wheels. It drew into a siding and its brakes set. The cars jarred together, the ending stood wheezing and panting.

Across the street from the right-of-way stood a line of dilapidated stores and restaurants with furnished rooms in their upper storeys. Mac glanced over his shoulder. The windows of the rooms were full of men's heads looking out. Mac said, "I don't like the looks of those guys."

"Why not?" Jim asked.

"I don't know. There ought to be some women there. There aren't any women at all."

In the doorways of the box-cars strike-breakers sat, and standing behind them were others. They stared uneasily. They made no move to get out on to the ground.

Then London stepped out in front, stepped so close to a guard that the shot-gun muzzle turned and pointed at his stomach, and the guard moved back a pace. The engine panted rhythmically, like a great, tired animal. London cupped his hands around his mouth. His deep voice roared, "Come on over, you guys. Don't fight against us. Don't help the cops." His voice was cut off by a shriek of steam. A jet of white leaped from the side of the engine, drowning London's voice, blotting out every sound but its own swishing scream. The line of strikers moved restively, bellied out in the middle, toward the guards. The shot-gun muzzles turned and swept the ranks. The guards' faces tightened, but their threat had stopped the line. The steam shrieked on, and its white plume rose up and broke into little pieces.

In the doorway of one of the box-cars a commotion started, a kind of a boiling of the men. A man squirmed through the seated scabs and dropped to the ground.

Mac shouted in Jim's ear, "My God! It's Joy!"

The misshapen, gnome-like figure faced the doorway, and the men. The arms waved jerkily. Still the steam screeched. The men in the doorway dropped to the ground and stood in front of the frantic, jerking Joy. He turned and waved his arm toward the strikers. His beaten face was contorted. Five or six of the men fell in behind him, and the whole group moved toward the line of strikers. The guards turned sideways, nervously trying to watch both sides at once.

And then—above the steam—three sharp, cracking sounds. Mac looked back at the stores. Heads and rifles were withdrawn quickly from the room windows and the windows dropped.

Joy had stopped, his eyes wide. His mouth flew open and a jet of blood rolled down his chin, and down his shirt. His eyes ranged wildly over the crowd of men. He fell on his face and clawed outward with his fingers. The guards stared unbelievingly at the squirming figure on the ground. Suddenly the steam stopped; and the quietness fell on the men like a wave of sound. The line of strikers stood still, with strange, dreaming faces. Joy lifted himself up with his arms, like a lizard, and then dropped again. A little thick river of blood ran down on the crushed rock of the roadbed.

A strange, heavy movement started among the men. London moved forward woodenly, and the men moved forward. They were stiff. The guards aimed with their guns, but the line moved on, unheeding, unseeing. The guards stepped swiftly sideways to get out of the way, for the box-car doors were belching silent men who moved slowly in. The ends of the long line curled and circled slowly around the center of the dead man, like sheep about a nucleus.

Jim clung shivering to Mac's arm. Mac turned and muttered, "He's done the first real, useful thing in his life. Poor Joy. He's done it. He'd be so glad. Look at the cops, Jim. Let go my arm. Don't lose your nerve. Look at the cops!"

The guards were frightened, riots they could stop, fighting they could stop; but this slow, silent movement of men with the wide eyes of sleep-walkers terrified them. They held to their places, but the sheriff started his car. The motorcycle police moved imperceptibly toward their parked machines.

The strike-breakers were out of the cars by now. Some of them crept between the box-cars or under the wheels and hurried away on the other side, but most of them moved up and packed tightly about the place where Joy lay.

Mac saw Dakin standing on the outskirts of the mob, his little pale eyes for once looking straight ahead and not moving. Mac walked over to him. "We better get him in your truck and take him out to the camp."

Dakin turned slowly. "We can't touch him," he said. "The cops'll have to take him."

Mac said sharply, "Why didn't the cops catch those guys in the windows? Look at the cops, they're scared to death. We've got to take him, I tell you. We've got to use him to step our guys up, to keep 'em together. This'll stick 'em together, this'll make 'em fight."

Dakin grimaced. "You're a cold-blooded bastard. Don't you think of nothing but 'strike'?"

Jim broke in, "Dakin, that little guy got shot trying to help us. D'you want to stop him now from doing it?"

Dakin's eyes moved slowly from Mac to Jim, and then to

Mac again. He said, "What do you know about what he was doin'? Couldn't hear nothing but that damn steam."

"We know him," Mac said. "He was a pal of ours."

Dakin's eyes were filled with dislike. "Pal of yours, and you won't let him rest now. You want to use him. You're a pair of cold-blooded bastards."

Mac cried, "What do you know about it? Joy didn't want no rest. Joy wanted to work, and he didn't know how." His voice rose hysterically, "and now he's got a chance to work, and you don't want to let 'im."

A number of the men had turned toward the voices, turned with a dull curiosity. Dakin peered at Mac for a moment longer. "Come on," he said. They pushed and jabbed their way into the tight mass of men, who gave way reluctantly.

Mac shouted, "Come on, you guys, let us in. We got to get this poor fellow out o' there." The men opened a narrow pathway, pushing violently backward to make it.

London joined them, and helped to force a way in. Joy was quite dead. When they had cleared a little space around him, London turned him over and started to wipe the bloody dirt from Joy's mouth. There was a foxy look in the open eyes; the mouth smiled terribly.

Mac said, "Don't do that, London. Leave it that way, just the way it is."

London lifted the little man in his arms. Joy looked very small against London's big chest. A path opened for them easily this time. London marched along, and the men arranged themselves into a crude column, and followed.

Beside Dakin's bright green truck the sheriff stood, surrounded by his deputies. London stopped, and the following men stopped. "I want that body," the sheriff said.

"No. You can't have it."

"You men shot a strike-breaker. We'll bring the charge. I want that body for the coroner."

London's eyes glowed redly. He said simply, "Mister, you know the guys that killed this little man; you know who did it. You got laws and you don't keep 'em." The mob was silent, listening.

"I tell you, I want that body."

London said plaintively, "Can't you see, mister? If you guys don't get the hell out of here, can't you see you're goin' get *killed*? Can't you see *that*, mister? Don't you *know* when you can't go no further?"

From the mob there came a rustle of released breath. The sheriff said, "I'm not through with you," but he backed away, and his deputies backed away. The mob growled, so softly that it sounded like a moan. London set Joy over the tailboard of the truck, and he climbed in and lifted the body forward, until it leaned against the back of the cab.

Dakin started his motor and backed around and rolled along the street, and the dull, menacing mob fell in behind. They made no noise. They walked with heavy, padding foot-steps.

No motorcycle police lined the road. The streets and the roads were deserted on their line of march. Mac and Jim walked a little to one side of the truck. "Was it vigilantes, Mac?"

"Yep. But they overdid it this time. Everything went wrong for them. That steam—if our guys could've heard the shoot-ing better, they'd probably have run away. But the steam was too loud. It was over too soon; our guys didn't have a chance to get scared. No, they made a mistake."

They trudged slowly along, beside the column of marching men. "Mac, who in hell are these vigilantes, anyway? What kind of guys are they?"

"Why, they're the dirtiest guys in any town. They're the same ones that burned the houses of old German people dur-ing the war. They're the same ones that lynch Negroes. They like to be cruel. They like to hurt people, and they always give it a nice name, patriotism or protecting the constitution. But they're just the old nigger torturers working. The owners use 'em, tell 'em we have to protect the people against reds. Y'see that lets 'em burn houses and torture and beat people with no danger. And that's all they want to do, anyway. They've got no guts; they'll only shoot from cover, or gang a man when they're ten to one. I guess they're about the worst scum in the world." His eyes sought the body of Joy, in the truck. He said, "During the war there was a little fat German tailor in my town, and a bunch of these patriotic bastards, about fifty of 'em, started his house on fire, and beat him to a pulp.

They're great guys, these vigilantes. Not long ago they shot tracer bullets through a kerosene tank and started a fire in a bunk house. They didn't even have the guts to do it with a match."

The column marched on through the country, raising a great dust. The men were coming slowly out of their dream. They talked together in low voices. Their feet scuffed heavily against the ground. "Poor Joy," Jim said. "He was a good little fellow. He'd been beaten so much. He reminded me of my old man, always mad."

Mac reproved him. "Don't feel sorry for Joy. If he could know what he did, he'd be cocky. Joy always wanted to lead people, and now he's going to do it, even if he's in a box."

"How about the scabs, Mac? We got a bunch of them with us."

"Sure, a bunch came over, but a lot of 'em beat it. Some of our guys beat it, too. We got just about the same number we started with. Didn't you see 'em crawling under the cars and running away?" Mac said, "Look at these guys. They're waking up. It's just as though they got a shot of gas for a while. That's the most dangerous kind of men."

"The cops knew it, too," said Jim.

"Damn right they did. When a mob don't make a noise, when it just comes on with dead-pans, that's the time for a cop to get out of the way."

They were nearing the Anderson place. Jim asked, "What do we do now, Mac?"

"Well, we hold the funeral, and we start picketing. It'll settle down now. They'll run in scabs with trucks."

"You still think we'll get beat, Mac?"

"I don't know. They got this valley organized. God, how they've got it organized. It's not so hard to do when a few men control everything, land, courts, banks. They can cut off loans, and they can railroad a man to jail, and they can always bribe plenty."

Dakin's truck pulled to the end of the line of cars and backed into place. The camp guards came streaming out, and the column of returning men deployed among them. Groups collected to hear the story, over and over. Dr. Burton trotted over to Dakin's truck. London stood up heavily. His wide blue shirt-front was streaked with Joy's blood. Burton took one look at Joy. "Killed him, eh?"

"Got him," said London.

Burton said, "Bring him to my tent. I'll look him over." From behind the tents a hoarse, bubbling scream broke out. All of the men turned, frozen at the sound. Burton said, "Oh, they're killing a pig. One of the cars brought back a live pig. Bring this body to my tent."

London bent over wearily and lifted Joy in his arms again. A crowd of men followed him, and stood clustered about the big troop tent. Mac and Jim followed Dr. Burton inside the tent. They watched silently while he unbuttoned the stiff, bloody shirt and disclosed a wound in the chest. "Well, that's it. That'd do it."

"Recognize him, Doc?"

Burton looked closely at the distorted face. "I've seen him before."

"Sure you have. It's Joy. You've set damn near every bone in his body."

"Well, he's through this time. Tough little man. You'll have to send his body to town. The coroner'll have to have it."

London said, "If we do that, they'll bury him, hide him."

Mac said, "We can send some guys in to see that he gets back here. Let 'em picket the morgue till they get the body back. Those damn vigilantes made a mistake; an' they know it by now."

Dakin lifted the flap and stepped into the big tent. "They're fryin' pork," he said. "They sure cut up that pig quick."

Mac said, "Dakin, can you have the guys build a kind of a platform? We'll want some place for the coffin to set. Y'ought to have a place to talk from, too."

"Want to make a show of it, do you?"

"You're damn right! You got me kinda wrong, Dakin. What we got to fight with? Rocks, sticks. Even Indians had bows an' arrows. But let us get one little gun to protect ourselves, an' they call out the troops to stop the revolution. We got damn few things to fight with. We got to use what we can. This little guy was my friend. Y'can take it from me he'd want to get used any way we can use him. We *got* to use him."

He paused. "Dakin, can't you see? We'll get a hell of a lot of people on our side if we put on a public funeral. We got to get public opinion."

London was nodding his head slowly up and down. "The guy's right, Dakin."

"O.K., if you want it too, London. I s'pose somebody's got to make a speech, but I ain't goin' to do it."

"Well, I will if I have to," London cried. "I seen the little guy start over to us. I seen him get it. I'll make the speech if you won't."

"Sounds like Cock Robin," Burton said.

"Huh?"

"Nothing. I was just talking. Better get the body taken in now, and turn it over to the coroner."

London said, "I'm going to send a flock of my own guys to stay with him."

Jim's voice came from outside the tent. "Oh, Mac, come on out. Anderson wants to see you."

Mac walked quickly outside. Anderson was standing with Jim. He looked tired and old. "You just played hell," he began fiercely.

"What's the matter, Mr. Anderson?"

"Said you'd protect us, didn't you?"

"Sure I did. The guys here'll take care of you. What's the matter?"

"I'll tell you what's the matter. Bunch of men burned up Al's lunch wagon last night. They jumped on Al' an' broke his arm an' six ribs. They burned his lunch wagon right down."

"Jesus!" Mac said. "I didn't think they'd do that."

"You didn't think, but they did it just the same."

"Where's Al now, Mr. Anderson?"

"He's over to the house. I had to bring him out from the hospital."

"I'll get the doctor. We'll go over and see him."

"Eighteen hundred dollars!" the old man cried. "He got some of it together, and I loaned him some, and then along you come. Now he hasn't got a thing."

"I'm awful sorry," Mac said.

"Sure, you're sorry. That don't unburn Al's wagon. That

don't mend his arm and his ribs. And what you doing to protect me? They'll burn my house next."

"We'll put a guard around your house."

"Guard, hell. What good's this bunch of bums? I wish I never let you on the place. You'll ruin me." His voice had risen to a high squeak. His old eyes were watering. "You just played hell, that's what you did. That's what we get for mixing up with a bunch of damn radicals."

Mac tried to soothe him. "Let's go over and see Al," he suggested. "Al's a swell guy. I want to see him."

"Well, he's all busted up. They kicked 'im in the head, too."

Mac edged him slowly away, for the men were beginning to move in, toward the shrill voice. "What you blaming us for?" he said. "We didn't do it. It was those nice neighbors of yours."

"Yes, but it wouldn't of happened if we didn't get mixed up with you."

Mac turned angrily on him. "Listen, mister, we know you got a sock in the teeth; little guys like you and me get it all the time. We're tryin' to make it so guys like you won't get it."

"That wagon cost eighteen hundred dollars. Why, man, I can't go in town without the kids throw rocks at me. You ruined us, that's what you did."

Mac asked, "How's Al feel about it?"

"I think Al's red as hell himself. Only people he's sore at are the men that did it."

"Al's got a good head," Mac said. "Al sees the whole thing. You would of been out on your can anyway. Now, if you get bounced, you got a big bunch of men in back of you. These men aren't going to forget what you're doing for 'em. And we'll put a guard around your house tonight. I'll have the doctor come over pretty soon and look at Al."

The old man turned tiredly, and walked away.

Smoke from the rusty stoves hung low over the camp. The men had begun to move in toward the smell of frying pork. Mac looked after the retreating figure of Anderson. "How's it feel to be a Party man now, Jim? It's swell when you read about it—romantic. Ladies like to get up and squawk about the 'boss class' and the 'downtrodden working man.' It's a heavy weight, Jim. That poor guy. The lunch wagon looks bigger than the world to him. I feel responsible for that. Hell," Mac continued. "I thought I brought you out here to teach you, to give you confidence; and here I spend my time belly-aching. I thought I was going to bolster you up, and instead—oh, what the hell! It's awful hard to keep your eyes on the big issue. Why the devil don't you say something?"

"You don't give me a chance."

"I guess I don't. Say something now! All I can think of is that poor little Joy shot up. He didn't have much sense, but he wasn't afraid of anything."

"He was a nice little guy," Jim said.

" 'Member what he said? Nobody was going to make him stop calling sons-of-bitches, 'sons-of-bitches.' I wish I didn't get this lost feeling sometimes, Jim."

"A little fried pork might help."

"By God, that's right. I didn't have much this morning. Let's go over."

A long delivery wagon drove up the road and stopped in front of the line of cars. From the seat a fussy little man stepped down and walked into the camp. "Who's in charge here?" he demanded of Mac.

"Dakin. He's over in that big tent."

"Well, I'm the coroner. I want that corpse."

"Where's your bodyguard?" Mac asked.

The little man puffed at him. "What do I want with a bodyguard? I'm the coroner. Where's that corpse?"

"In the big tent over there. It's all ready for you."

"Well, why didn't you say so?" He went puffing away like a small engine.

Mac sighed. "Thank God we don't have many like him to fight," he said. "That little guy's got guts. Came out all alone. He's kind of like Joy, himself." They walked on toward the stoves. Two men passed, carrying the body of Joy between them, and the coroner walked fussily along behind.

Men were walking away from the stoves with pieces of greasy fried pork in their hands. They wiped their lips with their sleeves. The tops of the stoves were covered with little slabs of hissing meat. "God, that smells good," said Mac. "Let's get some. I'm hungry as hell." The cooks handed out ill-cut, half-cooked pieces of pork to them, and they strolled away, gnawing at the soft meat. "Only eat the outside," Mac said. "Doc shouldn't let the men eat raw pork. They'll all be sick."

"They got too hungry to wait," said Jim.

10

An apathy had fallen on the men. They sat staring in front of them. They seemed not to have the energy to talk, and among them the bedraggled, discontented women sat. They were listless and stale. They gnawed thoughtfully at their meat, and when it was finished, wiped their hands on their clothes. The air was full of their apathy, and full of their discontent.

Mac, walking through the camp with Jim, grew discontented, too. "They ought to be doing something," Mac complained. "I don't care what it is. We can't let 'em sit around like this. Our strike'll go right out from under us. Christ, what's the matter with 'em? They had a man killed this morning; that ought to keep 'em going. Now it's just after noon, and they're slumped already. We got to get them working at something. Look at their eyes, Jim."

"They're not looking at anything—they're just staring."

"Yeah, they're thinking of themselves. Every man there is thinkin' how hurt he is, or how much money he made during the war. Just like Anderson. They're falling apart."

"Well, let's do something. Let's make them move. What is there to do?"

"I don't know. If we could make 'em dig a hole, it'd be as good as anything else. If we can just get 'em all pushing on something, or lifting something, or all walking in one direction—doesn't matter a hell of a lot. They'll start fighting each other if we don't move 'em. They'll begin to get mean, pretty soon."

London, hurrying past, caught the last words. "Who's goin' to get mean?"

Mac turned around. "Hello, London. We been talkin' about these here guys. They're all fallin' to pieces."

"I know it. I been around with these stiffs long enough to tell."

"Well, I just said they'd start fightin', if we didn't put 'em to work."

"They already did. That bunch we left in camp this morning

had a fuss. One of the guys tried to make another guy's woman. An' the first guy come in an' stuck him with a pair of scissors. Doc fixed him up. He like to bled to death, I guess."

"You see, Jim? I told you. Listen, London, Dakin's sore at me. He don't want to listen to nothing I tell him, but he'll listen to you. We got to move these guys before they get into trouble. Make 'em march in a circle—make 'em dig a hole and then fill it up. It don't make no difference."

"I know it. Well, how about picketin'?"

"Swell, but I don't think there's much work goin' on yet."

"What do we care, if it moves the guys off their ass."

"You got a head, London. See if you can get Dakin to send 'em out, about fifty in a bunch, out in different directions. Let 'em keep to the roads, and if they see any apple pickin', let 'em break it up."

"Sure I will," London said, and he turned and walked toward Dakin's brown tent.

Jim began, "Mac, you said I could go out with the pickets."

"Well, I'd rather have you with me."

"I want to get into it, Mac."

"O.K., go with one of the bunches, then. But stick close to them, Jim. They got our number here. You know that. Don't let 'em pick you off."

They saw Dakin and London come out of the tent. London talked rapidly. Mac said, "You know, I think we made a mistake about putting Dakin in. He's too tied up with his truck, and his tent, and his kids. He's too careful. London'ud have been the best man. London hasn't got anything to lose. I wonder if we could get the guys to kick Dakin out and put London in. I think the guys like London better. Dakin's got too much property. Did you see that folding stove of his? He don't even eat with the guys. Maybe we better start working and see if we can't get London in. I thought Dakin was cool, but he's too damn cool. We need somebody that can work the guys up a little."

Jim said, "Come on, Dakin's making up the pickets now."

Jim joined a picket group of about fifty men. They moved off along the road in a direction away from town. Almost as soon as they started the apathy dropped away. The straggling band walked quickly along.

The lean-faced Sam was in charge of it, and he instructed the men as he walked along. "Pick up rocks," he said. "Get a lot of good rocks in your pocket. And keep lookin' down the rows."

For a distance the orchards were deserted. The men began to sing tunelessly,

> "It was Christmas on the Island,
> "All the convicts they were there——"

They scuffed their feet in time. Across the intersecting road they marched, and a cloud of grey dust followed them. "Like France," a man said. "If it was all mud, it's just like France."

"Hell, you wasn't in France."

"I was so. I was five months in France."

"You don't walk like no soldier."

"I don't want to walk like no soldier. I walked like a soldier enough. I got schrap' in me, that's what I got."

"Where's them scabs?"

"Looks like we got 'em tied up. I don't see nobody workin'. We got this strike tied up already."

Sam said, "Sure, you got it win, fella. Just set on your can and win it, didn't you? Don't be a damn fool."

"Well, we sure scared hell out of the cops this mornin'. You don't see no cops around, do you?"

Sam said, "You'll see plenty before you get out of this, fella. You're just like all the stiffs in the world. You're king of hell, now. In a minute you'll start belly-achin', an' the *next* thing, you'll sneak out." An angry chorus broke on him.

"You think so, smart guy? Well, just show us somethin' to do."

"You got no call to be talkin' like that. What the hell'd you ever do?"

Sam spat in the road. "I'll tell you what I done. I was in 'Frisco on Bloody Thursday. I smacked a cop right off a horse. I was one of the guys that went in and got them night sticks from a carpenters' shop that the cops was gettin' made. Got one of 'em right now, for a souvenir."

"Tha's a damn lie. You ain't no longshoreman; you're a lousy fruit tramp."

"Sure I'm a fruit tramp. Know why? 'Cause I'm blacklisted with every shippin' company in the whole damn country, that's why." He spoke with pride. A silence met his assertion. He went on, "I seen more trouble than you can-heat bindle-stiffs ever seen." His contempt subjugated them. "Now keep your eyes down them rows, and cut out all this talk." They marched along a while.

"Look. There's boxes."

"Where?"

"Way to hell an' gone down that row."

Jim looked in the pointed direction. "There's guys down there," he cried.

A man said, "Come on, longshoreman, let's see you go."

Sam stood still in the road. "You guys takin' orders?" he demanded.

"Sure, we'll take 'em if they're any damn good."

"All right, then. Keep in hand. I don't want no rush at first, and then you guys runnin' like hell when anythin' busts. Come on, stick together."

They turned off the road and crossed a deep irrigation ditch, and they marched down the row between the big trees. As they approached the pile of boxes men began to drop out of the trees and to gather in a nervous group.

A checker stood by the box pile. As the pickets approached he took a double-barreled shot-gun from a box and advanced toward them a few steps. "Do you men want to go to work?" he shouted.

A chorus of derisive yells answered him. One man put his forefingers in his mouth and whistled piercingly.

"You get off this land," the checker said. "You've got no right on this land at all."

The strikers marched slowly on. The checker backed up to the box pile, where his pickers shifted nervously, and watched with frightened faces.

Sam said, over his shoulder, "All right. You guys stop here." He stepped forward alone a few paces. "Listen, you workers," he said. "Come over to our side. Don't go knifin' us guys in the back. Come on and join up with us."

The checker answered, "You take those men off this land or I'll have the whole bunch of you run in."

The derisive yell began again, and the shrill whistling. Sam turned angrily. "Shut up, you crazy bastards. Lay off the music."

The pickers looked about for a retreat. The checker reassured them. "Don't let him scare you, men. You've got a right to work if you want to."

Sam called again, "Listen, guys, we're givin' you this chance to come along with us."

"Don't let him bully you," the checker cried. His voice was rising. "They can't tell a man what he's got to do."

The pickers stood still. "You comin'?" Sam demanded. They didn't answer. Sam began to move slowly toward them.

The checker stepped forward. "There's a buckshot in this gun. I'll shoot you if you don't get off."

Sam spoke softly as he moved. "You ain't shootin' nobody, fella. You might get one of us, and the rest'd slaughter you." His voice was low and passionless. His men moved along, ten feet behind him. He stopped, directly in front of the checker. The quivering gun pointed at his chest. "We just want to talk," he said, and with one movement he stooped and dived, like a football tackle, and clipped the feet from under the checker. The gun exploded, and dug a pit in the ground. Sam spun over and drove his knees between the legs of the checker. Then he jumped up, leaving the man, writhing and crying hoarsely, on the ground. For a second both the pickers and the strikers had stood still. Too late the pickers turned to run. Men swarmed on them, cursing in their throats. The pickers fought for a moment, and then went down.

Jim stood a little apart; he saw a picker wriggle free and start to run. He picked up a heavy clod and hurled it at the man, struck him in the small of the back, and brought him down. The group surrounded the fallen man, feet working, kicking and stamping; and the picker screamed from the ground. Jim looked coldly at the checker. His face was white with agony and wet with the perspiration of pain.

Sam broke free and leaped at the kicking, stamping men. "Lay off, God-damn you, lay off," he yelled at them; and still they kicked, growling in their throats. Their lips were wet with saliva. Sam picked an apple box from the pile and smashed it over a head. "Don't kill 'em," he shouted. "Don't kill 'em."

The fury departed as quickly as it had come. They stood away from the victims. They panted heavily. Jim looked without emotion at the ten moaning men on the ground, their faces kicked shapeless. Here a lip was torn away, exposing bloody teeth and gums; one man cried like a child because his arm was bent sharply backward, broken at the elbow. Now that the fury was past, the strikers were sick, poisoned by the flow from their own anger glands. They were weak; one man held his head between his hands as though it ached terribly.

Suddenly a man went spinning around and around, croaking. A rifle-crack sounded from down the row. Five men came running along, stopping to fire now and then. The strikers broke and ran, dodging among the trees to be out of the line of fire.

Jim ran with them. He was crying to himself, "Can't stand fire. We can't stand fire." The tears blinded him. He felt a heavy blow on the shoulder and stumbled a little. The group reached the road and plunged on, looking back over their shoulders.

Sam was behind them, running beside Jim. "O.K.," he shouted. "They stopped." Still some of the men ran on in a blind panic, ran on and disappeared at the road intersection. Sam caught the rest. "Settle down," he shouted. "Settle down. Nobody's chasin' you." They came to a stop. They stood weakly at the side of the road. "How many'd they get?" Sam demanded.

The men looked at one another. Jim said, "I only saw one guy hit."

"O.K. He'll be all right, maybe. Got him in the chest." He looked more closely at Jim. "What's the matter with you, kid? You're bleedin'."

"Where?"

"All down your back."

"I ran into a limb, I guess."

"Limb, hell." Sam pulled the blue denim coat down from Jim's shoulder. "You got bored with a high-power. Can you move your arm?"

"Sure. It just feels numb."

"I guess it didn't get a bone. Shoulder muscle. Must of been a steel-jacket. You ain't even bleedin' much. Come on, guys, let's get back. There's goin' be cops thick as maggots around here."

They hurried along the road. Sam said, "If you get feelin' weak, I'll he'p you, kid."

"I'm all right. We couldn't take it, Sam."

Sam said bitterly, "We done noble when we was five to one; we made messes of them scabs."

Jim asked, "Did we kill any of 'em?"

"I don't think so. Some of 'em ain't ever goin' be the same again."

Jim said, "Jesus, it was pretty awful, wasn't it. Did you see that guy with his lip torn?"

"Hell, they'll sew his lip back on. We got to do it, kid. We just got to. If they won't come over, we just got to scare 'em."

"Oh. I know it," said Jim. "I'm not worrying about 'em."

Far ahead they heard a siren. Sam cried, "Jump for the ditch, you guys. Lie down in the ditch. Here comes the cops." He saw that they were all flat in a deep irrigation ditch along the road. The motorcycles roared by, and crossed the intersection, and an ambulance clanged after them. The men did not raise their heads until the motors had disappeared across the intersection. Sam jumped up. "Come on, now. We got to beat it fast."

They dog-trotted along the road. The sun was going down by now, and the road was in a blue evening shadow. A heavy cloud sailed like a ship toward the sun, and its dark edge reddened as it drew near. The men jumped for the ditch again when the ambulance came back. The motorcycles went by more slowly this time, the policemen looking down the rows as they went, but they did not search the ditch.

As the evening fell the pickets came back to the camp. Jim's legs were wobbling under him. His shoulder stung deeply, for the nerves were awakening after being stunned by the high-powered bullet. The men dispersed into the camp.

Mac walked over toward Jim, and when he saw how white Jim was, he broke into a trot. "What's the matter with you, Jim? Did you get hurt?"

"No, not much. Sam says I'm shot in the shoulder. I can't see it. It doesn't hurt much."

Mac's face turned red. "By God, I knew I shouldn't let you go."

"Why not? I'm no pansy."

"Maybe you aren't one, but you'll be pushing 'em up pretty soon, if I don't watch you. Come on, let Doc look at you. He was right here a minute ago. There he goes. Hi, Doc!" They took Jim into a white tent. "This one just came in. Doc's going to use it for a hospital," said Mac.

The autumn darkness was falling quickly, and the evening was hastened by the big black cloud, which spread out over the western sky. Mac held a lantern while Burton pulled Jim's shirt free of his shoulder. He washed the wound carefully, with hot, sterile water. "Lucky boy," he said. "A lead slug would have smashed your shoulder to pieces. You've just got a little auger-hole through the muscle. It'll be stiff for a while. Bullet went right on through." His deft hands cleansed the wound with a probe, applied a dressing and taped it on. "You'll be all right," he said. "Take it easy for a couple of days. Mac, I'm going over to see Al Anderson later. Want to come?"

"Sure, I'll be with you. I want to get Jim a cup of coffee." He shoved a tin can of black, ugly coffee in Jim's hand. "Come on, sit down," he said. He shoved a box out and sat Jim down on it, and reclined on the ground beside him. "What happened, Jim?"

"We went in after some scabs. Mac, our guys just kicked hell out of 'em. Kicked 'em in the heads."

Mac said softly, "I know, Jim. It's terrible, but it's the only thing to do if they won't come over. We've got to do it. It's not nice to see a sheep killed, either, but we've got to have mutton. What happened then?"

"Well, five men came running and shooting. Our guys ran like rabbits. They couldn't take it."

"Well, why should they, Jim, with nothing to fight with but their bare hands?"

"I hardly knew it when I got hit. One of our guys went down. I don't know whether he was killed or not."

"Nice party," Mac said. "The other crowds brought in about thirty scabs. They didn't have any trouble; just called 'em out, and they came along." He reached up and touched Jim's leg for a moment. "How's the shoulder feel now?"

"Hurts a little, not much."

"Oh say, Jim. Looks like we're goin' to have a new boss."

"Kicked Dakin out, you mean?"

"No, but he's out, all right. Dick sent word he had a load of blankets. Well, Dakin took six men and went in with his shiny truck. One of the six guys got away and came back and told how it was. They got their load and started back. A little way this side of town they ran over a bunch of nails, stopped to change a tire. Well, then a dozen men with guns jumped out and held them up. Well, six of them stand the guys up while they wreck Dakin's truck, smash the crank-case and set it on fire. Dakin stands there with a gun on him. He turns white, and then he turns blue. Then he lets out a howl like a coyote and starts for 'em. They shoot him in the leg, but that don't stop him. When he can't run any more, he crawls for 'em, slavering around the mouth like a mad dog—just nuts, he just went *nuts!* I guess he loved that truck better'n anything in the world. The guy that came back said it was just awful, the way he crawled for 'em. Tried to bite 'em. He was snarling—like a mad dog. Well, then, some traffic cops come along, and the vigilante boys fade. The cops pick Dakin up and take him in. The guy that came in and told about it was up a gum tree watching. He says Dakin bit a cop on the hand, and they had to stick a screw-driver back in his teeth to pry 'im loose. And that's the guy I said wouldn't lose his temper. He's in the can now. I guess the guys'll elect London in his place."

Jim said, "Well he sure looked cool enough to me. I'm glad I didn't lay a finger on his truck."

Mac heaped a little pile of dirt on the floor with his hand, and moulded it round, and patted a little flat top on it. "I'm kind of worried, Jim. Dick hasn't sent any food today. We haven't heard anything from him except those blankets. They're cooking up all the rest of the beans with pork bones, but that's all there is, except some mush. That's all there is for tomorrow."

"Do you suppose they knocked Dick off?"

Mac patted his mound flatter. "Dick's clever as a weasel. I don't think they could catch him. I don't know what's the matter. We've got to get food in. The minute the guys get hungry, they're through, I'm afraid."

"Maybe he didn't collect anything. He sent that pig this morning."

"Sure, and the pig's in the beans now. Dick knows how much it takes to feed these guys. Dick must have organized the sympathizers by now."

Jim asked, "How do the guys feel now?"

"Oh, they're better. They got a shot of life, this afternoon. I know it's quick, but we got to have that funeral tomorrow. That ought to steam 'em up for a while." He looked out the tent entrance. "God, look at that cloud!" He stepped outside and looked overhead. The sky was nearly dark with the thick black cloud. A skirmishing wind sprang up, blowing the dust along, blowing the smoke from the fires, flapping the canvases, whisking the apple trees that surrounded the camp. "That looks like a rain cloud," Mac said. "Lord, I hope it doesn't rain. It'll drown this bunch like rats."

Jim said, "You worry too much about what might happen, Mac. All the time you're worrying. These guys are used to the open. A little rain won't hurt 'em. You fidget all the time."

Mac sat down on the floor again. "Maybe that's right, Jim. I get so scared the strike'll crack, maybe I imagine things. I've been in so many strikes that got busted, Jim."

"Yeah, but what do you care if it's busted? It solidifies the unrest, you said so yourself."

"Sure, I know. I s'pose it wouldn't matter if the strike broke right now. The guys won't ever forget how Joy got killed; and they won't ever forget about Dakin's truck."

"You're getting just like an old woman, Mac."

"Well, it's my strike—I mean, I feel like it's mine. I don't want to see it go under now."

"Well, it won't, Mac."

"Huh? What do you know about it?"

"Well, I was thinkin' this morning. Ever read much history, Mac?"

"A little, in school. Why?"

"Well, you remember how the Greeks won the battle of Salamis?"

"Maybe I knew. I don't remember."

"Well, here's the Greeks with some ships, all boxed in a harbor. They want to run away to beat hell. And here's a whole slough of Persian ships out in front. Well, the Greek admiral knows his guys are going to run away, so he sends word to the enemy to box 'em in tight. Next morning the Greeks see they can't run away; they've got to fight to get away, and they win. They beat hell out of the Persian fleet." Jim fell silent.

Men began moving past, toward the stoves. Mac patted the ground hard with his open hand. "I see what you mean, Jim," he said. "We don't need it now, but if we do, by God, it's an idea, Jim," he said plaintively. "I bring you out here to teach you things, and right away you start teaching me things."

"Nuts," said Jim.

"O.K., then, nuts. I wonder how men know when food's ready. Kind of mind reading, I guess. Or maybe they've got that same kind of a sense that vultures have. Look, there they go. Come on, Jim. Let's eat."

II

THEY had beans, swimming in pork fat to eat. Mac and Jim brought their cans from the tent and stood in line until some of the mess was dumped into each of their cans. They walked away. Jim took a little wooden paddle from his pocket and tasted the beans. "Mac," he said, "I can't eat it."

"Used to better things, huh? You've got to eat it." He tasted his own, and immediately dumped the can on the ground. "Don't eat it, Jim. It'll make you sick, beans and grease! The guys'll raise hell about this."

They looked at the men sitting in front of the tents, trying to eat their food. The storm cloud spread over the sky and swallowed the new stars. Mac said, "Somebody'll try to kill the cooks, I guess. Let's go over to London's tent."

"I don't see Dakin's tent, Mac."

"No, Mrs. Dakin took it down. She went into town and took it along with her. Funny guy, Dakin; he'll have money before he's through. Let's find London."

They walked down the line to the grey tent of London. A light shone through the canvas. Mac raised the flap. Inside, London sat on a box, holding an open can of sardines in his hand. The dark girl, Lisa, crouched on the floor mattress nursing the baby. She drew a piece of blanket about the baby and the exposed breast as the men entered. She smiled quickly at them, and then looked down at the baby again.

"Just in time for dinner!" Mac said.

London looked embarrassed. "I had a little stuff left over."

"You tasted that mess out there?"

"Yeah."

"Well, I hope the other guys got some stuff left over. We got to do better than that, or them guys'll run out on us."

"Food kind of stopped comin' in," said London. "I got another can of sardines. You guys like to have it?"

"Damn right." Mac took the proffered can greedily, and twisted the key to open it. "Get out your knife, Jim. We'll split this."

"How's your arm?" London asked.

"Getting stiff," said Jim.

Outside the tent a voice said, "That's the place, that one with the light." The flap raised and Dick entered. His hair was combed neatly. He held a grey cap in his hand. His grey suit was clean, but unpressed. Only his dusty, unpolished shoes showed that he had been walking through the country. He stood in the tent entrance, looking about. "Hi, Mac. Hello, Jim," and to the girl, "Hi ya, baby?" Her eyes brightened. A spot of red came into her cheeks. She drew the piece of blanket coquettishly down around her shoulders.

Mac waved his hand. "This here's London—this here's Dick." Dick made a half salute. "H'ya?" he said. "Look, Mac, these babies in town have been taking lessons."

"What you mean? What you doin' out here anyways?"

Dick took a newspaper from his outside pocket and handed it over. Mac opened it and London and Jim looked over his shoulder. "Come out before noon," said Dick.

Mac exclaimed, "Son-of-a-bitch!" The paper carried a headline, "Supervisors vote to feed strikers. At a public meeting last night the Board of Supervisors voted unanimously to feed the men now striking against the apple growers."

"They sure took lessons," Mac said. "Did it start workin', yet, Dick?"

"Hell, yes."

London broke in, "I don't see no reason to kick. If they want to send out ham and eggs, it's O.K. by me."

"Sure," Mac said sarcastically, "*if* they want to. This paper don't tell about the other meeting right afterwards when they repealed the vote."

"What's the gag?" London demanded. "What the hell's it all about?"

"Listen, London," Mac said. "This here's an old one, but it works. Here's Dick got the sympathizers lined up. We got food and blankets and money comin'. Well, then *this* comes out. Dick goes the round. The sympathizers say, 'What the hell? The county's feeding 'em.' 'Th' hell it is,' says Dick. And the guy says, 'I seen it in the paper. It says they're sendin' food to you. What you gettin' out of this?' That's how it works, London. Did you see any county food come in to-day?"

"No——"

"Well, Dick couldn't get a rise either. Now you know. They figure to starve us out. And by God they can do it, too, if we don't get help." He turned to Dick. "You was goin' good."

"Sure," Dick agreed. "It was a push-over. Take me some time to work it all up again. I want a paper from this guy here saying you aren't getting any food. I want it signed by the strike chairman."

"O.K.," said London.

"Lots of sympathizers in Torgas," Dick went on. " 'Course the joint's organized by the Growers' Association, so the whole bunch is underground like a flock o' gophers. But the stuff is there, if I can get to it."

"You were doin' swell till this busted," Mac said.

"Sure I was. I had some trouble with one old dame. She wanted to help the cause somethin' terrible."

Mac laughed. "I never knew no maiden modesty to keep you out of the feed bag. S'pose she *did* want to give her all to the cause?"

Dick shuddered. "Her all was sixteen axe-handles acrost," he said.

"Well, we'll get your paper for you, and then I want you to get the hell out of here. They ain't got you spotted yet, have they?"

"I don't know," said Dick. "I kind of think they have. I wrote in for Bob Schwartz to come down. I got a feeling I'm going to get vagged pretty soon. Bob can take over then."

London rooted in a box and brought out a tablet of paper and a pencil. Mac took them from him and wrote out the statement. "You write nice," London said admiringly.

"Huh? Oh, sure. Can I sign it for you, London?"

"Sure. Go ahead."

"Hell," said Dick. "I could of done that myself." He took the paper and folded it carefully. "Oh, say, Mac. I heard about one of the guys gettin' bumped."

"Didn't you know, Dick? It was Joy."

"Th' hell!"

"Sure, he come down with a bunch of scabs. He was tryin' to bring 'em over when he got it."

"Poor bastard."

"Got him quick. He didn't suffer more'n a minute."

Dick sighed. "Well, it was in the books for Joy. He was sure to get it sooner or later. Going to have a funeral?"

"Tomorrow."

"All the guys goin' to march in it?"

Mac looked at London. "Sure they are," he said. "Maybe we can drag public sympathy our way."

"Well, Joy would like that," Dick said. "Nothing he'd like better. Too bad he can't see it. Well, so long. I got to go." He turned to leave the tent. Lisa raised her eyes. "Bye, baby. See you sometime," said Dick. The spots of color came into her cheeks again. Her lips parted a little and, when the tent flaps dropped behind Dick, her eyes remained there for some time.

Mac said, "Jesus, they got an organization here. Dick's a good man. If he can't get stuff to eat, it ain't to be got."

Jim asked, "How about that platform for the speech?"

Mac turned to London, "Yeah, did you get at it, London?"

"The guys'll put it up tomorrow mornin'. Couldn't get nothing but some old fence posts to make it. Have to be just a little one."

"Don't matter," Mac said, "just as long as it's high enough so every guy here can see Joy, that's enough."

A worried look came on London's face. "What t'hell am I goin' to say to the guys? You said I ought to make a speech."

"You'll get steamed up enough," said Mac. "Tell 'em this little guy died for 'em. And if he could do that they can at least fight for themselves."

"I never made no speeches much," London complained.

"Well, don't make a speech. Just talk to the guys. You done that often enough. Just tell 'em. That's better'n a speech, anyway."

"Oh. Like that. O.K."

Mac turned to the girl. "How's the kid?"

She blushed and pulled the blanket closer over her shoulders. Her lashes shadowed her cheeks. "Pretty good," she whispered. "He don't cry none."

The tent-flap jerked open and the doctor entered, his quick, brusque movements at variance with the sad, dog-like eyes. "I'm going over to see young Anderson, Mac," he said. "Want to come?"

"Sure I do, Doc." And to London, "Did you send the guys over to guard Anderson's place?"

"Yeah. They didn't want to go none, but I sent 'em."

"All right. Let's go, Doc. Come on, Jim, if you can make it."

"I feel all right," said Jim.

Burton looked steadily at him. "You should be in bed."

Mac chuckled. "I'm scared to leave him. He raises hell when I leave him alone for a minute. See you later, London."

Outside the darkness was thick. The big cloud had spread until it covered the sky, and all the stars were gone. A muffled quietness lay on the camp. Those men who sat around a few little fires spoke softly. The air was still and warm and damp. Doc and Mac and Jim picked their way carefully out of the camp and into the blackness that surrounded it. "I'm afraid it's going to rain," Mac said. "We'll have one hell of a time with the guys when they get wet. It's worse than gun-fire for taking the hearts out of men. Most of those tents leak, I guess."

"Of course they do," said Burton.

They reached the line of the orchard and walked down between two rows of trees. And it was so dark that they put their hands out in front of them.

"How do you like your strike now?" Doc asked.

"Not so good. They've got this valley organized like Italy. Food supply's cut off now. We're sunk if we can't get some food. And if it rains good and hard tonight the men'll be sneaking out on us. They just won't take it, I tell you. It's a funny thing, Doc. You don't believe in the cause, and you'll probably be the last man to stick. I don't get you at all."

"I don't get myself," Doc said softly. "I don't believe in the cause, but I believe in men."

"What do you mean?"

"I don't know. I guess I just believe they're men, and not animals. Maybe if I went into a kennel and the dogs were hungry and sick and dirty, and maybe if I could help those dogs, I would. Wouldn't be their fault they were that way. You couldn't say, 'Those dogs are that way because they haven't any ambition. They don't save their bones. Dogs always are that way.' No, you'd try to clean them up and feed them. I guess that's the way it is with me. I have some skill in helping men, and when I see some who need help, I just do it. I don't think about it much. If a painter saw a piece of canvas, and he had colors, well, he'd want to paint on it. He wouldn't figure why he wanted to."

"Sure, I get you. In one way it seems cold-blooded, standing aside and looking down on men like that, and never getting yourself mixed up with them; but another way, Doc, it seems fine as the devil, and clean."

"Oh, Mac, I'm about out of disinfectant. You'll get no more fine smell if I don't get some more carbolic."

"I'll see what I can do," said Mac.

A hundred yards away a yellow light was shining. "Isn't that Anderson's house?" Jim asked.

"I guess it is. We ought to pick up a guard pretty soon." They walked on toward the light, and they were not challenged. They came to the gate of the house-yard without being challenged. Mac said, "God-damn it, where *are* the guys London sent over? Go on in, Doc. I'm going to see if I can't find 'em." Burton walked up the path and into the lighted kitchen. Mac and Jim went toward the barn, and inside the barn they found the men, lying down in the low bed of hay smoking cigarettes. A kerosene lamp hung on a hook on the wall and threw a yellow light on the line of empty stalls and on the great pile of boxed apples—Anderson's crop, waiting to be moved.

Mac spluttered with anger, but he quickly controlled himself, and when he spoke his voice was soft and friendly. "Listen, you guys," he argued. "This isn't any joke. We got word the damn vigilantes is goin' to try something on Anderson to get back at him for lettin' us stay on his place. S'pose he never let us stay? They'd be kickin' us all over hell by now. Anderson's a nice guy. We hadn't ought to let nobody hurt him."

"There ain't nobody around," one of the men protested. "Jesus, mister, we can't hang around all night. We was out picketin' all afternoon."

"Go on, then," Mac cried angrily. "Let 'em raid this place. Then Anderson'll kick us off. Then where in hell would we be?"

"We could jungle up, down by the river, mister."

"You *think* you could. They'd run you over the county line so quick your ass'd smoke, and you know it!"

One of the men got slowly to his feet. "The guy's right," he said. "We better drag it out of here. My old woman's in the camp. I don't want to have her get in no trouble."

"Well, put out a line," Mac suggested. "Don't let nobody through. You know what they done to Anderson's boy— burned his lunch wagon, kicked hell out of Al."

"Al put out a nice stew," said one of the men. They stood up tiredly. When they were all out of the barn Mac blew out the lantern. "Vigilantes like to shoot at a light," he explained. "They take big chances like that. We better have Anderson pull down his curtains, too."

The guards filed off into the darkness. Jim asked, "You think they'll keep watch now, Mac?" he asked.

"I wish I thought so. I think they'll be back in that barn in about ten minutes. In the army they can shoot a guy if he goes to sleep. We can't do a thing but talk. God, I get sick of this helplessness! If we could only use guns! If we could only use punishment to keep discipline!" The sound of the guards' footsteps died away in the darkness. Mac said, "I'll rouse 'em out once more before we go back." They walked up on the kitchen porch and knocked on the door. Barking and growling dogs answered them. They could hear the dogs leaping around inside the house, and Anderson quieting them. The door opened a crack. "It's us, Mr. Anderson."

"Come on in," he said sullenly.

The pointers weaved about, whipping their thin, hard tails and whining with pleasure. Mac leaned over and patted each one and pulled the leathers. "You ought to leave the dogs outside, Mr. Anderson, to watch the place," he said. "It's so dark the guards can't see anything. But the dogs could smell anybody coming through."

Al lay on a cot by the stove. He looked pale and weak. He seemed to have grown thin, for the flesh on his jowls was loose. He lay flat on his back, and one arm was strapped down in front of him. Doc sat in a chair beside the cot.

"Hello, Al," Mac said quietly. "How's she go, boy?"

The eyes brightened. "O.K.," said Al. "It hurts quite a lot. Doc says it'll keep me down some time." Mac leaned over the cot and picked up Al's good hand. "Not too hard," Al said quickly. "There's busted ribs on that side."

Anderson stood by; his eyes were burning. "Now you see," he said. "You see what comes of it. Lunch wagon burned, Al hurt, now you see."

"Oh, for Christ's sake, Dad," Al said weakly. "Don't start that again. They call you Mac, don't they?"

"Right."

"Well, look, Mac. D'you think I could get into the Party?"

"You mean you want to go in active work?"

"Yeah. Think I could get in?"

"I think so—" Mac said slowly. "I'll give you an application card. What you want to come in for, Al?"

The heavy face twisted in a grimace. Al swung his head back and forth. "I been thinkin'," he said. "Ever since they beat me up I been thinkin'. I can't get those guys outa my head—my little wagon all burned up, an' them jumpin' on me with their feet; and two cops down on the corner watchin', and not doin' a thing! I can't get that outa my head."

"And so you want to join up with us, huh, Al?"

"I want to be against 'em," Al cried. "I want to be fightin' 'em all my life. I want to be on the other side."

"They'll just beat you up worse, Al. I'm tellin' you straight. They'll knock hell out of you."

"Well, I won't care then, because I'll be fightin' 'em, see? But there I was, just runnin' a little lunch wagon, an' givin' bums a handout now an' then——" His voice choked and tears squeezed out of his eyes.

Dr. Burton touched him gently on the cheek. "Don't talk any more, Al."

"I'll see you get an application card," Mac said. And he continued, "By God, it's funny. Guy after guy gets knocked into our side by a cop's night stick. Every time they maul hell out of a bunch of men, we get a flock of applications. Why, there's a Red Squad cop in Los Angeles that sends us more members than a dozen of our organizers. An' the damn fools haven't got sense enough to realize it. O.K., Al. You'll get your application. I don't know whether it'll go through, but it will if I can push it through." He patted Al's good arm. "I hope it goes through. You're a good guy, Al. Don't blame me for your wagon."

"I don't, Mac. I know who to blame."

Burton said, "Take it easy, Al. Just rest; you need it."

Anderson had been fidgeting about the room. The dogs circled him endlessly, putting up their liver-colored noses and sniffing, waving their stiff tails like little whips. "Well, I hope you're satisfied," he said helplessly. "You break up everything I've got. You even take Al away. I hope you take good joy of it."

Jim broke in, "Don't worry, Mr. Anderson. There's guards around your house. You're the only man in the Valley that has his apples picked."

Mac asked, "When are you going to move your apples?"

"Day after tomorrow."

"Well, do you want some guards for the trucks?"

"I don't know," Anderson said uneasily.

"I guess we better put guards on the trucks," said Mac, "just in case anybody tried to dump your crop. We'll get going now. Good night, Mr. Anderson. 'Night, Al. In one way I'm glad it happened."

Al smiled. " 'Night, you guys. Don't forget that card, Mac."

"I won't. Better pull your curtains down, Mr. Anderson. I don't think they'll shoot through your windows, but they might; they've done it before, other places."

The door closed instantly behind them. The lighted spot on the ground, from the window, shrank to darkness as the curtain was pulled down. Mac felt his way to the gate, and when they were out, shut it after them. "Wait here a minute," he said. "I'm going to look at those guards again." He stepped away into the darkness.

Jim stood beside the doctor. "Better take good care of that shoulder," Burton advised. "It might cause you some trouble later."

"I don't care about it, Doc. It seems good to have it."

"Yes, I thought it might be like that."

"Like what?"

"I mean you've got something in your eyes, Jim, something religious. I've seen it in you boys before."

Jim flared, "Well, it isn't religious. I've got no use for religion."

"No, I guess you haven't. Don't let me bother you, Jim. Don't let me confuse you with terms. You're living the good life, whatever you want to call it."

"I'm happy," said Jim. "And happy for the first time. I'm full-up."

"I know. Don't let it die. It's the vision of Heaven."

"I don't believe in Heaven," Jim said. "I don't believe in religion."

"All right, I won't argue any more. I don't envy you as much as I might, Jim, because sometimes I love men as much as you do, maybe not in just the same way."

"Do you get that, Doc? Like that—like troops and troops marching into you? And you closing around them?"

"Yes, something like that. Particularly when they've done something stupid, when a man's made a mistake, and died for it. Yes, I get it, Jim—pretty often."

They heard Mac's voice, "Where are you guys? It's so damn dark."

"Over here." They joined him and all three moved along into the orchard, under the black trees.

"The guards weren't in the barn," said Mac. "They were out on watch. Maybe they're going to stick it."

Far down the road they heard the mutter of a truck coming toward them. "I feel sorry for Anderson," Burton said quietly. "Everything he respects, everything he's afraid of is turning against him. I wonder what he'll do. They'll drive him out of here, of course."

Mac said harshly, "We can't help it, Doc. He happens to be the one that's sacrificed for the men. Somebody has to break if the whole bunch is going to get out of the slaughter-house. We can't think about the hurts of one man. It's necessary, Doc."

"I wasn't questioning your motives, nor your ends. I was just sorry for the poor old man. His self-respect is down. That's a bitter thing to him, don't you think so, Mac?"

"I can't take time to think about the feelings of one man?" Mac said sharply. "I'm too busy with big bunches of men."

"It was different with the little fellow who was shot," Doc

went on musingly. "He liked what he did. He wouldn't have had it any other way."

"Doc, you're breakin' my heart," Mac said irritably. "Don't you get lost in a lot of sentimental foolishness. There's an end to be gained; it's a real end, hasn't anything to do with people losing respect. It's people getting bread into their guts. It's *real*, not any of your high-falutin' ideas. How's the old guy with the broken hip?"

"All right, then, change the subject. The old man's getting mean as a scorpion. Right at first he got a lot of attention, he got pretty proud for a while; and now he's mad because the men don't come and listen to him talk."

"I'll go in and see him in the morning," said Jim. "He was a kind of a nice old fellow."

Mac cried, "Listen! Didn't that truck stop?"

"I think it did. Sounded as though it stopped at the camp."

"I wonder what the hell. Come on, let's hurry. Look out for trees." They had gone only a little distance when the truck roared, its gears clashed, and it moved away again. Its sound softened into the distance until it merged with the quiet. "I hope nothing's wrong," said Mac.

They trotted out of the orchard and crossed the cleared space. The light still burned in London's tent, and a group of men moved about near it. Mac dashed up, threw up the tent-flap and went inside. On the ground lay a long, rough pine box. London sat on a box and stared morosely up at the newcomers. The girl seemed to cower down on her mattress, while London's dark-haired, pale son sat beside her and stroked her hair. London motioned to the box with his thumb. "What the hell 'm I goin' to do with it?" he asked. "It's scared this here girl half to death. I can't keep it in here."

"Joy?" Mac asked.

"Yeah. They just brang him."

Mac pulled his lip and studied the coffin. "We could put it outside, I guess. Or we can let your kids sleep in the hospital tent tonight and leave it here, that is, unless it scares you, London."

"It don't mean nothing to me," London protested. "It's just another stiff. I seen plenty in my time."

"Well, let's leave it here, then. Jim an' me'll stay here with it. The guy was a friend of ours." Behind him the doctor chuckled softly. Mac reddened and swung around. "S'pose you do win, Doc? What of it? I knew the little guy."

"I didn't say anything," Burton said.

London spoke softly to the girl, and to the dark boy, and in a moment they went out of the tent, she holding the shoulder blanket tight about herself and the baby.

Mac sat down on one end of the oblong box and rubbed the wood with his forefinger. The coarse pine grains wriggled like little rivers over the wood. Jim stood behind Mac and stared over his shoulder. London moved nervously about the tent, and his eyes avoided the coffin. Mac said, "Nice piece o' goods the county puts out."

"What you want for nothing?" London demanded.

"Well," Mac replied, "I don't want nothing for myself but a bonfire, just a fire to get rid of me, so I won't lie around." He stood up and felt in his jeans pocket and brought out a big knife. One of the blades had a screwdriver end. He fitted it to a screw in the coffin-lid and twisted.

London cried, "What do you want to open it for? That won't do no good. Leave him be."

"I want to see him," said Mac.

"What for? He's dead—he's a lump of dirt."

The doctor said softly, "Sometimes I think you realists are the most sentimental people in the world."

Mac snorted and laid the screw carefully on the ground. "If you think this is sentiment, you're nuts, Doc. I want to see if it'd be a good idea for the guys to look at him tomorrow. We got to shoot some juice into 'em some way. They're dyin' on their feet."

Burton said, "Fun with dead bodies, huh?"

Jim insisted earnestly, "We've got to use every means, Doc. We've got to use every weapon."

Mac looked up at him appreciatively. "That's the idea. That's the way it is. If Joy can do some work after he's dead, then he's got to do it. There's no such things as personal feelings in this crowd. Can't be. And there's no such things as good taste, don't you forget it."

London stood still, listening and nodding his big head slowly up and down. "You guys got it right," he agreed.

"Look at Dakin. He let his damn truck make him mad. I heard he comes up for trial tomorrow—for assault."

Mac quickly turned out the screws and laid them in a line on the ground. The lid was stuck. He kicked it loose with his heel.

Joy looked flat and small and painfully clean. He had on a clean blue shirt, and his oil soiled blue jeans. The arms were folded stiffly across the stomach. "All he got was a shot of formaldehyde," Mac said. A stubble was growing on Joy's cheeks, looking very dark against the grey, waxy skin. His face was composed and rested. The gnawing bitterness was gone from it.

"He looks quiet," Jim remarked.

"Yes," said Mac. "That's the trouble. It won't do no good to show him. He looks so comfortable all the guys'll want to get right in with him." The doctor moved close and looked down at the coffin for a moment, and then he walked to a box and sat down. His big, plaintive eyes fastened on Mac's face. Mac still stared at Joy. "He was such a good little guy," he said. "He didn't want nothing for himself. Y'see, he wasn't very bright. But some way he got it into his head something was wrong. He didn't see why food had to be dumped and left to rot when people were starving. Poor little fool, he could never understand that. And he got the notion he might help to stop it. I wonder how much he helped? It's awful hard to say. Maybe not at all—maybe a lot. You can't tell." Mac's voice had become unsteady. The doctor's eyes stayed on his face, and the doctor's mouth was smiling a curious half-sardonic, half-kindly smile.

Jim interposed, "Joy wasn't afraid of anything."

Mac picked up the coffin-lid and set it in place again. "I don't know why we say 'poor little guy'. He wasn't poor. He was greater than himself. He didn't know it—didn't care. But there was a kind of ecstasy in him all the time, even when they beat him. And Jim says it—he wasn't afraid." Mack picked up a screw, and stuck it through the hole and turned it down with his knife.

London said, "That sounds like a speech. Maybe you better give the speech. I don't know nothin' about talkin'. That was a pretty speech. It sounded nice."

Mac looked up guiltily and searched London for sarcasm, and found none. "That wasn't a speech," he said quietly. "I guess it could be, but it wasn't. It's like tellin' the guy he hasn't been wasted."

"Why don't you make the speech tomorrow? You can talk."

"Hell, no. You're the boss. The guys'd be sore if I sounded off. They expect you to do it."

"Well, what do I got to say?"

Mac drove the screws in, one after another. "Tell 'em the usual stuff. Tell 'em Joy died for 'em. Tell 'em he was tryin' to help 'em, and the best they can do for him is to help 'emselves by stickin' together, see?"

"Yeah, I get it."

Mac stood up and regarded the grained wood of the lid. "I hope somebody tries to stop us," he said. "I hope some of them damn vigilantes gets in our way. God, I hope they try to stop us paradin' through town."

"Yeah, I see," said London.

Jim's eyes glowed. He repeated, "I hope so."

"The guys'll want to fight," Mac continued. "They'll be all sore inside. They'll want to bust something. Them vigilantes ain't got much sense; I hope they're crazy enough to start something tomorrow."

Burton stood up wearily from his box and walked up to Mac. He touched him lightly on the shoulder. "Mac," he said, "you're the craziest mess of cruelty and hausfrau sentimentality, of clear vision and rose-colored glasses I ever saw. I don't know how you manage to be all of them at once."

"Nuts," said Mac.

The doctor yawned. "All right. We'll leave it at nuts. I'm going to bed. You know where to find me if you want me, only I hope you won't want me."

Mac looked quickly at the tent ceiling. Fat, lazy drops were falling on the canvas. One—two—three, and then a dozen, patting the tent with a soft drumming. Mac sighed. "I hoped it wouldn't. Now by morning the guys'll be drowned rats. They won't have no more spirit than a guinea pig."

"I'm still going to bed," the doctor said. He went out and dropped the flaps behind him.

Mac sat down heavily on the coffin. The drumming grew

quicker. Outside, the men began calling to one another, and their voices were blurred by the rain. "I don't suppose there's a tent in the camp that don't leak," said Mac. "Jesus, why can't we get a break without getting it cancelled out? Why do we always have to take it in the neck—always?"

Jim sat gingerly down on the long box beside him. "Don't worry about it, Mac. Sometimes, when a guy gets miserable enough, he'll fight all the harder. That's the way it was with me, Mac, when my mother was dying, and she wouldn't even speak to me. I just got so miserable I'd've taken any chance. Don't you worry about it."

Mac turned on him. "Catching me up again, are you? I'll get mad if you show me up too often. Go lie down on the girl's mattress there. You've got a bad arm. It must hurt by now."

"It burns some, all right."

"Well, lie down there. See if you can't get some sleep." Jim started to protest, and then he went to the mattress on the ground and stretched out on it. The wound throbbed down his arm and across his chest. He heard the rain increase until it swept on the canvas, like a broom. He heard the big drops falling inside the tent, and then, when a place leaked in the center of the tent, he heard the heavy drops splash on the coffin box.

Mac still sat beside it, holding his head in his arms. And London's eyes, like the sleepless eyes of a lynx, stared and stared at the lamp. The camp was quiet again, and the rain fell steadily, out of a windless sky. It was not very long before Jim fell into a burning sleep. The rain poured down hour after hour. On the tent-pole the lamplight yellowed and dropped to the wick. A blue flame sputtered for a while, and then went out.

To Jim it seemed that he awakened out of a box. One whole side of him was encased in painful stiffness. He opened his eyes and looked about the tent. A grey and listless dawn had come. The coffin still lay where it had, but Mac and London were gone. He heard the pounding that must have awakened him, hammers on wood. For a time he lay quietly looking about the tent, but at last he tried to sit up. The box of pain held him. He rolled over and climbed up to his knees, and then stood up, drooping his hurt shoulder to protect it from tension.

The flap swung up and Mac entered. His blue denim jacket glistened with moisture. "Hi, Jim. You got some sleep, didn't you. How's the arm?"

"Stiff," said. "Is it still raining?"

"Dirty drizzle. Doc's coming to look at your shoulder in a minute. Lord, it's wet outside! Soon's the guys walk around a little bit, it'll be all slop."

"What's the pounding?"

"Well, we've been building the stand for Joy. Even dug up an old flag to go over him." He held up a small dingy package of cloth, and unrolled it, a threadbare and stained American flag. He spread it carefully on the coffin top. "No," he said. "I think that's wrong. I think the field should be over the left breast, like this."

"It's a lousy dirty flag," Jim said.

"I know, but it'll get over big. Doc ought to be along any minute now."

"I'm hungry as hell," said Jim.

"Who isn't? We're going to have rolled oats, straight, for breakfast, no sugar or no milk—just oats."

"Even that sounds good to me. You don't sound so low this morning, Mac."

"Me? Well, the guys aren't knocked out as much as I thought they would be. The women 're raising hell, but the guys are in pretty good shape, considering."

Burton hustled in. "How's it feel, Jim?"

"Pretty sore."

"Well, sit down over here. I'll put on a clean bandage." Jim sat on a box and braced himself against expected pain, but the doctor worked deftly, removed the old wrapping and applied a new one without hurting him. "Old Dan's upset," he said. "He's afraid he isn't going to get to go to the funeral. He says he started this strike, now everybody's forgetting him."

Mac asked, "Do you think we could put him on a truck and take him along, Doc? It'd be swell publicity if we could."

"You could, Mac, but it'd hurt him like the devil; and it might cause shock complications. He's an old man. Hold still, Jim. I'm nearly through. No, I'll tell you what we'd better do. We'll tell him we're going to take him, and then when we start to lift him, I think he'll beg off. His pride's just hurt. He thinks Joy stole the show from him." He patted the finished bandage. "There you are, Jim. How do you feel now?"

Jim moved his shoulder cautiously. "Better. Sure, that's lots better."

Mac said, "Why don't you go and see the old guy, Jim, after you eat. He's a friend of yours."

"I guess I will."

Burton explained, "He's a little bit off, Jim. Don't worry him. All this excitement has gone to his head a little bit."

Jim said, "Sure, I'll lead him along." He stood up. "Say, that feels lots better."

"Let's get some mush," said Mac. "We want to start this funeral in time so it'll tie up the noon traffic in town, if we can."

Doc snorted. "Always a friend to man. God, you're a scorpion, Mac! If I were bossing the other side I'd take you out and shoot you."

"Well, they'll do that some day, I guess," Mac replied. "They've done everything else to me."

They filed out of the tent. Outside the air was filled with tiny drops of falling water, a grey, misty drizzle. The orchard trees were dim behind a curtain of grey gauze. Jim looked down the line of sodden tents. The streets between the lines were already whipped to slushy mud by the feet of moving people, and the people moved constantly for there was no dry place to sit down. Lines of men waited their turns at the toilets at the ends of the streets.

Burton and Mac and Jim walked toward the stoves. Thick blue smoke from wet wood poured from the chimneys. On the stove-tops the wash-boilers of mush bubbled, and the cooks stirred with long sticks. Jim felt the mist penetrating down his neck. He pulled his jacket closer and buttoned the top button. "I need a bath," he said.

"Well, take a sponge bath. That's the only kind we have. Here, I brought your food can."

They stepped to the end of the line of men waiting by the stove. The cooks filled the containers with mush as the line filed by. Jim gathered some of it on his eating stick and blew it cool. "It tastes good," he said. "I'm half-starved, I guess."

"Well, you ought to be, if you aren't. London's over supervising the platform. Come on, let's go over." They slushed through the mud, stepping clear of the tracks when any untrampled ground showed. In back of the stoves the new platform stood, a little deck, constructed of old fence-posts and culvert planks. It was raised about four feet above the ground level. London was just nailing on a hand-rail. "Hello," he said. "How was breakfast?"

"Roast dirt would taste swell this morning," said Mac. "This is the last, ain't it?"

"Yep. They ain't no more when that's gone."

"Maybe Dick'll have better luck today," Jim suggested. "Why don't you let me go out and rustle food, Mac? I'm not doing anything."

Mac said, "You're stayin' here. Look, London, this guy's marked; they try to get him twice already, and here he wants to go out and walk the streets alone."

"Don't be a damn fool," said London. "We're goin' put you on the truck with the coffin. You can't walk none with that hurt. You ride on the truck."

"What th' hell?" Jim began.

London scowled at him. "Don't get smart with me," he said. "I'm the boss here. When you get to be boss, you tell me. I'm tellin' you, now."

Jim's eyes flared rebelliously. He looked quickly at Mac and saw that he was grinning and waiting. "O.K.," said Jim. "I'll do what you say."

Mac said, "Here's something you can do, Jim. See if you think it's all right, London. S'pose Jim just circulates and talks to the guys? Just finds out how they feel? We ought to know how far we can go. I think the guys'd talk to Jim."

"What do you want to know?" London asked.

"Well, we ought to know how they feel about the strike now."

"Sounds all right to me," said London.

Mac turned to Jim. "Go and see old Dan," he said. "And then just get to talkin' to a lot of the guys, a few at a time. Don't try and sell 'em nothing. Just 'yes' 'em until you find out how they feel. Can you do that, Jim?"

"Sure. Where do they keep old Dan?"

"Look. See down that second row, that tent that's whiter'n the rest? That's Doc's hospital tent. I guess old Dan'll be in there."

"I'll look in on him," said Jim. He scraped up the last of his mush on his paddle and ate it. At one of the water barrels he dipped water to wash the eating can, and, on passing his pup-tent threw the can inside. There was a little movement in the tent. Jim dropped on his knees and crawled inside. Lisa was there. She had been nursing the baby. She covered her breast hastily.

"Hello," said Jim.

She blushed and said faintly, "Hello."

"I thought you were going to sleep in the hospital tent."

"There was guys there," she said.

"I hope you didn't get wet here last night."

She pulled the shoulder blanket neatly down. "No, there wasn't no leak."

"What you scared of?" Jim asked. "I won't hurt you. I helped you once, Mac and I did."

"I know. That's why."

"What are you talking about?"

Her head almost disappeared under the blanket. "You seen me—without no clothes on," she said faintly.

Jim started to laugh, and then caught himself. "That doesn't mean anything," he said. "You shouldn't feel bad about that. We had to help you."

"I know." Her eyes rose up for a moment. "Makes me feel funny."

"Forget it," said Jim. "How's the baby?"

"All right."

"Nursing it all right?"

"Yeah." Then her face turned very red. She blurted, "I like to nurse."

" 'Course you do."

"I like to—because it—feels good." She hid her face. "I hadn't ought to told you."

"Why not?"

"I don't know, but I hadn't ought to of. It ain't—decent, do you think? You won't tell nobody?"

" 'Course not." Jim looked away from her and out the low doorway. The mist drifted casually down. Big drops slid down the tent slope like beads on a string. He continued to stare out of the tent, knowing instinctively that the girl wanted to look at him, and that she couldn't until he looked away.

Her glance went over his face, a dark profile against the light. She saw the lumpy, bandaged shoulder. "What's the matter 'th your arm?" she demanded.

He turned back, and this time her eyes held. "I got shot yesterday."

"Oh. Does it hurt?"

"Little bit."

"Just shot? Just up an' shot by a guy?"

"Fight with some scabs. One of the owners potted me with a rifle."

"You was fightin'? You?"

"Sure."

Her eyes stayed wide. She looked fascinatedly at his face. "You don't have no gun, do you?"

"No."

She sighed. "Who was that fella come in the tent last night?"

"Young fellow? That was Dick. He's a friend of mine."

"He looks like a nice fella," she said.

Jim smiled. "Sure, he's O.K."

"Kinda fresh, though," she said. "Joey, that's my hubby, he didn't like it none. I thought he was a nice fella."

Jim got to his knees and prepared to crawl out of the tent. "Had any breakfast?"

"Joey's out gettin' me some." Her eyes were bolder now. "You goin' to the funeral?"

"Sure."

"I can't go. Joey says I can't."

"It's too wet and nasty." Jim crawled out. " 'Bye, kid. Take care o' yourself."

" 'B-bye." She paused. "Don't tell nobody, will you?"

He looked back into the tent. "Don't tell 'em what? Oh, about the baby. No, I won't."

"Y'see," she explained, "you seen me that way, so I told you. I don't know why."

"I don't either. 'Bye, kid." He straightened up and walked away. Few men were moving about in the mist. Most of the strikers had taken their mush and gone back to the tents. The smoke from the stoves swirled low to the ground. A little wind blew the drizzle in a slow, drifting angle. As Jim went by London's tent, he looked in and saw a dozen men standing about the coffin, all looking down at it. Jim started to go in, but he caught himself and walked to the white hospital tent down the row. There was a curious, efficient neatness inside the tent, a few medical supplies, bandage, bottles of iodine, a large jar of salts, a doctor's bag, all arranged with precision on a big box.

Old Dan lay propped in a cot, and on the ground stood a wide-necked bottle for a urinal, and an old-fashioned chamber for a bed-pan. Old Dan's beard had grown longer and fiercer, and his cheeks were more sunken. His eyes glinted fiercely at Jim. "So," he said. "You finally come. You damn squirts get what you want, and then run out on a man."

"How you feeling, Dan?" Jim asked placatingly.

"Who cares? That doctor's a nice man; he's the only nice one in this bunch of lice."

Jim pulled up an apple box and sat down. "Don't be mad, Dan. Look, I got it myself; got shot in the shoulder."

"Served you damn well right," Dan said darkly. "You punks can't take care o' yourselves. Damn wonder you ain't all dead fallin' over your feet." Jim was silent. "Leave me lyin' here," Dan cried. "Think I don't remember nothing. Up that apple tree all you could talk was strike, strike. And who starts the strike? You? Hell, no. I start it! Think I don't know. I start it when I bust my hip. An' then you leave me here alone."

"We know it, Dan. All of us know it."

"Then why don't I get no say? Treat me like a God-damn baby." He gesticulated furiously, and then winced. "Goin' to leave me here an' the whole bunch go on a funeral! Nobody cares about me!"

Jim interposed, "That's not so, Dan. We're going to put you on a truck and take you right along, right at the head of the procession."

Dan's mouth dropped open, exposing his four long squirrel-teeth. His hands settled slowly to the bed. "Honest?" he said. "On a truck?"

"That's what the chief said. He said you were the real leader, and you had to go."

Dan looked very stern. His mouth became dignified and military. "He damn well ought to. He knows." He stared down at his hands. His eyes grew soft and child-like. "I'll lead 'em," he said gently. "All the hundreds o' years that's what the workin' stiffs needed, a leader. I'll lead 'em through to the light. All they got to do is just what I say. I'll say, 'You guys do this,' an' they'll do it. An' I'll say, 'You lazy bastards get over there!' an' by Christ, they'll git, 'cause I won't have no lazy bastards. When I speak, they got to jump, right now." And then he smiled with affection. "The poor damn rats," he said. "They never had nobody to tell 'em what to do. They never had no real leader."

"That's right," Jim agreed.

"Well, you'll see some changes now," Dan exclaimed. "You tell 'em I said so. Tell 'em I'm workin' out a plan. I'll be up and around in a couple days. Tell 'em just to have patience till I get out an' lead 'em."

"Sure I'll tell 'em," said Jim.

Dr. Burton came into the tent. " 'Morning, Dan. Hello, Jim. Dan, where's the man I told to take care of you?"

"He went out," Dan said plaintively. "Went out to get me some breakfast. He never come back."

"Want the pot, Dan?"

"No."

"Did he give you the enema?"

"No."

"Have to get you another nurse, Dan."

"Say, Doc, this young punk here says I'm goin' to the funeral on a truck."

"That's right, Dan. You can go if you want."

Dan settled back, smiling. "It's about time somebody paid some attention," he said with satisfaction.

Jim stood up from his box. "See you later, Dan." Burton went out with him. Jim asked, "Is he going nuts, Doc?"

"No. He's an old man. He's had a shock. His bones don't knit very easily."

"He talks crazy, though."

"Well, the man I told to take care of him didn't do it. He needs an enema. Constipation makes a man light-headed sometimes; but he's just an old man, Jim. You made him pretty happy. Better go in and see him often."

"Do you think he'll go to the funeral?"

"No. It'd hurt him, banging around in a truck. We'll have to get around it some way. How is your arm feeling?"

"I'd forgot all about it."

"Fine. Try not to get cold in it. It could be nasty, if you don't take care of it. See you later. The men won't shovel dirt in the toilets. We're out of disinfectant. Simply have to get some disinfectant—anything." He hurried away, muttering softly to himself as he went.

Jim looked about for someone to talk to. Those men who were in sight walked quickly through the drizzle from one tent to another. The slush in the streets was deep and black by now. One of the big brown squad tents stood nearby. Hearing voices inside, Jim went in. In the dim brown light he saw a dozen men squatting on their blankets. The talk died as he entered. The men looked up at him and waited. He reached in his pocket and brought out the bag of tobacco Mac had given him. "Hi," he said. The men still waited. Jim went on, "I've got a sore arm. Will one of you guys roll me a cigarette?"

A man sitting in front of him held out a hand, took the bag and quickly made the cigarette. Jim took it and waved it to indicate the other men. "Pass it around. God knows they ain't much in this camp." The bag went from hand to hand. A stout little man with a short mustache said, "Sit down, kid, here, on my bed. Ain't you the guy that got shot yesterday?"

Jim laughed. "I'm one of 'em. I'm not the dead one. I'm the one that got away."

They laughed appreciatively. A man with a lantern-jaw and shiny cheek-bones broke up the laughter. "What they goin' to bury the little guy today for?"

"Why not?" Jim asked.

"Yeah, but ever'body waits three days."

The stout little man blew a jet of smoke. "When you're dead, you're dead."

Lantern-jaw said somberly, "S'pose he ain't dead. S'pose he's just in a kind of a state? S'pose we bury him alive. I think we ought to wait three days, like ever'body else."

A smooth, sarcastic voice answered. Jim looked at a tall man with a white, unlined forehead. "No, he isn't sleeping," the man said. "You can be very sure of that. If you knew what an undertaker does, you'd be sure he isn't in any 'state.'"

Lantern-jaw said, "He might just be. I don't see no reason to take a chance."

White-forehead scoffed. "Well, if he can sleep with his veins full of embalming fluid, he's a God damn sound sleeper."

"Is that what they do?"

"Yes it is. I knew a man who worked for an undertaker. He told me things you wouldn't believe."

"I rather not hear 'em," said Lantern-jaw. "Don't do no good to talk like that."

The stout man asked, "Who was the little guy? I seen him try to get the scabs over, an' then I seen 'im start over, an' then, whang! Down he goes."

Jim held his unlighted cigarette to his lips for a moment. "I knew him. He was a nice little guy. He was a kind of a labor leader."

White-forehead said, "There seems to be a bounty on labor leaders. They don't last long. Look at that rattlesnake, Sam. Says he's a longshoreman. I bet he's dead inside of six months."

A dark boy asked, "How about London? Think they'll get him like they got Dakin?"

Lantern-jaw: "No, by God. London can take care of himself. London's got a head on him."

White-forehead: "If London has a head on him, why in hell are we sitting around here? This strike's screwy. Somebody's making money out of it. When it gets tough somebody'll sell out and leave the rest of us to take it on the chin."

A broad, muscular man got to his knees and crouched there like an animal. His lips snarled away from his teeth and his eyes blazed with a red light. "That's enough from you, wise guy," he said. "I've knew London for a long time. If you're gettin' around to sayin' London's fixin' to sell out, me an' you's goin' round and round, right now! I don't know nothin' about this here strike. I'm doin' it 'cause London says it's O.K. But you lay off the smart cracks."

White-forehead looked coldly at him. "You're pretty hard, aren't you?"

"Hard enough to beat the ass off you anyway, mister."

"Lay off," Jim broke in. "What do we want to get fighting for? If you guys want to fight, there's going to be plenty of it for everybody."

The square man grunted and sat back on his blankets. "Nobody's sayin' nothin' behind London's back when I'm there," he said.

The little stout man looked at Jim. "How'd you get shot, kid?"

"Running," said Jim. "I got winged running."

"I heard a guy say you all beat hell out of some scabs."

"That's right."

White-forehead said, "They say there are scabs coming in in trucks. And they say every scab has tear-gas bombs in his pocket."

"That's a lie," Jim said quickly. "They always start lies like that to scare the guys off."

White-forehead went on, "I heard that the bosses sent word to London that they won't deal as long as there's reds in camp."

The broad, muscular man came to life again. "Well, who's the reds? You talk more like a red than anybody I seen."

White-forehead continued, "Well, I think that doctor's a red. What's a doctor want out here? He doesn't get any pay. Well, who's paying him? He's getting his; don't worry about that." He looked wise. "Maybe he's getting it from Moscow."

Jim spat on the ground. His face was pale. He said quietly, "You're the God-damned meanest son-of-a-bitch I ever saw! You make everybody out the kind of a rat you are."

The square man got to his knees again. "The kid's right," he said. "He can't kick hell out of you, but I can. And by Christ I will if you don't keep that toilet seat of yours shut."

White-forehead got up slowly and went to the entrance. He turned back. "All right, you fellows, but you watch. Pretty soon London'll tell you to settle the strike. An' then he'll get a new car, or a steady job. You just watch."

The square man leaped to his knees again, but White-forehead dodged out of the tent.

Jim asked, "Who is that guy? Does he sleep in here?"

"Hell, no. He just come in a little while ago."

"Well did any of you guys ever see him before?"

They shook their heads. "Not me."

"I never."

Jim cried, "By Christ! Then they sent him in."

The fat man asked, "Who sent him?"

"The owners did. He's sent in here to talk like that an' get you guys suspecting London. Don't you see? It splits the camp up. Couple you guys better see he gets run out of camp."

The square man climbed to his feet. "I'll do it myself," he said. "They's nothin' I'd admire better." He went out of the tent.

Jim said, "You got to watch out. Guys like that'll give you the idea the strike's just about through. Don't listen to lies."

The fat man gazed out of the tent. "It ain't a lie that the

food's all gone," he said. "It ain't a lie that boiled cow food ain't much of a breakfast. It don't take no spies to spread that."

"We got to stick," Jim cried. "We simply got to stick. If we lose this, we're sunk; and not only us, either. Every other working stiff in the country gets a little of it."

The fat man nodded. "It all fits together," he agreed. "There ain't nothing separate. Guys think they want to get something soft for themselves, but they can't without every-body gets it."

A middle-aged man who had been lying down toward the rear of the tent sat up. "You know the trouble with workin' men?" he asked. "Well, I'll tell you. They do too God-damn much talkin'. If they did more sluggin' an' less arguin', they'd get someplace." He stopped. The men in the tent listened. From outside there came the sound of a little bustling, the mutter of footsteps, the murmur of voices, the sound of peo-ple, penetrating as an odor, and soft. The men in the tent sat still and listened. The sound of people grew a little louder. Footsteps were slushing in the mud. A group walked past the tent.

Jim stood up and walked to the entrance just as a head was thrust in. "They're goin' to bring out the coffin. Come on, you guys." Jim stepped out between the tent-flaps. The mist still fell, blowing sideways, drifting like tiny, light snowflakes. Here and there the loose canvas of a tent moved soddenly in the wind. Jim looked down the street. The news had traveled. Out of the tents men and women came. They moved slowly in together and converged on the platform. And as their group became more and more compact, the sound of their many voices blended into one voice, and the sound of their footsteps became a great restlessness. Jim looked at the faces. There was a blindness in the eyes. The heads were tipped back as though they sniffed for something. They drew in about the platform and crowded close.

Out of London's tent six men came, bearing the box. There were no handles on the coffin. Each pair of men locked hands underneath, and bore the burden on their forearms. They hes-itated jerkily, trying to get in step, and having established the swinging rhythm, moved slowly through the slush toward the platform. Their heads were bare, and the drops of moisture stood out on their hair like grey dust. The little wind raised a corner of the soiled flag, and dropped it, and raised it again. In front of the casket a lane opened through the people, and the bearers moved on, their faces stiff with ceremonial solemnity, necks straight, chins down. The people on the edge of the lane stared at the box. They grew quiet during the movement of its passage, and when it was by whispered nervously to one another. A few men surreptitiously crossed themselves. The bearers reached the platform. The leading pair laid the end on the planks, and the others pushed the box forward until it rested safely.

Jim hurried to London's tent. London and Mac were there. "Jesus, I wish you'd do the talkin', I can't talk."

"No. You'll do fine. 'Member what I told you. Try to get 'em answering you. Once you get responses started, you've got 'em. Regular old camp-meeting stuff; but it sure works on a crowd."

London looked frightened. "You do it, Mac. Honest to God I can't. I didn't even know the guy."

Mac looked disgusted. "Well, you get up there and make a try. If you fall down, I'll be there to pick it up."

London buttoned the collar of his blue shirt and turned up the flaps against his throat. He buttoned his old black serge coat over his stomach and patted it down. His hand went up to the tonsured hair and brushed it down, back and sides; and then he seemed to shake himself down to a tight, heavy solemnity. The lean-faced Sam came in and stood beside him. London stepped out of the tent, great with authority. Mac and Jim and Sam fell in behind him, but London walked alone, down the muddy street, and his little procession followed him. The heads of the people turned as he approached. The tissue of soft speech stopped. A new aisle opened to allow the leader to pass, and the heads turned with him as he passed.

London climbed up on the platform. He was alone, over the heads of the people. The faces pointed up at him, the eyes expressionless as glass. For a moment London looked down at the pine coffin, and then his shoulders squared. He seemed reluctant to break the breathing silence. His voice was remote and dignified. "I come up here to make some kind of speech," he said. "And I don't know no speeches." He paused and looked out over the upturned faces. "This little guy got killed yesterday. You all seen it. He was comin' over to our side, an' somebody plugged him. He wasn't doin' no harm to no-body." Again he stopped, and his face grew puzzled. "Well, what can a guy say? We're goin' to bury him. He's one of our own guys, an' he got shot. What can I say? We're goin' to march out and bury him—all of us. Because he was one of us. He was kind of like all of us. What happened to him is like to happen to any guy here." He stopped, and his mouth stayed open. "I—I don't know no speeches," he said uneasily. "There's a guy here that knowed this little fellow. I'm goin' to let him talk." His head turned slowly to where Mac stood. "Come on up, Mac. Tell 'em about the little guy."

Mac broke out of his stiffness and almost threw himself on the platform. His shoulders weaved like a boxer's. "Sure I'll tell 'em," he cried passionately. "The guy's name was Joy. He was a radical! Get it? A radical. He wanted guys like you to have enough to eat and a place to sleep where you wouldn't get wet. He didn't want nothing for himself. He was a radi-cal!" Mac cried. "D'ye see what he was? A dirty bastard, a danger to the government. I don't know if you saw his face, all beat to rags. The cops done that because he was a radical. His hands were broke, an' his jaw was broke. One time he got that jaw broke in a picket line. They put him in the can. Then a doctor come an' looked at him. 'I won't treat a God-damn red,' the doctor says. So Joy lies there with a busted jaw. He was dangerous—he wanted guys like you to get enough to eat." His voice was growing softer and softer, and his eyes watched expertly, saw faces becoming tense, trying to catch the words of his softening tone, saw the people leaning for-ward. "I knew him." Suddenly he shouted, "What are you going to do about it? Dump him in a mud-hole, cover him with slush. Forget him."

A woman in the crowd began to sob hysterically. "He was fightin' for you," Mac shouted. "You goin' to forget it?"

A man in the crowd yelled, "No, by Christ!"

Mac hammered on, "Goin' to let him get killed, while you lie down and take it?"

A chorus this time, "No-o-o!"

Mac's voice dropped into a sing-song. "Goin' to dump him in the mud?"

"No-oo." The bodies swayed a little bit.

"He fought for you. Are you going to forget him?"

"No-o-o."

"We're going to march through town. You going to let any damn cops stop us?"

The heavy roar, "No-oo." The crowd swayed in the rhythm. They poised for the next response.

Mac broke the rhythm, and the break jarred them. He said quietly, "This little guy is the spirit of all of us. We won't pray for him. He don't need prayers. And we don't need prayers. We need clubs!"

Hungrily the crowd tried to restore the rhythm. "Clubs," they said. "Clubs." And then they waited in silence.

"O.K.," Mac said shortly. "We're going to throw the dirty radical in the mud, but he's going to stay with us, too. God help anybody that tries to stop us." Suddenly he got down from the platform, leaving the crowd hungry and irritated. Eyes looked wondering into other eyes.

London climbed down from the platform. He said to the bearers, "Put him in Albert Johnson's truck. We'll get goin' in a few minutes now." He followed Mac, who was working his way out of the crowd.

Dr. Burton fell in beside Mac when he was clear of the bunched people. "You surely know how to work them, Mac," he said quietly. "No preacher ever brought people to the mourners' bench quicker. Why didn't you keep it up awhile? You'd've had them talking in tongues and holy-rolling in a minute."

Mac said irritably, "Quit sniping at me, Doc. I've got a job to do, and I've got to use every means to do it."

"But where did you learn it, Mac?"

"Learn what?"

"All those tricks."

Mac said tiredly, "Don't try to see so much, Doc. I wanted them mad. Well, they're mad. What do you care how it's done?"

"I know how it's done," said Burton. "I just wondered

how you learned. By the way, old Dan's satisfied not to go. He decided when we lifted him."

London and Jim caught up with them. Mac said, "You better leave a big guard here, London."

"O.K. I'll tell Sam to stay and keep about a hundred. That sure was a nice speech, Mac."

"I didn't have no time to figure it out ahead. We better get movin' before these guys cool off. Once they get goin' they'll be O.K. But we don't want 'em just to stand around and cool off."

They turned and looked back. Through the crowd the bearers came swinging, carrying the box on their forearms. The clot of people broke up and straggled behind. The light mist fell. To the west a rent in the cloud showed a patch of pale blue sky, and a high, soundless wind tore the clouds apart as they watched.

"It might be a nice day yet," Mac said. He turned to Jim. "I nearly forgot about you. How do you feel?"

"All right."

"Well, I don't think you better walk all that distance. You ride on the truck."

"No. I'll walk. The guys wouldn't like it if I rode."

"I thought of that," said Mac. "We'll have the pallbearers ride too. That'll make it all right. We all set, London?"

"All set."

13

THE COFFIN rested on the flat bed of an old Dodge truck. On each side of it the bearers sat, hanging their legs over. And Jim rode hanging his feet over the rear. The motor throbbed and coughed, Albert Johnson drove out of the park and stopped in the road until the line formed, about eight men to a file. Then he dropped into low gear and moved slowly along the road, and the long line of men shuffled after him. The hundred guards stood in the camp and watched the parade move away.

At first the men tried to keep step, saying, "Hep, hep," but they tired of it soon. Their feet scuffed and dragged on the gravel road. A little hum of talk came from them, but each man was constrained to speak softly, in honor to the coffin. At the concrete state highway the speed cops were waiting, a dozen of them on motorcycles. Their captain, in a roadster, shouted, "We're not interfering with you men. We always conduct parades."

The feet sounded sharply on the concrete. The ranks straggled along in disorder. Only when they reached the outskirts of the town did the men straighten up. In the yards and on the sidewalks the people stood and watched the procession go by. Many took off their hats to the casket. But Mac's wish was denied. At each corner of the line of march the police stood, re-routing the traffic, turning it aside, and opening the way for the funeral. As they entered the business district of Torgas the sun broke through and glittered on the wet streets. The damp clothes of the marching men steamed under the sudden warmth. Now the sidewalks were dense with curious people, staring at the coffin; and the marchers straightened up. The squads drew close together. The men fell into step, while their faces took on expressions of importance. No one interfered, and the road was kept clear of vehicles.

Behind the truck, they marched through the town, through the thinning town again, and out into the country, toward the county cemetery. About a mile out they came to it, weed-grown and small. Over the new graves were little galvanized posts, stamped with names and dates. At the back of the lot a pile of new, wet dirt was heaped. The truck stopped at the gate. The bearers climbed down and took the casket on their forearms again. In the road the traffic cops rested their machines and stood waiting.

Albert Johnson took two lengths of tow-rope from under his seat and followed the bearers. The crowd broke ranks and followed. Jim jumped down from the truck and started to join the crowd, but Mac caught him. "Let them do it now; the main thing was the march. We'll wait here."

A young man with red hair strolled through the cemetery gate and approached. "Know a guy they call Mac?" he asked.

"They call me Mac."

"Well, do you know a guy they call Dick?"

"Sure."

"Yeah? What's his other name?"

"Halsing. What's the matter with him?"

"Nothing, but he sent you this note."

Mac opened the folded paper and read it. "Hot damn," he said. "Look, Jim!"

Jim took the note. It said:

"The lady wins. She has got a ranch, R.F.D. Box 221, Gallinas Road. Send out a truck there right away. They have got two cows, old, and one bull calf and ten sks. lima beans. Send some guys to kill the cows.

                                        Dick.

P. S. I nearly got picked up last night.
P.P.S. Only twelve axe-handles."

Mac was laughing. "Oh, Jesus! Oh, Christ! Two cows and a calf and beans. That gives us time. Jim, run over and find London. Tell him to come here as quick as he can."

Jim plunged off, and walked through the crowd. In a moment he came back, with London hurrying beside him.

Mac cried, "Did he tell you, London? Did he?"

"He says you got food."

"Hell yes. Two cows and a calf. Ten sacks of beans! Why the guys can go right out in this truck now."

From the crowded side of the cemetery came the beating of mud thrown down on the pine casket. "Y'see," Mac said.

"The guys'll feel fine when they get their stomachs full of meat and beans."

London said, "I could do with a piece of meat myself."

"Look, London, I'll go on the truck. Give me about ten men to guard it. Jim, you can come with me." He hesitated. "Where we going to get wood? We're about out of wood. Look, London, let every guy pick up a piece or two of wood, fence picket, piece of culvert, anything. Tell 'em what it's for. When you get back, dig a hole and start a fire in it. You'll find enough junk in those damned old cars to piece out a screen. Get your fire going." He turned back to the red-haired young man. "Where is this Gallinas Road?"

" 'Bout a mile from here. You can drop me off on the way."

London said, "I'll get Albert Johnson and some men." He hurried over and disappeared in the crowd.

Mac still laughed softly to himself. "What a break!" he said. "New lease on life. Oh, Dick's a great guy. He's a great guy."

Jim, looking at the crowd, saw it stir to life, it swirled. An excited commotion overcame it. The mob eddied, broke and started back to the truck. London, in the lead, was pointing out men with his finger. The crowd surrounded the truck, laughing, shouting. Albert Johnson put his muddy ropes under the seat and climbed in. Mac got in beside him, and helped Jim in. "Keep the guys together, London," he shouted. "Don't let 'em straggle." The ten chosen men leaped on the bed of the truck.

And then the crowd played. They held the tailboard until the wheels churned. They made mud-balls and threw them at the men sitting on the truck. Outside, in the road, the police stood quietly and waited.

Albert Johnson jerked his clutch in and tore loose from the grip of the crowd. The motor panted heavily as he struck the road. Two of the cops kicked over their motors and fell in beside the truck. Mac turned and looked out through the rear window of the cab at the crowd. They came boiling out of the cemetery in a wave. They broke on the road, hurrying along, filling the road, while the cops vainly tried to keep a passage clear for automobiles. The jubilant men mocked them and pushed them and surged around them, laughing like children. The truck, with its escorts, turned a corner and moved quickly away.

Albert watched his speedometer warily. "I guess these babies'd like to pick me up for speeding."

"Damn right," said Mac. He turned to Jim. "Keep your head down if we pass anybody, Jim." And then to Albert, "If anybody tries to stop us, drive right over 'em. Remember what happened to Dakin's truck."

Albert nodded and dropped his speed to forty. "Nobody ain't goin' to stop me," he said. "I've drove a truck all my life when I could get it."

They did not go through the town, but cut around one end of it, crossed a wooden bridge over the river and turned into Gallinas Road. Albert slowed up to let the red-haired youth drop off. He waved his hand airily as they drove away. The road lay between the interminable apple trees. They drove three miles to the foothills before the orchards began to fall off, giving place to stubble fields. Jim watched the galvanized postboxes at the side of the road. "There's two-eighteen," he said. "Not very far now."

One of the cops turned back and went toward the town, but the other hung on.

"There it is," Jim said. "That big white gate there."

Albert headed in, and stopped while one of the men jumped down and opened the gate. The cop cut off his motor and leaned it against its stand.

"Private property," Mac called to him.

"I'll stick around, buddy," he said. "I'll just stick around."

A hundred yards ahead a little white house stood under a huge, spreading pepper tree, and behind it a big white barn reared. A stocky ranchman with a straw-colored mustache slouched out of the house and stood waiting for them. Albert pulled up. Mac said, "Hello, mister. The lady told us to come for some stuff."

"Yah," said the man. "She told me. Two old milk cow, little bully calf."

"Well, can we slaughter 'em here, mister?"

"Yah. You do it yourself. Clean up after. Don't make mess."

"Where are they, mister?"

"I got them in barn. You don't kill them there. Makes mess in the barn."

"Sure, mister. Pull around by the barn, Albert."

When the truck was stopped, Mac walked around it. "Any of you guys ever slaughter a cow?"

Jim broke in, "My old man was a slaughterhouse man. I can show 'em. My arm's too sore to hit 'em myself."

"O.K.," said Mac.

The farmer had walked around the house toward them. Jim asked, "You got a sledge-hammer?"

He pointed a thumb at a little shed that sloped off the barn. "And a knife?"

"Yah. I got goot knife. You give him back." He walked away toward the house.

Jim turned toward the men. "Couple of you guys go into the barn and bring out the calf first. He's probably the liveliest."

The farmer hurried back carrying a short-handled, heavy-headed hammer in one hand and a knife in the other. Jim took the knife from him and looked at it. The blade was ground away until it was slender and bright, and the point was needle-like. He felt the edge with his thumb. "Sharp," the farmer said. "He's always sharp." He took the knife back, wiped it on his sleeve and reflected the light from it. "Cherman steel. Goot steel."

Four men came running out of the barn with a red yearling bull calf between them. They clung to a rope around its neck and steered it by butting it with their shoulders. They dug their heels into the ground to stop it, and held it, plunging, between them.

"Over here," the farmer said. "Here the blood could go into the ground."

Mac said, "We ought to save the blood. It's good strong food. If only we had something to carry it in."

"My old man used to drink it," said Jim. "I can't drink it: makes me sick. Here, Mac, you take the hammer. Now, you hit him right here on the head, good and hard." He handed the knife to Albert Johnson. "Look. See where my hand is? Now that's the place to stick him, just as soon as Mac hits him. There's a big artery there. Get it open."

"How's a guy to know?"

"You'll know, all right. It'll shoot blood like a half-inch pipe. Stand back out of the way, you guys."

Two men on the sides held the plunging calf. Mac slugged it to its knees. Albert drove in the knife and cut the artery open and jumped back from the spurting blood. The calf leaped, and then settled slowly down. Its chin rented flat on the ground, and its legs folded up. The thick, carmine blood pool spread out on the wet ground.

"It's a damn shame we can't save it," Mac said. "If we only had a little keg we could."

Jim cried, "O.K. Bring out another. Bring her over here." The men had been curious at the first slaughter, but when the two old cows were killed, they did not press in so close to see. When all the animals were down and the blood oozed slowly from their throats, Albert wiped the sticky knife on a piece of sack and handed it back to the farmer. He backed his truck to the animals and the men lifted the limp, heavy creatures up on the bed, and let the heads hang loosely over so that they might bleed on the ground. Last, they piled the ten sacks of lima beans on the front of the truck bed and took their places on the sacks.

Mac turned to the farmer. "Thanks, mister."

"Not my place," he said. "Not my cow. I farm shares."

"Well, thanks for the loan of your knife." Mac helped Jim a little as he got into the truck and moved over against Albert Johnson. The shirt sleeve on Albert's right arm was red to the shoulder with blood. Albert started his slow, chugging motor and moved carefully over the rough road. At the gate the traffic cop waited for them, and when they got out on the county road he followed a little way behind.

The men on the sacks started to sing.

> "Soup, soup, give us some soup—
> We don't want nothing but just some soup."

The cop grinned at them. One of the men chanted at him,

> "Whoops my dear, whoops my dear,
> Even the chief of police is queer."

In the cab, Mac leaned forward and spoke across Jim. "Albert, we want to dodge the town. We got to get this stuff to the camp. See if you can sort of edge around it, will you, even if it's longer?"

Albert nodded morosely.

The sun shone now, but it was high, and there was no warmth in it. Jim said, "This ought to make the guys feel fine."

Albert nodded again. "Let 'em get their guts full of meat, and they'll go to sleep."

Mac laughed. "I'm surprised at you, Albert. Haven't you got no idears about the nobility of labor?"

"I got nothing," Albert said. "No idears, no money, no nothing."

"Nothing to lose but your chains," Jim put in softly.

"Bull," said Albert, "nothing to lose but my hair."

"You got this truck," Mac said. "How'd we get this stuff back without a truck?"

"This truck's got me," Albert complained. "The God-damned truck's just about two-bitted me to death." He looked sadly ahead. His lips scarcely moved when he talked. "When I'm workin' and I get three dollars to the good and I get set to look me up a floozy, somethin' on this buggy busts and costs three dollars. Never fails. God damn truck's worse'n a wife."

Jim said earnestly, "In any good system, you'd have a good truck."

"Yeah? In any good system I'd have a floozy. I ain't Dakin. If Dakin's truck could of cooked, he wouldn't of wanted nothing else."

Mac said to Jim, "You're talkin' to a man that knows what he wants, and it ain't an automobile."

"That's the idear," said Albert. "I guess it was stickin' them cows done it. I felt all right before."

They were back in the endless orchards now, and the leaves were dark and the earth was dark with the rain. In the ditches beside the road a little muddy storm water ran. The traffic cop rode behind them as Albert turned from road to road, making an angular circuit of the town. They could see among the trees the houses where the owners or the resident share-croppers lived.

Mac said, "If it didn't make our guys so miserable, I wish the rain'd go on. It isn't doin' those apples no good."

"It isn't doin' my blankets no good, neither," Albert said sullenly.

The men on the back were singing in chorus,

> "Oh, we sing, we sing, we sing
> Of Lydia Pinkham
> And her gift to the human race——"

Albert turned a corner and came into the road to Anderson's place. "Nice work," said Mac. "You didn't go near the town. It would of been hell if we'd got held up and lost our load."

Jim said, "Look at the smoke, Mac. They've got a fire going, all right." The blue smoke rolled among the trees, hardly rising above their tops.

"Better drive along the camp, near the trees," Mac advised. "They're going to have to cut up these animals, and there's nothing to hang them on but the apple trees."

Men were standing in the road, watching for them. As the truck moved along the men on the bean sacks stood up and took off their hats and bowed. Albert dropped into low gear and crawled through the crowd of men to the end of the camp, near the apple trees.

London, with Sam behind him, came pushing through the shouting mill of hysterical men and women.

Mac cried, "String 'em up. And listen, London, tell the cooks to cut the meat thin, so it'll cook quick. These guys are hungry."

London's eyes were as bright as those of the men around him. "Jesus, could I eat," he said. "We'd about give you up."

The cooks came through the crowd. The animals were hung to the lower branches of the trees, entrails scooped out, skins ripped off. Mac cried, "London, don't let 'em waste anything. Save all the bones and heads and feet for soup." A pan of hacked pieces of meat went to the pit, and the crowd followed, leaving the butchers more room to work. Mac stood on the running-board, overlooking the scene, but Jim still sat in the cab, straddling the gear-shift lever. Mac turned anxiously to him. "What's the matter, Jim? You feel all right?"

"Sure, I'm O.K. My shoulder's awful stiff, though. I darn near can't move it."

"I guess you're cold. We'll see if Doc can't loosen you up a little." He helped Jim down from the truck and supported him by the elbow as they walked across toward the meat pit. A smell of cooking meat hung over the whole camp, and the meat dripped fat on the coals so that fierce little flames leaped up and devoured each drop. The men crowded so densely about the pit that the cooks, who went about turning the meat with long pointed sticks, had to push their way through the throng. Mac guided Jim toward London's tent. "I'm going to ask Doc to come over. You sit down in there. I'll bring you some meat when it's done."

It was dusky inside the tent. What little light got through the grey canvas was grey. When Jim's eyes grew accustomed to the light, he saw Lisa sitting on her mattress holding the baby under her shoulder blanket. She looked at him with dark, questionless eyes. Jim said, "Hello. How you getting along?"

"All right."

"Well, can I sit down on your mattress? I feel a little weak."

She gathered her legs under her and moved aside. Jim sat down beside her. "What's that good smell?" she asked.

"Meat. We're going to have lots of meat."

"I like meat," she said. "I could just about live on meat." London's dark, slender son came through the tent flaps. He stopped and stared at the two of them. "He's hurt," Lisa said quickly. "He ain't doin' nothing. He's hurt in the shoulder."

The boy said, "Oh," softly. "I wasn't thinkin' he was." He said to Jim, "She always thinks I'm lookin' at her that way, and I ain't." He said sententiously, "I always think, if you can't trust a girl, it don't do no good to try to watch her. A tramp is a tramp. Lisa ain't no tramp. I got no call to treat her like a tramp." He stopped. "They got meat out there, lots of meat. They got limey beans, too. Not for now, though."

Lisa said, "I like them, too."

The boy went on, "The guys don't want to wait till the meat's done. They want to eat it all pink inside. It'll make 'em sick if they ain't careful."

The tent-flaps whipped open, admitting Dr. Burton. In his hands he carried a pot of steaming water. "This looks like the holy family," he said. "Mac told me you were stiffening up."

"I'm pretty sore," said Jim.

Doc looked down at the girl. "Do you think you could put that baby down long enough to hold some hot cloths on his shoulder?"

"Me?"

"Yes. I'm busy. Get his coat off and keep hot water on the stiff place. Don't get it in the wound if you can help."

"D'you think I could?"

"Well, why not? He did things for you. Come on, get his coat off and strip down his shirt. I'm busy. I'll put on a new bandage when you finish." He went out.

The girl said, "D'you want me to?"

"Sure. Why not? You can."

She handed the baby to Joey, helped Jim off with his blue denim jacket and slipped his shirt down. "Don't you wear no un'erclo's?"

"No."

She fell silent then, and put the hot cloths on the shoulder muscle until the sore stiffness relaxed. Her fingers pressed the cloth down and moved about, pressing and pressing, gently, while her young husband looked on. In a little while Dr. Burton returned, and Mac came with him, carrying a big piece of black meat on a stick.

"Feel better now?"

"Better. Much better. She did it fine."

The girl backed away, her eyes dropped with self-consciousness. Burton quickly put on a new bandage and Mac handed over the big piece of meat. "I salted it out there," he said. "Doc thinks you better not run around any more today."

Burton nodded. "You might catch cold and go into a fever," he said. "Then you couldn't do anything."

Jim filled his mouth with tough meat and chewed. "Guys like the meat?" he asked.

"Cocky'r'n hell. They think they run the world now. They're going out and clean up on somebody. I knew it would happen."

"Are they going out to picket today?"

Mac thought a moment. "You're not, anyhow. You're going to sit here and keep warm."

Joey handed the baby to his wife. "Is they plenty meat, mister?"

"Sure."

"Well, I'm goin' to get some for Lisa and I."

"Well, go ahead. Listen, Jim. Don't go moaning around. There's not going to be much going on. It's along in the afternoon now. London's going to send out some guys in cars to see how many scabs are working. They'll see how many and where, an' then, tomorrow morning, we'll start doing something about it. We can feed the guys for a coupla days now. Clouds are going. We'll have clear, cold weather for a change."

Jim asked, "Did you hear anything about scabs?"

"No, not much. Some of the guys say that scabs are coming in in trucks with guards on them, but you can't believe anything in a camp like this. Damnedest place in the world for rumors."

"The guys are awful quiet now."

"Sure. Why not? They've got their mouths full. Tomorrow we've got to start raising hell. I guess we can't strike long, so we've got to strike hard."

The sound of a motor came up the road and stopped. Outside the tent there was a sudden swell of voices, and then quiet again. Sam stuck his head into the tent. "London here?" he demanded.

"No. What's the matter?"

"There's a dressed-up son-of-a-bitch in a shiny car wants to see the boss."

"What about?"

"I don't know. Says he wants to see the chief of the strikers."

Mac said, "London's over by the pit. Tell him to come over. The guy probably wants to talk things over."

"O.K. I'll tell him."

In a moment London came into the tent, and the stranger followed him, a chunky, comfortable-looking man dressed in a grey business suit. His cheeks were pink and shaven, his hair nearly white. Wrinkles of good nature radiated from the corners of his eyes. On his mouth an open, friendly smile appeared every time he spoke. To London he said, "Are you the chairman of the camp?"

"Yeah," said London suspiciously. "I'm the elected boss."

Sam came in and took his place just behind London, his face dark and sullen. Mac squatted down on his haunches and balanced himself with his fingers. The newcomer smiled. His teeth were white and even. "My name's Bolter," he said simply. "I own a big orchard. I'm the new president of the Fruit Growers' Association of this valley."

"So what?" said London. "Got a good job for me if I'll sell out?"

The smile did not leave Bolter's face, but his clean, pink hands closed gently at his sides. "Let's try to get a better start than that," he begged. "I told you I was the *new* president. That means there's a change in policy. I don't believe in doing things the way they were being done." While he spoke Mac looked not at Bolter, but at London.

Some of the anger left London's face. "What you got to say?" he asked. "Spill it out."

Bolter looked around for something to sit on, and saw nothing. He said, "I never could see how two men could get anything done by growling at each other. I've always had an idea that no matter how mad men were, if they could only get together with a table between them, something good would come out of it."

London snickered. "We ain't got a table."

"You know what I mean," Bolter continued. "Everybody in the Association said you men wouldn't listen to reason, but I told them I know American working men. Give American working men something reasonable to listen to, and they'll listen."

Sam spat out, "Well, we're listenin', ain't we? Go on an' give us somethin' reasonable."

Bolter's white teeth flashed. He looked around appreciatively. "There, you see? That's what I told them. I said, 'Let me lay our cards down on the table,' and then let them lay theirs down, and see if we can't make a hand. American working men aren't animals."

Mac muttered, "You ought to run for Congress."

"I beg your pardon?"

"I was talkin' to this here guy," said Mac. London's face had grown hard again.

Bolter went on, "That's what I'm here for, to lay our cards on the table. I told you I own an orchard, but don't think because of that I haven't your interests at heart. All of us know we can't make money unless the working man is happy." He paused, waiting for some kind of answer. None came. "Well, here's the way I figure it; you're losing money and we're losing money because we're sitting growling at each other. We want you to come back to work. Then you'll get your wages, and we'll get our apples picked. That way we'll both be happy. Will you come back to work? No questions, no grudges, just two people who figured things out over the table?"

London said, "Sure we'll go back to work, mister. Ain't we American working men? Just give us the raise we want and kick out the scabs and we'll be up in those old trees tomorrow morning."

Bolter smiled around at them, one at a time, until his smile had rested on each face. "Well, I think you ought to have a raise," he said. "And I told everybody I thought so. Well, I'm not a very good business man. The rest of the Association explained it all to me. With the price of apples what it is, we're paying the top price we can. If we pay any more, we lose money."

Mac grinned. "I guess we ain't American workin' men after all," he said. "None of this sounds reasonable to me. So far it's sounded like a sock full of crap."

Jim said, "The reason they can't pay the raise is because that'd mean we win the strike; and if we did that, a lot of other poor devils'd go on strike. Isn't that it, mister?"

Bolter's smile remained. "I thought from the first you deserved a raise, but I didn't have any power. I still believe it, and I'm the president of the Association. Now I've told the Association what I'm going to do. Some of 'em don't like it, but I insisted you men have to have a raise. I'm going to offer you twenty cents, and no questions and no grudges. And we'll expect you back at work tomorrow morning."

London looked around at Sam. He laughed at Sam's scowling face, and slapped the lean man on the shoulder. "Mr. Bolter," he said, "like Mac says, I guess we ain't American workin' men. You wanted cards laid down, and then you laid yours down backs up. Here's ours, and by Christ, she's a full house. Your God damn apples got to be picked and we ain't picking 'em without our raise. Nor neither is nobody else pickin' 'em. What do you think of that, Mister Bolter?"

At last the smile had faded from Bolter's face. He said gravely, "The American nation has become great because everybody pitched in and helped. American labor is the best labor in the world, and the highest paid."

London broke in angrily, "S'pose a Chink does get half a cent a day, if he can eat on it? What the hell do we care how much we get, if we got to go hungry?"

Bolter put on his smile again. "I have a home and children," he said. "I've worked hard. You think I'm different from you. I want you to look on me as a working man, too. I've worked for everything I've got. Now we've heard that radicals are working among you. I don't believe it. I don't believe American men, with American ideals, will listen to radicals. All of us are in the same boat. Times are hard. We're all trying to get along, and we've got to help each other."

Suddenly Sam yelled, "Oh, for Christ's sake, lay off. If you got somethin' to say, say it; only cut out this God-damn speech."

Bolter looked very sad. "Will you accept half?"

"No," said London. "You wouldn't offer no half unless you was pressed."

"How do you know the men wouldn't accept, if you put it to a vote?"

"Listen, mister," London said, "them guys is so full of piss and vinegar they'll skin you if you show that slick suit outside. We're strikin' for our raise. We're picketin' your God damn orchards, and we're kickin' hell out of any scabs you run in. Now come on through with your 'or else.' Turn your damn cards over. What you think you're goin' to do if we don't go back?"

"Turn the vigilantes loose," said Mac.

Bolter said hurriedly, "We don't know anything about any

vigilantes. But if the outraged citizens band together to keep the peace, that's their affair. The Association knows nothing about that." He smiled again. "Can't you men see that if you attack our homes and our children we have to protect them? Wouldn't you protect your own children?"

"What the hell do you think we're doin'?" London cried. "We're trying to protect 'em from starving. We're usin' the only way a workin' stiff's got. Don't you go talkin' about no children, or we'll show you something."

"We only want to settle this thing peacefully," said Bolter. "American citizens demand order, and I assure you men we're going to have order if we have to petition the governor for troops."

Sam's mouth was wet. He shouted, "And you get order by shootin' our men from windows, you yellow bastard. And in 'Frisco you got order by ridin' down women. An' the newspapers says, 'This mornin' a striker was killed when he threw himself on a bayonet.' *Threw himself!*"

London wrapped his arm about the furious man and forced him slowly away from Bolter. "Lay off, Sam. Stop it, now. Just quiet yourself."

"Th' hell with you," Sam cried. "Stand there and take the lousy crap that big baloney hands you!"

London stiffened suddenly. His big fist lashed out and cracked into Sam's face, and Sam went down. London stood looking at him. Mac laughed hysterically. "A striker just threw himself into a fist," he said.

Sam sat up on the ground. "O.K., London. You win. I won't make no more fuss, but you wasn't in 'Frisco on Bloody Thursday."

Bolter stood where he was. "I hoped you would listen to reason," he said. "We have information that you're being influenced by radicals, sent here by red organizations. They are misleading you, telling you lies. They only want to stir up trouble. They're professional trouble-makers, paid to cause strikes."

Mac stood up from his haunches. "Well, the dirty rats," he said. "Misleadin' American workin' men, are they? Prob'ly gettin' paid by Russia, don't you think, Mr. Bolter?"

The man looked back at him for a long time, and the healthy red was gone from his cheeks. "You're going to make us fight, I guess," he said. "I'm sorry. I wanted peace. We know who the radicals are, and we'll have to take action against them." He turned imploringly to London. "Don't let them mislead you. Come back to work. We only want peace."

London was scowling. "I had enough o' this," he said. "You want peace. Well, what we done? Marched in two parades. An' what you done? Shot three of our men, burned a truck and a lunch wagon and shut off our food supply. I'm sick o' your God damned lies, mister. I'll see you get out without Sam gets his hands on you, but don't send nobody else again till you're ready to talk straight."

Bolter shook his head sadly. "We don't want to fight you men," he said. "We want you to come back to work. But if we do have to fight, we have weapons. The health authorities are pretty upset about this camp. And the government doesn't like uninspected meat moving in this county. The citizens are pretty tired of all this riot. And of course we may have to call troops, if we need them."

Mac got up and went to the tent-flaps and looked out. Already the evening was coming. The camp was quiet, for the men stood watching London's tent. All the faces, white in the gathering evening, were turned in toward the tent. Mac yelled, "All right, boys. We ain't goin' to sell you out." He turned back into the tent. "Light the lamp, London. I want to tell this friend of man a few things."

London set a match to the tin lantern and hung it on the tent pole, where it cast a pale, steady light. Mac took up a position in front of Bolter, and his muscled face broke into a derisive grin. "All right, Sonny Boy," he said. "You been talkin' big, but I know you been wettin' your pants the whole time. I admit you can do all the things you say you can, but look what happens after. Your health service burned the tents in Washington. And that was one of the reasons that Hoover lost the labor vote. You called out guardsmen in 'Frisco, and damn near the whole city went over to the strikers. Y' had to have the cops stop food from comin' in to turn public opinion against the strike. I'm not talkin' right an' wrong now, mister. I'm tellin' you what happens." Mac stepped back a pace. "Where do you think we're gettin' food and blankets an' medicine an' money? You know damn well where we're gettin' 'em. Your valley's lousy with sympathizers. Your 'outraged citizens' are a little bit outraged at you babies, and you know it. And you know, if you get too tough, the unions 'll go out. Truck drivers and restaurant men and field hands, everybody. And just because you do know it, you try to throw a bluff. Well, it don't work. This camp's cleaner'n the lousy bunk houses you keep for us on your ranches. You come here to try to scare us, an' it don't work."

Bolter was very pale. He turned away from Mac and faced London. "I've tried to make peace," he said. "Do you know that this man was sent out by red headquarters to start this strike? Watch out that when he goes to jail you don't go too. We have a right to protect our property, and we'll do it. I've tried to deal man to man with you, and you won't deal. From now on the roads are closed. An ordinance will go through tonight forbidding any parading on the county roads, or any gathering. The sheriff will deputize a thousand men, if he needs them."

London glanced quickly at Mac, and Mac winked at him. London said, "Jesus, mister, I hope we can get you out of here safe. When the guys out there hear what you just said, why they'll want to take you to pieces."

Bolter's jaw tightened and his eyelids drooped. He straightened his shoulders. "Don't get the idea you can scare me," he said. "I'll protect my home and my children with my life if I have to. And if you lay a hand on me we'll wipe out your strike before morning."

London's arms doubled, and he stepped forward, but Mac jumped in his way. "The guy's right, London. He don't scare. Plenty do, but he don't." He turned around. "Mister Bolter, we'll see you get out of the camp. We understand each other now. We know what to expect from you. And we know how careful you have to be when you use force. Don't forget the thousands of people that are sending us food and money. They'll do other things, if they have to. We been good, Mr. Bolter, but if you start any funny business, we'll show you a riot you'll remember."

Bolter said coldly, "That seems to be all. I'm sorry, but I'll have to report that you won't meet us halfway."

"Halfway?" Mac cried. "There ain't any halfway to no-where." His voice dropped to softness. "London you get on one side of him, and Sam on the other, and see that he gets away all right. Then I guess you'd better tell the guys what he said. But don't let 'em get out of hand. Tell 'em to tighten up the squads for trouble."

They surrounded Bolter and took him through the press of silent men, saw him into his coupe and watched him drive away down the road. When he was gone London raised his voice. "If you guys want to come over to the stand, I'll get up on it and tell you what the son-of-a-bitch said, and what we answered him back." He flailed his way through, and the men followed, excitedly. The cooks left the stoves where they were boiling beans and chunks of beef. The women crawled like rodents from the tents and followed. When London climbed up on the stand it was ringed closely with men, standing in the dusk looking up at him.

During the talk with Bolter Doc Burton had effaced him-self, had been so quiet that he seemed to have disappeared, but when the group went out, leaving only Jim and Lisa sit-ting on the mattress, he came out of his corner and sat down on the edge of the mattress beside them. His face was wor-ried. "It's going to be a mean one," he said.

"That's what we want, Doc," Jim told him. "The worse it is, the more effect it'll have."

Burton looked at him with sad eyes. "You see a way through," he said. "I wish I did. It all seems meaningless to me, brutal and meaningless."

"It has to go on," Jim insisted. "It can only stop when the men rule themselves and get the profits of their labor."

"Seems simple enough," Burton sighed. "I wish I thought it were so simple." He turned smiling to the girl. "What's your solution, Lisa?"

She started. "Huh?"

"I mean, what would you like to have to make you happy."

She looked self-consciously down at the baby. "I like to have a cow," she said. "I like to have butter an' cheese like you can make."

"Want to exploit a cow?"

"Huh?"

"I'm being silly. Did you ever have a cow, Lisa?"

"When I was a little kid we had one," she said. "Went out an' drunk it warm. Old man used to milk it into a cup-like, to drink. Tasted warm. That's what I like. Bet it would be good for the baby." Burton turned slowly away from her. She insisted, "Cow used to eat grass, an' sometimes hay. Not ever'-body can milk 'em, neither. They kick."

Burton asked, "Did you ever have a cow, Jim?"

"No."

Burton said, "I never thought of cows as counter-revolutionary animals."

Jim asked, "What are you talking about, Doc, anyway?"

"Nothing. I'm kind of unhappy, I guess. I was in the army in the war. Just out of school. They'd bring in one of our men with his chest shot away, and they'd bring in a big-eyed German with his legs splintered off. I worked on 'em just as though they were wood. But sometimes, after it was all over, when I wasn't working, it made me unhappy, like this. It made me lonely."

Jim said, "Y'ought to think only of the end, Doc. Out of all this struggle a good thing is going to grow. That makes it worthwhile."

"Jim, I wish I knew it. But in my little experience the end is never very different in its nature from the means. Damn it, Jim, you can only build a violent thing with violence."

"I don't believe that," Jim said. "All great things have violent beginnings."

"There aren't any beginnings," Burton said. "Nor any ends. It seems to me that man has engaged in a blind and fearful struggle out of a past he can't remember, into a future he can't foresee nor understand. And man has met and defeated every obstacle, every enemy except one. He cannot win over himself. How mankind hates itself."

Jim said, "We don't hate ourselves, we hate the invested capital that keeps us down."

"The other side is made of men, Jim, men like you. Man hates himself. Psychologists say a man's self-love is balanced neatly with self-hate. Mankind must be the same. We fight ourselves and we can only win by killing every man. I'm lonely, Jim. I have nothing to hate. What are you going to get out of it, Jim?"

Jim looked startled. "You mean me?" He pointed a finger at his breast.

"Yes, you. What will you get out of all the mess?"

"I don't know; I don't care."

"Well, suppose blood-poisoning sets in in that shoulder, or you die of lockjaw and the strike gets broken? What then?"

"It doesn't matter," Jim insisted. "I used to think like you, Doc, but it doesn't matter at all."

"How do you get that way?" Burton asked. "What's the process?"

"I don't know. I used to be lonely, and I'm not any more. If I go out now it won't matter. The thing won't stop. I'm just a little part of it. It will grow and grow. This pain in the shoulder is kind of pleasant to me; and I bet before he died Joy was glad for a moment. Just in that moment I bet he was glad."

They heard a rough, monotonous voice outside, and then a few shouts, and then the angry crowd-roar, a bellow like an animal in fury. "London's telling them," said Jim. "They're mad. Jesus, how a mad crowd can fill the air with madness. You don't understand it, Doc. My old man used to fight alone. When he got licked, he was licked. I remember how lonely it was. But I'm not lonely any more, and I can't be licked, because I'm more than myself."

"Pure religious ecstasy. I can understand that. Partakers of the blood of the Lamb."

"Religion, hell!" Jim cried. "This is men, not God. This is something you know."

"Well, can't a group of men be God, Jim?"

Jim wrenched himself around. "You make too damn many words, Doc. You build a trap of words and then you fall into it. You can't catch me. Your words don't mean anything to me. I know what I'm doing. Argument doesn't have any effect on me."

"Steady down," Burton said soothingly. "Don't get so excited. I wasn't arguing, I was asking for information. All of you people get angry when you're asked a question."

As the dusk turned into night the lantern seemed to grow brighter, to find deeper corners of the tent with its yellow light. Mac came in quietly, as though he crept away from the noise and shouting outside. "They're wild," he said. "They're hungry again. Boiled meat and beans tonight. I knew they'd get cocky on that meat. They'd like to go out and burn houses right now."

"How does the sky look?" Burton asked. "Any more rain in it?"

"Clear and stars. It'll be good weather."

"Well, I want to talk to you, Mac. I'm low in supplies. I need disinfectant. Yes, and I could use some salvarsan. If any kind of epidemic should break out, we'd be out of luck."

"I know," Mac said. "I sent word to town how it was. Some of the boys are out trying to get money. They're trying to get money to bail Dakin out now. I'd just as soon he stayed in jail."

Burton stood up from his seat on the mattress. "You can tell London what to do, can't you. Dakin wouldn't take everything."

Mac studied him. "What's the matter, Doc. Don't you feel well?"

"What do you mean?"

"I mean your temper's going. You're tired. What is it, Doc?"

Burton put his hands in his pockets. "I don't know; I'm lonely, I guess. I'm awfully lonely. I'm working all alone, towards nothing. There's some compensation for you people. I only hear heartbeats through a stethoscope. You hear them in the air." Suddenly he leaned over and put his hand under Lisa's chin and raised her head up and looked into her shrinking eyes. Her hand came slowly up and pulled gently at his wrist. He let go and put his hand back in his pocket.

Mac said, "I wish I knew some woman you could go to, Doc, but I don't. I'm new around here. Dick could steer you, in town. He prob'ly has twenty lined up by now. But you might get caught and jailed, Doc; and if you weren't taking care of us, they'd bounce us off this land in a minute."

Burton said, "Sometimes you understand too much, Mac.

Sometimes—nothing. I guess I'll go along and see Al Anderson. I haven't been there all day."

"O.K., Doc, if it'll make you feel any better. I'll keep Jim under cover tonight."

Doc looked down at Lisa once more, and then he went out.

The shouting had settled to talk by now, low talk. It made the night alive outside the tent.

"Doc doesn't eat," Mac complained. "Nobody's seen him sleep. I suppose he'll break, sooner or later, but he never has before. He needs a woman bad; someone that would like him for a night; you know, really like him. He needs to feel someone—with his skin. So do I. Lisa, you're a lucky little twirp, you just had a kid. You'd have me in your hair."

"Huh?"

"I say: How's the baby?"

"All right."

Mac nodded gravely at Jim. "I like a girl who doesn't talk too much."

Jim asked, "What went on out there? I'm sick of staying in already."

"Why, London told what Sonny Boy said, and asked for a vote of confidence. He sure as hell got it, too. He's out there now, talking to the squad leaders about tomorrow."

"What about tomorrow?"

"Well, Sonny Boy was telling the truth about that ordinance. By tomorrow it'll be against the law for the boys to march along the county road. I don't think they'll remember about trucks. So, instead of standing around orchards, we're going to send out flying squads in the cars. We can raid one bunch of scabs and get out, and raid another. It ought to work."

"Where we going to get gasoline?"

"Well, we'll take it out of all the cars and put it in the ones we use. That should last tomorrow. The next day we may have to try something else. Maybe we can hit hard enough tomorrow so we can rest up the next day, until they get in a new load of scabs."

Jim asked, "I can go tomorrow, can't I?"

Mac cried, "What good would you be? The guys that go have to be fighters. You just take up room with that bum arm. Use your head."

London pushed open the flaps and came in. His face was flushed with pleasure. "Them guys is sure steamed up," he said. "Jesus, they're belly-for-back to kick Torgas for a growler."

"Don't give 'em no headway," Mac advised. "They got their guts full of chow. If they go loose, we ain't never goin' to catch up with them."

London pulled up a box and sat down on it. "The chow's about ready, the guy says. I want to ast you, Mac, ever'body says you're a red. Them two guys that come to talk both said it. Seemed to know all about you."

"Yeah?"

"Tell me straight, Mac. Is you an' Jim reds?"

"What do you think?"

London's eyes flashed angrily, but he controlled himself. "Don't get mean, Mac. I don't take it nice if the guys on the other side know more about you'n I do. What the hell do I know? You come into my camp and done us a good turn. I never ast you no questions—never did. I wouldn't ast you any now, on'y I got to know what to expect."

Mac looked puzzled. He glanced at Jim. "O.K.?"

"O.K. by me."

"Listen, London," Mac began. "A guy can get to like you awful well. Sam'll kick the ass off any guy that looks crooked at you."

"I got good friends," said London.

"Well, that's why. I feel the same way. S'pose I was a red, what then?"

London said, "You're a friend of mine."

"O.K., then, I'm a red. There ain't a hell of a secret about it. They say I started this strike. Now get me straight. I would of started it if I could, but I didn't have to. It started itself."

London eyed him cautiously, as though his mind slowly circled Mac's mind. "What do you get out of it?" he asked.

"Money, you mean? Not a damn thing."

"Then what do you do it for?"

"Well, it's hard to say—you know how you feel about Sam

an' all the guys that travel with you? Well, I feel that way about all the workin' stiffs in the country."

"Guys you don't even know?"

"Yes, guys I don't even know. Jim here's just the same, just the same."

"Sounds crazy as hell," said London. "Sounds like a gag. An' you don't get no money?"

"You don't see no Rolls-Royces around, do you?"

"But how about after?"

"After what?"

"Maybe after this is over you'll collect."

"There ain't no after," Mac said. "When this one's done, we'll be in another one."

London squinted at him, as though he tried to read his thoughts. "I believe it," he said slowly. "You ain't give me no bum steers yet."

Mac reached over and struck him sharply on the shoulders. "I'd of told you before, if you asked me."

London said, "I got nothing against reds. Y'always hear how they're sons-of-bitches. Sam's kind of rattlesnake and whip tempered, but he ain't no son-of-a-bitch. Let's go over an' get some food."

Mac stood up. "I'll bring you and Lisa some, Jim."

London said, from the doorway, "Moon's comin' up nice. I didn't know it was full moon."

"It isn't. Where do you see it?"

"Look, see over there? Looks like moon-rise."

Mac said, "That ain't east—Oh, Jesus! It's Anderson's. *London,*" he shouted. "They've set fire to Anderson's! Get the guys. Come on, God damn it! Where are those guards? Get the guys quick!" He ran away toward the red, gathering light behind the trees.

Jim jumped up from the mattress. He didn't feel his wounded arm as he ran along, fifty yards behind Mac. He heard London's voice roaring, and then the drumming of many feet on the wet ground. He reached the trees and speeded up. The red light mushroomed out behind the trees. It was more than a glow now. A lance of flame cleared the tree-tops. Above the sound of steps there was a vicious crackling. From ahead came shrill cries and a muffled howling. The trees threw shadows away from the light. The end of the orchard row was blocked with fire, and in front of it black figures moved about. Jim could see Mac pounding ahead of him, and he could hear the increasing, breathy roar of the flames. He sprinted, caught up with Mac, and ran beside him. "It's the barn," he gasped. "Were the apples out yet?"

"Jim! Damn it, you shouldn't come. No, the apples are in the barn. Where the hell were the guards? Can't trust anybody." They neared the end of the row, and the hot air struck their faces. All the barn walls were sheathed in fire, and the strong flames leaped from the roof. The guards stood by Anderson's little house, quiet, watching the light, while Anderson danced jerkily in front of them.

Mac stopped running. "No go. We can't do a thing. They must of used gasoline."

London plunged past them, and his face was murderous. He drew up in front of the guards and shouted, "You God-damn rats! Where in hell were you?"

One of the men raised his voice above the fire. "You sent a guy to tell us you wanted us. We was halfway to the camp when we seen it start."

London's fury drained out of him. His big fists undoubled. He turned helplessly to where Mac and Jim stood, their eyes glaring in the light. Anderson capered close to them in his jerky, wild dance. He came close to Mac and stood in front of him and pushed his chin up into Mac's face. "You dirty son-of-a-bitch!" His voice broke, and he turned, crying, toward the tower of flame. Mac put his arm around Anderson's waist, but the old man flung it off. Out of the fire came the sharp, sweet odor of burning apples.

Mac looked weak and sad. To London he said, "God, I wish it hadn't happened. Poor old man, it's all his crop." A thought stopped him. "Christ Almighty! Did you leave anybody to look after the camp?"

"No. I never thought."

Mac whirled. "Come on, a flock of you. Maybe they're drawin' us. Some of you stay here so the house won't burn too." He sprinted back, the way he had come. His long black shadow leaped ahead of him. Jim tried to keep up with him, but a sick weakness set in. Mac drew away from him, and the men passed him, until he was alone, behind them, stumbling along giddily over the uneven earth. No flames broke from the camp ahead. Jim settled down to walk along the vague aisle between the rows. He heard the crash of the falling barn, and did not even turn to look. When he was halfway back, his legs buckled with weakness, and he sat down heavily on the ground. The sky was bright with fire over his head, and behind the low, rosy light the icy stars hung.

Mac, retracing his steps, found him there. "What's the matter, Jim?"

"Nothing. My legs got weak. I'm just resting. Is the camp all right?"

"Sure. They didn't get to it. There's a man hurt. Fell down, I think he busted his ankle. We've got to find Doc. What a damn fool easy trick that was! One of their guys tells the guards to get out while the rest splash gasoline around and throw in a match. Jesus, it was quick! Now we'll get *hell* from Anderson. Get kicked off the place tomorrow, I guess."

"Where'll we go then, Mac?"

"Say! You're all in. Here, give me your arm. I'll help you back. Did you see Doc at the fire?"

"No."

"Well, he said he was going over to see Al. I didn't see him come back. Come on, climb to your feet. I've got to get you bedded down."

Already the light was dying. At the end of the row lay a pile of fire, but the flames no longer leaped up in long streamers. "Hold on to me, now. Anderson was nearly crazy, wasn't he? Thank God they didn't get his house."

London, with Sam behind him, caught up. "How's the camp?"

"O.K. They didn't get it."

"Well what's the matter with the kid?"

"Just weak from his wound. Give 'im a lift on that side." Together they half-carried Jim down the row and across the open space to London's tent. They set him down on the mattress. Mac asked, "Did you see the Doc over there? A guy's bust his ankle."

"No. I never seen him."

"Well, I wonder where he is?"

Sam entered the tent silently. His lean face was ridged with tight muscles. He walked stiffly over and stood in front of Mac. "That afternoon, when that guy says what he'd do——"

"What guy?"

"That first guy that come, an' you told him."

"I told him what?"

"Told 'im what we'd do."

Mac started and looked at London. "I don't know, Sam. It might switch public sympathy. We should be getting it now. We don't want to lose it."

Sam's voice was thick with hatred. "You can't let 'em get away with it. You can't let the yellow bastards burn us out."

London said, "Come out of it, Sam. What do you want?"

"I want to take a couple guys—an' play with matches." Mac and London watched him carefully. "I'm goin'," Sam said. "I don't give a damn. I'm goin'. There's a guy name Hunter. He's got a big white house. I'm takin' a can of gasoline."

Mac grinned. "Take a look at this guy, London. Ever see him before? Know who he is?"

London caught it. "No, can't say I do. Who is he?"

"Search me. Was he ever in camp?"

"No, by God! Maybe he's just a guy with a grudge. We get all kind of things pinned on us."

Mac swung back on Sam. "If you get caught, you got to take it."

"I'll take it," Sam said sullenly. "I ain't sharin' no time. I ain't takin' nobody with me, neither. I changed my mind."

"We don't know you. You just got a grudge."

"I hate the guy 'cause he robbed me," said Sam.

Mac stepped close to him and gripped his arm. "Burn the bastard into the ground," he said viciously. "Burn every stick in the house. I'd like to go with you. Jesus, I would!"

"Stick here," said Sam. "This ain't your fight. This guy robbed me—an' I'm a fireburg. I always like to play with matches."

London said, "So long, Sam. Drop in some time."

Sam slipped quietly out of the tent and disappeared. London and Mac looked for a moment at the gently swaying tent-flap. London said, "I got a feelin' he ain't comin' back. Funny how you can get to like a mean man like that. Always got his chin stuck out, lookin' for trouble."

Jim had sat quietly on the mattress. His face was troubled. Through the tent walls the glow of the fire was still faintly visible, and now the shriek of sirens sounded, coming nearer and nearer, lonely and fierce in the night.

Mac said bitterly, "They gave it a good long time to get started before the trucks came out. Hell, we never did get anything to eat. Come on, London. I'll get some for you, Jim."

Jim sat waiting for them to come back. Lisa, beside him, was secretly nursing the baby under the blanket again. "Don't you ever move around?" Jim asked.

"Huh?"

"You just sit still. All these things go on around you, and you pay no attention. You don't even hear."

"I wisht it was over," she replied. "I wisht we lived in a house with a floor, an' a toilet close by. I don't like this fightin'."

"It's got to be done," Jim said. "It will be over sometime, but maybe not in our lives."

Mac came in carrying two steaming food cans. "Well, the fire trucks got there before it was all out, anyway. Here, Jim, I put the beef in with the beans. You take this one, Lisa."

Jim said, "Mac, you shouldn't've let Sam go."

"Why the hell shouldn't I?"

"Because you didn't feel right about it, Mac. You let your own personal hatred get in."

"Well, Jesus! Think of poor old Anderson, losing his barn and all his crop."

"Sure, I know. Maybe it's a good idea to burn Hunter's house. You got hot about it, though."

"Yeah? An' I guess you're goin' to be reportin' me, maybe. I bring you out to let you get some experience, an' you turn into a God damn school teacher. Who th' hell do you think you are, anyway? I was doin' this job when you were slobberin' your bib."

"Now wait a minute, Mac. I can't do anything to help but use my head. Everything's going on, and I sit here with a sore shoulder. I just don't want you to get mad, Mac. You can't think if you get mad."

Mac glared sullenly at him. "You're lucky I don't knock your can off, not because you're wrong, but because you're right. You get sick of a guy that's always right." Suddenly he grinned. "It's done, Jim. Let's forget it. You're turning into a proper son-of-a-bitch. Everybody's going to hate you, but you'll be a good Party man. I know I get mad; I can't help it. I'm worried as hell, Jim. Everything's going wrong. Where you s'pose Doc is?"

"No sign of him yet? Remember what he said when he went out?"

"Said he was going to see Al."

"Yes, but before that, how lonely he was. He sounded screwy, like a guy that's worked too hard. Maybe he went off his nut. He never did believe in the cause, maybe he's scrammed."

Mac shook his head. "I've been around with Doc plenty. That's one thing he didn't do. Doc never ran out on anybody. I'm worried, Jim. Doc was headed for Anderson's. S'pose he took those raiders for our guards, an' they caught him? They'd sure as hell catch him if they could."

"Maybe he'll be back later."

"Well, I'll tell you. If the health office gets out an order against us tomorrow, we can be damn sure that Doc was snatched. Poor devil! I don't know what to do about the man with the busted ankle. One of the guys set it, but he probably set it wrong. Oh, well, maybe Doc's just wanderin' around in the orchard. It's my fault for letting him start over there alone, all my fault. London's doing everything he can. I forget things. I'm getting a weight on me, Jim. Anderson's barn's right on top of me."

"You're forgetting the whole picture," Jim said.

Mac sighed. "I thought I was a tough baby, but you're a hell of a lot tougher. I hope I don't get to hate you. You better sleep in the hospital tent, Jim. There's an extra cot, and I don't want you sleeping on the ground until you feel better. Why don't you eat?"

Jim looked down at the can. "Forgot it, and I'm hungry,

too." He picked up a piece of boiled beef out of the beans and gnawed it. "You better get some yourself," he said.

"Yeah, I'm going now."

After he had gone, Jim quickly ate the beans, the big oval, golden beans. He speared three of them at a time on a sharpened stick, and when they were gone tilted the can and drank the juice. "Tastes good, doesn't it," he said to Lisa.

"Yeah. I always like limey beans. Don't need nothing but salt. Salt pork's better."

"The men are quiet, awfully quiet."

"They got their mouths full," said the girl. "Always talkin', except their mouths' full. Always talkin'. If they got to fight, why don' they fight an' get it over, 'stead o' talkin'?"

"This is a strike," Jim said defensively.

"Even you talk all the time," she said. "Talk don't turn no wheel."

"Sometimes it gets steam up to turn 'em, Lisa."

London came in, and stood picking his teeth with a sharpened match. The bald spot in his tonsure shone dully in the lamplight. "I been watchin' all over the country," he said. "Ain't seen no fire yet. Mebbe they caught Sam."

"He was a clever guy," said Jim. "The other day he knocked over a checker, and the checker had a gun, too."

"Oh, he's smart all right. Smart like a snake. Sam's a rattlesnake, only he don't never rattle. He went out alone, didn't take nobody with him."

"All the better. If he gets caught, he's just a nut. If three guys got caught, it'd be a plot, see?"

"I hope he don't get caught, Jim. He's a nice guy, I like him."

"Yeah, I know."

Mac came back in with his can of food. "Jesus I'm hungry. I didn't know it till I got the first bite. Have enough to eat, Jim?"

"Sure. Why don't the men build fires to sit by? They did last night."

"They got no wood," said London. "I made 'em put all the wood over by the stoves."

"Well, what makes 'em so quiet? You can hardly hear a thing," Jim said. "It's all quiet."

Mac mused, "It's damn funny about a bunch of men, how they act. You can't tell. I always thought if a guy watched close enough he might get to know what they're goin' to do. They get steamed up, an' then, all of a sudden, they're scared as hell. I think this whole damn camp is scared. Word's got out that Doc's been snatched. An' they're scared to be without 'im. They go an' take a look at the guy with the busted ankle, an' then they walk away. An' then, pretty soon, they go an' take a look at 'im again. He's all covered with sweat, he hurts so bad." Mac gnawed at a beef bone, tearing the white gristle with his teeth.

Jim asked, "D'you suppose anybody knows?"

"Knows what?"

"How a bunch o' guys'll act."

"Maybe London knows. He's been bossin' men all his life. How about it, London?"

London shook his head. "No," he said. "I've saw a bunch of guys run like rabbits when a truck back-fired. Other times, seems like nothin' can scare 'em. Y'can kind of feel what's goin' to happen before it starts, though."

"I know," said Mac. "The air gets full of it. I saw a nigger lynched one time. They took him about a quarter of a mile to a railroad over-pass. On th' way out that crowd killed a little dog, stoned it to death. Ever'body just picked up rocks. The air was just full of killin'. Then they wasn't satisfied to hang the nigger. They had to burn 'im an' shoot 'im, too."

"Well I ain't lettin' nothin' like that get started in this camp," London said.

Mac advised, "Well, if it does start, you better stand out of the way. Listen, there's a sound."

There was a tramp of feet outside the tent, almost a military rhythm. "London in there?"

"Yeah. What do you want?"

"We got a guy out here."

"What kind of a guy?" A man came in, carrying a Winchester carbine. London said, "Ain't you one of the guys I left to guard that house?"

"Yes. Only three of us came over. We saw this fellow moving around, and we kind of got around him and caught him."

"Well, who is it?"

"I don't know. He had this gun. The guys wanted to beat hell out of him, but I says we better bring him here, so we done it. We got him outside, tied up."

London looked at Mac, and Mac nodded toward Lisa. London said, "You better get out, Lisa."

She got slowly to her feet. "Where I'm goin' to go?"

"I don't know. Where's Joey?"

"Talkin' to a guy," said Lisa. "This guy wrote to a school that's goin' to get him to be a postman. Joey, he wants to be a postman too, so he's talkin' to this guy about it."

"Well, you go an' find some woman an' set with her."

Lisa shrugged up the baby on her hip and went out of the tent. London took the rifle from the man and threw down the lever. A loaded shell flipped out. "Thirty-thirty," said London. "Bring the guy in."

"O.K. Bring him in." Two guards pushed the prisoner through the flaps. He stumbled and recovered his balance. His elbows were bound together behind him with a belt, and his wrists were wrapped together with baling wire. He was very young. His body was thin and his shoulders narrow. He was dressed in corduroy trousers, a blue shirt and a short leather jacket. His light blue eyes were fixed with terror.

"Hell," said London. "It's a kid."

"Kid with a thirty-thirty," Mac added. "Can I talk to him, London?"

"Sure. Go ahead."

Mac stepped in front of the captive. "What are you doin' out there?"

The boy swallowed painfully. "I wasn't doing a thing." His voice was a whisper.

"Who sent you?"

"Nobody."

Mac struck him in the face with his open hand. The head jerked sideways, and an angry red spot formed on the white, beardless cheek. "Who sent you?"

"Nobody." The open hand struck again, harder. The boy lurched, tried to recover and fell on his shoulder.

Mac reached down and pulled him to his feet again. "Who sent you?"

The boy was crying. Tears rolled down his nose, into his bleeding mouth. "The fellows at school said we ought to."

"High school?"

"Yes. An' the men in the street said somebody ought to."

"How many of you came out?"

"Six of us."

"Where did the rest go?"

"I don't know, mister. Honest, I lost 'em."

Mac's voice was monotonous. "Who burned the barn?"

"I don't know." This time Mac struck with a closed fist. The blow flung the slight body against the tent-pole. Mac jerked him up again. The boy's eye was closed and cut.

"Be careful about that 'don't know' business. Who burned the barn?"

The boy could not speak; his sobs choked him. "Don't hit me, mister. Some fellows at the pool room said it would be a good thing. They said Anderson was a radical."

"All right, now. Did you kids see anything of our doctor?"

The boy looked at him helplessly. "Don't hit me, mister. I don't know. We didn't see anybody."

"What were you going to do with the gun?"

"Sh—sh-shoot through the tents an' try to scare you."

Mac smiled coldly. He turned to London. "Got any ideas what to do with him?"

"Oh hell," said London. "He's just a kid."

"Yes, a kid with a thirty-thirty. Can I still have him, London?"

"What you want to do with him?"

"I want to send him back to high school so no more kids with rifles will come out."

Jim sat on the mattress and watched. Mac said, "Jim, you gave me hell about losing my head a little while ago. I'm not losing it now."

"It's O.K. if you're cold," said Jim.

"I'm a sharpshooter," Mac said. "You feeling sorry for the kid, Jim?"

"No, he's not a kid, he's an example."

"That's what I thought. Now listen, kid. We can throw you out to the guys there, but they'll probably kill you. Or we can work you over in here."

The one open eye glared with fear.

"O.K. with you, London?"

"Don't hurt him too much."

"I want a billboard," said Mac, "Not a corpse. All right, kid. I guess you're for it." The boy tried to retreat. He bent down, trying to cower. Mac took him firmly by the shoulder. His right fist worked in quick, short hammer blows, one after another. The nose cracked flat, the other eye closed, and the dark bruises formed on the cheeks. The boy jerked about wildly to escape the short, precise strokes. Suddenly the torture stopped. "Untie him," Mac said. He wiped his bloody fist on the boy's leather jacket. "It didn't hurt much," he said. "You'll show up pretty in high school. Now shut up your bawling. Tell the kids in town what's waitin' for 'em."

"Shall I wash his face?" London asked.

"Hell, no! I do a surgeon's job, and you want to spoil it. You think I liked it?"

"I don't know," said London.

The prisoner's hands were free now. He sobbed softly. Mac said, "Listen to me, kid. You aren't hurt bad. Your nose is busted, but that's all. If anybody here but me did it, you'd of been hurt bad. Now you tell your little playmates that the next one gets his leg broke, and the next one after that gets both his legs broke. Get me——? I said, did you get me?"

"Yes."

"O.K. Take him down the road and turn him loose." The guards took the boy under the arms and helped him out of the tent. Mac said, "London, maybe you better put out patrols to see if there's any more kiddies with cannons."

"I'll do it," said London. He had kept his eyes on Mac the whole time, watching him with horror. "Jesus, you're a cruel bastard, Mac. I can unda'stand a guy gettin' mad an' doin' it, but you wasn't mad."

"I know," Mac said wearily. "That's the hardest part." He stood still, smiling his cold smile, until London went out of the tent; and then he walked to the mattress and sat down and clutched his knees. All over his body the muscles shuddered. His face was pale and grey. Jim put his good hand over and took him by the wrist. Mac said wearily, "I couldn't of done it if you weren't here, Jim. Oh, Jesus, you're hard-boiled. You just looked. You didn't give a damn."

Jim tightened his grip on Mac's wrist. "Don't worry about it," he said quietly. "It wasn't a scared kid, it was a danger to the cause. It had to be done, and you did it right. No hate, no feeling, just a job. Don't worry."

"If I could only of let his hands go, so he could take a pop at me once in a while, or cover up a little."

"Don't think of it," Jim said. "It's just a little part of the whole thing. Sympathy is as bad as fear. That was like a doctor's work. It was an operation, that's all. I'd done it for you if I wasn't bunged up. S'pose the guys outside had him?"

"I know," Mac agreed. "They'd butchered him. I hope they don't catch anybody else; I couldn't do it again."

"You'd have to do it again," said Jim.

Mac looked at him with something of fear in his eyes. "You're getting beyond me, Jim. I'm getting scared of you. I've seen men like you before. I'm scared of 'em. Jesus, Jim, I can see you changing every day. I know you're right. Cold thought to fight madness, I know all that. God Almighty, Jim, it's not human. I'm scared of you."

Jim said softly, "I wanted you to use me. You wouldn't because you got to like me too well." He stood up and walked to a box and sat down on it. "That was wrong. Then I got hurt. And sitting here waiting, I got to know my power. I'm stronger than you, Mac. I'm stronger than anything in the world, because I'm going in a straight line. You and all the rest have to think of women and tobacco and liquor and keeping warm and fed." His eyes were as cold as wet river stones. "I wanted to be used. Now I'll use you, Mac. I'll use myself and you. I tell you, I feel there's strength in me."

"You're nuts," said Mac. "How's your arm feel? Any swelling? Maybe the poison got into your system."

"Don't think it, Mac," Jim said quietly. "I'm not crazy. This is real. It has been growing and growing. Now it's all here. Go out and tell London I want to see him. Tell him to come in here. I'll try not to make him mad, but he's got to take orders."

Mac said, "Jim, maybe you're not crazy. I don't know. But you've got to remember London is the chairman of this strike, elected. He's bossed men all his life. You start telling him what to do, and he'll throw you to the lions." He looked uneasily at Jim.

"Better go and tell him," said Jim.

"Now listen——'

"Mac, you want to obey. You better do it."

They heard a low wail, and then the rising scream of a siren, and then another and another, rising and falling, far away. "It's Sam," Mac cried. "He's set his fire."

Jim scrambled up. Mac said, "You better stay there. You're too weak, Jim."

Jim laughed mirthlessly. "You're going to find out how weak I am." He walked to the entrance and went out, and Mac followed him.

To the north the starred sky was black over the trees. In the direction of Torgas the city lights threw a pale glow into the sky. To the left of the town, over the high rampart of trees, the new fire put a dome of red light over itself. Now the sirens screamed together, and now one was up while another sunk its voice to a growl. "They don't waste any time now," Mac said.

The men came tumbling out of the tents and stood looking at the rising fire. The flames broke over the trees, and the dome of light spread and climbed. "A good start," Mac said. "If they put it out now, the house'll be ruined anyway. They can't use anything but chemicals out that far."

London hurried over to them. "He done it!" London cried. "Christ, he's a mean guy. I knew he'd do it. He wasn't scared of nothing."

Jim said calmly, "We can use him, if he comes back."

"Use him?" London asked.

"Yes, a man who could give a fire that good a start could do other things. It's burning fine. London, come into the tent. We've got to figure some things out."

Mac broke in, "What he means, London——"

"I'll tell him what I mean. Come into the tent, London." Jim led the way inside and seated himself on a box.

"What's the idear?" London demanded. "What's this you're talkin' about."

Jim said, "This thing is being lost because there's no authority. Anderson's barn was burned because we couldn't trust the guards to obey orders. Doc got snatched because his bodyguard wouldn't stick with him."

"Sure. An' what we goin' to do about it?"

"We're going to create authority," said Jim. "We're going to give orders that stick. The men elected you, didn't they? Now they've got to take it whether they like it or not."

Mac cried, "For Christ's sake, Jim! It won't work. They'll just fade out. They'll be in the next county in no time."

"We'll police 'em, Mac. Where's that rifle?"

"Over there. What do you want with it?"

"That's authority," said Jim. "I'm damn sick of this circle-running. I'm going to straighten it out."

London stepped up to him. "Say, what the hell is this 'I'm goin' to straighten things out'? You're goin' to jump in the lake."

Jim sat still. His young face was carven, his eyes motionless; his mouth smiled a little at the corners. He looked steadily and confidently at London. "Sit down, London, and put on your shirt," he said gently.

London looked uneasily at Mac. "Is this guy gone screwy?"

Mac missed his eyes. "I don't know."

"Might as well sit down," said Jim. "You will sooner or later."

"Sure, I'll sit down."

"O.K. Now you can kick me out of the camp if you want to. They'll make room for me in jail. Or you can let me stay. But if I stay, I'm going to put this over, and I can do it."

London sighed. "I'm sick of it. Nothin' but trouble. I'd give you the job in a minute, even if you ain't nothing but a kid. I'm the boss."

"That's why," Jim broke in. "I'll put out the orders through you. Don't get me wrong, London; it isn't authority I want, it's action. All I want is to put over the strike."

London asked helplessly, "What d'you think, Mac? What's this kid puttin' over?"

"I don't know. I thought it might be poison from that shot, but he seems to talk sense," Mac laughed, and his laugh dropped heavily into silence.

"The whole thing sounds kind of Bolshevik," London said.

"What do you care what it sounds like, if it works?" Jim replied. "You ready to listen?"

"I don't know. Oh, sure, shoot."

"All right, tomorrow morning we're going to smack those scabs. I want you to pick the best fighters. Give the men clubs. I want two cars to go together, always in pairs. The cops'll probably patrol the roads, and put up barricades. Now we can't let 'em stop us. If they put up barricades, let the first car knock 'em off the road, and the second pick up the men from the wreck and go on through. Understand? Anything we start goes through. If we don't succeed, we're farther back than when we started."

"I'm goin' to have a hell of a time with the guys if you give orders," London said.

"I don't want to give orders. I don't want to show off. The guys won't know. I'll tell you, and you tell them. Now the first thing is to send out some men to see how that fire's getting on. We're going to get a dose of trouble tomorrow. I wish Sam hadn't set it; but it's done now. We've got to have this camp plenty guarded tonight, too. There's going to be reprisals, and don't forget it. Put out two lines of guards and have them keep in touch. Then I want a police committee of five to beat hell out of any guy that goes to sleep or sneaks away. Get me five tough ones."

London shook his head. "I don't know if I ought to smack you down or let you go ahead. The whole thing's so damn much trouble."

"Well, put out guards while you think it over. I'm afraid we're going to have plenty of trouble before morning."

"O.K., kid. I'll give it a try."

After he had gone out, Mac still stood beside the box where Jim sat. "How's your arm feel, Jim?" he asked.

"I can't feel it at all. Must be about well."

"I don't know what's happened to you," Mac went on. "I could feel it happen."

Jim said, "It's something that grows out of a fight like this. Suddenly you feel the great forces at work that create little troubles like this strike of ours. And the sight of those forces does something to you, picks you up and makes you act. I guess that's where authority comes from." He raised his eyes.

Mac cried, "What makes your eyes jump like that?"

"A little dizzy," Jim said, and he fainted and fell off the box.

Mac dragged him to the mattress and brought a box for his feet. In the camp there was a low murmur of voices, constant and varying and changing tone like the voice of a little stream. Men passed back and forth in front of the tent. The sirens raised their voices again, but this time there was no excitement in them, for the trucks were going home. Mac unbuttoned Jim's shirt. He brought a bucket of water that stood in a corner of the tent, and splashed water on Jim's head and throat.

Jim opened his eyes and looked up into Mac's face. "I'm dizzy," he said plaintively. "I wish Doc would come back and give me something. Do you think he'll come back, Mac?"

"I don't know. How do you feel now?"

"Just dizzy. I guess I've shot my wad until I rest."

"Sure. You ought to go to sleep. I'm going out and try to rustle some of the soup that meat was cooked in. That'll be good for you. You just lie still until I bring it."

When he was gone, Jim looked, frowning, at the top of the tent. He said aloud, "I wonder if it passed off. I don't think it did, but maybe." And then his eyes closed, and he went to sleep.

When Mac came in with the soup, he set it on the ground. He took the box from under Jim's legs and then sat down on the edge of the mattress and watched the drawn, sleeping face.

The face was never still. The lips crept back until the teeth were exposed, until the teeth were dry; and then the lips drew down and covered them. The cheeks around the eyes twitched nervously. Once, as though striving against weight, Jim's lips opened to speak and worked on a word, but only a growling mumble was said. Mac pulled the old coverlets over Jim's body.

Suddenly the lamp flame was sucked down, the wick and darkness crept in toward the center of the tent. Mac jumped up and found a spout-can of kerosene. He unscrewed the lantern cap and filled the reservoir. Slowly the flame grew up again, and its edges spread out like a butterfly's wings.

Outside, the slow footsteps of patrolling men went by. In the distance there could be heard the grumble of the great night cargo trucks on the highway. Mac took down the lantern from the tent-pole and carried it to the mattress and set it on the ground. From his hip pocket he brought out a packet of folded papers and a mussy stamped envelope and a broken piece of pencil. With the paper on his knee he wrote slowly, in large, round letters:

Dear Harry:

Christ sake get some help down here. Doc Burton was snatched last night. I think he was. Doc was not a man to run out on us, but he is gone. This valley is organized like Italy. The vigilantes are raising hell. We need food and medicine and money. Dick is doing fine, only if we don't get some outside help I am afraid we are sunk. I never ran into a place that was so God damn organized. About three men control the situation. For all I know Dick may be in the can now.

Jim is sure coming through. He makes me look like a pin. Tomorrow I expect that we will get kicked out of this place. The V's. burned the owner's barn, and he is awfully sore. With Doc Burton gone, the county health officers will bounce us. So try to think of something. They are after Jim's and my scalp all the time. There ought to be somebody down here in case they get us.

I am howling for help, Harry. The sympathizers are scared, but that's not the worst.

He picked up a new piece of paper.

The men are touchy. You know how they get. Tomorrow morning they might go down and burn the city hall, or they might bolt for the mountains and hide for six months. So for Christ's sake, Harry, tell everybody we have to have help. If they run us out of here, we'll have trouble finding a spot. We are going to picket in trucks. We can't find out much that's going on.

Well, so long. Jack will hand this to you. And for the love of God try to get some help here.

                                                      Mac

He read the letter over, crossed a neglected t, folded the paper and put it in the dirty envelope. This he addressed to John H. Weaver, *esq.*

Outside he heard a challenge. "Who is it?"

"London."

"O.K."

London came into the tent. He looked at Mac, and at the sleeping Jim. "Well, I got the guards out like he said."

"That's good. He's all in. I wish Doc was here. I'm scared of that shoulder. He says it don't hurt, but he's a fool for punishment." Mac turned the lantern back to the tent-pole and hung it on its nail.

London sat down on a box. "What got into him?" he asked softly. "One minute he's a blabber-mouth kid, and the next minute, by Christ, he just boots me out and takes over."

Mac's eyes were proud. "I don't know. I've saw guys get out of theirself before, but not like that. Jesus, you *had* to do what he said. At first I thought he was off his nut. I still don't know if he was. Where's the girl, London?"

"I bedded her and my kid down in an empty tent."

Mac looked up sharply. "Where did you get an empty tent?"

"Some of the guys scrammed, I guess, in the dark."

"Maybe it's only the guards."

"No," London said. "I figured on them. I guess some of the guys run off."

Mac rubbed his eyes hard with his knuckles. "I thought it was about time. Some of 'em just can't take it. Listen, London, I got to sneak in an' try to get a letter in the mailbox. I want to take a look around, too."

"Whyn't you let me send one of the guys?"

"Well, this letter's got to get there. I better go myself. I been watched before. They won't catch me."

London regarded his thick hands. "Is—is it a *red* letter?" he asked.

"Well, I guess so. I'm trying to get some help, so this strike won't flop."

London spoke constrainedly. "Mac—like I said, you always hear about reds is a bunch of son-of-bitches. I guess that ain't true, is it, Mac?"

Mac chuckled softly. "Depends on how you look at it. If you was to own thirty thousand acres of land and a million dollars, they'd be a bunch of sons-of-bitches. But if you're just London, a workin' stiff, why they're a bunch of guys that want to help you live like a man, and not like a pig, see? 'Course you get your news from the papers, an' the papers is owned by the guys with land and money, so we're sons-of-bitches, see? Then you come acrost us, an' we ain't. You got to make up your own mind which it is."

"Well, could a guy like I work in with you guys? I been doin' kind o' like that, lookin' out for the guys that travel with me."

"Damn right," said Mac eagerly. "You're damn right. You got leadership, London. You're a workin' stiff, but you're a leader, too."

London said simply, "Guys always done what I told 'em. All my life they done it."

Mac lowered his voice. He moved close and put his hand on London's knee. "Listen," he said. "I guess we're goin' to lose this strike. But we raised enough hell so maybe there won't be a strike in the cotton. Now the papers say we're just causing trouble. But we're getting the stiffs used to working together; getting bigger and bigger bunches working together all the time, see? It doesn't make any difference if we lose. Here's nearly a thousand men who've learned how to strike. When we get a whole slough of men working together, maybe—maybe Torgas Valley, most of it, won't be owned by three men. Maybe a guy can get an apple for himself without going to jail for it, see? Maybe they won't dump apples in the river to keep up the price. When guys like you and me need a apple to keep our God damn bowels open, see? You've got to look at the whole thing, London, not just this little strike."

London was staring painfully at Mac's mouth, as though he tried to see the words as they came out. "That's kind of reva—revolution, ain't it?"

"Sure it is. It's a revolution against hunger and cold. The three guys that own this valley are going to raise hell to keep that land, and to keep dumping the apples to raise the price. A guy that thinks food ought to be eaten is a God damned red. D'you see that?"

London's eyes were wide and dreaming. "I heard a lot of

radical guys talkin'," he said. "Never paid much attention. They always got mad. I ain't got no faith in a mad guy. I never seen it the way you say it before, never."

"Well, keep on seeing it, London. It'll make you feel different. They say we play dirty, work underground. Did you ever think, London? We've got no guns. If anything happens to us, it don't get in the newspapers. But if anything happens to the other side, Jesus, they smear it in ink. We've got no money, and no weapons, so we've got to use our heads, London. See that? It's like a man with a club fighting a squad with machine guns. The only way he can do it is to sneak up and smack the gunners from behind. Maybe that isn't fair, but hell, London, this isn't any athletic contest. There aren't any rules a hungry man has to follow."

"I never seen it," London said slowly. "Nobody never took time out to tell me. I like to see some of the guys that talk nice an' quiet. Always, when I hear them, they're mad. 'God damn the cops,' they say. 'T'hell with the government.' They're goin' to burn down the government buildings. I don't like that, all them nice buildings. Nobody never told me about that other."

"They didn't use their heads, then," said Mac.

"Mac, you said you guessed we'd lose this strike. What makes you think like that?"

Mac considered. "No—" he said, as though to himself, "You wouldn't pull out now. I'll tell you why, London. Power in this valley is in very few hands. The guy that came out yesterday was trying to get us to quit. But now they know we won't quit. The only thing left is to drive us out or to kill us off. We could stand 'em off a while if we had food and a doctor, and if Anderson would back us up. But Anderson's sore. They'll kick us out if they have to use cannons. Once they get a court order, they'll kick us right out. Then where are we going to go? Can't jungle up, because there'll be ordinances. They'll split us up, an' beat us that way. Our guys aren't any too strong as it is. I'm afraid we can't get any more stuff to eat."

London said, "Whyn't we just tell the guys to beat it, an' the whole bunch of us get out?"

"Don't talk so loud. You'll wake up the kid. Here's why.

They can scare our guys, but we can throw a scare into them, too. We'll take one last shot at them. We'll hang on as long as we can. If they kill some of us the news'll get around even if the papers don't print it. Other guys'll get sore. And we've got an enemy, see? Guys work together nice when they've got an enemy. That barn was burned down by our own kind of men, but they've been reading the papers, see? We've got to get 'em over on our side as quick as we can." He took out a slim, limp bag of tobacco. "I've been saving this. I want a smoke. You smoke, London?"

"No. I chew when I can get it."

Mac rolled himself a slender cigarette in the brown paper. He raised the lantern chimney to light the cigarette. "You ought to get in a nap, London. Christ knows what's going to happen tonight. I've *got* to go in town and find a mailbox."

"You might get caught."

"No, I won't. I'll go in through the orchards. I won't even get seen." He stared past London, at the back of the tent. London swung around. The tent wall bellied up from the bottom, and Sam wriggled in, and stood up. He was muddy, and his clothes were torn. A long cut extended down his lean cheek. His lips were drawn back with fatigue, and his eyes were sunken.

"I on'y got a minute," he said softly. "Jesus, what a job! You got a lot of guards out. I didn't want nobody to see me. Somebody'd double-cross us sure."

"You done it nice," Mac said. "We seen the fire."

"Sure. Damn near the whole house gone. But that ain't it." He looked nervously at Jim, sleeping on the mattress. "I — got caught."

"Th' hell!"

"Yeah, they grabbed me and got a look at me."

"You oughtn't to be here," London said severely.

"I know. I wanted to tell you, though. You ain't never seen me or heard of me. I had to — I kicked his brains out. I got to go now. If they get me again, I don't want nothing, see? I'm nuts, see. I'm screwy. I talk about God told me to do it, see? I wanted to tell you. Don't take no risk for me. I don't want it."

London went over to him and took his hand. "You're a

good guy, Sam. They don't make 'em no better. I'll see you sometime."

Mac had his eye on the tent-flap. He said very quietly, over his shoulder, "If you get to town, forty-two Center Avenue. Say Mabel sent you. It's only a meal. Don't go more than once."

"O.K., Mac. G'bye." He was on his knees, with his head out, looking into the dark. In a second he squirmed out, and canvas dropped back into place.

London sighed. "I hope he makes it, Mac. He's a good guy. They don't make 'em no better."

Mac said, "Don't give it a thought. Somebody'll kill him sometime, like that little guy Joy. He was sure to get popped off. Me an' Jim'll go that way, sooner or later. It's almost sure, but it doesn't make any difference."

London's mouth was open. "Jesus, what a hell of a way to look at it. Don't you guys get no pleasure?"

"Damn right," said Mac. "More than most people do. It's an important job. You get a hell of a drive out of something that has some meaning to it, and don't you forget it. The thing that takes the heart out of a man is work that doesn't lead any place. Ours is slow, but it's all going in one direction. Christ, I stand here shooting off my face. I've got to go."

"Don't let 'em get you, Mac."

"I won't, but listen, London, there's nothing those guys would like better than to rub me and Jim out. I can take care of myself. Will you stay right here and not let anything happen to Jim? Will you?"

"Sure I will. I'll set right here."

"No, lie down on part of the mattress and get some sleep. But don't let 'em get the kid. We need him, he's valuable."

"O.K."

"So long," said Mac. "I'll get back as soon as I can. I'd like to find out what's going on. Maybe I can get a paper."

"So long."

Mac went silently out of the doorway. London heard him speak to a guard, and then, farther off, to another. Even after he was gone, London listened to the sounds of the night. It was quiet outside, but there was no feeling of sleep. The footsteps of the prowling guards came and went, and their voices sounded in short greetings when they met. The roosters crowed, one near, and far away the deep voice of an old, wise cock—train bell and spurt of steam and pounding of a starting engine. London sat down on the mattress, beside Jim, one folded leg flat, and the other standing up and clasped between his hands. He bowed his head over his knee and rested his chin, and his eyes questioned Jim and probed him.

Jim moved restlessly. One arm flung out and dropped again. He said, "Oh—and—water." He breathed heavily. "Tar over everything." His eyes opened and blinked quickly, sightlessly. London unclasped his hands as though to touch Jim, but he didn't touch him. The eyes closed and were quiet. A great transport truck rumbled into hearing. London heard a muffled cry outside the tent, some distance away. "Hey," he cried softly.

One of the patrol came up. "What's the matter, Boss?"

"Well who's doin' the yellin'?"

"That? Didn't you hear that before? That's the old guy with the busted hip. He's crazy. They're holdin' him down. Fightin' like a cat, an' bitin'. They got a rag in his mouth."

"Ain't you Jake Pedroni? Sure you are. Look, Jake, I heard Doc say if the old guy didn't get soap and water up him to keep him cleared out, he'd get like that. I got to stay here. You go over and get it done, will you, Jake?"

"Sure, boss."

"O.K. Get along. It ain't doin' his hip no good to fight. How's the guy with the busted ankle?"

"Oh, him. Somebody give 'im a slug of whiskey. He's O.K."

"Call me if anything happens, Jake."

"All right, I will."

London went back to the mattress and lay down beside Jim. Far away, the engine pounded, faster and faster in the night. The old tough rooster crowed first, and the young one answered. London felt heavy sleep creeping into his brain, but he rose up on his elbow and looked at Jim once more before he let the sleep wash over him.

14

THE DARK was just beginning to thin when Mac looked into the tent. On the central post the lantern still burned. London and Jim were sleeping, side by side. Mac stepped in, and as he did London jerked upright and peered about. "Who is it?"

"Me," said Mac. "Just got in. How's the kid?"

"I been asleep," said London. He yawned and scratched the round bald spot on his head.

Mac stepped over and looked down at Jim. The tired lines were gone out of the boy's face, and the nervous muscles were relaxed. "He looks fine. He got a good rest."

London stood up. "What time is it?"

"I don't know. It's just starting to get light."

"The guys building the fires yet?"

"I saw somebody moving around over there. I smelled wood smoke. It might be Anderson's barn smouldering."

"I didn't leave the kid a minute," said London.

"Good for you."

"When you goin' to get some sleep?"

"Oh, Christ knows. I don't feel it much yet. I got some last night, or rather the night before, it was. Seems a week ago. We just buried Joy yesterday, just yesterday."

London yawned again. "I guess it's beef and beans this morning. God, I'd like a cup of coffee!"

"Well, let's go in and get coffee and ham and eggs in town."

"Oh, go to hell. I'm goin' to get them cooks movin'." He stumbled sleepily outside.

Mac pulled a box under the light and took a rolled newspaper out of his pocket. As he opened it, Jim said, "I've been awake, Mac. Where have you been?"

"Had to go mail a letter. I picked a paper off a lawn. We'll see what's going on."

"Mac, did I make a horse's ass of myself last night?"

"Hell, no, Jim. You made it stick. You had us eating out of your hand."

"It just came over me. I never felt that way before."

"How do you feel this morning?"

"Fine. But not like that. I could of lifted a cow last night."

"Well, you sure lifted us around. That's a good gag about the two trucks, too. The owner of the car that has to bust the barricade may not like it much. Now let's see what's going on in town. Oh—oh, headlines for the scrapbook! Listen, Jim:

STRIKERS BURN HOUSES—KILL MEN!

Last night at ten o'clock fire destroyed the suburban home of William Hunter. Police say the men now on strike from the apple orchards are responsible. A suspect, captured, assaulted his captor and escaped. The injured man, Olaf Bingham, special deputy, is not expected to live.

Now let's see, farther down:—

Earlier in the evening strikers, either through carelessness or malice, burned the barn on the Anderson farm. Mr. Anderson had previously given the men permission to camp on his land.

It's a long story, Jim. You can read it if you want to." He turned the page. "Oh boy, oh boy. Listen to this editorial:

We believe the time has come to take action. When transient laborers tie up the Valley's most important industry, when fruit tramps, led and inspired by paid foreign agitators (That's us, Jim), carry on a campaign of violence and burning, bringing Red Russia into peaceful America, when our highways are no longer safe for American citizens, nor their homes safe from firebrands, we believe the time for action has come!

This county takes care of its own people, but these strikers do not belong here. They flout the laws, and destroy life and property. They are living on the fat of the land, supplied by secret sympathizers. This paper does not, and has never believed in violence; but it does believe that when law is not sufficient to cope with these malcontents and murderers, an aroused citizenry must take a hand. The incendiary deserves no mercy. We must drive out these paid trouble-makers. This paper recommends that citizens inquire into the sources of luxuries these men have been given. It is reported that three prime steers were slaughtered in their camp yesterday."

Mac smashed the paper down on the ground. "And that last means that tonight a flock of pool-room-Americans will start slinging rocks through the windows of poor devils who said they wished times might get better."

Jim was sitting up. "Jesus Christ, Mac! Do we have to take all the blame?"

"Every damn bit."

"How about that guy they say was murdered."

"Well, Sam did it. They caught him. He had to get away. The guy had a gun; all Sam had was his feet."

Jim lay back again. "Yeah," he said. "I saw him use his feet the other day. But God, it sounds bad. Sounds awful!"

"Sure. That editor used some dollar-an'-a-half words, all right. 'Paid foreign agitators.' Me, born in Minneapolis! An' granpaw fought in the Battle of Bull Run. He always said he thought it was a bull-fight instead of a battle he was goin' to 'til they started shootin' at him. An' you're about as foreign as the Hoover administration. Oh, hell, Jim. That's the way it always is. But—" he brought out the last of his tobacco— "it's closing in, Jim. Sam shouldn't of set that fire."

"You told him to go ahead."

"I know, I was mad about the barn."

"Well, what do we do now?"

"Just go ahead, just go ahead. We start those cars out at the scabs. We keep it up as long as we can fight, and then we get away, if we can. Are you scared, Jim?"

"N-no-o."

"It's closing in on us, Jim. I can feel it, closing in." He got up from his box and walked to the mattress and sat down. "Maybe it's because I need sleep. On the way out from town just now it seemed to me there was a bunch of guys waiting for me in the shadow under every tree. I got so scared, I'd of run if a mouse moved."

"You're all tired," Jim said gently. "Maybe I could of been some use around here, if I hadn't got myself hurt. I just lie around, and get in the way."

Mac said, "The hell you do. Every time I get low you steam me up, and, baby, I need steam this morning. My guts are just water! I'd take a drink if I could get it."

"You'll be all right when you get something to eat."

Mac said, "I wrote to Harry Nilson; told him we had to have help and supplies. But I'm afraid it's too late." He stared strangely at Jim. "Listen, Jim, I found Dick last night. Now you listen close. Remember the night we came in?"

"Sure."

"Well, you remember when we turned left at that bridge and went to the jungle?"

"Yeah."

"Well, listen close. If hell should pop and we get separated, you get to that bridge and go underneath, clear up under the arch, on the side away from town. You'll find a pile of dead willows there. Lift 'em aside. There's a deep cave underneath. Get inside, and pull the willows over the hole. You can go in about fifteen feet, see? Now Dick's putting blankets in there, an' canned goods. If they dynamite us, you go there an' wait for me a couple o' days. If I don't come, you'll know something's happened to me. You get back to town. Travel at night till you're clear of this county. They've got nothing on us that'll get us more than six months unless they pad up a murder charge about that guy last night. I don't think they will, because it'd be too much publicity. I.L.D.'d come through and break that upstairs shooting of Joy. Now will you remember, Jim? Go there and wait for a couple of days. I don't think they'll root you out of there."

Jim asked, "What do you know, Mac? You're keeping something back."

"I don't know a thing," Mac said. "I've just got a feeling this joint's closing in on us—just a feeling. A lot of the guys took it on the lam last night, mostly the guys with women and kids. London's O.K. He'll be a Party member pretty soon. But right now I wouldn't trust the rest of these guys with a road-apple at a banquet. They're so God damn jumpy they might knife us themselves."

"You're jumpy yourself, Mac. Calm down." Jim got to his knees and stood carefully up, his head cocked as though he listened for pain. Mac watched him in alarm. "It's swell," said Jim. "Shoulder's a little bit heavy, but I feel swell. Not even light-headed. I ought to get around some today."

"That bandage ought to be changed," said Mac.

"Oh, yeah, say, did Doc come back?"

"No, I guess they got him. What a nice guy he was."

"Was?"

"No. I hope not. Maybe they'd only beat hell out of him. But so many of our guys just disappear and never show up again."

"You're a fine, happy influence," said Jim.

"I know. If I wasn't sure you could take it, I'd shut up. Makes me feel better to get it off my chest. I want a cup of coffee so bad I could bust into tears. Just think of all the coffee we used to have in town. Three cups if we wanted. All we wanted."

Jim said sternly, "Maybe a little bit of that might be good for you. You better pull up now. You'll get feeling sorry for yourself."

Mac tightened his loose face. "O.K., kid. I'm all right now. You want to go outside? Can you walk all right?"

"Sure I can."

"Well, blow out that lantern. We'll go see about some beef and beans."

The shade screeched when Jim raised it. The dawn grey leapt into the tent, grey like a wash of ink. Jim lifted the tent-flaps and tied them back. "Let's air this place out," he said. "It's getting strong. The whole damn bunch of us could do with a bath."

Mac agreed. "I'll try to get a bucket of warm water, and we'll sponge off after we eat."

The dawn had come into the sky. The trees were still black against the light east, and a colony of crows, flapping east-ward, were etched heavily against it. Under the trees a dusk still held, and the earth was dark, as though the light had to be sucked in slowly. Now that they could see, the guards had given up their pacing. They stood in tired groups, hands in pockets, coats turned up and buttoned over their throats. And they talked in the soft monotone of men who only talk to stay awake.

Mac and Jim approached a group of them on their way to the stove. "Anything happen last night?" Mac asked.

Talk stopped. The men looked at him with weary, blood-shot eyes. "Not a thing, buddy. Frank was just sayin'—sayin' he had a feelin' there was people movin' around all night. I had that feelin' too, just creepin' around; but we didn't hear nothing. We went around two together."

Mac laughed, and his voice seemed to penetrate deep into the air. "I was in the army," he said, "trained in Texas. By Christ, when I'd go on guard duty I could hear Germans all around me, could hear 'em whispering in German." The men chuckled softly, without amusement.

One said, "London told us we could sleep today. Soon's I get somethin' in my stomach, I'm goin' to roll in."

"Me too. Roll right in. I got gravel in my skin, like a hop-head. Ever seen a hop-head when he's got bugs in his skin? Make you laugh to watch him."

Mac asked, "Why'n't you come over to the stoves an' warm up?"

"Well, we was just talkin' about doin' that."

Jim said, "I'm going down to the can, Mac. See you over at the stove." He walked down the line of tents, and each tent was a little cave of darkness. Snores came from some, and in the entrances of others men lay on their stomachs and looked out at the morning, and their eyes were full of the inwardness of sleep. As he walked along, some men came into the air and hunched their shoulders and drew down their necks against the cold. He heard an irritable, sleepy voice of a woman de-tailing how she felt. "I want to get out o' this dump. What good we doin' here? An' I got a lump in my stomach big's your fist. It's a cancer, that's what it is. Card-reader tol' me two years ago I'd get a cancer if I din' watch out. Said I was the cancer type. Sleepin' on the ground, eatin' garbage." An inaudible grumble answered.

As Jim passed another tent, a tousled head stuck out. "Come on in quick, kid. He's gone."

"Can't," said Jim.

Two tents down a man kneeling on his blankets said, "Got the time, buddy?"

"No. Must be after six, I guess, though."

"I heard her give you the come-on. God damn lucky you didn' go. She's caused more trouble in this camp'n the scabs. They ought to run her out. Gets ever'body fightin'. They got a fire goin' over there?"

"Yes," said Jim. He passed out from between the row of tents. Fifteen yards away, in the open, stood the square canvas screen. Inside there was a two-by-four supported at each end, over a hole. There was room on board for three men. Jim picked up a box of chloride of lime and shook it, but it was empty. One man sat hunched up on the board. "Sompin' ought to be done about it," he said. "Where in hell is 'at doctor? He ain't done nothing about it since yesterday."

"Maybe we could shovel in a little dirt," said Jim. "That'd help."

"It ain't my business. That doctor ought to do sompin' about it. The guys are liable t'get sick."

Jim's voice was angry. "Guys like you that won't do anything damn well deserve to get sick." He kicked dirt into the hole with the side of his foot.

"You're a smart punk, ain't you?" the man said. "Wait till you been around a little and got dry behind the ears, 'n'en maybe you'll know sompin'."

"I know enough right now to know you're a lazy bastard."

"You wait till I get my pants up; I'll show you who's a lazy bastard." But he made no move.

Jim looked down at the ground. "I can't take you on. I'm shot in the shoulder."

"Sure, an' when you know you're safe from a sportin' man, you miscall a man. You lousy punks got sompin' comin' to you."

Jim controlled his voice. "I didn't mean to miscall you, mister. I wouldn't fight you. We got all the fighting to do we can take care of, without fighting each other."

"Well, now, that's better," said the man. "I'll he'p you kick some dirt in when I get through. What's goin' on today? You know?"

Jim began, "We're——" and then he remembered. "Damn' if I know. I guess London'll tell us when he gets ready."

"London ain't done nothing yet," said the man. "Hey, don't sit so near the middle. You're liable to break that two-by-four. Get over near the edge. London ain't done nothing. Just walks around lookin' big. Know what a guy told me? London's got cases an' cases of can' goods in his tent—ever 'thing. Corn-beef, an' sardines, an' can' peaches. He won't eat what us poor stiffs got to eat, not him. He's too God damn good."

"And that's a God damn lie," said Jim.

"Got smart again, have you? There's plenty guys seen them can' goods. How do you know it's a lie?"

"Because I've been in that tent. He let me sleep in there last night because I was hurt. There's an old mattress and two empty boxes in that tent, and not another damn thing."

"Well, a whole slough o' guys says there's can' peaches an' sardines in there. Some of the boys was goin' to bust in an' get some last night."

Jim laughed hopelessly. "Oh, Jesus, what a bunch of swine! You get a good man, and you start picking him to pieces."

"There you go, miscalling guys again. Wait 'll you get well an' somebody's goin' slap that smart puss right off you."

Jim got up from the plank and buttoned his jeans and went outside. The short stove-pipes of the cook stoves puffed grey smoke into the air, still, straight columns that went up fifty feet before they mushroomed at the top and spread out evenly. The eastern sky was yellow now, and the sky overhead had turned eggshell blue. From the tents men came rapidly. The awakening silence of the camp was replaced with the rustling footsteps, the voices, the movement of people.

A dark-haired woman stood in front of a tent, her head thrown back; and her throat was white. She combed her hair with long, beautiful sweeps of her arm. When Jim walked by she smiled wisely and said, "Good morning," and the combing didn't pause. Jim stopped. "No," she said. "Only good morning."

"You make me feel good," he said. For a moment he looked at the long white throat and the sharply defined jaws. "Good morning again," he said, and he saw her lips form to a line of deep and delicious understanding. And when he passed along, and the tousled head darted out and the husky voice whispered, "Come on in, quick, he's gone now," Jim only glanced, and went quickly on without responding.

Men were gathering about the old stoves, stretching their hands to the warmth, waiting patiently until the beef and beans in the big wash-boilers should be hot. Jim stepped to a water-barrel and dipped some water into a tin basin. He threw the cold water into his face, and into his hair, and he rubbed his hands together without soap. He let the water cling in drops to his face.

Mac saw him and walked over, holding out a food can. "I rinsed it out," he said. "What's the matter, Jim? You look tickled to death."

"I saw a woman——"

"You couldn't. Didn't have time."

"I just *saw* her," said Jim. "She was combing her hair. It's a funny thing—sometimes a person gets into an ordinary position, and it seems wonderful, it just stays in your mind all your life."

"If I saw a decent looking woman, I'd go nuts," said Mac.

Jim looked down into the empty can. "She had her head back. She was combing her hair—she had a funny kind of a smile on her face. You know, Mac, my mother was a Catholic. She didn't go to church Sundays because my old man hated churches as bad as we do. But in the middle of the week, sometimes, she'd go into the church when my old man was working. When I was a little kid she took me in sometimes, too. The smile on that woman—that's why I'm telling you this—— Well, there was a Mary in there, and she had the same kind of a smile, wise and cool and sure. One time I asked my mother why she smiled like that. My mother said, 'She can smile because she's in Heaven.' I think she was jealous, a little." His voice tumbled on, "And one time I was there, looking at that Mary, and I saw a ring of little stars in the air, over her head, going around and around, like little birds. Really saw them, I mean. It's not funny, Mac. This isn't religion—it's kind of what the books I've read call wish-fulfillment, I guess. I saw them, all right. They made me feel happy, too. My old man would have been sore if he knew. He never took any position that lasted. Everything was wasted in him."

Mac said, "You're going to be a great talker some time, Jim. You got a kind of a persuasive tone. Jesus, just now you made me think it'd be nice to sit in church. Nice! That's good talking. If you can talk guys over to our side, you'll be good." He took a little clean tin can that hung on a nail on the side of the water-barrel, and he filled the can and drank from it. "Let's go over and see if the slum is hot."

The men were forming in a line, and as they passed the stoves, the cooks ladled lima beans and lumps of boiled beef into the cans. Mac and Jim got on the end of the line and eventually passed the boilers. "Is that all the food?" Mac asked a cook.

"There's beans and beef enough for one more meal. We're out of salt, though. We need more salt."

They drifted along, eating as they went. A lance of sunlight shot over the trees and fell on the ground of the clearing, fell on the tents and made them seem less dingy. At the line of old cars London was talking to a group of men. "Let's see what's doing," Mac suggested. They walked toward the road, where the old cars stood. A light rust was settling on radiators, and some of the worn tires were down, and all of the cars had the appearance of having stood there a long while.

London saluted with a wave of his hand. "Hello, Mac. H'ya, Jim?"

"Fine," said Jim.

"Me and these guys is lookin' over the heaps. Tryin' to see which ones to send out. There ain't none of 'em worth a hoot in hell."

"How many'd you figure to send out?"

" 'Bout five couples. Two together, so if anything went wrong with one the other'd pick our guys up and go on." He pointed down the line. "That old Hudson's all right. There's five four-cylinder Dodges, and them old babies will go to hell on their bellies after you knock the wheels off. My model T's all right—runs, anyway. Let's see, we don't want no closed cars; y'can't heave a rock out of a closed car. Here's a shovel-nose. Think she'll run?"

A man stepped up. "Damn right she'll run. I brung her straight through Louisiana in winter. She never even warmed up, even comin' over the mountains."

They walked down the row, picking out prospects in the line of wrecks. "These guys is squad leaders," London explained. "I'm goin' give one of 'em charge of each bus, an' let 'em pick their own guys, five or six apiece. Guys they can trust, good fighters, see?"

"Sounds swell," said Mac. "I don't see how anybody's goin' to stop 'em."

One of the men turned on him. "And they *ain't* nobody goin' to stop us, neither," he said.

"Feelin' pretty tough, huh?"

"Just give us a show, an' see."

Mac said, "We'll walk around a little bit, London."

"Oh, wait a minute, the guys come back from Anderson's a little while ago. They says Anderson cussed 'em all night. An' this mornin' he started in town, still cussin'."

"Well, I thought he would. How about Al?"

"Al?"

"Yeah, Anderson's boy, the one that got smacked."

"Well, the guys went in an' seen him. He wanted to come over here, but they didn't want to move him. Couple guys stayed with him."

London stepped close and lowered his voice so the other men could not hear. "Where do you think Anderson's goin', Mac?"

"I guess he's goin' in town to put in a complaint and get us kicked off. He'll probably claim we burned his barn now. He's so scared he'll do anything to get in good with the other side."

"Uh-huh. Think we ought to fight here?"

"I'll tell you how I think it'll be," said Mac. "I think first they might send out a few guys to try to scare us off. We'll stand up to 'em. After that, they'll come out with a mob. We'll see how our guys feel. If they're sore and mean, we'll fight. But if they look yellow, we'll clear out, if we can." He tapped London on the shoulder. "If that happens, you and me and Jim have to go quick and far. That mob's going to want a chicken to kill, and they won't care much who it is."

London called to the men, "Drain the gas out of all the tanks, and put it in them cars we picked out. Start up the motors 'n' see if they're all right, but don't waste no gas." He turned back. "I'll walk along. I want to talk this out. What you think about our guys? Them babies over by the heaps 'll fight. How about the others?"

Mac said, "If I could tell in advance what a bunch of guys'd do, I'd be president. Some things I do know, though. A smell of blood seems to steam 'em up. Let 'em kill somethin', even a cat, an' they'll want to go right on killin'. If there's a fight, an' our guys get first blood, they'll put up a hell of a battle. But if we lose a man first, I wouldn't be surprised to see them hit for the trees."

"I know," London agreed. "Take one guy that you know ever'thing about him, an' take ten more the same, an' you can't tell what in hell they'll do. What you think of doin'? Just waitin' to see?"

"That's it," said Mac. "When you're used to mobs, you can tell, just a little bit ahead of time. You can feel it in the air. But remember, if our guys crack, get under somethin', an' stay there. Listen, under the Torgas River bridge there's a dug-out covered with dead willows. It's got food and blankets in it. That's the place to hit for. A mob don't stay crazy long. When you get in town, go to forty-two Center Avenue and say I sent you."

"I wish they was some way to get the kid and Lisa out. I don't want 'em to get hurt."

Jim broke in on them. "You guys talk like it was sure to happen. Nothing's happened yet, maybe nothing will. Maybe Anderson only went in to stay with somebody."

"I know it sounds like I'm calamity-howling," Mac said apologetically. "Maybe it won't happen. But London's a valuable guy. We need him. I don't like to get these stiffs killed off; they're good guys. But we need London. This whole strike's worth it if London comes over."

London looked pleased. "You been in plenty strikes, Mac. Always do they go this way?"

"Hell, no. This place is organized, I tell you. None of the other workers came out on strike with us. The owners cut us off out here with nothing to eat. If this bunch of raiders gets stopped today, we'll catch it good. You weren't planning to go out, were you, London?"

"Sure. I ain't been in a fight yet."

"I don't think you'd better go," Mac advised. "We're goin' to need you here. They'll try to root us out today. If you aren't here the guys might get scared and beat it. You're still the boss, London. The boss's got to stick in the center of the biggest group till the last minute. Let's get those cars on the move, shall we? There's plenty of scabs out, and they'll be working by now."

London turned and hurried back to the cars. "Come on, you guys. Step on it. Let's get rollin'."

The squad leaders trotted to the tents and picked their men, men armed with rocks and pieces of wood, and here and there a knife. The whole crowd moved out to the edge of the road, talking loudly and giving advice.

"Give 'em hell, Joe."

"Knock their can off."

The motors started and struggled against their age. The chosen men climbed in and took their places. London held up both hands to stop the noise. He shouted, "Three pairs go that way, and two this way." The gears dropped in. The cars crawled across the ditch and lined up in the road. Raiders stood up and waved their hats furiously, and shook their fists and made murderous cuts in the air with their clubs. The cars moved away slowly, in two directions, and the mob left in the camp shrieked after them.

When they had gone, the shouting stopped suddenly. The men stood, wondering and uneasy. They looked down the road and saw the cars jog out of sight. Mac and Jim and London walked back into the camp side by side.

"I hope to Christ they do some damage," Mac said. "If everything happens to us and nothing to anybody else, we aren't goin' to last much longer. Come on, Jim. Let's take a look at the old guy Dan. An' then maybe we can get some guys together and go over and see Al. I promised Al some-thing. He'll need some encouragement."

London said, "I'm goin' to see about gettin' some water. The barrel's low."

Jim led the way to the hospital tent. The flaps were tied back to let in the morning sunshine. In a pool of sun old Dan lay. His face was transparent white and waxen, and heavy black veins puffed out on his cheeks. "How you feeling, Dan?" Jim asked.

The old man mumbled weakly.

"What's that you say?" Mac bent over to hear.

Dan's lips worked carefully this time. "I ain't had nothing to eat."

Jim cried, "You poor devil. I'll get you something." He stepped out of the door. "Mac," he shouted, "they're coming back."

From the direction of the town four cars drew up and stopped in the road. London came running and flung himself through the crowd. "What th' hell's the matter?"

The driver of the first car smiled foolishly. The crowd fell completely silent. "We couldn't get through," the driver said, and he smiled again. "There's a barricade across the road."

"I thought I told you to crash it if it was there."

"You don't unda'stan'," the driver said dully. "They was two cars ahead of us. We come to the barricade. There's about twenty guys with guns behind it." He swallowed nervously. "A guy with a star on to him gets up on top an' he says, 'It's unlawful to picket in this county. Get back.' So that old Hud-son tried to go around, an' it tips over in a ditch, an' the guys spill out. So, like you said, the guys run an' get in the shovel-nose." The men in the other seats nodded solemnly at his words.

"Go on." London's voice was subdued.

"So then the shovel-nose starts to try to knock over the barricade. So then those guys start the tear gas an' shoot the tires off the shovel-nose. Then our guys start coughin', an' there's so much gas you can't see. So then those guys got on gas masks, an' they come in, an' they got 'bout a thousan' hand-cuffs." He smiled again. "So we come back. We couldn't do nothing. We didn' even have a decent rock to throw. They grabbed all the guys in the shovel-nose. Hell, I never seen so much gas." He looked up. "There's the other bunch comin'," he said hopelessly. "I guess they got the road blocked at both ends."

A curious, long sigh escaped from the crowd. Some of the men turned and walked slowly back toward the tents, walked glidingly, with their heads down, as though they were in deep thought.

London turned to Mac, and his face was perplexed. Mac said, "Do you suppose we could get the cars across the orchard, and out that way? They can't have all the roads blocked."

London shook his head. "Too wet. A car'd squat down in the mud before we could get it ten feet."

Mac leaped on the running-board of one of the cars. "Listen, you guys," he cried. "There's one way we can get through. Let's the whole bunch of us go down there and knock those barricades off the road. They can't block us in, God damn it!" He paused for a response, a quickening. But the men looked away from him, each waiting for another to speak.

At last a man said, "We got nothing to fight with, mister. We can't fight guns an' gas with our han's. Give us guns, an' we'll fight."

Mac's speech turned into fury. "You let 'em shoot our guys, an' burn the buildings of our friends, an' you won't fight. Now they got you trapped, an' still you won't fight. Why even a God damn rat'll fight when he's in a trap."

The hopelessness hung in the air like a gas itself. The same man repeated, "Mister, we can't fight guns and gas with our han's."

Mac's voice broke with rage. "Will any six of you yellow bastards fight *me* with your hands? *Will you?*" His mouth worked helplessly. "Try to help you—try to get something for you——" he shrieked.

London reached up and pulled him firmly off the running-board. Mac's eyes were mad. He tried to jerk free. "I'll kill the yellow bastards myself," he cried.

Jim stepped over and took his other arm. "Mac," he said. "Mac, for Christ's sake, you don't know what you're saying."

Between them, Jim and London turned him and led him through the crowd, and the men looked shame-facedly at the ground. They told each other softly, "But we can't fight guns and gas with our hands."

The raiders climbed stiffly down from their cars and joined the crowd, and left the automobiles standing in the road.

Mac was limp now. He allowed himself to be led into London's tent, and settled down on the mattress. Jim soaked a rag in the water bucket and tried to wash his face, but Mac took the cloth from him and did it for himself. "I'm all right now," he said quietly. "I'm no good. The Party ought to get rid of me. I lose my head."

"You're dead for sleep," said Jim.

"Oh, I know. But it isn't that. They won't help themselves. Sometimes I've seen men just like these go through a machine-gun nest with their hands. And here today they won't fight a few green deputy-sheriffs. Just scared to death." He said, "Jim, I'm as bad as they are. I'm supposed to use my head. When I got up on that running-board, I was going to try to steam them up. An' then the God damn sheep made me mad. I didn't have any right to get mad. They ought to kick me out of the Party."

London said in sympathy, "I got pretty damn mad myself."

Mac looked at each of his fingers carefully. "Makes me want to run away," he said ruefully. "I'd like to crawl down in a haystack and go to sleep, and to hell with the whole damn bunch of them."

Jim said, "Just as soon as you get rested up, you'll feel strong again. Lie down and get some sleep, Mac. We'll call you if we need you, won't we, London?"

"Sure," said London. "You just stretch out. There ain't nothing you can do now. I'm goin' to go out an' talk to them squad leaders. Maybe we could take a few good guys an' sneak up on the barricades."

"I'm scared they've got us now," Mac said. "They took the heart out of the guys before they could get going." He lay down on the mattress. "What they need is blood," he muttered. "A mob's got to kill something. Oh, Christ, I guess I've bungled everything right from the start." He closed his eyes, then suddenly opened them again. "Listen, they'll pay us a visit pretty soon, the sheriff or somebody. Be sure and wake me up. Don't let 'em get away with anything. Be sure and call me." He stretched like a cat and clasped his hands over his head. His breathing became regular.

The sun threw shadows of the tent-ropes on the canvas, and in the open entrance a piece of sunlight lay on the foot-beaten earth. Jim and London walked quietly outside. "Poor guy," London said. "He needs it. I never seen a guy so far gone for sleep. I heard how the cops keep a guy awake till he goes crazy."

"He'll be different when he wakes up," said Jim. "Lord, I said I'd take something to old Dan. An' then those cars came up. I better do it now."

"I'll go see how Lisa's getting along. Maybe she better go an' take care of the old duck."

Jim walked to the stove and ladled some beans into a can and carried them to the hospital tent. The idle men, standing about, had collected into little groups. Jim looked into the hospital tent. The triangular sunny place had shortened and fallen off the cot. Old Dan's eyes were closed, and his breathing was slow and light. A curious musty, rancid odor filled the tent, the breath from a congested and slowly dying body. Jim leaned over the cot. "Dan, I brought you something to eat."

Dan opened his eyes slowly. "I don't want none. I ain't got the strength to chew."

"You have to eat, Dan. Have to eat to get strong. Look, I'll put a pillow under your head, and I'll feed you."

"Don't want to get strong." His voice was langorous. "Just want to lay here. I been a top-faller." His eyes closed again. "You'd go up the stick, way up, way up, an' you could see all the little trees, second, third growth timber down below. Then you fix your safety belt." He sighed deeply, and his mouth went on whispering. A shadow fell in the spot of sunlight. Jim looked up.

Lisa stood in the door of the tent, and her baby was under the shoulder blanket. "I got enough to do, takin' care of the baby. He says I got to come an' take care of a old man, too."

Jim said, "Sh-h." He stood from the cot so she could see Dan's sunken face.

She crept in and sat down on the extra cot. "Oh, I di'n' know. What you want me to do?"

"Nothing. Just stay with him."

She said, "I don't like 'em like that. I can smell 'em. I know that smell." She shifted nervously, covered the baby's round face to protect it from the smell.

"Shh-h," Jim said. "Maybe he's going to be all right."

"Not with that smell. I know that smell. Part of 'im's dead already."

"Poor devil!" Jim said.

Something in the words caught at her. Her eyes grew wet with tears. "I'll stay. I seen it before. It don't hurt nobody."

Jim sat down beside her. "I like to be near you," he said softly.

"Don't you come none of that."

"No, I won't. I just wondered why it was warm beside you."

"I ain't cold."

He turned his face away. "I'm going to talk to you, Lisa. You won't understand, and it won't matter, not a bit. Everything's crumbling down and washing away. But this is just a little bit of the whole thing. This isn't anything, Lisa. You and I aren't much in the whole thing. See, Lisa? I'm telling it to myself, but I understand it better with you listening. You don't know what I'm talking about, do you, Lisa?"

He saw a blush creep up the side of her neck. "I jus' had a baby," she said. "Besides, I ain't that kind." She lifted her shamed eyes. "Don't talk that way. Don't get that tone on you," she begged. "You know I ain't that kind." He reached out his hand to pat her, but she shrank away from him. "No."

He stood up. "Be nice to the old guy. See? There's water and a spoon on the table. Give him a little, now and then." He raised his head tensely to listen to a stir of voices in the camp, a gradually increasing stir. And then, over the bass of voices, a haranguing voice sounded, a voice that rose and fell angrily. "I've got to go," Jim said. "Take care of him." He hurried out of the tent.

By the stoves he saw men collecting around some central object, all faces inward. The angry voice came from the center. As Jim watched, the crowd moved sideways toward the naked little stand that had been built for Joy's body. The mob touched the stand and flowed around it, but out of the group one man shot up and took his position in the stand. Jim ran over. He could see, now. It was the sullen, scowling Burke. His arms gesticulated. His voice bellowed over the heads of the crowd. Jim saw London hurrying in from the road.

Burke grasped the hand-rail. "There he is now," he shouted. "Look at 'im. That's the guy that's spoiled ever'-thing. What the hell's he done? Set in his tent an' et canned peaches while we got wet and lived on garbage a pig wouldn' touch."

London's mouth was open with astonishment. "What's goin' on here?" he cried.

Burke leaned forward over the rail. "I'll tell you what's goin' on. Us guys decided we wanted a real leader. We decided we want a guy that won't sell out for a load o' canned goods."

London's face paled, and his shoulders dropped. With a roar he charged the unresisting crowd, flung men aside, burrowed through the mass of men. He came to the stand and grasped the hand-rail. As he pulled himself up, Burke kicked at his head, missed, struck the shoulder and tore one hand loose from the rail. London roared again. He was under the rail and on his feet. Burke struck at his face, and missed. And then, with the terrible smooth speed of a heavy man, London lanced with his left hand and, as Burke ducked, the great right fist caught him on the side of the jaw, lifted him clear, and dropped him. His head hung over the edge of the platform, broken jaw torn sideways, shattered teeth hanging loosely between his lips. A thin stream of blood flowed from his mouth, beside his nose and eye, and disappeared into his hair.

London stood, panting, over him, looking down. He raised his head slowly. "Does any more sons-of-bitches think I double-crossed 'em?"

The men nearest Burke's hanging head stared, fascinated. From the other sides of the stand the people began to mill, to press in, standing on tip-toes for a look. Their eyes were bright and angry. A man said, "Bust his jaw clean off. That's blood out o' his brain." Another shouted hysterically, "Killed 'um. Busted his head off."

Women swam through the crowd and looked woodenly at the hanging head. A heavy, sobbing gasp went up from the mob. The eyes flared. All the shoulders were dropped, and the arms bowed dangerously. London still stood panting, but his face was perplexed. He looked down at his fist, at the split and bleeding knuckles. Then he looked out over the crowd for help, and he saw Jim standing on the outskirts. Jim shook his clasped hands together over his head. And then he pointed to the road, where the cars stood, and down the road, and to the cars again, and down the road again. London looked back at the snarling mob. The perplexity left his face and he scowled.

"All right, you guys," he yelled. "Why ain't I done nothing? Because you ain't helped me. But by Christ, now you're ready! Nothin' can stop you now." A long, throaty animal howl went up. London held up his hands. "Who'll follow now, and knock hell out o' that barricade?" The crowd was changing rapidly. The eyes of the men and women were entranced. The bodies weaved slowly, in unison. No more lone cries came from lone men. They moved together, looked alike. The roar was one voice, coming from many throats.

"Some of you bring cars," London shouted. "Come on, the rest of you. Come on, we'll see. Come, come on." He vaulted down from the stand and fought his way through to the head of the mob. Quickly the cars were started. The crowd poured into the road, and it was no longer loose and listless. It had become a quick, silent and deadly efficient machine. It swung down the road at a dog-trot, controlled and directed. And behind it the cars moved slowly along.

Jim had watched the start. He commanded himself aloud, "Don't get caught. Don't get caught. Don't let it catch you. Use your head."

Most of the women were running with the departing men, but a few who remained behind looked strangely at Jim, for his eyes, too, were entranced as he stared down the road after the terrible mechanism. When it had disappeared he sighed shudderingly and turned away. His hand went up to the hurt shoulder and pressed it, to make a steadying pain. He walked slowly to London's tent, went in silently, and sat down on a box.

Mac looked at him under lowered eyelids. Only a shiny slit showed that he was awake. "How long've I been sleeping, Jim?"

"Just a little while. I don't think it's even noon yet, near noon."

"I dreamed a lot, but I'm rested. I think I'll get up now."

"Better get some more sleep if you can."

"What's the use? I'm rested now." He opened his eyes wide. "Lost the sandy feeling. You sleep hard when you're that tired. I dreamed commotion."

"Better go to sleep again."

"No." He sat up and stretched. "Anything happen while I was asleep? It's awful quiet out there."

"Plenty happened," Jim said. "Burke tried to kick London out, and London smashed him—nearly killed him, and—Christ! I forgot Burke." He ran to the door, and around the back to the tent, and looked toward the stand. Then he went into the tent again. "Somebody took him in," he said.

Mac was up now, and excited. "Tell me."

"Well, when the crowd saw the blood they went nuts, and London started 'em down to break the barricade."

Mac cried, "Didn't I tell you? They need blood. That works. That's what I told you. Well then—what?"

"They're down there now. God, Mac, you ought to of seen them. It was like all of them disappeared, and it was just one big—animal, going down the road. Just all one animal. I nearly was there. I wanted to go, and then I thought, 'You can't. You've got to use your head.'"

"Right!" said Mac. "People think a mob is wasteful, but I've seen plenty; and I tell you, a mob with something it wants to do is just about as efficient as trained soldiers, but tricky. They'll knock that barricade, but then what? They'll want to do something else before they cool off." And he went on, "That's right, what you said. It *is* a big animal. It's different from the men in it. And it's stronger than all the men put together. It doesn't want the same things men want—it's like Doc said—and we don't know what it'll do."

"It'll get that barricade," said Jim.

"That's not what I mean. The *animal* don't want the barricade. I don't know what it wants. Trouble is, guys that study people always think it's men, and it isn't men. It's a different kind of animal. It's as different from men as dogs are. Jim, it's swell when we can use it, but we don't know enough. When it gets started it might do anything." His face was alive and excited, and slightly fearful.

Jim said, "Listen, I think I hear——" He ran to the entrance. "Coming back," he cried. "It's different now. It's spread out now, not the same."

Mac stood beside him. The road was full of the returning men. London broke out ahead and trotted heavily toward them. And when he came near enough he yelled, "Get back in the tent. Get back in the tent."

"What's he mean?" Jim asked. But Mac pushed him inside the tent, untied the strings and dropped the flaps.

"He knows," Mac said. "Just keep quiet and let him handle it. No matter what happens, don't go out there."

They heard the rain of footsteps on the ground, and shouting voices. Then they saw London's squat black shadow on the canvas and heard him yell, "Now you guys cool off."

"We'll show 'im who's yellow bastards!"

London cried, "You're sore because we told you off. Now you go an' get a drink an' cool down. You just done fine, but you ain't a'gonna get my friend. He's your friend, too. I tell you he's been workin' for you till he's dead tired."

Mac and Jim, in the tent, could feel the thrust change, break up, lose itself in a hundred cries. "We know, London."

"Sure, but he called us yellow."

Mac's breath came out, heavily. "That was close, Jim. Jesus, that was close." London's square shadow still stood on the tent wall, but the many excited voices drifted and lost their impact.

London stretched the subject. "If any of you guys think I got canned peaches, you can come in and look."

"Hell, no, London. We never thought that."

"It was that son-of-a-bitch Burke."

"He's been workin' against you, London. I heard him."

"Well, you guys clear out, then. I got work to do." The shadow stayed still on the tent wall until the voices had dwindled until no crowd faced the tent. London lifted the flap and stepped tiredly inside.

"Thanks," said Mac. "You don't know how close it was any better than I do. You handled 'em, London. Oh, you handled 'em."

London said, "I was scared. You won't think no worse of me, Mac, for that. On the way back I caught myself wantin' to come an' kill you myself." He grinned. "I don't know why."

"Nobody does," said Mac. "But that's the way it is. Tell us what happened down the road."

"We ironed 'em out," said London. "We just rolled over 'em like they wasn't there. They give us the gas, an' some of the guys coughed an' cried, but, hell, them green cops didn't stand a chance. Some of 'em got away—I guess most of 'em did. But the rest of 'em got kicked to pieces like cheese. God, the guys was sore."

"Any shooting?"

"No. Too quick for 'em. They shot over us, thought we'd stop, I guess. But we come right on. Some cops like to shoot guys, but most of 'em don't, I guess. An' then we just rolled 'em out, an' tore down the barricade."

"Well, did the cars get out?"

"Hell, yes, eight of 'em went through, loaded with guys cuttin' hell loose."

"Kill any of the cops?" Mac demanded.

"Huh? Kill 'em? I don't know. I didn't look. Maybe we did. We might of. I bet machine-guns wouldn't of stopped us."

"That's swell," said Mac. "If we could turn on the heat like that when we wanted it, and turn if off when we were through, we'd have our God damn revolution tomorrow, and all over tomorrow night. The guys got over it pretty quick."

"It was all that runnin' that did it," London said. "Damn near a mile. Time they got back, they was clear winded. I feel sick myself. I ain't used to runnin'."

"I know," said Mac. "It's not the running, so much, though. A thing like that gets you all messed up inside. I bet a lot of the guys are losing their breakfast right now."

London seemed suddenly to see Jim. He went over and banged him a clap on the back. "You pulled it, Jim. I was standin' up there after I cold-cocked Burke; I didn't know what the hell to do. An' them guys in the circle didn't know what to do, neither. They was all ready to get me, or any-body. An' I look out, and I seen you pointin', an' I know what to do with 'em."

Jim's face was alight with pleasure. "I'm not much use, with my bum shoulder. I was thinking what Mac said about a little blood setting the guys off. You remember saying that, Mac?"

"Sure I remember. But I'm not sure I would of thought of it out there. I don't know how you do it, Jim. Everybody loses their head except you. I heard about your old man; he wasn't a genius, all he knew was fight. I don't know where you learned to use your bean and keep clear."

"I've got to be some use," Jim said. "My father was like you say, but my mother was so cool she'd make you shiver."

London flexed his hand at his side, and then he looked in astonishment at his crushed knuckles. "Holy Christ! Look at that!"

"You sure smashed 'em," said Mac.

"I smashed 'em on that son-of-a-bitch Burke. How is he, Jim? Felt like I knocked his head clear off when I socked 'im."

Jim said, "I don't know how he is. Somebody took 'im off the stand."

"Guess I better see," said London. "Funny I never felt that hand till now."

"When you get mixed up with the animal, you never feel anything," said Mac.

"What animal?"

"Oh, it's just a kind of a joke. Be a good idea if you look at Burke. And see how the guys feel. They'll feel pretty rocky by now, I think."

London said, "I don't trust 'em no more. I can't tell what they'll do no more. I'm glad I wasn't back of that barricade."

Mac said, "Well, I'm glad you was in front of this tent. Jim an' me might be hangin' up on an apple tree by now."

"There was a minute there——" said London. He gath-ered the tent-flaps and tied them back. The sun did not enter the tent, it had passed its meridian. Mac and Jim watched London walk away, and then they faced each other again.

Mac flopped down on the mattress. Jim looked at him until Mac said, "You accusing me of something?"

"No, I was just wondering—seems to me now we've won a fight an' got our guys through we're more in danger of losing than ever. We came out here to do something, Mac. Have we messed up everything?"

Mac said sharply, "You think we're too important, and this little bang-up is too important. If the thing blew up right now it'd be worth it. A lot of the guys've been believing this crap about the noble American working-man, an' the partner-ship of capital and labor. A lot of 'em are straight now. They know how much capital thinks of 'em, and how quick capital would poison 'em like a bunch of ants. An' by Christ, we showed 'em two things—what they are, an' what they've got to do. And this last little ruckus showed 'em they could do it. Remember what the 'Frisco strike did to Sam? Well, all these guys'll get to be a little like Sam."

"But do you think they've got brains enough to see it?"

"Not brains, Jim. It don't take brains. After it's all over the thing'll go on working down inside of 'em. They'll know it without thinking it out."

"Well, what do you think's going to happen now?"

Mac rubbed his front teeth with a finger. "I guess they'll just have to steam-roller us out of here, Jim. Might be this afternoon, might be tonight."

"Well, what do you think; had we better just fade, or put up a fight?"

"Fight, if we can make the guys do it," said Mac. "If they sneak off, they get a bad feeling out of it, but if they fight and get licked, well, they still fought; and it's worth doing."

Jim settled down on one knee. "Look, if they come through with guns they're going to kill a lot of our guys."

Mac's eyes grew slitted and cold. "We keep switching sides, Jim. Suppose they do kill some of our men? That helps our side. For every man they kill ten new ones come over to us. The news goes creeping around the country and men all over hear it and get mad. Guys that are just half-warm get hot, see? But if we sneak off and the word gets around, and men say 'They didn't even put up a fight,' why all the working stiffs will be unsure of themselves. If we fight, an' the news gets around, other men in the same position'll fight too."

Jim put down the other knee and squatted on his heels. "I wanted to get the thing straight. But will the guys fight?"

"I don't know. Right now they won't. They're pretty sick. Maybe later. Maybe if we could throw 'em another chicken like Burke they would. Burke stepped on the third rail just in time, just when we needed him. Maybe somebody else'll spill a little blood for the cause."

Jim said, "Mac, if blood's all we need, I could pull off this bandage and start the hole bleeding."

"You're kind of funny, Jim," Mac said kindly. "You're so God damn serious."

"I don't see anything funny."

"No. Remember the lady that was buying a dog? She asks, 'Are you sure he's a bloodhound?' The owner says, 'Sure he is. Bleed for the lady, Oscar.'"

Jim smiled thinly. Mac went on, "No, Jim, you're more use to the cause than a hundred of these guys."

"Well, a little loss of blood won't hurt me."

Mac stroked his lower lip nervously. "Jim," he said. "Did you ever see four or five dogs all fighting?"

"No."

"Well, if one of those dogs gets hurt or goes down, all the rest'll turn on him and kill him."

"So what?"

"So—men do that sometimes, too. I don't know why. It's kind of like Doc says to me one time, 'Men hate something in themselves.'"

"Doc was a nice guy, but he didn't get anywhere with his high-falutin' ideas. His ideas didn't go anywhere, just around in a circle."

"All the same, I wish he was here. Your shoulder feel all right?"

"Sure. I'm not using it any more than I can help."

Mac got up. "Come on, let's look at it. Take off that coat." Jim worked the coat off. Mac pulled the plaster loose and carefully raised the bandage. "Looks pretty good. It's a little bit angry. I'll throw away a couple of layers of this gauze. I'll be glad when we get in town. You can get it taken care of. Now I'll put this clean part back." He pressed the plaster down in place and held it firmly until the body heat made it take hold.

"Maybe we'll find Doc in town," said Jim. "He talked awful funny just before he disappeared. Maybe he got disgusted, or scared, and beat it."

"Here, I'll help you with your coat. You can forget that. If Doc was goin' to get disgusted, he'd of got years ago. An' I've seen him under fire. He don't get scared."

London came in and stood quietly in the doorway. He looked serious and frightened. "I didn't kill 'im, but damn near. His jaw's busted terrible. I'm scared he'll die if he don't get a doctor."

"Well, we can ship him to town, but I don't think they'd take very good care of him in there."

London went on, "That woman of his is raisin' hell. Says she's goin' to have the whole bunch of us up for murder. Says the whole strike was just to get Burke."

Mac said, "It'd almost be worth it, at that. I never liked the bastard. I always thought he was the stool-pigeon. How do the guys feel?"

"They're just sittin' around, like you said. Look sick, like a bunch of kids that broke into a candy store."

"Sure," said Mac. "They used up the juice that should of lasted 'em about a week. We better get some food into 'em if we can. Maybe they'll sleep it off then. You're sure right, London. We need a doctor. How's the guy that hurt his ankle?"

"Well, he's raisin' merry hell too. Says it ain't set right, an' it hurts. An' he won't never be able to walk no more. All this howlin' around ain't helpin' the way the guys feel none."

"Yeah, an' there's Al," said Mac. "I wonder how Al is? We ought to go over an' see him. Think the guys you told to stay there stayed?"

London shrugged. "I don't know."

"Well, could we get half a dozen guys to go over with us?"

London said, "I don't think you'll get none of these guys to go no place. They just want to set there an' look at their feet."

"Well, by Christ, I'll go alone, then. Al's a good guy."

"I'll go with you, Mac," Jim broke in.

"No. You stay here."

London said, "I don't think there's nobody to bother you."

Mac begged, "Jim, I wish you'd stay. S'pose they got both of us? There'd be nobody here to go on. Stay here, Jim."

"I'm going. I've sat around here and nursed myself long enough. Why don't you stay and let me go?"

"All right, kid," Mac said resignedly. "We'll just be careful, and keep our eyes open. Try to keep the guys alive till we get back, London. Try to get a little of that beef and beans into 'em. They're sick of it, but it's food. We ought to be hearing something about those cars pretty soon."

London grunted, "I guess I'll just open me up a can of them peaches, an' some sardines. The guys said I had a flock of 'em, piled right up to the roof. I'll have some ready for you when you get back."

15

THEY walked out into the clear yellow sunshine. The camp looked bedraggled and grey in the clean light. A litter had accumulated since Burton was gone, bits of paper, strings, overalls hung on the guy-ropes of the tents. Mac and Jim walked out of the camp and across the surrounding field, to the edge of the orchard. At the line of trees Mac stopped. His eyes moved slowly across the horizontal fields of vision. "Look close, Jim," he advised. "It's probably a damn fool thing to go over alone. I know it isn't good sense." He studied the orchard. The long, sun-spotted aisles were silent. There was no movement. "It's so quiet. Makes me suspicious. It's too quiet." He reached to a limb and took down a small, misshapen apple the pickers had left. "God, that tastes good. I'd forgot about apples. Always forget what's so easy."

"I don't see anybody moving," said Jim. "Not a soul."

"Well look, we'll edge down in line with the trees. Anybody looking down a row won't see us, then." They stepped slowly in under the big apple trees. Their eyes moved restlessly about. They walked through shadows of branches and leaves, and the sun struck them with soft, warm blows.

Jim asked, "Mac, do you s'pose we could get a leave of absence some time and go where nobody knows us, and just sit down in an orchard?"

" 'Bout two hours of it, and you'd be raring to go again."

"I never had time to look at things, Mac, never. I never looked how leaves come out. I never looked at the way things happen. This morning there was a whole line of ants on the floor of the tent. I couldn't watch them. I was thinking about something else. Some time I'd like to sit all day and look at bugs, and never think of anything else."

"They'd drive you nuts," said Mac. "Men are bad enough, but bugs'd drive you nuts."

"Well, just once in a while you get that feeling—I never look at anything. I never take time to see anything. It's going to be over, and I won't know—even how an apple grows."

They moved on slowly. Mac's restless eyes roved about

among the trees. "You can't see everything," he said. "I took a leave and went into the woods in Canada. Say, in a couple of days I came running out of there. I wanted trouble, I was hungry for a mess."

"Well, I'd like to try it sometime. The way old Dan talks about timber——"

"Damn it, Jim, you can't have everything! We've got something old Dan hasn't got. You can't have everything. In a few days we'll be back in town, and we'll be so damned anxious to get into another fuss we'll be biting our nails. You've got to take it easy till that shoulder heals. I'll take you to a flophouse where you can watch all the bugs you want. Keep back of the line of trees. You're standing out like a cow on a sidehill."

"It's nice out here," said Jim.

"It's too damn nice. I'm scared there's a trap someplace."

Through the trees they could see Anderson's little white house, and its picket fence, and the burning geraniums in the yard. "No one around," said Jim.

"Well, take it easy." At the last row Mac stopped again and let his eyes travel slowly across the open. The great black square on the ground, where the barn had been, still sent up a lazy, pungent smoke. The white tank-house looked tall and lonely. "Looks O.K.," Mac said. "Let's go in the back way." He tried to open the picket gate quietly, but the latch clicked and the hinges growled. They walked up the short path to the porch with its yellowing passion vine. Mac knocked on the door.

A voice from inside called, "Who is it?"

"Is that you, Al?"

"Yeah."

"Are you alone?"

"Yeah. Who are you?"

"It's Mac."

"Oh, come on in, Mac. The door ain't locked."

They went into the kitchen. Al lay on his narrow bed against the wall. He seemed to have grown gaunt in the few days. The skin hung loosely on his face. "Hi, Mac. I thought nobody'd ever come. My old man went out early."

"We tried to get over before, Al. How's all the hurts?"

"They hurt plenty," said Al. "And when you're all alone they hurt worse. Who burned the barn, Mac?"

"Vigilantes. We're sorry as hell, Al. We had guards here, but they got a fast one pulled on 'em."

"My old man just raised hell all night, Mac. Talked all night. Give me hell about four times an hour, all night."

"We're damn sorry."

Al cleared one hand from the bedclothes and scratched his cheek. "I'm still with you, Mac. But the old man wants to blast you. He went in this morning to get the sheriff to kick you off'n the place. Says you're trespassin', an' he wants you off. Says he's punished for listenin' to guys like you. Says I can go to hell if I string along with you. He was mad as a hornet, Mac."

"I was scared he would be, Al. Listen, we know you're with us, see? It don't do no good to make that old man any sorrier than he is. If it'd do any good, it'd be different. You just pretend to come around to his side. We'll understand that, Al. You can keep in touch with us. I'm awful sorry for your old man."

Al sighed deeply. "I was scared you'd think I double-crossed you. If you know I ain't, I'll tell him t'hell with you."

"That's the stuff, Al. And we'll give you a boost in town, too. Oh, say, Al, did Doc look in on you last night?"

"No. Why?"

"Well, he started over here before the fire, an' he ain't been back."

"Jesus! What do you think happened to him?"

"I'm scared they snatched the poor devil."

"They been pushing you all around, ain't they?"

"Yeah. But our guys got in some good licks this morning. But if your old man turns us in, I guess they'll roll over us tomorrow."

"Whole thing flops, huh, Mac?"

"That don't mean anything. We done what we came to do. The thing goes right on, Al. You just make peace an' pretend you ain't ever goin' to get burned no more." He listened. "Is that somebody coming?" He ran through the kitchen and into the front of the house, and looked out a window.

"It's my old man, I recognize his step," said Al.

Mac returned. "I wanted to see if anybody was with him. He's all alone. We could make a sneak, I guess. I'd rather tell him I'm sorry."

"You better not," Al advised. "He won't listen to nothing from you. He hates your guts."

There were steps on the porch and the door burst open. Anderson stood, surprised and glaring. "God damn it," he shouted. "You bastards get out of here. I've been and turned you in. The sheriff's goin' kick the whole smear of you off my land." His chest swelled with rage.

Mac said, "We just wanted to tell you we're sorry. We didn't burn the barn. Some of the boys from town did."

"What th' hell do I care who burned it? It's burned, the crop's burned. What do you damn bums know about it? I'll lose the place sure, now." His eyes watered with rage. "You bastards never owned nothing. You never planted trees an' seen 'em grow an' felt 'em with your hands. You never owned a thing, never went out an' touched your own apple trees with your hands. What do you know?"

"We never had a chance to own anything," Mac said. "We'd like to own something and plant trees."

Anderson ignored his words. "I listened to your promises. Look what happened. The whole crop's burned, there's paper coming due."

Mac asked, "How about the pointers?"

Anderson's hands settled slowly to his sides. A look of cold, merciless hatred came into his eyes. He said slowly, softly, "The kennel was—against—the barn."

Mac turned to Al and nodded. For a moment Al questioned with his eyes, and then he scowled. "What he says goes. You guys get the hell out, and don't never come back."

Anderson ran to the bed and stood in front of it. "I could shoot you men now," he said, "but the sheriff's goin' to do it for me, an' damn quick."

Mac touched Jim on the arm, and they went out and shut the door. They didn't bother to look around when they went out the gate. Mac set out so rapidly that Jim had to stretch his stride to keep up. The sun was cutting downward now, and the shadows of whole trees lay between the rows, and the wind was stirring in the branches, so that both trees and ground seemed to quiver nervously.

"It keeps you hopping, keeping the picture," Mac said. "You see a guy hurt, or somebody like Anderson smashed, or you see a cop ride down a Jew girl, an' you think, what the hell's the use of it. An' then you think of the millions starving, and it's all right again. It's worth it. But it keeps you jumping between pictures. Don't it ever get you, Jim?"

"Not very much. It isn't long ago I saw my mother die; seems years, but it wasn't long ago. She wouldn't speak to me, she just looked at me. She was hurt so bad she didn't even want a priest. I guess I got something burned out of me that night. I'm sorry for Anderson, but what the hell. If I can give up my whole life, he ought to be able to give up a barn."

"Well, to some of those guys property's more important than their lives."

Jim said, "Slow down, Mac. What's your hurry? I seem to get tired easy."

Mac did slow his steps a little. "I thought that's what he went to town for. I want to get back before anything happens. I don't know what this sheriff'll do, but he'll be happy as hell to split us up." They walked silently over the soft, dark earth, and the shadows flickered on them. At the clearing they slowed down. Mac said, "Well, nothing's happened yet, anyway."

The smoke rose slowly from the stoves. Jim asked, "Where do you s'pose all the guys are?"

"In sleeping off the drunk, I guess. It wouldn't be a bad idea if we got some sleep, too. Prob'ly be up all night."

London moved over and met them. "Everything all right?" Mac asked.

"Just the same."

"Well, I was right. Anderson's been in and asked the sheriff to kick us off."

"Well?"

"Well, we wait. Don't tell the guys about it."

"Maybe you was right about that," London said, "but you was sure wrong about what them guys would eat. They cleaned us out. There ain't a damn drop o' beans left. I saved you a couple of cans, over in my tent."

"Maybe we won't need anything more to eat," said Mac.

"How do you mean?"

"We prob'ly won't any of us be here tomorrow."

In the tent London pointed to the two food cans on the box. "D'you s'pose the sheriff'll try to kick us off?" he asked.

"Damn right. He won't let a chance like that go by."

"Well, will he come shootin', d'you suppose? Or will he give the guys a warnin'?"

Mac said, "Hell, I don't know. Where's all the men?"

"All under cover, asleep."

Mac said, "I heard a car. May be our guys coming back."

London cocked his head. "Too big," he said. "That's one of them big babies."

They ran outside. Up the road from Torgas a huge Mack dump-truck rolled. It had a steel bed and sides, supported by two sets of double tires. It pulled up in front of the camp and stopped. A man stood up in the steel bed, and in his hands he held a submachine-gun with a big cartridge cylinder behind the forward grip. The heads of other men showed above the truck sides. Strikers began to boil out of the tents.

The standing man shouted, "I'm sheriff o' this county. If there's anyone in authority I want to see him." The mob approached closer and looked curiously at the truck.

Mac said softly, "Careful, London. They may pop us off. They could do it now if they wanted to." They walked forward, to the edge of the road, and stopped; and the mob was lining the road now, too.

London said, "I'm the boss, mister."

"Well, I've got a trespass complaint. We've been fair to you men. We've asked you to go back to work, or, if you wanted to strike, to do it peacefully. You've destroyed property and committed homicide. This morning you sent out men to destroy property. We had to shoot some of those men, and we caught the rest." He looked down at the men in the truck, and then up again. "Now we don't want any bloodshed, so we're going to let you out. You have all night tonight to get out. If you head straight for the county line, nobody'll bother you. But if this camp is here at daylight tomorrow, we're going through it."

The men stood silently and watched him. Mac whispered to London. London said, "Trespassin' don't give you no right to shoot guys."

"Maybe not, but resisting officers does. Now I'm talking fair with you, so you'll know what to expect. At daylight to-morrow a hundred men, in ten trucks like this, are coming out. Every man will have a gun, and we have three cases of Mills bombs. Some of you men who know can tell the others what a Mills bomb is. That's all. We're through fooling with you. You have till daylight to get out of the county. That's all." He turned forward. "Might as well drive along, Gus." He sank from sight behind the steel truck side. The wheels turned slowly, and gathered speed.

One of the strikers leaped into the shallow ditch and picked up a rock. And he stood holding it in his hand and looking at it as the truck rolled away. The men watched the truck go, and then they turned back into the camp.

London sighed. "Well, that sounds like orders. He didn't mean no funny business."

Mac said impatiently, "I'm hungry. I'm going to eat my beans." They followed him back into the tent. He gobbled his food quickly and hungrily. "Hope you got some, London."

"Me? Oh, sure. What we goin' to do now, Mac?"

"Fight," said Mac.

"Yeah, but if he brings the stuff he said, pineapples an' stuff, it ain't goin' to be no more fight than the stockyards."

"Bull," said Mac, and a little jet of chewed beans shot from his mouth. "If he had that stuff, he wouldn't need to tell us about it. He just hopes we'll get scattered so we can't put up a fight. If we move out tonight, they'll pick us off. They never do what they say."

London looked into Mac's face, hung on to his eyes. "Is that straight, Mac? You said I was on your side. Are you put-tin' somethin' over?"

Mac looked away. "We got to fight," he said. "If we get out without a scrap ever'thing we've been through'll be wasted."

"Yeah, but if we fight, a lot of guys that ain't done no harm is goin' get shot."

Mac put his unfinished food down on the box. "Look," he said. "In a war a general knows he's going to lose men. Now this is a war. If we get run out o' here without a fight, it's losing ground." For a moment he covered his eyes with his hand. "London," he said. "It's a hell of a responsibility. I know what we should do; you're the boss; for Christ's sake, do what you want. Don't make me take all the blame."

London said plaintively, "Yeah, but you know about things. You think we ought to fight, really?"

"Yes, we ought."

"Well, hell then, we'll fight—that is, if we can get the guys to fight."

"I know," said Mac. "They may run out on us, every one of 'em. The ones that heard the sheriff will tell the others. They may turn on us and say we caused the trouble."

London said, "Some ways, I hope they clear out. Poor bastards, they don't know nothing. But like you say, if they're ever goin' to get clear, they got to take it now. How about the hurt guys?" London went on, "Burke and old Dan, and the guy with the busted ankle?"

"Leave 'em," said Mac. "It's the only thing we can do. The county'll have to take care of 'em."

"I'm going to take a look around," London said. "I'm gettin' nervous as a cat."

"You ain't the only one," said Mac.

When he was gone, Jim glanced at Mac, and then began to eat the cold beans and strings of beef. "I wonder if they'll fight?" he asked. "D'you think they'd really let the guys through if they wanted to run?"

"Oh, the sheriff would. He'd be only too damn glad to get rid of 'em, but I don't trust the vigilante boys."

"They won't have anything to eat tonight, Mac. If they're scared already, there won't be any dinner to buck 'em up."

Mac scraped his can and set it down. "Jim," he said. "If I told you to do something, would you do it?"

"I don't know. What is it?"

"Well, the sun's going down pretty soon, and it'll be dark.

They're going to lay for you and me, Jim. Don't make any mistake about that. They're going to want to get us, bad. I want you to get out, soon as it gets dark, get clear and go back to town."

"Why in hell should I do that?"

Mac's eyes slid over Jim's face and went to the ground again. "When I came out here, I thought I was hell on wheels. You're worth ten of me, Jim. I know that now. If anything happened to me, there's plenty of guys to take my place, but you've got a genius for the work. We can't spare you, Jim. If you was to get knocked off in a two-bit strike— well, it's bad economy."

"I don't believe it," said Jim. "Our guys are to be used, not saved. I couldn't run out. Y'said yourself this was a part of the whole thing. It's little, but it's important."

"I *want* you to go, Jim. You can't fight with that arm. You'd be no damn good here. You couldn't help at all."

Jim's face was rigid. "I won't go," he said. "I might be of some use here. You protect me all the time, Mac. And sometimes I get the feeling you're not protecting me for the Party, but for yourself."

Mac reddened with anger. "O.K. then. Get your can knocked off. I've told you what I think's the best thing. Be pig-headed, if you want. I can't sit still. I'm going out. You do anything you damn please." He went out angrily.

Jim looked up at the back wall of the tent. He could see the outline of the red sun on the canvas. His hand stole up and touched his hurt shoulder, and pressed it gently, all around, in a circle that narrowed to the wound. He winced a little as his exploring fingers neared the hurt. For a long time he sat quietly.

He heard a step in the door and looked around. Lisa stood there, and her baby was in her arms. Jim could see past her, where the line of old cars stood against the road; and on the other side of the road the sun was on the treetops, but in the rows the shade had come. Lisa looked in, with a bird-like interest. Her hair was damp, plastered against her head, and little, uneven finger-waves were pressed into it. The short blanket that covered her shoulders was draped and held to one side with a kind of coquetry. "I seen you was alone," she said. She went to the mattress and sat down and arranged her gingham dress neatly over her legs. "I heard guys say the cops'll throw bombs, an' kill us all," she said lightly.

Jim was puzzled. "It doesn't seem to scare you much."

"No. I ain't never been ascared o' things like that."

"The cops wouldn't hurt you," Jim said. "I don't believe they'll do all that. It's a bluff. Do you want anything?"

"I thought I'd come an' set. I like to—just set here."

Jim smiled. "You like me, don't you Lisa?"

"Yes."

"I like you, too, Lisa."

"You he'ped me with the baby."

Jim asked, "How's old Dan? Did you take care of him?"

"He's all right. Just lays there mumblin'."

"Mac helped you more than I did."

"Yes, but he don't look at me—nice. I like t'hear you talk. You're just a young kid, but you talk nice."

"I talk too much, Lisa. Too much talk, not enough doing things. Look how the evening's coming. We'll light the lantern before long. You wouldn't like to sit here in the dark with me."

"I wouldn't care," she said quickly.

He looked into her eyes again, and his face grew pleased. "Did you ever notice, in the evening, Lisa, how you think of things that happened a long time ago—not even about things that matter? One time in town, when I was a little kid, the sun was going down, and there was a board fence. Well, a grey cat went up and sat on that fence for a moment, long-haired cat, and that cat turned gold for a minute, a gold cat."

"I like cats," Lisa agreed softly. "I had two cats onct, two of them."

"Look. The sun's nearly gone, Lisa. Tomorrow we'll be somewhere else. I wonder where? You'll be on the move, I guess. Maybe I'll be in jail. I've been in jail before."

London and Mac came quietly into the tent together. London looked down at the girl. "What you doing here, Lisa? You better get out. We got business." Lisa got up and clutched her blanket close. She looked sideways at Jim as she passed. London said, "I don't know what's goin' on. There's about ten little meetin's out there, an' they don't want me at none o' them."

"Yeah, I know," Mac said. "The guys're scared. I don't know what they'll do, but they'll want to scram tonight." And then the conversation died. London and Mac sat down on boxes, facing Jim. They sat there while the sun went down and the tent grew a little dusky.

At last Jim said softly, "Even if the guys get out, it won't all be wasted. They worked together a little."

Mac roused himself. "Yeah, but we ought to make a last stand."

"How you goin' to get guys to fight when they want to run?" London demanded.

"I don't know. We can talk. We can try to make 'em fight talkin' to 'em."

"Talk don't do much good when they're scared."

"I know."

The silence fell again. They could hear the low talk of many voices outside, scattered voices that gradually drew together and made a babble like water. Mac said, "Got a match, London? Light the lantern."

"It ain't dark yet."

"Dark enough. Light it up. This God damn half-light makes me nervous."

The shade screeched as London raised it, and screeched when he let it down.

Mac looked startled. "Something happened. What's wrong?"

"It's the men," said Jim. "They're quiet now. They've all stopped talking." The three men sat listening tensely. They heard footsteps coming closer. In the doorway the two short Italian men stood. Their teeth showed in self-conscious grins.

"C'n we come in?"

"Sure. Come on in, boys."

They stood in the tent like pupils preparing to recite. Each looked to the other to begin. One said, "The men out there—they want to call a meeting."

"Yeah? What for?"

The other answered quickly, "Those men say they vote the strike, they can vote again. They say 'What's the use all the men get killed?' They say they can't strike no more." They were silent, waiting for London's answer.

London's eyes asked advice from Mac. "Of course you'll call a meeting," Mac said. "The men are the bosses. What they say goes." He looked up at the waiting emissaries. "Go out and tell the guys London calls a meeting in about half an hour, to vote whether we fight or run."

They looked at London for corroboration. He nodded his head slowly. "That's right," he said. "In a half hour. We do what the guys vote to do." The little men made foreign bows, and wheeled and left the tent.

Mac laughed loudly. "Why that's fine," he said. "Why that makes it better. I thought they might sneak out. But if they want to vote, that means they're still working together. Oh, that's fine. They can break up, if they do it by their own consent."

Jim asked, "But aren't you going to try to make them fight?"

"Oh, sure. We have to make plans about that. But if they won't fight, well anyway they don't just sneak off like dogs. It's more like a retreat, you see. It isn't just getting chased."

"What'll we do at the meeting?" London demanded.

"Well, let's see. It's just about dark now. You talk first, London. Tell 'em why they should fight, not run. Now I better not talk. They don't like me too well since I told 'em off this morning." His eyes moved to Jim. "You're it," he said. "Here's your chance. You do it. See if you can bring 'em around. Talk, Jim. Talk. It's the thing you've been wanting."

Jim's eyes shone with excitement. "Mac," he cried, "I can pull off this bandage and get a flow of blood. That might stir 'em up."

Mac's eyes narrowed and he considered the thought. "No—" he decided. "Stir 'em up that way, an' they got to hit something quick. If you make 'em sit around, they'll go way down. No, just talk, Jim. Tell 'em straight what a strike means, how it's a little battle in a whole war. You can do it, Jim."

Jim sprang up. "You're damn right I can do it. I'm near choking, but I can do it." His face was transfigured. A furious light of energy seemed to shine from it.

They heard running footsteps. A young boy ran into the

tent. "Out in the orchard," he cried. "There's a guy says he's a doctor. He's all hurt."

The three started up. "Where?"

"Over the other side. Been lyin' there all day, he says."

"How'd you find him?" Mac demanded.

"I heard 'im yell. He says come and tell you."

"Show us the way. Come on now, hurry up."

The boy turned and plunged out. Mac shouted, "London, bring the lantern." Mac and Jim ran side by side. The night was almost complete. Ahead, they saw the flying figure of the boy. Across the open space they tore. The boy reached the line of trees and plunged among them. They could hear him running ahead of them. They dashed into the dark shadow of the trees.

Suddenly Mac reached for Jim. "Jim! Drop, for Christ' sake!" There was a roar, and two big holes of light. Mac had sprawled full length. He heard several sets of running footsteps. He looked toward Jim, but the flashes still burned on his retinas. Gradually he made Jim out. He was on his knees, his head down. "You sure got down quick, Jim."

Jim did not move. Mac scrambled over to him, on his knees. "Did you get hit, Jim?" The figure kneeled, and the face was against the ground. "Oh, Christ!" Mac put out his hand to lift the head. He cried out, and jerked his hand away, and wiped it on his trousers, for there was no face. He looked slowly around, over his shoulder.

The lantern bounced along toward him, lighting London's running legs. "Where are you?" London shouted.

Mac didn't answer. He sat back on his heels, sat very quietly. He looked at the figure, kneeling in the position of Moslem prayer.

London saw them at last. He came close, and stopped; and the lantern made a circle of light. "Oh," he said. He lowered the lantern and peered down. "Shot-gun?"

Mac nodded and stared at his sticky hand.

London looked at Mac, and shivered at his frozen face. Mac stood up, stiffly. He leaned over and picked Jim up and slung him over his shoulder, like a sack; and the dripping head hung down behind. He set off, stiff-legged, toward the camp. London walked beside him, carrying the lantern.

The clearing was full of curious men. They clustered around, until they saw the burden. And then they recoiled. Mac marched through them as though he did not see them. Across the clearing, past the stoves he marched, and the crowd followed silently behind him. He came to the platform. He deposited the figure under the hand-rail and leaped to the stand. He dragged Jim across the boards and leaned him against the corner post, and steadied him when he slipped sideways.

London handed the lantern up, and Mac set it carefully on the floor, beside the body, so that its light fell on the head. He stood up and faced the crowd. His hands gripped the rail. His eyes were wide and white. In front he could see the massed men, eyes shining in the lamplight. Behind the front row, the men were lumped and dark. Mac shivered. He moved his jaws to speak, and seemed to break the frozen jaws loose. His voice was high and monotonous. "This guy didn't want nothing for himself—" he began. His knuckles were white, where he grasped the rail. "Comrades! He didn't want nothing for himself——"

OF MICE AND MEN

I

A FEW MILES south of Soledad, the Salinas River drops in close to the hillside bank and runs deep and green. The water is warm too, for it has slipped twinkling over the yellow sands in the sunlight before reaching the narrow pool. On one side of the river the golden foothill slopes curve up to the strong and rocky Gabilan mountains, but on the valley side the water is lined with trees—willows fresh and green with every spring, carrying in their lower leaf junctures the debris of the winter's flooding; and sycamores with mottled, white, recumbent limbs and branches that arch over the pool. On the sandy bank under the trees the leaves lie deep and so crisp that a lizard makes a great skittering if he runs among them. Rabbits come out of the brush to sit on the sand in the evening, and the damp flats are covered with the night tracks of 'coons, and with the spread pads of dogs from the ranches, and with the split-wedge tracks of deer that come to drink in the dark.

There is a path through the willows and among the sycamores, a path beaten hard by boys coming down from the ranches to swim in the deep pool, and beaten hard by tramps who come wearily down from the highway in the evening to jungle-up near water. In front of the low horizontal limb of a giant sycamore there is an ash pile made by many fires; the limb is worn smooth by men who have sat on it.

Evening of a hot day started the little wind to moving among the leaves. The shade climbed up the hills toward the top. On the sand banks the rabbits sat as quietly as little gray, sculptured stones. And then from the direction of the state highway came the sound of footsteps on crisp sycamore leaves. The rabbits hurried noiselessly for cover. A stilted heron labored up into the air and pounded down river. For a moment the place was lifeless, and then two men emerged from the path and came into the opening by the green pool.

They had walked in single file down the path, and even in the open one stayed behind the other. Both were dressed in denim trousers and in denim coats with brass buttons. Both wore black, shapeless hats and both carried tight blanket rolls slung over their shoulders. The first man was small and quick, dark of face, with restless eyes and sharp, strong features. Every part of him was defined: small, strong hands, slender arms, a thin and bony nose. Behind him walked his opposite, a huge man, shapeless of face, with large, pale eyes, with wide, sloping shoulders; and he walked heavily, dragging his feet a little, the way a bear drags his paws. His arms did not swing at his sides, but hung loosely.

The first man stopped short in the clearing, and the follower nearly ran over him. He took off his hat and wiped the sweat-band with his forefinger and snapped the moisture off. His huge companion dropped his blankets and flung himself down and drank from the surface of the green pool; drank with long gulps, snorting into the water like a horse. The small man stepped nervously beside him.

"Lennie!" he said sharply. "Lennie, for God' sakes don't drink so much." Lennie continued to snort into the pool. The small man leaned over and shook him by the shoulder. "Lennie. You gonna be sick like you was last night."

Lennie dipped his whole head under, hat and all, and then he sat up on the bank and his hat dripped down on his blue coat and ran down his back. "Tha's good," he said. "You drink some, George. You take a good big drink." He smiled happily.

George unslung his bindle and dropped it gently on the bank. "I ain't sure it's good water," he said. "Looks kinda scummy."

Lennie dabbled his big paw in the water and wiggled his fingers so the water arose in little splashes; rings widened across the pool to the other side and came back again. Lennie watched them go. "Look, George. Look what I done."

George knelt beside the pool and drank from his hand with quick scoops. "Tastes all right," he admitted. "Don't really seem to be running, though. You never oughta drink water when it ain't running, Lennie," he said hopelessly. "You'd drink out of a gutter if you was thirsty." He threw a scoop of water into his face and rubbed it about with his hand, under his chin and around the back of his neck. Then he replaced his hat, pushed himself back from the river, drew up his knees and embraced them. Lennie, who had been watching, imitated George exactly. He pushed himself back, drew up his knees, embraced them, looked over to George to see whether he had it just right. He pulled his hat down a little more over his eyes, the way George's hat was.

George stared morosely at the water. The rims of his eyes were red with sun glare. He said angrily, "We could just as well of rode clear to the ranch if that bastard bus driver knew what he was talkin' about. 'Jes' a little stretch down the highway,' he says. 'Jes' a little stretch.' God damn near four miles, that's what it was! Didn't wanta stop at the ranch gate, that's what. Too God damn lazy to pull up. Wonder he isn't too damn good to stop in Soledad at all. Kicks us out and says, 'Jes' a little stretch down the road.' I bet it was *more* than four miles. Damn hot day."

Lennie looked timidly over to him. "George?"

"Yeah, what ya want?"

"Where we goin', George?"

The little man jerked down the brim of his hat and scowled over at Lennie. "So you forgot that awready, did you? I gotta tell you again, do I? Jesus Christ, you're a crazy bastard!"

"I forgot," Lennie said softly. "I tried not to forget. Honest to God I did, George."

"O.K.—O.K. I'll tell ya again. I ain't got nothing to do. Might jus' as well spen' all my time tellin' you things and then you forget 'em, and I tell you again."

"Tried and tried," said Lennie, "but it didn't do no good. I remember about the rabbits, George."

"The hell with the rabbits. That's all you ever can remember is them rabbits. O.K! Now you listen and this time you got to remember so we don't get in no trouble. You remember settin' in that gutter on Howard street and watchin' that blackboard?"

Lennie's face broke into a delighted smile. "Why sure, George. I remember that . . . . but . . . . what'd we do then? I remember some girls come by and you says . . . . you say . . . ."

"The hell with what I says. You remember about us goin'

into Murray and Ready's, and they give us work cards and bus tickets?"

"Oh, sure, George. I remember that now." His hands went quickly into his side coat pockets. He said gently, "George . . . . I ain't got mine. I musta lost it." He looked down at the ground in despair.

"You never had none, you crazy bastard. I got both of 'em here. Think I'd let you carry your own work card?"

Lennie grinned with relief. "I . . . . I thought I put it in my side pocket." His hand went into the pocket again.

George looked sharply at him. "What'd you take outa that pocket?"

"Ain't a thing in my pocket," Lennie said cleverly.

"I know there ain't. You got it in your hand. What you got in your hand—hidin' it?"

"I ain't got nothin', George. Honest."

"Come on, give it here."

Lennie held his closed hand away from George's direction. "It's on'y a mouse, George."

"A mouse? A live mouse?"

"Uh-uh. Jus' a dead mouse, George. I didn' kill it. Honest! I found it. I found it dead."

"Give it here!" said George.

"Aw, leave me have it, George."

"Give it here!"

Lennie's closed hand slowly obeyed. George took the mouse and threw it across the pool to the other side, among the brush. "What you want of a dead mouse, anyways?"

"I could pet it with my thumb while we walked along," said Lennie.

"Well, you ain't petting no mice while you walk with me. You remember where we're goin' now?"

Lennie looked startled and then in embarrassment hid his face against his knees. "I forgot again."

"Jesus Christ," George said resignedly. "Well—look, we're gonna work on a ranch like the one we come from up north."

"Up north?"

"In Weed."

"Oh, sure. I remember. In Weed."

"That ranch we're goin' to is right down there about a

quarter mile. We're gonna go in an' see the boss. Now, look—I'll give him the work tickets, but you ain't gonna say a word. You jus' stand there and don't say nothing. If he finds out what a crazy bastard you are, we won't get no job, but if he sees ya work before he hears ya talk, we're set. Ya got that?"

"Sure, George. Sure I got it."

"O.K. Now when we go in to see the boss, what you gonna do?"

"I . . . . I," Lennie thought. His face grew tight with thought. "I . . . . ain't gonna say nothin'. Jus' gonna stan' there."

"Good boy. That's swell. You say that over two, three times so you sure won't forget it."

Lennie droned to himself softly, "I ain't gonna say nothin' . . . . I ain't gonna say nothin' . . . . I ain't gonna say nothin'."

"O.K.," said George. "An' you ain't gonna do no bad things like you done in Weed, neither."

Lennie looked puzzled. "Like I done in Weed?"

"Oh, so ya forgot that too, did ya? Well, I ain't gonna remind ya, fear ya do it again."

A light of understanding broke on Lennie's face. "They run us outa Weed," he exploded triumphantly.

"Run us out, hell," said George disgustedly. "We run. They was lookin' for us, but they didn't catch us."

Lennie giggled happily. "I didn't forget that, you bet."

George lay back on the sand and crossed his hands under his head, and Lennie imitated him, raising his head to see whether he were doing it right. "God, you're a lot of trouble," said George. "I could get along so easy and so nice if I didn't have you on my tail. I could live so easy and maybe have a girl."

For a moment Lennie lay quiet, and then he said hopefully, "We gonna work on a ranch, George."

"Awright. You got that. But we're gonna sleep here because I got a reason."

The day was going fast now. Only the tops of the Gabilan mountains flamed with the light of the sun that had gone from the valley. A water snake slipped along on the pool, its head held up like a little periscope. The reeds jerked slightly in the current. Far off toward the highway a man shouted something, and another man shouted back. The sycamore limbs rustled under a little wind that died immediately.

"George—why ain't we goin' on to the ranch and get some supper? They got supper at the ranch."

George rolled on his side. "No reason at all for you. I like it here. Tomorra we're gonna go to work. I seen thrashin' machines on the way down. That means we'll be bucking grain bags, bustin' a gut. Tonight I'm gonna lay right here and look up. I like it."

Lennie got up on his knees and looked down at George. "Ain't we gonna have no supper?"

"Sure we are, if you gather up some dead willow sticks. I got three cans of beans in my bindle. You get a fire ready. I'll give you a match when you get the sticks together. Then we'll heat the beans and have supper."

Lennie said, "I like beans with ketchup."

"Well, we ain't got no ketchup. You go get wood. An' don't you fool around. It'll be dark before long."

Lennie lumbered to his feet and disappeared in the brush. George lay where he was and whistled softly to himself. There were sounds of splashings down the river in the direction Lennie had taken. George stopped whistling and listened. "Poor bastard," he said softly, and then went on whistling again.

In a moment Lennie came crashing back through the brush. He carried one small willow stick in his hand. George sat up. "Awright," he said brusquely. "Gi'me that mouse!"

But Lennie made an elaborate pantomime of innocence. "What mouse, George? I ain't got no mouse."

George held out his hand. "Come on. Give it to me. You ain't puttin' nothing over."

Lennie hesitated, backed away, looked wildly at the brush line as though he contemplated running for his freedom. George said coldly, "You gonna give me that mouse or do I have to sock you?"

"Give you what, George?"

"You know God damn well what. I want that mouse."

Lennie reluctantly reached into his pocket. His voice

broke a little. "I don't know why I can't keep it. It ain't no-body's mouse. I didn't steal it. I found it lyin' right beside the road."

George's hand remained outstretched imperiously. Slowly, like a terrier who doesn't want to bring a ball to its master, Lennie approached, drew back, approached again. George snapped his fingers sharply, and at the sound Lennie laid the mouse in his hand.

"I wasn't doin' nothing bad with it, George. Jus' strokin' it."

George stood up and threw the mouse as far as he could into the darkening brush, and then he stepped to the pool and washed his hands. "You crazy fool. Don't you think I could see your feet was wet where you went acrost the river to get it?" He heard Lennie's whimpering cry and wheeled about. "Blubberin' like a baby! Jesus Christ! A big guy like you." Lennie's lip quivered and tears started in his eyes. "Aw, Lennie!" George put his hand on Lennie's shoulder. "I ain't takin' it away jus' for meanness. That mouse ain't fresh, Len-nie; and besides, you've broke it pettin' it. You get another mouse that's fresh and I'll let you keep it a little while."

Lennie sat down on the ground and hung his head deject-edly. "I don't know where there is no other mouse. I remem-ber a lady used to give 'em to me—ever' one she got. But that lady ain't here."

George scoffed. "Lady, huh? Don't even remember who that lady was. That was your own Aunt Clara. An' she stopped givin' 'em to ya. You always killed 'em."

Lennie looked sadly up at him. "They was so little," he said, apologetically. "I'd pet 'em, and pretty soon they bit my fingers and I pinched their heads a little and then they was dead—because they was so little.

"I wish't we'd get the rabbits pretty soon, George. They ain't so little."

"The hell with the rabbits. An' you ain't to be trusted with no live mice. Your Aunt Clara give you a rubber mouse and you wouldn't have nothing to do with it."

"It wasn't no good to pet," said Lennie.

The flame of the sunset lifted from the mountaintops and dusk came into the valley, and a half darkness came in among the willows and the sycamores. A big carp rose to the surface of the pool, gulped air and then sank mysteriously into the dark water again, leaving widening rings on the water. Overhead the leaves whisked again and little puffs of willow cotton blew down and landed on the pool's surface.

"You gonna get that wood?" George demanded. "There's plenty right up against the back of that sycamore. Floodwater wood. Now you get it."

Lennie went behind the tree and brought out a litter of dried leaves and twigs. He threw them in a heap on the old ash pile and went back for more and more. It was almost night now. A dove's wings whistled over the water. George walked to the fire pile and lighted the dry leaves. The flame cracked up among the twigs and fell to work. George undid his bindle and brought out three cans of beans. He stood them about the fire, close in against the blaze, but not quite touching the flame.

"There's enough beans for four men," George said.

Lennie watched him from over the fire. He said patiently, "I like 'em with ketchup."

"Well, we ain't got any," George exploded. "Whatever we ain't got, that's what you want. God a'mighty, if I was alone I could live so easy. I could go get a job an' work, an' no trouble. No mess at all, and when the end of the month come I could take my fifty bucks and go into town and get whatever I want. Why, I could stay in a cat house all night. I could eat any place I want, hotel or any place, and order any damn thing I could think of. An' I could do all that every damn month. Get a gallon of whisky, or set in a pool room and play cards or shoot pool." Lennie knelt and looked over the fire at the angry George. And Lennie's face was drawn with terror. "An' whatta I got," George went on furiously. "I got you! You can't keep a job and you lose me ever' job I get. Jus' keep me shovin' all over the country all the time. An' that ain't the worst. You get in trouble. You do bad things and I got to get you out." His voice rose nearly to a shout. "You crazy son-of-a-bitch. You keep me in hot water all the time." He took on the elaborate manner of little girls when they are mimicking one another. "Jus' wanted to feel that girl's dress—jus' wanted to pet it like it was a mouse—— Well, how the hell did she know you jus' wanted to feel her dress? She jerks back and you hold on like it was a mouse. She yells and we got to hide in a irrigation ditch all day with guys lookin' for us, and we got to sneak out in the dark and get outta the country. All the time somethin' like that—all the time. I wisht I could put you in a cage with about a million mice an' let you have fun." His anger left him suddenly. He looked across the fire at Lennie's anguished face, and then he looked ashamedly at the flames.

It was quite dark now, but the fire lighted the trunks of the trees and the curving branches overhead. Lennie crawled slowly and cautiously around the fire until he was close to George. He sat back on his heels. George turned the bean cans so that another side faced the fire. He pretended to be unaware of Lennie so close beside him.

"George," very softly. No answer. "George!"

"Whatta you want?"

"I was only foolin', George. I don't want no ketchup. I wouldn't eat no ketchup if it was right here beside me."

"If it was here, you could have some."

"But I wouldn't eat none, George. I'd leave it all for you. You could cover your beans with it and I wouldn't touch none of it."

George still stared morosely at the fire. "When I think of the swell time I could have without you, I go nuts. I never get no peace."

Lennie still knelt. He looked off into the darkness across the river. "George, you want I should go away and leave you alone?"

"Where the hell could you go?"

"Well, I could. I could go off in the hills there. Some place I'd find a cave."

"Yeah? How'd you eat. You ain't got sense enough to find nothing to eat."

"I'd find things, George. I don't need no nice food with ketchup. I'd lay out in the sun and nobody'd hurt me. An' if I foun' a mouse, I could keep it. Nobody'd take it away from me."

George looked quickly and searchingly at him. "I been mean, ain't I?"

"If you don' want me I can go off in the hills an' find a cave. I can go away any time."

"No—look! I was jus' foolin', Lennie. 'Cause I want you to stay with me. Trouble with mice is you always kill 'em." He paused. "Tell you what I'll do, Lennie. First chance I get I'll give you a pup. Maybe you wouldn't kill *it*. That'd be better than mice. And you could pet it harder."

Lennie avoided the bait. He had sensed his advantage. "If you don't want me, you only jus' got to say so, and I'll go off in those hills right there—right up in those hills and live by myself. An' I won't get no mice stole from me."

George said, "I want you to stay with me, Lennie. Jesus Christ, somebody'd shoot you for a coyote if you was by yourself. No, you stay with me. Your Aunt Clara wouldn't like you running off by yourself, even if she is dead."

Lennie spoke craftily, "Tell me—like you done before."

"Tell you what?"

"About the rabbits."

George snapped, "You ain't gonna put nothing over on me."

Lennie pleaded, "Come on, George. Tell me. Please, George. Like you done before."

"You get a kick outta that, don't you? Awright, I'll tell you, and then we'll eat our supper. . . ."

George's voice became deeper. He repeated his words rhythmically as though he had said them many times before. "Guys like us, that work on ranches, are the loneliest guys in the world. They got no family. They don't belong no place. They come to a ranch an' work up a stake and then they go inta town and blow their stake, and the first thing you know they're poundin' their tail on some other ranch. They ain't got nothing to look ahead to."

Lennie was delighted. 'That's it—that's it. Now tell how it is with us."

George went on. "With us it ain't like that. We got a future. We got somebody to talk to that gives a damn about us. We don't have to sit in no bar room blowin' in our jack jus' because we got no place else to go. If them other guys gets in jail they can rot for all anybody gives a damn. But not us."

Lennie broke in. *"But not us! An' why? Because . . . ."*

because I got you to look after me, and you got me to look after you, and that's why." He laughed delightedly. "Go on now, George!"

"You got it by heart. You can do it yourself."

"No, you. I forget some a' the things. Tell about how it's gonna be."

"O.K. Someday—we're gonna get the jack together and we're gonna have a little house and a couple of acres an' a cow and some pigs and——"

"An' live off the fatta the lan'," Lennie shouted. "An' have *rabbits.* Go on, George! Tell about what we're gonna have in the garden and about the rabbits in the cages and about the rain in the winter and the stove, and how thick the cream is on the milk like you can hardly cut it. Tell about that, George."

"Why'n't you do it yourself? You know all of it."

"No . . . . you tell it. It ain't the same if I tell it. Go on . . . . George. How I get to tend the rabbits."

"Well," said George, "we'll have a big vegetable patch and a rabbit hutch and chickens. And when it rains in the winter, we'll just say the hell with goin' to work, and we'll build up a fire in the stove and set around it an' listen to the rain comin' down on the roof—Nuts!" He took out his pocket knife. "I ain't got time for no more." He drove his knife through the top of one of the bean cans, sawed out the top and passed the can to Lennie. Then he opened a second can. From his side pocket he brought out two spoons and passed one of them to Lennie.

They sat by the fire and filled their mouths with beans and chewed mightily. A few beans slipped out of the side of Lennie's mouth. George gestured with his spoon. "What you gonna say tomorrow when the boss asks you questions?"

Lennie stopped chewing and swallowed. His face was concentrated. "I . . . . I ain't gonna . . . . say a word."

"Good boy! That's fine, Lennie! Maybe you're gettin' better. When we get the coupla acres I can let you tend the rabbits all right. 'Specially if you remember as good as that."

Lennie choked with pride. "I can remember," he said.

George motioned with his spoon again. "Look, Lennie. I want you to look around here. You can remember this place, can't you? The ranch is about a quarter mile up that way. Just follow the river?"

"Sure," said Lennie. "I can remember this. Di'n't I remember about not gonna say a word?"

" 'Course you did. Well, look. Lennie—if you jus' happen to get in trouble like you always done before, I want you to come right here an' hide in the brush."

"Hide in the brush," said Lennie slowly.

"Hide in the brush till I come for you. Can you remember that?"

"Sure I can, George. Hide in the brush till you come."

"But you ain't gonna get in no trouble, because if you do, I won't let you tend the rabbits." He threw his empty bean can off into the brush.

"I won't get in no trouble, George. I ain't gonna say a word."

"O.K. Bring your bindle over here by the fire. It's gonna be nice sleepin' here. Lookin' up, and the leaves. Don't build up no more fire. We'll let her die down."

They made their beds on the sand, and as the blaze dropped from the fire the sphere of light grew smaller; the curling branches disappeared and only a faint glimmer showed where the tree trunks were. From the darkness Lennie called, "George—you asleep?"

"No. Whatta you want?"

"Let's have different color rabbits, George."

"Sure we will," George said sleepily. "Red and blue and green rabbits, Lennie. Millions of 'em."

"Furry ones, George, like I seen in the fair in Sacramento."

"Sure, furry ones."

" 'Cause I can jus' as well go away, George, an' live in a cave."

"You can jus' as well go to hell," said George. "Shut up now."

The red light dimmed on the coals. Up the hill from the river a coyote yammered, and a dog answered from the other side of the stream. The sycamore leaves whispered in a little night breeze.

2

THE BUNK HOUSE was a long, rectangular building. Inside, the walls were whitewashed and the floor unpainted. In three walls there were small, square windows, and in the fourth, a solid door with a wooden latch. Against the walls were eight bunks, five of them made up with blankets and the other three showing their burlap ticking. Over each bunk there was nailed an apple box with the opening forward so that it made two shelves for the personal belongings of the occupant of the bunk. And these shelves were loaded with little articles, soap and talcum powder, razors and those Western magazines ranch men love to read and scoff at and secretly believe. And there were medicines on the shelves, and little vials, combs; and from nails on the box sides, a few neckties. Near one wall there was a black cast-iron stove, its stovepipe going straight up through the ceiling. In the middle of the room stood a big square table littered with playing cards, and around it were grouped boxes for the players to sit on.

At about ten o'clock in the morning the sun threw a bright dust-laden bar through one of the side windows, and in and out of the beam flies shot like rushing stars.

The wooden latch raised. The door opened and a tall, stoop-shouldered old man came in. He was dressed in blue jeans and he carried a big push-broom in his left hand. Behind him came George, and behind George, Lennie.

"The boss was expectin' you last night," the old man said. "He was sore as hell when you wasn't here to go out this morning." He pointed with his right arm, and out of the sleeve came a round stick-like wrist, but no hand. "You can have them two beds there," he said, indicating two bunks near the stove.

George stepped over and threw his blankets down on the burlap sack of straw that was a mattress. He looked into his box shelf and then picked a small yellow can from it. "Say. What the hell's this?"

"I don't know," said the old man.

"Says 'positively kills lice, roaches and other scourges.'

What the hell kind of bed you giving us, anyways. We don't want no pants rabbits."

The old swamper shifted his broom and held it between his elbow and his side while he held out his hand for the can. He studied the label carefully. "Tell you what—" he said finally, "last guy that had this bed was a blacksmith—hell of a nice fella and as clean a guy as you want to meet. Used to wash his hands even *after* he ate."

"Then how come he got graybacks?" George was working up a slow anger. Lennie put his bindle on the neighboring bunk and sat down. He watched George with open mouth.

"Tell you what," said the old swamper. "This here black-smith—name of Whitey—was the kind of guy that would put that stuff around even if there wasn't no bugs—just to make sure, see? Tell you what he used to do— At meals he'd peel his boil' potatoes, an' he'd take out ever' little spot, no matter what kind, before he'd eat it. And if there was a red splotch on an egg, he'd scrape it off. Finally quit about the food. That's the kinda guy he was—clean. Used ta dress up Sundays even when he wasn't going no place, put on a neck-tie even, and then set in the bunk-house."

"I ain't so sure," said George skeptically. "What did you say he quit for?"

The old man put the yellow can in his pocket, and he rubbed his bristly white whiskers with his knuckles. "Why . . . . he . . . . just quit, the way a guy will. Says it was the food. Just wanted to move. Didn't give no other reason but the food. Just says 'gimme my time' one night, the way any guy would."

George lifted his tick and looked underneath it. He leaned over and inspected the sacking closely. Immediately Lennie got up and did the same with his bed. Finally George seemed satisfied. He unrolled his bindle and put things on the shelf, his razor and bar of soap, his comb and bottle of pills, his liniment and leather wristband. Then he made his bed up neatly with blankets. The old man said, "I guess the boss'll be out here in a minute. He was sure burned when you wasn't here this morning. Come right in when we was eatin' break-fast and says, 'Where the hell's them new men?' An' he give the stable buck hell, too."

George patted a wrinkle out of his bed, and sat down. "Give the stable buck hell?" he asked.

"Sure. Ya see the stable buck's a nigger."

"Nigger, huh?"

"Yeah. Nice fella too. Got a crooked back where a horse kicked him. The boss gives him hell when he's mad. But the stable buck don't give a damn about that. He reads a lot. Got books in his room."

"What kind of a guy is the boss?" George asked.

"Well, he's a pretty nice fella. Gets pretty mad sometimes, but he's pretty nice. Tell ya what—know what he done Christmas? Brang a gallon of whisky right in here and says, 'Drink hearty boys. Christmas comes but once a year.'"

"The hell he did! Whole gallon?"

"Yes sir. Jesus, we had fun. They let the nigger come in that night. Little skinner name of Smitty took after the nigger. Done pretty good, too. The guys wouldn't let him use his feet, so the nigger got him. If he coulda used his feet, Smitty says he woulda killed the nigger. The guys said on account of the nigger's got a crooked back, Smitty can't use his feet." He paused in relish of the memory. "After that the guys went into Soledad and raised hell. I didn't go in there. I ain't got the poop no more."

Lennie was just finishing making his bed. The wooden latch raised again and the door opened. A little stocky man stood in the open doorway. He wore blue jean trousers, a flannel shirt, a black, unbuttoned vest and a black coat. His thumbs were stuck in his belt, on each side of a square steel buckle. On his head was a soiled brown Stetson hat, and he wore high-heeled boots and spurs to prove he was not a laboring man.

The old swamper looked quickly at him, and then shuffled to the door rubbing his whiskers with his knuckles as he went. "Them guys just come," he said, and shuffled past the boss and out the door.

The boss stepped into the room with the short, quick steps of a fat-legged man. "I wrote Murray and Ready I wanted two men this morning. You got your work slips?" George reached into his pocket and produced the slips and handed them to the boss. "It wasn't Murray and Ready's fault. Says right here on the slip that you was to be here for work this morning."

George looked down at his feet. "Bus driver give us a bum steer," he said. "We hadda walk ten miles. Says we was here when we wasn't. We couldn't get no rides in the morning."

The boss squinted his eyes. "Well, I had to send out the grain teams short two buckers. Won't do any good to go out now till after dinner." He pulled his time book out of his pocket and opened it where a pencil was stuck between the leaves. George scowled meaningfully at Lennie, and Lennie nodded to show that he understood. The boss licked his pencil. "What's your name?"

"George Milton."

"And what's yours?"

George said, "His name's Lennie Small."

The names were entered in the book. "Le's see, this is the twentieth, noon the twentieth." He closed the book. "Where you boys been working?"

"Up around Weed," said George.

"You, too?" to Lennie.

"Yeah, him too," said George.

The boss pointed a playful finger at Lennie. "He ain't much of a talker, is he?"

"No, he ain't, but he's sure a hell of a good worker. Strong as a bull."

Lennie smiled to himself. "Strong as a bull," he repeated.

George scowled at him, and Lennie dropped his head in shame at having forgotten.

The boss said suddenly, "Listen, Small!" Lennie raised his head. "What can you do?"

In a panic, Lennie looked at George for help. "He can do anything you tell him," said George. "He's a good skinner. He can rassel grain bags, drive a cultivator. He can do anything. Just give him a try."

The boss turned on George. "Then why don't you let him answer? What you trying to put over?"

George broke in loudly, "Oh! I ain't saying he's bright. He ain't. But I say he's a God damn good worker. He can put up a four hundred pound bale."

The boss deliberately put the little book in his pocket. He

hooked his thumbs in his belt and squinted one eye nearly closed. "Say—what you sellin'?"

"Huh?"

"I said what stake you got in this guy? You takin' his pay away from him?"

"No, 'course I ain't. Why ya think I'm sellin' him out?"

"Well, I never seen one guy take so much trouble for another guy. I just like to know what your interest is."

George said, "He's my . . . . cousin. I told his old lady I'd take care of him. He got kicked in the head by a horse when he was a kid. He's awright. Just ain't bright. But he can do anything you tell him."

The boss turned half away. "Well, God knows he don't need any brains to buck barley bags. But don't you try to put nothing over, Milton. I got my eye on you. Why'd you quit in Weed?"

"Job was done," said George promptly.

"What kinda job?"

"We . . . . we was diggin' a cesspool."

"All right. But don't try to put nothing over, 'cause you can't get away with nothing. I seen wise guys before. Go on out with the grain teams after dinner. They're pickin' up barley at the threshing machine. Go out with Slim's team."

"Slim?"

"Yeah. Big tall skinner. You'll see him at dinner." He turned abruptly and went to the door, but before he went out he turned and looked for a long moment at the two men.

When the sound of his footsteps had died away, George turned on Lennie. "So you wasn't gonna say a word. You was gonna leave your big flapper shut and leave me do the talkin'. Damn near lost us the job."

Lennie stared hopelessly at his hands. "I forgot, George."

"Yeah, you forgot. You always forget, an' I got to talk you out of it." He sat down heavily on the bunk. "Now he's got his eye on us. Now we got to be careful and not make no slips. You keep your big flapper shut after this." He fell morosely silent.

"George."

"What you want now?"

"I wasn't kicked in the head with no horse, was I, George?"

"Be a damn good thing if you was," George said viciously. "Save ever'body a hell of a lot of trouble."

"You said I was your cousin, George."

"Well, that was a lie. An' I'm damn glad it was. If I was a relative of yours I'd shoot myself." He stopped suddenly, stepped to the open front door and peered out. "Say, what the hell you doin' listenin'?"

The old man came slowly into the room. He had his broom in his hand. And at his heels there walked a dragfooted sheepdog, gray of muzzle, and with pale, blind old eyes. The dog struggled lamely to the side of the room and lay down, grunting softly to himself and licking his grizzled, moth-eaten coat. The swamper watched him until he was settled. "I wasn't listenin'. I was jus' standin' in the shade a minute scratchin' my dog. I jus' now finished swampin' out the wash house."

"You was pokin' your big ears into our business," George said. "I don't like nobody to get nosey."

The old man looked uneasily from George to Lennie, and then back. "I jus' come there," he said. "I didn't hear nothing you guys was sayin'. I ain't interested in nothing you was sayin'. A guy on a ranch don't never listen nor he don't ast no questions."

"Damn right he don't," said George, slightly mollified, "not if he wants to stay workin' long." But he was reassured by the swamper's defense. "Come on in and set down a minute," he said. "That's a hell of an old dog."

"Yeah. I had 'im ever since he was a pup. God, he was a good sheep dog when he was younger." He stood his broom against the wall and he rubbed his white bristled cheek with his knuckles. "How'd you like the boss?" he asked.

"Pretty good. Seemed awright."

"He's a nice fella," the swamper agreed. "You got to take him right."

At that moment a young man came into the bunk house; a thin young man with a brown face, with brown eyes and a head of tightly curled hair. He wore a work glove on his left hand, and, like the boss, he wore high-heeled boots. "Seen my old man?" he asked.

The swamper said, "He was here jus' a minute ago, Curley. Went over to the cook house, I think."

"I'll try to catch him," said Curley. His eyes passed over the new men and he stopped. He glanced coldly at George and then at Lennie. His arms gradually bent at the elbows and his hands closed into fists. He stiffened and went into a slight crouch. His glance was at once calculating and pugnacious. Lennie squirmed under the look and shifted his feet nervously. Curley stepped gingerly close to him. "You the new guys the old man was waitin' for?"

"We just come in," said George.

"Let the big guy talk."

Lennie twisted with embarrassment.

George said, "S'pose he don't want to talk?"

Curley lashed his body around. "By Christ, he's gotta talk when he's spoke to. What the hell are you gettin' into it for?"

"We travel together," said George coldly.

"Oh, so it's that way."

George was tense, and motionless. "Yeah, it's that way."

Lennie was looking helplessly to George for instruction.

"An' you won't let the big guy talk, is that it?"

"He can talk if he wants to tell you anything." He nodded slightly to Lennie.

"We jus' come in," said Lennie softly.

Curley stared levelly at him. "Well, nex' time you answer when you're spoke to." He turned toward the door and walked out, and his elbows were still bent out a little.

George watched him out, and then he turned back to the swamper. "Say, what the hell's he got on his shoulder? Lennie didn't do nothing to him."

The old man looked cautiously at the door to make sure no one was listening. "That's the boss's son," he said quietly. "Curley's pretty handy. He done quite a bit in the ring. He's a lightweight, and he's handy."

"Well, let him be handy," said George. "He don't have to take after Lennie. Lennie didn't do nothing to him. What's he got against Lennie?"

The swamper considered. . . . . "Well . . . . tell you what. Curley's like a lot of little guys. He hates big guys. He's alla time picking scraps with big guys. Kind of like he's mad at 'em because he ain't a big guy. You seen little guys like that, ain't you? Always scrappy?"

"Sure," said George. "I seen plenty tough little guys. But this Curley better not make no mistakes about Lennie. Lennie ain't handy, but this Curley punk is gonna get hurt if he messes around with Lennie."

"Well, Curley's pretty handy," the swamper said skeptically. "Never did seem right to me. S'pose Curley jumps a big guy an' licks him. Ever'body says what a game guy Curley is. And s'pose he does the same thing and gets licked. Then ever'body says the big guy oughtta pick somebody his own size, and maybe they gang up on the big guy. Never did seem right to me. Seems like Curley ain't givin' nobody a chance."

George was watching the door. He said ominously, "Well, he better watch out for Lennie. Lennie ain't no fighter, but Lennie's strong and quick and Lennie don't know no rules." He walked to the square table and sat down on one of the boxes. He gathered some of the cards together and shuffled them.

The old man sat down on another box. "Don't tell Curley I said none of this. He'd slough me. He just don't give a damn. Won't ever get canned 'cause his old man's the boss."

George cut the cards and began turning them over, looking at each one and throwing it down on a pile. He said, "This guy Curley sounds like a son-of-a-bitch to me. I don't like mean little guys."

"Seems to me like he's worse lately," said the swamper. "He got married a couple of weeks ago. Wife lives over in the boss's house. Seems like Curley is cockier'n ever since he got married."

George grunted, "Maybe he's showin' off for his wife."

The swamper warmed to his gossip. "You seen that glove on his left hand?"

"Yeah. I seen it."

"Well, that glove's fulla vaseline."

"Vaseline? What the hell for?"

"Well, I tell ya what—Curley says he's keepin' that hand soft for his wife."

George studied the cards absorbedly. "That's a dirty thing to tell around," he said.

The old man was reassured. He had drawn a derogatory

statement from George. He felt safe now, and he spoke more confidently. "Wait'll you see Curley's wife."

George cut the cards again and put out a solitaire lay, slowly and deliberately. "Purty?" he asked casually.

"Yeah. Purty . . . . but——"

George studied his cards. "But what?"

"Well—she got the eye."

"Yeah? Married two weeks and got the eye? Maybe that's why Curley's pants is full of ants."

"I seen her give Slim the eye. Slim's a jerkline skinner. Hell of a nice fella. Slim don't need to wear no high-heeled boots on a grain team. I seen her give Slim the eye. Curley never seen it. An' I seen her give Carlson the eye."

George pretended a lack of interest. "Looks like we was gonna have fun."

The swamper stood up from his box. "Know what I think?" George did not answer. "Well, I think Curley's married . . . . a tart."

"He ain't the first," said George. "There's plenty done that."

The old man moved toward the door, and his ancient dog lifted his head and peered about, and then got painfully to his feet to follow. "I gotta be settin' out the wash basins for the guys. The teams'll be in before long. You guys gonna buck barley?"

"Yeah."

"You won't tell Curley nothing I said?"

"Hell no."

"Well, you look her over, mister. You see if she ain't a tart." He stepped out the door into the brilliant sunshine.

George laid down his cards thoughtfully, turned his piles of three. He built four clubs on his ace pile. The sun square was on the floor now, and the flies whipped through it like sparks. A sound of jingling harness and the croak of heavy-laden axles sounded from outside. From the distance came a clear call. "Stable Buck—ooh, sta-able Buck!" And then, "Where the hell is that God damn nigger?"

George stared at his solitaire lay, and then he flounced the cards together and turned around to Lennie. Lennie was lying down on the bunk watching him.

"Look, Lennie! This here ain't no set up. I'm scared. You gonna have trouble with that Curley guy. I seen that kind before. He was kinda feelin' you out. He figures he's got you scared and he's gonna take a sock at you the first chance he gets."

Lennie's eyes were frightened. "I don't want no trouble," he said plaintively. "Don't let him sock me, George."

George got up and went over to Lennie's bunk and sat down on it. "I hate that kinda bastard," he said. "I seen plenty of 'em. Like the old guy says, Curley don't take no chances. He always wins." He thought for a moment. "If he tangles with you, Lennie, we're gonna get the can. Don't make no mistake about that. He's the boss's son. Look, Lennie. You try to keep away from him, will you? Don't never speak to him. If he comes in here you move clear to the other side of the room. Will you do that, Lennie?"

"I don't want no trouble," Lennie mourned. "I never done nothing to him."

"Well, that won't do you no good if Curley wants to plug himself up for a fighter. Just don't have nothing to do with him. Will you remember?"

"Sure, George. I ain't gonna say a word."

The sound of the approaching grain teams was louder, thud of big hooves on hard ground, drag of brakes and the jingle of trace chains. Men were calling back and forth from the teams. George, sitting on the bunk beside Lennie, frowned as he thought. Lennie asked timidly, "You ain't mad, George?"

"I ain't mad at you. I'm mad at this here Curley bastard. I hoped we was gonna get a little stake together—maybe a hundred dollars." His tone grew decisive. "You keep away from Curley, Lennie."

"Sure I will, George. I won't say a word."

"Don't let him pull you in—but—if the son-of-a-bitch socks you—let 'im have it."

"Let 'im have what, George?"

"Never mind, never mind. I'll tell you when. I hate that kind of a guy. Look, Lennie, if you get in any kind of trouble, you remember what I told you to do?"

Lennie raised up on his elbow. His face contorted with

thought. Then his eyes moved sadly to George's face. "If I get in any trouble, you ain't gonna let me tend the rabbits."

"That's not what I meant. You remember where we slep' last night? Down by the river?"

"Yeah. I remember. Oh, sure I remember! I go there an' hide in the brush."

"Hide till I come for you. Don't let nobody see you. Hide in the brush by the river. Say that over."

"Hide in the brush by the river, down in the brush by the river."

"If you get in trouble."

"If I get in trouble."

A brake screeched outside. A call came, "Stable—Buck. Oh! Sta-able Buck."

George said, "Say it over to yourself, Lennie, so you won't forget it."

Both men glanced up, for the rectangle of sunshine in the doorway was cut off. A girl was standing there looking in. She had full, rouged lips and wide-spaced eyes, heavily made up. Her fingernails were red. Her hair hung in little rolled clusters, like sausages. She wore a cotton house dress and red mules, on the insteps of which were little bouquets of red ostrich feathers. "I'm lookin' for Curley," she said. Her voice had a nasal, brittle quality.

George looked away from her and then back. "He was in here a minute ago, but he went."

"Oh!" She put her hands behind her back and leaned against the door frame so that her body was thrown forward. "You're the new fellas that just come, ain't ya?"

"Yeah."

Lennie's eyes moved down over her body, and though she did not seem to be looking at Lennie she bridled a little. She looked at her fingernails. "Sometimes Curley's in here," she explained.

George said brusquely, "Well he ain't now."

"If he ain't, I guess I better look some place else," she said playfully.

Lennie watched her, fascinated. George said, "If I see him, I'll pass the word you was looking for him."

She smiled archly and twitched her body. "Nobody can't

blame a person for lookin'," she said. There were footsteps behind her, going by. She turned her head. "Hi, Slim," she said.

Slim's voice came through the door. "Hi, Good-lookin'."

"I'm tryin' to find Curley, Slim."

"Well, you ain't tryin' very hard. I seen him goin' in your house."

She was suddenly apprehensive. " 'Bye, boys," she called into the bunk house, and she hurried away.

George looked around at Lennie. "Jesus, what a tramp," he said. "So that's what Curley picks for a wife."

"She's purty," said Lennie defensively.

"Yeah, and she's sure hidin' it. Curley got his work ahead of him. Bet she'd clear out for twenty bucks."

Lennie still stared at the doorway where she had been. "Gosh, she was purty." He smiled admiringly. George looked quickly down at him and then he took him by an ear and shook him.

"Listen to me, you crazy bastard," he said fiercely. "Don't you even take a look at that bitch. I don't care what she says and what she does. I seen 'em poison before, but I never seen no piece of jail bait worse than her. You leave her be."

Lennie tried to disengage his ear. "I never done nothing, George."

"No, you never. But when she was standin' in the doorway showin' her legs, you wasn't lookin' the other way, neither."

"I never meant no harm, George. Honest I never."

"Well, you keep away from her, 'cause she's a rat-trap if I ever seen one. You let Curley take the rap. He let himself in for it. Glove fulla vaseline," George said disgustedly. "An' I bet he's eatin' raw eggs and writin' to the patent medicine houses."

Lennie cried out suddenly—"I don' like this place, George. This ain't no good place. I wanna get outa here."

"We gotta keep it till we get a stake. We can't help it, Lennie. We'll get out jus' as soon as we can. I don't like it no better than you do." He went back to the table and set out a new solitaire hand. "No, I don't like it," he said. "For two bits I'd shove out of here. If we can get jus' a few dollars in the poke we'll shove off and go up the American River and pan gold. We can make maybe a couple of dollars a day there, and we might hit a pocket."

Lennie leaned eagerly toward him. "Le's go, George. Le's get outta here. It's mean here."

"We gotta stay," George said shortly. "Shut up now. The guys'll be comin' in."

From the washroom nearby came the sound of running water and rattling basins. George studied the cards. "Maybe we oughtta wash up," he said. "But we ain't done nothing to get dirty."

A tall man stood in the doorway. He held a crushed Stetson hat under his arm while he combed his long, black, damp hair straight back. Like the others he wore blue jeans and a short denim jacket. When he had finished combing his hair he moved into the room, and he moved with a majesty only achieved by royalty and master craftsmen. He was a jerkline skinner, the prince of the ranch, capable of driving ten, sixteen, even twenty mules with a single line to the leaders. He was capable of killing a fly on the wheeler's butt with a bull whip without touching the mule. There was a gravity in his manner and a quiet so profound that all talk stopped when he spoke. His authority was so great that his word was taken on any subject, be it politics or love. This was Slim, the jerkline skinner. His hatchet face was ageless. He might have been thirty-five or fifty. His ear heard more than was said to him. and his slow speech had overtones not of thought, but of understanding beyond thought. His hands, large and lean, were as delicate in their action as those of a temple dancer.

He smoothed out his crushed hat, creased it in the middle and put it on. He looked kindly at the two in the bunk house. "It's brighter'n a bitch outside," he said gently. "Can't hardly see nothing in here. You the new guys?"

"Just come," said George.

"Gonna buck barley?"

"That's what the boss says."

Slim sat down on a box across the table from George. He studied the solitaire hand that was upside down to him. "Hope you get on my team," he said. His voice was very gentle. "I gotta pair of punks on my team that don't know a barley bag from a blue ball. You guys ever bucked any barley?"

"Hell, yes," said George. "I ain't nothing to scream about, but that big bastard there can put up more grain alone than most pairs can."

Lennie, who had been following the conversation back and forth with his eyes, smiled complacently at the compliment. Slim looked approvingly at George for having given the compliment. He leaned over the table and snapped the corner of a loose card. "You guys travel around together?" His tone was friendly. It invited confidence without demanding it.

"Sure," said George. "We kinda look after each other." He indicated Lennie with his thumb. "He ain't bright. Hell of a good worker, though. Hell of a nice fella, but he ain't bright. I've knew him for a long time."

Slim looked through George and beyond him. "Ain't many guys travel around together," he mused. "I don't know why. Maybe ever'body in the whole damn world is scared of each other."

"It's a lot nicer to go around with a guy you know," said George.

A powerful, big-stomached man came into the bunk house. His head still dripped water from the scrubbing and dousing. "Hi, Slim," he said, and then stopped and stared at George and Lennie.

"These guys jus' come," said Slim by way of introduction.

"Glad ta meet ya," the big man said. "My name's Carlson."

"I'm George Milton. This here's Lennie Small."

"Glad ta meet ya," Carlson said again. "He ain't very small." He chuckled softly at his joke. "Ain't small at all," he repeated. "Meant to ask you, Slim—how's your bitch? I seen she wasn't under your wagon this morning."

"She slang her pups last night," said Slim. "Nine of 'em. I drowned four of 'em right off. She couldn't feed that many."

"Got five left, huh?"

"Yeah, five. I kept the biggest."

"What kinda dogs you think they're gonna be?"

"I dunno," said Slim. "Some kinda shepherds, I guess.

That's the most kind I seen around here when she was in heat."

Carlson went on, "Got five pups, huh. Gonna keep all of 'em?"

"I dunno. Have to keep 'em a while so they can drink Lulu's milk."

Carlson said thoughtfully, "Well, looka here, Slim. I been thinkin'. That dog of Candy's is so God damn old he can't hardly walk. Stinks like hell, too. Ever' time he comes into the bunk house I can smell him for two, three days. Why'n't you get Candy to shoot his old dog and give him one of the pups to raise up? I can smell that dog a mile away. Got no teeth, damn near blind, can't eat. Candy feeds him milk. He can't chew nothing else."

George had been staring intently at Slim. Suddenly a triangle began to ring outside, slowly at first, and then faster and faster until the beat of it disappeared into one ringing sound. It stopped as suddenly as it had started.

"There she goes," said Carlson.

Outside, there was a burst of voices as a group of men went by.

Slim stood up slowly and with dignity. "You guys better come on while they's still something to eat. Won't be nothing left in a couple of minutes."

Carlson stepped back to let Slim precede him, and then the two of them went out the door.

Lennie was watching George excitedly. George rumpled his cards into a messy pile. "Yeah!" George said, "I heard him, Lennie. I'll ask him."

"A brown and white one," Lennie cried excitedly.

"Come on. Le's get dinner. I don't know whether he got a brown and white one."

Lennie didn't move from his bunk. "You ask him right away, George, so he won't kill no more of 'em."

"Sure. Come on now, get up on your feet."

Lennie rolled off his bunk and stood up, and the two of them started for the door. Just as they reached it, Curley bounced in.

"You seen a girl around here?" he demanded angrily.

George said coldly. " 'Bout half an hour ago maybe."

"Well what the hell was she doin'?"

George stood still, watching the angry little man. He said insultingly, "She said—she was lookin' for you."

Curley seemed really to see George for the first time. His eyes flashed over George, took in his height, measured his reach, looked at his trim middle. "Well, which way'd she go?" he demanded at last.

"I dunno," said George. "I didn' watch her go."

Curley scowled at him, and turning, hurried out the door.

George said, "Ya know, Lennie, I'm scared I'm gonna tangle with that bastard myself. I hate his guts. Jesus Christ! Come on. They won't be a damn thing left to eat."

They went out the door. The sunshine lay in a thin line under the window. From a distance there could be heard a rattle of dishes.

After a moment the ancient dog walked lamely in through the open door. He gazed about with mild, half-blind eyes. He sniffed, and then lay down and put his head between his paws. Curley popped into the doorway again and stood looking into the room. The dog raised his head, but when Curley jerked out, the grizzled head sank to the floor again.

3

ALTHOUGH there was evening brightness showing through the windows of the bunk house, inside it was dusk. Through the open door came the thuds and occasional clangs of a horseshoe game, and now and then the sound of voices raised in approval or derision.

Slim and George came into the darkening bunkhouse together. Slim reached up over the card table and turned on the tin-shaded electric light. Instantly the table was brilliant with light, and the cone of the shade threw its brightness straight downward, leaving the corners of the bunk house still in dusk. Slim sat down on a box and George took his place opposite.

"It wasn't nothing," said Slim. "I would of had to drowned most of 'em anyways. No need to thank me about that."

George said, "It wasn't much to you, maybe, but it was a hell of a lot to him. Jesus Christ, I don't know how we're gonna get him to sleep in here. He'll want to sleep right out in the barn with 'em. We'll have trouble keepin' him from getting right in the box with them pups."

"It wasn't nothing," Slim repeated. "Say, you sure was right about him. Maybe he ain't bright, but I never seen such a worker. He damn near killed his partner buckin' barley. There ain't nobody can keep up with him. God awmighty I never seen such a strong guy."

George spoke proudly. "Jus' tell Lennie what to do an' he'll do it if it don't take no figuring. He can't think of nothing to do himself, but he sure can take orders."

There was a clang of horseshoe on iron stake outside and a little cheer of voices.

Slim moved back slightly so the light was not on his face. "Funny how you an' him string along together." It was Slim's calm invitation to confidence.

"What's funny about it?" George demanded defensively.

"Oh, I dunno. Hardly none of the guys ever travel together. I hardly never seen two guys travel together. You know how the hands are, they just come in and get their bunk and work a month, and then they quit and go out alone. Never seem to give a damn about nobody. It jus' seems kinda funny a cuckoo like him and a smart little guy like you travelin' together."

"He ain't no cuckoo," said George. "He's dumb as hell, but he ain't crazy. An' I ain't so bright neither, or I wouldn't be buckin' barley for my fifty and found. If I was bright, if I was even a little bit smart, I'd have my own little place, an' I'd be bringin' in my own drops, 'stead of doin' all the work and not getting what comes up outa the ground." George fell silent. He wanted to talk. Slim neither encouraged nor discouraged him. He just sat back quiet and receptive.

"It ain't so funny, him an' me goin' aroun' together," George said at last. "Him and me was both born in Auburn. I knowed his Aunt Clara. She took him when he was a baby and raised him up. When his Aunt Clara died, Lennie just come along with me out workin'. Got kinda used to each other after a little while."

"Umm," said Slim.

George looked over at Slim and saw the calm, God-like eyes fastened on him. "Funny," said George. "I used to have a hell of a lot of fun with 'im. Used to play jokes on 'im 'cause he was too dumb to take care of 'imself. But he was too dumb even to know he had a joke played on him. I had fun. Made me seem God damn smart alongside of him. Why he'd do any damn thing I tol' him. If I tol' him to walk over a cliff, over he'd go. That wasn't so damn much fun after a while. He never got mad about it, neither. I've beat the hell outa him, and he coulda bust every bone in my body jus' with his han's, but he never lifted a finger against me." George's voice was taking on the tone of confession. "Tell you what made me stop that. One day a bunch of guys was standin' around up on the Sacramento River. I was feelin' pretty smart. I turns to Lennie and says, 'Jump in.' An' he jumps. Couldn't swim a stroke. He damn near drowned before we could get him. An' he was so damn nice to me for pullin' him out. Clean forgot I told him to jump in. Well, I ain't done nothing like that no more."

"He's a nice fella," said Slim. "Guy don't need no sense to be a nice fella. Seems to me sometimes it jus' works the other way around. Take a real smart guy and he ain't hardly ever a nice fella."

George stacked the scattered cards and began to lay out his solitaire hand. The shoes thudded on the ground outside. At the windows the light of the evening still made the window squares bright.

"I ain't got no people," George said. "I seen the guys that go around on the ranches alone. That ain't no good. They don't have no fun. After a long time they get mean. They get wantin' to fight all the time."

"Yeah, they get mean," Slim agreed. "They get so they don't want to talk to nobody."

" 'Course Lennie's a God damn nuisance most of the time," said George. "But you get used to goin' around with a guy an' you can't get rid of him."

"He ain't mean," said Slim. "I can see Lennie ain't a bit mean."

" 'Course he ain't mean. But he gets in trouble alla time because he's so God damn dumb. Like what happened in Weed——" He stopped, stopped in the middle of turning over a card. He looked alarmed and peered over at Slim. "You wouldn't tell nobody?"

"What'd he do in Weed?" Slim asked calmly.

"You wouldn' tell? . . . . No, 'course you wouldn'."

"What'd he do in Weed?" Slim asked again.

"Well, he seen this girl in a red dress. Dumb bastard like he is, he wants to touch ever'thing he likes. Just wants to feel it. So he reaches out to feel this red dress an' the girl lets out a squawk, and that gets Lennie all mixed up, and he holds on 'cause that's the only thing he can think to do. Well, this girl squawks and squawks. I was jus' a little bit off, and I heard all the yellin', so I comes running, an' by that time Lennie's so scared all he can think to do is jus' hold on. I socked him over the head with a fence picket to make him let go. He was so scairt he couldn't let go of that dress. And he's so God damn strong, you know."

Slim's eyes were level and unwinking. He nodded very slowly. "So what happens?"

George carefully built his line of solitaire cards. "Well, that girl rabbits in an' tells the law she been raped. The guys in

Weed start a party out to lynch Lennie. So we sit in a irrigation ditch under water all the rest of that day. Got on'y our
heads sticking outa water, an' up under the grass that sticks
out from the side of the ditch. An' that night we scrammed
outa there."

Slim sat in silence for a moment. "Didn't hurt the girl
none, huh?" he asked finally.

"Hell, no. He just scared her. I'd be scared too if he
grabbed me. But he never hurt her. He jus' wanted to touch
that red dress, like he wants to pet them pups all the time."

"He ain't mean," said Slim. "I can tell a mean guy a mile
off."

" 'Course he ain't, and he'll do any damn thing I——"

Lennie came in through the door. He wore his blue denim
coat over his shoulders like a cape, and he walked hunched
way over.

"Hi, Lennie," said George. "How you like the pup now?"

Lennie said breathlessly, "He's brown an' white jus' like I
wanted." He went directly to his bunk and lay down and
turned his face to the wall and drew up his knees.

George put down his cards very deliberately. "Lennie," he
said sharply.

Lennie twisted his neck and looked over his shoulder.
"Huh? What you want, George?"

"I tol' you you couldn't bring that pup in here."

"What pup, George? I ain't got no pup."

George went quickly to him, grabbed him by the shoulder
and rolled him over. He reached down and picked the tiny
puppy from where Lennie had been concealing it against his
stomach.

Lennie sat up quickly. "Give 'um to me, George."

George said, "You get right up an' take this pup back to the
nest. He's gotta sleep with his mother. You want to kill him?
Just born last night an' you take him out of the nest. You take
him back or I'll tell Slim not to let you have him."

Lennie held out his hands pleadingly. "Give 'um to me,
George. I'll take 'um back. I didn't mean no harm, George.
Honest I didn't. I jus' wanted to pet 'um a little."

George handed the pup to him. "Awright. You get him
back there quick, and don't you take him out no more. You'll

kill him, the first thing you know." Lennie fairly scuttled out of the room.

Slim had not moved. His calm eyes followed Lennie out the door. "Jesus," he said. "He's jes' like a kid, ain't he."

"Sure he's jes' like a kid. There ain't no more harm in him than a kid neither, except he's so strong. I bet he won't come in here to sleep tonight. He'd sleep right alongside that box in the barn. Well—let 'im. He ain't doin' no harm out there."

It was almost dark outside now. Old Candy, the swamper, came in and went to his bunk, and behind him struggled his old dog. "Hello, Slim. Hello, George. Didn't neither of you play horseshoes?"

"I don't like to play ever' night," said Slim.

Candy went on, "Either you guys got a slug of whisky? I gotta gut ache."

"I ain't," said Slim. "I'd drink it myself if I had, an' I ain't got a gut ache neither."

"Gotta bad gut ache," said Candy. "Them God damn turnips give it to me. I knowed they was going to before I ever eat 'em."

The thick-bodied Carlson came in out of the darkening yard. He walked to the other end of the bunk house and turned on the second shaded light. "Darker'n hell in here," he said. "Jesus, how that nigger can pitch shoes."

"He's plenty good," said Slim.

"Damn right he is," said Carlson. "He don't give nobody else a chance to win——" He stopped and sniffed the air, and still sniffing, looked down at the old dog. "God awmighty, that dog stinks. Get him outa here, Candy! I don't know nothing that stinks as bad as an old dog. You gotta get him out."

Candy rolled to the edge of his bunk. He reached over and patted the ancient dog, and he apologized, "I been around him so much I never notice how he stinks."

"Well, I can't stand him in here," said Carlson. "That stink hangs around even after he's gone." He walked over with his heavy-legged stride and looked down at the dog. "Got no teeth," he said. "He's all stiff with rheumatism. He ain't no good to you, Candy. An' he ain't no good to himself. Why'n't you shoot him, Candy?"

The old man squirmed uncomfortably. "Well—hell! I had him so long. Had him since he was a pup. I herded sheep with him." He said proudly, "You wouldn't think it to look at him now, but he was the best damn sheep dog I ever seen."

George said, "I seen a guy in Weed that had an Airedale could herd sheep. Learned it from the other dogs."

Carlson was not to be put off. "Look, Candy. This ol' dog jus' suffers hisself all the time. If you was to take him out and shoot him right in the back of the head—" he leaned over and pointed, "—right there, why he'd never know what hit him."

Candy looked about unhappily. "No," he said softly. "No, I couldn' do that. I had 'im too long."

"He don't have no fun," Carlson insisted. "And he stinks to beat hell. Tell you what. I'll shoot him for you. Then it won't be you that does it."

Candy threw his legs off his bunk. He scratched the white stubble whiskers on his cheek nervously. "I'm so used to him," he said softly. "I had him from a pup."

"Well, you ain't bein' kind to him keepin' him alive," said Carlson. "Look, Slim's bitch got a litter right now. I bet Slim would give you one of them pups to raise up, wouldn't you, Slim?"

The skinner had been studying the old dog with his calm eyes. "Yeah," he said. "You can have a pup if you want to." He seemed to shake himself free for speech. "Carl's right, Candy. That dog ain't no good to himself. I wisht somebody'd shoot me if I get old an' a cripple."

Candy looked helplessly at him, for Slim's opinions were law. "Maybe it'd hurt him," he suggested. "I don't mind takin' care of him."

Carlson said, "The way I'd shoot him, he wouldn't feel nothing. I'd put the gun right there." He pointed with his toe. "Right back of the head. He wouldn't even quiver."

Candy looked for help from face to face. It was quite dark outside by now. A young laboring man came in. His sloping shoulders were bent forward and he walked heavily on his heels, as though he carried the invisible grain bag. He went to his bunk and put his hat on his shelf. Then he picked a pulp magazine from his shelf and brought it to the light over the table. "Did I show you this, Slim?" he asked.

"Show me what?"

The young man turned to the back of the magazine, put it down on the table and pointed with his finger. "Right there, read that." Slim bent over it. "Go on," said the young man. "Read it out loud."

" 'Dear Editor' ": Slim read slowly. " 'I read your mag for six years and I think it is the best on the market. I like stories by Peter Rand. I think he is a whing-ding. Give us more like the Dark Rider. I don't write many letters. Just thought I would tell you I think your mag is the best dime's worth I ever spent.' "

Slim looked up questioningly. "What you want me to read that for?"

Whit said, "Go on. Read the name at the bottom."

Slim read, " 'Yours for success, William Tenner.' " He glanced up at Whit again. "What you want me to read that for?"

Whit closed the magazine impressively. "Don't you remember Bill Tenner? Worked here about three months ago?"

Slim thought. . . . "Little guy?" he asked. "Drove a cultivator?"

"That's him," Whit cried. "That's the guy!"

"You think he's the guy wrote this letter?"

"I know it. Bill and me was in here one day. Bill had one of them books that just come. He was lookin' in it and he says, 'I wrote a letter. Wonder if they put it in the book!' But it wasn't there. Bill says, 'Maybe they're savin' it for later.' An' that's just what they done. There it is."

"Guess you're right," said Slim. "Got it right in the book."

George held out his hand for the magazine. "Let's look at it?"

Whit found the place again, but he did not surrender his hold on it. He pointed out the letter with his forefinger. And then he went to his box shelf and laid the magazine carefully in. "I wonder if Bill seen it," he said. "Bill and me worked in that patch of field peas. Run cultivators, both of us. Bill was a hell of a nice fella."

During the conversation Carlson had refused to be drawn in. He continued to look down at the old dog. Candy watched him uneasily. At last Carlson said, "If you want me to, I'll put the old devil out of his misery right now and get it over with. Ain't nothing left for him. Can't eat, can't see, can't even walk without hurtin'."

Candy said hopefully, "You ain't got no gun."

"The hell I ain't. Got a Luger. It won't hurt him none at all."

Candy said, "Maybe tomorra. Le's wait till tomorra."

"I don't see no reason for it," said Carlson. He went to his bunk, pulled his bag from underneath it and took out a Luger pistol. "Le's get it over with," he said. "We can't sleep with him stinkin' around in here." He put the pistol in his hip pocket.

Candy looked a long time at Slim to try to find some reversal. And Slim gave him none. At last Candy said softly and hopelessly, "Awright—take 'im." He did not look down at the dog at all. He lay back on his bunk and crossed his arms behind his head and stared at the ceiling.

From his pocket Carlson took a little leather thong. He stooped over and tied it around the old dog's neck. All the men except Candy watched him. "Come boy. Come on, boy," he said gently. And he said apologetically to Candy, "He won't even feel it." Candy did not move nor answer him. He twitched the thong. "Come on, boy." The old dog got slowly and stiffly to his feet and followed the gently pulling leash.

Slim said, "Carlson."

"Yeah?"

"You know what to do."

"What ya mean, Slim?"

"Take a shovel," said Slim shortly.

"Oh, sure! I get you." He led the dog out into the darkness.

George followed to the door and shut the door and set the latch gently in its place. Candy lay rigidly on his bed staring at the ceiling.

Slim said loudly, "One of my lead mules got a bad hoof. Got to get some tar on it." His voice trailed off. It was silent outside. Carlson's footsteps died away. The silence came into the room. And the silence lasted.

George chuckled, "I bet Lennie's right out there in the barn with his pup. He won't want to come in here no more now he's got a pup."

Slim said, "Candy, you can have any one of them pups you want."

Candy did not answer. The silence fell on the room again. It came out of the night and invaded the room. George said, "Anybody like to play a little euchre?"

"I'll play out a few with you," said Whit.

They took places opposite each other at the table under the light, but George did not shuffle the cards. He rippled the edge of the deck nervously, and the little snapping noise drew the eyes of all the men in the room, so that he stopped doing it. The silence fell on the room again. A minute passed, and another minute. Candy lay still, staring at the ceiling. Slim gazed at him for a moment and then looked down at his hands; he subdued one hand with the other, and held it down. There came a little gnawing sound from under the floor and all the men looked down toward it gratefully. Only Candy continued to stare at the ceiling.

"Sounds like there was a rat under there," said George. "We ought to get a trap down there."

Whit broke out, "What the hell's takin' him so long? Lay out some cards, why don't you? We ain't going to get no euchre played this way."

George brought the cards together tightly and studied the backs of them. The silence was in the room again.

A shot sounded in the distance. The men looked quickly at the old man. Every head turned toward him.

For a moment he continued to stare at the ceiling. Then he rolled slowly over and faced the wall and lay silent.

George shuffled the cards noisily and dealt them. Whit drew a scoring board to him and set the pegs to start. Whit said, "I guess you guys really come here to work."

"How do ya mean?" George asked.

Whit laughed. "Well, ya come on a Friday. You got two days to work till Sunday."

"I don't see how you figure," said George.

Whit laughed again. "You do if you been around these big ranches much. Guy that wants to look over a ranch comes in Sat'day afternoon. He gets Sat'day night supper an' three meals on Sunday, and he can quit Monday mornin' after breakfast without turning his hand. But you come to work Friday noon. You got to put in a day an' a half no matter how you figure."

George looked at him levelly. "We're gonna stick aroun' a while," he said. "Me an' Lennie's gonna roll up a stake."

The door opened quietly and the stable buck put in his head; a lean negro head, lined with pain, the eyes patient. "Mr. Slim."

Slim took his eyes from old Candy. "Huh? Oh! Hello, Crooks. What's'a matter?"

"You told me to warm up tar for that mule's foot. I got it warm."

"Oh! Sure, Crooks. I'll come right out an' put it on."

"I can do it if you want, Mr. Slim."

"No. I'll come do it myself." He stood up.

Crooks said, "Mr. Slim."

"Yeah."

"That big new guy's messin' around your pups out in the barn."

"Well, he ain't doin' no harm. I give him one of them pups."

"Just thought I'd tell ya," said Crooks. "He's takin' 'em outa the nest and handlin' them. That won't do them no good."

"He won't hurt 'em," said Slim. "I'll come along with you now."

George looked up. "If that crazy bastard's foolin' around too much, jus' kick him out, Slim."

Slim followed the stable buck out of the room.

George dealt and Whit picked up his cards and examined them. "Seen the new kid yet?" he asked.

"What kid?" George asked.

"Why, Curley's new wife."

"Yeah, I seen her."

"Well, ain't she a looloo?"

"I ain't seen that much of her," said George.

Whit laid down his cards impressively. "Well, stick around

an' keep your eyes open. You'll see plenty. She ain't concealin' nothing. I never seen nobody like her. She got the eye goin' all the time on everybody. I bet she even gives the stable buck the eye. I don't know what the hell she wants."

George asked casually, "Been any trouble since she got here?"

It was obvious that Whit was not interested in his cards. He laid his hand down and George scooped it in. George laid out his deliberate solitaire hand—seven cards, and six on top, and five on top of those.

Whit said, "I see what you mean. No, they ain't been nothing yet. Curley's got yella-jackets in his drawers, but that's all so far. Ever' time the guys is around she shows up. She's lookin' for Curley, or she thought she lef' somethin' layin' around and she's lookin' for it. Seems like she can't keep away from guys. An' Curley's pants is just crawlin' with ants, but they ain't nothing come of it yet."

George said, "She's gonna make a mess. They's gonna be a bad mess about her. She's a jail bait all set on the trigger. That Curley got his work cut out for him. Ranch with a bunch of guys on it ain't no place for a girl, specially like her."

Whit said, "If you got idears, you ought ta come in town with us guys tomorra night."

"Why? What's doin'?"

"Jus' the usual thing. We go in to old Susy's place. Hell of a nice place. Old Susy's a laugh—always crackin' jokes. Like she says when we come up on the front porch las' Sat'day night. Susy opens the door and then she yells over her shoulder, 'Get yor coats on, girls, here comes the sheriff.' She never talks dirty, neither. Got five girls there."

"What's it set you back?" George asked.

"Two an' a half. You can get a shot for two bits. Susy got nice chairs to set in, too. If a guy don't want a flop, why he can just set in the chairs and have a couple or three shots and pass the time of day and Susy don't give a damn. She ain't rushin' guys through and kickin' 'em out if they don't want a flop."

"Might go in and look the joint over," said George.

"Sure. Come along. It's a hell of a lot of fun—her crackin'

jokes all the time. Like she says one time, she says, 'I've knew people that if they got a rag rug on the floor an' a kewpie doll lamp on the phonograph they think they're running a parlor house.' That's Clara's house she's talkin' about. An' Susy says, 'I know what you boys want,' she says. 'My girls is clean,' she says, 'an' there ain't no water in my whisky,' she says. 'If any you guys wanta look at a kewpie doll lamp an' take your own chance gettin' burned, why you know where to go.' An' she says, 'There's guys around here walkin' bow-legged 'cause they like to look at a kewpie doll lamp.' "

George asked, "Clara runs the other house, huh?"

"Yeah," said Whit. "We don't never go there. Clara gets three bucks a crack and thirty-five cents a shot, and she don't crack no jokes. But Susy's place is clean and she got nice chairs. Don't let no goo-goos in, neither."

"Me an' Lennie's rollin' up a stake," said George. "I might go in an' set and have a shot, but I ain't puttin' out no two and a half."

"Well, a guy got to have some fun sometime," said Whit.

The door opened and Lennie and Carlson came in together. Lennie crept to his bunk and sat down, trying not to attract attention. Carlson reached under his bunk and brought out his bag. He didn't look at old Candy, who still faced the wall. Carlson found a little cleaning rod in the bag and a can of oil. He laid them on his bed and then brought out the pistol, took out the magazine and snapped the loaded shell from the chamber. Then he fell to cleaning the barrel with the little rod. When the ejector snapped, Candy turned over and looked for a moment at the gun before he turned back to the wall again.

Carlson said casually, "Curley been in yet?"

"No," said Whit. "What's eatin' on Curley?"

Carlson squinted down the barrel of his gun. "Lookin' for his old lady. I seen him going round and round outside."

Whit said sarcastically, "He spends half his time lookin' for her, and the rest of the time she's lookin' for him."

Curley burst into the room excitedly. "Any you guys seen my wife?" he demanded.

"She ain't been here," said Whit.

Curley looked threateningly about the room. "Where the hell's Slim?"

"Went out in the barn," said George. "He was gonna put some tar on a split hoof."

Curley's shoulders dropped and squared. "How long ago'd he go?"

"Five—ten minutes."

Curley jumped out the door and banged it after him.

Whit stood up. "I guess maybe I'd like to see this," he said. "Curley's just spoilin' or he wouldn't start for Slim. An' Curley's handy, God damn handy. Got in the finals for the Golden Gloves. He got newspaper clippings about it." He considered. "But jus' the same, he better leave Slim alone. Nobody don't know what Slim can do."

"Thinks Slim's with his wife, don't he?" said George.

"Looks like it," Whit said. " 'Course Slim ain't. Least I don't think Slim is. But I like to see the fuss if it comes off. Come on, le's go."

George said, "I'm stayin' right here. I don't want to get mixed up in nothing. Lennie and me got to make a stake."

Carlson finished the cleaning of the gun and put it in the bag and pushed the bag under his bunk. "I guess I'll go out and look her over," he said. Old Candy lay still, and Lennie, from his bunk, watched George cautiously.

When Whit and Carlson were gone and the door closed after them, George turned to Lennie. "What you got on your mind?"

"I ain't done nothing, George. Slim says I better not pet them pups so much for a while. Slim says it ain't good for them; so I come right in. I been good, George."

"I coulda told you that," said George.

"Well, I wasn't hurtin' 'em none. I jus' had mine in my lap pettin' it."

George asked, "Did you see Slim out in the barn?"

"Sure I did. He tol' me I better not pet that pup no more."

"Did you see that girl?"

"You mean Curley's girl?"

"Yeah. Did she come in the barn?"

"No. Anyways I never seen her."

"You never seen Slim talkin' to her?"

"Uh-uh. She ain't been in the barn."

"O.K.," said George. "I guess them guys ain't gonna see no fight. If there's any fightin', Lennie, you keep out of it."

"I don't want no fights," said Lennie. He got up from his bunk and sat down at the table, across from George. Almost automatically George shuffled the cards and laid out his solitaire hand. He used a deliberate, thoughtful, slowness.

Lennie reached for a face card and studied it, then turned it upside down and studied it. "Both ends the same," he said. "George, why is it both end's the same?"

"I don't know," said George. "That's jus' the way they make 'em. What was Slim doin' in the barn when you seen him?"

"Slim?"

"Sure. You seen him in the barn, an' he tol' you not to pet the pups so much."

"Oh, yeah. He had a can a' tar an' a paint brush. I don't know what for."

"You sure that girl didn't come in like she come in here today?"

"No. She never come."

George sighed. "You give me a good whore house every time," he said. "A guy can go in an' get drunk and get ever'thing outa his system all at once, an' no messes. And he knows how much it's gonna set him back. These here jail baits is just set on the trigger of the hoosegow."

Lennie followed his words admiringly, and moved his lips a little to keep up. George continued, "You remember Andy Cushman, Lennie? Went to grammar school?"

"The one that his old lady used to make hot cakes for the kids?" Lennie asked.

"Yeah. That's the one. You can remember anything if there's anything to eat in it." George looked carefully at the solitaire hand. He put an ace up on his scoring rack and piled a two, three and four of diamonds on it. "Andy's in San Quentin right now on account of a tart," said George.

Lennie drummed on the table with his fingers. "George?"

"Huh?"

"George, how long's it gonna be till we get that little place an' live on the fatta the lan—an' rabbits?"

"I don' know," said George. "We gotta get a big stake together. I know a little place we can get cheap, but they ain't givin' it away."

Old Candy turned slowly over. His eyes were wide open. He watched George carefully.

Lennie said, "Tell about that place, George."

"I jus' tol' you, jus' las' night."

"Go on—tell again, George."

"Well, it's ten acres," said George. "Got a little win'mill. Got a little shack on it, an' a chicken run. Got a kitchen, orchard, cherries, apples, peaches, 'cots, nuts, got a few berries. They's a place for alfalfa and plenty water to flood it. They's a pig pen——"

"An' rabbits, George."

"No place for rabbits now, but I could easy build a few hutches and you could feed alfalfa to the rabbits."

"Damn right, I could," said Lennie. "You God damn right I could."

George's hands stopped working with the cards. His voice was growing warmer. "An' we could have a few pigs. I could build a smoke house like the one gran'pa had, an' when we kill a pig we can smoke the bacon and the hams, and make sausage an' all like that. An' when the salmon run up river we could catch a hundred of 'em an' salt 'em down or smoke 'em. We could have them for breakfast. They ain't nothing so nice as smoked salmon. When the fruit come in we could can it— and tomatoes, they're easy to can. Ever' Sunday we'd kill a chicken or a rabbit. Maybe we'd have a cow or a goat, and the cream is so God damn thick you got to cut it with a knife and take it out with a spoon."

Lennie watched him with wide eyes, and old Candy watched him too. Lennie said softly, "We could live offa the fatta the lan'."

"Sure," said George. "All kin's a vegetables in the garden, and if we want a little whisky we can sell a few eggs or something, or some milk. We'd jus' live there. We'd belong there. There wouldn't be no more runnin' round the country and gettin' fed by a Jap cook. No, sir, we'd have our own place where we belonged and not sleep in no bunk house."

"Tell about the house, George," Lennie begged.

"Sure, we'd have a little house an' a room to ourself. Little fat iron stove, an' in the winter we'd keep a fire goin' in it. It ain't enough land so we'd have to work too hard. Maybe six, seven hours a day. We wouldn't have to buck no barley eleven hours a day. An' when we put in a crop, why, we'd be there to take the crop up. We'd know what come of our planting."

"An' rabbits," Lennie said eagerly. "An' I'd take care of 'em. Tell how I'd do that, George."

"Sure, you'd go out in the alfalfa patch an' you'd have a sack. You'd fill up the sack and bring it in an' put it in the rabbit cages."

"They'd nibble an' they'd nibble," said Lennie, "the way they do. I seen 'em."

"Ever' six weeks or so," George continued, "them does would throw a litter so we'd have plenty rabbits to eat an' to sell. An' we'd keep a few pigeons to go flyin' around the win'-mill like they done when I was a kid." He looked raptly at the wall over Lennie's head. "An' it'd be our own, an' nobody could can us. If we don't like a guy we can say, 'Get the hell out,' and by God he's got to do it. An' if a fren' come along, why we'd have an extra bunk, an' we'd say, 'Why don't you spen' the night?' an' by God he would. We'd have a setter dog and a couple stripe cats, but you gotta watch out them cats don't get the little rabbits."

Lennie breathed hard. "You jus' let 'em try to get the rabbits. I'll break their God damn necks. I'll . . . . I'll smash 'em with a stick." He subsided, grumbling to himself, threatening the future cats which might dare to disturb the future rabbits.

George sat entranced with his own picture.

When Candy spoke they both jumped as though they had been caught doing something reprehensible. Candy said, "You know where's a place like that?"

George was on guard immediately. "S'pose I do," he said. "What's that to you?"

"You don't need to tell me where it's at. Might be any place."

"Sure," said George. "That's right. You couldn't find it in a hundred years."

Candy went on excitedly, "How much they want for a place like that?"

George watched him suspiciously. "Well—I could get it for six hundred bucks. The ol' people that owns it is flat bust an' the ol' lady needs an operation. Say—what's it to you? You got nothing to do with us."

Candy said, "I ain't much good with on'y one hand. I lost my hand right here on this ranch. That's why they give me a job swampin'. An' they give me two hunderd an' fifty dollars 'cause I los' my hand. An' I got fifty more saved up right in the bank, right now. Tha's three hunderd, and I got fifty more comin' the end a the month. Tell you what——" He leaned forward eagerly. "S'pose I went in with you guys. Tha's three hunderd an' fifty bucks I'd put in. I ain't much good, but I could cook and tend the chickens and hoe the garden some. How'd that be?"

George half-closed his eyes. "I gotta think about that. We was always gonna do it by ourselves."

Candy interrupted him, "I'd make a will an' leave my share to you guys in case I kick off, 'cause I ain't got no relatives nor nothing. You guys got any money? Maybe we could do her right now?"

George spat on the floor disgustedly. "We got ten bucks between us." Then he said thoughtfully, "Look, if me an' Lennie work a month an' don't spen' nothing, we'll have a hunderd bucks. That'd be four fifty. I bet we could swing her for that. Then you an' Lennie could go get her started an' I'd get a job an' make up the res', an' you could sell eggs an' stuff like that."

They fell into a silence. They looked at one another, amazed. This thing they had never really believed in was coming true. George said reverently, "Jesus Christ! I bet we could swing her." His eyes were full of wonder. "I bet we could swing her," he repeated softly.

Candy sat on the edge of his bunk. He scratched the stump of his wrist nervously. "I got hurt four years ago," he said. "They'll can me purty soon. Jus' as soon as I can't swamp out no bunk houses they'll put me on the county. Maybe if I give you guys my money, you'll let me hoe in the garden even after I ain't no good at it. An' I'll wash dishes an' little chicken stuff like that. But I'll be on our own place, an' I'll be let to work on our own place." He said miserably, "You seen what they done to my dog tonight? They says he wasn't no good to himself nor nobody else. When they can me here I wisht somebody'd shoot me. But they won't do nothing like that. I won't have no place to go, an' I can't get no more jobs. I'll have thirty dollars more comin', time you guys is ready to quit."

George stood up. "We'll do her," he said. "We'll fix up that little old place an' we'll go live there." He sat down again. They all sat still, all bemused by the beauty of the thing, each mind was popped into the future when this lovely thing should come about.

George said wonderingly, "S'pose they was a carnival or a circus come to town, or a ball game, or any damn thing." Old Candy nodded in appreciation of the idea. "We'd just go to her," George said. "We wouldn't ask nobody if we could. Jus' say, 'We'll go to her,' an' we would. Jus' milk the cow and sling some grain to the chickens an' go to her."

"An' put some grass to the rabbits," Lennie broke in. "I wouldn't never forget to feed them. When we gon'ta do it, George?"

"In one month. Right squack in one month. Know what I'm gon'ta do? I'm gon'ta write to them old people that owns the place that we'll take it. An' Candy'll send a hunderd dollars to bind her."

"Sure will," said Candy. "They got a good stove there?"

"Sure, got a nice stove, burns coal or wood."

"I'm gonna take my pup," said Lennie. "I bet by Christ he likes it there, by Jesus."

Voices were approaching from outside. George said quickly, "Don't tell nobody about it. Jus' us three an' nobody else. They li'ble to can us so we can't make no stake. Jus' go on like we was gonna buck barley the rest of our lives, then all of a sudden some day we'll go get our pay an' scram outa here."

Lennie and Candy nodded, and they were grinning with delight. "Don't tell nobody," Lennie said to himself.

Candy said, "George."

"Huh?"

"I ought to of shot that dog myself, George. I shouldn't ought to of let no stranger shoot my dog."

The door opened. Slim came in, followed by Curley and Carlson and Whit. Slim's hands were black with tar and he was scowling. Curley hung close to his elbow.

Curley said, "Well, I didn't mean nothing, Slim. I just ast you."

Slim said, "Well, you been askin' me too often. I'm gettin' God damn sick of it. If you can't look after your own God damn wife, what you expect me to do about it? You lay offa me."

"I'm jus' trying' to tell you I didn't mean nothing," said Curley. "I jus' thought you might of saw her."

"Why'n't you tell her to stay the hell home where she belongs?" said Carlson. "You let her hang around bunk houses and pretty soon you're gonna have som'pin on your hands and you won't be able to do nothing about it."

Curley whirled on Carlson. "You keep outta this les' you wanta step outside."

Carlson laughed. "You God damn punk," he said. "You tried to throw a scare into Slim, an' you couldn't make it stick. Slim throwed a scare inta you. You're yella as a frog belly. I don't care if you're the best welter in the country. You come for me, an' I'll kick your God damn head off."

Candy joined the attack with joy. "Glove fulla vaseline," he said disgustedly. Curley glared at him. His eyes slipped on past and lighted on Lennie; and Lennie was still smiling with delight at the memory of the ranch.

Curley stepped over to Lennie like a terrier. "What the hell you laughin' at?"

Lennie looked blankly at him. "Huh?"

Then Curley's rage exploded. "Come on, ya big bastard. Get up on your feet. No big son-of-a-bitch is gonna laugh at me. I'll show ya who's yella."

Lennie looked helplessly at George, and then he got up and tried to retreat. Curley was balanced and poised. He slashed at Lennie with his left, and then smashed down his nose with a right. Lennie gave a cry of terror. Blood welled from his nose. "George," he cried. "Make 'um let me alone, George." He backed until he was against the wall, and Curley followed, slugging him in the face. Lennie's hands remained at his sides; he was too frightened to defend himself.

George was on his feet yelling, "Get him, Lennie. Don't let him do it."

Lennie covered his face with his huge paws and bleated with terror. He cried, "Make 'um stop, George." Then Curley attacked his stomach and cut off his wind.

Slim jumped up. "The dirty little rat," he cried, "I'll get 'um myself."

George put out his hand and grabbed Slim. "Wait a minute," he shouted. He cupped his hands around his mouth and yelled, "Get 'im, Lennie!"

Lennie took his hands away from his face and looked about for George, and Curley slashed at his eyes. The big face was covered with blood. George yelled again, "I said get him."

Curley's fist was swinging when Lennie reached for it. The next minute Curley was flopping like a fish on a line, and his closed fist was lost in Lennie's big hand. George ran down the room. "Leggo of him, Lennie. Let go."

But Lennie watched in terror the flopping little man whom he held. Blood ran down Lennie's face, one of his eyes was cut and closed. George slapped him in the face again and again, and still Lennie held on to the closed fist. Curley was white and shrunken by now, and his struggling had become weak. He stood crying, his fist lost in Lennie's paw.

George shouted over and over, "Leggo his hand, Lennie. Leggo. Slim, come help me while the guy got any hand left."

Suddenly Lennie let go his hold. He crouched cowering against the wall. "You tol' me to, George," he said miserably.

Curley sat down on the floor, looking in wonder at his crushed hand. Slim and Carlson bent over him. Then Slim straightened up and regarded Lennie with horror. "We got to get him in to a doctor," he said. "Looks to me like ever' bone in his han' is bust."

"I didn't wanta," Lennie cried. "I didn't wanta hurt him."

Slim said, "Carlson, you get the candy wagon hitched up. We'll take 'um into Soledad an' get 'um fixed up." Carlson hurried out. Slim turned to the whimpering Lennie. "It ain't your fault," he said. "This punk sure had it comin' to him. But—Jesus! He ain't hardly got no han' left." Slim hurried out, and in a moment returned with a tin cup of water. He held it to Curley's lips.

George said, "Slim, will we get canned now? We need the stake. Will Curley's old man can us now?"

Slim smiled wryly. He knelt down beside Curley. "You got your senses in hand enough to listen?" he asked. Curley nodded. "Well, then listen," Slim went on. "I think you got your han' caught in a machine. If you don't tell nobody what happened, we ain't going to. But you jus' tell an' try to get this guy canned and we'll tell ever'body, an' then will you get the laugh."

"I won't tell," said Curley. He avoided looking at Lennie.

Buggy wheels sounded outside. Slim helped Curley up. "Come on now. Carlson's gonna take you to a doctor." He helped Curley out the door. The sound of wheels drew away. In a moment Slim came back into the bunk house. He looked at Lennie, still crouched fearfully against the wall. "Le's see your hands," he asked.

Lennie stuck out his hands.

"Christ awmighty, I hate to have you mad at me," Slim said.

George broke in, "Lennie was jus' scairt," he explained. "He didn't know what to do. I told you nobody ought never to fight him. No, I guess it was Candy I told."

Candy nodded solemnly. "That's jus' what you done," he said. "Right this morning when Curley first lit intil your fren', you says, 'He better not fool with Lennie if he knows what's good for 'um.' That's jus' what you says to me."

George turned to Lennie. "It ain't your fault," he said. "You don't need to be scairt no more. You done jus' what I tol' you to. Maybe you better go in the wash room an' clean up your face. You look like hell."

Lennie smiled with his bruised mouth. "I didn't want no trouble," he said. He walked toward the door, but just before he came to it, he turned back. "George?"

"What you want?"

"I can still tend the rabbits, George?"

"Sure. You ain't done nothing wrong."

"I di'n't mean no harm, George."

"Well, get the hell out and wash your face."

4

CROOKS, the negro stable buck, had his bunk in the harness room; a little shed that leaned off the wall of the barn. On one side of the little room there was a square four-paned window, and on the other, a narrow plank door leading into the barn. Crooks' bunk was a long box filled with straw, on which his blankets were flung. On the wall by the window there were pegs on which hung broken harness in process of being mended; strips of new leather; and under the window itself a little bench for leather-working tools, curved knives and needles and balls of linen thread, and a small hand riveter. On pegs were also pieces of harness, a split collar with the horsehair stuffing sticking out, a broken hame, and a trace chain with its leather covering split. Crooks had his apple box over his bunk, and in it a range of medicine bottles, both for himself and for the horses. There were cans of saddle soap and a drippy can of tar with its paint brush sticking over the edge. And scattered about the floor were a number of personal possessions; for, being alone, Crooks could leave his things about, and being a stable buck and a cripple, he was more permanent than the other men, and he had accumulated more possessions than he could carry on his back.

Crooks possessed several pairs of shoes, a pair of rubber boots, a big alarm clock and a single-barreled shotgun. And he had books, too; a tattered dictionary and a mauled copy of the California civil code for 1905. There were battered magazines and a few dirty books on a special shelf over his bunk. A pair of large gold-rimmed spectacles hung from a nail on the wall above his bed.

This room was swept and fairly neat, for Crooks was a proud, aloof man. He kept his distance and demanded that other people keep theirs. His body was bent over to the left by his crooked spine, and his eyes lay deep in his head, and because of their depth seemed to glitter with intensity. His lean face was lined with deep black wrinkles, and he had thin, pain-tightened lips which were lighter than his face.

It was Saturday night. Through the open door that led into

the barn came the sound of moving horses, of feet stirring, of teeth champing on hay, of the rattle of halter chains. In the stable buck's room a small electric globe threw a meager yellow light.

Crooks sat on his bunk. His shirt was out of his jeans in back. In one hand he held a bottle of liniment, and with the other he rubbed his spine. Now and then he poured a few drops of the liniment into his pink-palmed hand and reached up under his shirt to rub again. He flexed his muscles against his back and shivered.

Noiselessly Lennie appeared in the open doorway and stood there looking in, his big shoulders nearly filling the opening. For a moment Crooks did not see him, but on raising his eyes he stiffened and a scowl came on his face. His hand came out from under his shirt.

Lennie smiled helplessly in an attempt to make friends.

Crooks said sharply, "You got no right to come in my room. This here's my room. Nobody got any right in here but me."

Lennie gulped and his smile grew more fawning. "I ain't doing nothing," he said. "Just come to look at my puppy. And I seen your light," he explained.

"Well, I got a right to have a light. You go on get outta my room. I ain't wanted in the bunk house, and you ain't wanted in my room."

"Why ain't you wanted?" Lennie asked.

" 'Cause I'm black. They play cards in there, but I can't play because I'm black. They say I stink. Well, I tell you, you all of you stink to me."

Lennie flapped his big hands helplessly. "Ever'body went into town," he said. "Slim an' George an' ever'body. George says I gotta stay here an' not get in no trouble. I seen your light."

"Well, what do you want?"

"Nothing—I seen your light. I thought I could jus' come in an' set."

Crooks stared at Lennie, and he reached behind him and took down the spectacles and adjusted them over his pink ears and stared again. "I don't know what you're doin' in the barn anyway," he complained. "You ain't no skinner. They's no call for a bucker to come into the barn at all. You ain't no skinner. You ain't got nothing to do with the horses."

"The pup," Lennie repeated. "I come to see my pup."

"Well, go see your pup, then. Don't come in a place where you're not wanted."

Lennie lost his smile. He advanced a step into the room, then remembered and backed to the door again. "I looked at 'em a little. Slim says I ain't to pet 'em very much."

Crooks said, "Well, you been takin' 'em out of the nest all the time. I wonder the old lady don't move 'em someplace else."

"Oh, she don't care. She lets me." Lennie had moved into the room again.

Crooks scowled, but Lennie's disarming smile defeated him. "Come on in and set a while," Crooks said. " 'Long as you won't get out and leave me alone, you might as well set down." His tone was a little more friendly. "All the boys gone into town, huh?"

"All but old Candy. He just sets in the bunk house sharpening his pencil and sharpening and figuring."

Crooks adjusted his glasses. "Figuring? What's Candy figuring about?"

Lennie almost shouted, " 'Bout the rabbits."

"You're nuts," said Crooks. "You're crazy as a wedge. What rabbits you talkin' about?"

"The rabbits we're gonna get, and I get to tend 'em, cut grass an' give 'em water, an' like that."

"Jus' nuts," said Crooks. "I don't blame the guy you travel with for keepin' you outa sight."

Lennie said quietly, "It ain't no lie. We're gonna do it. Gonna get a little place an' live on the fatta the lan'."

Crooks settled himself more comfortably on his bunk. "Set down," he invited. "Set down on the nail keg."

Lennie hunched down on the little barrel. "You think it's a lie," Lennie said. "But it ain't no lie. Ever' word's the truth, an' you can ast George."

Crooks put his dark chin into his pink palm. "You travel aroun' with George, don't ya?"

"Sure. Me an' him goes ever' place together."

Crooks continued. "Sometimes he talks, and you don't

know what the hell he's talkin' about. Ain't that so?" He leaned forward, boring Lennie with his deep eyes. "Ain't that so?"

"Yeah . . . . sometimes."

"Jus' talks on, an' you don't know what the hell it's all about?"

"Yeah . . . . sometimes. But . . . . not always."

Crooks leaned forward over the edge of the bunk. "I ain't a southern negro," he said. "I was born right here in California. My old man had a chicken ranch, 'bout ten acres. The white kids come to play at our place, an' sometimes I went to play with them, and some of them was pretty nice. My ol' man didn't like that. I never knew till long later why he didn't like that. But I know now." He hesitated, and when he spoke again his voice was softer. "There wasn't another colored family for miles around. And now there ain't a colored man on this ranch an' there's jus' one family in Soledad." He laughed. "If I say something, why it's just a nigger sayin' it."

Lennie asked, "How long you think it'll be before them pups will be old enough to pet?"

Crooks laughed again. "A guy can talk to you an' be sure you won't go blabbin'. Couple of weeks an' them pups'll be all right. George knows what he's about. Jus' talks, an' you don't understand nothing." He leaned forward excitedly. "This is just a nigger talkin', an' a busted-back nigger. So it don't mean nothing, see? You couldn't remember it anyways. I seen it over an' over—a guy talkin' to another guy and it don't make no difference if he don't hear or understand. The thing is, they're talkin', or they're settin' still not talkin'. It don't make no difference, no difference." His excitement had increased until he pounded his knee with this hand. "George can tell you screwy things, and it don't matter. It's just the talking. It's just bein' with another guy. That's all." He paused.

His voice grew soft and persuasive. "S'pose George don't come back no more. S'pose he took a powder and just ain't coming back. What'll you do then?"

Lennie's attention came gradually to what had been said. "What?" he demanded.

"I said s'pose George went into town tonight and you

never heard of him no more." Crooks pressed forward some kind of private victory. "Just s'pose that," he repeated.

"He won't do it," Lennie cried. "George wouldn't do nothing like that. I been with George a long time. He'll come back tonight——" But the doubt was too much for him. "Don't you think he will?"

Crooks' face lighted with pleasure in his torture. "Nobody can't tell what a guy'll do," he observed calmly. "Le's say he wants to come back and can't. S'pose he gets killed or hurt so he can't come back."

Lennie struggled to understand. "George won't do nothing like that," he repeated. "George is careful. He won't get hurt. He ain't never been hurt, 'cause he's careful."

"Well, s'pose, jus' s'pose he don't come back. What'll you do then?"

Lennie's face wrinkled with apprehension. "I don' know. Say, what you doin' anyways?" he cried. "This ain't true. George ain't got hurt."

Crooks bored in on him. "Want me ta tell ya what'll happen? They'll take ya to the booby hatch. They'll tie ya up with a collar, like a dog."

Suddenly Lennie's eyes centered and grew quiet, and mad. He stood up and walked dangerously toward Crooks. "Who hurt George?" he demanded.

Crooks saw the danger as it approached him. He edged back on his bunk to get out of the way. "I was just supposin'," he said. "George ain't hurt. He's all right. He'll be back all right."

Lennie stood over him. "What you supposin' for? Ain't nobody goin' to suppose no hurt to George."

Crooks removed his glasses and wiped his eyes with his fingers. "Jus' set down," he said. "George ain't hurt."

Lennie growled back to his seat on the nail keg. "Ain't nobody goin' to talk no hurt to George," he grumbled.

Crooks said gently, "Maybe you can see now. You got George. You *know* he's goin' to come back. S'pose you didn't have nobody. S'pose you couldn't go into the bunk house and play rummy 'cause you was black. How'd you like that? S'pose you had to sit out here an' read books. Sure you could play horseshoes till it got dark, but then you got to read books. Books ain't no good. A guy needs somebody—to be near him." He whined, "A guy goes nuts if he ain't got nobody. Don't make no difference who the guy is, long's he's with you. I tell ya," he cried, "I tell ya a guy gets too lonely an' he gets sick."

"George gonna come back," Lennie reassured himself in a frightened voice. "Maybe George come back already. Maybe I better go see."

Crooks said, "I didn't mean to scare you. He'll come back. I was talkin' about myself. A guy sets alone out here at night, maybe readin' books or thinkin' or stuff like that. Sometimes he gets thinkin', an' he got nothing to tell him what's so an' what ain't so. Maybe if he sees somethin', he don't know whether it's right or not. He can't turn to some other guy and ast him if he sees it too. He can't tell. He got nothing to measure by. I seen things out here. I wasn't drunk. I don't know if I was asleep. If some guy was with me, he could tell me I was asleep, an' then it would be all right. But I jus' don't know." Crooks was looking across the room now, looking toward the window.

Lennie said miserably, "George wun't go away and leave me. I know George wun't do that."

The stable buck went on dreamily, "I remember when I was a little kid on my old man's chicken ranch. Had two brothers. They was always near me, always there. Used to sleep right in the same room, right in the same bed—all three. Had a strawberry patch. Had an alfalfa patch. Used to turn the chickens out in the alfalfa on a sunny morning. My brothers'd set on a fence rail an' watch 'em—white chickens they was."

Gradually Lennie's interest came around to what was being said. "George says we're gonna have alfalfa for the rabbits."

"What rabbits?"

"We're gonna have rabbits an' a berry patch."

"You're nuts."

"We are too. You ast George."

"You're nuts." Crooks was scornful. "I seen hunderds of men come by on the road an' on the ranches, with their bindles on their back an' that same damn thing in their heads. Hunderds of them. They come, an' they quit an' go on; an' every damn one of 'em's got a little piece of land in his head. An' never a God damn one of 'em ever gets it. Just like heaven. Ever'body wants a little piece of lan'. I read plenty of books out here. Nobody never gets to heaven, and nobody gets no land. It's just in their head. They're all the time talkin' about it, but it's jus' in their head. He paused and looked toward the open door, for the horses were moving restlessly and the halter chains clinked. A horse whinnied. "I guess somebody's out there," Crooks said. "Maybe Slim. Slim comes in sometimes two, three times a night. Slim's a real skinner. He looks out for his team." He pulled himself painfully upright and moved toward the door. "That you, Slim?" he called.

Candy's voice answered. "Slim went in town. Say, you seen Lennie?"

"Ya mean the big guy?"

"Yeah. Seen him around any place?"

"He's in here," Crooks said shortly. He went back to his bunk and lay down.

Candy stood in the doorway scratching his bald wrist and looking blindly into the lighted room. He made no attempt to enter. "Tell ya what, Lennie. I been figuring out about them rabbits."

Crooks said irritably, "You can come in if you want."

Candy seemed embarrassed. "I do' know. 'Course, if ya want me to."

"Come on in. If ever'body's comin' in, you might just as well." It was difficult for Crooks to conceal his pleasure with anger.

Candy came in, but he was still embarrassed. "You got a nice cozy little place in here," he said to Crooks. "Must be nice to have a room all to yourself this way."

"Sure," said Crooks. "And a manure pile under the window. Sure, it's swell."

Lennie broke in, "You said about them rabbits."

Candy leaned against the wall beside the broken collar while he scratched the wrist stump. "I been here a long time," he said. "An' Crooks been here a long time. This's the first time I ever been in his room."

Crooks said darkly, "Guys don't come into a colored man's

room very much. Nobody been here but Slim. Slim an' the boss."

Candy quickly changed the subject. "Slim's as good a skinner as I ever seen."

Lennie leaned toward the old swamper. "About them rabbits," he insisted.

Candy smiled. "I got it figured out. We can make some money on them rabbits if we go about it right."

"But I get to tend 'em," Lennie broke in. "George says I get to tend 'em. He promised."

Crooks interrupted brutally. "You guys is just kiddin' yourself. You'll talk about it a hell of a lot, but you won't get no land. You'll be a swamper here till they take you out in a box. Hell, I seen too many guys. Lennie here'll quit an' be on the road in two, three weeks. Seems like ever' guy got land in his head."

Candy rubbed his cheek angrily. "You God damn right we're gonna do it. George says we are. We got the money right now."

"Yeah?" said Crooks. "An' where's George now? In town in a whore house. That's where your money's goin'. Jesus, I seen it happen too many times. I seen too many guys with land in their head. They never get none under their hand."

Candy cried, "Sure they all want it. Everybody wants a little bit of land, not much. Jus' som'thin' that was his. Som'thin' he could live on and there couldn't nobody throw him off of it. I never had none. I planted crops for damn near ever'body in this state, but they wasn't my crops, and when I harvested 'em, it wasn't none of my harvest. But we gonna do it now, and don't you make no mistake about that. George ain't got the money in town. That money's in the bank. Me an' Lennie an' George. We gonna have a room to ourself. We're gonna have a dog an' rabbits an' chickens. We're gonna have green corn an' maybe a cow or a goat." He stopped, overwhelmed with his picture.

Crooks asked, "You say you got the money?"

"Damn right. We got most of it. Just a little bit more to get. Have it all in one month. George got the land all picked out, too."

Crooks reached around and explored his spine with his

hand. "I never seen a guy really do it," he said. "I seen guys nearly crazy with loneliness for land, but ever' time a whore house or a blackjack game took what it takes." He hesitated. ". . . . If you . . . . guys would want a hand to work for nothing—just his keep, why I'd come an' lend a hand. I ain't so crippled I can't work like a son-of-a-bitch if I want to."

"Any you boys seen Curley?"

They swung their heads toward the door. Looking in was Curley's wife. Her face was heavily made up. Her lips were slightly parted. She breathed strongly, as though she had been running.

"Curley ain't been here," Candy said sourly.

She stood still in the doorway, smiling a little at them, rubbing the nails of one hand with the thumb and forefinger of the other. And her eyes traveled from one face to another. "They left all the weak ones here," she said finally. "Think I don't know where they all went? Even Curley. I know where they all went."

Lennie watched her, fascinated; but Candy and Crooks were scowling down away from her eyes. Candy said, "Then if you know, why you want to ast us where Curley is at?"

She regarded them amusedly. "Funny thing," she said. "If I catch any one man, and he's alone, I get along fine with him. But just let two of the guys get together an' you won't talk. Jus' nothing but mad." She dropped her fingers and put her hands on her hips. "You're all scared of each other, that's what. Ever' one of you's scared the rest is goin' to get something on you."

After a pause Crooks said, "Maybe you better go along to your own house now. We don't want no trouble."

"Well, I ain't giving you no trouble. Think I don't like to talk to somebody ever' once in a while? Think I like to stick in that house alla time?"

Candy laid the stump of his wrist on his knee and rubbed it gently with his hand. He said accusingly, "You gotta husban'. You got no call foolin' aroun' with other guys, causin' trouble."

The girl flared up. "Sure I gotta husban'. You all seen him. Swell guy, ain't he? Spends all his time sayin' what he's gonna do to guys he don't like, and he don't like nobody. Think I'm gonna stay in that two-by-four house and listen how Curley's gonna lead with his left twict, and then bring in the ol' right cross? 'One-two' he says. 'Jus the ol' one-two an' he'll go down.'" She paused and her face lost its sullenness and grew interested. "Say—what happened to Curley's han'?"

There was an embarrassed silence. Candy stole a look at Lennie. Then he coughed. "Why . . . . Curley . . . . he got his han' caught in a machine, ma'am. Bust his han'."

She watched for a moment, and then she laughed. "Baloney! What you think you're sellin' me? Curley started som'pin' he didn't finish. Caught in a machine—baloney! Why, he ain't give nobody the good ol' one-two since he got his han' bust. Who bust him?"

Candy repeated sullenly, "Got it caught in a machine."

"Awright," she said contemptuously. "Awright, cover 'im up if ya wanta. Whatta I care? You bindle bums think you're so damn good. Whatta ya think I am, a kid? I tell ya I could of went with shows. Not jus' one, neither. An' a guy tol' me he could put me in pitchers. . . ." She was breathless with indignation. "—Sat'iday night. Ever'body out doin' som'pin'. Ever'body! An' what am I doin'? Standin' here talkin' to a bunch of bindle stiffs—a nigger an' a dum-dum and a lousy ol' sheep—an' likin' it because they ain't nobody else."

Lennie watched her, his mouth half open. Crooks had retired into the terrible protective dignity of the negro. But a change came over old Candy. He stood up suddenly and knocked his nail keg over backward. "I had enough," he said angrily. "You ain't wanted here. We told you you ain't. An' I tell ya, you got floozy idears about what us guys amounts to. You ain't got sense enough in that chicken head to even see that we ain't stiffs. S'pose you get us canned. S'pose you do. You think we'll hit the highway an' look for another lousy two-bit job like this. You don't know that we got our own ranch to go to, an' our own house. We ain't got to stay here. We gotta house and chickens an' fruit trees an' a place a hunderd time prettier than this. An' we got fren's, that's what we got. Maybe there was a time when we was scared of gettin' canned, but we ain't no more. We got our own lan', and it's ours, an' we c'n go to it."

Curley's wife laughed at him. "Baloney," she said. "I seen

too many you guys. If you had two bits in the worl', why you'd be in gettin' two shots of corn with it and suckin' the bottom of the glass. I know you guys."

Candy's face had grown redder and redder, but before she was done speaking, he had control of himself. He was the master of the situation. "I might of knew," he said gently. "Maybe you just better go along an' roll your hoop. We ain't got nothing to say to you at all. We know what we got, and we don't care whether you know it or not. So maybe you better jus' scatter along now, 'cause Curley maybe ain't gonna like his wife out in the barn with us 'bindle stiffs.'"

She looked from one face to another, and they were all closed against her. And she looked longest at Lennie, until he dropped his eyes in embarrassment. Suddenly she said, "Where'd you get them bruises on your face?"

Lennie looked up guiltily. "Who—me?"

"Yeah, you."

Lennie looked to Candy for help, and then he looked at his lap again. "He got his han' caught in a machine," he said.

Curley's wife laughed. "O.K., Machine. I'll talk to you later. I like machines."

Candy broke in. "You let this guy alone. Don't you do no messing aroun' with him. I'm gonna tell George what you says. George won't have you messin' with Lennie."

"Who's George?" she asked. "The little guy you come with?"

Lennie smiled happily. "That's him," he said. "That's the guy, an' he's gonna let me tend the rabbits."

"Well, if that's all you want, I might get a couple rabbits myself."

Crooks stood up from his bunk and faced her. "I had enough," he said coldly. "You got no rights comin' in a colored man's room. You got no rights messing around in here at all. Now you jus' get out, an' get out quick. If you don't, I'm gonna ast the boss not to ever let you come in the barn no more."

She turned on him in scorn. "Listen, Nigger," she said. "You know what I can do to you if you open your trap?"

Crooks stared hopelessly at her, and then he sat down on his bunk and drew into himself.

She closed on him. "You know what I could do?"

Crooks seemed to grow smaller, and he pressed himself against the wall. "Yes, ma'am."

"Well, you keep your place then, Nigger. I could get you strung up on a tree so easy it ain't even funny."

Crooks had reduced himself to nothing. There was no personality, no ego—nothing to arouse either like or dislike. He said, "Yes, ma'am," and his voice was toneless.

For a moment she stood over him as though waiting for him to move so that she could whip at him again; but Crooks sat perfectly still, his eyes averted, everything that might be hurt drawn in. She turned at last to the other two.

Old Candy was watching her, fascinated. "If you was to do that, we'd tell," he said quietly. "We'd tell about you framin' Crooks."

"Tell an' be damned," she cried. "Nobody'd listen to you, an' you know it. Nobody'd listen to you."

Candy subsided. "No . . . ." he agreed. "Nobody'd listen to us."

Lennie whined, "I wisht George was here. I wisht George was here."

Candy stepped over to him. "Don't you worry none," he said. "I jus' heard the guys comin' in. George'll be in the bunk house right now, I bet." He turned to Curley's wife. "You better go home now," he said quietly. "If you go right now, we won't tell Curley you was here."

She appraised him coolly. "I ain't sure you heard nothing."

"Better not take no chances," he said. "If you ain't sure, you better take the safe way."

She turned to Lennie. "I'm glad you bust up Curley a little bit. He got it comin' to him. Sometimes I'd like to bust him myself." She slipped out the door and disappeared into the dark barn. And while she went through the barn, the halter chains rattled, and some horses snorted and some stamped their feet.

Crooks seemed to come slowly out of the layers of protection he had put on. "Was that the truth what you said about the guys come back?" he asked.

"Sure. I heard 'em."

"Well, I didn't hear nothing."

"The gate banged," Candy said, and he went on, "Jesus Christ, Curley's wife can move quiet. I guess she had a lot of practice, though."

Crooks avoided the whole subject now. "Maybe you guys better go," he said. "I ain't sure I want you in here no more. A colored man got to have some rights even if he don't like 'em."

Candy said, "That bitch didn't ought to of said that to you."

"It wasn't nothing," Crooks said dully. "You guys comin' in an' settin' made me forget. What she says is true."

The horses snorted out in the barn and the chains rang and a voice called, "Lennie. Oh, Lennie. You in the barn?"

"It's George," Lennie cried. And he answered, "Here, George. I'm right in here."

In a second George stood framed in the door, and he looked disapprovingly about. "What you doin' in Crooks' room. You hadn't ought to be here."

Crooks nodded. "I tol' 'em, but they come in anyways."

"Well, why'n't you kick 'em out?"

"I di'n't care much," said Crooks. "Lennie's a nice fella."

Now Candy aroused himself. "Oh, George! I been figurin' and figurin'. I got it doped out how we can even make some money on them rabbits."

George scowled. "I thought I tol' you not to tell nobody about that."

Candy was crestfallen. "Didn't tell nobody but Crooks."

George said, "Well you guys get outta here. Jesus, seems like I can't go away for a minute."

Candy and Lennie stood up and went toward the door. Crooks called, "Candy!"

"Huh?"

" 'Member what I said about hoein' and doin' odd jobs?"

"Yeah," said Candy. "I remember."

"Well, jus' forget it," said Crooks. "I didn' mean it. Jus' foolin'. I wouldn't want to go no place like that."

"Well, O.K., if you feel like that. Good-night."

The three men went out of the door. As they went through the barn the horses snorted and the halter chains rattled.

Crooks sat on his bunk and looked at the door for a moment, and then he reached for the liniment bottle. He pulled out his shirt in back, poured a little liniment in his pink palm and, reaching around, he fell slowly to rubbing his back.

5

ONE END of the great barn was piled high with new hay and over the pile hung the four-taloned jackson fork suspended from its pulley. The hay came down like a mountain slope to the other end of the barn, and there was a level place as yet unfilled with the new crop. At the sides the feeding racks were visible, and between the slats the heads of horses could be seen.

It was Sunday afternoon. The resting horses nibbled the remaining wisps of hay, and they stamped their feet and they bit the wood of the mangers and rattled the halter chains. The afternoon sun sliced in through the cracks of the barn walls and lay in bright lines on the hay. There was the buzz of flies in the air, the lazy afternoon humming.

From outside came the clang of horseshoes on the playing peg and the shouts of men, playing, encouraging, jeering. But in the barn it was quiet and humming and lazy and warm.

Only Lennie was in the barn, and Lennie sat in the hay beside a packing case under a manger in the end of the barn that had not been filled with hay. Lennie sat in the hay and looked at a little dead puppy that lay in front of him. Lennie looked at it for a long time, and then he put out his huge hand and stroked it, stroked it clear from one end to the other.

And Lennie said softly to the puppy, "Why do you got to get killed? You ain't so little as mice. I didn't bounce you hard." He bent the pup's head up and looked in its face, and he said to it, "Now maybe George ain't gonna let me tend no rabbits, if he fin's out you got killed."

He scooped a little hollow and laid the puppy in it and covered it over with hay, out of sight; but he continued to stare at the mound he had made. He said, "This ain't no bad thing like I got to go hide in the brush. Oh! no. This ain't. I'll tell George I foun' it dead."

He unburied the puppy and inspected it, and he stroked it from ears to tail. He went on sorrowfully, "But he'll know. George always knows. He'll say, 'You done it. Don't try to put nothing over on me.' An' he'll say, 'Now jus' for that you don't get to tend no rabbits!' "

Suddenly his anger arose. "God damn you," he cried. "Why do you got to get killed? You ain't so little as mice." He picked up the pup and hurled it from him. He turned his back on it. He sat bent over his knees and he whispered, "Now I won't get to tend the rabbits. Now he won't let me." He rocked himself back and forth in his sorrow.

From outside came the clang of horseshoes on the iron stake, and then a little chorus of cries. Lennie got up and brought the puppy back and laid it on the hay and sat down. He stroked the pup again. "You wasn't big enough," he said. "They tol' me and tol' me you wasn't. I di'n't know you'd get killed so easy." He worked his fingers on the pup's limp ear. "Maybe George won't care," he said. "This here God damn little son-of-a-bitch wasn't nothing to George."

Curley's wife came around the end of the last stall. She came very quietly, so that Lennie didn't see her. She wore her bright cotton dress and the mules with the red ostrich feathers. Her face was made up and the little sausage curls were all in place. She was quite near to him before Lennie looked up and saw her.

In a panic he shoveled hay over the puppy with his fingers. He looked sullenly up at her.

She said, "What you got there, sonny boy?"

Lennie glared at her. "George says I ain't to have nothing to do with you—talk to you or nothing."

She laughed. "George giving you orders about everything?"

Lennie looked down at the hay. "Says I can't tend no rabbits if I talk to you or anything."

She said quietly, "He's scared Curley'll get mad. Well, Curley got his arm in a sling—an' if Curley gets tough, you can break his other han'. You didn't put nothing over on me about gettin' it caught in no machine."

But Lennie was not to be drawn. "No, sir. I ain't gonna talk to you or nothing."

She knelt in the hay beside him. "Listen," she said. "All the guys got a horseshoe tenement goin' on. It's only about four o'clock. None of them guys is goin' to leave that tenement.

Why can't I talk to you? I never get to talk to nobody. I get awful lonely."

Lennie said, "Well, I ain't supposed to talk to you or nothing."

"I get lonely," she said. "You can talk to people, but I can't talk to nobody but Curley. Else he gets mad. How'd you like not to talk to anybody?"

Lennie said, "Well, I ain't supposed to. George's scared I'll get in trouble."

She changed the subject. "What you got covered up there?"

Then all of Lennie's woe came back on him. "Jus' my pup," he said sadly. "Jus' my little pup." And he swept the hay from on top of it.

"Why, he's dead," she cried.

"He was so little," said Lennie. "I was jus' playin' with him . . . . an' he made like he's gonna bite me . . . . an' I made like I was gonna smack him . . . . an' . . . . an' I done it. An' then he was dead."

She consoled him. "Don't you worry none. He was jus' a mutt. You can get another one easy. The whole country is fulla mutts."

"It ain't that so much," Lennie explained miserably. "George ain't gonna let me tend no rabbits now."

"Why don't he?"

"Well, he said if I done any more bad things he ain't gonna let me tend the rabbits."

She moved closer to him and she spoke soothingly. "Don't you worry about talkin' to me. Listen to the guys yell out there. They got four dollars bet in that tenement. None of them ain't gonna leave till it's over."

"If George sees me talkin' to you he'll give me hell," Lennie said cautiously. "He tol' me so."

Her face grew angry. "Wha's the matter with me?" she cried. "Ain't I got a right to talk to nobody? Whatta they think I am, anyways? You're a nice guy. I don't know why I can't talk to you. I ain't doin' no harm to you."

"Well, George says you'll get us in a mess."

"Aw, nuts!" she said. "What kinda harm am I doin' to you? Seems like they ain't none of them cares how I gotta live. I tell you I ain't used to livin' like this. I coulda made somethin' of myself." She said darkly, "Maybe I will yet." And then her words tumbled out in a passion of communication, as though she hurried before her listener could be taken away. "I lived right in Salinas," she said. "Come there when I was a kid. Well, a show come through, an' I met one of the actors. He says I could go with that show. But my ol' lady wouldn' let me. She says because I was on'y fifteen. But the guy says I coulda. If I'd went, I wouldn't be livin' like this, you bet."

Lennie stroked the pup back and forth. "We gonna have a little place—an' rabbits," he explained.

She went on with her story quickly, before she should be interrupted. "'Nother time I met a guy, an' he was in pitchers. Went out to the Riverside Dance Palace with him. He says he was gonna put me in the movies. Says I was a natural. Soon's he got back to Hollywood he was gonna write to me about it." She looked closely at Lennie to see whether she was impressing him. "I never got that letter," she said. "I always thought my ol' lady stole it. Well, I wasn't gonna stay no place where I couldn't get nowhere or make something of myself, an' where they stole your letters. I ast her if she stole it, too, an' she says no. So I married Curley. Met him out to the Riverside Dance Palace that same night." She demanded, "You listenin'?"

"Me? Sure."

"Well, I ain't told this to nobody before. Maybe I ought'n to. I don' *like* Curley. He ain't a nice fella." And because she had confided in him, she moved closer to Lennie and sat beside him. "Coulda been in the movies, an' had nice clothes—all them nice clothes like they wear. An' I coulda sat in them big hotels, an' had pitchers took of me. When they had them previews I coulda went to them, an' spoke in the radio, an' it wouldn'ta cost me a cent because I was in the pitcher. An' all them nice clothes like they wear. Because this guy says I was a natural." She looked up at Lennie, and she made a small grand gesture with her arm and hand to show that she could act. The fingers trailed after her leading wrist, and her little finger stuck out grandly from the rest.

Lennie sighed deeply. From outside came the clang of a horseshoe on metal, and then a chorus of cheers. "Somebody made a ringer," said Curley's wife.

Now the light was lifting as the sun went down, and the sun streaks climbed up the wall and fell over the feeding racks and over the heads of the horses.

Lennie said, "Maybe if I took this pup out and throwed him away George wouldn't never know. An' then I could tend the rabbits without no trouble."

Curley's wife said angrily, "Don't you think of nothing but rabbits?"

"We gonna have a little place," Lennie explained patiently. "We gonna have a house an' a garden and a place for alfalfa, an' that alfalfa is for the rabbits, an' I take a sack and get it all fulla alfalfa and then I take it to the rabbits."

She asked, "What makes you so nuts about rabbits?"

Lennie had to think carefully before he could come to a conclusion. He moved cautiously close to her, until he was right against her. "I like to pet nice things. Once at a fair I seen some of them long-hair rabbits. An' they was nice, you bet. Sometimes I've even pet mice, but not when I could get nothing better."

Curley's wife moved away from him a little. "I think you're nuts," she said.

"No I ain't," Lennie explained earnestly. "George says I ain't. I like to pet nice things with my fingers, sof' things."

She was a little bit reassured. "Well, who don't?" she said. "Ever'body likes that. I like to feel silk an' velvet. Do you like to feel velvet?"

Lennie chuckled with pleasure. "You bet, by God," he cried happily. "An' I had some, too. A lady give me some, an' that lady was—my own Aunt Clara. She give it right to me—'bout this big a piece. I wisht I had that velvet right now." A frown came over his face. "I lost it," he said. "I ain't seen it for a long time."

Curley's wife laughed at him. "You're nuts," she said. "But you're a kinda nice fella. Jus' like a big baby. But a person can see kinda what you mean. When I'm doin' my hair sometimes I jus' set an' stroke it 'cause it's so soft." To show how she did it, she ran her fingers over the top of her head. "Some people got kinda coarse hair," she said complacently. "Take Curley. His hair is jus' like wire. But mine is soft and fine. 'Course I brush it a lot. That makes it fine. Here—feel right here." She took Lennie's hand and put it on her head. "Feel right aroun' there an' see how soft it is."

Lennie's big fingers fell to stroking her hair.

"Don't you muss it up," she said.

Lennie said, "Oh! That's nice," and he stroked harder. "Oh, that's nice."

"Look out, now, you'll muss it." And then she cried angrily, "You stop it now, you'll mess it all up." She jerked her head sidways, and Lennie's fingers closed on her hair and hung on. "Let go," she cried. "You let go!"

Lennie was in a panic. His face was contorted. She screamed then, and Lennie's other hand closed over her mouth and nose. "Please don't," he begged. "Oh! Please don't do that. George'll be mad."

She struggled violently under his hands. Her feet battered on the hay and she writhed to be free; and from under Lennie's hand came a muffled screaming. Lennie began to cry with fright. "Oh! Please don't do none of that," he begged. "George gonna say I done a bad thing. He ain't gonna let me tend no rabbits." He moved his hand a little and her hoarse cry came out. Then Lennie grew angry. "Now don't," he said. "I don't want you to yell. You gonna get me in trouble jus' like George says you will. Now don't you do that." And she continued to struggle, and her eyes were wild with terror. He shook her then, and he was angry with her. "Don't you go yellin'," he said, and he shook her; and her body flopped like a fish. And then she was still, for Lennie had broken her neck.

He looked down at her, and carefully he removed his hand from over her mouth, and she lay still. "I don't want ta hurt you," he said, "but George'll be mad if you yell." When she didn't answer nor move he bent closely over her. He lifted her arm and let it drop. For a moment he seemed bewildered. And then he whispered in fright, "I done a bad thing. I done another bad thing."

He pawed up the hay until it partly covered her.

From outside the barn came a cry of men and the double clang of shoes on metal. For the first time Lennie became conscious of the outside. He crouched down in the hay and listened. "I done a real bad thing," he said. "I shouldn't of did that. George'll be mad. An' . . . . . he said . . . . . an' hide in the brush till he come. He's gonna be mad. In the brush till he come. Tha's what he said." Lennie went back and looked at the dead girl. The puppy lay close to her. Lennie picked it up. "I'll throw him away," he said. "It's bad enough like it is." He put the pup under his coat, and he crept to the barn wall and peered out between the cracks, toward the horseshoe game. And then he crept around the end of the last manger and disappeared.

The sun streaks were high on the wall by now, and the light was growing soft in the barn. Curley's wife lay on her back, and she was half covered with hay.

It was very quiet in the barn, and the quiet of the afternoon was on the ranch. Even the clang of the pitched shoes, even the voices of the men in the game seemed to grow more quiet. The air in the barn was dusky in advance of the outside day. A pigeon flew in through the open hay door and circled and flew out again. Around the last stall came a shepherd bitch, lean and long, with heavy, hanging dugs. Halfway to the packing box where the puppies were she caught the dead scent of Curley's wife, and the hair arose along her spine. She whimpered and cringed to the packing box, and jumped in among the puppies.

Curley's wife lay with a half-covering of yellow hay. And the meanness and the plannings and the discontent and the ache for attention were all gone from her face. She was very pretty and simple, and her face was sweet and young. Now her rouged cheeks and her reddened lips made her seem alive and sleeping very lightly. The curls, tiny little sausages, were spread on the hay behind her head, and her lips were parted.

As happens sometimes, a moment settled and hovered and remained for much more than a moment. And sound stopped and movement stopped for much, much more than a moment.

Then gradually time awakened again and moved sluggishly on. The horses stamped on the other side of the feeding racks and the halter chains clinked. Outside, the men's voices became louder and clearer.

From around the end of the last stall old Candy's voice came. "Lennie," he called. "Oh, Lennie! You in here? I been figuring some more. Tell you what we can do, Lennie." Old

Candy appeared around the end of the last stall. "Oh, Lennie!" he called again; and then he stopped, and his body stiffened. He rubbed his smooth wrist on his white stubble whiskers. "I di'n't know you was here," he said to Curley's wife.

When she didn't answer, he stepped nearer. "You oughten to sleep out here," he said disapprovingly; and then he was beside her and— "Oh, Jesus Christ!" He looked about help-lessly, and he rubbed his beard. And then he jumped up and went quickly out of the barn.

But the barn was alive now. The horses stamped and snorted, and they chewed the straw of their bedding and they clashed the chains of their halters. In a moment Candy came back, and George was with him.

George said, "What was it you wanted to see me about?"

Candy pointed at Curley's wife. George stared. "What's the matter with her?" he asked. He stepped closer, and then he echoed Candy's words. "Oh, Jesus Christ!" He was down on his knees beside her. He put his hand over her heart. And finally, when he stood up, slowly and stiffly, his face was as hard and tight as wood, and his eyes were hard.

Candy said, "What done it?"

George looked coldly at him. "Ain't you got any idear?" he asked. And Candy was silent. "I should of knew," George said hopelessly. "I guess maybe way back in my head I did."

Candy asked, "What we gonna do now, George. What we gonna do now?"

George was a long time in answering. "Guess . . . . we gotta tell the . . . . guys. I guess we gotta get 'im an' lock 'im up. We can't let 'im get away. Why, the poor bastard'd starve." And he tried to reassure himself. "Maybe they'll lock 'im up an' be nice to 'im."

But Candy said excitedly, "We oughtta let 'im get away. You don't know that Curley. Curley gon'ta wanta get 'im lynched. Curley'll get 'im killed."

George watched Candy's lips. "Yeah," he said at last, "that's right, Curley will. An' the other guys will." And he looked back at Curley's wife.

Now Candy spoke his greatest fear. "You an' me can get that little place, can't we, George? You an' me can go there an' live nice, can't we, George? Can't we?"

Before George answered, Candy dropped his head and looked down at the hay. He knew.

George said softly, "—I think I knowed from the very first. I think I knowed we'd never do her. He usta like to hear about it so much I got to thinking maybe we would."

"Then—it's all off?" Candy asked sulkily.

George didn't answer his question. George said, "I'll work my month an' I'll take my fifty bucks an' I'll stay all night in some lousy cat house. Or I'll set in some poolroom till ever'-body goes home. An' then I'll come back an' work another month an' I'll have fifty bucks more."

Candy said, "He's such a nice fella. I didn' think he'd do nothing like this."

George still stared at Curley's wife. "Lennie never done it in meanness," he said. "All the time he done bad things, but he never done one of 'em mean." He straightened up and looked back at Candy. "Now listen. We gotta tell the guys. They got to bring him in, I guess. They ain't no way out. Maybe they won't hurt 'im." He said sharply, "I ain't gonna let 'em hurt Lennie. Now you listen. The guys might think I was in on it. I'm gonna go in the bunk house. Then in a minute you come out and tell the guys about her, and I'll come along and make like I never seen her. Will you do that? So the guys won't think I was in on it?"

Candy said, "Sure, George. Sure I'll do that."

"O.K. Give me a couple minutes then, and you come run-nin' out an' tell like you jus' found her. I'm going now." George turned and went quickly out of the barn.

Old Candy watched him go. He looked helplessly back at Curley's wife, and gradually his sorrow and his anger grew into words. "You God damn tramp," he said viciously. "You done it, di'n't you? I s'pose you're glad. Ever'body knowed you'd mess things up. You wasn't no good. You ain't no good now, you lousy tart." He sniveled, and his voice shook. "I could of hoed in the garden and washed dishes for them guys." He paused, and then went on in a sing-song. And he repeated the old words: "If they was a circus or a baseball game . . . . we would of went to her . . . . jus' said 'ta hell with work,' an' went to her. Never ast nobody's say so. An' they'd of been a pig and chickens . . . . an' in the winter

. . . . the little fat stove . . . . an' the rain comin' . . . . an' us jus' settin' there." His eyes blinded with tears and he turned and went weakly out of the barn, and he rubbed his bristly whiskers with his wrist stump.

Outside the noise of the game stopped. There was a rise of voices in question, a drum of running feet and the men burst into the barn. Slim and Carlson and young Whit and Curley, and Crooks keeping back out of attention range. Candy came after them, and last of all came George. George had put on his blue denim coat and buttoned it, and his black hat was pulled down low over his eyes. The men raced around the last stall. Their eyes found Curley's wife in the gloom, they stopped and stood still and looked.

Then Slim went quietly over to her, and he felt her wrist. One lean finger touched her cheek, and then his hand went under her slightly twisted neck and his fingers explored her neck. When he stood up the men crowded near and the spell was broken.

Curley came suddenly to life. "I know who done it," he cried. "That big son-of-a-bitch done it. I know he done it. Why—ever'body else was out there playin' horseshoes." He worked himself into a fury. "I'm gonna get him. I'm going for my shot gun. I'll kill the big son-of-a-bitch myself. I'll shoot 'im in the guts. Come on, you guys." He ran furiously out of the barn. Carlson said, "I'll get my Luger," and he ran out too.

Slim turned quietly to George. "I guess Lennie done it, all right," he said. "Her neck's bust. Lennie coulda did that."

George didn't answer, but he nodded slowly. His hat was so far down on his forehead that his eyes were covered.

Slim went on, "Maybe like that time in Weed you was tellin' about."

Again George nodded.

Slim sighed. "Well, I guess we got to get him. Where you think he might of went?"

It seemed to take George some time to free his words. "He—would of went south," he said. "We come from north so he would of went south."

"I guess we gotta get 'im," Slim repeated.

George stepped close. "Couldn' we maybe bring him in an'

they'll lock him up? He's nuts, Slim. He never done this to be mean."

Slim nodded. "We might," he said. "If we could keep Curley in, we might. But Curley's gonna want to shoot 'im. Curley's still mad about his hand. An' s'pose they lock him up an' strap him down and put him in a cage. That ain't no good, George."

"I know," said George. "I know."

Carlson came running in. "The bastard's stole my Luger," he shouted. "It ain't in my bag." Curley followed him, and Curley carried a shotgun in his good hand. Curley was cold now.

"All right, you guys," he said. "The nigger's got a shotgun. You take it, Carlson. When you see 'um, don't give 'im no chance. Shoot for his guts. That'll double 'im over."

Whit said excitedly, "I ain't got a gun."

Curley said, "You go in Soledad an' get a cop. Get Al Wilts, he's deputy sheriff. Le's go now." He turned suspiciously on George. "You're comin' with us, fella."

"Yeah," said George. "I'll come. But listen, Curley. The poor bastard's nuts. Don't shoot 'im. He di'n't know what he was doin'."

"Don't shoot 'im?" Curley cried. "He got Carlson's Luger. 'Course we'll shoot 'im."

George said weakly, "Maybe Carlson lost his gun."

"I seen it this morning," said Carlson. "No, it's been took."

Slim stood looking down at Curley's wife. He said, "Curley—maybe you better stay here with your wife."

Curley's face reddened. "I'm goin'," he said. "I'm gonna shoot the guts outa that big bastard myself, even if I only got one hand. I'm gonna get 'im."

Slim turned to Candy. "You stay here with her then, Candy. The rest of us better get goin'."

They moved away. George stopped a moment beside Candy and they both looked down at the dead girl until Curley called, "You George! You stick with us so we don't think you had nothin' to do with this."

George moved slowly after them, and his feet dragged heavily.

And when they were gone, Candy squatted down in the

hay and watched the face of Curley's wife. "Poor bastard," he said softly.

The sound of the men grew fainter. The barn was darkening gradually and, in their stalls, the horses shifted their feet and rattled the halter chains. Old Candy lay down in the hay and covered his eyes with his arm.

6

THE DEEP GREEN POOL of the Salinas River was still in the late afternoon. Already the sun had left the valley to go climbing up the slopes of the Gabilan mountains, and the hilltops were rosy in the sun. But by the pool among the mottled sycamores, a pleasant shade had fallen.

A water snake glided smoothly up the pool, twisting its periscope head from side to side; and it swam the length of the pool and came to the legs of a motionless heron that stood in the shallows. A silent head and beak lanced down and plucked it out by the head, and the beak swallowed the little snake while its tail waved frantically.

A far rush of wind sounded and a gust drove through the tops of the trees like a wave. The sycamore leaves turned up their silver sides, the brown, dry leaves on the ground scudded a few feet. And row on row of tiny wind waves flowed up the pool's green surface.

As quickly as it had come, the wind died, and the clearing was quiet again. The heron stood in the shallows, motionless and waiting. Another little water snake swam up the pool, turning its periscope head from side to side.

Suddenly Lennie appeared out of the brush, and he came as silently as a creeping bear moves. The heron pounded the air with its wings, jacked itself clear of the water and flew off down river. The little snake slid in among the reeds at the pool's side.

Lennie came quietly to the pool's edge. He knelt down and drank, barely touching his lips to the water. When a little bird skittered over the dry leaves behind him, his head jerked up and he strained toward the sound with eyes and ears until he saw the bird, and then he dropped his head and drank again.

When he was finished, he sat down on the bank, with his side to the pool, so that he could watch the trail's entrance. He embraced his knees and laid his chin down on his knees.

The light climbed on out of the valley, and as it went, the tops of the mountains seemed to blaze with increasing brightness.

Lennie said softly, "I di'n't forget, you bet, God damn. Hide in the brush an' wait for George." He pulled his hat down low over his eyes. "George gonna give me hell," he said. "George gonna wish he was alone an' not have me botherin' him." He turned his head and looked at the bright mountain tops. "I can go right off there an' find a cave," he said. And he continued sadly, "—an' never have no ketchup—but I won't care. If George don't want me . . . . I'll go away. I'll go away."

And then from out of Lennie's head there came a little fat old woman. She wore thick bull's-eye glasses and she wore a huge gingham apron with pockets, and she was starched and clean. She stood in front of Lennie and put her hands on her hips, and she frowned disapprovingly at him.

And when she spoke, it was in Lennie's voice. "I tol' you an' tol' you," she said. "I tol' you, 'Min' George because he's such a nice fella an' good to you.' But you don't never take no care. You do bad things."

And Lennie answered her, "I tried, Aunt Clara, ma'am. I tried and tried. I couldn' help it."

"You never give a thought to George," she went on in Lennie's voice. "He been doin' nice things for you alla time. When he got a piece a pie you always got half or more'n half. An' if they was any ketchup, why he'd give it all to you."

"I know," said Lennie miserably. "I tried, Aunt Clara, ma'am. I tried and tried."

She interrupted him. "All the time he coulda had such a good time if it wasn't for you. He woulda took his pay an' raised hell in a whore house, and he coulda set in a pool room an' played snooker. But he got to take care of you."

Lennie moaned with grief. "I know, Aunt Clara, ma'am. I'll go right off in the hills an' I'll fin' a cave an' I'll live there so I won't be no more trouble to George."

"You jus' say that," she said sharply. "You're always sayin' that, an' you know sonofabitching well you ain't never gonna do it. You'll jus' stick around an' stew the b'Jesus outa George all the time."

Lennie said, "I might jus' as well go away. George ain't gonna let me tend no rabbits now."

Aunt Clara was gone, and from out of Lennie's head there

came a gigantic rabbit. It sat on its haunches in front of him, and it waggled its ears and crinkled its nose at him. And it spoke in Lennie's voice too.

"Tend rabbits," it said scornfully. "You crazy bastard. You ain't fit to lick the boots of no rabbit. You'd forget 'em and let 'em go hungry. That's what you'd do. An' then what would George think?"

"I would *not* forget," Lennie said loudly.

"The hell you wouldn'," said the rabbit. "You ain't worth a greased jack-pin to ram you into hell. Christ knows George done ever'thing he could to jack you outa the sewer, but it don't do no good. If you think George gonna let you tend rabbits, you're even crazier'n usual. He ain't. He's gonna beat hell outa you with a stick, that's what he's gonna do."

Now Lennie retorted belligerently, "He ain't neither. George won't do nothing like that. I've knew George since—I forget when—and he ain't never raised his han' to me with a stick. He's nice to me. He ain't gonna be mean."

"Well, he's sick of you," said the rabbit. "He's gonna beat hell outa you an' then go away an' leave you."

"He won't," Lennie cried frantically. "He won't do nothing like that. I know George. Me an' him travels together."

But the rabbit repeated softly over and over, "He gonna leave you, ya crazy bastard. He gonna leave ya all alone. He gonna leave ya, crazy bastard."

Lennie put his hands over his ears. "He ain't, I tell ya he ain't." And he cried, "Oh! George—George—George!"

George came quietly out of the brush and the rabbit scuttled back into Lennie's brain.

George said quietly, "What the hell you yellin' about?"

Lennie got up on his knees. "You ain't gonna leave me, are ya, George? I know you ain't."

George came stiffly near and sat down beside him. "No."

"I knowed it," Lennie cried. "You ain't that kind."

George was silent.

Lennie said, "George."

"Yeah?"

"I done another bad thing."

"It don't make no difference," George said, and he fell silent again.

Only the topmost ridges were in the sun now. The shadow in the valley was blue and soft. From the distance came the sound of men shouting to one another. George turned his head and listened to the shouts.

Lennie said, "George."

"Yeah?"

"Ain't you gonna give me hell?"

"Give ya hell?"

"Sure, like you always done before. Like, 'If I di'n't have you I'd take my fifty bucks——' "

"Jesus Christ, Lennie! You can't remember nothing that happens, but you remember ever' word I say."

"Well, ain't you gonna say it?"

George shook himself. He said woodenly, "If I was alone I could live so easy." His voice was monotonous, had no emphasis. "I could get a job an' not have no mess." He stopped.

"Go on," said Lennie. "An' when the enda the month come——"

"An' when the end of the month come I could take my fifty bucks an' go to a . . . . cat house . . . ." He stopped again.

Lennie looked eagerly at him. "Go on, George. Ain't you gonna give me no more hell?"

"No," said George.

"Well, I can go away," said Lennie. "I'll go right off in the hills an' find a cave if you don' want me."

George shook himself again. "No," he said. "I want you to stay with me here."

Lennie said craftily—"Tell me like you done before."

"Tell you what?"

" 'Bout the other guys an' about us.

George said, "Guys like us got no fambly. They make a little stake an' then they blow it in. They ain't got nobody in the worl' that gives a hoot in hell about 'em——"

"But not us," Lennie cried happily. "Tell about us now."

George was quiet for a moment. "But not us," he said.

"Because——"

"Because I got you an'——"

"An' I got you. We got each other, that's what, that gives a hoot in hell about us," Lennie cried in triumph.

The little evening breeze blew over the clearing and the

leaves rustled and the wind waves flowed up the green pool. And the shouts of men sounded again, this time much closer than before.

George took off his hat. He said shakily, "Take off your hat, Lennie. The air feels fine."

Lennie removed his hat dutifully and laid it on the ground in front of him. The shadow in the valley was bluer, and the evening came fast. On the wind the sound of crashing in the brush came to them.

Lennie said, "Tell how it's gonna be."

George had been listening to the distant sounds. For a moment he was business-like. "Look acrost the river, Lennie, an' I'll tell you so you can almost see it."

Lennie turned his head and looked off across the pool and up the darkening slopes of the Gabilans. "We gonna get a little place," George began. He reached in his side pocket and brought out Carlson's Luger; he snapped off the safety, and the hand and gun lay on the ground behind Lennie's back. He looked at the back of Lennie's head, at the place where the spine and skull were joined.

A man's voice called from up the river, and another man answered.

"Go on," said Lennie.

George raised the gun and his hand shook, and he dropped his hand to the ground again.

"Go on," said Lennie. "How's it gonna be. We gonna get a little place."

"We'll have a cow," said George. "An' we'll have maybe a pig an' chickens . . . . an' down the flat we'll have a . . . . little piece alfalfa——"

"For the rabbits," Lennie shouted.

"For the rabbits," George repeated.

"And I get to tend the rabbits."

"An' you get to tend the rabbits."

Lennie giggled with happiness. "An' live on the fatta the lan'."

"Yes."

Lennie turned his head.

"No, Lennie. Look down there acrost the river, like you can almost see the place."

Lennie obeyed him. George looked down at the gun.

There were crashing footsteps in the brush now. George turned and looked toward them.

"Go on, George. When we gonna do it?"

"Gonna do it soon."

"Me an' you."

"You . . . . an' me. Ever'body gonna be nice to you. Ain't gonna be no more trouble. Nobody gonna hurt nobody nor steal from 'em."

Lennie said, "I thought you was mad at me, George."

"No," said George. "No, Lennie. I ain't mad. I never been mad, an' I ain't now. That's a thing I want ya to know."

The voices came close now. George raised the gun and listened to the voices.

Lennie begged, "Le's do it now. Le's get that place now."

"Sure, right now. I gotta. We gotta."

And George raised the gun and steadied it, and he brought the muzzle of it close to the back of Lennie's head. The hand shook violently, but his face set and his hand steadied. He pulled the trigger. The crash of the shot rolled up the hills and rolled down again. Lennie jarred, and then settled slowly forward to the sand, and he lay without quivering.

George shivered and looked at the gun, and then he threw it from him, back up on the bank, near the pile of old ashes.

The brush seemed filled with cries and with the sound of running feet. Slim's voice shouted, "George. Where you at, George?"

But George sat stiffly on the bank and looked at his right hand that had thrown the gun away. The group burst into the clearing, and Curley was ahead. He saw Lennie lying on the sand. "Got him, by God." He went over and looked down at Lennie, and then he looked back at George. "Right in the back of the head," he said softly.

Slim came directly to George and sat down beside him, sat very close to him. "Never you mind," said Slim. "A guy got to sometimes."

But Carlson was standing over George. "How'd you do it?" he asked.

"I just done it," George said tiredly.

"Did he have my gun?"

"Yeah. He had your gun."

"An' you got it away from him and you took it an' you killed him?"

"Yeah. Tha's how." George's voice was almost a whisper. He looked steadily at his right hand that had held the gun.

Slim twitched George's elbow. "Come on, George. Me an' you'll go in an' get a drink."

George let himself be helped to his feet. "Yeah, a drink."

Slim said, "You hadda, George. I swear you hadda. Come on with me." He led George into the entrance of the trail and up toward the highway.

Curley and Carlson looked after them. And Carlson said, "Now what the hell ya suppose is eatin' them two guys?"

CHRONOLOGY

NOTE ON THE TEXTS

NOTES

Chronology

1902 Born John Ernst Steinbeck on February 27 in Salinas, California; the third child and only son (sisters are Esther, b. 1892, and Beth, b. 1894) of Olive Hamilton Steinbeck, a former schoolteacher, and John Ernst Steinbeck, manager of a flour mill. (Paternal grandfather, John Adolph Grossteinbeck, a German cabinetmaker from Düsseldorf, moved to Jerusalem with his brother Frederic in 1854 and married Almira Dickson, daughter of Sarah Eldridge Dickson and evangelist Walter Dickson, Americans who had gone to the Holy Land to convert the Jews. After Arab raiders killed Frederic and raped Sarah Dickson and her daughter, Mary, in 1858, John and Almira came to the United States, where they used the name Steinbeck. They settled in New England and then in Florida, where John Ernst Steinbeck was born, before moving to California after the Civil War. Maternal grandfather, Samuel Hamilton, born in northern Ireland, immigrated to the United States at age 17 and settled in New York City, where he married Elizabeth Fagen, an American of northern Irish ancestry; they soon moved to California, where Hamilton homesteaded a ranch and was a skilled blacksmith.)

1903–9 Spends summers by the sea in Pacific Grove near Monterey and on uncle Tom Hamilton's ranch near King City. Sister Mary is born in 1905. Steinbeck enjoys roaming in fields and along seashore; from father learns to love gardening. Receives a red Shetland pony named Jill from family in 1906, and cares for her himself. Home is full of books; parents and older sisters read out loud to him, and he becomes acquainted at an early age with novels of Robert Louis Stevenson and Walter Scott, the Bible, Greek myths, *The Pilgrim's Progress*, and *Paradise Lost*. Begins reading books himself and especially enjoys Sir Thomas Malory's *Le Morte d'Arthur* (later writes, "The Bible and Shakespeare and *Pilgrim's Progress* belonged to everyone. But this was mine—secretly mine . . . Perhaps a passionate love for the English language opened to me from this one book"). Attends public schools in Salinas; does well in school and skips fifth grade. Enjoys reading Mark

Twain and Jack London. Often cared for by older sisters while mother takes active part in town affairs.

1910   When the mill is closed in Salinas, father decides against taking job offer with a company farther north because it would mean uprooting the family. Father opens a feed and grain store which fails, and works briefly as accountant for sugar refinery before being appointed treasurer of Monterey County (holds position, through continual re-election, until shortly before his death).

1918   In junior year of high school Steinbeck develops pleural pneumonia and nearly dies; nursed by mother on ranch farther south in Salinas Valley. Writes stories and reads them out loud to close friends.

1919–24   Graduates from Salinas High School. Begins sporadic attendance at Stanford University in October as an English major. Meets Carlton "Dook" Sheffield and Carl Wilhelmson, who become lifelong friends. In spring 1920 undergoes operation for acute appendicitis. After working as surveyor in mountains above Big Sur, works in the summer as carpenter's helper at Spreckels Sugar Mill (continues to work over the next several years at the mill and on its many sugar beet ranches, where his duties include running chemical tests on sugar beets and supervising day laborers). Returns to Stanford full-time in January 1923; studies English versification with William Herbert Carruth in spring 1923, and enrolls for summer study at Stanford-affiliated Hopkins Marine Station in Pacific Grove, where he takes courses in English and zoology. Studies creative writing with Edith Mirrielees at Stanford for two terms in 1924. Influenced by philosophy lectures of Harold Chapman Brown. Publishes stories "Fingers of Cloud: A Satire on College Protervity" and "Adventures in Arcademy: A Journey into the Ridiculous" in the February and June issues of *The Stanford Spectator*, student literary magazine.

1925–26   Leaves Stanford without a degree in June 1925, having completed less than three years of coursework. After working during the summer as caretaker of a lodge near Lake Tahoe, sails on a freighter by way of the Panama Canal to New York City. Settles in Brooklyn (moves to

Gramercy Park area of Manhattan in 1926). Works as laborer on the construction of Madison Square Garden and as reporter for the *New York American*. Submits short stories to Robert M. McBride & Company, New York publishing firm, which rejects them. Returns to California by freighter in summer 1926, working as assistant steward in return for passage. Hired in the fall to work as caretaker of Lake Tahoe estate of Mrs. Alice Brigham.

1927 Lives alone on Brigham estate during winter. Story "The Gifts of Iban" appears in *The Smoker's Companion* in March under pseudonym "John Stern." Works with close friend Webster (Toby) Street on Street's play "The Green Lady" (material becomes the basis for *To a God Unknown*).

1928 Finishes first novel, *Cup of Gold*, in January. Leaves caretaker job in May and begins work at fish hatchery in Tahoe City in June. Meets Carol Henning, a tourist visiting the hatchery, during summer. Fired from hatchery job for wrecking superintendent's truck. In September moves to San Francisco, where he lives in "a dark little attic" on Powell Street and gets job as warehouse worker for company owned by sister Mary's husband, Bill Dekker.

1929 With help of college acquaintance Amasa (Ted) Miller, *Cup of Gold* is accepted for publication by Robert M. McBride. Gives up warehouse job and with father's financial help spends most of year writing in Pacific Grove and Palo Alto (father frequently sends money during the next several years). *Cup of Gold* published in August. Moves back to San Francisco in the fall and shares an apartment with Carl Wilhelmson.

1930 Marries Carol Henning in January. They stay briefly with Dook Sheffield and his wife in Eagle Rock, near Los Angeles, and then, successively, in a shack and two rented houses in the vicinity, before moving in September to family's three-room cottage in Pacific Grove where they live rent-free and feed themselves in part through fishing and raising vegetables. Manuscript of *To a God Unknown* rejected by Robert M. McBride. Meets marine biologist Edward F. Ricketts, owner of Pacific Biological Laboratory, who becomes close friend and major intellectual influence. Writes experimental novella "Dissonant

Symphony" and, under pseudonym Peter Pym, crime novel "Murder at Full Moon"; neither is accepted for publication, and he later destroys manuscript of "Dissonant Symphony."

1931 Works on series of related stories, *The Pastures of Heaven*. Begins lifelong association with New York literary agency McIntosh & Otis (agent Elizabeth Otis becomes close friend).

1932 *The Pastures of Heaven* accepted for publication by Cape and Smith in February. Through Ricketts, becomes acquainted with religious scholar Joseph Campbell. Carol works part-time as bookkeeper-secretary at Ricketts' laboratory in spring and summer; after she loses job because Ricketts cannot afford to pay her, Steinbeck and Carol move to Montrose area, north of Eagle Rock, staying with the Sheffields until they find a house to rent. Following bankruptcy of Cape and Smith, *The Pastures of Heaven* published by Brewer, Warren, and Putnam (where Cape and Smith editor Robert O. Ballou had moved).

1933 Despite father's financial help, Steinbeck and Carol are unable to make ends meet and are forced in February to give up the Montrose house. Mother becomes seriously ill in March, and after being hospitalized, suffers massive stroke; Steinbeck and Carol move to family home in Salinas. Steinbeck spends most of his time taking care of his mother at hospital and, after her release in June, at home. Writes the first of the four stories later joined together as *The Red Pony*. Father collapses in August and remains incapacitated for nearly a year; cared for by Carol at Pacific Grove cottage while Steinbeck spends much time in Salinas caring for mother. *To a God Unknown* published in September by Robert O. Ballou under his own imprint. During summer and fall completes first draft of *Tortilla Flat*, partly based on anecdotes told to him by Susan Gregory, a high school Spanish teacher in Monterey. Meets journalist Lincoln Steffens and his wife, Ella Winter, who are living in Carmel (continues to visit them until Steffens' death in 1936). "The Red Pony" (later titled "The Gift") and "The Great Mountains" appear in *North American Review*, November–December (both later become part of *The Red Pony*).

1934   Mother dies in February. Steinbeck and Carol live with
        father in Pacific Grove cottage, until arrangements are
        made for father to move back into Salinas home with care-
        takers in March. Steinbeck meets fugitive labor organizers
        Cicil McKiddy and Carl Williams in Seaside, California;
        interviews them about their involvement with 1933 cotton
        workers' strike in the San Joaquin Valley, organized by
        Communist-led Cannery and Agricultural Workers' Indus-
        trial Union, and about strike leader Pat Chambers. Manu-
        script of *Tortilla Flat* rejected by Robert O. Ballou and by
        Louis Kronenberger at Knopf. During summer completes
        nine short stories, eight of which are later collected in *The
        Long Valley*. Begins writing *In Dubious Battle*, based in
        part on interviews with McKiddy and Williams, in Au-
        gust. *Tortilla Flat* is accepted for publication by Pascal
        Covici of Covici-Friede. Enunciates "aggregation" theory
        of groups in unpublished essay "Argument of Phalanx":
        "Men are not final individuals but units in the greater
        beast, the phalanx . . . The nature of the phalanx is not
        the sum of the natures of unit-men, but a new individual
        having emotions and ends of its own, and these are for-
        eign and incomprehensible to unit-men."

1935   *In Dubious Battle* accepted by Covici-Friede. Father dies in
        May. *Tortilla Flat*, published in May, becomes Steinbeck's
        first commercially successful book. Forms friendship with
        Joseph Henry Jackson, book reviewer for *San Francisco
        Chronicle*. Meets Pascal Covici for the first time in August.
        With royalties from *Tortilla Flat*, travels with Carol to
        Mexico in September; they rent an apartment in Mexico
        City (writes to friend: "This well of just pure life is charg-
        ing us up again"). Meets painter Diego Rivera. Learns
        that film rights for *Tortilla Flat* have been sold to Para-
        mount for $4,000. Returns to United States at year's end,
        traveling to New York to sign Paramount contract and
        then to Pacific Grove before Christmas.

1936   *In Dubious Battle* published by Covici-Friede in January.
        Begins work on children's book (project eventually leads
        him to write *Of Mice and Men*); much of manuscript is
        destroyed by his dog in May. Visited by John O'Hara,
        who had contracted to write a dramatic adaptation (even-
        tually abandoned) of *In Dubious Battle*; O'Hara becomes
        lifelong friend. In May begins to build house in Los Gatos,

north of Monterey. Goes on six-day trip with Ricketts collecting octopuses along Baja California coast. Moves into Los Gatos house, completed at end of July. Completes *Of Mice and Men* in August. Commissioned by *San Francisco News* to write articles on migrant farm workers; after meeting with federal officials at Resettlement Administration in San Francisco, tours San Joaquin Valley in bakery truck, accompanied by former preacher Eric H. Thomsen, regional director of federal migrant camp program. At Arvin Sanitary Camp ("Weedpatch") in Kern County, meets camp director Tom Collins, and from his conversation and written reports on migrant workers gathers material later incorporated into *The Grapes of Wrath*. Articles published as "The Harvest Gypsies" in seven installments in October. Begins researching and writing novel about migrants (later referred to as "The Oklahomans"). Limited editions of *Nothing So Monstrous* (excerpt from *The Pastures of Heaven*, with a new epilogue) and *Saint Katy the Virgin* published by Covici-Friede.

1937   *Of Mice and Men* published in March; becomes a bestseller and Book-of-the-Month Club selection. Sails in March with Carol through Panama Canal to Philadelphia; after two-and-a-half-week stay in New York, they travel to Denmark, Sweden, Finland, and the Soviet Union, returning to New York in July. Works with director George S. Kaufman on dramatic adaptation of *Of Mice and Men*. Visits Farm Security Administration office in Washington, D.C., and talks with deputy administrator Dr. Will Alexander. Stories "The Promise," "The Gift," and "The Great Mountains" published as *The Red Pony* in a limited edition by Covici-Friede. Travels in California in October doing research on migrants; joined at migrant camp in Gridley by Tom Collins, who accompanies him on rest of trip. *Of Mice and Men* opens on Broadway November 23, starring Wallace Ford and Broderick Crawford; it runs for 207 performances (Steinbeck never sees the production).

1938   Dramatic adaptation of *Tortilla Flat* by Jack Kirkland opens on Broadway in January (closes after four performances). Meets documentary filmmaker Pare Lorentz. Makes two trips to San Joaquin Valley in February and March, where he joins Tom Collins in investigating condition of migrant workers in the wake of devastating floods in Visalia. Article based on trips is rejected by *Life*. Invited by Lorentz, travels to Hollywood where he meets film directors King Vidor, Lewis Milestone, and Mervyn Le Roy and actor James Cagney. Article on floods published in April as "Starvation Under the Orange Trees" in the *Monterey Trader*. *Their Blood Is Strong*, expanded version of "The Harvest Gypsies," published as pamphlet by Simon J. Lubin Society of California to raise money for migrant workers. In May abandons unfinished satirical novel ("L'Affaire Lettuceberg") about vigilantes, suggested by brutal Salinas lettuce strike of September 1936. Learns that *Of Mice and Men* has won the New York Drama Critics' Circle Award as best play of 1937. In late May begins 100-day period of work on novel that becomes *The Grapes of Wrath*. Keeps journal of novel's composition (published posthumously in 1989 as *Working Days*); of the title, suggested by Carol, Steinbeck writes: "I like it because it is a march and this book is a kind of march—because it is in our own revolutionary tradition and because in reference to this book it has a large meaning." Visited unexpectedly by Charlie Chaplin, who is living in Pebble Beach, near Carmel, and they establish friendship. Purchases 47-acre ranch (the "Old Biddle Ranch") outside Los Gatos; begins construction of new house on property in September. In July, Covici-Friede goes bankrupt and Pascal Covici joins Viking Press as senior editor; short story collection *The Long Valley* is published by Viking in September and sells well. (Viking becomes the publisher of all of Steinbeck's subsequent books.) Physically exhausted, completes manuscript of *The Grapes of Wrath* in November.

1939   Suffers for most of the year from sometimes crippling leg pain. Elizabeth Otis, his agent, urges him to make changes in the language of *The Grapes of Wrath*; during two days of intensive work agrees to some revisions. Later writes to Covici, "This book wasn't written for delicate ladies. If they read it at all they're messing in something not their business. I've never changed a word to fit the prejudices of a group and I never will." Argues further with Covici over proposal to change the novel's ending: "You know that I have never been touchy about changes, but I have too many thousands of hours on this book, every incident has been too carefully chosen and its weight judged and fitted.

The balance is there. One other thing—I am not writing a satisfying story. I've done my damndest to rip a reader's nerves to rags, I don't want him satisfied." In March hears rumor that he is being investigated by the FBI; worries about possible violence against him by Associated Farmers organization. *The Grapes of Wrath*, published in April by Viking with large advance sale, becomes the number one national bestseller; screen rights are sold for $75,000. Novel is banned or burned in Buffalo, New York, East St. Louis, Illinois, and Kern County, California, is denounced in Congress by Oklahoma representative Lyle Boren, and is the subject of a protest meeting at the Palace Hotel in San Francisco. Steinbeck is overwhelmed by flood of public attention and correspondence. Travels to Chicago in April to work with Pare Lorentz on *The Fight for Life*, documentary about Chicago Maternity Center. Rents apartment in Hollywood in June. Through old friend Max Wagner, now working in Hollywood, meets singer Gwendolyn ("Gwyn") Conger, and begins affair with her. Forms friendships with songwriter Frank Loesser and his wife, Lynn Loesser, actor Burgess Meredith, Nunnally Johnson (screenwriter for *The Grapes of Wrath*), and writer Robert Benchley. Difficulties with Carol lead to temporary separation; they reconcile and go on car trip in Pacific Northwest, visiting Vancouver in company with composer John Cage and his wife, Xenia. Travels with Carol in September to Chicago, visiting Lorentz and science writer Paul de Kruif in connection with *The Fight for Life*. Plans to devote himself to study of science and to write science textbooks in collaboration with Ricketts; spends much time at Ricketts' laboratory, and makes marine collecting trips with him in San Francisco Bay area. In December sees previews of John Ford's film version of *The Grapes of Wrath* ("No punches were pulled—in fact . . . it is a harsher thing than the book") and Lewis Milestone's film of *Of Mice and Men* ("Milestone has done a curious lyrical thing. It hangs together and is underplayed").

1940 In March, embarks with Ricketts, Carol, and small crew on marine collecting expedition in Gulf of California on boat *Western Flyer*, returning to Monterey April 20. Writes Eleanor Roosevelt, thanking her for remarking after her visit to a migrant workers camp in April that she had "never believed that *The Grapes of Wrath* was exaggerated." Wins Pulitzer Prize for *The Grapes of Wrath* (gives prize money to friend Ritchie Lovejoy to enable him to complete a novel). Impressed by singer Woody Guthrie, who records "The Ballad of Tom Joad," based on *The Grapes of Wrath*. Travels with Carol to Mexico in May to work on script for *The Forgotten Village*, an independent feature film produced and directed by Herbert Kline, about the struggle to bring modern medicine to a remote village. Meets with Lewis Milestone in Hollywood about film version of *The Red Pony*. Disturbed by influence of German propaganda in Latin America, writes to President Franklin D. Roosevelt, who receives him for brief visit in which Steinbeck proposes the formation of a propaganda office focusing on the Western hemisphere. Visits Roosevelt again in September and proposes scheme to undermine Axis powers by distributing counterfeit German money in occupied countries of Europe. Takes flying lessons. Returns to Mexico in October to work on *The Forgotten Village*.

1941 Buys small house on Eardley Street in Monterey. Tells Carol in April about affair with Gwyn Conger. Separates from Carol at end of April; lives in Eardley Street house. *The Forgotten Village*, book version of film script, illustrated with stills, published in May. Works on book about Gulf of California trip, describing it to Pascal Covici as "a new kind of writing," and completes manuscript in July. Sells Los Gatos ranch at end of August. Works on screenplay for *The Red Pony*. In autumn moves to East Coast with Gwyn; they stay in a house on Burgess Meredith's farm in Suffern, New York, before moving in November into Bedford Hotel in Manhattan. Writes radio speeches for Foreign Information Service under direction of Robert E. Sherwood; travels frequently between New York and Washington. *Sea of Cortez: A Leisurely Journey of Travel and Research*, narrative by Steinbeck with a detailed scientific appendix by Ricketts, published in December. Film of *The Forgotten Village* banned for indecency by New York State Board of Censors because of scenes of childbirth and breast-feeding (ban lifted after public hearing).

1942 *The Moon Is Down*, set in occupied Norway, published in March; opens as play on Broadway in April. Moves into rented house at Sneden's Landing in Rockland County,

New York, in April. Becomes friendly with playwright Maxwell Anderson, singer Burl Ives, and radio comedian Fred Allen. Sells film rights to *The Moon Is Down*. Appointed special consultant to the Secretary of War and accepts assignment from the Army Air Forces to write book about the training of bomber crews. Visits 20 air bases across the United States with photographer John Swope; their work is published as *Bombs Away: The Story of a Bomber Team*. Rents house in Sherman Oaks, California, in September to work on film based on *Bombs Away*, but production is plagued by difficulties and film is never made. With old friend Jack Wagner (brother of Max Wagner), writes script for film *A Medal for Benny*. Film of *Tortilla Flat*, directed by Victor Fleming and starring Spencer Tracy, released.

1943   Writes novella (unpublished) as basis for film *Lifeboat*, directed by Alfred Hitchcock. Moves into apartment on East 51st Street in New York City with Gwyn. Divorce from Carol becomes final on March 18. Marries Gwyn on March 29 in New Orleans. Accredited as war correspondent for New York *Herald Tribune*, following intensive security investigation by army counterintelligence. Travels to England on troop ship in June; meets photographer Robert Capa, renews acquaintance with foreign correspondent William L. Shirer, and spends time with Burgess Meredith. Receives clearance in early August to go to North Africa; travels in Algeria and Tunisia, writing reports and working on an army film project. Sails on PT boat from Tunisia to Sicily as part of special operations unit commanded by actor Douglas Fairbanks Jr. that carries out coastal raids designed to harass and mislead the Germans. Reports from Salerno beachhead in Italy in mid-September. Rejoins Fairbanks' unit and participates in operations, including capture of Italian island of Ventotene. After a few weeks in London returns to New York City in early October, suffering from effects of combat, including burst eardrums and partial amnesia. Begins *Cannery Row* in November. *The Portable Steinbeck*, edited by Pascal Covici, published by Viking Press. Film of *The Moon Is Down*, directed by Irving Pichel, released.

1944   Sees screening of Hitchcock's *Lifeboat*; angered by changes in his original story and tries unsuccessfully to have his name removed from the credits. Travels with Gwyn to Mexico by way of Chicago and New Orleans in mid-January. Begins to develop film project *The Pearl* (based on Mexican folktale briefly recounted in *Sea of Cortez*), to be directed by Emilio Fernandez. Returns to New York in March. Has busy social life with friends, including Robert Capa and John O'Hara; meets Ernest Hemingway but is dismayed by his boorish behavior. Discusses plans for a musical comedy, "The Wizard of Maine," with Frank Loesser. Receives Academy Award nomination for best original story for *Lifeboat*. Finishes *Cannery Row* in July, with central character modeled on Ricketts. Writes to Dook Sheffield about the book: "One thing—it never mentions the war—not once . . . The crap I wrote over seas had a profoundly nauseating effect on me. Among other unpleasant things modern war is the most dishonest thing imaginable." Son Thom born August 2. In October moves back to California, settling in Soto House, large 19th-century adobe house near waterfront in Monterey.

1945   *Cannery Row* published; it sells well despite poor reviews. Completes draft of novella *The Pearl* and goes to Mexico with Gwyn in February to work with Fernandez on the film; they return in mid-March. Troubled by resentment he has experienced in Monterey, writes to Covici: "You remember how happy I was to come back here. It really was a home coming. Well there is no home coming nor any welcome. What there is is jealousy and hatred and the knife in the back . . . Our old friends won't have us back . . . And the town and the region—that is the people of it—just pure poison." Returns to Mexico in April with Jack Wagner, followed by Gwyn and Thom; works on shooting script for *The Pearl* in luxurious rented house in Cuernavaca. Does research in Mexican archives for proposed film about Emiliano Zapata. With Jack Wagner, receives Academy Award nomination for best original story for *A Medal for Benny* (directed by Irving Pichel). Begins to work on *The Wayward Bus*. Gwyn leaves Mexico for New York because of ill health; Steinbeck visits her there for over a month, then returns to Cuernavaca in October for filming of *The Pearl*. Having sold Monterey house, Steinbeck and Gwyn buy pair of adjacent brownstones on East 78th Street in New York City; he drives back to New York in early December.

1946   Settles into new home. (Rents out second brownstone to Nathaniel Benchley and wife, Marjorie, who become close friends of Steinbeck and Gwyn.) Son John born June 12. After difficult pregnancy, Gwyn continues to be in poor health. Steinbeck returns to Mexico in August for further work on film of *The Pearl*. After finishing *The Wayward Bus*, sails to Europe with Gwyn in October, visiting Sweden, Denmark, Norway, and France. Awarded King Haakon Liberty Cross in Norway for *The Moon Is Down*.

1947   Works on play "The Last Joan" (abandoned by April). *The Wayward Bus* published in February. Amid marital difficulties Gwyn goes to California for a month. With Robert Capa, Steinbeck plans trip to Russia for the New York *Herald Tribune*. Hospitalized after seriously injuring knee and foot when second-story railing in apartment breaks. Still walking with a cane, travels to France in June with Gwyn and Capa; after Gwyn returns home in July, goes on with Capa for brief stay in Sweden before proceeding to Soviet Union; visits Moscow, Stalingrad, Ukraine, and Georgia; returns by way of Prague and Budapest. Begins research for novel *The Salinas Valley* (later *East of Eden*). *The Pearl* published in November.

1948   Invests in World Video, television venture which collapses after a few months. Film of *The Pearl* released in the United States. Goes to Monterey for several weeks in February to research *East of Eden*. *A Russian Journal*, with text by Steinbeck and photographs by Capa, published in April. Hospitalized in April for removal of varicose veins. Ed Ricketts is severely injured in automobile accident on May 7 and dies on May 11; Steinbeck writes to friend Bo Beskow, "there died the greatest man I have known and the best teacher. It is going to take a long time to reorganize my thinking and my planning without him." After returning from funeral in Monterey, is told by Gwyn that she wants a divorce; moves into Bedford Hotel. Spends much of summer in Mexico, researching screenplay for *Viva Zapata!*, to be directed by Elia Kazan. Returns to California in September, settling again in Pacific Grove house. Divorce becomes final in October. Devotes himself to gardening and home repairs; drinks heavily, and suffers from deep depression. Travels to Mexico in November with Kazan. Learns in December that he has been elected to the American Academy of Arts and Letters.

1949   Film of *The Red Pony*, directed by Lewis Milestone and with screenplay by Steinbeck, released. Returns briefly to Mexico in February. Over Memorial Day weekend meets Elaine Scott, wife of actor Zachary Scott; sees her frequently thereafter while working in Hollywood on *Zapata* screenplay. Sons come to stay for two months in summer, first in series of annual visits mandated by custody agreement. Begins work on *Everyman* (later *Burning Bright*), play in novella form. Finishes draft of *Viva Zapata!* screenplay. Elaine Scott files for divorce; Steinbeck moves to New York City and Elaine joins him there with her daughter Waverly; they settle in large apartment on East 52nd Street.

1950   Finishes *Burning Bright* in January. Leads active social life, meeting Elaine's many friends in the theater (she had previously worked as stage manager and in casting for the Theatre Guild and as stage manager for the original production of *Oklahoma!*). In February works with Kazan in Los Angeles on *Zapata*. Travels with Elaine to Texas in the spring to meet her family in Fort Worth (her father, Waverly Anderson, is a prominent oilman). Rents house for summer in Rockland County, near Burgess Meredith, Maxwell Anderson, and cartoonist Bill Mauldin. *Burning Bright*, produced by Richard Rodgers and Oscar Hammerstein II and starring Kent Smith and Barbara Bel Geddes, opens on Broadway in October to generally poor reviews; novel version published in November. Resumes work on *East of Eden*. Marries Elaine on December 28, and they honeymoon in Bermuda.

1951   Writes in *East of Eden* journal addressed to Pascal Covici: "The form will not be startling, the writing will be spare and lean, the concepts hard, the philosophy old and yet new born. In a sense it will be two books—the story of my county and the story of me." Steinbeck and Elaine move in February into brownstone on East 72nd Street (their home for the next 13 years). Summers in Nantucket with Elaine and sons. *The Log from the Sea of Cortez*, edition of the narrative portion of *Sea of Cortez*, with new

introductory memoir "About Ed Ricketts," published in
September. Completes draft of *East of Eden* in November.

1952   Renews acquaintance with playwright Arthur Miller, with
whom he forms close friendship. *Viva Zapata!* released.
Travels from March to September in Morocco, Algeria,
Spain, France, Switzerland, Italy, England, Scotland, and
Ireland, writing articles for *Collier's*, with Elaine collabo-
rating as photographer. Attacked by Italian Communist
newspaper *L'Unita* while in Rome for failure to denounce
U.S. policy in Korea, and writes lengthy retort (incident
recounted in *Collier's* article "Duel Without Pistols"). *East
of Eden* is published in September; receives mixed reviews
but sells well. Writes and delivers on-camera introduction
to omnibus film *O. Henry's Full House*. Writes speeches for
supporters of Adlai Stevenson's presidential campaign.

1953   Travels with Elaine and writer Barnaby Conrad to the Virgin Islands, for first of nine annual Caribbean vacations.
Receives Academy Award nominations for best story and
best screenplay for *Viva Zapata!* Collaborates with Cy
Feuer and Ernest Martin, who are to produce musical
Bear Flag, a continuation of *Cannery Row*; works on novel
derived from idea for the musical, later titled *Sweet Thursday*. In September rents cottage in Sag Harbor, Long Island, where he consults with neighbor Ernest Martin on
progress of musical. Suffers from depression and consults
psychologist Gertrudis Brenner.

1954   During Virgin Islands vacation enjoys company of econo-
mist John Kenneth Galbraith and his wife, Catherine.
Richard Rodgers and Oscar Hammerstein take over both
writing and production of *Bear Flag* (now titled *Pipe
Dream*). Sails with Elaine to Europe in March; they travel
in Portugal and Spain, and in May begin four-month stay
in Paris; suffers minor stroke on his way to Paris. Shocked
by news that Robert Capa has been killed by a land mine
in Vietnam. *Sweet Thursday* published in June. Travels to
Munich to visit facilities of Radio Free Europe; writes
statement on freedom of expression for broadcast behind
the Iron Curtain. Writes weekly articles for literary supple-
ment of *Le Figaro*; honored at dinner given by the Aca-
démie Française. Leaves Paris in September to travel in
England (where he meets editor Malcolm Muggeridge

and agrees to contribute occasional pieces to *Punch*), southern France, Italy, and Greece; returns with Elaine to America in December on the *Andrea Doria*.

1955   Invites William Faulkner to dinner in New York, but Faulkner drinks heavily and is uncommunicative (later they become friendly). Buys house in Sag Harbor, Long Island. Film of *East of Eden*, directed by Elia Kazan, with screenplay by Paul Osborn based on the novel's final segment, opens in March. Joins staff of *Saturday Review* as "Editor-at-Large" (contributes 17 articles and editorials by 1960). *Pipe Dream* opens on Broadway in September.

1956   Flies with Elaine to Trinidad in January. Covers Democratic and Republican political conventions in Chicago and San Francisco for Louisville *Courier-Journal* and its syndicated papers. Meets Adlai Stevenson, who becomes close friend; again contributes speech material to Stevenson campaign. Beginning in November serves on writers' committee (chaired by William Faulkner) of government-sponsored People to People program. Finishes comic novel *The Short Reign of Pippin IV* in November. Begins version of Sir Thomas Malory's *Morte d'Arthur* in modern English (never completed; it is published posthumously in 1976 as *The Acts of King Arthur and His Noble Knights*). Collection of essays in French written for *Le Figaro Littéraire* and other magazines published in Paris as *Un Américain à New York et à Paris*.

1957   Reads Malory intensively; does medieval research in Morgan Library in New York, assisted and advised by bookstore manager Chase Horton. Writes defense of Arthur Miller, then standing trial for contempt of Congress as a result of House Un-American Activities Committee investigation: "The Congress is truly on trial along with Arthur Miller . . . I feel profoundly that our country is better served by individual courage and morals than by the safe and public patriotism which Dr. Johnson called 'the last refuge of scoundrels.'" Sails in March to Italy with Elaine and sister Mary Dekker, partly under auspices of United States Information Agency, staying mostly in Florence and Rome. Continues Arthurian research, including investigation of Thomas Malory's life. Writes about the trip for Louisville *Courier-Journal*. *The Short Reign of*

Pippin IV published in April. After leaving Italy, travels in France, England, Denmark, and Sweden. Meets leading Malory scholar Eugène Vinaver in Manchester, England, and sees Dag Hammarskjöld and Soviet novelist Mikhail Sholokhov in Stockholm. Flies to Tokyo in September with John Hersey and John Dos Passos to attend P.E.N. conference; becomes ill with severe influenza shortly after arrival.

1958 Travels to the Bahamas with Burgess Meredith and others as part of unsuccessful treasure salvage project. Spends June in England with Elaine. Sees Vinaver again and meets playwright Robert Bolt; continues Malory research. Works on novella "Don Keehan," based on *Don Quixote* (eventually abandoned). *Once There Was a War*, collection of war dispatches from 1943, published in September.

1959 Sails with Elaine to England in February; meets novelist Erskine Caldwell on board ship. Spends next eight months in rented cottage near Bruton, Somerset. Works on Malory project. Discouraged by unsympathetic response of Elizabeth Otis and Chase Horton to Malory book. In August goes on motor trip through Wales. Returns to United States in October. Suffers an undiagnosed attack (possibly from a small stroke) and is briefly hospitalized. Letter to Adlai Stevenson on destructive aspects of American affluence creates controversy when it is published in the press ("If I wanted to destroy a nation, I would give it too much, and I would have it on its knees, miserable, greedy, and sick").

1960 Puts aside Malory book, intending to return to it later. Begins novel eventually titled *The Winter of Our Discontent* in March; completes first draft in mid-July. Becomes involved in unsuccessful effort to draft Adlai Stevenson for Democratic presidential nomination. In September sets out on eleven-week journey ("Operation Windmills") with dog Charley across America, in pick-up truck he names Rocinante. Travels through New England, the Great Lakes region, and the Dakotas to the West Coast, where he is joined temporarily by Elaine in Seattle, then returns to New York by way of California, Texas, and Louisiana.

1961   Attends inauguration of President John F. Kennedy. Continues working on *Travels with Charley*, account of his cross-country journey, in February during vacation on Barbados. Sons Thom and John move in permanently with Steinbeck and Elaine because of difficulties with Gwyn. Accompanies Mohole expedition off the Mexican coast and writes account that appears in *Life* in April (project attempted to drill hole through the oceanic crust into the earth's mantle). *The Winter of Our Discontent* published in spring; Steinbeck is depressed by reviews, "even the favorable ones." In September begins ten-month stay in Europe with wife, sons, and their tutor, future playwright Terrence McNally. On arrival in London shocked by news of death of Dag Hammarskjöld in plane crash. Tours England, Wales, and Scotland in rented car, and after brief stay in Paris continues on through southern France to Italy; in Milan, at end of November, suffers attack (either a small stroke or heart attack). Family spends Christmas in Rome.

1962   Stays on Capri with Elaine, recuperating for several months, while sons travel with McNally. Pays tribute to his Stanford creative writing teacher Edith Mirrielees in preface to Viking reissue of her book *Story Writing*. Resumes travels in Italy and Greece in April; gives speech to Greek students at American College in Athens. *Travels with Charley in Search of America* published in midsummer. Through McNally meets playwright Edward Albee, with whom he forms friendship. Learns on October 25 that he has won Nobel Prize for Literature. Writes to Swedish friend Bo Beskow: "I suppose you know of the attack on the award to me not only by Time Magazine with which I have had a long-time feud but also from the cutglass critics, that grey priesthood which defines literature and has little to do with reading. They have never liked me and now are really beside themselves with rage." Travels to Stockholm for award ceremonies; makes short visit to London.

1963   Attends honorary dinner in New York for longtime friend Carl Sandburg in January. Moves with Elaine out of brownstone into high-rise apartment on same block in March. Dog Charley dies in April. Undergoes surgery for detached retina in June; while recuperating in hospital, visited regularly and read to by John O'Hara. At the suggestion of President Kennedy, makes two-month cultural exchange visit to Eastern Europe; in October travels with Elaine to Finland, the Soviet Union (including visits to Ukraine, Armenia, and Georgia), Poland, Austria, Hungary, Czechoslovakia, and West Germany. Tour joined (as Steinbeck had requested) by Edward Albee in Moscow. Steinbeck publicly protests pirating of Western books in the Soviet Union; sees Soviet writers including Ilya Ehrenburg, Victor Nekrasov, and Yevgeny Yevtushenko, and visits grave of Boris Pasternak despite official interference. Spends time with Erskine Caldwell, also staying in Moscow. Learns in Warsaw of assassination of President Kennedy. In West Berlin meets German writers Günter Grass and Uwe Johnson. Travels with Elaine to Washington in December for State Department debriefing; they attend private dinner with President Lyndon Johnson and Lady Bird Johnson (Elaine had known Lady Bird at University of Texas), establishing friendship.

1964   Asked by Jacqueline Kennedy to write book about John F. Kennedy; has long correspondence with her, but declines project. Estranged from sons, who return to live with Gwyn and bring suit with her for additional child support (large increase denied by New York Family Court in April). Spends Easter in Rome with Elaine. Begins work on text originally designed to accompany collection of photographs of America (eventually published as essay collection *America and Americans*). Helps write Lyndon Johnson's speech accepting the Democratic presidential nomination. Receives Presidential Medal of Freedom in September. Resumes work on Malory book. Pascal Covici dies October 14; Steinbeck speaks at memorial service along with Arthur Miller and Saul Bellow. Attends reunion with relatives in Watsonville, California. Works on President Johnson's inaugural address. Spends Christmas in County Galway, Ireland, with film director John Huston.

1965   Spends several weeks in London and Paris in early January; in Paris learns of sister Mary Dekker's death. Asked by President Johnson to make trip to Vietnam as special emissary, but declines. Writes to Elizabeth Otis proposing publication of journal written during composition of *East of Eden* (published posthumously in 1969 as *Journal of a Novel*). Begins regular column for *Newsday* (it runs, with some interruptions, from November 1965 to May 1967). Travels with Elaine to England in December; accompanied by Eugène Vinaver and his wife on tour of libraries in northern England. Spends Christmas with John Huston in Ireland.

1966   Travels with Elaine to Israel in February for *Newsday*; visits graves of relatives there. Appointed by President Johnson to council of the National Endowment for the Arts in April. *America and Americans* published. Son John finishes basic training and asks father's help in getting assigned to serve with American forces in Vietnam; Steinbeck writes, "I was horrified when you asked me to get you orders to go out, but I couldn't have failed you there . . . But if I had had to request that you *not* be sent, I think I would have been far more unhappy." Writes to Lyndon Johnson in May in support of his Vietnam policy. After *The New York Times* publishes poem by Yevtushenko attacking Steinbeck's failure to oppose the Vietnam War, Steinbeck writes public letter describing war as "Chinese-inspired" and criticizing the Soviet Union for arming North Vietnam. Makes unsuccessful attempt to start new novel, "A Piece of It Fell on My Tail." Sees Yevtushenko, who is on reading tour of America, in November; they are partially reconciled. In December goes to Southeast Asia as reporter for *Newsday* with Elaine; met in Saigon by son John. Over six-week period tours wide area of South Vietnam, frequently going on combat missions and reporting sympathetically on American war effort.

1967   Visits Thailand, Laos, Indonesia, Hong Kong, where he suffers slipped disk, and Japan; returns home in April. Spends weekend at White House in May, and at President Johnson's request discusses his journey with Vice-President Hubert Humphrey, Secretary of State Dean Rusk, and Secretary of Defense Robert McNamara. Suffers debilitating pain as a result of back injury, and in October enters hospital for surgery. While awaiting operation, learns of son John's arrest in Washington, D.C., in connection with marijuana found in his apartment; John visits his father in hospital, but rejects offer of legal assistance.

(While still in the army, John had written a magazine article about widespread marijuana use among soldiers in Vietnam; following his arrest, his comments on the subject are given wide press exposure; he is acquitted of the drug charge in mid-December.) Steinbeck undergoes successful back operation and spinal fusion on October 23; released from hospital in early December. Flies to Grenada with Elaine for Christmas.

1968   After a month in Grenada, recuperates in New York apartment. Goes to Sag Harbor in spring. Suffers minor stroke on Memorial Day weekend in Sag Harbor, followed by heart attack later in July. Enters New York Hospital July 17, and suffers another heart attack while there. Leaves hospital and returns to Sag Harbor in August. Writes to Elizabeth Otis: "I am pretty sure by now that the people running the war have neither conception nor control of it . . . I know we cannot win this war, nor any war for that matter." Returns to city apartment in November. Dies at home of cardiorespiratory failure at 5:30 P.M. on December 20. Funeral service is held at St. James Episcopal Church on Madison Avenue. Elaine takes ashes to Pacific Grove; after family service at Point Lobos on December 26, they are later buried in the family plot in Garden of Memories Cemetery, Salinas.

Note on the Texts

This volume contains five early works by John Steinbeck, the linked short story collection *The Pastures of Heaven* (1932) and the novels *To a God Unknown* (1933), *Tortilla Flat* (1935), *In Dubious Battle* (1936), and *Of Mice and Men* (1937).

In May 1931, Steinbeck wrote to his friend Amasa Miller that he was at work on "a thing called The Pastures of Heaven . . . a series of related stories." In the same month he informed his agent, Mavis McIntosh of McIntosh & Otis, that the "manuscript is made up of stories, each one complete in itself, having its rise, climax and ending. Each story deals with a family or an individual. They are tied together only by the common locality and by the contact with Morans." (The Morans were the family on whom the Munroes of *The Pastures of Heaven* were modeled; Steinbeck wrote in his letter to McIntosh that "in their whole history I cannot find that they have committed a really malicious act . . . But about the Morans there was a flavor of evil. Everyone they came in contact with was injured. Every place they went dissension sprang up.") In the middle of December 1931 Steinbeck sent the completed manuscript to his agents, and it was accepted in the early spring of 1932 by Robert O. Ballou of Cape and Smith. Only weeks afterward, however, Cape and Smith went bankrupt, and Ballou moved to Brewer, Warren, and Putnam, where the book was accepted for publication. In October 1932 Brewer, Warren, and Putnam printed 2,500 copies; this firm, too, went bankrupt during the book's publication and left about 1,850 copies unbound. Ballou purchased the unbound sheets and unsold bound volumes and issued approximately 1,000 copies under his own imprint in late 1932. The remaining volumes and sheets were bought by Pascal Covici and issued under the Covici-Friede imprint in 1935. All three issues are therefore from the same printing, and the text of that printing is the one presented here. (In 1936, Covici-Friede published 370 copies of the sixth chapter separately, under the title *Nothing So Monstrous*. On this occasion, Steinbeck wrote a short epilogue that was not included in subsequent editions of *The Pastures of Heaven*; it is printed in the notes to this volume.)

To a God Unknown had its origins in "The Green Lady," a play written by Steinbeck's friend Webster (Toby) Street, who first showed Steinbeck his manuscript in 1927. Unable to complete the play, Street entrusted the manuscript to Steinbeck, who drafted part of a novel based on the play the following year, with authorial credit shared on the manuscript by Steinbeck and Street. Steinbeck continued to work on the book, making major alterations in the story. In the fall of 1931, at a time when he was also at work on *The Pastures of Heaven*, he described the novel as "torn down like a Duzenberg having its valves ground," and in February 1932 he wrote that he had "changed the place, characters, time, theme, and thesis." He sent the completed novel to McIntosh & Otis in February 1933, and it was published in the fall of 1933 by Robert O. Ballou under his own imprint. The remaining unbound sheets were later bought by Pascal Covici, who substituted a new title page and issued the book under the Covici-Friede imprint in the fall of 1935. Both these issues are therefore from the same printing, and the text of that printing is the one presented here. Steinbeck made no changes in the work subsequently.

Tortilla Flat was written fairly rapidly in the summer and fall of 1933. Robert O. Ballou had contracted to publish Steinbeck's next two books after *The Pastures of Heaven* but, concerned over the fragmentary form of the narrative, rejected the manuscript. Steinbeck then offered the book to Louis Kronenberger at Knopf, who had expressed interest in his work, but Kronenberger's response was also negative. Steinbeck's friend Mahlon Blaine subsequently showed the manuscript to a number of other New York publishers, all of whom rejected it. In late 1934, Steinbeck was contacted by Pascal Covici, who had been impressed by Steinbeck's work; Covici offered to publish *Tortilla Flat*, take an option on future books, and reissue *Cup of Gold*, *The Pastures of Heaven*, and *To a God Unknown* under the Covici-Friede imprint. *Tortilla Flat* was published in May 1935, in an edition of 4,000 copies. The book was Steinbeck's first popular success; there were at least eight printings between May 1935 and April 1937. In 1937, Steinbeck wrote a foreword for the Modern Library edition of *Tortilla Flat*, but he made no changes to the text. (The foreword is printed in the notes to this volume.) The text printed here is that of the first printing of the first edition.

In early 1934 Steinbeck met two labor organizers, Cicil McKiddy and Carl Williams, who were hiding out in Seaside, California, after participating in the San Joaquin Valley cotton strike of October 1933. He interviewed them with a view toward writing an account of the strike and of its leader, Pat Chambers, but was encouraged by Mavis McIntosh to recast the project as a novel. He began work on *In Dubious Battle* in early September 1934 and completed the first draft in five months; the novel was accepted by Pascal Covici and published by Covici-Friede in January 1936. No changes were made by Steinbeck in subsequent editions. The text printed here is that of the first edition.

The novel that eventually became *Of Mice and Men* was begun in January 1936, as a children's book. After several false starts, Steinbeck began serious work in March and, after suffering a setback when his dog tore up much of the manuscript in May, completed the book in mid-August 1936. It was published in February 1937 by Covici-Friede. In the first copies printed, the sentence that ends on page 798, line 10, of the present volume concluded with the words: "and only moved because the heavy hands were pendula." These words were removed and the entire page was reset, with the sentence now ending: "but hung loosely." The text printed here is that of the second state of the first edition, which contains this revision.

This volume presents the texts of the original printings chosen for inclusion here, but it does not attempt to reproduce features of their typographic design, such as display capitalization of chapter openings. The texts are printed without change, except for the correction of typographical errors. Spelling, punctuation, and capitalization are often expressive features, and they are not altered, even when inconsistent or irregular. The following is a list of typographical errors corrected, cited by page and line number: 13.9, Jimmy; 17.21, said,; 80.29, him,"; 87.2, California.' ; 97.24, *home?" Where's*; 118.25, Jimmy'll; 120.32, ground); 138.39, threshhold; 153.19, cleaned; 163.34, Jimmy; 163.38, Jimmy; 177.5, mused,; 182.28, repaciousness; 186.2, contemptuously.; 188.38, lay,; 193.29, little Juanito?; 204.36, "Why; 207.6, alter; 237.38, its; 238.25, said.; 239.6, uneasily.; 245.38, said.; 247.8, irresistable; 249.19, ducks; 249.35, him,; 252.39, slowly,; 255.34, "My; 257.14, nothing.; 270.7, It's; 276.6, He; 298.25, passionately.; 299.18, then; 310.39, "Can't; 323.33, handerkerchief; 324.20, use; 325.10, Im; 326.4, said.; 326.21, eyes,; 327.13, sad, "Joseph; 327.14, it.; 333.32, said.; 335.31, "like; 341.3, asked.; 342.27, yard; 345.40, us.; 349.27, it's; 351.14, asked.; 353.26, know señor; 355.34, least; 361.13, I; 383.9, A pile; 393.25, added.; 435.32, treasure?"; 506.4, ' That; 513.9, steathily; 525.28–29, to the Danny's; 526.10, "Why; 580.25, "We; 589.22, he man; 732.3, Mac,; 787.36, said, "If; 803.32, little."; 829.36, gone.; 833.1, come; 848.35, said, "But; 866.36, mens'.

Notes

In the notes below, the reference numbers denote page and line of this volume (the line count includes headings). No note is made for material included in standard desk-reference books such as Webster's *Collegiate*, *Biographical*, and *Geographical* dictionaries. For references to other studies, and further biographical background than is contained in the Chronology, see Jackson J. Benson, *The True Adventures of John Steinbeck, Writer* (New York: Viking Press, 1984); *Steinbeck: A Life in Letters* (New York: Viking Press, 1975), edited by Elaine Steinbeck and Robert Wallsten; John Steinbeck, *Working Days: The Journals of The Grapes of Wrath, 1938–1941* (New York: Viking Penguin, 1989), edited by Robert DeMott; Thomas Fensch, *Steinbeck and Covici: The Story of a Friendship* (Middlebury, Vt.: Paul S. Eriksson, 1979); Peter Lisca, *The Wide World of John Steinbeck* (New Brunswick: Rutgers University Press, 1958; new edition, New York: Gordian Press, 1981); Robert DeMott, *Steinbeck's Reading: A Catalogue of Books Owned and Borrowed* (New York & London: Garland Publishing, 1984); Tetsumaro Hayashi, *A New Steinbeck Bibliography, 1929–1971* and *A New Steinbeck Bibliography: 1971–1981* (Metuchen, N.J.: Scarecrow Press, 1973 & 1983); John Steinbeck, *Zapata* (New York: Penguin Books, 1993), edited by Robert E. Morsberger; *Conversations with John Steinbeck* (Jackson & London: University Press of Mississippi, 1988), edited by Thomas Fensch; and *Letters to Elizabeth: A Selection of Letters from John Steinbeck to Elizabeth Otis* (San Francisco: Book Club of California, 1978), edited by Florian J. Shasky and Susan F. Riggs.

THE PASTURES OF HEAVEN

3.2   Carmelo Mission] Mission San Carlos Borromeo del Rio Carmelo (or Carmel Mission), established in 1771 by Franciscan missionary Junipero Serra. Its presidio chapel was constructed in 1775.

4.8   *Las Pasturas del Cielo*] In a letter to Amasa (Ted) Miller in May 1931, Steinbeck wrote: "I am doing a thing called The Pastures of Heaven which takes its name from an enclosed valley in the mountains named by the Spanish discoverers Las Pasturas del Cielo. This is a mythical place but it is only mythical in name. The place is the Corral de Tierra and I would keep that name except for the fact that I am writing about actual people who live there." Corral de Tierra is located approximately 12 miles from Monterey and eight miles from Salinas.

11.13   modern artist . . . blue popular]   Pablo Picasso in his "blue period" (1901–4).

12.34   Merry Widows]   A brand of condom.

63.23   Velasquez' *Cardinal*]   Diego Rodríguez de Silva y Velázquez's portrait *Cardinal Camillo Astalli* (1650).

64.11   *Adventures in Contentment*]   Essays on the benefits of farm life published in 1907 by Ray Stannard Baker (1870–1946) under the pseudonym David Grayson.

72.2–3   "There . . . ourselfs."]   Cf. Robert Louis Stevenson, "Virginibus Puerisque" (1881): "There is nothing so monstrous but we can believe it of ourselves. About ourselves, about our aspirations and delinquencies, we have dwelt by choice in a delicious vagueness from our boyhood up."

77.4–6   mercenaries . . . Thermopylae]   At the end of the First Punic War in 241 B.C., unpaid mercenaries in the Carthaginian army revolted and laid siege to the city. The rebellion was finally crushed by the Carthaginian commander Hamilcar Barca in 237 B.C. In Book Seven of his *Histories*, Herodotus wrote that a Persian spy watched the vastly outnumbered Spartans (Lacedaemonians) comb their hair before the battle of Thermopylae in 480 B.C. Their behavior bewildered the emperor Xerxes, who was then told by a Greek that it was customary for Spartan warriors to pay careful attention to their hair before risking their lives in battle. In the subsequent fighting, the Spartans were annihilated after they refused to concede the Thermopylae pass to the invading Persians.

82.19   alone."]   For a limited edition of Chapter VI, published under the title *Nothing So Monstrous* (Pynson Press, 1936), Steinbeck wrote the following epilogue:
"It is some years now since Junius Maltby and Robbie climbed on the bus to go to San Francisco to get a job. I've often wondered whether Junius got a job and whether he kept it. He was strong in spirit when he went away. I for one should find it difficult to believe he could go under.
"I think rather he might have broken away again. For all I know he may have come back to the Pastures of Heaven. Somewhere in the brush-thick canyons there may be a cave looking out on a slow stream, shaded by sycamores. And in the cave Junius may live and Robbie with him. This cave would be secret, mind you, and curtained with vines, the entrance concealed. And to this cave young farmers who were little boys when Junius was here before, may come secretly, slipping through the brush, splashing across the stream in the night. Yes they may leave their warm comfortable wives in bed and creep out to sit in Junius' cave, a whole raft of them around a little fire. Each man would fill his hand with the dry sand of the floor and let the sand sift out of his closed palm while Junius talks, and each man would study his hand and not see it.
"But they may sit there on the floor while Junius tells how ants as big as

cows pulled down the camels in the desert as Herodotus shows, and how
Solomon was buried secretly in a cavern as big and very like a church. And
Junius may wonder just what the Lotus was and what manner of gas came
out of the crevasse at Delphi. The young farming men may listen and be glad
he came back. And well after midnight when the sky is black and the roosters
have started crowing long before the light, they may slip quietly away and
creep into their houses and ease into their beds beside their warm wives.

"I don't know that this is true. I only hope to God it is.

"*November 1936*

"*Los Gatos, California*"

83.31   adelante!] Forward!

103.34   the bandit Vasquez] Tiburcio Vasquez (1835–75), a stagecoach
robber, rustler, and bandit leader, was born in Monterey County and became
a popular symbol of Mexican resistance to Anglo domination. He was captured near Los Angeles in 1874 and executed in San Jose.

155.36–37   Georgics . . . farming] Virgil's *Georgics*, a didactic poem on
farming, and *De Re Rustica*, a treatise by Marcus Terentius Varro.

TO A GOD UNKNOWN

173.1–27   *TO . . . VEDA*] An adaptation of the hymn to the god Praja-
pati from the ancient Hindu scripture *Rig-Veda*; Steinbeck's source was a
version by F. Max Müller (1823–1900).

214.12   "*Maxwellton's . . . bonnie—*"] Scottish song, with words by William Douglas, altered and set to music as *Annie Laurie* (1838) by Lady John
Scott (Alicia Anne Spottiswoode Scott).

214.25   cholo] Half-breed.

214.31   *Sobre las Olas*] "Over the Waves."

216.14   Pacific Grove] Community on Monterey Bay, founded by the
Methodist Episcopal Church in 1874 as a summer tent camp and religious
retreat.

222.30–31   "*Estando . . . Simon—*"] "As they were drinking wine/Pedro,
Rodarte and Simon—"; opening lines of a Mexican ballad about three young
men who fight over a woman.

235.24–25   "*Ven . . . viene.*"] "Come here, look! look! The new Mrs.
Wayne is here."

272.33   "*Corono . . . mia—*"] A wreath of flowers that is mine.

350.36   *piojo*] Louse.

TORTILLA FLAT

369.1   TORTILLA FLAT] When the novel was reissued by the Modern
Library in 1937, Steinbeck added a dedication, "To SUSAN GREGORY of

Monterey," which appears in most subsequent editions and reprintings of *Tortilla Flat*; he also added the Foreword printed below, which appeared only in the Modern Library edition:

"When this book was written, it did not occur to me that the paisanos were curious or quaint, dispossesed or underdoggish. They are people whom I know and like, people who merge successfully with their habitat. In men this is called philosophy, and it is a fine thing.

"Had I known these stories and these people would be considered quaint, I think I never should have written them.

"I remember a little boy, a school friend. We called him the *piojo*, and he was a nice, kind, brown little boy. He had no mother or father—only an elder sister whom we loved and admired. We called her, with a great deal of respect, a hoor-lady. She had the reddest cheeks in town, and she made to- mato sandwiches for us sometimes. Now in the little house where the *piojo* and his sister the hoor-lady lived, the faucet at the sink was broken off. A wooden plug had been pounded into the pipe to keep it from leaking. The water for cooking and drinking was drawn from the toilet. There was a tin dipper on the floor to get it out. When the water was low, you simply flushed the toilet and there was a new supply. No one was allowed to use this toilet as a toilet. Once when we sequestered a colony of pollywogs in the bowl, the hoor-lady gave us hell and then flushed them down the sewer.

"Perhaps this is shocking. It doesn't seem so to me. Perhaps it is quaint— God help it. I have been subjected to decency for a long time, and still I can't think of the hoor-lady as (that nastiest of words) a prostitute, nor of *piojo*'s many *uncles*, those jolly men who sometimes gave us nickels, as her clients.

"All of this gets around to the point that this is not an introduction, but a conclusion. I wrote these stories because they were true stories and be- cause I liked them. But literary slummers have taken these people up with the vulgarity of duchesses who are amused and sorry for peasantry. These stories are out, and I cannot recall them. But I shall never again subject to the vulgar touch of the *decent* these good people of laughter and kindness, of honest lusts and direct eyes, of courtesy beyond politeness. If I have done them harm by telling a few of their stories, I am sorry. It will not happen again.

"Adios, Monte.

"John Steinbeck"

377.22   *"Chinga . . . Piojo."*]   "Go fuck your mother, louse."

377.27–28   *"Pon . . . cabeza."*]   "Go put a condom on your head."

391.1   *"Su servidor,"*]   "Your servant."

397.33   *"Que tomas?"*]   "What are you drinking?"

398.5   "Madre . . . *vino!"*]   "Mother of God, what wine!"

403.17   Hotel del Monte]   Luxury hotel in Swiss Gothic style established in 1880 in a 126-acre park; it was rebuilt in a different style after its destruction by fire in 1924.

430.3   *St. Andrew's Eve*]   November 29; Andrew is the patron saint of fishermen.

446.21–22   "Ai, . . . vas?"]   "Hey, buddy, where are you going?"

449.35   pasatiempo]   Pastime.

462.14   *puta*]   Whore.

469.6   Bowditch]   Nathaniel Bowditch's *The New American Practical Navigator*, published in 1802 and frequently reprinted.

477.9–10   bad wolf . . . sister larks.]   Anecdotes in *Fioretti di San Francesco* (*The Little Flowers of St. Francis*, 14th c.), chapters 16, 21, and 22.

523.33   Donner Party]   A California-bound party of 82 immigrants, led by Jacob and George Donner, that was trapped in the Sierra Nevada mountains in late October 1846. Thirty-five members of the party perished before the spring of 1847; many of the survivors resorted to cannibalism during the winter.

IN DUBIOUS BATTLE

531.10   PARADISE LOST]   Book I, lines 101–9.

547.4   *New Masses*]   Weekly magazine (1927–48) devoted to politics, literature, and art, affiliated with the American Communist Party.

599.3   pants rabbits]   Lice.

666.33   Bloody Thursday]   On July 5, 1934, during an International Longshoremen's Association strike on San Francisco's docks, police killed two pickets and wounded approximately 80 other people.

721.34–36   health service . . . labor vote.]   Between 15,000 and 20,000 unemployed World War I veterans gathered in Washington, D.C., in the spring of 1932 to demand from Congress payment of their military bonus certificates (issued in 1924 but not redeemable until 1945). On July 28, 1932, President Herbert Hoover ordered federal troops led by General Douglas MacArthur to destroy the campsites and shelters set up by the "Bonus Army" and forcibly evict the protestors. Hoover lost the 1932 presidential election to Franklin D. Roosevelt by a wide margin.

721.36–37   You called out guardsmen . . . the strikers.]   Four days after the Bloody Thursday killings (see note 666.33), more than 10,000 people turned out in San Francisco for a peaceful funeral march in honor of the slain workers; the procession was followed by a four-day city-wide general strike.

755.29   I.L.D]   International Labor Defense (organized 1925), legal branch of the American Communist Party.

786.10   Mills bombs]   A type of hand-grenade, invented by Sir William Mills in 1915.

OF MICE AND MEN

795.1   OF MICE AND MEN]   Cf. Robert Burns, "To a Mouse": "The best laid schemes o' Mice an' Men, / Gang aft agley, / An' lea'e us nought but grief an' pain, / For promis'd joy!"

810.2   pants rabbits]   See note 599.3.

810.9   graybacks]   Bedbugs.

836.15   goo-goos]   Filipinos or other Asians.

Cataloging Information

Steinbeck, John. 1902–1968.
  [Selections. 1994]
  Novels and stories, 1932–1937 / John Steinbeck.
  Edited by Robert DeMott and Elaine A. Steinbeck.
  (The Library of America ; 72)
  Contents: The Pastures of heaven—To a god unknown—Tortilla flat—In
dubious battle—Of mice and men.
  I. Title. II. The pastures of heaven. III. To a god unknown. IV. Tortilla
flat. V. In dubious battle. VI. Of mice and men. VII Series.
PS3537.T3234A6   1994   94–2943
813'.52—dc20
ISBN 1–883011–01–9 (alk. paper)

This book is set in 10 point Linotron Galliard,
a face designed for photocomposition by Matthew Carter
and based on the sixteenth-century face Granjon. The paper
is acid-free Ecusta Nyalite and meets the requirements for permanence of the American National Standards Institute. The binding
material is Brillianta, a 100% woven rayon cloth made by
Van Heek-Scholco Textielfabrieken, Holland. The composition is by Haddon Craftsmen, Inc., and The
Clarinda Company. Printing and binding
by R. R. Donnelley & Sons Company.
Designed by Bruce Campbell.

THE LIBRARY OF AMERICA SERIES

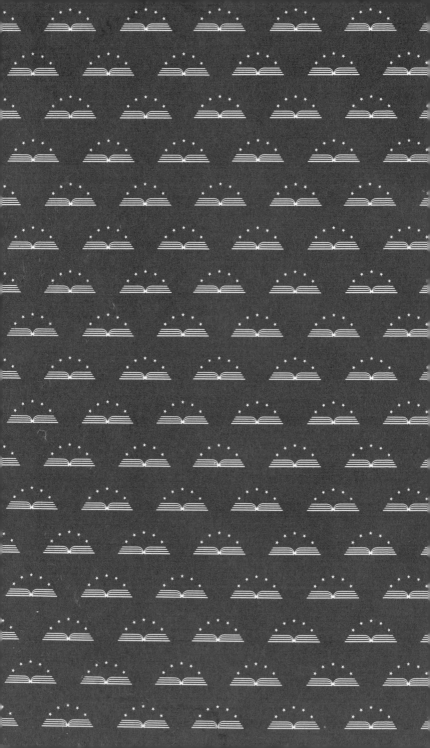